THE OBSIDIAN SAGA BOOK ①
BLACKWOOD

JESSA CROSS

- *Follow Jessa Cross on social media @AuthorJessaCross*
- *Cover Artist: Alex McLaughlin at Nox Cover Designs*

Paperback ISBN: 979-8-9937600-1-8
E-Book ISBN: 979-8-9937600-0-1

For those who saw my darkness,
and loved me anways.
This is for you. 🖤

AUTHOR NOTE

Dear Readers,

This is not a safe book. It was never meant to be. The Obsidian Saga dives into the darkest parts of human nature and doesn't flinch. It explores trauma, survival, obsession, and revenge. Some scenes may be disturbing, upsetting, or triggering for certain readers.

Please read with care if you're sensitive to:
- Childhood trauma and abuse
- Self-harm, suicide, and emotional instability
- PTSD, panic attacks, and mental health struggles
- Loss of loved ones, including children
- Obsession, stalking, and psychological manipulation
- Human trafficking and captivity
- Torture, gun violence, and graphic murder
- Underground fight clubs and brutal physical violence
- Vulgar language
- Sexual assault (on-page and referenced)
- Explicit sexual content, including MMF relationships
- Institutional and criminal corruption
- Snake phobia

This story may be fiction, but its weight is real.
You are not weak for skipping a chapter, putting it down, or walking away entirely.

Your mental health matters.
Always.

With love,
JESSA CROSS 🖤

PROLOGUE
NEW YORK CITY
20 AND A HALF YEARS AGO

October in New York City arrived with a sharp bite. Gray skies hung low over the rain-slicked pavement. The streets shimmered with reflections of red lights and taxi headlights, distorted by puddles and shadow. Trees lining the sidewalks wore their final blaze of glory, leaves in hues of crimson, amber, and gold clinging desperately to branches before the storm swept them away.

Inside the hospital, the storm outside mirrored the one unfolding within. The rain hammered relentlessly at the windows, demanding to be let in.

Raina screamed. Her voice cracked against the walls as her body convulsed. The overhead lights were too bright, buzzing faintly as they drowned her in heat and pain and panic. Sweat plastered onyx strands to her pale face. Latex and bleach burned her nose. The smell clashing with the iron of blood on her tongue. Every breath tasted like metal.

She clenched the white linen sheets, now stained a coppery tinge. Her nails tore at the fabric, desperate to anchor herself to something, anything, as her body quickly betrayed her.

Her chest rose and fell in ragged bursts, her ribs aching, her heart pounding and trying to tear its way out. A sob clawed up her throat, but she swallowed it. There was no room for weakness right now.

Though there was no time for fear, it still crept in. Fear of the shadow still chasing her. Fear of the man who haunted her every step. Fear that her baby girl, the one person she had left to love, would be swallowed by the world she'd risked everything to escape.

"Contractions are worsening. We're losing her!" someone shouted.

She didn't see their faces. Just shifting shapes in bluish-green scrubs moving like ghosts through the white haze. Voices overlapped in a frantic chorus, muffled by the screaming inside her head.

Pain pulsed through her in brutal waves. Each one carving her open from the inside out. She couldn't feel her legs. Couldn't remember what air tasted like. Her body was no longer hers. It was an aching battlefield. A dying vessel with one final purpose: to bring her daughter into the world.

Tears slid sideways, mixing with sweat and unearned grief. She was slipping. She could feel it. Feel her heartbeat skipping, her lungs catching. Death was waiting just beyond the next contraction.

But she couldn't go yet. Not until Isabella was safe. Not until she was free. A hand touched hers, grounding her.

She heard a woman's voice.

"Raina. Look at me, sweetheart."

She blinked through the blur. A face swam into focus. Auburn hair pulled back in a loose bun, hazel eyes burning with urgency and soft with fear.

Dr. Claire Donnelly.

"She's coming," Claire said. "We need to move fast."

"Please," Raina rasped, her Italian accent breaking through cracked lips before her voice caught. "My baby,"—*a sharp screech of pain*—" Isabella, you have to get her out."

Claire nodded, misunderstanding the urgency. "We're trying, Raina. We're going to get the baby out. Just hang on."

But Raina shook her head weakly, tears streaking her face. "No... not just out of me. Out of here. Out of this city. He can't ever find her."

Her eyes were glassy now, panic overtaking the pain, wild and unfocused. "He's still looking," she choked out, her fingers tightening in Claire's grasp. "He'll never stop. He won't rest until he finds her. You don't know what he's capable of. What he's already done."

Her voice cracked, hysteria edging in. "Please... please, promise me. You must save her. You must keep her hidden. Don't let him take her."

"Who is he, Raina?" Claire asked, voice barely above a whisper. "Who are you so afraid of?"

Raina's lips trembled. She beckoned Claire closer with a weak flick of her fingers, her breath rattling. When Claire leaned in, Raina pressed her mouth to her ear, her voice a ghost.

"He's the devil in a silk suit," she breathed. "He doesn't forgive. He doesn't forget. If he finds her, please don't let him find her."

Then, with what little strength she had, Raina whispered his name into Claire's ear. A name soaked in fear and blood.

Claire's eyes went wide.

She knew that name. Knew the stories. Her husband had spoken of him in hushed tones over late-night whiskey and case files half-hidden under their kitchen table. A man who moved in shadows and bought silence with blood. A man who could not be outrun.

"I swear," she whispered. "I'll protect her."

Raina's lips moved into the faintest smile, and for a second, she looked at peace. Not like a woman dying but like a girl who once danced beneath club lights, full of dreams she was never allowed to keep.

Slowly, the light faded behind her eyes. The machines screamed. The silence that followed was louder than death itself. Those few seconds lasting a lifetime until finally, another sound.

A cry.

Small.

High.

Furious.

Claire held the child, slippery, bloodied, already fighting with a fire that didn't match her tiny size. She let out another sharp, indignant cry, legs kicking and fists flailing. Claire's breath hitched at the sound. Her heart clenched so tightly it hurt.

This was no ordinary delivery. This was a last wish. A dying prayer wrapped in six pounds of new life. Claire looked down at the little girl, so small and angry at the world already, and then up at the woman who had given everything to bring her here. Raina's chest no longer moved. Her mouth hung open, her final breath carrying her soul away.

Tears blurred Claire's vision. "I've got you," she whispered to the baby, cradling her against her chest with trembling arms. "I've got you, Isabella."

"She's beautiful," the nurse whispered.

Claire's voice broke. "She's in danger."

She stayed long after the body was covered. The others had left. Claire stood alone under flickering lights, holding the tiny little one in her arms. Her gloves were stained. Her shoulders shaking.

She'd delivered dozens of babies, but none like this. None that came with a whispered name. None who'd be hunted the moment she was claimed.

She looked down at the baby again. Her tiny face scrunched and her fists curled against the pink cotton blanket.

"You're beautiful," she whispered to the child. "Just like your mother."

But beauty wouldn't protect her. Power wouldn't save her. And the name that should've been inked on her birth certificate would destroy her long before she ever learned to speak it. Claire's thoughts spun, but one voice cut through the storm.

Her sister, Elise Harrington. She lived with her husband in a quiet, beautiful lake house in Arkansas. One where morning mist curled off the water and trees glowed amber in the fall. Their home was filled with laughter, music, and love. A safe haven. Warm, steady, and far from this cold, blood-stained city.

They'd wanted a child for years. Tried every test, every treatment, rode the emotional roller coaster of hope and heartbreak more times than Claire could count. And yet, they never gave up. Not on the dream. Not on the possibility.

Elise had the kind of love that could rewrite destinies. And maybe, just maybe, this was the child her sister had been waiting for.

Claire took a breath and made her choice.

She thought of Jack, NYPD, with his endless backdoors and favors owed. Between them, they could bend the rules just enough to make Isabella disappear. They could give her safety. A new life rewritten in silence and love.

It was dangerous. Illegal. But it was right.

That night, the cameras glitched for thirteen full seconds. Files went missing. A new name was scribbled in elegant, unfamiliar handwriting.

Isabella Marie Harrington was born.

Isabella, for Raina's final wish. A name whispered through blood and breath.

Marie, after the woman who raised Claire and Elise, whose kindness would live on in the little girl's heart.

Harrington, the name of the family that would protect her with every ounce of love and fire they had left.

By dawn, she wasn't lost.

She wasn't stolen.

She was saved.

PART 1

CHAPTER ①
BELLA
AGE 5
FAYETTEVILLE, ARKANSAS

The Fayetteville Square smells like peppermint and hot cocoa—sweet, warm, and perfect. It feels like stepping into a snow globe. Christmas lights wrap every tree like candy canes, glowing red, green, and gold beneath the December sky.

I hold onto Daddy's hand. His big, calloused fingers swallowing mine as we walk the brick-lined path. My other arm hugging my Razorback stuffed animal, the one Daddy bought me at the last home game.

Snowflake lights blink across shop windows. Holiday music floats from hidden speakers, mixing with the jingling bells on horse-drawn carriages. Kids squeal past light-up reindeer and giant candy canes. Everything feels dipped in sugar and sparkle.

"Daddy, can we get cookies next?" I ask, puffing tiny clouds with my breath.

He looks down and grins. His dark brown hair is messy and his warm chocolate eyes crinkle the way they always do when he smiles. He's wearing his fire department jacket and smells like cinnamon and smoke. It's the kind of scent that never washes off and always makes me feel safe.

"Course we can, Sugar Bear. But only if you promise not to eat five again like last time."

"Did not!" I huff.

Mama laughs, balancing two cups of cocoa. "You did, baby. You just stopped counting after three."

I gasp. "Rude!"

Daddy chuckles. "She gets that from you."

As we pass the last row of glowing trees, I look up at them with sugar on my cheeks and cocoa on my lips and ask, "Daddy, do you think Uncle Jack and Aunt Claire are gonna make it to my Christmas dance recital?"

He scoops me into his arms with a playful grunt. "Course they are, Sugar Bear. Their plane lands first thing in the morning. Aunt Claire packed her sparkly sign and ten tissues."

I giggle. "Uncle Jack too?"

Daddy grins. "Yep. And you've got just enough time to give Razorback a proper Christmas bath before showtime. That pig's starting to smell like peppermint and trouble."

I gasp again. "His name is Mr. Piggles and he does not smell like trouble!"

Mama laughs into her cocoa. "He kind of smells like frosting and mischief."

I stick my tongue out and snuggle deeper into Daddy's coat.

"Well, I think he's perfect."

We gather in the living room, celebrating my recital together like we always do. Just us, no fuss, wrapped up in love bigger than any fancy theater could hold. The fireplace crackles, casting a soft orange light across the floor and warming the house in that cozy, cinnamon-sweater kind of way.

The tree sparkles in the corner, dressed in red ribbons and glittering ornaments I'm not supposed to touch but do anyway. Twinkle lights line the mantle and the whole house smells like Mama's homemade cider: cloves, oranges, and something that makes the air feel like a hug.

Pink and silver balloons bob near my chair. A glittery sign that says, *"Ballet Star!"* is taped crookedly to the fridge. Mr. Piggles sits proudly in my lap. He's still wearing the tiny tutu Mama had made just for him.

I'm sitting cross-legged on the rug with my sparkly recital costume still on, even though it itches. I'm not ready to let go of the magic just yet.

Uncle Jack kneels by the coffee table, squinting at my new dollhouse instructions like they're written in some sort of secret code. But when I start telling the story of my final spin again, he looks up and smiles like it's the first time he's hearing it. He laughs in all the right places, even as he drops a miniature door under the couch and pretends not to notice the pink sticker I'd snuck onto his arm.

"She nailed her landing," Daddy says proudly, lounging on the couch with a steaming mug. "Didn't even wobble."

"Probably all those afternoons practicing with the Razorback cheerleaders," Aunt Claire adds with a wink, perched by the fire.

"Must be nice," Uncle Jack says while raising his brows at me. "Season tickets and field access? Spoiled rotten."

Mama laughs, shaking her head. "Well, her daddy is Razorback royalty, Jack. Quarterback legend, remember?"

"She's got game day spirit in her blood," Daddy adds. "Just like her mama."

Mama's smile softens. "She's a Razorback baby. That stadium's practically her second home."

Mama always says Daddy spotted her first on the sideline, pom-poms flying, and decided right then he'd marry her. Daddy swears it was her sparkle. Mama says it was his throwing arm. I think it was both.

"Razorback Stadium is the best place," I chime in, hugging Mr. Piggles tight. "Except here. I like the lake the most. But games are a little more fun 'cause of the fireworks and pom-poms and yelling."

Daddy chuckles. "You've perfected calling the hogs, Sugar Bear."

"Good lungs," Mama says with a smile. "She gets that from you."

He winks. "And she gets the sparkle from you, babe."

Aunt Claire's eyes flick toward Mama, just for a second. Daddy sees it too. He reaches over and gently squeezes Mama's knee. His thumb moving in slow circles, pulling her back from whatever shadow she was drifting toward.

"Aunt Claire, wanna see Mr. Piggles do his big finale bow?" I ask, scooting toward the fireplace.

She smiles and nods. "Hey babe," she says to Uncle Jack. "Why don't you take Bella and Mr. Piggles over by the tree and let her show you the whole routine."

I grab Mr. Piggles and skip across the room. The Christmas lights blinking behind me as I find my spot for my big finish. But just as I twirl into my starting pose, I catch the low whisper of voices behind me.

"I keep feeling like someone's watching us," Mama says.

"We did everything right," Aunt Claire says softly. "Jack called in favors at the precinct. I handled the medical records. There's nothing left, Elise. No trail."

Daddy's voice drops to something hard and low. "We've kept her safe for five years, changed her name and her records. Her whole damn life. But if he ever finds out, if he even starts looking again, none of it will matter. You know what kind of power he has, Claire. If he wants her, no forged paper is going to stop him."

I freeze mid-spin. The sugar on my lips suddenly feeling sour.

Uncle Jack kneels beside me. He makes Mr. Piggles do a grand, wobbly bow and says in a dramatic tone, "Your Highness, might I request a performance from the Star of the Tutu Kingdom?"

I squeal. The tightness eases.

He scoops me up, kisses my cheek, and twirls me in front of the fireplace like a ballerina superhero. His whiskers scratch my skin, but I giggle so hard I hiccup. And when we dips low into the firelight, the magic comes back.

CHAPTER ②
BELLA
AGE 8
FAYETTEVILLE, ARKANSAS

The dance studio smells like hairspray and floor polish. I love it. Mirrors line the walls, the wood floor squeaks under our shoes, and the bass thumps softly from another classroom. I burst through the door, hair in a tight ponytail, my glitter backpack bouncing behind me.

"Sorry we're late!" Mama calls, handing my dance bag to Miss Allie.

Miss Allie is the coolest. The kind of dancer you could only dream of becoming. Long brown hair that fades into a violet ombré, edgy outfits, joggers, cropped tanks, and Nikes that squeak when she hits her turns just right. Mama says she's like fire and poetry. I just think she's magic.

"She's right on time," Miss Allie says with a wink.

I plop onto the bench to change shoes, already chatting with the older girls about school, dance, and Mr. Piggles. We laugh so hard my stomach hurts.

When the music starts, everything else falls away.

My body moves like it remembers something older, like rhythm had lived in my bones before I ever learned to walk. I don't just dance. I tell stories. I cast spells. I become light and fire and feeling. Every flick of my wrist, every breath, every turn is a part of something bigger.

Through the observation window I catch a glimpse of Mama. One hand on her chest, the other curled in her lap. Her eyes are glassy but she smiles.

Dinner is pizza tonight. Two boxes on the counter, still warm when Daddy opens them. Mama didn't have the energy to cook tonight, and nobody asked her to. We don't care. Pizza and paper plates on the couch is sometimes even better.

She's curled up in the corner of the couch, wrapped in her favorite quilt, a half-eaten slice on her plate. She smiles as I recite the routine move by move, but her eyes aren't shiny anymore. They look like the Christmas lights at the square after you unplug them, still there, but dark.

I notice that. I always notice.

After bedtime, with Mr. Piggles tucked under my arm, I hear them outside on the back patio.

"You didn't eat much," Daddy says softly.

"I wasn't hungry," Mama whispers.

"It's getting worse, isn't it?"

"Something's not right, Henry. The fatigue. The chest pain. I feel like I'm slipping. Like I'm here, but barely. I'm screaming underwater, but no one can hear me."

Daddy's voice shakes. "You're just tired. That's all."

"What if I'm not here when she needs me? What if he finds her and I'm not strong enough to stop it? What if I've already failed her?"

"I don't care what it takes," Daddy's low voice booms. "Hospitals, specialists, even goddamn voodoo. I'll chase every miracle this world has to offer. I'll knock on the devil's door if I must and make his ass listen."

His voice cracks. "And *him*? That bastard doesn't get near her. Not now. Not ever. I don't care if I have to burn every system to the ground. You and Bella are my whole life, Elise. My breath. My purpose. If the universe wants a fight—"

He leans closer.

"I'll give it one it'll never fucking forget."

"Henry," Mama whispers. "Watch your mouth."

He exhales. "Sorry, baby."

CHAPTER ③
B E L L A
AGE 10
F A Y E T T E V I L L E ,   A R K A N S A S

The autumn dance recital is a few days away. My name is printed in glitter on the program, right next to *Soloist*. That should mean everything. But it doesn't. Not right now.

Rehearsals are supposed to be my world. All full of music, laughter, and counting to eight. But I keep turning toward the door mid-spin, hoping I'll see Mama watching. Hoping she'll clap and call me her little star. Half-hoping. Half-dreading what it means when she isn't here.

Deep down, I know it. Mama is fading.

The mornings are quieter. No more humming over pancakes. No more playful spins between the fridge and the sink. She still smiles. Still kisses my forehead. Still packs lunches with sticky notes that say things like, *Keep your heart in the music, Sugar Bear*. Her hugs are longer now, almost like she's afraid to let me go.

"Want me to braid it for you tonight?" she asked softly the other night.

I nodded and sat between her knees, just like I had a hundred times before. Her fingers moved through my hair slower than usual. She paused halfway through.

"Mama?" I asked.

"I'm okay, sweetheart," she whispered, pressing a kiss to the top of my head.

But she wasn't okay.

She isn't okay.

Daddy has stopped stomping around in his work boots like the floor might shatter beneath him. Aunt Claire and Uncle Jack show up without calling, their smiles tight. They are over all the time now. It's like they're trying to hold the world together with good intentions and fraying hope.

And one night, through the wall of my bedroom, I heard Mama

cry. Not the loud kind you let someone hear. The kind that leaks out quiet and raw. The kind you try to keep hidden, but can't.

The day I found clumps of her hair in the bathroom trash, something inside me shattered. I didn't ask. I didn't want to. I just crawled into bed with her and curled up close, wrapping my fingers around hers like I could somehow hold her in place.

We fell asleep like that.

Uncle Jack's old scar curls down his left forearm. He gives me a small smile. He doesn't usually pick me up from school, so I know something is wrong.

"Hey, kiddo," he says, crouching next to me as his emerald eyes meet mine. "Change of plans. Your mom had a little scare. Nothing to panic about, but I'm taking you to the hospital."

We don't talk on the drive. No music. No jokes. The window is cracked and the air is cold, but I don't roll it up. I count the leaves we pass, orange and burgundy blurs, pretending if I make it to a hundred everything will be okay.

I stare without seeing, fingers clenched in Uncle Jack's hand. His thumb traces soft circles on my palm. Not enough to stop the fear climbing up my chest. But enough to remind me I'm not alone.

My heart thuds louder with every mile. "Uncle Jack," my voice shakes. "Is she gonna be okay?"

He doesn't answer right away. Just shuts off the engine, turns to face me, and brushes a stray hair from my face.

"She's strong, Bells. Stronger than anyone I know."

That's not a yes.

I follow him through the sterile maze of the hospital, my shoes scuffing faintly against the too-clean linoleum. The air smells of disinfectant and something sour underneath.

Fluorescent lights buzz overhead, casting stretched shadows that cling to the floor like whispers. My chest aches. Every breath is shallow. Panic simmers just under my skin.

The nurses behind the counter smile that rehearsed smile. All pity and no comfort. It makes something inside me angry. I want to run. To turn back time.

When we reach Mama's room, Uncle Jack kneels beside me.

"She's tired. But she wants to see you."

Daddy and Aunt Claire are already there. Daddy sits hunched beside the bed. His large, calloused hand is trembling as he brushes hair from Mama's forehead. His eyes are bloodshot, his jaw locked. Every breath he takes sounds thick, like it hurts just to breathe.

Aunt Claire stands at the foot of the bed, one hand pressed to Mama's chart. Her face is pale, lips tight, and her eyes are glassy and rimmed in unshed tears.

Just as I step inside, a man walks in.

Dr. Callahan.

He gives me a small nod, turns to Daddy and Aunt Claire with something heavy in his eyes. "Can I speak with you both in the hallway for a moment?"

Daddy looks from me to Mama, reluctant, like leaving her for even a second will break him. Aunt Claire touches his arm.

He leans down and kisses Mama's forehead.

"I'll be right back."

I turn back to Mama, my chest tight with fear. "Mama?"

She opens her eyes and smiles soft, small but real.

"Hi, Sugar Bear. Come here."

I crawl into bed beside her and rest my head against her chest.

"I missed you today," I whisper.

"I missed you more." Her fingers stroke my hair. "How was school?"

"It was ok. At recess, I showed my friends the new routine. It was hard, but I danced really good, Mama."

"That's my girl," she whispers. "Keep dancing. No matter what. You hear me?"

I nod and close my eyes. From the hallway, I hear Daddy's voice rise, sharp, raw, and angry.

"What do you mean there's nothing else you can do?" he roars. "You're a goddamn hospital, don't just stand there! DO SOMETHING! That's my wife in there. The woman I built my world with. You don't get to shrug and walk away!"

"Henry, please," Aunt Claire says. "Calm down. Let him talk. Yelling isn't going to help."

"I don't need calm, Claire. I need fucking answers! What am I supposed to tell Bella?"

Their voices echo down the hallway tangled with grief, panic, and rage.

I stay curled beside Mama. And even though her hand still moves through my hair, even though I'm still holding on, I can't stop the tears from falling.

CHAPTER ④
BELLA
AGE 10
FAYETTEVILLE, ARKANSAS

The smell of lillies and sadness fills the old church. I sit in the front pew in a satin black dress, a black bow tied in my long onyx hair. Mr. Piggles is tucked inside my backpack, the zipper barely closed around his fuzzy red snout.

Mama's photo sits framed on the altar. She looks so alive in it. Her eyes bright, hair soft, and smile like sunlight. But that woman isn't here anymore. That woman won't be singing in the car or twirling in the kitchen.

That woman is gone.

People say a lot of nice things. That she was kind. Brave. The kind of person who lit up every room.

I don't care about the rooms she lit up. I just want her back in mine. I want her humming in the kitchen. Her warm hands in my hair. Her whispers saying everything will be okay, even if it wasn't. I want her laugh. I want her.

Not the memory.

Not the stupid photo in the gold frame.

Her.

Daddy holds my hand the whole time, never letting go. Even when the music starts. Even when the casket rolls down the aisle. I look up and see his face, stone-set, eyes rimmed in red, but dry. No tears. Only pain.

We drive to the cemetery in silence. Just the low hum of tires and the lump in my throat I can't seem to swallow.

Mama's casket now rests beneath a white tent. The roses from the church already wilting and curling at the edges like they know she isn't coming back. I hate those flowers.

The sun hangs low, creating long shadows across the grass. A breeze brushes my dress. It's cool against my legs, but I barely feel it.

My fingers clutch Mr. Piggles. I'd taken him out on the drive. I don't care if anyone thinks I am too old. I need him.

Aunt Claire stands behind me, her hand warm and steady on my shoulder. I don't turn. I can't. If I met her eyes, I'll shatter into pieces too sharp and too wide to ever fix again.

Daddy stands at the head of the grave like a soldier. All stiff and still. His fists are bound so tight I think his skin might split. His eyes are locked on the casket, like if he stares hard enough, he can undo it all.

When the pastor finishes, Daddy steps forward and lays a single white lily across the coffin. It looks lonely on the dark wood. His favorite, not hers. Maybe because he couldn't stand the thought of giving her something she loved when she wasn't here to love it back.

Then comes the sound. The first thud of dirt hitting wood. Then another. And another. Each one a cruel drumbeat inside my chest.

Aunt Claire whispers a prayer, but her voice feels far away, lost beneath the roaring ache in my ears.

Uncle Jack's hand slides over mine, squeezing tight. When a tear slips down my cheek, he brushes it away with his thumb before I can.

The pastor keeps saying that she's at peace now. That Mama isn't hurting anymore. But how can it be peaceful if I'm not with her? If she's not with me?

I want to scream. To jump in and pull the dirt back out with my hands until Mama can breathe again.

But I don't. I stand there, quiet and small, while they bury the only person who's ever truly seen me.

An eerie chill scrapes down my spine.

A shadow moves where shadows shouldn't. At the edge of the cemetery, half-hidden by trees, a black SUV idles. No plates. A man sitting in silence and hidden behind tinted windows as he watches us.

"Daddy," I whisper, tugging his sleeve. "Who's that?"

His hand tightens around mine, then lets go. "Stay here," he says, voice low and rough enough to scar. "Hey, Jack."

Before they can take a step, the SUV eases back, tires crunching slow over gravel almost like it wanted us to see it leave. Wanted us to remember.

"Probably someone lost," Aunt Claire says, but her hand presses harder against my back like a shield.

She's lying.

I don't know how I know. Only that I do. Something has changed. Something has started.

And my Mama isn't here anymore to stop it.

CHAPTER ⑤
BELLA
AGE 10
FAYETTEVILLE, ARKANSAS

The new year is starting with words I know but don't fully understand. Big, cold words spoken at the front door—*custody, violation, investigation.* My stomach hurts like when you eat too much candy. Only worse.

I slip off my bed. My heart is thudding. Mr. Piggles is clutched in one hand and my other fisting in the hem of my purple sweater.

From the hallway shadows, I see them. Two strangers in stiff clothes. A man and a woman. The man has a clipboard. The woman keeps glancing past Aunt Claire like she already knows exactly where I am.

"I don't understand," Aunt Claire says, her voice tight with panic. "You can't just show up and—"

"Ma'am," the woman firmly cuts in. "We have legal cause. There's been a flag in the system. The child—"

"Her name is Bella," Aunt Claire snaps.

The woman sighs. "We need to speak to the legal guardian. Is he home?"

"He's at work. But you can't just—"

Then I hear it, the roar of Daddy's truck. A second later, the front door slams open. "What the hell is going on here?"

The strangers turn, but Daddy is already storming forward.

"Who are you?" he barks. "Why are you in my house?"

"Mr. Harrington," the man says, still trying to stay calm. "We're with Child Protective Services. We received a tip regarding forged birth records and falsified document—"

"What?" Daddy's voice raises. "Get the hell out of my house."

"Sir, we have legal cause to be here. Isabella is not your biological child. There is no medical record of your wife's pregnancy or delivery. The paperwork appears—"

"She doesn't need paperwork. She needs a family!" Daddy roars, stepping so close the man flinches. "Get the hell out of my house. NOW!"

"I'm sorry, sir. We're required to place her in emergency foster care for her safety."

"Safety," Daddy's voice breaks. "You think strangers are safer than her own damn father?"

He's shaking now, chest heaving and eyes burning. "You won't fucking take my daughter."

Aunt Claire steps in between them with trembling hands. "Please don't do this. Elise, her mother, she just passed. Henry's the only parent she has left."

"We understand this is difficult," the man says quietly.

"Difficult?!" Daddy's face goes red. "She's my daughter! You want difficult? I'll give you difficult! Where do you think you're taking her?"

"I'm sorry, sir. The location is—"

"Oh no, no, no. You're not taking her anywhere. You don't get to just..." Daddy runs a hand through his hair. "Jesus Christ you can't do this!"

I step into the doorway. "Daddy?"

His head whips around. His eyes lock on mine and they break. I've never seen his face look like this. Not even when Mama died.

The woman turns toward me with a practiced smile. "Hi, Isabella sweetheart. We're going to take a little trip, okay?"

"No," I whisper, backing away and clutching Mr. Piggles in my arms.

"Isabella," she reaches for me gently. "It's going to be alright."

"NO!" I scream, running toward Daddy. "Daddy!"

He lunges for me, but the male agent steps between us.

"Sir, don't make this harder than it has to be. Don't let her remember you like this."

Aunt Claire grabs my shoulder, trying to pull me back.

"I'll fucking kill you both!" Daddy roars as he strains to reach me. "Let her go. She's all I have left!"

The room goes crazy. Everyone is yelling, pushing, and words are flying so sharp they make my ears sting.

"Please," Daddy finally stutters. "Just... just let me say good-bye to my baby."

Everything goes still for one breath. The man steps aside.

Daddy drops to his knees in front of me, hands trembling, eyes red and shining like I've never seen. He reaches into his pocket and pulls out Mama's locket. The golden one she always wore, still faintly scented with lavender.

His hands shake as he fastens it around my neck. "Mama wanted you to have this, Sugar Bear," he whispers. "She said it'd keep you safe when we couldn't."

Aunt Claire is sobbing, frantically shoving clothes and Mr. Piggles into my old backpack. She keeps saying, *'I'll call Uncle Jack, I'll call Uncle Jack,'* like the words themselves can fix it.

But nothing can.

The woman steps forward and takes my hand. "It's time, Isabella."

"I DON'T WANT TO GO!" I kick and sob. "DADDY!"

He slams his fists into the wall, punching straight through the drywall as the fury pours out of him in a wildfire.

"I'll find you!" he shouts after the car. "Bella, I'm coming for you, baby! You hear me? I'M COMING!"

The car door slams. I press my face to the glass until it hurts. His voice gets smaller as the driveway disappears. I try to trap it inside my head before it goes away.

CHAPTER ⑥
BELLA
AGE 10
MIAMI, FLORIDA

The Miami air in January isn't cold like I thought winter should be. It's humid in a lazy, sticky way, like the sky couldn't decide if it wanted to rain or sweat.

As the car curves up a smooth stone drive, dread twists in my belly. The house that comes into view is stunning. White stucco walls and a red tile roof. Palm trees swaying against a bright blue sky. Bougainvillea vines frame arched windows and curl around ornate columns. A gold-plated fountain bubbles in the circular drive.

It looks like something out of a magazine. But something about it feels wrong. Too perfect. Too polished. Like when you see a doll smiling but its eyes don't look right. Pretty, but scary underneath.

Carlos doesn't say a word as he parks his sleek black Mercedes beside the fountain and yanks open my door.

"Get out," he grunts.

I clutch my backpack tighter. I want to scream. To cry. To run.

But I step out because I don't have a choice.

Where could I possibly run to?

The foyer smells like lemon polish and fresh orchids. Marble floors stretch in every direction, gleaming like glass. A grand staircase sweeps up one side of the entrance lined with gold trim and massive portraits. Everything is elegant and beautiful, but deadly silent.

A woman stands at the far end of the hallway poised in a pale pink silk blouse, white slacks, and dark red heels. Her chestnut hair is pinned up, lipstick is perfect, but her smile is brittle.

She's holding a little boy on her hip. He's got messy curls and big, anxious eyes. He buries his face in her shoulder as we get closer.

Carlos doesn't introduce them. Doesn't care. He just flicks his eyes toward the stairs.

"Upstairs. Second door on the left. Lights out at nine. Don't touch anything that ain't yours. Don't eat unless I say so. Don't cry.

And for the love of God, don't fucking bother me. You understand?"

I whimper. "When can I see my—"

CRACK.

Fire blooms across my cheek.

"Get your little ass up to your fucking room," he snarls.

My head snaps sideways. My ears ring and the chandelier above blurs into a thousand spinning lights. The taste of pennies fills my mouth.

For a second, I can't move. I can't breathe. No one has ever hit me before. Finally, my legs obey, shaky and slow as they carry me up the stairs and to the left like I'm sleepwalking through a nightmare.

With the echo of his voice still in my skull, I realize something deep in my bones. Whatever *home* had meant before, it didn't live here.

The door creaks when I push it open. The room inside is beautiful. A full-size bed with a velvet headboard. White silky linens. A pink velvet chair in the corner sitting next to a white nightstand. A window with gauzy pink curtains and a distant view of the ocean.

If it were any other circumstance, I would've loved it.

I sit on the edge of the bed, arms wrapped around my knees and wonder how a girl who once danced under Arkansas sunsets had ended up here. Alone in a place that looked like paradise but feels like a trap.

"Don't look him in the eye when he's drinking. Don't go near the kitchen after dark. Matter fact, don't eat nothin' unless Mariela puts it in your hand. And if you hear the door creak past midnight close your eyes and fake sleep like your life depends on it. 'Cause it might."

I turn fast, my heart in my throat.

A boy in dark jeans and a black hoodie stands in the doorway. Tall and lean, older than me by a few years. His skin is a rich, deep brown, and his jaw is tight like he's used to clenching it just to stay quiet.

But it's his eyes that freeze me. Dark brown, nearly black and heavy. Almost like they'd seen too much and refused to look away.

He doesn't come closer. Just leans against the door frame

like he's been carved into it. His eyes don't blink as he watches me. Trying to decide if I'm worth the risk.

"I'm the reason this door don't got a lock," he mutters, pulling his hood down. "Last time that bastard tried locking someone in here, I snapped it clean off. Carlos lost his damn mind but he ain't fixed it since."

He doesn't say it to impress me. He says it like a promise. Like A warning.

Like he'd do it again.

He never asks how old I am. Or why I am here. He already knows. He just looks at me with the intensity of someone trying to solve a puzzle no one else can see.

"What's your name?"

"Isabella Marie Harrington," I whisper.

His face twitches. Barely, but I see it. I see the flicker in his dark eyes. But instead of asking questions, he just nods and steps forward.

"I'm Ezekiel. Ezekiel Malik Carter. Named after my Dad," he says, softer now like he doesn't want to scare me more. "But everyone calls me Zeke."

He crouches beside me, his shadow shielding mine.

"You're not alone no more, Isabella. Not ever again. I got you. Whatever it takes." His voice is strong and steady. A hand reaching out in a storm.

"He's not sellin' you. Not touchin' you either. I swear on everything I won't let that happen."

"S-sell me?" I whisper, the words trembling out like cracked glass. My fingers clutch tighter at the sheet beneath me. "Why would he sell me?"

Zeke curses under his breath and looks away, jaw tense. "Nah, scratch that. You don't need to worry about it. That's my shit to handle not yours."

"But—"

He turns back to me. "You're safe now, Isabella. Promise. Just try to get some rest, yeah?"

He says it like a vow. Almost like he owes me something I don't understand yet.

"Bella," I whisper, my voice barely holding together. "It's just Bella."

The tears come. Spilling over before I can stop them. My chest shakes with the weight of everything I don't understand, everything I don't want to feel. The name that doesn't even feel like mine anymore. Just something I said to prove I still existed.

Zeke doesn't ask me anymore questions. He pulls me into him. Arms tightening around me as if he's been holding broken things his entire life.

"It's gonna be okay," he promises. "Not tonight. But soon."

I bury my face in his hoodie and let the sobs rip through me.

There's a creak at the door and small footsteps patter on the marble floor.

"C'mere, Dylan," Zeke says.

The little boy I saw earlier peeks in, wide-eyed and cautious. He doesn't speak. Just walks over, climbs into Zeke's lap, and rests his little hand on mine.

"This is Dylan," Zeke says real soft, brushing the kid's hair out of his face. "He don't talk much 'til he knows you're solid. But he's brave as hell. Way braver than he should have to be."

And so we sit, the three of us. Pressed close in a room that smells like salt and secrets. Where the silence creeps through the curtains and the shadows don't need to scream.

A boy already scarred by fire and ghosts.

A girl already breaking before she knew how to heal.

And a little child with scraped knees and more heart than the world deserved.

It isn't safety.

Not yet.

But it's something.

A sliver of hope in a house built on nightmares.

CHAPTER ⑦
B E L L A
AGE 13
M I A M I ,   F L O R I D A

Carlos slams the cabinet door so hard the marble counter top trembles. I flinch, every muscle locking up as the echo of his voice ricochets off the vaulted ceilings, rattling inside my chest like a warning bell that won't stop ringing.

Outside, spring shimmers like a postcard. The ocean breeze drifts in through the arched kitchen window, laced with the scent of orange blossoms from the manicured garden. Birds chirp as if nothing is wrong. Like the world is soft. Safe.

But inside, this house is a perfectly curated gallery. Beautiful on the surface but hollow underneath. And if you stare too long, you'll start to see the cracks behind the gold.

It's hell in a designer skin. A place where sunlight can't reach past the spotless windows and pristine decor. Where silence swallows even the loudest sound. And the walls, no matter how white and gleaming, can't hide the rot underneath. Nothing blooms inside here except yesterday's bruises and broken promises.

I shouldn't have talked back. God, I know better. Zeke taught me the rules. How to keep my head down. How to disappear inside myself. How to choke down every scream before it reaches my throat.

Silence is survival. Stillness is safety. Every bruise had taught me that. Every slammed door. Every muffled sob in the middle of the night reminded me that *quiet girls don't bleed.*

But today, something inside me split wide open. Maybe it was the subtle mind games, slicing like paper cuts you don't see 'til you're bleeding.

Or maybe it was the bruises carefully hidden under the prettiest dresses. The way governors and senators come over and smile while telling us how lucky we are to live in a house with such *loving* foster parents.

Maybe it was the way Carlos can gut you with a smile. The way

Mariela serves French toast with syrup and sorrow. Maybe it was the scent beneath the perfume, the rot hiding under lemon polish and sea breeze diffusers. That sour bite of something wrong in a house that looks too right.

Or maybe it was the way Carlos looks at Dylan. Like he's already named a price. Like Dylan isn't a child anymore. Just a countdown. Just property.

And I couldn't take it. Not one more second of pretending I don't see it. Not one more breath of silence that tastes of complicity.

Carlos's gaze slides over me like slime, slow and claiming, already deciding where I'll be sent. What I'll be worth.

I hate him. I hate the walls that hold us and the floors that never creak when he walks. The air that never moves unless he lets it. I hate the fear that curls like smoke inside my lungs, whispering the same old lullaby: *Stay small. Stay silent. Stay safe.*

I know the price of disobedience in this house. But today, my voice betrays me.

"It's just a glass."

And now I'm going to pay for it.

"Then pick it up!" he barks, pointing to the shattered glass on the floor.

My hands tremble as I reach for the shards of the crystal glass I'd dropped. Carlos steps forward and slams his boot down on my hand, grinding the shards deeper into my skin. Pain explodes through my palm. Bright, warm blood blooms almost instantly, staining the white marble floor in thick crimson streaks.

I bite my tongue until I taste copper. I keep moving and keep collecting the shards one by one. If I stop, I'll cry. And if I cry, he'll call me weak. Or worse, he'll remind me just how powerless I really am in this perfect house of horrors.

"Clumsy little bitch," he sneers.

I don't say anything. I don't even look at him. I just scoop up the last piece into my hand, throw it in the trash, and turn away hoping that he'll lose interest.

He doesn't.

A hand clamps around my arm like a steel trap, yanking me

backwards so violently I barely catch my breath. My hip slams into the corner of the counter, pain flashing white-hot up my side. The sharp edge bites deep and I swear I feel something crack. Tears well up, but I bite down hard on my tongue and swallow the scream.

I've learned the hard way that making noise will only make it worse.

"You're not gonna last long," he growls into my ear, his sour breath against my skin as he leans in, inhaling the scent of my hair like a predator savoring the moment before the kill. "They'll break you just like the rest. But if they don't..."

He lets the silence linger, dragging it out like a blade over skin. "...I'll be more than happy to take my time doing it myself, pretty girl."

He shoves me again. Not hard enough to knock me down, but enough to tell me he could. And he can.

The sound of his belt sliding free says everything.

I know it is time.

"Please," I whisper, but my voice is nothing. I'm nothing here.

Dylan rings out, panicked. "No! No, don't hurt her!"

Mariela sobs something in Spanish. A prayer, maybe. Or a warning.

"Stop." A voice so low and calm slices through the room.

Zeke.

He steps into the kitchen like a shadow that has found its fury, shoulders squared, jaw tight. Fire smoldering behind his dark eyes.

"It was me."

Carlos turns, nostrils flaring, hand still gripping tightly around my arm. "You think I'm stupid?"

"Oh, I know exactly what you are. I was just feelin' generous and figured I'd try this thing called *manners*. Just for today."

Zeke jerks his chin toward me and Dylan. "Seeing as there's actual kids in the room. Didn't wanna traumatize them more than your busted-ass face already has."

Carlos's grip tightens. "You've got a real smart mouth, boy."

"And there it is. That ugly-ass vein in your five-head. Pops out every time you start fantasizing about hurting one of us," Zeke says, voice low, like a loaded gun.

"You know what I've learned about monsters like you?"

He tilts his head, just barely. "You all think you're untouchable. Invisible. Like nobody notices how your breath catches when Dylan cries. Or how your eyes drag when Bella walks into the room."

Zeke stalks forward. "But I see it. Every single tick. Every little twitch. All those disgusting habits you think you're hiding."

Another step.

"You reek of weakness dressed up like power."

His voice drops. "Yeah, you got people in your pocket right now. But one day they'll be gone."

A beat of silence.

"And when they are?"

Zeke's smile is all teeth. "I'm coming for you."

I choke on a breath I didn't know I was holding, caught somewhere between terror and awe.

Zeke takes another slow step forward, unfazed. "Now let go of my sister, asshole. Right the fuck now."

Carlos's eyes dart between us. His anger rising.

"You lookin' to swing, fuckface? Try me. I broke your glass and I'll break another. Hell, maybe I'll start with that sad little nose job you wasted money on."

He grins. "Damn, Carlos. A nose job? At your age? Who you tryna impress, your own reflection, or your little crew of creeps down at the club?"

Zeke tilts his head, eyes dragging over him with unfiltered disgust. "Should've skipped the nose and gone for a tummy tuck. You're gettin' thick, my guy, and not in a good way."

Carlos drops my arm like it burned him, nostrils flaring, lips curling back. A seething dog about to bite.

Zeke doesn't look away. My big brother just stands tall, unmoved. Defiant. And for a second I think Carlos is going to back down.

"Turn around, boy."

Zeke obeys. Silent. Shoulders squared.

The belt cracks.

Once.

Twice.

Three times.

Four.

I watch in horror, frozen in place as my own body refuses to move. To speak up. To save him.

Crimson bleeds through the thin white cotton of Zeke's shirt, slowly spreading like ink in water. Each lash leaving a shudder beneath his skin, but he never makes a sound. His silence is more powerful than any scream. A defiance carved as deep as the wounds.

He takes it.

Because of me.

Because he always does.

Carlos tosses the belt aside like this was nothing. Like Zeke's skin isn't split and stinging. He straightens his shirt and turns to leave. He pauses near the edge of the kitchen, one hand resting on the back of a high-backed barstool.

"You're about to age out soon boy," he sneers, cracking his knuckles. "Less than a year by my count."

He steps back toward us, slow and smug with that sick gleam in his eyes.

"I always wondered why none of the deals for you ever stuck. Every time I had a buyer, it fell through. Like some sort of bad luck followed you around like a fucking curse."

He snorts, half-amused, half-frustrated. "All worked out in the end I guess. Now I get to watch you leave. Ezekiel Malik Carter, a little scared boy with nowhere to go. How tragic."

Carlos's gaze slithers past Zeke and lands on me, curling hot and filthy at the edges. "You'll leave her here. And the best part?"

His smile sharpens into something out of a horror movie. "You'll spend every fucking day for the rest of your miserable excuse of a life wondering where I took her. What I did to her. Who I sold her to. Or even better, if I decided to keep her for myself."

Carlos narrows his eyes at Zeke. "And you won't be here to stop it."

Then he turns and walks off, boots tapping across the marble. No slamming doors. No yelling. Only the echo of him fading down the hall.

Zeke doesn't move. His fists are so tight I think his bones might break through his skin. His back rises and falls like every breath costs him.

But when he finally turns, it isn't rage on his face. Something worse is plastered there.

Grief.

Like he'd failed me. Like I was the only one bleeding and he couldn't stop it.

His eyes drop to my hand, still shaking from where the glass had sliced across the base of my palm. Blood dripping down my wrist, painting lines over skin that already feels bruised.

"Shit, Bells," he breathes, voice cracking just a little. "Here. Sit."

He pulls out a barstool and I sink onto it without thinking.

"I'm fine," I whisper even though the room is tilting.

He doesn't argue. He rips a thread of fabric from his shirt and takes my hand, wraps it in up, and secures it tight with a knot.

"You're not fine," he says, his voice low. "But you will be."

"I broke it," I choke out, tears stinging my eyes. "I broke it and you—"

"Shhh." His hands gather mine, careful not to brush the raw parts. Blood from both of us staining the space between. "You didn't deserve that, Bells. Not today. Not ever."

His voice gets softer. "And hey, you've got that recital next weekend, remember? No way I'm lettin' you walk in with belt marks. You're gonna show up like a star. Not like you crawled out of a damn war zone."

"But you—"

"Look at me."

I do.

"I've been through worse. You don't gotta carry this, Bells. Not by yourself."

I sob harder as he pulls me into his arms. I cling to my big brother like a lifeline, like if I let go, I'll drown in everything I can't say.

The hug is cut off by soft footsteps. "Zeke, Bella?"

Zeke lifts his head. "Come here, dude."

Dylan grabs one of the elegant kitchen stools and drags it next to mine, the wooden legs scraping across the icy marble.

He sits down and lets out a quiet breath as he leans his narrow shoulder against mine. His hand finds mine beneath the gleaming stone island, fingers brushing hesitantly at first, then gripping tighter.

We don't look at each other, we don't talk. That quiet pressure of his hand says everything: *I'm here. I've got you. We're not breaking today.*

And that's when it hits me. Dylan doesn't feel so little anymore. Eight, almost nine, and already holding the weight of too much. He should still be clinging to stuffed animals, not bracing his big sister's heart or learning how to be brave in the dark.

Not growing up this fast.

"I hate him," Dylan whispers.

"Yeah," Zeke rasps, still focused on my hand. "We all got scars 'cause of him. But he doesn't get to win. Not while I'm still breathing. Not while we've got each other."

CHAPTER ⟨8⟩
BELLA
AGE 13
MIAMI, FLORIDA

The air is thick with summer, the heat suffocating. The sun had finally slipped below the horizon, bleeding pink and gold across the sky, too beautiful for a night like this. Too soft for the nightmare we live in.

It's late, Zeke and I are sitting in my room talking as a terrified, high-pitched scream tears through the house.

"Dylan," I gasp, already on my feet.

Zeke moves faster than I've ever seen, ripping open my bedroom door and sprinting down the hall. I'm right behind him, my heart racing and lungs already burning.

We hit Dylan's room at the same time.

He's cornered. Pressed against the wall, eyes wide and bloodshot, body trembling like a leaf in a hurricane. His little hands are clenched into fists, but he's too small. Too frozen. And behind him, looming and smirking, is Vince.

I've seen him around the house before. That piece of shit. He is too close. His hands too low. His eyes gleaming with something vile.

"Back the fuck off him!" Zeke roars, voice tearing through the air.

Dylan whimpers.

I scream.

Zeke launches.

He hits Vince like a wrecking ball, fists flying with years of rage behind them. They crash to the floor, Zeke on top, punching, and snarling wild with fury. Blood sprays with every hit. Vince tries to cover his face, but Zeke isn't letting up.

I don't wait to see more. I bolt forward, grab Dylan's arm, and pull him into motion. He's shaking so hard he can barely walk, legs stumbling under him, but I get him down the hall and into my room.

I slam the door shut behind us and turn to face him.

"Dylan listen to me." I grip his shoulders, getting him to focus. "I need you to stay here. Don't leave my room, no matter what."

His chest is heaving, little eyes still wide and wet. "What's happening?"

"I don't know yet," I say, trying to stay calm even as panic claws at my throat. "But I'm going to go get Zeke and then we're getting the hell out of here. Do you understand?"

He nods fast and terrified.

"You're safe here in my room," I say, brushing a curl off his forehead. "I'll be right back. Just stay here, Dylan."

Then I slam the door shut and run.

When I get back to Dylan's room, Zeke is still on Vince, covered in blood. His face twisted in a rage. Vince is coughing, groaning, and his arms are limp. Zeke's knuckles are raw, one eye swollen shut.

"Zeke, stop!" I scream. "You'll kill him!"

He doesn't even hear me.

Carlos bursts in. "What the fuck is going on in here?!"

Zeke's fist slam down one more time right as Carlos lunges. He grabs him by the shoulders, yanking him off Vince like he weighs nothing. "Get off him, goddamnit!"

Zeke struggles but Carlos shoves him hard. Zeke hits the wall panting, his fists bloody. I rush in and grab him, pulling him back into the hallway.

"Zeke, it's okay. I got him. We need to go, now!" I breathlessly ramble.

A gunshot.

For a second, the house goes silent. Like the walls themselves couldn't believe what they heard.

"Ahhh!" Mariela wails.

Zeke and I run toward the screaming. We get to the master bedroom and Dylan's on the floor.

Small.

Still.

Blood spread beneath him, a dark halo against the cream carpet. The gun still clutched in his little hand. Too big. Too heavy.

Mariela is sobbing in Spanish. She's collapsed against the wall, hands over her face. Zeke lets out a noise I've never heard before—part gasp, part growl, part broken plea—and drops to his knees.

"No," I whisper, stumbling forward. "No, no, no, no."

But I know. Even before I touch him, I know. His eyes are open. Empty. His chest doesn't rise.

My hands hover over his body. I don't know what to do. What to fix. What to scream. Zeke presses his forehead to the floor beside Dylan's body, his bloodied fists balled so tight they shake.

"I hid him," I choke out. "I told him to hide. I told him we were going to get out. Zeke why would he—"

"Because he was fuckin' terrified," Zeke rasps. "And he thought that was all he had left."

Tears blur everything. I can feel the numbness setting in. He'd taken the gun. He'd taken the choice. Because we hadn't made it back fast enough.

Raised voices echo down the hall. Carlos and Vince cursing at each other. Something crashes. A door violently slams.

Silence.

The bedroom door bursts open. Carlos storms in like a loaded weapon, all twitching fury and barely leashed violence. His shirt is unbuttoned, stained with sweat and alcohol.

He looks into the room. His eyes land on Dylan's body and widen. A beat of shock. Then... nothing. No sadness or grief. Just cold calculation.

He turns to Zeke, picks up the gun, and points it at him. Mariela cries out. I scream. Zeke doesn't move.

"You just cost me the biggest sale of my fucking life, boy," Carlos hisses, slurring around the stench of whiskey. "Lost me a real important ally. Vince was a major customer. A major connection."

He stalks forward, pistol still aimed at Zeke's chest. "If I can't fix things with Vince," he says, lips curling back, "it'll be you sitting in a pool of blood next time. You understand?"

Zeke stays still. Carlos tilts his head, lips curving into a grotesque, slow smile.

"And once you're gone." His eyes slide to me. "There won't be anyone left to keep me from that sweet little ass of a sister you've been playing bodyguard for."

Carlos laughs. "No more big, scary protector. No more rules. Just me..." He licks his lips. "And Isabella."

Zeke moves so fast I barely see it. One second, he's frozen in shock, the next he lunges and cracks his fist across Carlos's face. The sickening crunch echos through the room as Carlos stumbles back, blood spraying from his nose.

"You slimy, twisted piece of shit," Zeke snarls, breath hitching with rage. "Say her name like that one more time, go ahead. I'll shove your teeth so far down your throat, you'll be choking on 'em."

Carlos raises the gun to Zeke's face. Zeke freezes.

"Brave now, aren't you, boy?" Carlos sneers, blood running down his lip. "You think you're some little hero?"

He steps closer. "You're not a man. You're not even a real threat. Just another mouth I'm legally required to feed. And trust me, the clock's ticking."

Zeke just stares him down. Face as cold as ice.

"I should put you down like the stray mutt you are," Carlos hisses, pressing the barrel forward, his finger ghosting the trigger.

"Next time you swing, boy." He laughs as he wipes his lip. "You better make it count. Because I will shoot back and I don't miss."

He holds Zeke's gaze for one blistering second, finger still brushing the trigger, before lowering the gun like he's not even worth the bullet.

"The two of you get the fuck out of my sight. You've cost me enough for one day. Mariela, call the cleaner. Let's get this shit cleaned up."

Zeke stands there, shaking. His fist still curled, blood drying on his knuckles. Rage rippling through him like heat off asphalt. He turns, grabs my hand, and leads me to my room without a word.

I sink onto the bed, clutching my mother's locket so tight it cuts into my palm. I curl inward and press my knees knees to my chest just trying to disappear.

Zeke doesn't speak at first. He just crosses the room, yanks the velvet chair from the corner, and jams it under the doorknob. Then he drops down in front of it, arms crossed, dark eyes locked on mine.

"I'm not leavin' you," he grits, voice raw and shaking. "I'm moving' into this goddamn room. You hear me?"

His chest rises hard and fast like he can't breathe.

"You're not alone. You'll never be alone again. I swear it on Dylan's fuckin' name," he says, tears cutting down his face. "That bastard may have taken Dylan. But he won't get to take you too. I won't let that happen. I won't."

I want to believe him. God, I want to believe him so badly it hurts.

He leans back against the door. "I should've gotten to him faster," he whispers, his voice barely holding. "Should've seen it. Should've known—"

His words break, breath catching in his chest. "But I'll die before I let him lay a finger on you, Bells. That's a promise."

And in that moment, drowning in grief and fury and heartbreak, I believe him. Because he's not just promising me safety. He's promising me a *war*.

And Zeke doesn't lose twice.

CHAPTER ⑨
ZEKE
AGE 17
MIAMI, FLORIDA

Carlos Lucero has always been a monumental sack of shit. But tonight, he graduated. Magna fucking cum laude with tassels and a standing ovation for services to human garbage.

It's been nine months since Dylan got hold of Carlos's gun and made a choice we never should've let cross his mind. Nine months since we found him on that bedroom floor—*bloody, broken, gone*— because we were too slow. Too late.

Carlos didn't pull the trigger. But he may as well have handed him the bullet. I've been waiting ever since. Waiting for the slip-up. The crack. The breath in the wrong direction. Just one excuse to snap his neck like the roach he is.

I don't sleep anymore. That luxury died with Dylan. Now I crash on the floor of Bella's room. Back to the wall. Chair jammed under the doorknob with my knife under the pillow. Laptop humming beside me.

She thinks I do it to help her feel safe.

And maybe I do. But mostly it's about control. Control of proximity. Control of protection. Control of the fact that Carlos and his slimy-ass friends can't walk through that goddamn door.

I mean they can. They'll just have to go through *me* first.

And let's be real. Carlos is scared of me now. I see it in the way his eyes twitch when I move too fast. The way he flinches when I reach for my plate at the dinner table.

God, I live for that. For the squirm.

He and Mr. Fancypants Vince have been thick as thieves lately, whispering like snakes in a pit. Vince, the new DA with his slick suits, shiny shoes, and a closet full of bones. Apparently, that promotion came gift-wrapped with a fat-ass donation from Carlos.

Real cute.

Vince plays the game, cocktail charm, power smiles, and all

that clean-cut predator bullshit. But I see past it. Men like him don't wear their monsters on their sleeves. They bury 'em behind legal briefs and empty courtrooms.

The two of them have been plotting. Whispering timelines. Buyer lists. Talking about her. About what happens once I'm gone.

It's a miracle I haven't gutted them both yet. They think when I turn eighteen, I'll just walk away into the sunset with my hoodie and my laptop. Like I'd ever fucking leave my sister behind.

Idiots.

It's late. Bella's not asleep. I can tell by the way she moves.

She's thinking.

Plotting.

Pissed.

She doesn't cry anymore. There's no softness left inside her. She's fourteen. Fourteen and already burned to ash on the inside.

"Zeke?"

I glance up from the glow of my screen. "Yeah?"

She turns toward me, one eye barely open. "Carlos said he's gonna get rid of you tomorrow."

My jaw tightens. "Yeah. Heard that."

"Said you won't be in their way anymore."

I fully look up from my laptop, my eyes cold as they meet hers. "I'll always be in their way, Bells."

She sits up, fire sparking in her steel-gray eyes. "Good. Because if I wake up and you're gone, I'm setting the kitchen on fire. I already stashed two lighters under the sink."

"That's my girl."

She shrugs. A half-smile flickers across her face. She's gotten stronger since Dylan. Gone is the kid who used to flinch at footsteps.

Now she throws matches.

Downside is she's got the attitude of a full-blown prima donna. Snark and all. Not that I'm completely mad about it. She's becoming a pint-sized me and I'd be lying if I said I wasn't a little proud.

"Carlos was outside our door last night," she says. "While you were in the shower."

My spine goes stiff. "You should've come and got me," I snap.

"Outta the shower?" She wrinkles her nose. "Yeah, no fucking thanks. I'd rather the first dick I see not be my big brother's."

"The first dick you see, little sister, is getting cut off by yours truly. I don't give a damn how romantic you think it is."

She scrunches her face again. "Gross, bro. You're full of rage tonight."

"You bring it outta me, little psycho. And watch your mouth."

"Takes one to raise one," she shoots back, grinning like the little devil child she is.

I shake my head, settling back against the wall. My hand resting on the blade under the pillow. "So what'd he say?" I ask.

"Nothing worth repeating. Just him and Vince with their, *'Zeke's almost out, yay the bitch'll finally be alone'* crap. You know, the usual."

"That's not usual, Bells. That's sick." My fingers return to the keyboard. "Try to get some sleep, sis."

"You too," she says around a yawn she tries to hide. "Hey, Zeke?"

"Yeah?"

"Happy early birthday."

11:59 PM

She's out. Finally.

Moonlight spills through the window, silver streaks slice across the marble like a prison dressed in pearls. The breeze slips through the cracks, soft but useless.

This room feels like a cage. I mean it's polished, quiet, and some might even say beautiful. But still a fucking cage.

Bella is curled up on her side. Her fists balled like she's ready to fight in her sleep. Even unconscious she doesn't let her guard down.

I glance at the clock glowing off my laptop screen.

Midnight. Eighteen.

"Happy birthday, Zeke," I mutter and close my eyes.

1:03 AM

Voices.

I'm up in a flash, knife in hand, laptop kicked aside, chair still jammed under the knob. I press my ear to the door. Carlos and Vince.

Of fucking course.

Vince's smooth voice drips through the wood. "...and I'm ready for tonight. Every time she walks by, I see her on her knees. That perfect little mouth all swollen and obedient."

He groans. "I want her broken. Bleeding. Knowing no one's coming. My balls have been blue just thinking about it."

Carlos laughs. "Glad we could work something out after the incident."

The incident? Oh. He means Dylan. This motherfucker just called my little brother an incident.

Vince hums like he's sipping wine. "Wasn't ideal, but it worked. One less mouth to worry about. Did Krolek get in touch about replacements?"

Carlos snorts. "Yeah. Met with his guy, Piotr, last week. Got a new shipment lined up by end of the month. But you let me worry about that," he laughs. "No more Zeke in the way so you can just focus on Bella. Paperwork's clean. The deal's done."

"Good," Vince says, sharper now. "Once he's gone, she's mine. And I want him to know it. Want him to leave this house knowing what I'm going to do to her."

"Hell Vince, let's give him a sendoff. Strap him to a chair. Make him watch while you break her in. I'll even hold her down for you."

I don't remember opening the door. Don't remember stepping into the hall. But I remember the words.

Strap him to a chair. Break her in.

After that, just red.

"Hey, Carlos," I say, voice calm as death. "Still breathing?"

He turns, his eyes wide.

"Let's fix that."

I slam him into the wall before he can make a sound. The blade slides under his ribs slow and mean. I drag it sideways like I'm gutting a pig at the fucking slaughter.

He screams.

I grin.

"What's wrong, my guy? No bedtime story this time? No creepy commentary about little girls?"

I twist the blade and yank it out. His shirt blooms red. "You like fear and power, don't ya? Let's see how brave you are with your intestines on the tile."

I stab lower this time and lean close to his ear. "Newsflash, Carlos, you don't have power. You never did."

Vince comes charging over with a lamp like he's in some damn Lifetime movie.

"Cute," I laugh as I duck, sweep his legs, and stomp on his hand until bones crunch under my boot like eggshells. He wails as I grab him by the hair and slam his face into the glass table.

Twice.

It shatters.

Sorry Mariela.

"Blue balls, right?" I growl in his ear. "Said you got blue balls just thinking about her?"

CRACK.

His nose caves. Blood sprays everywhere.

"You're lucky I don't cut your dick off and paint the walls with it."

He's choking now. Bleeding and barely conscious, but that's not good enough. I grab the back of his head and smash it into the marble floor. Again. And again.

"You don't get to breathe around her."

When I finally stop, he's twitching in a puddle of blood and teeth. Carlos is crawling. Or trying to crawl. I crouch beside Carlos real calm.

"You're not a predator. Not a king. Not even a man. You're just a maggot playing dress-up in a skin suit."

I raise the knife. He gurgles—blood bubbling like a clogged drain. I lean in close enough for him to see my eyes.

"Don't worry," I whisper. "You're not dying tonight."

I bite my lip, trying to hold back the cruel smile working its way out. "That's the punishment."

Then I drive the knife in one last time. "And that one's for Dylan."

"Zeke?!"

Bella. Shit. Here we go, cue dramatic teen in three, two, one.

"Oh my God. What the hell?!" we both yell in unison.

I wipe the blade off on Carlos's shirt. "Just takin' out the trash, sis."

"I can see that." She glances at Vince. "You missed some teeth. You're slipping."

She looks at Carlos, passed out in a puddle of blood. "Is he dead?"

"No. Not yet. I was just—"

"Dios mío, what did you do?"

Mariela appears out of nowhere. She sees the scene and gasps with her hand covering her mouth.

"They were gonna hurt Bella," I snap. "Planned it. Talked through every step like it was a team project. Scheduled it like some twisted business meeting, with snacks and fucking small talk."

Her face drains. "Go," she whispers. "Take my car. You must leave."

"Come with us."

She hesitates. "No. You go. Be free."

"You really think the cops are gonna roll up and hand you a medal for cleaning up their mess again? Wake up, Mariela. You're not safe here."

She drops her gaze. One hand rests on her stomach. Circles.

"Shit. You're pregnant?"

She nods, tears in her eyes. "This will be my penance. For all the times I didn't stop him. I'm so sorry, Zeke. Take her. Take your sister and run."

Bella grabs her hand. "Come with us. Please. You can't stay here. Not with him."

I run back to the room, grab the go-bag I've had packed for months. Laptop. Mr. Piggles. We meet back at the stairs. Mariela and

Bella are still hugging. I tug my sister's arm.

"Time to go, sis."

Mariela's white BMW is waiting for us. Bella slides into the passenger seat. I toss the bag in the back, climb in, and start the engine.

"Please tell me you have a plan," she mutters.

"No, I thought we'd wing it," I say, flipping on the headlights.

"So that's a yes?"

"Yes. I have a fucking plan."

We peel down the driveway. The gates swing open—*thanks, Mariela*—and we hit the empty road.

We make all of two blocks in silence before Bells pipes up.

"Where are we going?" she asks.

"To some people I trust."

"How safe is it?"

"Safe enough, I mapped this route out months ago. Granted, it was supposed to be tomorrow after I picked you up from school. But hey, improv."

She stares at me. "Months?"

"Since Dylan. Look, there's a lot you don't know, Bells. I'll tell you everything once we're somewhere safe."

"I knew it," she says, turning to look at me. "You were too calm lately. Was this what all the laptop-clicking was about? Your big plan?"

"Plans." I grin, tapping the steering wheel. "I've got plans. This one. The one behind it. And two more stacked under that."

She sighs. "Of course you do. Nerd."

We hit a stretch of road with no lights. Just trees and dark. She pulls her knees to her chest. "You were never gonna leave me behind."

I shake my head. "Never."

She leans her head against the glass. "Good. 'Cause I was already making a list of people's throats to slit."

"That's... sweet and deeply concerning, Bells."

"Learned from the best." She salutes.

"Psycho."

"Takes one to raise one."

CHAPTER ⑩
ZEKE
AGE 18
FORT MEYERS, FLORIDA

The tires crunch across gravel as the airstrip creeps into view. No signs. No lights, except a few hazy ones lining the runway. Just cracked asphalt, a rusted-ass hangar, and a shiny black jet sitting there like a loaded gun nobody's claiming.

I reach over and nudge Bella's shoulder. "Yo, sis. We're here."

She stirs, hugging Mr. Piggles as if he's luxury bedding, then blinks at the jet. "You stole a plane?"

I roll my neck, everything in me aching. "Didn't steal it. Paid for it."

"With what?" she snaps. "A punch and a dream?"

I shoot her a look. "No, smart-ass. I used their money. Drained it from creeps who deserved worse. Hacked the accounts and rerouted the funds. Long story."

Her eyebrows go up but she stays quiet.

"Basically, I'm a vigilante philanthropist. You're welcome."

"Yeah, if Robin Hood had a god complex and unresolved rage issues."

I shrug. "He probably did. Fucker wore tights and robbed rich people. I'm just better dressed."

"Debatable," she mutters.

"Keep runnin' that mouth and you're walking to New York."

"Wait, why the fuck are we going to New York?"

"Watch your mouth, Bells."

She crosses her arms. "Seriously. You pull me out of hell, bleed all over everything, magically conjure a damn jet, and now we're just moving across the country like this is some family road trip?"

"Glad to see you're catching on."

The wind cuts deep as we walk toward the jet. The smell of jet fuel in the air mixes with the weird, metallic taste of freedom. At the bottom of the stairs, three silhouettes wait.

One of them steps forward. His polished black shoes click on the tarmac. Gray suit, shoulder holster, hazel scanners for eyes. Every breath controlled. He walks like a guy who gives orders, not suggestions.

Nate.

He never told me which part of the alphabet soup he works for and I don't care. Pretty sure it's the FBI. One of their stupid embedded codes flagged me, and boom, Nate popped up like a ghost with a badge. Doesn't really matter. All that matters is that he's on my side. Helping me take scum off the earth one Black Book at a time.

"You're early."

"Plans changed. Punches were thrown. Carlos caught a knife to the gut." I shrug. "Unfortunately, a little drywall was harmed in the making of our escape."

Nate exhales, dragging a hand down his face. "Jesus, Zeke."

His eyes shift to Bella. "This her?"

"I have a name," Bella says, arms crossed like she's already over it.

Nate almost smiles. Almost. "Noted."

His voice drops. "Carlos?"

I shake my head. "Alive. Barely. Vince too. They'll wake up with concussions, broken ribs... maybe a collapsed trachea, and a definite need for stitches. Give or take."

Nate raises a brow. "So merciful. You do realize he's a fucking D.A., Zeke?"

"I was rushed."

And then there's Tex. Posted up by the wing, arms crossed, boots planted like the pavement owes him money. Late thirties, early forties maybe. Buzz cut dusted with silver. The kind of man who doesn't flinch when someone pulls a gun because he's already aiming two back.

His stare's locked on Bella. Hasn't said a word, hasn't moved a muscle. Just stands there radiating ex-hitman energy like it's a goddamn cologne.

Bella notices, of course she does. "You gonna keep eye-fucking me," she snaps, "or introduce yourself?"

"Mouth!" I growl, tossing her a glare.

She rolls her eyes like I'm the one out of pocket. Teenagers. I swear to God.

"Just making sure you're not a threat," Tex says.

Bella steps forward with her chin high. "Spoiler alert, I am."

I wedge myself between them before Bella decides to throw hands with the human version of a damn head shot.

"Tex doesn't talk much, Bells. Don't take it personal."

"I'm not," she mutters. "I just don't enjoy being looked at like I'm next on the menu."

From behind us, Nate chimes in. "He doesn't eat people. He just eliminates them. Quietly."

Bella raises a brow. "Wow. You surrounded yourself with really stable people."

I nod. "Welcome to the team."

"Yay," she says, voice dripping with sarcasm. "I feel so safe."

Nate claps his hands once. "Alright, snark squad load up. Wheels up before someone starts sniffing around. Eric, you ready?"

A voice fires back from the bottom of the stairs. "Was born ready. You're the ones dragging ass."

I glance over. Eric's leaning on the rail like it's a magazine cover shoot, full Top Gun mode. Black jeans. Scuffed boots. Faded Zeppelin tee under a leather jacket that's seen more years than Bella.

He's got a black tattoo curling up the side of his neck, something winged and sharp like it'd bite you back if you touched it. Aviators, of course, because subtlety is officially dead.

Bella slows her step. "That's our pilot?" she says not even trying to hide the judgment.

Eric pushes off the rail and strolls toward. "You want smooth, fast, and invisible? I'm your guy."

Bella eyes him up and down. "You sure?"

He grins like the devil just gave him a five-star rating. "Honey, I've flown through sandstorms, cartel airspace, and one hell of an ex-wife's divorce party. This? This is a damn coffee run."

I nod. "He's chaos. But he's efficient chaos."

"Air Chaos. Trademark pending," Eric laughs as he pulls something small and sleek from his jacket. "Gotta deal with your loose end. Give me a sec."

Bella frowns. "Loose end?"

Nate tilts his head. "Say goodbye to Mariela's car."

"Wait, he's gonna—" Bella starts.

A dull thud shakes the ground as heat flashes across the tarmac.

I shrug. "It was either that or leave behind a *please arrest us* starter kit."

"Plus the two of you have to die," Nate adds.

Eric strolls back over, casually brushing ash from his jacket like he just flicked a cigarette and didn't set a whole damn car on fire.

"Handled," he says. "Two dead teenagers. Let's fly."

Bella looks at me as if I've officially lost my mind.

I grin. "It'll be fine. I promise."

CHAPTER ⑪
BELLA
AGE 14
FORT MEYERS, FLORIDA

The plane's got buttery leather seats, a few recliners, a sleek little bar in the corner, and enough room to seat maybe twelve. There is a flat screen on the wall, drinks tucked into crystal-clear holders, and a low table set with snacks like someone thought this was some sort of party.

I slide into a seat across from Zeke and shoot a look at the suit guy.

"Alright," I say, folding my arms. "Let's play a game. It's called *Who the Hell Are You People?* You first, Men's Warehouse. FBI? CIA? PTA?"

"Whatever acronym you need me to be," the guy Zeke called, *Nate*, answers back.

I narrow my eyes. "So that's a yes."

He shrugs, annoyingly calm. "You asked who I am. Not what I file under."

I turn to Zeke, deadpan. "Is he always like this?"

"Yup," Zeke says. "All mystery and murder."

The quiet sniper dude finally lifts a finger like he's in class. "Not CIA."

"Awesome," I say, leaning back with a scoff. "So we've got a maybe-fed, a sniper statue that hasn't blinked since we got on the plane, a Batman-wannabe for a brother, and a pilot who for sure has bodies hidden in the trunk of his car. Totally normal."

"Told you I had a plan," Zeke smirks like I didn't just name-drop every reason I'll need meds by the time I'm twenty.

I kick my feet up on the seat across from me, not giving a single damn about manners. "Yeah? Now would be a great time to share it, mastermind."

Zeke nods at Mr. Acronym, who hands me a black folder. I flip it open. Two passports. Two IDs. They're still warm like they just came off a secret printer hidden in the basement of the Pentagon. My eyes skim the names.

Isabella Marie Blackwood.

Ezekiel Malik Blackwood.

"It's my mom's maiden name," Zeke says, quieter now.

I pause for a second. Just a second. Then I nod. I don't ask anything else. Don't make a joke.

Not this time.

"Cool," I say quietly. "Guess I'm somebody new now."

Zeke leans back. "Started laying the groundwork before Dylan... but that night?" he pauses, eyes dark. "That's when everything snapped into place. That's when I stopped waiting."

I look at him for a beat.

He's different now. He's sharper, angrier. I see it in his eyes. The promise he made. The one he thinks he owes Dylan.

"So what now?" I ask.

"Now," he says, "We disappear. New names. Better lives. You train and learn how to move in the shadows. Nate's got the gear. Tex'll watch your six."

"And you?"

Zeke grins like he's already picked his first target. "I'm gonna teach you how to gut monsters in silk suits hiding in penthouses wrapped in bulletproof glass. How to bankrupt 'em so deep their great-grandkids are born broke."

His eyes darken. "We're gonna burn it all down. For Dylan. For every kid nobody looked for."

He leans forward just slightly. "And don't worry, we have help. From our... let's just say newly acquired criminal associates."

I raise an eyebrow. "You have associates?"

"I have leverage," he says. "You'll see later."

"Good enough, I'm too tired to question it anyway."

I close the folder, lean back, and let my head hit the seat.

Manhattan, New York

The plane lands with a jolt that jerks me so hard I nearly bite through my tongue.

Rude.

So much for mister *'this is a damn coffee run'*. Gold star officially revoked. I blink awake, neck wrecked, and my spine screaming in five different languages.

My breath fogs the window as I glare out at the skyline. New York. Gray sky. Glass towers cutting through low-hanging clouds.

We get off the plane and a gust of wind hits me like it's trying to pick a fight. I tug my hoodie over my head, middle finger already mentally extended at the weather.

Waiting for us is—*shocker*—a sleek blacked-out SUV. Because apparently Zeke's entire new aesthetic is *Batman, but make it extra*.

Tex slides into the driver's seat without a word. Silent and surgical like he was the entire flight.

God, if I didn't know Zeke's parents died in that plane crash, I'd honestly think Tex was his dad. They've got the same dark eyes and deep brown skin, the same strong jaw, and that whole don't-mess-with-me face that looks carved out of stone. His quiet, deadly, protective thing is giving overqualified parental sniper energy.

Mr. Acronym takes the passenger side, probably mapping out every exit and escape route in Manhattan.

Zeke and I climb into the back. The seats are heated. Which, thank God, because my soul is frozen from the wind.

Outside the tinted windows, New York starts to wake. Steam rises from grates like the city's exhaling secrets. Street carts sputter to life. Horns blare their battle cries. And people charge through crosswalks with caffeine and zero regard for human decency.

We come to a stop in front of a building, all black glass, steel, and sharp edges. Forty-one stories of pure flex. It looks like it whispers power and signs its emails with a kill count. It's the kind of place that screams penthouse villain energy minus the fluffy white cat.

Zeke leans forward, voice low. "Top floor's ours."

I squint at him. "I'm sorry you own a Manhattan penthouse?

You're seventeen."

"We," he corrects. "And, I'm eighteen now. Happy birthday to me, remember?"

"Right," I mutter. "Because that makes this way less insane."

He just chuckles. "And this isn't just a penthouse, Bells. This is a *Daniel Barinov* building."

I blink. "Okay, two things. One, *we*? And two, what the hell is a *Daniel Barinov* building?"

Zeke sighs. "Yes, we own the penthouse, Bells."

He pinches the bridge of his nose. "And Daniel Barinov is only one of the biggest architects on the planet. Guys a certified genius. His buildings are fortresses with museum-level aesthetics. Security, structure, silence, all the things we need."

I just stare at him.

He rolls his eyes like I've officially offended him. "He builds safe houses disguised as luxury, Bells. So, when a penthouse opened up in one of his properties, I had Nate wire the money and had the guys fix it up just how I wanted."

I gape at him. "What money, man?! You keep saying that like you've got a checking account at the Bank of Vengeance."

He lifts a brow. "I mean... you're not wrong."

I blink again. "Zeke."

"I've been draining Carlos and his buyers since the first time I realized they were selling kids. I was twelve. Megan, my first little foster sister, was six."

"Six?" I ask quietly. I shouldn't be surprised. Carlos was always a fucking creep.

He nods, gaze steady. "Yeah. He listed her like property. I found the wire transfer. That's when it started. Every account I hacked. Every deal I tanked. Every shell company I blew up from the inside. All of it."

"You're telling me you're using stolen money from creepy children buyers to buy us a plane and an apartment in New York?"

"Poetic, right?"

I pause. "Dark."

"Fair," he agrees. "Also, it turns out my parents had more

money than God. So that helped."

My eyes narrow. "Wait, what?"

"Carlos had it hidden. Some secret account overseas. I hacked it last year and took back every dollar."

He looks at me, eyes steady. "It was never his to begin with. So yeah... this place? It's ours now."

I stare at him. "You bought a plane, a penthouse, and probably a small country with trafficker scumbag money and mystery inheritance cash?"

"Yep."

"Jesus."

"You're welcome."

When the doors slide open, I seriously forget how to breathe. Double-height ceilings with floor-to-ceiling windows that swallow the entire skyline. The sun's casting gold over the fog and clearly trying to impress us. A beautiful freaking spiral staircase, gleaming dark wood floors, and furniture that looks like the place dreams go to sleep.

The fireplace crackles low, filling the room with a cozy warmth. There is art on the walls. Real art. The kind that tells a story and not just fills a space.

"So, you had the guys build us the actual Batcave," I mumble.

Zeke drops his bag by the couch. "It's secure. Sensors on every entrance. Triple encryption on the system. Panic room in the master closet if shit hits the fan."

He shoots me a look before I can even open my mouth. "And drop the Batman jokes. You're not as funny as you think, Bells."

"Whatever you say, Bruce Wayne." I salute, already collapsing onto the couch. "I'm gonna nap here on your vigilante furniture, and when I wake up, you're answering everything. And giving me the tour of the Batcave."

Zeke rolls his eyes but grins, "Deal."

I wake up a few hours later, warm and disoriented, cocooned in what might be the softest white plushy blanket on earth with Mr.

Piggles in my arms. For a second, I forget where I am. Then the skyline punches into view through the giant window and everything clicks.

Right. Gotham tower. Zeke's insane penthouse. I'm sorry, *our* insane penthouse, in a fancy Daniel Bari-something building.

Zeke's at the table across the room, typing on one of his laptops like he's decoding the matrix in real time. Tex is by the window, arms crossed. His eyes scanning the skyline like he expects it to shoot back. Mr. Acronym's nowhere in sight, probably busy alphabetizing weapons or whatever the man does for fun.

I stretch, yawn, then say loud enough to echo, "Okay. I'm rested. I want the tour, the plan, and pancakes. Preferably in that order."

Zeke doesn't even look up. "Morning, sunshine."

"Don't test me," I say, tossing the blanket off. "You promised answers. Start talking, Bruce Wayne."

He finally glances up, one eyebrow raised. "Tour first?"

"Obviously. I need to know which room I'm claiming before I commit to this vigilante sleepover."

Mr. Acronym and Tex give me the actual tour, not Zeke.

"Zeke came up with the design," Mr. Acronym says as he leads me toward the kitchen. "We just followed his specs. He wanted it ready. Said it had to be perfect when the three of you got here."

He says it like it's no big deal. As if wiring a surveillance hub, installing a massive panic room, and building a hidden armory was just another weekly errand.

The kitchen and living room is first on the tour. Double island. Built-in espresso bar. A fridge that could totally fit a body inside. There's an armory tucked behind a fingerprint-locked wine cabinet.

Like these guys actually drink wine. Should have put it behind a whiskey barrel or some shit like that.

I raise an eyebrow. Tex shrugs. "Multi-functional."

A hidden surveillance command center, reminiscent of something you'd find at NASA, is concealed behind a bookshelf in the living room.

The view of New York from the living room is incredibly beautifu. But it pales in comparison to the rooftop.

Zeke has created an urban oasis up there. A terrace complete with a pool, string lights, elegant loungers, and tables that all overlook the entire, sprawling city. It's a spectacular sight that genuinely steals your breath straight out of your lungs.

"I could totally live up here," I say.

We come back inside. But before we continue, I stop.

"Why now?" I ask quieter. "Why didn't you get us out earlier? You said this place was supposed to be for the three of us."

"We had to make sure everything was in place," Mr. Acronym says after a quick pause. "Pulling you out too early could've tipped off the entirely wrong people. Carlos and Vince had ties. Real ones. Big ones that we still need to find. Carlos was being wa—"

"Zeke was still a minor," Tex cuts him off. "The plan was always to get the three of you out when he turned eighteen. That was the safest window."

He gives Mr. Acronym a grumpy look.

"Zeke is good at what he does, Bella," Tex continues. "You don't understand how important the intel he's gathering really is to the final goal. Dylan's death was unexpected and it escalated things. Quickly."

Something about the way he cut him off and the rehearsed sound in his voice seems off. I narrow my eyes for a second, but neither of them move. They're not lying. Not exactly. But I can feel it. They're hiding something.

We get to the last door on the tour. My room. It's gorgeous. Big windows with light wood floors. The kind of bed you throw yourself into face-first and never leave.

I glance at the wall and it punches me in the gut.

One whole side is a hand-painted mural. Razorback Stadium. Crimson and white roaring through the crowd. The bleachers are packed, the sky overhead a deep navy fading into twilight with stadium lights casting a golden glow over the field.

The Razorback mascot charges across the turf and flags wave high above the scoreboard. The colors bleed together, bold reds, smoky shadows, and that electric shimmer of game night magic. You can almost hear the band, the cheerleaders, the hogs being called.

It feels like home.

"He remembered," I whisper, fingertips brushing my lips. "I can't believe it."

Mr. Acronym nods back in silence.

I stand there staring. A small smile tugging at my mouth.

"Of all the things, he remembered this," I whisper, a single tear escaping down my cheek.

I find Zeke back in the main room, sitting at the long marble table with a half-empty mug in front of him. He looks up when I walk in, and for once he doesn't joke.

"You good?"

I nod, sliding into the chair across from him. "Yeah. Your psycho sniper and Mr. Acronym gave a killer tour. The mural was..."

I stop myself and look out the window for a second. "Thanks, Zeke."

"You're welcome," he says, a flicker behind his eyes. Then he leans forward, arms braced on the table. "You wanted answers," he says as he shuts his laptop. "So here they are."

Then, he just lets it all out. No warm-up. No sugar-coating. The whole damn thing dropped on the table like a live grenade.

There are these Black Books of criminal families. Each one packed with the kind of dirt that could ruin legacies, bury empires, and start wars. Names, money trails, deals, everything the powerful want buried. Zeke has all of them.

But that's not the point.

"They're leverage," he explains. "I'm not trying to run their world. I don't give a shit about their empires. I'm using them to blow the real one to pieces."

His eyes stay locked on mine. "The Black Books buy us access. Buy us protection. Buy us time. We squeeze them, and in return they give us what we need—intel, logistics, clean routes, secure jobs. They hand us the worst of the worst, Bells. The ones who don't even deserve to breathe."

Zeke doesn't hesitate. "To find the people like Vince and Carlos. The traffickers. The buyers. The ghosts hiding in the cracks while everyone looks the other way."

His jaw flexes. "The families that swear they're not part of it, but they are. Every damn one of them."

He leans back slightly, eyes still sharp. "I use the Black Book families to hunt worse ones."

Zeke pauses just long enough to let it sink in. "As long as they play nice, I don't release their books. They run small ops for us, intel, location drops, sometimes cleanups. Mostly muscle when we're pulling kids out of bad situations."

His tone drops to something more calculated. "I give 'em just enough pieces of their books back to make them feel like they're still in control."

He shrugs. "They're not."

From across the room, Mr. Acronym coughs under his breath.

Tex lets out a low laugh. "They think he's generous."

"Yeah, well... they think they're getting their books back," he mutters, leaning forward. "I keep a copy."

Then he shrugs again, casual as hell. "I'm not a fucking idiot."

I stare at him. "You're blackmailing crime families and running an underground war all while failing trig?"

"Pretty much yeah. Except I passed trig," he says with a devilish grin.

"You're insane."

He leans in and winks at me. "Takes one to raise one."

"It's not about revenge anymore, Bells. It's a mission. A war." He looks at me. "We're building something. For Dylan. For the kids nobody saved. And the ones no one's even looking for."

I sit back trying to take it all in. The books. The families. The money. The quiet war Zeke's been fighting while I thought he was just keeping us alive.

"And how did they come in?" I ask nodding towards the others.

"O'Malley's book," Zeke says. "That's what flagged me. Some code buried deep in their financial statements." He nods towards Nate. "Instead of shutting me down, Nate reached out. Started messaging me. Testing me. Then the planning started."

A quick nod toward Tex. "He was already working with him as his personal guard, sniper, whatever title you want to give it. Together, we built the network."

Zeke's eyes meet mine. "And Project Dylan was born."

Tex smirks. "Not at first. Don't let him get away with rewriting history. What was it again...?" He tilts his head like he's scrolling through a mental file. "*Operation ZeroTrace.* That's what you tried to name it before Dylan, right? Sounded like a sweaty gamer clan."

"Wait, you actually named it that?" My eyes widen and I can't help but laugh. "Oh my God, please tell me there's a logo. Did you make merch? PowerPoint slides?"

Tex grins, the bastard. "Bet he had a theme song."

Zeke scowls, his jaw ticking. "I was fourteen."

"So, what made you pick them?" I ask. "Why those families?"

"Because I did my homework," he says. "Picked the families with baggage. Ones who lost daughters. Got burned by trafficking ops. People who already hate that world because it cost them."

He glances toward the skyline. "They agreed to help to earn their books back. On our terms with our conditions."

His voice hardens. "We don't touch their other business— drugs, weapons, smuggling. As long as it doesn't touch kids, we let it slide."

"You're serious?"

"They stay in their lane," he says, hard as stone. "No children getting hurt. No exceptions. The second they cross that line, I fucking bury them."

I look at Mr. Acronym and wait for the moral outrage. But it isn't there. Just a clenched jaw and an exhale that feels like it's been sitting in his lungs for years.

"My sister was taken," he whispers through a sniffle. "Seventeen. She was raped. Sold. Made it home but... not really. She killed herself a week before her eighteenth birthday."

The words drop like a hammer.

"I'm so sorry."

He nods once, eyes fixed on nothing. "I don't give a damn about drugs or art heists or blood diamonds. I care about what they do to kids like her. Kids like you."

I look between them, "So your grand plan was to what? Hand

a teenage hacker with a god complex a Glock and call it good?"

Tex raises an eyebrow, not even fazed. "To be fair, we didn't give him a gun until he turned seventeen."

I gasp, hand to my chest in full dramatic horror. "Oh. Wow. That makes it so much better."

Tex huffs a laugh. "Wasn't exactly the plan. But let's not pretend your brother isn't a brilliant little asshole."

Mr. Acronym adds, "He's also saved lives. A lot of them. With Zeke, the outcomes outweigh the ethics most days."

"We can't save the whole world, Bells. Never could," Zeke says looking at me, tired but steady. "But we can save the kids they try to erase. The ones nobody's looking for. And that's enough for me."

I let it sit. Let the silence stretch while my brain catches up with my heart. Then another question hits me sideways.

"Why New York?"

Zeke exhales. "Because New York's a cesspool."

"That's not an answer. That's an insult."

He half-smiles, just barely. "Millions of people always moving with constant turnover, noise, and chaos. You can disappear here, Bells. You can hunt here."

"And that makes it perfect for you?" I ask.

Zeke nods. "Exactly. Bigger the crowd, easier it is for monsters to hide." He glances out the window. "And easier for us to catch 'em when they slip."

There's something they're not saying. I file it away.

And then I nod, quiet.

"For Dylan," I say. "I'm in."

CHAPTER ⑫
BELLA
AGE 16
MANHATTAN, NEW YORK

Outside, the city is cloaked in autumn. Trees dripping in amber and rust, crunchy leaves skittering under boots like tiny paper secrets.

Inside, the penthouse glows. Not because it needed the help. Zeke lives in luxury, just the the stripped-down and bulletproof kind. No clutter. No softness. He'd still rather chew glass than buy a throw pillow.

But thanks to Ellie, it's been upgraded beautifully for my birthday. She's got vanilla-and-rain scented candles scattered all around the penthouse. She put ivory pumpkins ribboned in black velvet along the mantel and a slim black banner in golden script that simply reads *Sixteen!*

Over the table, she has a sculptural arch of matte-black and champagne balloons climbing like evening wear. It's threaded with silk ribbon and a few smoked-glass bats so delicate they look hand-blown.

There's even a tower of Fifth Avenue cupcakes on an onyx stand, dark chocolate and blackberry under a whisper of gold leaf.

It's extra.

It's beautiful.

It's Ellie.

"Um, El... I think Vogue's fall issue would like its lighting back."

Ellie's perched on my couch like she owns the deed. Her blonde curls are loose and glossy. Her sweater dress is Gucci, of course, and her knee-high boots scream *Daddy paid for this.*

She's rich, spoiled, dramatic, and my best friend in the entire world.

"You like it?" she asks, practically vibrating. "I was going for Upper East Side Halloween goddess, but with just a hint of emotional damage. You know, to honor your brand."

I raise a brow. "You commissioned a balloon sculpture."

"I commissioned three," she squeals. "One just wasn't enough."

"You're crazy."

"And you're sixteen!" she declares, pitching a velvet pillow at my head. "Which means you're legally required to start sneaking out for dangerous makeouts and questionable decisions."

"Define dangerous."

She winks. "Anything involving tongue and/or a motorcycle."

Zeke hated the idea of me going to school. He wanted me locked away in Gotham Tower, safe behind firewalls and bulletproof glass, learning how to dismantle pedo rings in between spelling tests. He gritted his teeth so hard I thought he'd crack a molar.

But eventually, I wore him down. He gave in. Made me swear that I'd keep training if he sent me to school.

I agreed and he enrolled me at St. Lyra's Prep. A school so elite it probably has its own Black Amex. Legacy last names roamed the marble halls like royalty. Every girl had a signature blowout, a curated trauma, and an Instagram following bigger than most European nations.

That's where I met Ellie Whitmore. Back row of our freshman philosophy elective, quietly trying to exist. New notebook. Fresh pens. Chipped pink nail polish I'd redone three times the night before, like if I could just get the edges perfect maybe I wouldn't feel like I was about to unravel.

Then she appeared. Blonde curls. Gucci sweater dress. An energy so unapologetically bright it made the air around her feel warmer. She slid into the seat beside me as if we'd been doing this forever.

"*Sooo,*" she said, eyeing me like I was a limited-edition bag she already decided to buy, "*you've got that whole mysterious loner thing going. Deadpan stare, silence, excellent boots. I'm intrigued.*"

"*I bite. Occasionally.*"

Her eyes lit up. "*Ugh, finally someone with bite and cheekbones.*"

I glanced at her, more amused than I wanted to be. "*You always sit next to girls who look like they might fake a seizure to get out of a group discussion?"*

"Only the ones with potential," she said with a wink.

Then she held out her hand like she was offering me a Chanel contract. *"Ellie Whitmore. Soon to be the next Vixens' dance team captain. Trust fund certified. Your new bestie, unless you've got two left feet, in which case, this won't work."*

"I used to dance," I said. *"Haven't in a while."*

She arched a perfectly groomed brow. *"Tragic. We're fixing that. Tryouts are next week. Show up, shake your ass, and blow them away."*

I didn't say yes but I showed up. We both made the team, danced our asses off, became co-captains, and somewhere along the way became best friends.

She doesn't know what I really do when I skip sleepovers or sneak out after parties. She thinks I'm dancing, or dating, or just being chaotic. And that's okay. Because she sees the version of me that I sometimes forget is real. The one who's just... Bella.

Tex is at the stove, flipping pancakes and humming under his breath. Mr. Acronym's by the window, reading something on his tablet with the same expression he'd probably use to dismantle a government.

I'm halfway through my second pancake when Zeke tosses a black velvet box through the air. I catch it without flinching.

"Happy sixteen, Bells. Let's keep the body count low till at least noon."

Inside is a slim, balanced, matte-black blade with my initials carved into the hilt. A new beginning disguised as a birthday gift.

"You said when I turned sixteen—"

"You shadow tonight," Zeke cuts in, voice dropping low so Ellie can't hear. "That's it. No contact. No freelancing. You stay close and you follow my word like it's the fucking gospel, you hear me?"

"I won't screw it up."

"You'd better not," Tex calls over. "I just polished your gear."

Ellie walks over and claps like it's a movie ending. "Hate to break up whatever intense brooding vibe this is, but we need to get ready for your party."

"El, the party doesn't start for like... twelve hours."

She gasps. "Exactly. Hair. Nails. Outfit changes. Emotional prep. Do you think perfection happens on accident?"

The last of the laughter fades around eleven. There's cupcake crumbs on the counter, a trail of black glitter on the floor, and two girls from St. Lyra's still giggling by the elevator and taking selfies like it's some exclusive club. One of them waves. I fake a smile.

Ellie is doing her rounds and being a proper hostess—hugging, air-kissing, whispering secrets no one will remember in the morning. Her heels clicking on the marble.

Zeke's in the corner looking like he's regretting every decision that led to this moment, including letting Ellie convince him to host the party here.

He said no guests. Ellie heard *let's make it chic.*

She doesn't get it. Not fully. She knows the broad strokes. We came from a bad foster home, we got out, and that Zeke does something in tech with Nate and makes a shit ton of money. She's convinced Tex is in finance, like her dad.

"I mean, he's got the whole mysterious ex-military hedge fund thing going," she whispered once like it was a conspiracy theory. *"Silent. Intense. Probably manages billion-dollar portfolios and doesn't believe in therapy."*

I didn't correct her.

She thinks this place is just a moody penthouse filled with high-functioning introverts and one guarded girl who refuses to talk about the time before freshman year. Sometimes she jokes that it's like some dark, minimalist Upper East Side reboot of *New Girl.*

"Three broody hot guys, one dancing baddie, and a killer view? Honestly, Netflix should call," she said once, curling up on the couch.

But she doesn't understand why Zeke always positions himself facing the door. Why Tex scans the room like he's cataloging threats. Why Nate doesn't blink for long stretches of time. Or why none of them ever talk about what they do.

She's never seen the weapons. Never stumbled onto a mission file or caught sight of anything suspicious. They're careful around her. Always have been.

She just wanted tonight to be beautiful. For me. And it was.

"Okay," Ellie says, swaying toward me with a soft smile and slightly smudged lipstick. "Everyone's out, I managed to clean up without breaking a nail. No one cried or got arrested, so I'm feeling pretty good about myself."

I huff a quiet laugh.

"You good?" she says squeezing my arms gently.

"I'm good."

"You sure? You get quiet like this when something's eating at you."

"Just tired," I say, not even a lie.

"Text me tomorrow," she replies. "Or tonight if you go out. I want updates. I'm talking full detail and outfit pics."

"Promise."

She pulls me into a long, warm and tight hug. "I love you, Bella," she whispers.

"I love you too."

Zeke waits until the elevator doors close behind her before moving. "Finally," he mutters, sweeping through the room and unlocking the wine cabinet armory. "What part of no civilians was unclear?"

Tex shrugs, "Could've been worse. No one tripped an alarm, nobody died, and Ellie didn't find the gun safe."

"Yet."

Mr. Acronym doesn't say a word. He just stands, buttons his suit jacket, and nods once like we just flipped a switch from family to mission.

Zeke turns to me. "Go change, it's time to go."

12:30 AM
Undisclosed Warehouse
Brooklyn, New York

The chill punches the breath from my lungs the second I step out of the SUV. Gone is the warmth, the glitter, the soft pulse of birthday music. Now it's concrete, steel, and shadows.

Tex leads us through the side door of the warehouse, silent as a ghost. Fluorescent lights buzz above, casting long, shadows on the floor. We turn a corner and walk down a long corridor. At the end of it, Tex opens a metal door into what looks like an old office.

Inside there's a man tied to a chair under a single overhead light. He is bleeding. Streaks of blood turning his blonde hair a little strawberry. Hands zip-tied behind his back. One of his eyes is already swollen shut.

The guy doesn't look scared, he looks pissed.

Zeke walks in slowly, pulling off his gloves with deliberate calm. Mr. Acronym's near the back wall, tapping something into his tablet like he's logging inventory. Tex stands in the corner, arms folded, one foot pressed against the wall just waiting for a green light.

I hang back in the shadows.

The man in the chair lifts his head and spits blood at Zeke's feet. Zeke stops. Looks down. Then slow, almost lazy, he draws his gun from his waistband. The guy opens his mouth to speak. Something in German comes out.

BANG.

Zeke shoots him in the knee. The sound is thunder in the silence. The man screams, his whole body jerking against the chair.

Zeke tilts his head. "Wrong language."

The man curses, screaming in German. I catch *Mädchen*. Girl, I think? Probably need to brush up on my German.

BANG.

Zeke fires again. The second knee. Gross. The scream turns into something raw, something feral.

He crouches in front of him. "You moved them through Newark. I already know that."

He leans in just slightly, eyes like knives. "What I don't know is where they're going next, and where they're being held. And you're gonna tell me, because this time?"

His voice drops to a razor's edge. "I'm not fucking playing."

The man is sobbing now, choking on his own spit. Zeke grabs his chin, forcing eye contact.

"Where are the girls?"

Silence.

Blood is pooling beneath the chair, slick and fast. His legs are ruined, useless slabs of meat, and the pain's finally carved through whatever bravado he's got left.

Zeke points his gun at the man's crotch. "One more time. Where are the girls?"

The man's entire body shakes. "Q-Queens," he stammers. "Warehouse 27-B off Hunters Point. Please, oh God. I-I swear please, I told you everything."

"How many?"

"E-e-eight I think."

"Ages?"

"I don't know man, it was a mixed bag," he says like these girls are just a bag of potato chips.

"Think harder," Zeke says, shoving the gun closer to the man.

"Ok, ok, ok, please. The oldest is probably seventeen, youngest maybe seven."

"When's the sale?"

"Two days from now. Nine o'clock."

Zeke straightens. Dusts off his jeans.

"Now see," he says lightly. "That wasn't so hard, was it?"

The man whimpers. Zeke looks at Tex and gives him a small nod. Tex moves, silent as death. The man starts praying in German.

Zeke turns to me, unbothered, voice flat. "You get all that?"

I nod.

"Good." He holsters his gun, already moving. "We're not done yet. Now you get to learn how to plan an op."

We turn. Behind me, light. Just a clean, controlled flash. I barely hear the shot, but I feel the silence that follows.

CHAPTER ⑬
ZEKE
AGE 19
WAREHOUSE 27-B
QUEENS, NEW YORK

There's a reason I never wanted her here. Not because she couldn't handle it. Because she could. And that's what scares the living shit out of me. Warehouse 27-B looks like every other godforsaken hole we've hit—rotting siding, busted cameras, and the smell of desperation baked into the walls. But tonight, it's different.

Tonight, she's here.

Two guards down. Two left. One buyer. One seller.

"East corridor's clear," Tex says in my ear. *"Last two are yours."*

I slow my steps just enough to catch their voices. Morales and the seller are still arguing over shipment weight and payment splits like this is a goddamn stock exchange and not a trafficking deal.

Bella's breath hitches in my ear. She isn't out here with me. She's in the van, headset on and watching every hijacked feed we could rip from their system. I wasn't about to bring her into a mission where the target wasn't already zip-tied and crying.

"Morales on the left," Nate mutters over the comms. *"Suit. Smug asshole. Cartel crest tattooed on his neck. Seller's the twitchy one near the crate. Go slow."*

I step out of the shadows, gun raised. "Evening, gentlemen."

They both spin. Morales sizes me up with the kind of look that's gotten men killed in parking lots. I let him have it. The moment, the illusion, the last breath.

"You're Elias Morales," I say. "Cartel accountant, part-time bottom-feeder, soon-to-be floor decoration."

He scoffs. "You think you're funny?"

"I think I'm hilarious," I shrug. "And I also think that your head exploding might be the highlight of my night."

He lifts his gun.

CRACK.

Tex's shot slices through the air from across the street. One bullet, left eye. Morales drops.

"Told you," I mutter.

I hear Bella gasp over the comm.

The seller stumbles back like a busted Roomba, keys rattling as he spins to run. I lift my Glock. "Ah-ah. Take one more step and I'll turn your kneecaps into confetti."

He freezes. Smart rat.

"See that door?" I nod toward the container. "Open it."

He fumbles with the keys and misses the lock once. Twice. Third time, *CLICK.* The metal groans open as the stench hits. Rot. Sweat. Human waste. Misery sealed in steel. I step up behind him and press the muzzle to the back of his skull.

"Congrats. You've officially entered the worst moment of your life. And lucky for you, I'm your tour guide."

"Zeke," Nate cuts in over comms. *"For the love of God stop playing with your food."*

"Not playing. Just letting it marinate."

The guy whimpers. Fucking pussy.

Eight girls. Cramped. Filthy. Silent. Eyes wide and limbs trembling. The smallest one's curled in the lap of the oldest like a broken doll. She's got blood smeared across her bare legs, staining the hem of a tattered Minnie Mouse nightgown.

She can't be more than *six.*

I raise my voice just enough to carry through comms. "Nate," I say, eyes locked on the seller. "You getting this?"

There's a beat of silence. Then Nate's voice comes through, low, cold, no hesitation. *"Well, at least we don't have to make a second stop tonight. You know what to do. For Dylan."*

I nod once. No filters. No mercy. Just reality. Brutal. Unedited. And now, fucking personal.

"We need medics, clean clothes, hot food. You know the drill," I say calmly.

"Already on it," he replies.

I step closer to the seller, slow and steady. He's trembling, eyes darting toward the open container. Toward the blood, the stench. The wreckage of what he sold. I lean in just inches from his ear. Pretty sure he just pissed his fucking pants.

"That little one in the corner," I say quietly. "The one in the Minnie Mouse nightgown."

He doesn't answer. Just shakes.

"She can't be more than six."

His mouth opens, excuse, denial, plea. I don't care.

"Dylan was *nine*," I say

He freezes. Confused. Scared.

"That's the line," I whisper. "That's the rule."

I lean in, voice steady as the barrel against his skull. "You don't come back from breaking it. You don't get to go to our lovely little bunker and play chess with all your sick pedo buddies that we've collected over the years. You just get removed."

Before he can run or cry or beg, Tex grits through the comms. *"Zeke, hurry up. Medics two minutes out. You and Bella need to vanish. Right fucking now."*

I nod once. Then grab the seller by the collar and drag him behind a crate. "Guess I don't get to play with my food tonight."

No speech. No theatrics. Only one silenced shot straight through the fuckface's skull. I step over the body, blood ruining my boots, and head for the van.

"Bells," I say, reaching for her wrist as I climb in. "Let's go."

She stares at the screens, frozen. Eyes locked on the blood. On the girls. On what I just did.

"Zeke, wait," she breathes. "We can't just leave. What about the girls? What about him?"

"We don't have time," I mutter, grabbing her wrist.

She plants her feet and won't budge. "No!" She jerks free, voice cracking, chest heaving. "Why aren't we staying? They need—"

"They need to live," I snap. "And we're the reason they get that chance. That's enough."

She doesn't move. I grind my teeth, pulse spiking. Fucking teenage drama and of course it picks now to show up.

"Bella, this isn't a movie! There's no time for breakdowns. You don't understand we have to move."

Her lips part. "Then help me understand!"

Nate's voice punches through, "Isabella Marie Blackwood." His tone could stop a freight train. "You don't need to understand. You need to go. Right fucking now!"

Bella flinches.

"This op's over. The medics are inbound, the FBI cover is in place, and you and Zeke can't be on the scene when it hits. If you stay, you compromise everything. Go! That's an order."

She stands there, knuckles white, breathing like she might explode. Then she looks at me. And I see it, that storm in her eyes.

Fear. Fury. Fire.

But she moves.

We sprint to the second car and the engine roars to life. Tires scream against pavement. In the rear view mirror, the warehouse shrinks. The girls. The blood. The man I left behind. Bella's gripping my hand like it's the only thing keeping her grounded.

Neither of us look back.

BELLA - Age 16
Our Penthouse – Later that night

The city hums below, loud and endless, like it has no idea what just happened. Inside, everything's quieter. Dim firelight illuminating whiskey glasses. The faint click of laptop keyboards.

Mr. Acronym finally speaks. "For the record," he says, glancing my way, "I meant what I said in the van. But I probably shouldn't have shouted."

I look over at him.

"When I told you to move," he adds. "That tone wasn't personal."

"Oh." I nod, slow. "Right. When you used my full name and dropped an f-bomb like a pissed-off dad at Disneyland."

Tex chuckles low. "You should've heard him when Zeke blew a

power grid in Singapore. That did get personal."

"Tex! That was classified," he mutters.

Zeke smirks into his glass.

"I get it," I say. "You were right."

He gives me a small nod. "You didn't freak, completely. You didn't interfere. That's a win in my book."

Zeke leans forward just enough to meet my eyes. "You were solid."

"I didn't do anything."

"Exactly," Mr. Acronym says. "You didn't fuck it up. That's the whole point."

Tex raises his glass. "Here's to not fucking it up."

I laugh under my breath as Zeke clinks his glass against Tex's.

"High bar, huh?"

"We're a team of highly armed problem solvers," Tex says. "Not overachievers."

"Speak for yourself," Zeke says.

I smile, a little real this time. The tension's still in my chest, but it's duller now. Wrapped in sarcasm and firelight and the kind of silence that feels earned.

"Alright," Mr. Acronym says after a long sip. "We'll finish the full report in the morning. He gets up, stretching like a cat, and disappears down the hall.

Tex pushes to his feet with a grunt. "Don't touch my bourbon, Zeke."

Zeke flips him off.

Tex winks at me as he passes. "You did good, kid."

Zeke doesn't move. Just watches the flames.

"Go to bed," he says without looking at me.

"I'm not tired."

"Yeah, you are. Your bones just haven't figured it out yet."

"I'm not tired."

He leans forward, elbows on his knees, "Are you okay?"

I look up. Meet his eyes. And there it is, beneath the sarcasm and scars, the firelight and shadows. My brother. Not the fighter or the hacker, just Zeke.

"I don't know," I whisper.

He nods once like that's an answer he understands. "That's fair."

For a second we just sit there. This strange, heavy quiet wrapping around the edges of everything we don't say.

He tilts his head toward the staircase and says, "Get some sleep. I'll be here."

I stand slowly, the blanket slipping off my shoulders.

"If you need me... don't knock. Just come in."

I take a few steps toward the stairs before I stop. "Zeke?"

He looks up from the fire, eyes shadowed and quiet. Waiting.

"I need to ask you something."

He doesn't say anything, just shifts in his seat.

I swallow. "Can I see him?"

His jaw tenses. Just slightly. But it's enough.

"You know who I mean."

"Yeah," he says quietly. "I do."

I step closer. "Please."

He stands and crosses the room until he's just in front of me. An unmovable wall of safety he always becomes when things go sideways.

"No," he says gently. "Not yet."

"Why not?"

"Because it's not safe."

"Carlos is in prison," I snap. "He can't touch us."

"One. He's not in *prison*," he fires back. "He's in one of those Club Fed facilities where they serve quinoa, offer yoga, and probably give blowjobs with their breakfast smoothies."

"Disgusting."

"Accurate. And two, Vince is still out there, free and pissed. You think he's just gonna let what we did slide?"

I cross my arms. "They think we died in that explosion, Zeke. Mariela's car went up with two charred bodies. That bought us time."

"Yeah, well, time isn't forever," he says, tone flat. "Vince isn't stupid. If he ever starts doubting that fire... if anyone decides to really look into it? Fayetteville's the first place they'll look."

He takes a deep breath. "You think he won't check your old dance studio? Henry's front porch?"

My mouth presses into a line.

"We burned a very powerful man. We also humiliated a District Attorney who ran for Senate and lost because of us. This isn't just about Miami anymore, Bells. You don't get to walk back into your old life like we didn't start a war."

"Vince doesn't know that was us, Zeke. And, the lake house is—"

"It doesn't matter," Zeke snaps, then lowers his voice again. "It's not about where he is. It's about who he is to you. And if someone finds out, if they connect the dots, he's leverage. And you're exposed. You could be putting him in danger, not just yourself."

"I'm not asking to go back. I'm not trying to run away and play house," I whisper, voice shaking. "I just want to see him. That's all. Just once. I just want to see my Dad."

"I know," he says. "But it's not time yet."

My throat tightens. "Will it ever be?"

He's quiet for a long moment. "I hope so," he says honestly. "If the network holds. If we can find Vince and eliminate that threat."

I nod, lips pressed tight to hold back the emotion trying to claw its way out. Zeke brushes a knuckle down my cheek and tucks a strand of hair behind my ear. Then he leans in and presses a kiss to my forehead.

"I'll get you there one day."

He pulls back, and I see it, all the weight he's carrying. All the pain he doesn't let out. Every wall he's built around both of us to keep us breathing. He walks away, footsteps silent as he vanishes up the staircase without looking back.

I stand there for a while, letting the firelight flicker across the floor until it doesn't feel warm anymore. Then I turn off the lights and head to bed.

ZEKE - Age 19
The next morning

Tex is at the coffee machine, watching it as if it's going to pull a weapon. Nate's already locked-in at the table, sleeves rolled, files open, and dissecting the op like it'll confess if he presses hard enough. I take the first mug.

Nate breaks the silence. "We need to talk about the city."

"Fucking hell. Here we go," I say as I sip my coffee.

Tex doesn't even look surprised. "We've been dancing around it for weeks. Maybe New York was too much of a risk."

I exhale through my nose, lean against the window, eyes on the skyline as it flickers to life behind the fog.

"This was never about comfort," I say. "We didn't pick Manhattan because it's safe. We picked it because it's a lion's den."

"That's exactly the problem," Nate snaps. "We are in *his* lion's den."

"Exactly. He's here. Which means we can keep eyes on him. Track every move he makes while he's too busy chasing ghosts to see what's right in front of him."

Tex crosses his arms. "And what if he stops chasing ghosts, Zeke? What happens when he starts looking in his own backyard?"

I set the mug down hard, before I break it in my hand. "Then we finish it."

I suck in a deep breath.

"He doesn't know she's alive!" I grit. "Doesn't know I've got his book. He doesn't know a damn thing."

Nate leans forward, eyes locked on mine. "But if he connects the dots. If he finds out Bella's alive and—"

"I know," I cut in. "Trust me. I know."

No one moves.

"He isn't going to find anything. Isabella Marie Harrington died in a car explosion at a private airstrip near Fort Myers. Years ago. We made sure of it."

My voice stays level. Cold. "And that's if he ever found a trail to Bells as a Harrington in the first place, which he didn't. There's never been a single fucking breadcrumb. No one was ever sent to Arkansas to find her. Not by *him*, anyway."

"Fine. How's she doing?" Tex asks. "How was she after we went to bed last night?"

I pause.

"She asked about Henry," I say, quieter now. "We were by the fire, and she just looked at me. Dead in the eye and asked, '*Can I see him?*'"

Tex mutters a curse under his breath.

"I told her no. Because it's not time."

"Maybe it should be," Tex grumbles. "She's not a little kid anymore, not really. She's earned that much. Survived more shit than half the people on this team."

I shake my head. "Not with Vince breathing, and sure as hell not with you know who walking free."

I look up, eyes burning. "Fayetteville's the first place he'd look if he even suspected she was alive. You think he wouldn't go after Henry? You think he wouldn't kill him just to pull her out of hiding?"

My voice dips lower. "What do you think that would do to her?"

Nate's stern baritone cuts through the fog. "So what? We keep her locked in this tower forever?"

"We keep her alive," I snap. "That's the job."

"You're not the only one protecting her, Zeke," Tex says. "We're in this with you. She's our family too, you both are."

I nod. "I know. But if something happens to her?" I glance between them. "It won't be on your conscience. It'll be on mine. She's been my responsibility ever since she got dumped by Krolek's agents in Miami."

The silence hangs. Heavy.

Nate drops his gaze to the laptop. "Shit," he breathes spinning the laptop toward me. "Looks like Krolek's been busy."

New file. Surveillance photos. Timestamped calls. Encrypted transfers. One headline blinking at the top:

OPERATION GHOST: KROLEK MOVEMENT
Confirmed. 22 minors. Target: Newark.

Tex whistles low. "That's not a shuffle. That's a fucking ship-ment."

Nate scrolls. "Intel confirms them tagged for an offshore sale. Private plane out of Newark. Two nights from now. Midnight."

"Where's the plane headed?"

"Unclear," Nate says. "Logs say Dubai. Red Silk's intercepts say Poland."

"Money's on Poland if Krolek is involved," Tex adds.

"Twenty-two kids," I repeat under my breath. My throat tastes like rust. "This one's ours."

Tex nods. "We need the full team for this, or at least half of them."

"Call in Khoza and Ivan," I say. "O'Malley, too"

Nate looks up. "We pulling Bella in?"

I hesitate. "No. Not for this one. We don't know what we're walking into yet. She stays grounded. We can't risk Krolek seeing her. Or Vince if he's somehow involved in this one."

"She'll fight you on that," Tex says.

"She can fight me all she wants," I mutter. "She's not going anywhere near that plane."

A long silence. Then Tex pipes up, "Twenty-two."

I nod. "Let's bring them home."

"Bella may not be the mission," Nate says, voice softer now. "But she's why it matters."

I glance toward the staircase. Then at the skyline. Then down at my phone. There's a photo on the screen. Me and her on the field at St. Lyra's right after her Homecoming game halftime show. She's still in uniform, glitter on her face, ponytail swinging, grinning like she just took over the world.

Ellie's somewhere in the background yelling about lighting or angles, I don't remember. All I remember is her. Bella, flushed from the performance, eyes wild and bright, dragging me out of the shad-ows like I wasn't actively trying to avoid every camera on the East Coast.

I told her no. She took the picture anyway. Brat never listens. Made some poor senior take it while I stood there in a Vixen t-shirt, arms crossed like a bouncer at a princess party. Hoodie ditched for once because she asked me to. I looked completely out of place and I didn't give a shit. Not this time. Because she was glowing and I was proud as hell.

She'd danced like she owned that field. Like everything we'd been through—all of the pain, the blood, the nightmares—it hadn't touched her. Like the fire hadn't carved her hollow.

And in that second, standing beside her with stadium lights in our eyes and glitter stuck to my damn arm, I didn't feel like a bodyguard. Or a ghost. I felt like her brother. And it was enough.

I stare at the photo. The grin. The glitter. That moment. I don't get many of those with her. Not anymore. Now it's blades and bruises and black site raids. Rigs and recon and revenge.

The girl in this photo, she's still in there somewhere. But she's tired. She's scarred. And she's carrying way too much shit I should've protected her from.

Maybe it's time.

Not for normal. That ship sailed along time ago.

Not for safety. That's a goddamn fairy tale.

Not even for closure. She knows too much for that.

But maybe if I can give her him, just once. Her dad. Her safe place. Her *real* anchor before all of this. Maybe she'll keep going. Maybe she'll believe she still deserves a little light. And maybe, if I'm lucky, she'll be okay.

There's just one problem. If I give her him, I risk losing her.

And I don't know if I'm ready for that.

CHAPTER (14)
BELLA
AGE 18
MANHATTAN, NEW YORK

The boutique takes up the entire floor of an unmarked building just off Madison. The kind of address whispered between stylists and heiresses. There's no sign, no storefront, just a sleek brass call box and a doorman in what has to be a twenty-thousand-dollar suit. The room is carpeted with soft lighting and crystal vases filled with white roses. It's not flashy. It doesn't need to be. Here, luxury is inherited, not announced.

Ellie glides across the boutique like she's on a damn runway. Five-inch heels, silent on the carpet, her golden gown catching the light like it had been poured onto her by a Greek god. She pauses in front of a mirror, lips pursed.

She turns with a flick of her wrist toward the stylist, the seamstress, and the woman steaming a rack of dresses by the wall.

"I'm not looking for compliments," she says. "I want silence. Boys forgetting their last names. Girls rethinking their sexuality. If there's not at least one scandal by midnight, we've truly failed Bells."

"Subtle as always, darling." Savannah Whitmore, grace incarnate in a cream silk blouse and pearls that probably have their own security detail, sips her rosé and smiles. Her honey-blonde hair is swept into a flawless chignon, not a strand out of place. Her skin glows with the kind of radiance only generational wealth and daily facials can buy. Even seated, she has this Upper East Side elegance that makes you want to straighten your posture and fix your eyeliner.

"Please." Ellie waves a hand. "You didn't raise me to be subtle. You raised me to be iconic."

"I did no such thing. You came out dramatic."

"She came out demanding a damn tiara," I mutter, emerging from the dressing room in a Dior gown the stylist had insisted I try.

Savannah tilts her head graciously. "It's... sweet."

Ellie looks like she's about to throw her shoe at me. "No. Absolutely not. That's a dress for a divorcée attending her third charity luncheon. In Connecticut."

"It's Dior," the stylist offers gently.

"And it's beige," Ellie snaps. "Bells, no. We're not going to your godmother's garden brunch. We're throwing a party that starts in couture and ends in scandal. This is our villain era. You need something that says: *Yes, I just stole your heart, your inheritance, and I looked flawless doing it.*"

She hands me a new dress. "Try this before I cry."

I stare at it. Deep crimson satin cut with a threat, sharp lines, and wicked intent. The bodice is sculpted to lift, cinch, and ruin lives. The slit climbs so high it feels like a challenge and the neckline dips low enough to make even a priest flinch. This dress is a loaded weapon wrapped in silk.

"El—"

"If Zeke kills me for this," Ellie says sweetly, "just make sure my eulogy is fabulous. And blame yourself, because if you show up to our graduation party in *beige,* I will haunt you. Loudly. In vintage Valentino. Preferably after sneaking out of Zeke's bed."

"Did you seriously just sexualize my brother mid-threat?"

She shrugs, unbothered. "What? I'm heartbroken, reckless, and your brother looks like violence in a suit. Let me live."

Savannah chuckles, unbothered as ever. "She's a touch dramatic," she says, rising from her chair with her rosé in hand. "But she's not wrong."

She turns to me with a glint in her eye. "Beige is not your color, sweetheart."

I obey and I step into the dress.

Ellie lets out a gasp so loud it echos. "Oh my God. Shut up. Shut. The hell up." She looks genuinely offended by how good I look.

Savannah stares. One hand comes to her mouth, the way elegant women react to car crashes or couture miracles.

"Bella," she breathes.

Ellie crosses the floor like a woman on a mission and circles me, humming as if she's inspecting a new Ferrari.

"You look like heartbreak. You look like you know things. Like you bite."

"She looks... grown," Savannah whispers.

I glance up, startled. There are tears in her eyes. Savannah Whitmore's crying. Over me.

"I remember when you first arrived at St. Lyra's. So poised. So quiet. Like you didn't quite believe you were allowed to take up space. You were the best friend I could've ever hoped for my Ellie," she says, thick with emotion.

"And somewhere along the way," her voice catches. "You didn't just become Ellie's best friend. You became family, my second daughter."

I freeze.

"Now you're graduating. Headed to Wexley. Dancing for The Legacy at Ashmoor Hall. Living in Rosethorne Mansion, like I did. And I just..." Her voice trembles, elegant and raw. "I've never been so proud. You didn't just become everything I hoped. You became more."

Ellie blinks fast. "Okay Mom, I was not emotionally prepared for mom tears."

I'm speechless, because under all the silk and champagne, Savannah meant every word. She doesn't see scars or silence or a trail of broken things behind me. She just sees me.

Ellie loops her arm through mine, grinning at our reflection. "We're going to look so good they'll name storms after us."

"Zeke's going to lose his shit."

"Oh, absolutely," Ellie says, eyes sparkling. "He's gonna go postal. Maybe break something. But it'll be worth it. He'll throw a trench coat over you, ban cameras, start yelling in five languages. And maybe if the lighting hits just right, he'll finally look at me like I'm not just your unhinged sexy best friend, but the girl who can make Pete regret everything."

I choke. "Ellie. Please don't use my brother in your revenge fantasy."

She shrugs. "What? He's hot. Pete's stalking my socials. If your brother wants to scowl protectively in my direction and look like a Calvin Klein assassin doing it, who am I to stop fate?"

Savannah raises an eyebrow, but says nothing. She just sips her rosé like she's seen this play out a thousand times at a thousand different tables.

"He may try to shut the whole party down," Ellie continues, fanning herself like the drama queen she is. "But he can't stop us from being the hottest girls in the room."

CHAPTER ⑮
BELLA
AGE 18
GRADUATION DAY
ST. LYRA'S PREP

The auditorium shimmers with gold trim and history, sunlight pouring through stained glass like the room itself was blessing the moment. Every seat is full of pearls and pocket squares. Legacy families wrapped in elegance and quiet ambition.

Front row, Savannah Whitmore looks every inch the empire matriarch. Dressed in an ivory silk dress, perfect posture, and a soft smile that hasn't left her lips all morning. Her husband, Wall Street's very own Clay Whitmore, rests a proud hand over hers.

A few seats down, Ellie's twin brothers, Callum and Cade, sit in silent observation. They graduated last year and are currently attending Wexley University.

But it was the row behind them that makes my throat tighten.

Sitting next to Mr. Acronym and Tex, is my big brother. Zeke's in all black, sharp, tailored, and expensive. Armani, obviously. He'd gone full Bruce Wayne for the occasion and I love it. Fresh fade so clean it came with a warning label. Diamond-cut watch. Jaw set. Dark brown eyes locked on me like I'm the only thing that matters in the room.

For once the guys aren't on a mission. They're not lurking in the shadows. They're just here to see me.

The headmaster adjusts the microphone with the precision of a man that has practiced it in the mirror every day for the last twenty years. Names roll out like clockwork. Girls stand. Bursts of polite clapping, shouts from proud families. Some names get whistles, some get wild cheers.

Ellie leans over and whispers, "I swear I heard someone hired a violinist."

"Isabella Marie Blackwood."

Silence.

Then Zeke stands. Full height, full volume, "That's my girl!"

His voice cracks halfway through, loud, raw, and undeniably proud. His hands hit like thunder, clapping hard enough to echo. And right beside him, Tex stands too, broad and stoic, letting out a sharp whistle that makes half the room jump. Mr. Acronym actually whoops, throwing one fist in the air like they're at the damn Super Bowl.

Savannah stands, gracefully and glowing with pride. She claps delicately, and for the first time all morning, the room follows her lead. The applause swells, hesitant at first but then real.

"Eleanor Elizabeth Whitmore."

Ellie slowly rises like a starlet at a film premiere, draped in black and gold. She throws a wink at the crowd, twirls, and poses for the flash of a camera that hadn't even gone off yet.

Applause roars. Someone whistles. Someone else screams her name like she was headlining a concert. A flower lands on the stage from somewhere. She blows a kiss, curtsies like she's on the Met Gala carpet, and waltzes forward as if this was all a scene she'd scripted herself.

The rooftop terrace of our penthouse has never looked like this. This is more than a party, it's a damn a spectacle. Luxury chaos curated by a Whitmore with no budget cap and zero chill. Gold dripping from every corner. String lights tangling with the stars. Glass fire pits glowing beside velvet loungers.

Ellie had gone nuclear.

There's a live DJ in a crystal booth spinning like we're in Ibiza, fog machines rolling like a movie set, LED panels flashing our names in molten gold script, and enough champagne to flood the building if someone trips. The pool has been covered in glass and turned into a back-lit dance floor that pulses with every beat drop.

Ellie's golden dress clings like it's been airbrushed on by a team of runway stylists with something to prove. She's dancing barefoot now, heels swinging from two fingers, curls wild, highlighter catching every spotlight. If the goal was making Pete jealous, then mission fucking accomplished, babe.

Savannah and Clay find me near one of the outdoor lounge beds lit by floating candles and motion Ellie off the dance floor.

"You two..." Savannah says, voice steady but eyes glinting. "We're so proud of you."

Clay chuckles. "Be nice to your brothers next semester, El. Try not to steal their car, Bella."

Ellie and I laugh. "It was one time, Dad."

Cal strolls up with his hands in his pockets, the standard Whitmore smirk carved on his face. Tall, broad-shouldered, with sun-kissed skin and tousled light chestnut hair that looks styled even when it isn't.

Quarterback. King of The Order and Carrington Row. The kind of strong, spoiled, stupidly hot guy who ruled athletes, trust fund brats, and half the social calendar without breaking a sweat.

We used to get into so much trouble together when we were younger. Sneaking out, stealing his dad's bourbon, and talking our way out of shit we absolutely shouldn't have gotten away with. Cal's always been anarchy in a varsity jacket. And I guess I've always been just reckless enough to follow.

His twin, Cade, had dipped out earlier to catch his boyfriend's fight. Quieter, more intense. The one who used to drive Ellie and me home after parties back in high school. Always had ink on his hands and a sketchbook tucked under his arm.

I used to think there was something between us, especially after Nashville. But then he went off to college and got himself a boyfriend. Apparently, my gaydar was clearly way the fuck off.

"Heard you're in Legacy dance?" Cal says, eyes dragging slow. "Those girls are hot. Hope to see you at some Carrington Row parties this fall. I'm sure The Order would love to have you give us a dance, Bella."

Ellie makes a gagging noise. "Gross."

Cal just smirks. "Relax, princess. It's tradition. Legacy girls usually dance for us. Row parties are where it's at. You'll see soon enough." He glances at me again. "Bells, you've really got what it takes." He winks and strolls off, probably to go ruin someone's night in the VIP corner.

"Ugh, can you believe I have to go to school with my brothers?" Ellie groans, dragging me onto the dance floor. "I swear to God, if I see Cal's smug face before coffee, I will throw myself off the Rosethorne balcony in protest."

The bass vibrates through my ribs. "This year is going to be insane," Ellie says over the music, twirling me once. "Legacy rehearsals. Rosethorne room setups. Oh! And the masquerade party! You have to start planning your outfit now."

I laugh, breathless. "That's months away, El."

"Exactly," she says, wide-eyed. "And the theme is rumored to be *Decadent Devotion*, whatever that means, but it sounds like couture and poor choices."

"You just want an excuse to wear a feathered mask and make out with someone mysterious."

"I want an excuse to look hot and maybe ruin a politician's son. That's called balance, Bells."

We dance for awhile and then I spot him near the terrace edge. Alone, quiet, and watching like he always does. He doesn't blend in, even when he tries.

I stroll over. "You hiding from Ellie or the army of drunk socialites trying to flirt with you?"

"Both. One tried to hand me a vape and asked my fucking sign," Zeke laughs.

"Did you tell her you're an Aries with a God complex?"

"I told her I'm her worst decision and to keep walking."

I laugh. "Did it work?"

He drags a hand down his face. "No. I think it just turned her on more. She asked if I meant emotionally or financially."

"God, you're like pheromones for unhinged women."

"I attract feral energy like it's my damn job."

We both turn to the dance floor just in time to see Ellie draped all over a Wall Street clone with too much gel and not enough self-preservation.

Zeke squints toward the dance floor. "Is that Pete 2.0?"

"It's like Pete 5.0 at this point. She's chewing through Wall

Street interns like they're seasonal flavors."

"Goddamn, she's gonna eat him alive," he says.

"She already has. He just thinks the edge of death is foreplay."

Zeke barks out a laugh. "Poor bastard doesn't even know he's the appetizer."

We crack up, and for a second, it's just us again. The way it used to be.

I bump his shoulder. "So... not checking in on an op?"

"Not tonight." But something in his face tightens, just a small flicker. I know him too well not to notice.

"What is it?"

"Nothing," he says, a little too fast.

I turn to face him fully. "Ezekiel Malik Blackwood."

He exhales, eyes skimming past me. "Your real present's downstairs. In the penthouse. Come with me, I want you to see it."

I narrow my eyes. "What kind of present?"

His lips twitch. "The kind you don't open in front of a crowd of drunk socialites."

I give him a look, but he's already stepping back, nodding toward the elevator.

"Come on."

The door slides open and my heart stops. Zeke doesn't say a word. Just places a hand on my back and gently guides me inside. The penthouse is still. Just the soft hum of the city beyond the glass and the pounding of my heartbeat in my ears.

Someone is standing by the window, facing the skyline. My chest caves as he turns and looks at me.

"Daddy?"

CHAPTER ⑯
B E L L A
AGE 18
O U R   P E N T H O U S E

I've got to be dreaming. Or maybe someone spiked the champagne tower with something much stronger than Dom, because there is no fucking way this is real. No way he's actually here, in my living room of all places, looking at me with those same warm, chocolate-brown eyes that raised me.

Time has kissed his skin with sun and age, deepened the lines around his eyes and peppered his hair with gray. He's older now, yes. But not smaller. Not faded. Just as strong, stronger even.

"Daddy?" I say again because that's literally all I can get out.

"Hi Sugar Bear," he says, voice raspy and strong.

My knees buckle and hit the floor before my brain can register what's going on. All the years I held myself together just snapped in half. The sound that tears from me isn't a cry, not really. It is everything I never got to say. Every bedtime story I lost. Every hug that never came.

He runs to me, drops to the floor and wraps his arms around me. Pulling me into him like no time has passed.

"I've got you, baby" he whispers as he kisses the top of my head. His hands shake, one buried in my hair, the other clutching my back as if he's afraid I'm going to disappear again.

I pull back just enough to see his face. "You're real," I whisper.

He gives a soft, cracked laugh. "Of course I am."

"How?" My voice barely a sound.

Daddy smiles, soft and teary. He brushes away one of my tears with his calloused fingers.

"Your brother," he says, nodding toward Zeke, now leaning against the arm of the couch like he didn't just upend my entire world.

"Sort of. Technically, this fed shows up on my porch—suit, badge, the whole nine. Thought I was getting arrested or audited or both. Before I knew it, I was on a plane without so much as a toothbrush."

Zeke scoffs. "Jesus, Henry. You make it sound like we zip-tied you and tossed you in the luggage bay. It was a damn private jet."

Daddy chuckles, "Felt a little like it."

He stands, voice gentler now as he helps me off the ground. "Then he showed me a picture. My little girl. Grown, beautiful, and alive. I swear, I'd have walked barefoot across broken glass just to hold you again."

His eyes shimmer as he steadies me.

"After that, your brother sat me down and told me everything. All of it." His voice thickens. "Miami. Dylan. That god-awful house. What you lived through. What you and Zeke built from the wreckage. The kids you've saved. The lives you've changed."

He rubs the back of his neck. "I can't even wrap my head around most of it, but Jesus, Bella. I'm so damn proud." His hands ball into fists. "And also furious. I'm glad that bastard Carlos is in prison. Because if he wasn't, I'd have lit the son of a bitch on fire myself."

Zeke snorts from the couch. "I mean, it was on the table. Right next to poisoning and wood chipper. We just couldn't figure out how to sneak one into Cell Block D."

My chest stutters with a watery laugh as Daddy shakes his head, but his voice breaks when he looks at me again.

"You got out. You held on. And you didn't just make it, baby you fought back. You became something no one could ever touch again."

He reaches up, wipes the tear from my cheek with his thumb. "You're everything, Sugar Bear. Everything I ever hoped you'd grow up to be. I just wish your mama was here to see it too."

I feel my throat tighten, but I push through. "Zeke?" I whisper. "What about Vince?"

"He won't be a problem, Bells," Zeke says, voice steady but edged with warning. "Far as the world's concerned, the FBI just pulled Henry in for routine questioning. He'll be back at the lake house by tomorrow night. No trails. No heat. Vince won't know a damn thing."

"*Tomorrow*?" Daddy's voice cracks hard with disbelief. "You expect me to walk away after this? After all this time?"

He steps forward, chest rising like a storm building. "I finally have her back and you want me on a flight before the sun sets? No. Fuck no. Not happening, son."

Zeke's expression hardens in an instant. "One, I'm not your fucking son, so don't call me that. Two. Yeah, you are leaving. Tomorrow. We talked about this on the plane. It's the only way to keep her safe."

Daddy's eyes flare. "Safe? She shouldn't even be in—"

"Not another word," Zeke snaps. "I swear to fucking God, Henry."

A shriek rings out from the hallway. "Move it, Nathaniel, I know she's in there!"

Zeke closes his eyes. "Shit."

The door bursts open. Ellie storms in like a hurricane in gold sequins, heels swinging from one hand, blue eyes narrowed and feral.

"How long does it take to open a freaking present, Bella? If you think you can skip out on our—"

She freezes mid-step. Eyes landing on Daddy. Then drifting to Zeke. Then back again. Her face twisting slowly, like her brain is buffering.

"Oh my God. Is this some sort of weird age-gap, forbidden brother kink?" She gestures wildly between Daddy and Zeke. "Because I know I said we wanted *scandal* but damn girl this is a bit much, even for me."

Nate and Tex rush in behind her, scowling. "We tried to stop her."

Ellie just walks over and points a French-tipped finger at Daddy, "Seriously. Who is that?"

"Ellie," I say, my voice a little shaky. "This is my dad."

Ellie stares, eyes narrowing like the math isn't quite mathing. "Your what?"

"My dad."

"Yeah, heard that. But I thought you were an orphan. Grew up in foster care and met Batman over there during it?"

"I am," I say quietly. "This is my foster dad. Well... my first foster dad."

Ellie throws her hands up. "Okay, no. There is so much more to this story than any of you are letting on. Spill it. Now."

I look at Zeke and shrug. "She deserves to know. I'm going to be living with her soon at Rosethorne. I can't keep it a secret forever."

Zeke shakes his head, one hand dragging down his face. "She's the last person we should loop into this," he mutters. "Trust fund socialite with a verified account and a phone addiction. That's a liability waiting to happen."

"Hey, I can keep a secret," Ellie snaps, stepping forward, arms crossed. "Just because my selfies get more likes than your brooding ever will doesn't mean I can't handle classified intel."

"Sweetheart, your version of classified intel is which investment banker's son took you to dinner before ghosting you."

"At least I get asked to dinner," she says, lifting her chin. "When's the last time you actually got laid? You're so tightly wound it's a miracle you haven't combusted."

"Careful, Whitmore. You poke the bear too many times and he starts thinking you want to be chased."

"God help us all," Tex mutters and makes for the whiskey.

"That's enough you two," I sigh. "Ellie sit down," I say, motioning to the couch.

She drops onto the cushions with the grace of someone expecting tea and war.

I take a breath. "This is Henry. My first foster dad. He and his wife Elise got me when I was a baby. They raised me in Arkansas. It was... happy. They were amazing. But then Elise got sick. Cancer."

I take a deep breath and push through. "She died when I was ten. And because of some screwed-up paperwork, CPS came and took me."

I glance at Daddy who looks like he wants to set fire to the world all over again. "They dropped me in Miami. New family. It was... not amazing."

"Foster dad was a fucking monster," Zeke adds flatly.

I nod. "Yeah. So, long story short, Zeke and I met. He figured out a way to get us out. We ran. Came to New York and built a new life."

Ellie's brows are practically in her hairline. "Wait wait wait, so you're telling me you grew up happy, got stolen by the government, dumped off with a psychopath, broke out with your hacker brother, and now live in a secret Gotham penthouse with Armani Batman and his two henchmen."

She looks over to Daddy.

"Then you get this very emotionally loaded, Daddy-daughter reunion and no one thought to come upstairs and get me?"

"Basically, yeah."

"She left out the part where she stabbed a guy with a pencil at fourteen."

"Zeke," I snap.

Ellie points, wild-eyed. "Okay, no more plot twists without warning. But first, we have to go back upstairs and make our dramatic exit before people think we died or eloped or something equally scandalous."

She stands up and flips her hair. "Then we can come back and unpack this soap opera properly, from the beginning. I need a Power-Point, a wine spritzer, and a personal assistant to help me process."

Zeke crosses his arms. "What you need Whitmore, is a leash."

"You offering, Zeke?"

Daddy smiles softly and tucks a stray piece of hair behind my ear. "Go on, Sugar Bear. I'll be right here when you get back."

Ellie blinks. "Wait, you're not coming?"

Zeke tilts his head back and runs a hand over his face. "Secret, remember? Jesus, Whitmore. You'd think someone with a private jet and a thousand-dollar skincare routine could follow basic op-sec."

Ellie gasps and puts a hand over her heart. "Excuse you, this routine cost twelve hundred, and don't act like you haven't been staring."

I loop my arm through hers, dragging her toward the elevator.

"Come on, girl. Let's get you back upstairs before Cal turns a champagne bottle into a felony and hijacks your spotlight. Again."

As the elevator doors slide shut behind us, Ellie fans herself with one hand and whispers, "Holy shit, Bells. You've been sitting on the scandal of the century and didn't even leak a teaser trailer?"

ZEKE - Age 22

"Time to get our fucking story straight," I say as soon as the girls leave the penthouse.

Henry doesn't miss a beat. "We wouldn't need a story if you'd just told Bella the truth from the beginning."

"We went over this on the plane. I was a kid when I found her file. I didn't know what it meant. Didn't know who she was. I've been cleaning up that fallout ever since."

I meet his glare dead-on. "But she is not finding out about her biological father. Not now. Not ever."

"She got taken away from me because of you," Henry spits out, chest rising fast. "You opened that fucking door. You triggered the whole damn thing."

He's not entirely wrong. After my parents died and I ended up in Miami all I had was my dad's old laptop and his words. *"Everything in this world bends, Zeke. Laws, people, promises. The one thing that doesn't bend is code. It tells the truth, even when no one else will."*

I was eleven when I cracked the folder, just some encrypted archive buried in the drive. Thought it was some digital diary from a dead man.

It wasn't.

It was the first Black Book I'd ever seen. It was names. Bank wires. Surveillance footage that made my skin crawl. Including thirteen seconds of grainy video. A baby being carried out the back of a hospital. I didn't know who she was. Didn't know what I was watching.

"This isn't helping," Tex mutters. "Y'all need to breathe before someone gets thrown through a wall."

Henry ignores him, eyes locked on mine like I'm a loaded weapon. "You didn't know," he says, low and bitter. "And still you cost me everything."

I don't move.

"I lost years, Ezekiel. Watching the clock, wondering if she was dead. If she was scared. Hurt. Alone."

His voice cracks, but he doesn't stop. "You think a fancy apartment and stolen money makes it even? You think that all of this is some sort of penance? Think again."

Nate cuts through the air. "Enough."

He steps between us, eyes hard, shoulders squared.

"Henry, I get it. You're pissed. You're heartbroken. But so is he. So is she. And guess what?"

He points a finger toward me. "Zeke shows the fuck up. Every time."

He turns on Henry, voice rising. "You want to talk about loss? Pain? This kid built a war machine out of a trauma response and used it to save *hundreds* of children. And your daughter's been right there beside him every step of the way."

Nate's tone drops in finality. "The man who made her thinks she's dead. We made sure of that. That's why we keep secrets. That's why this story stays straight. You want to blow that up because you're hurting? Because you want a few more minutes with the fantasy version of her you had to let go of?"

He leans closer, nose to nose. "Not going to happen. So drop it. Or walk. But understand this, Bella's not that ten-year-old you remember. She's fire now. She's purpose. And she's family."

His tone hardens. "Our family. Whether you can stomach it or not."

Henry doesn't speak.

"Well, this is going great," Tex exhales. "Look I don't mean to change the subject or anything, but we've got one big-golden-Gucci-problem."

"Fuck," I mutter. "Whitmore."

"Yep, the glitter bomb of Wall Street. What are we going to do about her?" Tex responds, raising a hand before I can speak. "And before you say it, no. We are not killing Bella's best friend."

"I wasn't—"

"You were thinking it."

CHAPTER ⑰
BELLA
AGE 18
OUR PENTHOUSE

Ellie's gaze sweeps the room like a sniper picking her target.

"Okay, someone better start talking before I start assigning characters and inventing my own backstory. Spoiler alert, it will involve a secret affair and at least one illegitimate heir."

Zeke groans, rubbing his temples like he regrets every life decision that got him here. "Jesus fucking Christ, Whitmore."

Nate mutters under his breath, "Should've drugged her."

Ellie turns to him slowly, smiling like a debutante about to commit a felony. "Try it, and I'll lace your kale smoothies with estrogen and ruin your credit score."

"I don't drink smoothies."

"I'll adapt," she says sweetly, tossing her hair.

"Okay!" I shoot to my feet, hands out ready to break up this fight. "Everyone breathe. Ellie, please try to chill for like five seconds. Guys, maybe don't threaten my best friend."

"I am totally chill," Ellie mumbles under her breath.

"I'm not really sure how to explain it. Or where to start," I admit, shifting nervously under the weight of everyone's eyes.

Zeke cuts in, "Just say it fast before she tries to pitch the rights to HBO."

Ellie shoots him a glare. "Say what you want, Broody Spice, but I know drama when I see it and this is Emmy-level."

Tex nods to me. "Just tell her the version that won't get us all arrested."

I draw a breath, heart pounding. "Okay. Just... let me talk. No interruptions. No judging. No selling this to the New York Times."

Ellie raises a brow. "Rude. I was thinking Vanity Fair. Seriously though, get talking."

Zeke rolls his eyes so hard I think he might detach a retina.

I tell her about Arkansas. About the warm, golden years when life still felt safe. Game nights at Razorback Stadium, screaming *Woo Pig* until my little voice gave out. Quiet mornings at the lake house where everything smelled like pancakes and pine.

Ellie's lips curve. "That actually sounds... kind of perfect."

"It was," I say softly. "Until my mom's cancer got worse. That's when the cracks started." My throat tightens, but I keep going.

"And then one morning CPS just showed up. Ripped me out of my Daddy's arms like I was luggage, not a little girl."

Ellie's face falls. "Jesus, Bella..."

I tell her about Miami. About Carlos. About the way he made deals like we were cattle, the punishments he handed out like he got off on the sound of kids crying. And about Zeke, barely more than a kid himself, taking every hit meant for me so I could keep breathing.

Her hand flies to her mouth. "Zeke..."

"Yeah," I say quietly. "I wouldn't have survived without him."

Then I tell her about Dylan. Her face changes when I do. It softens in that way people do when they hear about a child who never got the chance to grow up.

"God," she whispers. "He was just a baby."

I take a breath. "But here's the thing, Zeke was already hacking before Dylan. He'd found trails, money, all of it. Families hiding rot under diamonds. That's how he cracked the Black Books, ledgers of power and corruption, names people would kill to protect. He was already in them. Already building a plan."

Ellie blinks, stunned. "You're telling me he was, what? Running some kind of underground war?"

"Yeah."

My voice drops. "But after Dylan, the grief, it turned into fuel. Zeke stopped waiting. He pushed harder. Went darker. And I followed him."

She sits back like I'd just knocked the wind out of her.

I press on. "Carlos and Vince. That last night in that house. The name change. Blowing up the car. Our death. None of it was some neat plan, El. It was survival that turned into a war."

Ellie takes in a deep breath.

"Our life since then has been safe houses and ghost signals.

Late-night runs and whispered codes. Zeke and I pulling kids out of basements and crates. Some made it out. Some didn't."

My throat burns. "Every mission leaves a mark. Every name in Project Dylan's database feels personal because it is personal."

For once, Ellie doesn't have a comeback. She just stares at me, lips parted, breath catching somewhere in her throat.

Zeke steps in away from the wall. "Holy fucking shit. Whitmore's speechless. Someone grab a camera."

Tex laughs. "Make sure you frame it. We might never see it again."

Nate doesn't even look up, "Mark the date. Historic moment."

Ellie flips them off. "Shut up."

Then her ocean-blue eyes find mine again, and the teasing stops, just for a second. Her voice drops, softer now.

"I just... I had no idea, Bella. I mean, I knew you had secrets. But this? You were just a kid. And you've been carrying all of this alone?"

"I haven't been alone," I say quietly, glancing toward Zeke. "Not really."

Ellie follows my gaze, then lets out a breathy laugh and wipes under her eyes. "Ugh. I hate crying. It ruins my lashes."

She reaches out and takes my hand. "I'm really proud of you, Bells. I just I need you to promise me one thing."

"Anything."

"No matter how scary shit gets, I want to be in it with you. Okay? Don't shut me out."

I squeeze her hand. "Okay."

Zeke groans. "Perfect. Now she's emotionally invested. We're never getting rid of her ass."

Ellie beams. "Damn right you're not. Oooh! Does this mean I get a gun? And if so, can it be pink?"

"No!" Zeke, Tex and Nate all shout at once.

CHAPTER ⑱
B E L L A
AGE 18
R O S E T H O R N E   M A N S I O N
W E X L E Y   U N I V E R S I T Y

The first week of August is move-in week at Wexley Universi-ty. They do it this way on purpose. Give the seniors time to clear out, while letting the incoming freshman feel somewhat important. By the time school officially starts on the Thursday after Labor Day, the cam-pus is already buzzing. Territory claimed. Alliances formed. Crowns unofficially passed.

And nowhere is that more obvious than Rosethorne Mansion. The chandelier in the lobby probably costs more than my soul itself. It glitters like a damn disco ball, suspended above marble floors so polished I can see my reflection staring right back at me.

Zeke grunts behind me dragging two massive Louis Vuitton suitcases. Clay follows, equally over it, juggling another suitcase in one hand and balancing an entire dress rack with the other.

"Why the hell do you girls need so many shoes?" Zeke curses under his breath.

Savannah, perfectly composed in cream heels and a silky green blouse, breezes past them and links her arm through mine.

"Because they're fabulous and I taught them well."

Ellie twirls ahead of us in a light blue sundress. "Can you be-lieve this place?" she gushes. "Rosethorne is a whole lifestyle. It smells like lavender and generational wealth. Ah! I love it!"

A bellhop-looking guy in a navy suit with the Wexley Universi-ty crest—a snarling black wolf framed by a burgundy shield and gold-en laurels—on his chest pocket jogs over and offers to help with the bags.

Ellie flutters her lashes. "Oh, you're such a doll."

We walk up the stairs and down the hall. At the door, Ellie turns to me, practically bouncing. "This is it. The next chapter. Col-lege. Freedom. Hot guys. And me as your roommate. You're so welcome."

I give her a look. "You're exhausting."

"You love it."

Our room is massive. One breathtaking, impossibly perfect bedroom that looks more like a luxury suite. Cream wallpaper with rose gold inlay shimmers in the soft light. A blush velvet couch is tucked beneath a wide bay window, covered by sheer silk curtains that whisper when the breeze moves through. Two ornate vanities stand like thrones against the far wall, each framed in carved gold leaf and surrounded by mirror lights.

A custom walk-in closet stretches deeper than expected, easily rivaling the wardrobe of a Carrington heiress or some Fifth Avenue legacy bride. At the far end, two over-sized canopy beds stand draped in layers of ivory and blush with plush duvets practically begging you to ruin your GPA.

The bathroom is a marble dream of polished floors, a double vanity veined in rose-gold quartz, pure gold fixtures, a walk-in rain shower with ten separate body jets... and a sauna.

Ellie lets out a delighted scream and throws herself onto the couch. "We have a velvet lounge area! I'm never leaving."

Zeke drops the suitcases with a grunt. "Good. Saves us from having to carry this shit back out."

Clay sets the last box down, looks around, and lets out a low whistle. "Damn. Bit of a step up from when you went here, huh honey?"

Savannah smiles, her eyes sweeping over the space. "It's stunning. These girls are going to rule this place. I can feel it now."

We stand there a moment, all of us. The silence soft and full. The kind that holds everything you don't say.

Then the goodbyes start.

Savannah hugs me tight. "You've got this, sweetheart."

Clay gives me a bear hug and whispers, "Make good choices. Or at least clever ones."

I smile, blinking faster than I want to. "Thanks Mom and Dad."

Savannah freezes for half a second and then pulls me in for another bone-crushing hug.

Zeke squeezes me and doesn't let go right away. When he finally steps back, his voice drops low and quiet, but dead serious. "If anyone gives you shit let me know. If you go missing, we'll know before the cops do. And just so we're clear..."

He turns to Ellie, his expression flat. "This whole room? Bugged. Chandelier, smoke detector, even the damn candle itself. So maybe don't confess to any felonies near that lavender one."

Ellie freezes mid-lip gloss application. "I'm sorry, WHAT?"

I roll my eyes. "You're insane."

Zeke grins. "Takes one to raise one."

The door clicks shut behind them and for the first time since we stepped foot in Rosethorne, we're alone.

Ellie flops onto one of the canopy beds with a groan. "We're officially on our own. Like, adulting."

I smile faintly and pull my phone out of my backpack. "I'm going to go call my dad really quick."

We've been texting all summer. Quick check-ins. I've Face-Timed him from the penthouse a few times and Zeke even flew him in for a few hours on the Fourth of July. But other than that, it's stayed... distant. Not because he doesn't want to see me. But until we find Vince, it's just safer this way.

I'm just about to hit the FaceTime button when the door bursts open.

"Bitches! I have arrived!"

Haley.

Tall, tan, green-eyed, redheaded chaos dripping in sex. Her long, fiery waves spill down her back. Fendi crop top, black leather skirt barely clinging to her hips, and heels that are sharp enough to kill a man.

She saunters in like she owns the place, a bottle of Veuve clutched in one hand and zero shame in the other. Lip gloss gleaming, perfume trailing behind her like smoke, she's the kind of beautiful that makes people stupid.

We met her at the start of summer rehearsals when Coach Javi threw the three of us together for a trial set. A few dances later, he clutched his necklace, kissed the air, clapped his hands, and declared,

"This is it. This is the future of The Legacy."

The Trifecta was born.

Haley is the heartthrob, undeniably hot and magnetic. The kind of girl frat boys dare each other to talk to. Totally taken but totally doesn't care. She demands attention and gets it.

Ellie is the sweetheart. Smiling, sparkling, and effortlessly lovable.

I apparently get to be center stage. Javi made it clear from day one that he wanted me to be the leader. He pushed me harder, handed me choreography duties, and even whispered about plans to have us mic'd up during football games. He said it's so we can dance and command the crowd in real time.

Coach Javi is all Latin flair wrapped in muscle and a perfect tan. Broad-shouldered, late 30s, with dark hair slicked back like he just walked off a telenovela set. His jawline's sharp, his voice smoother than top-shelf tequila, and his presence is dominant. Commanding.

When he enters the room the energy changes completely. Dancers snap straighter and the music obeys. When he smiles, which is rare and always earned, it lights up the whole studio.

Javi isn't just some basic, boring dance coach. He is dance. Salsa, bachata, hip-hop, contemporary, he'll show you how it's done, and then make you do it sexier. Every routine drips with heat. Fast hips and even faster footwork. All with plunging necklines and just enough scandal to make the Wexley board sweat.

He moved here from Barcelona last year with his husband, Rico. Where Javi is command, Rico is sparkle. He's our costume designer, obsessed with making us "unforgettable." Legacy uniforms? Him. The Trifecta's sexed-up masterpieces? Also him. Every slit, every shimmer, every strap... Rico.

Designing for us has become his summer religion and we're his very hot, very bendy disciples. Ellie's already asked if he'll design her wedding dress one day. Girl has zero boundaries. None.

Rico's even assigned us our own signature colors. Two each, so we can flex across styles depending on the routine.

Ellie: Bright yellow and hot pink.

Haley: Emerald green and deep teal.

Me: Cherry red and royal purple.

Statement colors. Bold. Unapologetic. Like us.

Haley's boyfriend, Knox, runs all of our lighting and sound, syncing every cue perfectly with Rico's hand-picked color palettes.

He also handles our entire social media presence, turning every rehearsal into a cinematic moment and every performance into instant viral gold. A tech god with a camera in one hand and a light board in the other.

He makes us look like the baddest bitches in every frame. Every filter? Knox. Every beat drop timed to a hair flip or hip pop? Knox. Every backstage reel that somehow looks like a scene out of Euphoria? Also Knox.

He built our aesthetic from the ground up—moody reds, flickering strobes, fire transitions, and captions that slap. At this point, we're more than just dancers, we're an entire brand. A movement. And Knox is the engine running the machine.

He's always cocky with a smirk, a vape pen tucked behind his ear, and those stupidly-perfect dirty-blonde curls he's always pushing back with long fingers. Blue eyes bright as a summer sky, lashes criminally unfair. Haley really is one lucky bitch. The man is fine as fuck.

We've even got merch now! All designed by Rico and dropping soon at home games. Hoodies, posters, even a Trifecta calendar. My personal favorite is a shirt that says Property of Bella Blackwood with a very sexy picture of me on it.

Savannah's so proud. Tex already put in an order. Nate too. And Zeke? He filed the copyright himself. He's proud. He just won't admit it.

"Ahh! First weekend without a rehearsal since summer started," Haley announces, grinning like sin. "Let's party bitches!"

She pops the bottle, sits down on the couch, and points the neck at Ellie. "Oh, Callum and August called. Said The Trifecta is officially summoned to perform at The Row tonight."

"Of course he did." Ellie rolls her eyes.

Callum Whitmore and August Kingsley. Kings of Carrington Row. Wexley's star quarterback and wide receiver. Kingsley Field was named after August's dad, a former quarterback who led the Wolves to their first-ever national championship back in the day. August never lets anyone forget it.

Ever.

"Actually, Callum's exact words were, *'Uh hey Hales, The Order expects The Tri to dance tonight at The Row. Be there, be hot, and for fuck's sake, don't be late.'*"

She rolls her dark green eyes. "First off, *The Tri?* The fuck is that? Second, he's such a cocky asshole. The other one like that too?"

Ellie shakes her head immediately, already digging through a pile of shoes. "No. Cade is everything Cal isn't."

I raise my drink. "Well, let's give The Order a show they won't forget."

Haley clinks the bottle to mine. "Trifecta style."

CHAPTER ⑲
BELLA
AGE 18
CARRINGTON ROW
WEXLEY UNIVERSITY

Carrington Row is way more than a dorm. It's an entire kingdom. Three massive modern mansions curved into a sleek horseshoe claiming an entire city block in glass and stone. At the center stands the main house—bigger, bolder, built like a fortress. It's home to the football and basketball elite where captains like Cal and August rule with muscle, money, and magnetic power.

To the north sits the athlete overflow, housing star recruits and future draft picks in waiting. To the south, the Cash House pulses with trust fund prodigies and hedge fund heirs like Knox.

Between them sprawls the courtyard. Polished stone walkways, a huge stage, crimson cabanas, and a black-tiled pool that glows like liquid obsidian. A built-in marble bar lines the edge, and stadium seating wraps around turning it into a private amphitheater.

At night, The Row becomes a private club, pulsing with bass and booze. And behind the DJ booth, Knox rules like a warlord, controlling the music, the lights, and the crowd.

The bass rattles through the foundation, lights low and golden. Top-shelf whiskey pours like water. Imported tequila chills on ice sculptures carved with The Order's crest. A margarita bar glitters under Edison bulbs while trays of glowing shots balances on golden platters.

Javi and Rico stand near Knox at the DJ booth, dressed in all black like the fashion-forward gods of backstage chaos. Javi has that no-bullshit stance, arms crossed, headset on, hair slicked back. Beside him, Rico looks like he belongs on a Milan runway, tight black tee, tailored pants, silver rings flashing as he waves at Knox about light cues and skirt angles.

"You know what to do," Javi orders. "Start the night with a fucking explosion."

Done.

Knox cuts the music and grabs his mic, voice low and smug. The blue back light catching the sharp edge of his jaw and the glint of the silver hoop in his brow.

"Ladies. Gentlemen," he drawls out. "Please... take your seats." A few guys whistle. Most just freeze.

"Wexley's finest are about to lose their minds. Give it up for the hottest Wolves in the building, The Trifecta!"

Lights cut. Bass drops. Music booms. We step out. Me. Ellie. Haley. All three of us in oversized Wexley football jerseys, numbers barely covering what's underneath. Hair down. Eyes locked. Heels high.

The crowd roars.

Three gold-trimmed thrones sit center stage, already occupied. Cal in the middle. His legs are spread, jaw tight, smirk cocky. To his left, August. To his right, the tight end, Jalen. All shirtless. All grinning from ear to ear.

On the first beat, we stop in front of the guys.

The next beat, the jerseys hit the floor. Underneath is a Rico special: custom black two-piece sets, lingerie reimagined for war. Lace clinging to curves, high-cut and scandalous. Under strobes the fabric shimmers like smoke and shadow.

Then we move.

Three girls.

Three chairs.

One routine.

We circle the chairs, fingertips gliding and teasing.

One beat. Two. Straddle.

My knees frame Cal's thighs as I sink into his lap. My hips roll with precision, hands sliding up his chest. I don't break eye contact. His hazel eyes track every move. He tries to stay cool, but fails miserably.

My fingers ghost down his chest. I lean in, lips near his jaw but not touching. Then roll again, deep, slow, and steady. Cal's grip tightens on the chair. Then I feel it, Callum Whitmore is hard as granite underneath me.

Ellie teases August with sugar-sweet precision. Haley rocks Jalen like a storm in heels.

Three bodies in perfect sync. Arched backs. Parted lips.

Final beat.

Freeze.

One inhale.

Then we turn and walk away like we didn't just set the place on fire as the applause explodes.

We change fast. Heels kicked off, lashes adjusted, and lace swapped. Ellie adds glitter. Haley throws on a blazer with nothing underneath. I go with a black crop top and a leather mini.

We make it back down just as Knox's backup DJ drops a remix and the crowd surges.

"Trifecta," Cal says, voice smooth, smug, unmistakably amused. I turn. He strolls up, drink in hand with an arm around a Barbie in pink.

"Hell of a performance," he says, gaze still lingering. "I used to think The Order ran this place. But after that? I'm starting to think we're just the warm-up act."

Haley scoffs. "You finally caught up."

Ellie bats her lashes. "That chair okay, bro? It looked like it survived something biblical."

August steps in, sun-kissed curls, mischievous eyes, and charm for days. "If that routine was meant to intimidate, then it worked."

"Good," I say. "Then we choreographed it right."

Cal chuckles. "Careful, Bells. Keep moving like that and someone might think you're dangerous."

I lean in, close enough to draw a glare from Barbie. "Oh sweetheart, I am dangerous. You just don't know how to handle it."

Before he can reply, Javi swoops in. "¡Dios mío, cabronas!" he screeches, pulling us into a group hug. "That was art. Pure, filthy art. I want this energy bottled and sold."

Knox follows, phone raised. "Already posted. Over two thousand likes already."

Ellie gasps. "You icon."

"Truly," Javi says. "If Wexley doesn't frame this moment in

gold, I swear I'm defecting to USC." He pulls Rico toward the exit. "See you divas tomorrow."

Haley beams. "Alright, bitches. Let's get a drink."

Ellie nods. "Tequila. Now."

We head to the marble bar. As they order, a tall, blonde guy in a crimson polo steps up behind me.

"Hell of a dance."

I turn to see a blue-eyed, clean cut, preppy guy. Probably a tennis player or maybe basketball.

"I'm Wes," he says, flashing an easy smile. "Starting forward for the Wolves. You're Bella, right? That was the hottest thing I've ever seen. Didn't know that The Legacy danced like that."

I smirk. "The Legacy doesn't. The Trifecta does."

He leans in. "So... what do you think of Carrington Row so far?"

"It's—"

"THIS IS OUR SONG!" Ellie shrieks, yanking me away.

Wes blinks, amused.

I shrug, grinning back at him. "Guess I'll have to tell you later."

He smiles back. "I'll hold you to it."

CHAPTER 20
BELLA
AGE 19
WEXLEY UNIVERSITY

The school year is flying by at a rapid rate. It's a week before fall break and I'm running on fumes. Between classes, Row parties, Masquerade Prep, Trifecta rehearsals, and late-night Project Dylan ops I'm stretched so thin it feels like even breathing takes effort.

And keeping it all from Wes is the hardest part. He is so sweet. Steady. The first real boyfriend I've ever had.

But secrets don't mix with normal. I want to tell him. I want to show him the real me. The part that doesn't sleep. The part that hunts monsters at midnight.

Haley and Knox understood. Eventually. Totally freaked them out at first. But now, Knox helps with the tech side of things and somehow has become Zeke's unofficial bestie.

Haley says it's hot. Ellie's just jealous that Zeke talks to Knox more than her. Their sexual tension is getting out of control.

"Alright, we crushed that," Haley says, practically bouncing down the gym steps. "Full house for the tonight's basketball game. Sold out Trifecta booth! We're on top, babes."

Knox tosses her a protein shake and kisses the side of her head.

Wes slides an arm around my waist. "You okay, babe?"

I force a smile. "I'm just tired."

We're halfway to the lot laughing about something Ellie just said when I see him.

Tex. Leaning against a blacked-out SUV. He doesn't smile. Doesn't move. Just looks at me. I stop walking.

"Bella. Who is that?" Wes asks.

Tex pushes off the car and walks toward me slow. Controlled. "Zeke's gone."

♥♥♥

Health class at St. Lyra's had taught us that the brain protects itself from shock. Slows things down. Muffles sound. Pulls the world away so it doesn't hit you all at once.

Clinical.

Predictable.

Biological.

And that's exactly what's happening to me. Everything blurs. The parking lot, trees, Ellie's boots on pavement. It's like I've been dropped to the bottom of the ocean. Tex's mouth moves, but the words don't reach me.

A golden blur drops into my vision, screaming.

"Bella! Babe, snap out of it! Oh my God." Ellie's face comes into view, ocean-blue eyes wide and wet.

"Let's sit her down," Knox says.

"No," my voice cracks. "I'm fine."

I blink through the fog, tears stinging. "Tex, what do you mean Zeke's gone?"

Tex's eyes drop, jaw locked tight. "Chicago, last night," he rasps. "Ivan's tip must've been bad. We thought the warehouse was clear."

Something in me breaks. "What happened?"

"There was an explosion."

I shake my head before he finishes. "No."

"Zeke was inside," he says quietly. "Running point."

My knees buckle. Knox grabs me and holds me tighter.

"But you, h-h-how did you and Nate get out?"

"I was in the sky. Far enough out I didn't catch the blast." He hesitates. "Nate wasn't as lucky. The van took a hit. He'll live. Really banged up, but alive. Chicago General."

Nate's alive.

And Zeke. Zeke isn't.

"We were set up, Bells." His voice cracks just enough to make my heart lurch. "I don't know if it was Ivan. Someone else. Maybe both. But it wasn't a mistake. Someone didn't want us leaving Chicago alive."

"He's dead?"

"I'm sorry, Bella."

"No," I whisper.

Zeke.

Gone.

I think I scream, or maybe I just fall.

Either way, the world fractures, and I go down with it.

PART 2

CHAPTER (21)
BELLA
SAN FRANCISCO, CALIFORNIA
517 DAYS SINCE ZEKE'S DEATH

Nate is halfway in my personal space, threading the mic wire through my jacket collar with his usual laser focus, steady hands and no small talk. Across from us Knox taps through the camera feeds, eyes flicking from screen to screen and already ten steps into the mission.

Laing sits near the back, adjusting his comm in calm and unreadable silence. Six-foot-five and carved like a myth. Broad shoulders, lean muscle, and long fingers that have made me moan his name more times than I care to admit. Jet-black hair tousled just enough to look effortless and warm golden-brown skin that catches the low light like brushed bronze.

And then there's that fucking dragon tattoo curling up the left side of his neck and disappearing beneath his shirt collar as if it's got a secret to keep.

Focus, bitch.

It was the Red Silk Triad's intel that led us to these kids. Laing Wei took over when he was only twenty-four after his father was shot and killed by a rival gang in broad daylight on the streets of downtown Hong Kong.

Laing is lethal, brutal, and fucking brilliant. Since taking over, he's gutted and rebuilt the entire RST from the inside out. Some of his encryption techniques make even Knox do a double take.

With Zeke gone, Laing's been running more missions with us. Honestly, a lot of the Black Book families have. Whether it's guilt, strategy, or straight-up leverage, I don't care. They're useful and that's enough. I've even built actual relationships with a few of them.

Strange twisted bonds forged through shared blood and secrets. I still own their asses so they'll do anything for me. For access to their Black Book. For the hope of getting into my pants. Sometimes both. Either way, I always get what I want.

Laing and I've been shacking up sometimes after ops. Nothing emotional. No promises made to each other under the sheets. Just pain burned off in the fastest way I know how.

Absolutely not love.

Only a release.

Dr. Monroe calls it, *avoidant coping behavior wrapped in dissociative intimacy.* I call it a damn good night's sleep.

Tex is outside with Kenji—Laing's lean, silent, and precise sniper. The two of them move like ghosts, checking their weapons with the kind of coordination that only comes from years of high-body-count ops.

"Alright, let's do a comm check," Knox says, eyes on his tablet. He goes through the team, everyone's seemed to be in working order.

"Boss?"

"It's good Knox. I can hear you loud and clear," I reply.

He doesn't budge. Just gives me that fucking look.

I sigh. "Really?"

"Magic word, please, Blackwood."

I roll my eyes. "Jackass, fine... *Problem Child* present."

That earns me a quiet little grin. He's been calling me that since Zeke died. Not because he's a dick. I mean he *is* a dick, but that's not why he does it.

He says if I'm going to act like a problem child, he's going to call me one. Just like Zeke would have. When Zeke died, I couldn't process it. I shut down. Like *full-on shell-of-myself-lights-on-no-body-home shut down.*

For weeks.

Tex and Nate tried to fix me. So did the girls. They all looked at me like I was some fragile little glass vase about to shatter at any minute.

But not Knox. Knox made me focus. Pulled me out of the fog. He made me face it. Zeke's death. Head-on. No hiding from it. He made me break. Really break. *Hysterical-screaming-nothing-left-in-side* kind of break. He made me relive it, every second, over and over until I eventually stopped crying.

Haley called it cruel punishment. But somehow, it worked.

Knox got through and he's been a rock for me ever since.

Dr. Monroe doesn't approve of Knox's methods. He can shove it up his Stanford University ass for all I care.

The doc means well, he did wonders with Nate during his recovery. And he's completely bought and paid for by Project Dylan so he keeps his mouth shut when we talk about missions. I'm just not a fan.

God though, if I have to sit through one more group therapy session with him, me, Tex, and Nate, I might just throw myself off a building.

Nate glances up from his screens. "Comms are clean. Cameras are good. We're a go." His tone clipped and calm. Always so fucking calm. The man could literally be standing on a landmine and still sound like he's reading the stock reports.

I lean back slightly, letting the tension slip from my shoulders. "Alright, boys. What's the word of the day?" I say, cracking my knuckles. "We going with sports, colors, or horoscopes today? Laing, your turn to choose."

"Let's do sports."

I grin. "Excellent choice. Since we're in San Fran, let's go with... Niners."

Tex cuts through the comms, dry as ever. *"Figures. Leave it to you to pick the most disappointing franchise in California."*

"You heard her," Nate says without missing a beat. "Word of the day is Niners. Everyone move out."

I turn to Laing and tilt my head to the SUV waiting at the curb. He pushes off the wall without a word and follows me in.

Laing found the op. Intel came from a Triad source buried deep in a Hong Kong-linked cargo chain. He got us in the door.

Knox got us the rest of the way. Fake IDs, burner phones, and wire transfers that vanish into thin air. He's good at that part, setting the stage and making it all look real.

This time, I'm going in as a rep from a private child wellness foundation. Which is a fancy way of saying that I'm posing as a corrupt social worker who pulls kids from bad homes and funnels them into worse ones.

Carlos-style homes. Ones with locks on the outside of the bedroom doors.

Laing drives silently next to me, all coiled tension and shadow. In today's production of *To Catch a Pedo*, he's just the muscle. Quiet, intimidating, and on my leash.

For a second his hand reaches across the center console, fingers brushing toward mine. I pull back without looking.

"Hey Tex, you in place?" I say through the comms.

His voice comes through a beat later, low and steady. *"Eyes on the prize. One container. He only brought one muscle. Must think a little girl like yourself isn't a threat."*

I hear Knox snicker in my ear. Fucking assholes.

"Dr. Monroe wouldn't approve of that comment, Tex." I say sweetly over the comms. "Or you laughing Knox."

Tex laughs, *"Sorry Bells. You're clear to approach. Be safe."*

"Always am." I reply.

Laing kills the engine and we step out into the cold metal maze of the docks. The smell of rust and salt fills the air. The container's already there. Positioned as if it was waiting for us. So is the seller. Slick suit, ugly face, and a bodyguard who's built like a refrigerator. He's staring at me like I don't belong.

I stare right back. "If you keep looking at me like that, I'm going to start charging rent."

He looks away first.

The seller steps forward, aiming straight for Laing. "Mr. Wei," he says, reaching out like I'm not even here. "Pleasure to finally meet you in person."

Laing just smiles and nods toward me. "Nice to meet you too, Andre. However, I just brought the bitch here. You're gonna have to deal with her."

"Rude," I mutter, then flash Andre a too-sweet smile. "But he's right. Now, can I see my merchandise? I've got some loving families lined up and ready to meet these cuties." I about gag on my own words.

He laughs, sharp and ugly, and jerks his chin toward his muscle. The guy moves to unlock the container.

I motion to Laing with a tilt of my head. "Go on, handsome. Make sure the merchandise matches the invoice."

Taking his sweet time, he strolls over and steps up to the container. The muscle unlocks it and swings the door open just enough for him to peek inside. Laing scans it, glances back at me, then shuts the door and nods.

"Everything looks to be in order," he says. "You want me to start the transfer?"

I nod. "Go ahead."

Laing pulls out his phone, thumb tapping across the screen in an impressively convincing performance of wire fraud.

I turn back to Andre, keeping my voice light, almost flirtatious.

"You know this is my first real time in the Bay Area."

He raises a brow. "Yeah?"

"Mm-hmm," I say, smiling. "Too bad it isn't football season. I would have loved to catch a Niners game."

The second Niners leaves my lips, both Andre and his muscle drop in sync, blood spraying the container walls behind them.

"Nice shootin', Tex," I say through the comms. "Although Kenji, I think you were a half of a second slow this time."

"Don't be a bitch, Iz," Laing smirks as he walks back toward the container.

Eleven kids. Seven girls and four boys huddled together in the dark. Thin arms. Haunted faces. Most of them don't even move.

But the smallest one in the back corner stops me cold. He can't be more than four, five at the most.

"Dylan," I whisper.

Or... he looks like he could be a Dylan clone. If I hadn't seen Dylan die in front of me. If I hadn't seen the blood on Zeke's shirt and hands as he calmed me down that night, I'd swear this was him. Curly hair. Wide, terrified eyes. Exactly like the first time I saw Dylan in Mariela's arms the day I arrived in Miami.

I step into the container, boots echoing off the steel. I walk past the older children, my eyes locked on him.

I kneel slowly until I'm eye-level. "Hey," I say gently. "It's okay. I'm not going to hurt you. You're safe now."

He doesn't speak. Just stares, frozen. His little arm is twisted at a wrong angle, bruised and swollen. Shipping container with no straps. God knows how far they moved him. Probably broken.

I reach out slowly. "I've got you now, buddy. You're gonna be okay."

He doesn't move. Doesn't cry. Just stares with hollow eyes like he already left his body behind. I slide my arms under him carefully, mindful of the arm. He winces and tears start to well in his eyes.

"I know, buddy," I whisper. "Let's get you fixed up."

I carry him out of the container just as headlights cut through the dock haze. Nate and Knox roll up in the van, doors already open. Tex and Kenji materialize from the shadows, rifles slung, faces unreadable.

"Ambulance is about five minutes out," Nate says.

Knox tosses him a med kit. "Let's start pulling them out. Waters are in the back. Trauma blankets too."

Tex is beside me in seconds. "You good?"

I nod, holding the boy tighter. "He needs to be seen first. His little arm is definitely broken."

Tex nods. He turns and starts helping Kenji and Laing guide the other kids out. Nate pops the side door open wider and lays out a blanket.

He still hasn't spoken. Still hasn't let go.

"I guess we're just going to sit together then," I say quietly.

He stays quiet. Doesn't flinch when the ambulance pulls up, sirens fading into the dock noise like static in the background. He just clings to me like I'm the only solid thing left in the world.

I sit with him in my lap while the medics examine him. They shine lights in his eyes, check vitals, whisper things like *"clean break"* and *"dehydration."* I just keep holding him.

Outside it's chaos. Controlled, but chaos all the same.

The feds are here now. So is Child Services. Though, not the usual CPS vultures. These are our people. Project Dylan has vetted and placed child service agents in every region of the U.S. They'll track down the real families if they exist. And if not, they'll place the kids somewhere safe. Somewhere good. Where they'll actually get help.

Therapy. Healing.

I spot Laing and Kenji slipping into the shadows the second badges start flashing. They can't be here. Not officially. Not legally. They can't risk the wrong person seeing them here.

I don't blame them.

A guy in a Bureau windbreaker approaches me like he owns the oxygen around us. Clipboard. Mirrored sunglasses and government-grade attitude.

"I'm gonna need to ask you a few questions," he says. "What's your name, who authorized this op, and why we weren't notified in advan—"

"Back the fuck off."

He blinks, taken aback. "Excuse me?"

"She's with me," Nate says, stepping in as he was summoned by my sheer rage. He flashes a badge with the confidence of a man who's used it to walk into hell and back. "Homeland Security."

The agent mutters something but walks off, clearly pissed. Nate gives me a quick nod and then heads straight toward Mr. Official.

The medics finish bandaging the little boy's arm. One of them murmurs something about transport options, but I barely hear them.

The boy's still in my lap, still clinging, still silent. I shift slightly, brush the hair off his forehead.

"Hey," I whisper, soft and steady. "Can you tell me your name baby?"

His lips part, barely a breath. "Ollie."

"Hi, Ollie," I whisper. "You did so good, okay? You were so brave."

He just blinks at me, lip trembling.

A familiar voice approaches from the open doors. "Bella"

I look up. It's Alyssa Park, dark blazer, soft voice, and blue eyes that don't miss anything. She's one of ours. Embedded. Trusted. She's pulled more kids out of hell than most people even know exist.

"I've got him from here," she says gently. "He's on a missing persons list, taken from a park in Santa Monica three weeks ago. We've already contacted his parents."

She smiles. "He's going home."

"Did you hear that, buddy? They're going to take you to your mommy and daddy. You're going to be safe now, I promise."

Ollie doesn't move at first. Keeps looking up at me and trying to decide if I mean it.

I nod. "It's okay. You can go. Alyssa's going to keep you safe. She's nice, you can trust her. And you want to know a secret? She always finds the best ice cream shops."

Ollie hesitates, and then finally lets go. Tiny fingers slide off my jacket as he reaches for Alyssa's hand.

She wraps her arm around him and lifts him off of the ground.

"I'll stay with him all the way home," she says over her shoulder.

And just like that, he's gone.

CHAPTER (22)
BELLA
SAN FRANCISCO, CALIFORNIA
517 DAYS SINCE ZEKE'S DEATH

I shut the hotel door behind me with a soft click, sliding the bolt into place. The suite is dark, too dark. I know I left the bathroom light on. And I never close the blackout curtains all the way. I like the view of the Bay. Like knowing what's outside.

CLICK.

A soft glow spills from the side table lamp. I turn, gun raised in a breath. He doesn't even blink.

"Laing," I snap, heart slamming against my ribs. "What the fuck are you doing here? This is exactly how you get yourself shot."

Without answering me, Laing leans back in the armchair, legs spread, one arm slung over the side like he's posing for a sin-stained Renaissance painting. Shadows dance behind him, curling like smoke. His shirt is unbuttoned just enough to make me want to curse.

That damn tattoo.

The dragon, black ink and menace, starts low on his hip and cuts a path up across the carved ridges of his abs. It coils around his ribs staking a claim, muscles flexing beneath its scaled body. The beast slithers up the column of his neck warning you that he's dangerous even when he's silent.

And fuck, it works. He looks like sex and sabotage. My pulse is a goddamn traitor.

"How's the boy?" Laing asks, voice rough enough to make me clench my thighs.

I hesitate. My grip eases on the gun.

"Safe. Alyssa has him. She found his parents."

Laing nods once, then slowly stands. "You did good tonight."

I open my mouth to throw a smart-ass comment back, but he's already closing the space between us.

"I'm not here to fucking talk, Iz."

I barely get out a gasp before he's got me pinned against the wall, gun dropped on the carpet. Laing's hands lock around my wrists before slamming them up over my head. His mouth is demanding, rough and claiming—teeth scraping and tongue plunging. He's all heat, hunger, and command with zero softness.

"Back at the docks," he growls against my lips, "you said I was rude."

"You called me a bitch," I shoot back, breathless.

"Because you are."

His thigh slides between mine, forcing them apart as my breath stutters.

"You like being treated like one, don't you?"

My hips betray me, grinding into the pressure of his leg before I can stop them.

"That's what I thought."

He lifts me without warning. His strong hands gripping under my thighs, slamming my back into the wall. My legs wrap around his waist on instinct, just as his mouth finds my neck and bites. Hard. Our tongues clash like a damn war, biting and sucking.

He sets me down just enough to shove my jeans down and to take off his own. His fingers slip beneath the lace of my underwear, dragging through wet heat.

"Soaked," he growls. "You always like this after a mission? Or is this wetness just for me, Iz?"

I don't answer. I can't. Not when he pushes two fingers deep inside me, curling them just right to hit that perfect spot. My head thumps back against the wall.

He pumps them slow. Painfully slow, like he wants to feel every reaction and every tremble. He looks down to watch his work as his thumb circles my throbbing clit once, twice. Three times.

"Ah... Laing." He picks up his pace and I gasp as my pussy clenches around his fingers. "I'm so close."

"Shh." He kisses me again, brutal and deep, yanking his fingers free right as I'm about to explode.

"Asshole," I bite out.

"Turn around," he says, licking my arousal off his fingers one by one.

I hesitate.

"I said. Turn the fuck around, Iz."

He flips me fast, smashing my chest against the wall. One hand rips my panties off with enough force I'm sure will leave a mark tomorrow. The other finds the back of my neck, pressing me forward.

I feel him. His thick, pierced, tatted monster of a cock already dripping and pressing against the curve of my ass.

"You want me?" he asks.

I nod.

"Then you're going to have to work for it, Iz. You're going to count every one of them for me tonight."

"Count them?"

"Each fucking piercing, Iz."

I swallow, trying to calm myself down.

He pulls me back into him and starts to push himself inside. The burn as the first piercing scrapes against my walls makes me gasp.

"What did I say?"

"One," I moan.

"Good girl."

He keeps going, pushing in at a slow and punishing speed that forces me to feel the stretch, the sting. Forces me to feel him fucking ruin me.

"Two."

"Keep going."

"Ah! Laing," I cry. "Three."

"Almost there, Iz."

"Four."

"One more," he says as he thrusts his cock the rest of the way in, sending a jolt through my entire body.

"Ahh... five!"

"That's it, Iz. You feel that?" he starts to pick up his pace, dragging the piercings through my pussy.

My cries draw out a growl from somewhere deep inside him.

"Fuck," I cry out, nails scraping the wall.

He groans low behind me. "Fucking tight as always."

His hand closes around my throat, tightening just enough to make the edges of my vision go fuzzy. The drag of his cock, the slight burn of those damn piercings, it's everything.

"You want it rough," he snarls. "All that fire. All that fight."

He fucks me harder with every word, every vicious thrust deeper than the last. My knees nearly give out.

"That what you need, Iz? Huh? Someone to fuck the rage out of you?"

"Yes. God, yes."

He releases my throat and fists my hair, yanking me back against his chest, his breath hot against my ear. His other hand slips around us, finding my clit again, rubbing tight, punishing circles that make my knees tremble.

"I'm gonna come, Laing. Oh!"

"No you won't," he commands, voice like steel. "You'll only come when I fucking say you can. You understand me, Iz?"

He pulls out, just long enough to make me whimper. He yanks me around so I'm facing him and then slams back in, harder, deeper, filling me so brutally I gasp.

His grip shifts, one hand locking around my throat again, squeezing it tight enough that I see stars.

The pressure. That delicious stretch. The way he owns every inch of my body, it's too much. He thrusts again. And again. The filthy sound of skin on skin quickly filling the quiet room.

"You like this," he mutters against my neck, teeth dragging. "Like being used. Owned."

I can't even answer, all I can do is nod.

His rhythm is relentless. My hands claw at his back. My thighs burn, pussy tensing so tight it hurts. He bites down on my shoulder, hard enough to bruise.

"Beg for it," he hisses. "Give me a good fucking reason to let you come, Iz."

My throat tightens under his hand. My eyes roll back. "Laing please," I gasp, every word ripped from me. "Please let me come. I need it. Fuck, I need you."

He doesn't ease up. Doesn't slow.

"That all you've got?" he growls.

"Please," I cry again, voice breaking. "I've been so fucking good. I took everything you gave me. I counted them all. I need it, Laing. I need to come. Please."

He groans, filthy and low. "You want to come for me, Iz?" he mutters, voice rough in my ear. "Want to soak my cock while I'm buried in you so deep you forget your own name?"

"Yes," I whimper. "Please. Let me come, I'm begging you."

"Then do it," he snarls. "Come for me, Iz. Now."

And I break.

My climax rips through me like a fucking grenade.

He follows with a guttural growl against my neck. One last thrust, one last drag, and then he spills into me, body locked and shaking.

My legs collapse. He catches me before I hit the floor. But he doesn't kiss me. Doesn't ask to stay. He gets dressed, grabs his jacket, and walks out the door like he didn't just fuck the sanity out of me.

And that's exactly how I like it.

The door clicks shut. The suite goes silent. I tug down my shirt and head toward the bed.

My phone vibrates on the dresser.

INSTAGRAM

New Message Request.

@LucaWasHere

Profile pic: a grainy shot of the New York City skyline at night. No posts. No followers. No bio.

@LucaWasHere

Nice work tonight, my sweet Blackwood,
Though I had hoped you'd choose someone good.
Your plaything's dull, his edge is fake.
I've seen wolves with more at stake.

Oh and Ollie's cries? A lullaby.
A quiet sound as you walked by.
Sleep tight, Izzy. Don't ask why,
I never watch without goodbye.

CHAPTER ㉓
BELLA
DR. MONROE'S OFFICE
MANHATTAN, NEW YORK
528 DAYS SINCE ZEKE'S DEATH

Therapy Homework Assignment
Name: Bella Blackwood
Date: 528 days since my brother was murdered.
Session #: Who the fuck knows. Too many.

1. How have you been feeling since our last session?

Shitty. We lost to the Brazilian bitches at Worlds. Got second fucking place. Total bullshit. We saved some kids, took down some bad guys like always. I fucked Laing, again. I know what you are going to say but the damn dragon tattoo doc. Gets me every time!

2. What would you like to focus on in our next session?

Honestly, I think we should dive deep into why my coping mechanisms make you more uncomfortable than me. Or we can just sit in awkward silence while you write notes about my "avoidant behavior." Dealer's choice.

Dr. Monroe flips the paper with care, expression unreadable behind his glasses. He lets out a quiet breath, something between a sigh and a resigned exhale.

"Well, Bella, I see you put a lot of heart into this."

I cross my arms and kick my legs up on the edge of the couch. "Thought I'd spice it up. Keep things fresh."

"Of course you did," he says, calm and clipped. "Start at the top then, let's talk about Worlds."

I don't answer.

He glances up over the rim of his glasses. "Bella."

Still nothing.

He leans back in his chair. "Look, I'm getting paid whether you sit here and glare at me or sit here and talk to me. It's your money. Dealer's choice, remember?"

I roll my eyes. "Fine. I feel like I let them down."

Dr. Monroe waits patiently, doesn't respond.

"Second fucking place. Trifecta worked our asses off. We gave everything and it still wasn't enough."

He nods once like he's waiting for more.

"Javi keeps saying it's a huge deal just to get to Worlds. Says Wexley's never even made it that far before and we should be proud, blah blah rah-rah bullshit."

I pause. "But, I wanted it. I really fucking wanted it."

Silence.

"I don't think the girls blame me. But I do. I was center. It was my routine. My choreography. And I couldn't win us the damn thing."

Dr. Monroe taps his pen against the clipboard once, then looks up. "Sounds like you've got a bit of a savior complex."

"Oh great, here we go."

"You choreographed the routine. You lead the team. But you don't perform alone, Bella. There are three of you. Four, if we're counting Javi. Hell, six if you count Rico and Knox. And then there's a panel of biased, probably underpaid international judges you have zero control over."

I don't say anything.

"You didn't lose Worlds," he says. "You placed second at the highest level of competitive dance in the world. That's not failure. That's pressure distorting your perspective."

I scoff. "It's not pressure. It's expectations."

"No," he says, setting the clipboard down with a quiet finality. "It's grief. In a leotard."

I just stare at him.

He shrugs. "You're not mad about second place. You're mad that something you led didn't fix what's broken. You thought winning would make it all make sense. That it would silence everything else."

I don't respond.

"Tell me I'm wrong," he says calmly.

I look away and cross my arms. "Rico would shit his pants if we showed up in a leotard."

Dr. Monroe lifts a brow.

"His designs are way too fashionable," I add, tone dry. "Think couture mesh, rhinestones, and dramatic back cutouts. Not a single boring-ass leotard in sight."

He gives the faintest huff of amusement. "So what I'm hearing is, grief but make it runway."

"Exactly."

He doesn't miss a beat. "Also, quit deflecting."

I roll my eyes.

"Okay fine, no more dance talk. What was next? You said you saved some kids. That's good."

My eyes drift to the window behind him. It's blue-sky bright outside, but all I see is red. Miami. The blood pooling underneath my little brother's body. Zeke's rage. All fucking red.

My fingers move to my wrist like they always do. I start rubbing the inside where the ink lives, tracing each line that holds me together. Dylan. Same as Zeke's. Same as it's always been.

"Bella?"

I don't look at him. My leg's bouncing. My stomach turns and everything inside me starts to hum.

"He looked just like Dylan," I finally say, barely above a whisper.

Silence.

"The kid. Ollie."

I blink fast, trying to shake it, but it's too late. I'm already there again. Miami. Carlos and Mariela's bedroom. The scream in my throat that never made it out.

"All I see is Dylan's little body," I say, staring straight ahead. "Eyes, open but gone in a pool of red." My voice snaps off, breath catching. "He didn't move. His body was so small."

"Bella," Monroe coaxes. "Breathe."

I try. But it's like there's glass in my lungs. The kind that cuts going in and out. Where the fuck is Knox when I need him?

He waits. Doesn't push.

I swallow the burn in my throat. Try again. "I know Ollie's not him," I manage. "But I held him and my brain didn't know the difference. Not right away."

"You were triggered," Monroe says, gently now. "That's not weakness. That's memory. Remember that trauma doesn't ask permission."

I clench my hands into fists but the tremble won't stop. "He wouldn't let go of me," I say. "Just wrapped his arm around my neck. And he didn't speak until we were already in the ambulance."

"What did he say?" he asks.

I glance down at my wrist again. "Just that his name was Ollie," I manage, voice breaking on the name.

"And where is he now?"

"He's home," I whisper. "With his real parents. Alyssa tracked them from Santa Monica. He's safe now."

Monroe nods. "You helped save him."

I shake my head. "We did. The team did. It wasn't just me."

He watches me for a moment, then says gently, "But you're the one that Ollie held onto."

"Next." I say sharply. "I'm done talking about the mission."

"Fine. You said you fucked Laing." He looks up, deadpan. "I'd say I'm shocked, but I'm not, Bella. More... disappointed."

I shrug, unapologetic. "I'm not. Laing's great in the sack."

"You need more than that. You need real emotional connection. Not just sex. Not just a warm body after a mission. You need someone who sees you."

I cross my arms. "I have the girls. We talk all the time. Ellie, Hal—"

"Nathaniel says you're pretending with the girls," Monroe cuts in.

My jaw tightens.

"He says you smile, you perform. That you're hiding behind this version of yourself that looks fine on the outside, but is rotting underneath."

"Well, Nathaniel apparently needs to learn to keep his fat trap shut."

He leans forward, elbows on his knees. "You've built walls so high even the people who love you can't reach you anymore. You compartmentalize. You sleep with Laing and then go dance, smile, and play house with your best friends like none of it touches you. But it does."

I look at the window, chewing on the inside of my cheek.

"Sex isn't the problem," he says. "The problem is you've convinced yourself it's the only thing you're allowed to feel. Like if you let yourself love someone, really love someone, you'll lose them."

I glance at him. Quiet. He's not wrong. He's never wrong. Fucking hate that about him.

"You think if you love someone, they'll die," he says gently.

I don't respond.

"Zeke. Dylan. Elise."

Still nothing.

"Bella, if there was someone out there who could give you both—the release and the connection—wouldn't that be worth letting in? Even just a little?"

I scoff. "If they exist, I'll send them a thank-you card. But no. I'd still probably run."

He waits.

I meet his gaze. "Emotions get messy. Attachments get broken. Look, I've buried half the people I've ever loved. The ones I fuck seem to be the ones who survive."

"Bella," he observes, voice dropping an octave. "You're using sex like a tourniquet. It might stop the bleeding temporarily, but that'll never truly heal the wound."

"Good thing I'm not trying to heal," I mutter.

"Then what are you trying to do?"

I glance away. Again, I don't answer. Because if I say it out loud, it makes it real. And I don't think I'll survive that.

Dr. Monroe just watches me. Patiently waiting for the crack to finally split wide open.

"Bella."

And it does.

"I'm trying," I snap, breath catching. "I'm trying to find the fucking person responsible for taking my family away."

The bitter words rip out of me before I can stop them. "The person who killed my brother. The person who... who ripped Zeke away from me like he was nothing. The person who turned me into this cold bitch everyone loves to whisper about behind my back."

I bolt from the chair, my skin prickling with a sudden, stinging heat as I pace the narrow strip of carpet.

"I've got my mission," I spit. "That's it. That's all I fucking have. I wake up, I train, I dance, I kill, I fuck, and I keep moving. Because if I stop. If I let myself feel anything for too long, I'll fall apart again and I'm afraid that even Knox won't be able to bring me back this time."

I stop moving. Just stand there. Frozen. Shaking.

Tears sting but I refuse to let them fall.

Dr. Monroe's voice is steady, low. "You can't keep holding yourself together with rage, Bella. It's not armor, it's acid. And it's eating you alive."

By the time I make it back to Wexley my head's pounding and my tolerance for human interaction is at zero. The second I step into the Rosethorne Mansion suite, I kick off my heels and sigh.

Since Haley's great-great-great-something grandmother founded Rosethorne Mansion, the university basically treats her like royalty, which means The Trifecta got a serious upgrade Sophomore year.

And when I say upgrade, I mean master suite.

Not the oh wow, this dorm has a private bathroom kind of master. I'm talking a full three-bedroom, two-bath, walk-in closet, velvet sectional, skyline-view type situation. Hardwood floors, chandelier lighting, and a full marble bar for "hydration."

Technically it's still considered campus housing, but it's giving luxury penthouse with a side of estrogen frenzy.

Knox loves it because he has a key and an excuse to crash without guilt. Ellie loves it because the revolving door of Wall Street wannabes gives her a new ego boost every weekend. Honestly, I'm shocked she hasn't been referred to Dr. Monroe yet. I'm sure he'd have plenty to say about her ever-evolving emotional exploration phase.

I toss my purse on the dresser and stretch, ready to take a hot shower and maybe pretend I didn't just almost cry in front of a therapist when my phone buzzes.

@LucaWasHere
No mention of me in your little chat?
Tsk, Izzy. We both know better than that.
Keep pretending, keep playing brave,
But I'll be the thought you can't quite shave.

Therapy won't fix what's already mine.
You'll bleed the truth to me, in time.
Your doctor listens, takes his notes,
But I hear more between your quotes.

CHAPTER (24)
BELLA
ROSETHORNE MANSION
WEXLEY UNIVERSITY
541 DAYS SINCE ZEKE'S DEATH

"Ellie, I swear to God if you touch that curling iron one more time."

"I just need to do one more piece, Hales!" Ellie shrieks, chasing a loose golden curl. "It's frizzy!"

Haley laughs, lip gloss wand between her fingers. "We are already late El, we really have to go."

I'm leaning in the bathroom doorway watching the soon-to-be cat fight unfold when my phone buzzes.

@LucaWasHere
Happy Cinco, Izzy. The end draws near.
Just days remain of your sophomore year.
Have a drink. Flash that grin.
Let them think they'll ever win.

But tell that quarterback to watch his hands,
Or I'll burn down the Wolves and all their plans.
One wrong move, one second too slow,
And he'll learn what it means when I let go.

"He still messaging you?" Knox says sneaking up behind me.

I jump, click my phone screen off, and whip around. "Jesus, Knox. Get a bell. Don't sneak up on people like that."

"I'll take that as a yes. Any luck figuring out who this Luca douche is?"

"No, she's on the struggle bus," Ellie blurts from across the bathroom. "She stayed up half the night trying to crack it. No luck. This guy's good. Like total Ze—"

"Ellie!" Haley cuts her off with a glare.

"No, it's okay," I say. "I can't be afraid to say his name forever." I exhale. "And yeah, Knox. She's right. No luck. Not even a bread-crumb."

"You want me to take a stab at it?" he offers, already pulling out his phone.

"You can try," I say, shrugging. "But I've already run it through our entire server. Used every tool we've got, even Laing's arsenal. Nothing. It's like this Luca guy's a ghost."

Ellie's phone rings. She groans, answers. "Yes, Cal. We're on our way. Calm the fuck down."

She hangs up with a dramatic sigh. "Boys. Zero chill. Come on, bitches, we gotta go."

Carrington Row is already thumping by the time we pull up. Latin beats pulsing through the marble entrance. Bodies everywhere with glittering lights bouncing off glass, sweat, and too many tequila shots. This isn't your average frat party, it's Wexley elite. Cinco de Mayo: Carrington Row style. And we're the main event.

Ellie shimmers in hot pink trimmed with gold, her curves hugged like a second skin. Blonde curls bouncing around her shoulders like she just stepped out of a Vogue shoot in Havana.

Haley is a weapon in deep teal, strappy mesh bodysuit, glitter flashing at her collarbones, and a ponytail that cracks like a whip every time she turns.

I'm in deep purple, shimmering under the strobes with skin-baring cutouts, plunging neckline, and rhinestoned fabric brushed onto my hips.

We match without matching. A statement. A Rico masterpiece. One look and the crowd knows that we didn't come to play. We came to conquer.

"Let's make it quick," Haley mutters, smoothing her hips. "Dance, slay, tequila. In that order."

We move toward the stage and get in to position behind the curtain. The lights dim. A low whistle slices through the noise, followed by Knox's voice blaring through the speakers like he owns the goddamn city.

"Yo, yo, yo! Welcome to the fuckin' Row!"

The crowd erupts. Drinks slosh. Someone yells Trifecta before we've even hit the floor.

Knox keeps going, hyped as hell from the DJ booth. "Y'all didn't think we'd throw a Cinco de Mayo party without a little heat, right?"

He lets it breathe for a second, the beat crawling in like tension before a kiss. "Alright, Wexley, hope you're ready to lose your damn minds. Straight from the heart of this savage little kingdom... give it up for the one, the only, The Trifecta!"

Ellie peeks out from behind the curtain and mouths, *Oh my god, he's so dramatic,* just before Knox booms again.

"First up is the sweetheart of the group, our little chaos in pink, Ellie Whitmore!"

She spins out like she's on fire. The crowd eats it up.

"Next, the heartthrob in teal. My baby, and heiress to the Rosethorne Mansion, Haley Rosethorne!"

Haley struts out, pure sex and power in motion. Every step hits perfectly synced to the beat drop, her gaze locked and lethal. One hand drags slowly down the curve of her waist, the other flicks her ponytail over one shoulder. Someone in the front row chokes on their drink.

"Goddamn, baby," Knox says fanning his face and smiling at Haley.

"And last but never fuckin' least," Knox says, voice curling with heat. "The one who keeps us all on our toes. The Problem Child herself, Bella Blackwood."

I walk out into that spotlight like it's my birthright. Purple bodysuit glittering, heels slicing the floor. Ellie and Haley fall into formation beside me. We don't just dance, we dominate.

The Trifecta has arrived.

The music fades out in a rush of cheers and whistles. The floor practically vibrates from the aftermath.

Knox's voice reverberates through the speakers, smooth and hyped. "How about those girls?"

The crowd roars.

He laughs into the mic, loving every second of it. "Wexley's finest. Ellie Whitmore, Haley Rosethorne, and Bella Blackwood. The Trifecta, baby."

Whistles and applause fills the air. Someone even howls from the upper balcony.

Knox grins. "But don't sit your pretty asses down just yet," he says, spinning back to us. "Because it's Cinco de Mayo and we're just getting started."

Then he pauses, hand cupping his ear dramatically.

"Girls, you ready?"

We nod. But before we can move, "Wait, wait, wait..." Knox throws up a hand like he's about to stop traffic. "I've got an idea! Let's crank up the heat." Knox twists a dial and suddenly the room is filled with color. Pink. Teal. Purple. Matching the lights to our bodysuits.

"Let's hear it for the men who help make The Trifecta unstoppable. Give it up for your favorite dance partners. The ones who hold it down, flip it up, and keep up with every twist: Josh, Sam, and Drake!"

The crowd loses it as the guys emerge from the wings, grinning, confident, and matching our energy stride for stride. Josh takes his place beside me, hand brushing mine. Sam steps behind Ellie, already syncing with her rhythm. Drake shoots Haley a wink as he slides into place.

Knox's voice lowers, teasing and electric. "This next one? It's not just a dance. It's foreplay with footwork. Hold onto your drinks, Wolves, because things are about to get real sexy."

"Hey Baby" by Pitbull starts. The music pulses low and deep, thick with Latin heat. Josh's hand slides around my waist, fingers splaying against my lower back like he owns it. My leg hooks over his hip, heels clicking as we move in perfect rhythm—chest to chest, breath to breath.

Ellie's already spinning, hair flying as Sam dips her so low the crowd gasps. Drake catches Haley mid-turn, their bodies locking in a slow grind that oozes danger and desire. Every move is sharp, intentional, and way too filthy for a school-sponsored event.

But this is The Row, and at The Row, rules don't apply.

We twist. We drop. We flip. Perfectly in sync.

The guys lift us like we weigh nothing, pressing us tight before spinning us away, only to yank us right back in. Heat builds in the space between our bodies, in the friction of hands sliding down curves and hips snapping to the beat.

And right as Pitbull drops that line about Dade County, the other four freeze in place.

Our turn.

Josh slides one hand up my thigh, the other gripping my waist as he spins me into him, fast and fluid, like we've danced this dance a hundred times in another life. Our chests collide, breath catching, but the rhythm doesn't break.

His lips brush my cheek, not a kiss, a small tease of a kiss. I hook my arm around the back of his neck, and then we're moving. Fast feet. Faster hips. Every twist a dare, every step a challenge. I roll my body with sultry precision, grinding down with a flick of my hips, snapping back into a tight cha-cha pivot. Josh dips me so low my hair nearly touches the floor before pulling me up with a force that makes my thighs clench.

The heat between us is electric. Dangerous.

I ride the beat like I was forged in Miami fire, shaped by its heat and its scars. It's not just showmanship. It's release. It's rage in rhythm.

The crowd sees a girl dancing like she owns the night. They think it's because I'm from Miami. They think that's why I always dance to the parts of the song where Pit talks about the 305.

They don't know I bled there. They don't know I burned there. They don't know I'm exorcising demons with every fucking step.

Javi and Knox made that plan for me when Zeke died. They made me the Miami focus on every Pitbull routine. To dance out my grief, my rage. To face it and not hide.

Josh's hands never stop moving, one sliding up my spine, the other slipping under the curve of my ass. Feeding off the fire I never asked for but learned how to wield.

The crowd loses it as The Trifecta snaps back in. All six of us hit the next beat like they never left to finish out the song.

Knox laughs breathlessly through the speakers. "Fuck that was hot." He drags a hand through his hair, needing to cool down just watching. "Okay, okay, let's get the rest of this show on the road."

He grins and steps forward, voice booming. "Welcome to The Row. My name's Knox. Those are my girls, The Trifecta, and it's Cinco de fucking Mayo."

He throws his arms up.

"Now let's get this party started!"

Music cranks. Lights flash. The whole mansion feels as if it's about to ignite.

Cal and August stroll up like royalty. High-fiving, fist bumping and winking at every girl they pass. Cal's got that shit-eating grin on full display and a tray of tequila shots balanced in one hand like a pro.

"Here's to The Trifecta," Cal says, pausing for dramatic effect. "And to The Order officially having the hottest dancers in Wexley history."

Ellie twirls a blonde curl. "As if there was ever any doubt."

"And," August says with a smug grin, "here's to Cal and me kicking off our senior year. Football gods. Order royalty. Living legends in the making."

"You're insufferable," Ellie fires back, grinning as she takes her shot glass.

"But charming," August winks.

"That's debatable, Augie," Haley mutters, grabbing hers.

I lift mine. "To The Trifecta."

"To The Row," Cal adds, winking at me as he tilts his glass.

"To senior year," August says with a hand on his chest like he's just been knighted.

We clink. We shoot. The tequila burns like hell, but it's the kind of hell we all welcome.

Ellie coughs once and laughs. "Okay. That one had evil in it."

"Or flavor," August counters. "Same difference."

My phone buzzes in my hand and instinct kicks before reason. I glance down.

@LucaWasHere
Tell Josh to not to cling too tight,
You're not his to hold, not his by right.
He's playing a part, but I wrote the play,
And you, Izzy, were mine before he ever looked your way.

He's attached a screenshot. One Knox must've posted to The Trifecta's Instagram stories. It's from the final beat of our dance with the guys. Josh has his hand on my waist, my leg hooked up his hip, our faces too close to be innocent.

Ellie leans over. "Who is it?"

I click my phone off. "Nobody. Let's go dance."

CHAPTER (25)
CADE
CARRINGTON ROW
WEXLEY UNIVERSITY
541 DAYS SINCE ZEKE'S DEATH

I don't do Row parties. Never have. Too loud. Too drunk. Too full of testosterone and bad decisions. However, it's about to be my senior year and something told me to show up tonight. Maybe it was Cal. Maybe it was August. Maybe it was some unhinged whisper in my head that said, *go see what all the damn fuss is about.*

And I'm so glad I did. Because there she is.

She's in deep purple, curves framed by slits and cutouts that scream confidence without begging. Hair long and black, cheeks flushed, and those damn steel eyes. Every move she makes is sharp and sinfully fluid, like the music's part of her blood. I've never seen anything like it. She dances like the floor belongs to her. And fuck me, maybe it does.

Ellie's best friend. Her shadow. The girl who stole a jet ski on our family vacation and nearly got us banned from the entire resort. The girl I used to pick up from parties at two a.m. barefoot, laughing, and begging me for fries and mint chocolate chip like it was life or death.

I didn't really see her then. Not until Nashville. And even then... not like this.

God, she's beautiful.

Ellie's beside her, golden and chaotic like always. Haley's on the other side, sexy and untamed. Together they're The Trifecta. But it's her. The girl in the middle. The one I can't look away from.

Cal's arm slides around her waist as the crowd roars. He tips back a shot with her, smug as hell, wearing that stupid grin like he knows he's touching something sacred. My jaw tightens.

I shouldn't care. I shouldn't want. But I do. Because it's her. I feel it in my chest. I feel it in the sharp punch of breath I lose every time she laughs. When her head tilts back and that smile flashes like a damn firework, something inside me breaks. She's the one Lex and I swore we'd find.

And the craziest part is that I've known her since before I could fucking drive.

I step off to the side, near the bar where the crowd thins and the view gets clearer. I grab a beer I won't drink, and let it sweat in my hand while I watch her. She's out there now, hips rolling to the beat, sweat glistening across her collarbone like diamonds. Her girls are with her, a synchronized mess of mayhem and sin.

She flips her hair over her shoulder, grinds low with one of the football players, then spins away before he can even touch her. Unbothered. Untouchable. Unaware that every part of me is currently wired to her.

I slip a hand into my pocket and pull out my phone, heart pounding like I've already jumped off a damn cliff.

ME: Babe. I think I found her.

LEX: Cade. I love you. But don't you fucking dare get my hopes up unless you're sure.

LEX: You bring home another maybe and I swear to God it's your ass on the line. Literally.

ME: It's Bella

LEX: Bella? As in Ellie's damn little glitter shadow you used to complain about all the fucking time? The one you had to drive to Philly to pick her drunk little ass up at three in the morning?

ME: Technically yes... but trust me. It's her. I know it is.

LEX: I hope you're right. Don't fuck it up. I mean it. Your fucking ass Cade.

LEX: See you at home. I love you.

I smile, rolling my eyes even as my chest tightens. Typical Lex. Blunt as hell and dramatic as ever, but I know the truth underneath it. He wants this just as much as I do. Maybe more. He just doesn't let himself hope anymore.

We met our freshman year. Wexley and Northvale aren't exactly sister schools. Hell, they're practically sworn enemies. And in the underground scene, the rivalry runs even deeper.

Meaner.

Bloodier.

They call it The Pit, Northvale's infamous fight ring. Fight nights are brutal, invite-only, and sanctioned by The Hollow Kings.

That night, it was Cal versus Lex. I didn't even want to go. I was there to support Cal, not fall in love with the enemy. But the second Lex walked in—tall, inked-up, all brute force and Russian fire—I was done for. We locked eyes across the ring and didn't look away.

Cal won that night. Mostly because Lex got distracted by me. He didn't even try to hide it. We talked after the fight. Then again the next night. By the end of the week he kissed me and then fucked me. Hard. Twice.

He's chaos wrapped in leather and scars. All Bratva blood and biker rage. Tattoos that crawl down his arms like warnings. Co-leader of The Hollow Kings. A born predator with a shitty attitude.

And then there's me, quiet, collected, and obsessive with my art. No one expected us to work. Not his world. Not mine. Especially not my parents.

At first they didn't understand. The tattoos. The fighting. The danger. His family. It didn't help that he's from Northvale and I'm a Whitmore. Wexley legacy through and through. That rivalry runs deep and my parents weren't exactly thrilled about me falling for the enemy.

But they're trying now. Slowly. They see the way he treats me. The way he loves me. And I think they're finally starting to get it.

We've been building this life together. Quietly. Fiercely. Ours.

But about a year ago, we started talking about adding a third. A *girl*. Someone who could hold her own between us. Someone who didn't flinch from heat or softness.

We thought maybe we'd find her. We looked. We waited. But it never felt right. And lately, Lex has been pulling back.

"Maybe it's just supposed to be us," he said last week, his voice low and raw in the dark. We were tangled together, skin on skin, his thigh between mine, his breath hot against my neck. *"You and me. Maybe that's enough, babe."*

A hand claps my shoulder, jolting me back to the present. I nearly drop my beer as August grins down at me, red-faced and three drinks past subtle.

"What the hell you lookin' at?" he slurs, then follows my gaze. "Oh. Shit. Bella?"

He barks out a laugh, loud and obnoxious. "Dude, aren't you like gay or something? And like dating that Northvale fighter dude?"

"Bisexual," I say flatly. "And none of your damn business, August."

He stumbles for a second but recovers with that usual shit-eating grin. "Damn. My bad. Didn't know you swung both ways."

"Now you do."

His eyes drift back to the floor, Bella in that deep purple, moving like pure temptation itself, laughing with Ellie like they own the damn night.

"She's a lot, man," he mutters. "Way outta your league."

I almost laugh. "You mean the girl I've known since she was fifteen? Who once crashed a golf cart into the side of a hotel because she was chasing a raccoon with a churro?"

His smirk falters. Just for a beat.

"Thanks for your unsolicited opinion," I add.

"I'm just saying," he shrugs, trying to play it off. "Cal's been into her forever. Pretty sure he's already called dibs."

"Dibs?" I glance at him. "Did we time-travel back to middle school?"

"Bro-code."

"Cal treats bro-code like a damn buffet. Picks what he wants and skips the rest."

August snorts. "And what's your big brute of a boyfriend think about you drooling over some hot piece of ass? Where is he anyway?"

"One, Lex is at a Hollow Kings meeting."

"And you're not invited?" August mocks. "The shame."

"I'm not a King," I say simply. "Two, we've both agreed to keep our eyes open."

"For girls?"

"For a third. For her."

He whistles. "Jesus. That's some kinky shit, man. So what, you're just gonna stand here all night and pretend you're not obsessed?"

"Not pretending. Not obsessed."

"Nah man, you've got that look. Like you're already picking out a wedding date."

I take a slow sip of my beer. "Only if the cake's good."

"You're such a fucking Whitmore."

I glance at him, calm as ever. "Funny. You've spent the last how many years trying to be one of us?" My gaze moves to Ellie. "Or at least fuck one of us."

He opens his mouth, but I don't give him the chance.

"What's the saying?" I ask, letting my eyes drift back to Bella. "She's just not that into you."

We fall silent again but I don't stop watching her. Not because I'm desperate. Because I'm sure. There's something about her, about the way she moves and the way the whole room bends around her without even realizing it.

She's not the kind of girl you chase. She's the kind you meet at the right moment. When the timing's sharp enough to cut through doubt and the fire is already lit.

The kind of girl who once made me drive to Saratoga Springs because she lost her shoes at a party. The kind who always laughed when she was hungover. The kind who used to steal my hoodies and pretend she didn't.

Of all the moments we've already had, I intend to make sure this moment is the one that counts.

CHAPTER 26
CADE
WHITMORE FAMILY YACHT
547 DAYS SINCE ZEKE'S DEATH

It's Dad's birthday. A Whitmore holiday in every curated detail. Full of tradition and legacy, mimosas and entitlement.

It's the kind of spring heat that pretends its summer. Warm enough for linen shirts and cold beer, but not quite ready to burn. The breeze still bites if you're in the shade too long, but no one mentions it. Not today.

The water stretches out in brushstrokes, layered shades of cerulean and sapphire bleeding into one another, sun-glazed and infinite. It's the kind of view that makes your chest ache. The kind you want to capture but know you never could. The sea glimmers like polished glass, soft crests breaking into foam as the yacht slices through them.

Somewhere behind me my parents sip chilled rosé under the awning of the upper deck, all linen and legacy, framed by laughter and perfectly arranged charcuterie. Cal's shirtless, of course, double-fisting cocktails and bragging about god-knows-what. Ellie's probably off to the side, no doubt checking one of her infamous social accounts, thumbs flying like it's a competitive sport.

I'm sitting on a lounger, phone in hand, thinking about a girl who doesn't belong to this world at all.

The last few messages from Bella are still lit up on my screen.

> BELLA: So, do you want to maybe come to a Trifecta practice next week?

> BELLA: You coming or what?

I scroll up through our short thread. It's nothing, really. Just a few innocent messages. The first one from me, sent with way too much second-guessing.

> ME: Hey I know it's been a long time, but I just wanted to say I thought your dance at The Row party was incredible.

Her reply came fast.

> BELLA: Oh hey! Thank you! That night was wild.

A few more followed. Short. Easy. Safe. Until I overthought it, like I always do, and stopped replying. No reason. Just froze up, like if I kept texting, I might say something real. Something she'd see right through.

Now I'm here, floating somewhere off the Amalfi Coast surrounded by perfect water and perfect sun. And all I can think about is her.

Lex thinks I'm spiraling. That I fucked it up by giving her space. That I should've just gone for it. He says I'm wasting time chasing a girl who might not want us.

I haven't been painting. Barely sleeping. Lex caught me scrolling through our texts at three a.m. the other night and nearly snapped my phone in half. Called me pathetic. Then kissed me and said, *"Fine Cade. If she's worth it then fucking act like it, babe."*

And she is.

She always has been. Bella's been around forever. Since we were teenagers. She was the chaos in our guest room, the glitter trail in my Range Rover. The girl who used to sneak into my studio and pretend she wasn't watching me paint. I never saw her like this, not really. Maybe in Nashville, but that was so long ago.

Maybe I've been ignoring it for years. Maybe now it's too loud to ignore.

Jesus Christ, I don't *do* this. I don't chase. I don't unravel. I don't obsess. That's Lex's thing. Lex is the one that falls fast and holds on way too tight.

I don't even notice Ellie until she drops into the lounger next to Cal, curls wrapped in a silk scarf, sunglasses covering half her face.

"Cal, that's gross," she drawls, sipping something pink and probably illegal. "Bella will never go for you... or your dick."

Cal scoffs, stretched out shirtless like he's posing for a yacht magazine. "Why the hell not?"

Ellie snorts. "Because you're Callum. You're a walking thirst trap with a superiority complex. She'd chew you up and use your bones for contour."

"She flirts with me all the time, she always has."

"She flirts with everyone," Ellie fires back. "It's literally part of her job. She's the face of Legacy. The center of The Trifecta. Flirting is branding, Cal."

"She doesn't flirt with everyone like she flirts with me."

I close my eyes.

God, someone get me off this fucking boat.

"She's just playing the game, Cal," Ellie continues. "The Trifecta is a brand. Your Row parties elevate that brand. You? You're a pawn. A hot pawn, but still."

"Who wants Callum's dick?" Dad's deep voice cuts in, cool and amused.

We all turn and see Mom standing there with a tray of fruit and two champagne flutes, raising a brow. Behind her, Dad lowers his sunglasses and gives us his signature wink. The one that always means trouble.

"I mean," Dad says, "if we're talking dicks, I'm assuming someone lost a bet."

"Dad," I mutter. "Please stop."

"Just trying to stay informed," he says, settling in like this is perfectly normal.

Mom laughs, hands Dad his drink, and sets down the tray. "So, who started the dick conversation and why is it always Callum?"

Ellie doesn't miss a beat. "Because Cal thinks Bella wants him."

Mom lights up. "Oh, I love Bella. Callum, are you and Bella finally becoming an item?"

Ellie groans. "Mom. No. In no universe is my best friend going anywhere near my brother's dick."

Cal grins as if he's doing the world a favor. "Please. Bells should be honored to get a dick like mine."

Dad nearly chokes on his drink. "Damn right she should. Whitmore men are a premium package."

"Clay dear, stop encouraging him. He's already insufferable."

I get up, done with this whole conversation. I swear August has to be watching us from somewhere taking notes like we're his favorite soap opera. Our family isn't normal. We're a reality show that forgot to hire a therapist.

"Oh don't be salty, bro. Twins get the same face but clearly one of us got the deluxe edition."

I stare at him, brows raised. "You're proud of that sentence?"

"Facts are facts."

Mom waves him off. "Be nice to your brother."

"I am being nice," Cal says. "Just acknowledging my natural gifts."

"Oh my God," Ellie gripes. "I need to go bleach my brain."

Mom shakes her head. "Speaking of Bella, where is she? I miss her. And Lex too. Why did they miss your Dad's birthday?"

Ellie pauses, her drink halfway to her mouth. "She's just busy, Mom."

I jump in casually. "Lex and Damien are at the Hollow Kings send-off for the graduating seniors. Redspire stuff."

Cal snorts. "Theatrics for a bunch of guys who punch people in a basement."

Ellie side-eyes him. "Jealousy doesn't look good on you, Cal. Plus, you fight there all the time."

They keep going—bickering, jabbing, tossing egos around like it's a family sport—but I've already checked out.

All I can see is Bella's last message. Her name on my screen. The four little words that have been sitting there for hours now.

BELLA: You coming or what?

"Fuck this, Cade, quit being a little bitch," I mutter to myself as I begin to type.

ME: I'll be there.

CHAPTER ㉗
BELLA
NEW ORLEANS, LOUISIANA
547 DAYS SINCE ZEKE'S DEATH

CADE: I'll be there.

I read it once. Then again and again. And I smile.

What the hell am I doing?

This is Cade. Ellie's older brother. Cal's twin. The same guy who used to barely look at me when I was fifteen and practically living at their place. Who once told me glitter was a personality flaw and offered me a protein bar like that would somehow fix me.

The one who saw me puking behind their pool house after my first party, handed me a Gatorade, and didn't tell a soul. Just sat next to me in silence while I swore I'd never drink again.

Let's not forget the part that he's also gay. With a boyfriend. And I'm supposed to be focusing on a mission. Not melting over one text from a guy I've known forever.

Get it together, bitch.

"Somethin' good, chérie?"

I look up fast, slipping the phone into my pocket. "Fine," I lie. "Let's just make sure your men are where they're supposed to be."

Sabine arches a perfectly penciled brow, lips curling because she already knows I'm full of shit.

"They'll be there. Long as I get my piece like we agreed."

I nod once. "Stick to your end and everything will go fine."

We climb into the SUV, just the two of us. No Tex. No Nate. Not this time.

Sabine looks like something out of a dark fairy tale. The kind where the witch doesn't die, she wins. Head-to-toe black layers of silk and something sheer that moves like smoke. Gold rings on every finger, some sharp enough to draw blood. Her hair's twisted into this chaotic braided crown with feathers and beads threaded through. Eyes lined in gold and charcoal. Lips painted the color of dried roses.

And when she looks at you, it's like she already knows how you'll die.

Sabine Marchand is the head of *Le Serpent Noir* and a fellow Black Book of mine. The Serpents control elite auction houses and the chemical black market. Basically, if you need a stolen Van Gogh fenced for a private bidder or raw supplies for a dirty bomb, she's your girl. And bonus points, she makes the best damn jambalaya in the entire world. The best.

The leather creaks under us as the doors shut and she starts the engine. The scent of something earthy clings to her. Rosemary, if I had to guess.

"When I got your boy transferred outta there," she says, her dark-brown eyes still on the road. "I did it clean. But my men... well. They got a little excited."

"Yeah," I mutter. "A trail of corpses usually doesn't scream *clean*, Sabine."

She hums, low and lazy. "Made it look like he ran. Slicked the scene with just enough blood to make the feds think the ol' fool blew the doors and hit the road."

Her eyes glint as she cuts me a wicked smile.

"They're scouring highways and rest stops like damn fools. Meanwhile—" She leans in, voice syrupy-sweet. "—he's chained up in my bayou. Right where I want him. Waitin' on you chérie."

"You better be right about this, Sabine."

"Oh, sugar. I'm always right when it comes to *revenge*."

I look out the window, watching the moss-laced trees close in as we leave the city lights behind. My fingers twitch toward the blade tucked under my jacket.

We roll to a stop, gravel crunching beneath the tires as the last sliver of road disappears behind us. Sabine kills the engine and turns to me, eyes gleaming.

"We walk from here, honey."

"Of course we do."

The air outside is thick. Cypress trees loom overhead, branches draped with Spanish moss that sway like ghosts. The mud squelches beneath our feet as we step off the path, following a narrow trail through the swampy dark. Frogs croak in the distance. Something splashes near the bank.

"That better not be a gator," I whisper, narrowing my eyes at the water.

"If it is, let him watch. Gators carry souls, chérie, and this swamp's got stories to tell."

I shoot her a look. "Great. Just what I need. A soul-snatching reptile watching me."

We reach a cabin, or what used to be one. The thing looks stitched together from driftwood and bones, weather-beaten and warped. A single yellow bulb buzzes over the door, casting everything in a jaundiced glow. Wind chimes made from bullet casings clink softly in the breeze.

One of Sabine's men stands on the porch, casually leaning beside the door with a cigarette in his mouth and a shotgun in his hands. He straightens when he sees us.

"He's all tied up for you, ma'am. Just like you asked."

Sabine grins. "Thank ya, baby." She tosses him the keys. "You can go wait outside. Us girls have it from here."

He tips his head and saunters off, disappearing into the shadows without another word.

I climb the porch stairs behind her, my heart pounding harder than I want to admit. The wooden boards creak under our weight.

Sabine pushes open the door and there he is.

Carlos fucking Lucero.

Tied to a chair in the middle of the room, wrists and ankles bound tight, head slumped forward.

He stirs at the sound of us entering, slowly lifting his head. I can't help but grin when the asshole's eyes meet mine.

"Hi, Carlos," I say. "Miss me?"

Carlos thrashes in the chair as the door creaks shut behind us. He tries to speak through the gag—useless frantic and muffled sounds. His face is already slick with sweat.

Good. He's scared.

"Do you know why you're here, Carlos?" I tease.

He grunts again, panicked now, shaking his head like it might buy him mercy. It won't.

Sabine smiles as she strolls toward Carlos, the hem of her long black dress whispering over the warped floorboards. Carlos's eyes cut to her and then go wild when he sees what's coiled around her wrist.

A snake. Thick. Yellow. Smooth as shadow and nearly silent as it slides down her forearm.

"*Revenge*, baby," she purrs, eyes never leaving Carlos. "That's why you're here."

Carlos jerks in the chair, trying to lurch away, but he's bound tight. The chair creaks beneath him. His breathing goes ragged.

"Sabine! Where the fuck did that thing come from?"

Sabine chuckles. "Left it for me, he did. My man Jacques always knows what I need." She strokes the snake's head with one painted fingernail. "This little darling can sense the soul, you know. Knows if a man's good. Or dirty. Knows if he's got blood on his hands."

The snake flicks its tongue in Carlos's direction. Carlos lets out a muffled shriek, his whole body trembling now.

I glance at Sabine. "Your man left us a soul-sensing snake?"

I flash a wicked grin. "Perfect."

I step forward, arms crossed.

"Okay, Carlos, this is Sabine. Sabine, this is Carlos." I point lazily to the snake still curled around Sabine's arm. "And this... is also here for you."

Sabine lifts the snake gently, cradling it with eerie tenderness.

"Her name's Celeste," she says with a hint of reverence.

"Celeste," I echo flatly. "Lovely. Apparently, she's here to see if you have a soul."

Sabine leans in. "To see if it's a good soul... or a wicked one."

"Spoiler alert, babe. It's wicked."

Sabine shrugs. "Never hurts to check."

She steps closer and carefully lays the snake across Carlos's lap. He loses it. He tries to scream but it's muffled by the gag. His body thrashes in the chair. The ropes hold.

Celeste doesn't flinch. She begins to slither with the patience of a predator. Moving up his trembling chest and around his neck. His eyes roll as he tries to suck in a breath. Every inch of him straining away from the cool, scaled body now brushing his jaw.

"Let's see what my girl finds."

Celeste pauses at his throat, her smooth body coiled in a necklace of nightmares. Her head tilts back toward Sabine like she's asking permission.

I glance over, confused as hell. "Uh..."

Sabine just nods once. Celeste sticks her fangs deep into the flesh of Carlos's neck. He lets out a scream through the gag, jerking in the chair like he's been electrocuted.

"Shit!" I jump back, eyes wide. "Please tell me that thing didn't just take my revenge from me."

Sabine steps closer, admiring her little pet. "No, chérie. There's no venom in Celeste. But you were right."

She leans down and lifts it off of him. "His soul is pure evil."

"Great," I mutter, brushing invisible dust off my jeans. "Now that we got that out of the way." I step forward and yank the gag down from Carlos's mouth.

"You bitch," he spits immediately, face red and furious. "Fucking psycho slut—"

"Wow," I cut him off, my tone almost bored. "That is no way to talk to someone who literally has your life in her fucking hands. But okay." I motion toward the snake curling up Sabine's arm. "If you'd rather talk to Celeste."

"No, no!" Carlos panics, eyes flicking to the serpent like she's about to strike again.

"Then let's try this again." I crouch, voice dropping. "Where is Vince?"

He scoffs. "How the fuck should I know? You and your brother got me locked up, remember?"

The second he says *brother*, rage ignites in my chest. The blade slides into his thigh before I even register the motion. Carlos screams, body bucking and blood seeping through his pants.

"See, I just don't believe you, Carlos." I twist the handle slightly, just enough to make him wail again. "That's the thing about liars. They always forget the details."

"I haven't talked to Vince since I got in, I swear," he sobs. "I don't even know where he is."

I stare at him a beat longer, the copper tang of blood already coating the air. He looks pathetic and broken. But pathetic doesn't mean honest.

I glance sideways at Sabine. "Got any snakes that can tell if a man is lyin'?"

"No snakes like that here, sorry honey."

"Hmm. Okay, Carlos. Next question. Since you don't know where Vince is, answer me this, did you do it?"

"Did I do what, bitch?" he says and spits at the floor.

Wrong answer.

I rip the blade out of his thigh with one clean pull. His scream bounces off the cabin walls. I move it up and slice a thin, slow line straight down his chest. Blood blossoms immediately.

His scream turns to whimpering. I press the tip of the blade to his crotch, not hard, but enough to make the threat clear.

"Call me a bitch again," I whisper, smiling sweetly, "and your pathetic excuse for a cock goes *bye-bye*. You understand?"

"Please! No!" he cries, panic flooding his voice. "Please!"

"Then answer the fucking question!" My voice cracks like a whip. "Did you do it, Carlos?"

He gulps, voice lower now, almost careful. Looks like he's learning.

"I don't know what you're talking about."

"Zeke!" I yell the name like a curse. "Chicago. Did you send the tip that got my brother killed?"

Something shifts in his face, just for a second. Then the smile creeps back. My stomach drops. My breath catches. That grin, that look, it hits like a fucking freight train.

Panic. Rage. *Dylan.*

Sabine must see it—or feel it—because she's suddenly beside me. Calm. Present. She gently slides the knife from my hand and replaces it with cold steel.

A pistol.

My fingers curl around it automatically. Carlos freezes.

"I had no idea the mutt was dead," he grits. Then, that sick, rotten grin widens. "But I wish I'd been the one to kill him."

My finger grazes the trigger. I raise the gun, the barrel aimed straight at Carlos's forehead.

"Do it!" he screams, spit flying, eyes wild.

My finger tightens on the trigger.

"Isabella," Sabine says softly, a lullaby cutting through a war-zone. "Be smart now, baby. Don't waste your revenge on a head-shot."

I glance at her. She winks and dips her eyes towards Carlos's crotch. I nod. Then I shift my aim down a little lower and pull the trig-ger. The shot cracks like thunder. Blood sprays. His body jerks against the chair. He howls like an animal caught in a trap.

Sabine laughs behind me. "Good girl."

"You fucking bitches!" Carlos roars, spit and agony mangling every word.

Sabine clicks her tongue and steps forward. "May I?"

I nod, handing her the gun without a word.

She circles him slowly. "See here, little man," she says, crouch-ing to eye level. "I don't take kindly to anyone who hurts babies." Carlos trembles.

"And from what I hear?" She tilts her head. "You're one of the worst. Taking and selling little ones. Letting monsters into your house to touch and torture the children you were given to protect."

He whimpers.

Sabine lifts the pistol and takes two quick shots to both knees. Carlos's screams rip through the bayou like a banshee's wail.

I wince. "Damn."

Sabine just blows the smoke from the barrel. "Told you not to waste revenge on the head-shot." She turns me towards the door.

Carlos sobs behind us, his breath catching in ragged gasps. "Please," he cries. "Please don't leave me here alone like this."

Sabine pauses mid-step and turns back, smile curling with venom. "Oh honey," she says sweetly, "we're not leaving you here alone."

The door creaks open again. Two of her men step inside, both dressed in black, faces blank. One's carrying a can of gasoline. The other's holding a damn industrial torch.

Carlos sees it and loses whatever scrap of sanity he was still clinging to.

"No, no. PLEASE!"

We keep walking.

"Bella, please. Mariela. And my child."

I stop at the door. Slowly turn. He's pale now, panicked in a whole new way. "Please, Bella. Please don't hurt them."

I stare him down, voice sharp as a blade. "Mariela helped me and Zeke get out. Helped us disappear. She saved us, I would never hurt her. Or her child. Trust me, Mariela and her daughter will live a long, happy life without you, Carlos."

And then I walk out. Behind me, the screaming starts before we even reach the trees. Wet, raw, soul-deep screams that echo off the water like a damn funeral dirge.

We don't look back. By the time we make it to Sabine's car, the smoke is already rising in the distance. A low, orange glow flickers between the trees. The bayou has its revenge. I climb into the passenger seat, exhale slowly, and open my phone.

@LucaWasHere
Damn, Izzy. That shot was slick.
Nice work wrecking Carlos's dick.
Did it feel good? Watching him fall?
Hearing him beg? Seeing him crawl?

Told you, pet. You were built for war.
It's in your blood, deep in your core.
You're finally waking up to who you are.
My chaos. My violence. My rising star.

My fingers curl tight around the phone. Sabine slides into the driver's seat, glancing at me sideways.

"You good, chérie?"

I nod once, jaw locked. "Yeah."

Sabine taps her long nails on the steering wheel. "Now don't forget what I asked for, baby. I did you a favor, I expcct the same."

"Your data's being returned to you as we speak," I say smoothly, fingers tapping at the screen. "Pleasure as always, Sabine."

She smiles like she just won a hand of high-stakes poker. "Pleasure's mine. You let Sabine know if you ever need anything else, baby."

CHAPTER ㉘
C A D E
W E X L E Y   U N I V E R S I T Y
551 DAYS SINCE ZEKE'S DEATH

BELLA: So, do you want to maybe come
to a Trifecta practice next week?

That's the text that did it. Now I'm here on the front row. Sitting beside about twenty chicks and fifty other guys ranging from jocks, all the way to Wall Street interns, to a guy I'm pretty sure was in my sculpting class last year.

I shift in my seat, arms crossed, trying to act like I belong. Like this is normal. Like I'm not lowkey sweating under my damn henley.

Because I know exactly why I'm here. She invited me.

And that should feel innocent, friendly even. But it doesn't. Not when I see her walk in, all legs and fire and confidence in a tiny purple sports bra with *BELLA* across her chest. Her black shorts say *TRIFECTA*, same as the ones on Haley and Ellie.

The rest of the Legacy girls wear basic black. Their tops say *LEGACY*, not their names. I guess The Trifecta gets their own personalized gear.

Some guy is helping Bella stretch. I try not to stare, but of course I do. So does everyone else.

"What the fuck are you doing here?"

I glance up. Cal and August.

Of course.

"I was invited."

Cal scoffs. "Fuck right you were."

"Bella invited me."

That shuts him up. For exactly one second.

August barks a laugh. "No fucking way." He claps once, loud enough that one of the Legacy girls turns and glares. "Dude, I thought you were joking when you said that shit back at Cinco."

Cal's head whips toward him. "What shit?"

August grins like he's just pulled the pin on a grenade and can't wait to watch it blow us to pieces.

"Your brother and his Russian boytoy are on the hunt for a third. Apparently, they've got their sights set on Bella."

Cal jerks. "You're fucking kidding me."

"Nope," August says, way too pleased. "Looks like your brother's trying to make it a full-blown throuple."

I grind my teeth, ignoring the heat rising in my chest. I know that look on Cal's face. The same look he used to get back when Bella would curl up on the couch with me during family movie nights. The same look he had when we were in high school and she showed up drunk to a house party, and I was the one she texted for help.

The same look he gave me in Nashville.

"You're serious."

"I am," I say simply. "And I'm not here to fight, Cal."

His jaw flexes. "You know I've always liked her."

I nod once. "I know."

"So what, now you want her too?"

"Just drop it, Cal."

Cal lets out a bitter laugh. "You always say that. You always try to take what's mine."

I meet his eyes. "I didn't know she was yours."

"She's not, but that doesn't mean you get to swoop in like—"

"I'm not swooping in." I cut him off.

"Then what are you doing, Cade?"

"Trying not to lose her," I say quietly.

Before Cal can fire back or throw a punch, Coach Javi's voice cracks across the gym like a man on a mission.

"Thank you all for coming," he says, his Latin accent smooth and charismatic. He's standing mid-court with a clipboard and one dramatic hand raised.

Cal's mouth opens again but I shoot him a glare.

"Later," I mutter.

"I see some familiar faces this week." He throws a pointed wink toward Cal and August and then to a few of the basketball boys sitting nearby. "Football gods, Order royalty, and resident heart-breakers.

Welcome back, gentlemen."

Cal leans back in his seat, arms crossed and staring right at the girl of my dreams. August raises his beer like it's a toast.

"And some new faces," Javi continues, letting his gaze sweep over the rest of the bleachers, then pauses right on me. "Welcome, welcome. Consider yourselves lucky. Not everyone gets to witness greatness up close."

There's a ripple of laughter from the crowd. I manage a tight smile.

Javi flips to a new page on his clipboard and clicks his pen. "We are The Wexley Legacy. And this—" He gestures to the floor where Bella, Ellie, and Haley are now in formation, their matching sets practically glowing under the lights. "—is The Trifecta."

Coach Javi claps once. "Alright, Knox. You know what to do."

Knox steps up to the center with that easy, cocky grin of his. He's got his laptop under one arm, mic in the other, and somehow manages to look like both a DJ and a cult leader.

"Ladies," he drawls into his mic, "and fellow Wolves, welcome to the official Wexley Legacy rehearsal." A pause, dramatic and full of swagger. "But more importantly, as Javi said, welcome to The Trifecta."

The crowd hoots. Cal and August fist bump like jackasses. I just shift in my seat, trying to look casual.

Knox grins. "Now, let's set the tone. Problem Child?"

Bella steps forward, black shorts hugging her hips, that purple sports bra doing things to me I'm not proud of. Her ponytail swings with each step, but it's her eyes that lock me in place.

She's not the same girl from Cinco de Mayo. She's different now, focused. Fierce. Like she walked through hell and came back colder, meaner, and untouchable. There's power in her now. Not the showy kind. The kind that makes the room hold its breath.

"Okay," Bella says, radiating confidence as her voice fills the room. "We're here to dance, to practice, and to kick ass at Worlds. But that doesn't mean we don't get to have a little fun."

Ellie and Haley fall in behind her, matching energy like it's choreographed, which knowing them, it probably is.

"You'll see us dance. Sing. Lip sync. And yeah." She smirks, eyes skimming the front row. "There'll be a few chairs."

"Woo!" August yells like he's at a strip club.

"Not you, Augie."

The gym explodes in laughter, August included. She spins slowly, making sure she's got the room's attention.

She does.

"Now. If you're lucky enough to be picked for a chair dance, there are rules." Her voice sharpens. "We touch you. You don't touch us."

Instant silence.

"And if you break that rule or make any of us uncomfortable, Josh, Drake, and Sam—" She motions toward the three guys now stretching behind the group. "—will take you out."

"Literally," Ellie adds sweetly.

Cal lets out a low laugh. "Harsh."

Bella raises an eyebrow. "Not harsh, baby. Policy."

"Alright, ladies," Knox calls out, a devilish grin spreading across his face. "Let's start the night off sexy."

He raises one hand like a ringmaster calling in the lions. "With a chair!"

Cheers, whistles, and a few *oh shits* break out from the guys in the row behind us.

Knox chuckles into the mic. "Y'all asked for it."

One of the freshman dancers rushes forward, dragging a single black chair and places it dead center. The room hums with anticipation.

Knox grins. "Alright, gentlemen... who wants the first chair today?"

Shouts and whistles bounce off the walls. Hell, half the football team practically is jumping out of their sneakers. It's chaos, competitive, testosterone-fueled chaos.

Knox laughs. "Damn. Y'all are thirsty."

He turns toward the front row. "Callum Whitmore," he calls out like it's already decided.

Cal throws an arm around my shoulder and leans in. "Maybe

next time, bro," he says with that cocky quarterback grin I loathe so much.

He struts to the chair like its game day and he's already won. He drops into the seat, legs spread wide, and grins at Bella like he's waiting for dessert.

"Cal," she says, all sugary-sweet. "You know the rules. Shirts off. Now."

Cal stands, turns to face the crowd, and rips his shirt off in one dramatic motion. He tosses it back toward the bleachers where three girls nearly get into a fistfight catching it.

August leans in, voice dripping with mock sympathy. "So much for your throuple. Maybe next time, Whit."

I'm still trying to decide whether I'm going to murder August or just let Lex do it for me when Knox glances my way and winks.

"Whoa, whoa, whoa. Is your whole family here, bro?" He points at me. "Let's get the other Whitmore out here!"

I stand up.

"And Augie? What the hell, man. Come on down."

August jumps up, strips his shirt off, and whoops like he just won the damn lottery. Two freshmen sprint out with more chairs. They set them up beside Cal's.

Knox claps his hands and points like he's a game show host. "Whit twin, you sit in the middle here. Shirt off man, it's the rules." He pats the other chair, "August, you're here."

Bella starts gliding toward me. Perky breasts practically spilling out of that purple sports bra. Head tilted, eyes locked on me, teasing smile playing at the corner of her mouth like she already knows how this ends.

I know, without a doubt, she did this on purpose.

Beside me Cal looks like he's about to rupture a blood vessel. The King of The Row, dethroned in real time. August leans back as if he's watching the world's hottest soap opera, smirking like the chaos is his personal gift.

"Okay, boys. You know the rules." Bella paces in front of us. A general before the battle begins. "Hands behind your back. No touching. Just enjoy the ride."

She catches my eye before giving a small nod to Knox.

"Let's give them a show."

I don't even register the song. Pitbull I think, maybe. Doesn't matter. It's fast, hypnotic, and seductive as hell. But the truth is, I'm not even remotely listening to the sounds blaring through Knox's speaker.

I'm watching her.

They move together, Legacy and Trifecta in perfect sync. A masterpiece of motion, hips, legs, and torsos folding and unfolding like someone painted lust and power into human form and hit play.

Bella turns and her eyes lock on mine. She strolls up, places her hands firmly on my shoulders, and lowers herself onto my lap like it's her home.

I'm gone. Utterly, completely done for.

The weight of her, the heat of her, the curve of her spine as she arches her back.

That smile.

God, that smile. All fire and mischief and something deeper, something meant just for me. I could paint it a million times and never catch it as beautiful as the real thing.

And in this moment, I believe she can ruin me.

Hell, maybe I want her to.

When the music cuts and she rises, it feels like being yanked from a dream I never want to wake from. I drag in a breath and can't help but think that Lex would fucking love this.

Knox's voice cuts through the haze. "Alright! How about that first chair, huh?"

The crowd cheers.

"Thank you, boys. You can return to your seats... or if you need a few minutes to adjust we can do that too."

Cal grumbles something under his breath beside me. I don't hear it. I'm too busy watching her walk away.

We're back in our seats, the buzz still crackling in the air like static. Cal's fuming, arms crossed like he's seconds from punching a wall. August keeps laughing under his breath, nursing whatever is left in his beer.

From behind me, a hand claps my shoulder. "You lucky bastard," some guy mutters. I don't even turn. I can't. Because Bella's back out there and this time, it's not a chair routine.

It's something different. The music is slower, darker, like honey over a knife's edge. The lights drop, shadows stretching across the floor.

The entire Legacy team moves as one body, but my eyes find her instantly. She's telling a story and I don't know the plot, but I do know that I'd follow it anywhere. It's beauty, yes. But it's more than that. It's grief.

Lust. Rage. Power.

My phone buzzes.

LEX: How's the show, babe?

ME: She's the one, Lex. Trust me.

LEX: The one? You sure about this?

ME: I'm really sure. You're not here, Lex. You don't see her. She moves like a reckoning. And when she smiles? Babe, it's like watching lightning flirt with the sea.

LEX: Jesus Christ. You and your fucking metaphors. Fine. I trust you. Ask her out. Just don't bring her home until you're sure. I love you.

After what feels like an entire concert series of routines, Knox finally grabs the mic again, laughing like the smug little shit he is.

"Alright, alright," he calls out. "Welcome to Legacy. I'm Knox, your humble DJ-slash-hype-man. This is The Trifecta: Bella, Haley, and Ellie. Thank you for coming to watch my girls shake their asses today."

Chairs scrape and the guys scramble. Half the team looks like they're about to faint. Cal makes a direct line for Bella. She hugs him tight as if they're close. They are close.

I glance away for a second and then she's in front of me.

"Thanks for coming," she says, still a little breathless. "What'd you think?"

"That was..." I exhale. "Honestly, that was incredible. You're a real artist."

She bites her lip but there's something softer under it. "Thanks. That means a lot coming from an actual artist like yourself."

We stand there a second, not quite ready to walk away.

"You want to get coffee sometime?" I ask, trying not to sound like I've been dying to ask that.

"Um." She lingers on the word, which only makes my heart trip over itself. "Yeah. I'd love to."

Behind her, Cal looks like he's about to commit a felony. August is doing nothing to stop it, too busy laughing his ass off.

But she doesn't notice. Or maybe she does and doesn't care.

Either way. It's a date.

CHAPTER ㉙
BELLA
ROSETHORNE MANSION
WEXLEY UNIVERSITY
555 DAYS SINCE ZEKE'S DEATH

"I cannot believe you are going on a date with my brother," Ellie says, voice pitched halfway between disbelief and betrayal as she stares at me like I've just committed war crimes.

"Like... Cade Whitmore. My actual brother. Who I share DNA with."

I roll my eyes and flip my hair over one shoulder, trying to act unbothered even though my insides are spiraling like I'm fifteen again, sneaking into his art studio just to be near him.

"Okay, it's not a date. It's literally just coffee."

Haley spins in her vanity chair, legs crossed, and grins like a cat with a secret. "Oh, babe. It's totally a date. Did you see the way Callum and Cade looked like they were about to murder each other at practice? It was like a damn pissing contest with choreography."

Ellie groans and flops backward on the couch, blonde curls spilling over the side dramatically. "Gross. Ew. No. My best friend and my brother cannot be a thing. That is trauma I will not unpack in therapy."

I sip my water bottle, leaning against the wall and trying to ignore the way my pulse spikes just thinking about it. Cade Whitmore. The same guy who once called me Ellie's obnoxious sidekick. Who used to give me the silent treatment whenever I was too loud at family dinners. Who picked me up drunk from a party when I was sixteen and never told anyone.

"For the last time," I say, "it's not a thing. We're just hanging out."

Haley raises a brow. "Uh-huh. And he just happened to ask you to 'hang out' right after you gave him the chair routine of his life, all while Cal sat beside him foaming at the mouth."

Ellie groans. "Can we not talk about my brother foaming?"

I bite back a laugh. "You two are unhinged."

"And you." Haley points at me. "Are into him."

"My brother, Bella," Ellie says, her voice rising like she's about to break into song.

"Alright, El you need to chill," Haley cuts in. "At least it's not the womanizer one."

"Thank you!" I gesture dramatically. "Also, can we calm down. It's just coffee."

Haley narrows her eyes. "That's how it starts."

"Plus," I mutter, trying to sound casual. "He's already in a relationship."

Haley chucks a throw pillow at my face. "See! You do like him."

"Oh my God," I gripe, catching the pillow. "You girls are the worst."

Ellie sighs. "Fine. You're right, Hales. If she's gonna date one of my brothers, at least she picked the good one."

"I'm not dating anyone," I mumble. "He has a boyfriend. It's just coffee."

"Denial," Haley sings, kicking her feet. "First comes coffee, then comes well, you know."

"I hate all of you."

"You love us." Then Ellie squints at her phone, face morphing into a dangerous grin. "I wonder if Lex knows..."

My head snaps up. "What are you doing?"

She doesn't answer, just starts typing. A second later, her eyes widen.

"Oh. My. Fucking. God."

She immediately dials Cade. "What the hell, bro? Why didn't you tell me?"

A pause.

"Lex just told me your plans... with Bella!"

I cover my face. Haley looks like she's watching live theater.

Ellie gasps. "She's my best friend, Cade."

Haley and I exchange the most alarmed glance in history.

More silence.

"Ew, no! I do not want the details!" she screeches. "Yeah, she's on her way."

Then she hangs up and turns toward us like she's about to announce a royal wedding.

Haley leans forward. "What the hell was that?"

Ellie's ocean-blue eyes lock on me. "Bella..."

"Oh no," I mutter under my breath.

She leans in. "What is your opinion on a threesome?"

Haley chokes on her drink and grabs her phone. "I gotta call Knox."

I bury my face in a pillow. "I officially hate everyone in this room."

The Black and Burgundy - Wexley University

I should probably call Dr. Monroe.

Because walking into The Black and Burgundy, Wexley's coffee shop on the quad for a not-date with my best friend's brother while replaying *'What is your opinion on a threesome?'* on a loop in my brain definitely has to count as a psychotic break.

I'm nervous. Like, *about to fake my own death and flee the country*, nervous. This isn't me. I don't do coffee dates. I don't do any dates. I fuck and leave. In and out. And I sure as hell don't do sweet, artsy guys who come with family attachments and actual emotional availability.

It's just coffee. Normal people do this all the time. Caffeine. Conversation. Casual friendliness. Not the end of the world. Or is it?

What am I doing?

This is Cade. The same guy who once asked if I was lost when I wandered into his art studio at fifteen. Who used to call me Ellie's stray and swore Van Gogh would've hated my glitter eyeliner. He was just Ellie's hot, judgmental brother. Quiet, broody, always halfway covered in charcoal and pretending I didn't exist.

Nashville was the one time he saw me, I think. And even that felt like a glitch in the matrix. Since then, nothing. I've barely spoken to the guy in years.

But then I see him. Already at the corner table by the window, back lit by soft morning light as if the universe decided to stage the moment. Same messy light chestnut brown hair, but somehow it works now. Like he's grown into it. Worn leather jacket over a maroon hoodie, fingers ink-stained around a mug. He's still the artist, but sharper... hotter.

Fuck.

His hazel eyes sweep the room and then land on me with something softer and warmer than recognition. Like maybe he remembers everything I thought he forgot. And that smile he gives me? Yeah. That's definitely new. I inhale once and attempt steady myself.

You can do this.

He stands the second he sees me. Not out of obligation or for show. It's like it's instinct, like some black-and-white movie gentleman who never forgot how to treat a girl.

He doesn't say a word as he pulls out my chair, waits until I'm seated, then slides it. His cedar and ink scent fills the space between us. It's soft, familiar, and dangerous. It smells like late nights and sketchbooks and the boy I used to watch draw when he thought no one was looking.

Then he sits across from me and holds out a bouquet of daisies. My favorite. Bright, simple, and perfect.

"You remembered?"

"Of course I did."

Who does that? Not fucking Laing. Wes never did. No one I know. Not in my world. Most of the men in my life are fighters, soldiers, or ghosts. They don't hold chairs. They hold weapons. Secrets. Sins.

"Glad you could make it."

"Yeah... thanks for inviting me," I say, trying to sound chill.

Totally not chill. My pulse is sprinting. My brain still echoing *'What is your opinion on a threesome?'* and now I'm seriously wondering if I should've called Dr. Monroe instead of showing up.

Thank God the waitress appears. She's tall, gorgeous, definitely older, and completely ignores me. Her eyes lock on Cade like he's the prize in some Manhattan dating raffle.

"Good morning," she purrs. "What can I get you?"

Cade, to his credit, doesn't even look at her. "Just a black coffee. Thanks."

"Caramel latte," I say, bitchier than necessary. "Extra whip."

The waitress barely glances at me, gives Cade another smile like she's leaving her number in it, and then struts off like she's the one onstage.

"Okay. So, I have a question."

Cade pinches the bridge of his nose. "Ellie told you."

"Yeah..." I fidget with my mother's locket. "Um."

"I told her not to," he says quickly, leaning in a little. "I just wanted to get to know you again. That's all. It's... a long story."

I stare at him, trying to figure out if I should run or pull out a notebook. "Well, I've got about an hour and a half until I need to head to practice," I say dryly. "So... go."

"Okay. I guess I'll just get straight to it."

My pulse spikes. Maybe I should have ordered a chamomile tea.

"You know I have a boyfriend. Lex. We've been dating since our freshman year. But things have gotten complicated."

I narrow my eyes. "Complicated?"

He scratches the back of his neck, hazel eyes flicking down for a second. "Well, not complicated exactly. It's just that we both need more."

Thank God, the waitress shows up and drops off our drinks.

"What do you mean, more?" I ask, fingers tightening around my latte.

"Both of us agreed we wanted someone else to come into our relationship."

"And you thought I'd be a good option?" I try to keep it light, but it lands a little too defensive.

"Honestly? I wouldn't have ever guessed it would be you."

"Wow. Thanks."

"No wait," He laughs under his breath, shaking his head. "I just mean... you've always been around. Sneaking Pop-Tarts, raiding

Ellie's closet, dragging Cal into trouble. I remember the glitter, the sarcasm, and the way you used to argue with me over which Fast & Furious movie was the best."

"The fifth one is superior and you know it."

He grins. "See? That. You've always had this fire. But that night, Cinco de Mayo, I watched you dance and it was like seeing you for the first time. Not just as Ellie's friend. Not just the girl who once puked on my shoes after a party and still managed to flirt with the Uber driver.

You were something else. All power and grace and control. It wasn't just hot, it was art. I couldn't look away."

His eyes lock on mine, soft but intense. "So, I talked to Lex and told him how I felt. He's a little more skeptical about all of this. About bringing someone in, especially you." He gives a little shrug.

"Then he asked me to talk to you, get to know you, and see if this has anything real to it before we even think about going further," he finishes, gesturing between us.

Okay. Most forward *coffee-not-a-date* of all time.

I let out a breath, still gripping my caramel latte.

"Wow. Okay. That's a lot."

Cade groans and leans back. "I know. I wish Ellie hadn't said anything. I just wanted this to be a simple meet and greet. What's your favorite color? Football team? Song? That kind of thing."

"Blue. Razorbacks for college, Chiefs for pro, and "Nobody" by Dylan Scott," I say automatically, then take a long, slow sip of my latte like I didn't just answer like a damn Tinder response.

He flinches a little bit, probably at the choice of song and the memory of Nashville, but then he laughs and damn it, he has a nice smile. One of those easy, genuine ones that reaches his hazel eyes. The kind that makes it hard to stay annoyed.

Cade grins, still watching me. "See? That was way less terrifying."

I stir my latte, staring into the swirl of caramel like it's going to give me answers. Dr. Monroe's voice creeps in uninvited. *"Bella, if there was someone out there who could give you both—the release and the connection—wouldn't that be worth letting in? Even just a little?"*

I'd rolled my eyes when he said that. Thought it was romanticized bullshit wrapped in a copay.

I exhale slowly, a lopsided grin tugging at my mouth. "Okay, fine. Let's get to know each other."

His brows lift, searching my eyes.

"Favorite color?" I ask.

"Green," Cade answers.

"Team?"

"College, Wexley."

"Obviously, you Whitmore's and your legacy shit," I say.

"Pro, please don't hate me, The Bills."

I pretend to clutch my pearls. "That's disgusting, but it tracks. I remember being the only Chiefs fan on Sunday Nights at your parents' house."

He laughs again and my chest does this annoying flutter thing. "Song?"

"Far Away," he says without missing a beat.

"Nickelback?"

He grins. "Don't mock it. That song ruined me in high school."

I smile over the rim of my mug. "You're such a walking contradiction, Whitmore."

"What, because I like sad rock ballads and turn emotions into brushstrokes?"

"Because you like Nickelback and somehow made it sexy."

Cade smiles and leans forward, hands wrapped around his coffee cup. "So... what's the dream, Bella? After school. What do you want?"

To kill Vince. To destroy every man who sees a child as currency and sleeps just fine. But I probably shouldn't say that over lattes.

I tilt my head. "Honestly? Haven't thought that far ahead."

He raises a brow.

"If I had to guess." I swirl my spoon through the foam. "Something with dance. Maybe the KC Chiefs if I'm feeling extra sparkly. Or maybe open a studio one day. Teach little boys and girls how to kick ass in rhinestones."

He leans forward, forearms resting on the table, eyes locked on mine like I'm some kind of mystery he's determined to solve.

I clear my throat. "What about you? Going to carry the Whitmore torch into the nearest Wall Street boardroom?"

He laughs, leaning back in his chair. "God, no. That's Cal's dream, not mine. I just want to paint, draw."

He says it like it's obvious. Like it's always been there.

"I want to travel," he says. "See how light hits stone at Giotto's Bell Tower in Florence, sketch the shadows in Santorini, paint the skyline in Tokyo. I want to capture those moments, not to sell. Just to keep them. I don't know, maybe open a little gallery someday. Nothing fancy, just mine."

"That sounds perfect, Cade."

We talk for the rest of the hour, back and forth, easy. Shows. Music. Most embarrassing high school moments. All the things we somehow never talked about even when I was crashing in their guest room after practice.

Then he asks about my family and my smile slips.

Cade notices. "Sorry," he says, voice quiet. "Didn't mean to pry."

I shake my head. "It's okay. It's just not a happy story."

He nods. "Ellie told me enough to know it hurt. I remember when Zeke died, but she didn't tell me every—"

"Murdered," I cut in. "Zeke was murdered."

Cade's eyes widen, the words catching in his throat. "Shit. Bella, I'm so sorry."

I take a breath and sip my coffee. "It's okay. Just not really... first date talk."

He smiles, warm and a little sly. "So you do agree it's a date."

Despite myself, I laugh. Just a little. And just like that, some of the ache lifts. "I guess it is a date."

I glance at my phone and curse under my breath. "Shit. A date that's officially about to make me late for practice."

"What?"

"I'm so sorry, but I've got to go," I say, grabbing my bag.

"Hey, let me take you."

I hesitate. "It's okay, I can run."

"No, seriously," he says, pushing up from his seat and juggling his keys. "Wexley's got hills. And I'll get you there on time, trust me. My car is pretty fast."

"Careful, Whitmore. One of the last times I got into your car... it was technically stolen."

He huffs a laugh. "Yeah, well at least this time you won't be driving."

We head outside and he leads me to his car. Of course, it's not just a car. It's a brand-new Aston Martin Vantage, all matte black and wicked curves. Sleek, low to the ground, with blood-red brake calipers and carbon fiber trim.

A Whitmore-mobile if I've ever seen one.

He opens the door like a gentleman. "After you."

The short drive is quiet but warm, filled with little glances and charged silence. When we pull up outside the gym he puts the car in park but doesn't shut it off.

"I had a great time," he says, voice softer now.

"Me too."

He holds my gaze for a second longer. "Can I call you later?"

I nod, fingers tightening around the strap of my bag. "Sure." I turn and head up the stairs, heart still thumping like I'm mid-performance. But just as I reach the top, my phone vibrates in my hand.

@LucaWasHere
What do you think you're doing, Izzy?
Cafés and coy smiles? Don't get me dizzy.
He touched your wrist like he had a right.
Next time, I'll show him how I bite.

CHAPTER ㉚
BELLA
DR. MONROE'S OFFICE
MANHATTAN, NEW YORK
573 DAYS SINCE ZEKE'S DEATH

So, how have things been since our last session?" Dr. Monroe says, uncapping his pen.

I blow out a heavy breath. "I don't know. Complicated."

"Care to explain?"

"Not really."

"Bella."

"I know. We've talked about this. Vulnerability, connection, whatever." I wave a hand vaguely. "Fine. So... my mind's been all over the place. I started dating this guy. Cade."

"You've mentioned him before." More scribbling.

"I've technically known him forever," I add. "But we just re-connected. And it's good. Really good."

He finally looks up. "You're smiling."

"Am I?"

He nods once. "That sounds like a positive step."

"It is. I think. It's just, God, it's a lot."

His pen stills. "What's the part that feels like a lot?"

I glance at the ceiling. "He has a boyfriend."

His eyebrows lift slightly, judgment-free awareness in his gaze.

"And they, um, kind of want me to be with both of them," I say, rushing the words.

Monroe tilts his head. "I see."

"It's not a throuple," I add quickly. "I mean, I guess yeah it kind of is, but not in a weird way. Like, they're already together. For years. And now they want me to just... join?"

Monroe hums and writes something else. His expression doesn't change.

"And I know I sound crazy. I really like Cade, I think I have ever since I was a teen. And from what he's said about Lex, I know I'll like him too. And they seem to actually—God, I don't even know—want me. Like, for real."

"But?"

"But what if I'm just a phase?" My voice squeaks, embarrassing as hell. "What if I ruin it? What if they realize I don't fit? That I'm too dark, or too much, or too broken."

Monroe finally sets his pen down. "Why do you think they would want you in the first place if you didn't already fit?"

"Because I'm shiny on the outside," I mutter. "Because I know how to perform. But what happens when that fades and they're stuck with the reality?"

He studies me. "What is the reality, Bella?"

"I'm loud. I'm bitter. I'm obsessive. Fucking traumatized."

"You're also resilient. Focused. And highly capable of love, whether or not you believe it yet."

I snort. "Do you write those things in a little therapist affirmation journal?"

"No," Monroe replies evenly. "I write them in your file."

I laugh, too tired to care. "It's messing with everything. My dances, my missions. I literally almost got shot at a drop last night because I was too busy thinking about Cade's mouth down on me and Lex's stupid pictures I stalk on Instagram."

Monroe blinks. "That's quite an image."

"I'm serious. If O'Malley hadn't grabbed my vest, I'd be dead. And the last thought in my head would've been Cade going down on me and saying sweetheart like he wanted to ruin me."

He scribbles again. Probably under a heading like *hyper-sexual spiral, danger to self, and wants to be ruined.*

"Bella," he says calmly, "you've always carried stress well. But this is different. This is emotional stress. Intimacy. It's not just pressure, it's uncertainty."

"I don't like uncertainty."

"I know. You like precision. Perfection. Power."

"All the best P's."

"Here's a better one. Patience. Because this relationship won't be perfect. It'll be messy. Awkward. Human. It's going to take time and probably a lot of it."

I glance down at my hands. "So, what, I just jump in and hope I don't drown?"

"You survived foster care. A monster for a foster father. Multiple missions. Dylan's death. Zeke's death."

His voice softens. "I think you can survive two boys trying to love you."

I let that one sit.

"You always perform better under pressure," he adds dryly. "Maybe the universe decided it'll take two men to handle your dramatic ass."

"Are you calling me dramatic, doc?"

"Clinically. Yes."

I shake my head. "You might be right."

Monroe leans back. "Then stop spiraling. Let them try. Let yourself try."

I glance toward the window where the skyline's half-blurred in summer haze. "Maybe I will."

"And Bella?"

"Yeah?"

"If you get shot because you were distracted by anyone's mouth again, I'm calling your whole team in for a group session."

I groan. "You're the worst."

"You say that," Monroe says, already reaching for his next form, "and yet you'll be back next week."

CHAPTER ③①
BELLA
ROSETHORNE MANSION
WEXLEY UNIVERSITY
576 DAYS SINCE ZEKE'S DEATH

Cade's mouth is on me like he's ravenous, but not reckless. No, this is a slow, focused, delicious torture. One that I welcome with open arms—well, legs. The kind that says he's waited for this. His hands grip my thighs like they're his, as if he's staking a claim he's been dying to make since our first coffee-non-date, or maybe even Nashville.

My back arches off the bed, a strangled gasp slipping out, "Cade..."

He groans against me, sending a tremor through my core that feels like a breaking point.

We've been testing the edges of this thing, testing us, before he brings Lex into the picture. And I still can't believe I'm even saying that. I'm dating a guy with the hope of eventually adding another one.

At first, the whole throuple situation scared the shit out of me. But I'd be lying if I said I'm not excited about the possibility of it now.

But when it's Cade, when it's this? God, it almost feels inevitable.

So many nights tangled in rooftop conversations and late-night texts. So many coffees and dinners and inside jokes that go back years.

He knows my sarcasm. My coffee order. The way I hum when I'm thinking too hard and chew pens when I'm anxious. He knows the version of me that fit neatly into their family orbit, but not the parts that shattered and rebuilt themselves after.

He doesn't know about Dylan. Or the Black Books. Or Zeke, fully. Or what I really do after dance practice. To him, I'm just the girl from a bad foster situation with a dead brother and a past I don't talk about. A girl who loves to dance. A girl he wants to spoil. Protect. Worship.

Cade is the sweetest. He carries the conversation like a pro.

Opens doors and sends playlists. Shows up with daisies and asks how practice went like it's the most important question in the world.

He remembers things. Like how I used to steal his hoodies and fall asleep on the Whitmore's couch after too much sugar and too little sleep. How I always hated mornings but somehow never missed a single dance class. How I once made Ellie a glitter bomb that exploded in his car and he didn't speak to us for a week.

He remembers *me*, even the messy, chaotic, glitter-coated parts.

And right now, he's driving me insane in the best way possible.

I cry out as the pressure inside me fractures, sharp, aching, and unbearable. My fingers claw through his chestnut brown hair, anchoring me to something real, something solid, while the rest of me unravels beneath his mouth.

He doesn't let up. With a rhythmic, teasing heat, he strokes slow then fast until the trembling starts. My legs give way and my breath hitches, splintering into broken gasps.

The thick and addictive smell of cedar and ink wraps around me. It fills my lungs, clings to my skin, and marks me as his. I breathe him in and fall apart for him, again and again, until I'm not even sure where I end and he begins.

He groans against me like the taste of me is his only religion and this is the altar where he worships. Cade's hands grip my thighs, needing to keep me there, needing to own every inch of my surrender. And he does. God, he does.

He wraps his lips around my clit and sucks hard before thrusting two fingers deep inside me, curling them upward.

"Fuck! Cade, oh!" I cry out, my world shattering as a shuddering heat rips through me. My thighs clamp around his head, a desperate, crushing hold. Cade never pulls back. He stays, his mouth still moving as if he's drinking in the way I break apart just for him.

He tenderly kisses his way up my body. Like every inch of me deserves worship, and he's grateful for the privilege.

"You okay, sweetheart?" he murmurs, voice thick with adoration, lips brushing my ribs and sending goosebumps skittering across my stomach.

"Better than okay," I whisper, still trembling. "So much better."

He smiles against my skin and kisses me. It's deep, unhurried, and tastes like me. Then his mouth trails lower, warm and wet against my throat, my collarbone, until he reaches my breasts.

He takes his time, sucking each nipple into his mouth, flicking with his tongue while his hand toys with the other, gentle and teasing, applying just enough pressure to make me gasp.

"You're so beautiful," he says, voice rough as his hand comes up to cradle my jaw. "I could spend the rest of my life making you feel this good."

He rolls me gently, his hands steady on my hips, until I'm straddling him. His cock pressing hot and heavy between us. I wrap my hand around it, pumping slow strokes just to tease. He lets out a guttural groan, head dropping back into the pillows as his fingers dig into my thighs.

His hazel eyes roll back in his head, lashes fluttering as he breathes my name. "Fuck, Bella... just like that."

I lean forward and kiss his neck before lining him up with my entrance and sliding down. I take him in inch by inch, savoring every stretch, every delicious ache. My hands find his chest, grounding me as I start to move my hips in slow, steady circles, grinding down until we both gasp.

His eyes stay locked on mine the entire time, memorizing every second.

"Meet Lex," he moans, voice strained.

I freeze for a beat. "Are you seriously bringing up another guy while I'm riding your dick, Cade?" I moan, rolling my hips just right.

"Fuck," he pants. "It's time, sweetheart. I want you both. I need you both."

I arch a brow and slam down a little harder, dragging a moan from deep in his throat. "Then you better make a damn good case."

He sits up, wraps his arms around me, and kisses me like he's starving for my lips. His hands slide down to cup my ass, guiding me as I ride him slow and deep, his cock buried so perfectly inside me it's like my body was made for this.

Made for him.

"Lex wants you," he murmurs, voice wrecked, lips brushing my jaw.

I stare down at him. "How the hell could you possibly know that? I've never even met the guy."

Cade grins, lazy and sinfully confident, his thumb stroking over my hip as he rolls up into me again. "Because I've told him everything," he rasps. "Every time you moaned, every time you shook. I've been very... *detailed*."

"You what?" I say, trying to suppress a moan.

"There are no secrets between us, sweetheart."

He thrusts up again.

"Mmmm," his voice drops an octave. "He knows how you sound when you come, Bella."

Another thrust.

"How your thighs tremble when I taste you just right."

Thrust.

"The little whimper that escapes your throat when I suck your clit into my mouth."

Another.

"How you like to be kissed."

Thrust.

"Touched."

Another.

"Fucked."

He thrusts up quick and harder this time to prove his point and I gasp, digging my nails deeper into his chest.

"And now," Cade adds, lips grazing my ear, "he wants you too. He's waited long enough."

My body tightens unexpectedly at the thought.

"Say yes, Bella," he whispers against my lips.

"Yes, Bella," I tease, moaning when he thrusts up gently to meet me.

He chuckles, low and warm, and pulls one breast into his mouth again, sucking my nipple hard enough to make me yelp.

"Cade! Your sister's in the next room," I hiss between gasps.

"Then you better be quiet, sweetheart," he whispers, taking his attention back to my nipple.

"Oh," I moan.

He rolls us again, settling between my thighs, his body pressed tight to mine. He fucks me slow, moving in a punishing rhythm of deep strokes that leave me panting, clinging, and melting beneath him.

It is never rough with Cade. Only full of devotion. Like he's trying to carve his name into every inch of my goddamn soul.

When I come again, a tear slips down my cheek as I realize it. This is real. He kisses it away like he's been waiting for that moment his whole life.

And when he finally falls apart—hips jerking, breath catching against my skin—I realize I've never been touched like this. I've never been worshiped like this. Or loved like this.

"Yes," I whisper.

My phone vibrates over on the vanity.

I already know who it is. And I don't care. Let him watch. Let him see. Because all I care about right now is the man holding me as if I'm sacred and the man I get to meet soon.

CHAPTER ㉜
BELLA
ROSETHORNE MANSION
WEXLEY UNIVERSITY
577 DAYS SINCE ZEKE'S DEATH

Cade just left. My sheets still smell like cedar and ink and for once, the quiet isn't heavy. It's soft, almost peaceful. But peace never lasts long around here. I stare at my phone. The screen glows back at me, taunting.

@LucaWasHere
You're playing with fire, Izzy, it's true.
The painter. The parties. Your polished new crew.
I don't bend and I don't break.
Touch what's mine? That's your last mistake.

I heard your cries. I watched you come.
Pretty little gasps, each one made me numb.
Not from pain, but something worse.
A rage that comes with every curse.

You bled for him, you gave him more,
So now I'm kicking down the door.
Your painter's sweet, all charm and art,
But I know how to pull you apart.

He paints in red? I'll give him shades,
Of broken bones and unmarked graves.
His hands, his smile, his fucking voice,
Gone, because you made the choice.

The door swings open and Ellie waltzes in wearing a pink silk robe, vanilla iced coffee in hand.

"Ok seriously," she groans. "Next time you decide to fuck my brother, please send out a warning so I can book a hotel. Or a priest. Or both."

I shoot her a look but I'm not biting.

She pauses mid-dramatic-sip. "Wait, hey. I'm kidding. I mean, not about the warning—I definitely don't want to hear that—but you know I totally ship you and Cade together."

She softens. "What's up?"

I don't say anything. I just tilt the screen toward her.

She sets her cup down fast. "Again? Okay, what the actual fuck! Who is this guy and why the hell can't you find him?"

"I don't know," I mutter. "I've tried. Knox has tried. Nate's tried. No luck. Whoever this creep is, he's good."

Ellie sinks onto the bed beside me, eyes still glued to the screen. "And he's watching you. Like... watching *watching*. But from where? Mommy and daddy's basement?"

"Probably. Ugh, internet creeps!" I say as I start typing at lightning speed.

Ellie's eyes go wide. "Wait, what are you doing?"

"Messaging him," I say, fingers flying. "If this poet wants to play, fine. Let's play."

@BellaBlackwood
Ok fucker. You got my attention.
What do you want?

Ellie's eyebrows launch halfway up her forehead. "Babe, are you sure about this?"

"I literally have a criminal empire working for me. I shouldn't be scared of some creep probably hiding in his parents' basement just like you said."

@LucaWasHere
Got your attention, didn't I, pet?
You're a habit I'll never forget.
You know what I want, it's always been you.
So here's your warning, I always break through.

Mind, body, and soul, you gave him a taste.
Now I'll take mine, no time to waste.
Touch what's mine? I'll snap him in two.
You bleed for me. You always do.

Your pretty lies, your sweet facade,
Won't save the boy from what I've clawed.
He smiles. He paints. He doesn't see,
But I'll be there when you choose me.

@BellaBlackwood
Gross. I'm taken. Plus, I'd rather fuck a cactus.

"At least make it a spiky one, let him feel the rejection babe,"
Ellie laughs.

@LucaWasHere
That'll change. You'll beg me soon.
You'll break beneath a colder moon.
You're mine. For you've always been.
And no white knight's going to save you from sin.

@BellaBlackwood
I don't trust creeps who rhyme like failed poets.
And I sure as hell won't be yours, so choke on it.

@LucaWasHere
I see it all, Izzy, every blink.
Every breath you take, every time you sink.
I'm in the walls. I'm in your head.
Each scream you bite before you're in bed.

And that little artist who plays your shield?
One slip, baby girl, he'll be the next to yield.
He paints in light, but I deal in shade.
One crack, one twitch, and he'll be unmade.

@BellaBlackwood
Then enjoy the fucking show while you can.
Threaten Cade again and I'm coming for you.

"Ok, that's enough," Ellie snaps, grabbing the phone out of my hands like it's about to explode. "This guy gives me the ick on a soul level."

I lean back, breathing hard. "I'm meeting Lex soon."

Ellie blinks. "So?"

"So, I think I need you and Haley to come."

She recoils. "You want me and Haley to go on a date with you, my brother, and Lex? Sounds like a party, but no thanks."

"Not a date," I say, rolling my eyes. "Fight Night. I'm meeting Lex there and I want backup."

Ellie narrows her eyes. "You want me and Haley to roll into an underground fight club full of sweaty Titans, Bratva princes, and testosterone-fueled chaos as backup?"

I nod.

She exhales dramatically. "Ugh. Fine. But only because Haley's dying to wear those new boots and I heard that The Revenants perform. It'll be good to see what they're dancing to before Regionals. Oooh... did you know that Madison Rae Holloway apparently has a thing for Lex?"

Madison Rae Holloway. Tall, blonde, total Barbie prototype, Cal would love her. She's the leader of *The Revenants,* Northvale's version of The Trifecta. Big tits, no rhythm, and a bitch streak a mile wide. They've got a whole Northvale Legacy team. But honestly, we don't even bother learning their names.

Our rivalry with them runs thick, especially after that one Halloween when they tried to crash The Row party by throwing fake blood down from the rafters full on Carrie style. Let's just say, it didn't end well for them.

"Oh, Maddie Rae," I mutter, rolling my eyes so hard they practically click.

Ellie arches a brow.

"El, I have an idea," I say, already reaching for my phone.

"Oh no," she whines, dropping her head back. "You've got that look."

"What look?" I ask.

"The kind of look that means you have a crazy plan. The kind that usually ends with shots."

"Gunshots or tequila shots?"

She shrugs. "We really never know."

> ME: Hey, how fast can you make me a top or three?

> RICO: For you chica, give me an hour or two. What's the fantasy?

> ME: Something spicy... 🤜🖤 Fight night legends meets your dirty little mind?

> RICO: Oh yes babe! I'm on it!!!

I smirk, but inside I'm already calculating. The countdown to Fight Night has officially begun. And Luca wants a show? Good. Let's give him one. What the hell, Maddie Rae too.

> ME: Hey babe. So... I need you to do something for me.

> CADE: Anything sweetheart.

> ME: Other than Lex, do you have any contacts at the pit?

> CADE: His cousin Damien. Why?

> ME: Because I have an idea I need to run by you. Do you think you can come back to Rosethorne after your classes?

CHAPTER 33

BELLA

THE PIT
NORTHVALE UNIVERSITY
580 DAYS SINCE ZEKE'S DEATH

Cade's hand is wrapped around mine. His thumb strokes lazily over my knuckles like he's soothing something in me he can't see but feels anyway. Ellie, Haley, and Knox follow close behind us. We're walking into the belly of Redspire Mansion, down a set of stone stairs that leads to a door guarded by two men in suits with Hollow King rings glinting on their fingers. No one says a word as we pass, they just nod at Cade.

Apparently, we're expected.

"Why does this feel like we're walking into hell?" Haley says, glancing around The Pit. "A beautiful hell, but still."

The doors swing open. It hits me all at once, the heat, bass, and light. The Pit isn't what I expected. It's better.

The walls are jet-black, matte and seamless as if they swallowed the light and enjoyed it. Neon-red accents pulse behind sharp architectural cutouts, looking like veins under skin. Overhead, spotlights slice through faint trails of smoke, casting everything in crimson and shadow.

The floor is polished concrete, stained the color of dried blood. Elevated ringside seating curves around the four-sided ring in the center. Thick bands of black and red wrap the perimeter. A warning to turn back.

It's like a Roman coliseum redesigned by a billionaire sadist, all brutal elegance and high-stakes spectacle.

It's dark.

Violent.

Sexy.

We wind down closer to the ring, where black velvet ropes part for us. Cade leads me to our reserved seats, one of the best seats in the house. Dead center with a perfect view of the ring. Knox slides in next to Haley, already checking the lighting rig above.

Ellie sits on the other side of me, taking it all in, "Okay... this is not what I expected. It's giving billionaire fight club meets Satan's VIP lounge."

We're barely settled when she shows up. Madison Rae Holloway. And, of course, her two backup dancers, Barbie 2.0 and Botox Lite, flanking her like a clearance aisle Mean Girls reboot.

"Well, well, well," Madison mocks, stopping right in front of us with a sneer that makes my knuckles itch. "Who in the world let you bitches in here?"

Haley scoffs under her breath. Ellie just crosses one leg over the other, calm and unbothered like a rich cat at a peasant party.

I lean back slowly, arching a brow. "Wow. No warm-up? No hello? Straight to the hostility, Maddie Rae, that's not very hospitable of you."

She scowls. "This is Hollow Kings territory, sweetheart. Not some Wexley dance circle."

"Oh," I say, mockingly concerned. "Then what exactly are you doing here? You're not a King, Mads."

Her jaw ticks. Behind her, the blonde one glares at me like she wants to bite, but I'm pretty sure she couldn't even chew a protein bar without cracking a veneer.

Maddie steps closer. "You don't belong here."

"And yet, here I am. Front row. VIP. Funny how that works."

Her eyes drop to Cade's hand on my thigh, fingers curled possessively as he squeezes. Her laugh is sharp and fake as hell.

"You cannot be serious, Cade. You... with her?"

Before I can answer, Cade beats me to it. "Us with her Maddie. Lex wants Bella just as much as I do." Then he turns my chin and kisses me. Deep. Open. Tongue and heat and a little bit of showmanship just for her.

Maddie's face twists. "Ugh. You're lying," she screeches.

"Oh honey, my brother never lies." Ellie leans in, voice pure sugar with a bite of venom.

Maddie makes a disgusted noise and storms off in a cloud of hairspray and fury, her clones flouncing behind her like little mean-girl ducklings.

I settle back into my seat, lips tingling, and grin. "That was fun."

The lights strobe overhead, blinding white and pulsing like a heartbeat. The crowd hushes as a distorted voice crackles over the speakers.

"Welcome to Fight Night here at The Pit."

Cheers erupt from every corner, the energy is electric and charged. But the lighting and the theatrics, it's all so underwhelming.

Knox leans over, lips near Haley's ear but loud enough for all of us to hear. "God, can you imagine what I could do with an arena like this? This place would be fucking fire."

Ellie snorts and Haley lets out a low, "Preach," as she slips an arm through his.

Cade pulls me into his side. He presses a soft kiss to my temple and something tight in my chest loosens.

I lean back just enough to meet his eyes. "You ready for this?"

He nods once, sure and steady. "Everything's set, sweetheart. Trust me. Damien hates The Revenants just as much as you do."

I smirk. "Good. Because this night, is about to be legendary."

He leans in and brushes his lips over mine. It's just a whisper of a kiss but enough to leave a spark behind. "They're not ready for you, Bella."

The first fight ends with a brutal, bloody punch and a roar from the crowd. One guy gets carried out, the other raises his fists like he just conquered Rome. But before the crowd can settle, the DJ's voice roars over the speakers again.

"All right, who's ready for something sexy?" The DJ draws it out like a sleazy game show host. "Please welcome Northvale's very own... The Revenants!"

A few cheers, mostly from the NU side of the room. Then the opening beat of "Disco Inferno" by 50 Cent drops. Madison Rae and her two try-hard lackeys strut out like it's their Super Bowl.

Oh no. Don't laugh. Don't laugh. Don't. Fucking. Laugh.

Their outfits are tight, shiny, and completely mismatched. Madison's top looks like it was yanked out of a clearance bin at a stripper convention.

They start dancing, if you can call it that, and I'm instantly in pain. It's overdone. Off-beat. One of them nearly trips on her own heel. Maddie flicks her hair like she's headlining a Vegas burlesque show and starts air-humping the floor as if her life depends on it.

Haley leans in, unable to hide her grin. "Good lord, Maddie looks like she's trying to have an orgasm out there."

Cade chokes on his laugh, covering his mouth. Ellie looks personally offended.

That's when I notice a guy cutting through the crowd like a blade. He's huge, at least six-five, with broad shoulders and muscle for days. His hair is so blonde it's nearly white, cropped short on the sides and tousled up top like he just rolled out of bed and still somehow looks sexy as sin.

His eyes freeze me in place, icy-greenish-blue, almost otherworldly.

Mesmerizing.

Dangerous.

His left arm is a masterpiece of black and gray ink. Modern, architectural, and lethal in its precision. The centerpiece on his bicep is the Hollow Kings crest: a crowned skull framed by a laurel wreath, two crossed swords behind it, and the Latin phrase In Tenebris Regnat—He reigns in darkness—etched beneath like a battle standard. Faint, geometric outlines of Russian Orthodox domes rise just behind the crest as if drafted straight from a blueprint.

He stops at our row. "Whitmore."

Cade looks up. "Damien."

The guy raises an unimpressed brow. "Good God, man. Call me Rez. We've been over this shit."

His eyes turn to me. "And you must be Bella."

He takes my hand and kisses it with obnoxious flair.

Cade grumbles, "Bella, this is Dam—I mean, Rez. Lex's cousin. Co-leader of the Hollow Kings."

Rez flashes a grin. "Guilty."

Then he jerks his chin toward the disaster on stage. "Look, I'll just get right to it because I'm up soon. First, per your request, he is in the dark. Completely and utterly clueless."

I look at Cade and smile.

"And like I said on the phone," Rez continues. "We've been trying to hype this place back up. Fight Nights used to be insane. Now? Fights are still good, but... let's be honest."

Knox leans in, grinning from ear to ear, all cocky and smug as hell, "You mean you want Row-level shit up in here."

Rez sighs. "As much as I hate to admit it, yes. I've seen your Row parties on the live stream. That's the kind of energy we need. The lighting, the music, the fights, and the girls. We've got a major donor event in the fall and if we can't blow it out of the fucking water, it will not look good on me, or Lex. Do you think you are up for the challenge?"

I smile sweetly. "What all do you need from me?"

"We pull in the same fighters each week to fight The Hollow Kings. We need bigger names, bigger fighters. No offense to the schools around here but it's not cutting it. That and entertainment between fights."

"I think we can work something out. I have a few fighters in mind." I say, earning myself quite the side-eye from Knox.

"Glad to hear it, Izzy," Rez says.

My entire body goes still. "What did you just call me?"

Rez raises a brow, unfazed. "Izzy?"

Knox sits up straighter, muscles taut like he's ready to launch across the floor. Haley immediately drops a hand to his thigh, calming him. Ellie suddenly cannot sit still, eyes narrowing with razor precision.

Even Cade's looking around now completely confused. "Uh, am I miss—"

"Her fucking name is Bella," Knox's voice cuts him off.

Rez shrugs, all casual arrogance. "Eh. I like Izzy better. Has bite. Like you."

Cade grabs my leg again, clearly unimpressed. "Careful, Rez."

"Relax, Whitmore. I don't poach. Just admire." He winks at me. "You're a lot more interesting than Maddie Rae made you sound."

I cross my arms. "Let me guess. She said I'm crazy, slutty, and not Hollow Kings material?"

"Pretty much. But now that I've met you..."

He steps a little closer, just enough to test boundaries. "I'm thinking Maddie Rae might be even more full of shit than usual. Can't wait to see what you girls bring. Who knows..."

His mouth curls into something that toes the line between a smirk and a dare. "Maybe I'll let you girls replace The Revenants in The Pit. We could think of tonight as your official interview."

He winks, then adds, "I should go get ready. We'll be in touch about the fall, I've already got your number. Try not to get too distracted by all this." He motions vaguely to himself, then turns and disappears into the back.

The DJ's voice booms through the speakers. "How about those Revenants, huh? Give it up for Northvale's finest!"

Cade leans in, warm breath against my ear. "Hey, sweetheart. You okay?"

I force a smile. "Yeah. Everything's fine."

"What fighters are you thinking, Bells?" Knox leans over and whispers.

"Not now Knox, but you'll—"

My phone buzzes.

@LucaWasHere
Izzy, Izzy, still so blind.
Did you think that beast was mine?
The frostbit brute with vacant eyes,
He growls, but never satisfies.

You taste the wrong names in your mouth,
Choke on guesses, looking south.
You flinch at ghosts you can't define,
While I trace patterns down your spine.

My stomach drops. I jerk up instinctively, eyes scanning the crowd.

Cade frowns. "What is it? What's wrong?"

Knox leans over and snatches the phone from my hand. He reads it and mutters under his breath, "Seriously? The poet, again."

Cade's alarm bells go off immediately. "Bella, talk to me."

I glance at him, unsure how to even begin. "Okay, well, it's kind of a long story. Or... actually, not really—"

Ellie cuts in sharply, "She has a creepy Instagram stalker."

"What?" Cade says, louder than he probably meant to.

"Thanks, El."

Before I can say more, the DJ's voice blares again. "And now... stepping into the ring Northvale's own, leader of The Hollow Kings, the one and only, Damien 'Rez' Reznikov!"

"Sweetheart, just show me. Please." Cade leans in and whispers at my temple.

I hesitate, fingers tightening around my phone but I hand it over. The second it leaves my hand, I regret it.

He reads it once, then again, and scrolls up through the thread. His body goes rigid. Right leg bouncing uncontrollably. His jaw locks so tight I can hear the grind of his teeth. He lets out a slow exhale through his nose.

"Bella," he says, eyes still glued to the screen. "Who the fuck is this?"

I don't answer.

He finally looks at me and it's not anger I see. It's something far worse. It's hurt. Fear. That raw, protective panic I've only seen a few times before.

Once when I twisted my ankle at the lake. Once when I didn't come home from a party. Once when I cried on the Whitmore patio and he handed me a blanket and a strawberry milkshake like it was enough to fix the world.

"Tell me right now," he orders. "Who the hell is this, Bella?"

"I don't know," I admit quietly. "We've tried to find out."

"Bella, you need to take this to the police."

"No." I shake my head. "It's fine. He's just a creep. I'll be fine." I press a kiss to his cheek. "I promise."

"Bella, this is not fine. The stuff he said to you, what does it mean *Damn, Izzy. That shot was slick. Nice work wrecking Carlos's dick.* Who the hell is Carlos?"

He leans in closer, eyes searching mine. "Bella, talk to me. What is going on?"

I take a shaky breath and squeeze his hand. "It's almost time for our performance."

"Bella—"

"I promise," I whisper, cutting him off gently. "I will tell you everything. Just... not here. Not yet. Please trust me when I say we've got this under control."

His jaw works like he wants to argue, but he doesn't. He just nods once, tightly, eyes still burning with worry as the lights begin to dim again.

"And your winner... Rez!"

The crowd roars as Rez lifts both fists and basks in the frenzy.

"Alright, Northvale. We've come to the main event of the night. And it's going to be one hell of a show! First up, repping Wexley University, give it up for Callum Whitmore!"

The entire Row section erupts.

"WHITMORE!" Haley screams. Ellie's whistling like a damn banshee. Knox throws both fists in the air.

Cade cups his hands and shouts, "Let's go, Cal!"

"And his opponent... from Northvale University... Leader of The Hollow Kings and the undisputed King of The Pit... Aleksandr "Lex" Barinov!"

As us girls get into our places, Lex walks out from the shadows like pure fucking sex wrapped in black silk.

This isn't the first time I've seen him. I remember the first. Ellie's eighteenth birthday. He showed up late with Cade, all quiet confidence and brutal beauty, leaning against the wall like he was bored as fuck. I remember thinking he looked like a storm in a damn leather jacket. Dangerous. Untouchable. And I hated how jealous I was of the way he looked at Cade.

But his is a whole different breed of feral.

He's shirtless, just fight shorts slung low on his hips, clinging to every hard-cut line of muscle. Black gloves. Black boots. And those tattoos. God, why is it always the damn tattoos?

Both arms are sleeved in ink. Same Hollow Kings crest as Rez. Same Orthodox architecture mixed with deeper, darker lines, and geometric shapes. There's a bird on his chest, a phoenix forged from smoke and fire.

But it's the ink on his right bicep that stops my breath cold. Hidden in the geometry, bold and defiant, are two initials in Gothic black: CW.

Cade Whitmore.

My heart slams. There's a pulse between my legs that doesn't care about timelines or the fact that he still hasn't even looked at me.

His black hair is damp, pushed back from his forehead. Eyes that are ice-blue and cutting. Like they see through skin and soul. Like they've already undressed me, mapped me, and completely ruined me.

He looks like wrath carved out of stone. A myth made of violence and want. And the worst of all, I already know I'm completely, devastatingly fucked.

CHAPTER ⟨34⟩
LEX
THE PIT
NORTHVALE UNIVERSITY
ABOUT TO KICK CALLUM WHITMORE'S SMUG QUARTERBACK ASS.
580 DAYS SINCE ZEKE'S DEATH

"And his opponent... from Northvale University... Leader of The Hollow Kings and the undisputed King of The Pit... Aleksandr 'Lex' Barinov!"

The second I hear my name, I take off down the corridor. Cheers explode around me like a fucking war drum. The lights slam into my face the moment I step into the ring and I feed on it. All of it. The noise, the pressure, the bloodlust in the air. It's my oxygen.

But even with the crowd chanting my name, even with The Pit shaking from the sound of it, I'm scanning.

For her.

Cade won't shut up about her. Hasn't since Cinco de Mayo. Says she's going to tie us all together like some cherry-lipped fucking peace treaty. Sweet on the outside, chaos underneath. I've seen the pictures. Heard the stories. The girl who's supposed to be mine, even if no one's said it out loud yet.

But she's not here. Not in the VIP with Cade, not in the back row, not even in the shadows near the balcony. Nothing.

And that pisses me off.

I want her here. Watching me. Front and center. I want her eyes locked on what I do to the poor bastard stupid enough to stand across from me. Especially when the bastard is Callum fucking Whitmore. I want her to see the fists, the blood, the win, my name in the air like a war cry. I want her to know what she's walking into.

Rez climbs into the ring with a damn mic.

Oh for fuck's sake.

"Okay, gentlemen. There's been a slight change of plans."

I cock my head.

"We're going to add a little more entertainment before the two of you get your well-deserved rematch." He flashes that lazy grin of his. "Both of you men to your corners. Take a seat."

I glare at him as I head to my stool, wiping the sweat from my palms on my shorts.

The fuck are you doing, Rez?

He's lucky we're family. Unless this is some Maddie Rae and her Botox Barbies bullshit again. Then he can get bent.

I look up and notice that's not our usual DJ. Some blond dude is behind the booth now, putting on the headset, adjusting the dials, and plugging some USB drive into the booth.

I know I've seen this guy before.

Rez nods toward the new DJ. "As you all probably know, we are The Hollow Kings, Northvale's real pride and joy."

The crowd goes wild.

Damn straight.

Rez lifts the mic again, pacing slow like he's about to deliver a sermon instead of a fight intro. "Now, in the spirit of friendly competition—and because I'd rather not spend the rest of the night breaking up brawls between Row rats and Northvale psychos—let's try to keep it in the ring tonight, yeah?"

The crowd rumbles, a few laughs, a few hollers.

"And for your cooperation..." He lets the silence stretch, his voice dipping into that slow, lethal purr. "...I do have a little surprise for you."

The crowd stills and his smile goes wicked. "Tonight, we are also joined by Wexley's pride and joy."

Rez lifts a brow. "Knox, you wanna take it from here?"

Knox? Must be Blondie.

The guy flashes a cocky grin as he leans into the mic. "Thanks, Rez." His voice cuts smooth through the speakers.

"Yo, what's up, Northvale?" He grins. "I'm Knox, part-time DJ, full time shit-stirrer. And Rez wasn't lying, we do have some of Wexley's finest in the house tonight."

He pauses. "Sorry, Cal. We don't mean you tonight."

What the hell is going on?

I sit forward slightly on my stool, every muscle in my body locked.

Knox's voice rings out again, louder this time. "Ladies and gents, it is my absolute pleasure to introduce you to Wexley's sexiest, deadliest, and baddest bitches of The Row... my girls Ellie, Haley, and Bella. The Trifecta!"

The Pit fucking explodes. Apparently, my girl and her group are a lot more popular than I thought. I glance over at The Revenants. They all look like they all are about to have a damn stroke when the lights go dark before changing to red, pink, and teal.

When the fuck did we get colored ring lights?

And then I see them. First, the redhead, Haley. Black pants so tight they might as well be painted on, sliced up the thighs with deliberate slits that flash skin every time she moves. Black top cut so low it's practically porn. Trifecta flashes across her chest in deep red rhinestones. She knows exactly what she's doing.

Then it hits me, Knox. He's the DJ for Carrington Row and he's the one fucking the redhead of the group.

Thank God. That was going to bug the shit out of me.

Second, Little Whitmore. Black bikini top with The Trifecta logo stitched over her left tit. Leather pants slit down the sides daring everyone to look. Her grin is pure sass.

There she is, the girl of my fucking dreams. She's dead center of the chaos. Simple black tank clinging like a second skin. Tight black leather shorts riding low on her hips, hugging the kind of ass that makes men forget how to breathe. Black boots with blood-red heels, clicking with every step in a countdown to destruction.

Her hair's long, black, wild, like she walked through hell and didn't bother to brush off the ashes. And those eyes... steel gray. She's a vision. A weapon. A dare.

Bella Blackwood.

Mine and Cade's new girl.

'Bout time you showed up, baby.

So, I may or may not have stalked her socials the second I found out she fucked my boyfriend. Curiosity and all. I went down a spiral and also liked every single picture on her profile, even saved a few of them on my phone. Except the ones with fucking Callum or any of the other Row boys in it, those can rot.

I've also been following their group. Watched every performance they've posted. Call me a Trifecta super fan now. Shit, I should probably get me one of those fancy Trifecta t-shirts they advertised.

There's a name inked on her wrist, *Dylan*, or some shit. I'm going to have to get that fucker's name off my girl's skin, pronto. And a Z on her right shoulder blade, wrapped in clean, curving lines that move like smoke.

Like memory.

Like vengeance.

It's hot.

She struts across the ring and plops herself onto Callum's lap, wrapping her arm around his neck. He slides his arms around her waist and pulls her in close.

The fuck is this girl doing?

"Whoa, whoa, whoa?" Knox yells into the mic. "What the hell are you doing, Bella?"

Damn right, Knox. Love this guy. Get her ass off him.

She grins, lips painted cherry red. "Oh, sorry, Knox. Just wishing Cal good luck." She turns her head, nodding straight at me.

"From the looks of that guy over there..." She winks and then looks back at Callum. "You might need it, Cal."

You fucking know it, baby. He will need it.

I lean back into the ropes, muttering under my breath, "Dead man walking."

She's center ring now, arms crossed, all attitude and boots.

"Um, Problem Child?" Knox calls over the mic.

She groans. "We're really going with that again. I mean, it's so rude." She throws a hand toward Ellie. "Ellie gets Sweetheart. Which is what Cade calls me, you know, like in bed. So yeah... we really do need to change that." She looks at Cade and blows him a kiss.

Cade fucking smiles.

Knox groans. "Problem Child, focus."

She shrugs, exaggerated and smug. "Sorry. It gets me feeling things I really shouldn't be feeling down *there* when I'm trying to dance."

Okay. Now I'm jealous of my own fucking boyfriend.

She turns back to the crowd. "Haley gets Heartthrob and I get this bullshit?" Another groan. Full of drama. Full of fire.

Knox shrugs. "When you quit acting like one, I'll quit calling you one."

The crowd laughs. She stomps. Clearly the response they were looking for. It's all a perfectly scripted show and the Titans and Wolves are eating it up. The Revenants should really be taking notes. Somebody get Maddie Rae a damn notepad and pen.

"Problem Child?" he repeats.

"Yes, Satan's spawn?"

Roars.

"Bella," he sighs, "What are you wearing? Where is your Trifecta gear?"

She looks at her chests and shrugs. "Oh, yeah. Sorry."

She looks at the other girls, turns to me and winks before she rips her tank off. Underneath is a bright, cherry-red skimpy-ass top with *Property of Lex Barinov* stitched across the front in black rhinestones.

The Pit has never been this loud. Screaming, cheering, and a few dramatic shrieks from Maddie and her minions echoing off the concrete.

I think I'm having a goddamn heart attack, and I'm seriously rethinking my decision to wear these thinner shorts.

Knox's jaw drops. "There we go. Was that so hard?"

Something's hard.

Bella rolls her eyes. "Just play the track, Knox?"

Knox coughs. "Uh, well, bad news. Considering this was kinda last minute, I don't have all of our shit with me."

"Knox!" she screams. "What do you expect us to dance to?"

Knox leans into the mic, voice lazy and amused. "Calm down, Problem Child. Don't cause a scene. Frown lines, remember?" He points to his forehead. "It'll be fine. Just wing it, girls. You seriously can't be worse than what this place already had to endure tonight."

This guy's officially my new bestie.

She spins to the girls. "Fine. Hit it."

Disco. Fucking. Inferno. The same damn song Maddie Rae and her plastic bitches botched earlier.

Nice move, baby. Goddamn.

The redhead and little Whitmore are solid, yeah. Sexy as hell.

But Bella? Fucking Bella.

She's front and center and I can't take my eyes off her. This girl is fucking taunting me. Feeding off every beat, every snap of her hips. And she can't take her eyes off me either. Not for one goddamn second.

On the count of one-two-three, they rotate, switching places with precision that should not be legal in shorts and leather pants that tight. Bella drops low, ass to the floor, rolls her body up like a fucking wave, and pops her hip with a smile that could start wars.

Every goddamn person is on their feet and for good reason. I feel it in my chest. In my throat. In my dick. Bella's not just dancing to the song. She's dancing to me. She knows exactly what she's doing. And she's doing it in front of the whole damn world.

Right when I didn't think it could get any better... Bella does the un-fucking-thinkable. She spins on those sharp little black boots and sits. Right on my lap.

Ok, Little Lex. Be cool.

Her body's pressed against mine, a perfect fit. And for a few bars, she rides me to the beat. Her hips shifting slow, steel eyes pinned to mine like she's got me by the throat.

She totally does.

Then she leans in. Face dangerously close. And then—*fuck me*—this girl drags her tongue up from my collarbone to the edge of my cheek, before giving it a quick peck.

My eyes roll back. "Oh my God, baby, you're killing me."

Shit. That was supposed to be in my head.

And just like that, she's gone. Off my lap. Off my body.

She finishes the final chorus with the other girls but I'm not watching the other two. My eyes are locked on Bella. I glance over at Callum. He looks like he wants to throw me through a wall.

Good. Let him try.

The crowd is so loud I can't even hear Knox anymore... just roars, stomps, and chants. It's pure chaos in here.

Bella heads toward the edge of the ring, aiming for Cade. Rez stops her. Leans down and says something in her ear. She smiles and looks back at me. My entire body locks up. She turns back to Rez, nods once. Confident.

DING.

Callum storms forward, jaw tight, all that cocky quarterback rage finally boiling over. Good. I want it. He jabs. I dodge. He swings wide. I duck under and land a body shot that makes him grunt.

I glance to the side. She's there watching the fight with Rez, Chase, and DeShawn ringside. Not phased. Not blinking. Unlike Little Whitmore behind her who is watching the fight behind her hands, wincing every time a fist finds a face.

There's something dark in Bella's eyes. They're savage and completely focused. Like me.

CRACK.

Callum catches me clean across the jaw.

My back hits the mat. The air leaves my lungs.

Focus, Barinov.

I blink up and there she is, crouched down under the ropes ringside. "Get the fuck up, Lex." Bella says it like a challenge as she smacks both hands on the mat. "Don't you dare make me go cheer for Cal. Finish this. I've got places to be, *baby*."

Did she just call me baby?

That's all I need. I lunge up like a goddamn beast.

Left.

Right.

One more left.

Hook.

Knee.

Callum tries to recover but he's too fucking slow, too focused on Bella. A few more jabs and one final uppercut sends him sprawling back into the ropes. He hits the mat like a sack of broken pride.

The Pit erupts. I lift my arms, panting, blood dripping down my lip, sweat burning in my eyes.

Out of the corner of my eye I see Maddie Rae. Glittering in her knockoff crown, heels wobbling and ready to slither into the ring to play Queen of The Pit.

Rez steps in front of her. Shakes his head. Then nods to her, to my girl. Bella slides under the ropes like she was made for this. Boots hitting the mat, confidence bleeding from every step. She walks right up to me and raises my hand into the air.

Victory.

Claimed.

CHAPTER ⑤
CADE
THE PIT
NORTHVALE UNIVERSITY
580 DAYS SINCE ZEKE'S DEATH

Bella's in the ring. One hand gripped around Lex's wrist, raising it high in the air declaring him the winner like she's been living in that ring her whole life. The Pit is losing its mind—screaming, chanting, stomping.

But those two? It's like none of it exists. Not the blood still on Lex's jaw. Not Cal groaning on the mat. Not the hundreds of Titans and Wolves going absolutely batshit crazy.

Just Bella and Lex.

Locked in this electric, breathless stare that looks more like foreplay than a post-fight celebration. They're not smiling. Not talking. Not moving. Just watching each other like they're trying to memorize every scar, every look, every untold truth between them.

I know that look. I've felt that look. And I know that they're both about ten seconds away from tearing each other's clothes off in front of all of Northvale before Rez breaks it.

He jogs into the ring, laughing, wild with adrenaline, and throws an arm around Lex's shoulder. Lex drops his arm from Bella's grip and leans into his cousin, soaking in and fueling on the chaos. The Hollow Kings are loving this moment and Lex totally earned it.

Bella takes a step back. Just one. And then she turns her head, eyes scanning through the blur of people and color until they land on me. Her face softens instantly.

That smile, the one that only ever really belongs to me, pulls at her lips. Like she's grounding herself, reminding herself I'm here. That we are still us, even with Lex standing half-naked and victorious beside her.

And fuck, if that doesn't level me. The damn problem is her stupid phone. She handed it to me before the dance. Just tossed it in my lap like it wasn't a ticking goddamn time bomb.

But the more I read from *@LucaWasHere*, the more my stomach knots. He's probably just a creep. A sick one, yeah. Definitely not the first loser to obsess over a girl like Bella. She's visible, online, gorgeous, and powerful. That draws attention.

But if that wasn't bad enough, a new message popped up. Not Instagram. A text from some guy named *Nate*.

NATE: All set for tonight. Be ready by midnight. We'll be there to pick you up.

I stared at it like it was in a different language. But then another one came in right under it.

NATE: Lineup for tonight: Knox and I in the van. Tex in the sky. And don't shoot me, but Laing and you are on ground. I'm not comfortable sending you solo if Krolek shows for the buy.

Laing? Krolek? A buy? What the hell is she wrapped up in? My heart is pounding. I don't even know if I'm more confused, furious, or just fucking worried.

The ring is flooded with Hollow Kings now. Rez is still hyping Lex up, yelling something in Russian as a few more of their boys jump the ropes, hands slapping backs, throwing fists in the air. Celebration mode. The Pit is a madhouse, flashing lights and roaring voices.

In the middle of it all is Lex, shirtless and bloodied, looking like a goddamn gladiator. But he's not looking at Rez or the chaos surrounding him. He's looking at her.

Bella steps out of the ring, boots hitting the floor like she's still in full command of the entire arena. Her eyes find his and he moves toward her instinctively, like gravity. But the Kings grab him and pull him back to the center of the ring.

He jerks his chin, trying to keep her in sight. She gives him the smallest smile and keeps walking. Right to me.

I put her phone in my back pocket right before her body hits mine with no hesitation, arms locking around my neck. I catch her waist and pull her in close as she tips up to kiss me.

"You," I rasp against her lips, "just made history."

She grins up at me, breathless, that fire still dancing in those storm-colored eyes. "You like it?"

I laugh, low and full of every ounce of pride I've got in me. "Sweetheart, I loved it."

"Oh yeah?" Bella tilts her head, eyes twinkling under the lights.

"You all were perfect," I say, brushing her hair off her cheek. "And the shirt? Rico did incredible work with this one."

"I know. He's the best."

I shake my head, still grinning. "You should've seen Madison's face."

"That bad?"

"Oh, sweetheart, it was priceless." I lean in, lips brushing her ear. "And when you licked Lex?" I pull back just enough to raise a brow. "I'll admit. I got a little jealous."

"And a little hard?"

I groan. "Don't start."

Then I pull her in and kiss her slow and deep, my hands gripping her waist like I might never let go. I press my forehead to hers, breathing in her cherry-vanilla scent. My heart is still thumping out of my chest.

"That was one hell of a dance, Bella. I mean it. You stole the whole damn night."

"That was the point, Cade."

"And as much as I loved it. Sweetheart, we need to talk."

Bella stiffens. "Not now."

"Then when?" I step back just enough to look her in the eye. "Bella, you got more messages during the dance."

Her face falls. "From Luca?"

I shake my head. "No, sweetheart. Wanna share who the hell *Nate* is?"

Her entire body stills. Eyes wide. Color draining. She looks like she might faint. And right then—*perfect fucking timing*—Lex slides up behind her, one arm casually wrapping around her waist pulling her toward him.

"Well..." he drawls, glancing between us with that cocky grin I love so much. "That was one way to meet."

The color rushes back to Bella's face in a slow wave, like she's remembering how to breathe. She takes a small step toward me, fingers tugging at the hem of her shorts nervously.

"Yeah," she says lightly, voice threading the tension. "Sorry about that. The Trifecta and The Revenants rivalry runs pretty deep."

"No worries, baby," he says nonchalantly, brushing his fingers down her arm. "I thoroughly enjoyed the show." Then he leans over and kisses me.

When he pulls back, he gives us a wink. "I'm gonna hit the showers. You two stay here. I'll be right back."

As soon as Lex disappears down the hallway, I turn to her.

"Okay, sweetheart," I say, my voice lower now, steadier. "Who is Nate?"

Bella's jaw tightens. Her eyes flick away from mine. "Cade, please. Can we just drop it?"

"No," I snap, firmer than I mean to. "We cannot just drop it."

Her lips press together.

"You've got a stalker, Bella," I say, my voice rising with each word. "Someone who's clearly obsessed with you. And now I'm seeing texts from some guy talking about a 'buy' and picking you up at midnight?"

My jaw locks. "You expect me to just sit with that?"

I take a step closer, keeping my voice just between us. "Bella, is this about drugs or something?"

Her eyes shoot up, wide. "What? No. No, Cade, it's not—" she cuts herself off and takes a deep breath.

"It's not drugs, Cade," Bella snaps, but there's something fragile under the edge in her voice.

Before I can press again, her phone starts ringing. She glances down at the screen.

NATE.

Her throat bobs as she swallows, then she lifts her eyes to mine, pleading and desperate. "Please trust me," she whispers. "I have to take this."

She kisses my cheek and turns on her heel and walks off. I stand there staring after her, fists clenched at my sides. Torn between wanting to follow her and knowing if I do, I might lose my damn mind.

She's pacing and talking with her hands. Clearly frustrated. Every movement sharp and tense. She runs a hand through her hair as if the world is crashing around her and she's still pretending it's all under control.

Still the most beautiful thing I've ever fucking seen. Still keeping secrets.

Lex jogs up beside me, towel around his neck, hair damp from the shower. "Who's she talking to?" he asks, drying off his face.

I don't take my eyes off her. "We're about to find out."

We quickly stride over, just in time to hear her hiss into the phone, "That's fine. Just bring me a change of clothes. I'll be at Northvale."

My blood runs cold as I stop right behind her. "Bella," I say quietly. "What the hell is going on?"

She turns around slowly, phone still clutched in one hand, her other hand trembling slightly at her side. Bella looks between us. Eyes wide. Chest rising and falling like she's running out of air.

"Cade, no," she says softly, looking at Lex. "Not right now."

I shake my head. "Bella, there are no secrets in this. It can't work if there are."

Lex glances between the two of us, his brows pulling together. "What am I missing here?"

Her eyes flick to his, and I see it, the crack in her armor. The fear brewing. All of the guilt bubbling up inside her. The weight of whatever the hell she's been carrying on her own for way too long.

But I can't let it go. Not now. Not anymore.

"Bella?" Lex steps closer. His voice is quieter now. Gentler. "Talk to us."

She closes her eyes for a beat. Like she's praying for the right words, or praying for us to drop it.

"Sweetheart," I say, stepping in grabbing her trembling hands in mine. "Just tell us."

She bites her lip. And I realize that whatever this is, it's not just a secret. It's a huge storm about to break.

CHAPTER ⑶⑹
BELLA
THE PIT
NORTHVALE UNIVERSITY
580 DAYS SINCE ZEKE'S DEATH

"Sweetheart," Cade pushes, his low voice vibrating against my chest.

His thumbs trace slow circles over my knuckles. "Just tell us."

No...no... no fucking no.

I can't do this.

Not here. Not now. Not when Lex is standing two feet away. Not when I just met him. Not when I'm still high off the feeling of his lap under mine and his hand clenched in mine when I raised it in victory.

This isn't fucking happening. My heartbeat is so loud I can barely hear anything else. My lungs feel like they've turned to concrete.

Maybe I should faint. It works in the movies, right? Just full-on Disney princess it. A little sway, an eyelid flutter, and a dramatic collapse into Cade's arms. Although, Lex would probably catch me first.

Shit, maybe that's not the worst idea I've ever had.

If I tell them, everything changes. If I don't, I could lose them both. Fuck, and I haven't even had one of them yet.

Focus, Bella. Just think. What would Zeke do?

Well, bitch. Zeke would've never gotten himself tangled up in a situationship with an artsy version of a damn Esquire model and a Russian fighter who makes your brain short-circuit every time he looks at you with his damn icy eyes.

Zeke would've stayed focused. He would've stuck to the mission. He would've ghosted before feelings could complicate the plan.

Damn it, Bella.

No, fuck that shit. Not damn it, Bella. Damn it, Dr. Monroe and his *"You need real intimacy. Real connection. Real trust."* crap.

Tell that to the part of me currently debating whether to lie, cry, or pretend to pass the fuck out in front of the two most beautiful men I've ever seen in my life.

This is such bullshit. This is exactly why I don't do therapy. Or relationships. Or Russian fighters with tattoos on their fucking soul.

"Cade, please..."

His hands tighten around mine. Gentle. Solid. "Sweetheart, it's okay."

I swallow the knot in my throat. Then sigh. They obviously are not going to let this go.

"Okay. Fine." I glance at Lex, then back to Cade. "We should probably sit down," I mutter. "This is a pretty long story."

We sit side by side. My hands still feel shaky, but they're wrapped in Cade's and Lex is close enough I can feel his warmth like armor.

"Okay," I start. "So, you know that I was an orphan. Lived in Arkansas. Bad foster home. Brother got me out. Died. And now I'm here."

They both nod.

"All of that is true," I admit. "But there's a lot more."

I breathe out. "When I was little, I wasn't in a bad home, I was in a good one. My dad was an ex-Razorback quarterback and a firefighter. My mom was a teacher, but also used to dance. I got my love of dance from her. I was loved."

My southern accent slips out, soft and unguarded. "Really loved. Until my mama died of cancer and then my life blew up."

Lex leans in, voice a low rumble. "What happened, baby?"

I swallow, the memories catching like glass in my throat. "Apparently there was some kind of issue with my paperwork, I really don't know. Something with the records. CPS showed up out of nowhere and took me away. I still have nightmares about that day... being dragged out of my Daddy's arms. My aunt screaming. Begging them not to take me away."

I pause, breath shaking. "They didn't care. They put me in a new home in Miami."

I look down at my hands in Cade's. "On the outside, it looked perfect. Ocean view. White pillars. Beautiful garden. Smiling couple. Everything clean and quiet like a damn brochure."

I feel Lex tense next to me. Cade's thumb stills against my skin.

"But it was all a lie." I look up, throat tight. "Carlos was a monster. He took in kids knowin' his fancy, sick pedo friends would pay good money for a few minutes with us. Or better yet, just buy us straight out like we were nothing but property."

"What the fuck?!" Lex explodes.

Cade grabs my leg, his body's on autopilot and wired to shield me before his brain even catches up. There's panic in his touch, urgency in the way his fingers dig in, like if he holds me tight enough, nothing can touch me. Nothing can take me.

"It's okay," I whisper, holding up a hand as they both look ready to burn the world to ash. "No one touched me. They never got the chance."

I blink, hard. "I was protected by my foster brother. Zeke."

Lex's voice is quiet, almost reverent. "The Z on your shoulder?"

I nod. "He intercepted every deal meant to buy me or our little brother Dylan. Hacked systems, rerouted payments, faked medical emergencies. Took every punishment when Carlos found out."

My fingers trace the name on my wrist. Lex's eyes follow the motion.

"When Dylan died." My throat clamps around the words, but I force them out. "Everything changed." The tears come. I try to bite them back, swallow the grief like I've done a hundred times before, but it doesn't work.

"Dylan..."

My voice cracks. I swallow. Try again. "Fuck. Um... Dylan was nine."

I can feel Cade's grip tighten around my leg. Lex goes still beside me, but I don't dare look at either of them yet. I just stare straight ahead at the ring.

"Zeke and I were in my room when we heard him scream. We tore down the hall and...uh..." I run my hand on the back of my neck.

"One of Carlos's sleazy friends was standing behind him."

I feel my chest cave in like a sinkhole. "Zeke lost it."

The memory flashes—Zeke's roar, the way his fists didn't stop even when Vince dropped.

"I grabbed Dylan and ran. Took him back to my room and told him to stay put. Then I went back for Zeke."

My voice shakes harder now. "Zeke had nearly killed Vince by the time we heard the shot."

I pause. A tear slips down my cheek and I can't catch it in time. My left leg starts to tremble. I press my palm against my thigh, but it won't stop. Lex leans forward and covers my hand with his.

I whisper, "Dylan shot himself."

"Why didn't CPS do anything?" Lex asks.

"Because the system's rigged. Kids are a cash business. All it takes is a fake ID, a fake death, or enough money and nobody looks."

Cade's voice is barely above a whisper. "Oh, sweetheart, why didn't you ever tell me?"

I squeeze his hand, then let go. "Because that's not the whole story. See Vince had purchased Dylan. The incident, as Carlos so lovingly put it, caused Carlos to lose a lot of money and piss off a very wealthy client and friend."

Lex and Cade both go still. I take a breath that feels like sandpaper. "A few months later, Vince came back as a fucking District Attorney. Apparently, Carlos made a huge donation and they were besties again."

Lex's jaw clenches. Cade shifts like he's ready to stand.

"Carlos sold me to Vince at a discounted rate. It was Zeke's eighteenth birthday. He was going to age out and get kicked out of the house." I shake my head, voice splintering. "He heard them talking. What they were planning to do to me."

I meet their eyes. "He went insane. Full blackout rage."

Cade's breath catches. Lex's stare is lethal as he cracks his knuckles.

"It was a bloodbath," I whisper. "Mariela came in before Zeke could finish the job. She grabbed her keys and told us to run."

I pause.

"We did. We took her car, grabbed what we could, and left. We faked our deaths and then we disappeared. Changed our last names and came here."

Lex's brow pulls together. "So, you just, moved to New York? How, you were just kids?"

I glance down at my shaking hands, then back up. "I'm not done," I say softly.

CHAPTER ㉚
LEX
THE PIT
ABOUT TO LOSE MY DAMN MIND...
580 DAYS SINCE ZEKE'S DEATH

I can't fucking breathe. She's sitting between us, tears on her cheeks, voice shaking, and still she says, *I'm not done.* How the hell is there more? I've taken hits from men twice my size and never felt pain like this. Never felt rage like this. Cade looks wrecked, like someone just ripped out his heart.

"After the explosion, we boarded the plane. Our plane, I guess."

"What do you mean your plane, sweetheart?" Cade asks.

She exhales as if it hurts. "Remember how I said Zeke was stopping the buys?"

We both nod.

"Well, he'd been working on that for a while. Taking money from corrupt politicians, billionaires, anyone who paid to hurt kids. He was robbing them blind."

Fucking genius man.

She swallows. "And he, uh, also hacked into some criminal families. Stole their Black Books."

I suck in a breath.

Her voice calms, now personal. "That's how Nate came into the picture." She looks at Cade.

"Nate's ex-something. Acronym type. FBI maybe. CIA. I don't really know, but he's brilliant. His sister was kidnapped and..."

She stops. Takes a breath. "...she didn't make it."

A long silence.

Her voice steadies. "Zeke, Tex, and Nate built Project Dylan. We get kids out of foster hellholes, save them from abusive parents, and yank them out of trafficking rings. We pull them out and drop the sellers and buyers in a hole so deep they can't crawl out of. We use the Black Books as leverage, blackmail, pressure, and muscle."

That blazing fire in her is back. A different kind of rage.

Purpose.

"I was trained but didn't get to go on my first mission until my sixteenth birthday," she adds quietly, like it still haunts her.

Cade cuts in, voice quiet but strained. "So, you've been going on these missions since you were sixteen?"

She nods. "Yeah. Zeke, Nate, and Tex pretty much raised me. Trained me to be a weapon for Project Dylan."

"And you're still doing these missions? Saving children?" Cade asks.

"Yes, Cade. I'm still saving kids."

But then her voice flattens and her eyes go cold. "Our mission changed my Freshman year. Zeke was on a mission in Chicago. We got a tip. Thought it was solid." Her shoulders rise and fall once, like she's trying to stay steady. "It was a trap. There was an explosion and... and..." Her lip quivers. "My brother was murdered."

Cade looks gutted. I just want names. She keeps going.

"Knox—"

"The DJ?" I ask.

She nods. "Yeah. He pulled me out of a bad state and got me to face it. In a very cruel and unusual way for sure, but it worked better than the shrink."

She glances at me. "Nate was near the blast. He still gets a little shaken up from time to time. Knox is a great hacker, almost Zeke level. He's a major asset to the team."

Cade's voice cuts through the quiet, low and shaky. "If Knox knows all of this, then—"

She nods once. "The girls do too."

He leans back like the wind got knocked out of him. "Dad's birthday? When you missed the yacht outing?"

Her silence is the answer. But it's the way she won't meet his eyes that really says it. And I see it. The years of built-up closeness neither of them ever named. The kind of bond you don't get from just dating. This shit runs deeper. Shared summers, family trips, midnight pick-ups, late-night texts when she wouldn't talk to anyone else.

Cade's jaw flexes. "You told them. But not me."

"I told them before we were ever a thing," she says, shoulders dropping. "Ellie at St. Lyra's graduation, and Hales and Knox the summer before freshman year."

Cade blinks, like the timeline just shifted under his feet. His brows pull together. "That long ago?"

She nods. "They were my roommates, Cade. My team. My family."

I watch Cade swallow hard, like he's trying to make space in his chest for that truth. For everything he didn't know. Everything she carried before they ever touched. Before he ever kissed her like she was his.

"Where were you on Dad's birthday, Bella?" Cade asks again.

"I was in New Orleans." She looks down. "The Black Book families want their data back, and they will do just about anything to get it. I made a trade for some pieces of one, and their leader got me what I asked for. My revenge on Carlos."

That name is gasoline. I shift forward, something feral curling in my chest. "What kind of revenge, baby?"

Her eyes meet mine. And for the first time tonight, she smiles. But it's not sweet. It's dark.

"I should back up. First, Zeke and I got Carlos put in prison. Mariela was pregnant and there was no way in hell we were letting that baby girl grow up with him as a father. So we bankrupted him. Zeke stripped away the cops, politicians, all of it. He leaked Carlos's failed sales to the feds, enough they couldn't bury. Carlos went down. Afterward, we sent Mariela cash, IDs, a way out. A safe new life for her and her daughter."

She shifts in her seat. "So now... back to the New Orleans part. Sabine got Carlos transferred from Miami to New Orleans," she continues, calmer now. No longer trembling.

"Her men attacked the transport van. Made it look like Carlos ran. And then they sat him in the bayou to wait for me," she says letting out a huff.

Her voice is different now. It's like me when I get into one of my rage spirals and don't come out until someone's broken or bleeding. She looks like she could kill a god and then go sleep like a damn baby.

Cade, on the other hand, looks like he's about to faint. His mouth opens. Closes. Opens again.

"Carlos didn't make it out of that swamp."

Cade's voice barely cooperates. "You... you killed a man?"

Ok calm the fuck down, Cade. Fucker had it coming.

Bella's head tilts. "Not exactly."

Cade blinks fast. "The message. From Luca. Is this that Carlos?"

She nods once. "Yeah."

"Okay. What aren't you telling me?" I ask. "I haven't seen these messages. What happened in that bayou, baby?"

"Well..." she says like she's about to tell us the ending of some twisted bedtime story. "Sabine—who, by the way, totally looks like a voodoo priestess—is a beautiful genius. And she lives for revenge. She has this snake that she swears can tell if a soul is rotten."

She shrugs. "Turns out Carlos's was."

Cade looks like he's going to be sick.

"She told me not to waste my revenge on a head-shot. Said that'd be too merciful. To be smart, savor it." She shrugs again, all casual carnage. "So, since he had talked about all the nasty things he wanted to do to me with his dick, I shot him in it."

I wince.

"Sabine shot him in the kneecaps and then we left him there."

"Fuck, baby," I mutter. "That's... brutal."

Cade looks green. Like, *billionaire-heir-vomits-on-his-loafers,* kind of green.

She stands and something in her breaks. Her fire is gone. That sharp, fearless energy she carries like armor just flickers out.

"And this," she says softly, gaze locked on Cade, "this is exactly why I didn't want to say anything."

We both rise instantly. I catch her hand. "Bella, wait."

She stops but she's not looking at me. Just him. Cade. And he fucking freezes. Doesn't say a word. And that's all it takes.

Her chin trembles. "The way you're looking at me right now, Cade, like the girl you've been kissing, sleeping with, and laughing with these past few weeks just ripped her mask off and underneath is something dark and twisted. Like I'm a stranger or worse, some kind of monster."

Cade's jaw tightens. His fists clench like he wants to scream, but he doesn't.

"This is what I was afraid of," she whispers, like it's the last secret she has left. "This is why I never told you. Not in Nashville, not ever. I just knew the second I fell in love with you, Cade, I was just biding my time."

Cade flinches. The words physically hitting him.

"Because every time I let myself love someone... really love them, I lose them." Her voice is barely a whisper now. "Zeke. Dylan. My parents. Every damn time I choose love. It gets ripped away from me."

Cade's voice cracks the silence. "Bella, I don't think you're a monster."

But he won't look at her.

Her arms fold tight, but her voice stays calm. Too calm. "Yes. Yes you do, Cade."

He still wont meet her eyes.

"You know how I know?" she says, stepping back. "Because you haven't looked me in the eyes once since I told you I left Carlos in that chair."

Cade drags a hand through his hair, pacing and trying to outrun the truth. "I'm sorry, Bella. But what the hell did you expect? That I'd just nod and say, 'cool, you killed a guy,' and go back to kissing your shoulder while you hum yourself to sleep?"

She barely flinches, but I see it.

He keeps pacing. "Jesus, how am I supposed to process that you've... that you murdered someone?"

I take a step forward. I'm one more dumbass sentence away from throwing him into a wall, but Bella lifts her hand without looking and stops me cold.

Her voice cuts the air. "I didn't kill him, Cade."

Silence.

"I maimed him. For what he did. For what he would've done. And then I walked away. Left him alive and bleeding."

The harsh, brutal truth my boyfriend doesn't want to hear.

And yet, Cade still can't shut the fuck up. "What happened to Carlos after you left, Bella?" he asks.

She blinks. "What do you mean?"

"You know what I mean." He's not yelling but the heat is there. "You said you left him but I know you. Maybe better than you think. What really happened after you and Sabine walked out?"

"Cade," I snap, low and dangerous. "Enough."

Bella stops me again. She looks at him.

"You want the truth?" she says. "Fine."

Her voice is fire and ash. "We walked to the door. He asked what would happen to his kid. I told him the truth, that his wife and daughter would live a long, happy life without him. Then Sabine's men walked in behind us and they burned the fucking house to the ground."

Cade's expression hardens. He looks wounded. Deep. Like this version of her doesn't fit the memory he's been holding onto.

"And in case you somehow forgot, Zeke was murdered. Dylan took his own life all because of that man."

She steps toward Cade, gaze locked. No more fear. Just fury and grief and that terrifying strength that only comes from surviving hell.

"And Carlos? He laughed when he found out Zeke was dead."

A beat passes.

"So yeah," she bites out, "I got my revenge." Her breath shakes, but her spine stays straight. Her eyes never leave his.

"And you want to know something, Cade?" she says, softer now, deadlier. "I fucking loved it."

She leans in. "Do you even know what revenge looks like? It's a girl with a gun in her hand, a body full of trauma, and not a single soul left to stop her."

"You talk about revenge like it's survival," he says quietly. "And maybe for you it is. I get that. I do."

He runs a hand through his hair, that old nervous tic. "But for me? It's... it's a darkness I don't know how to live in. I don't know how to love someone who doesn't want to come back into the light."

Her whole face crumples. Like he just proved her worst fear, that the second she handed him the truth, he'd flinch.

He'd flee.

He takes a breath like it hurts to speak. "I just... I need some time, Bella."

And fuck me, I want to kill him for that.

Her phone rings.

"What Nate?!" she literally screams in the phone. "Ok, yeah. I'm sorry... No, I'm fine... Yeah, I'm on my way out."

She puts her phone back into her pocket. "I have to go."

Cade steps up like he's finally decided to grow a pair. "Now? Bella, we need to finish talking about all of this. We still haven't even started talking about Luca."

"No, Cade. We don't." Her voice is steady. "You said enough. You want time. I get that. Take it. Do what you need to do."

She turns, grabbing her bag. "But what I need to do right now, is to go do my job."

"Bella, please wait."

"Look!" she yells, stepping closer, fire trembling beneath every word. "There's no version of this where I'm the girl you thought I was."

I see it then, what he sees.

The girl who used to pass out on the couch next to him watching old movies with Ellie. The one who used to give him shit about his sketchbooks, but stay and watch him draw anyway. The one he never touched back then because she was young and hurting and off-limits.

"I'm the girl who grew up in hell," she says. "Who clawed her way out with blood under her nails and no map to follow. I tried to give you the version of me that wasn't soaked in all of it. The version who smiled easier, laughed louder. The version I used to be when I was fifteen and stupid enough to believe I could somehow be normal."

Cade's still not talking. Just staring at her like he's watching her slip through his fingers.

"But she's not all of me," Bella continues, voice breaking and fierce all at once. "And the part you don't want, the part you looked at like it might burn you alive? That's the part that's saving kids, Cade."

She looks at him one last time. "So, take whatever time you need. But I have to go. Those kids need me more than you do right now."

She looks at me, tears staining her steel eyes as she nears the exit. "I'm sorry I messed this up, Lex. I know you had your hopes up." She turns and walks out.

"What the fuck, Cade?" I grit, laced with disbelief. "You're really just going to let the best thing that ever happened to us walk out of this fucking Pit?"

He turns, his jaw tight. "What do you want me to do, Lex? Just pretend none of this happened?"

"I want you to see her," I snap, stepping into Cade's space without even realizing it. "See her the way I do. The way you used to before she ripped herself open to give *you* the truth you demanded." His jaw clenches, but he doesn't speak. So, I keep going.

"You asked for this, Cade. You. You pushed. You kept digging, kept prying, like you needed to see how deep the wounds went. And now what, you just shut down?"

My voice drops, rough and razor-edged. "Don't stand there like you're the victim in this. She trusted you with the worst parts of her and you looked at her like she was a stranger."

"I just wanted the truth, Lex," he says running a hand over his neck.

"Well congratulations, you got it. Now tell me, is this something you're gonna get the fuck over? Because everything she's done, *everything*, has been completely fucking justified."

"Justified?" he snaps, eyes wide. "She killed a man, Lex. She let him burn like it was nothing. That's not normal. That's not just some dark secret she forgot to mention."

"And how the fuck is that any different than my family?" I step in, heat rising. "You know what my mom and uncle do. You know about the guns they bring in every goddamn week, whats hiding in all the Barinov bunkers."

He says nothing, chest rising and falling like he's trying to find the right words and keeps choking on them.

"So what now, *Whitmore*?" I throw the name at him like a

challenge. "You gonna let your pride fuck this up? You gonna walk because she isn't your picture-perfect fantasy anymore?"

Silence. The guy won't even blink.

I lean in, deadly calm now. "Do you love her?"

"What?"

"Do you love her, Cade?" My voice cracks like a whip through the space between us. "Because she just stood there, shaking and falling apart, admitted she loved you and you said nothing. *Nothing.* Just whined about the fact that she shot a guy in the dick who, by the way, absolutely had it fucking coming."

He doesn't respond right away. Just stares at the floor like it might hold the answers he's too afraid to say out loud.

And I can't take it. I step in, furious now. "You were the one who said she was it for us. You're the one who got my hopes up, Cade. Not just for her, but for the family that you and I have wanted for a long time, babe."

Cade's throat works around a breath. "Yes."

My chest goes still.

"Yes," he says again, firmer this time. "I love her. But—"

"No buts, Cade!" I cut him off, stepping forward, fury and heartbreak coiled in my throat.

"If you love her, prove it. You already love me with all my darkness. Now it's Bella's turn. Jesus Christ Cade, you don't just get to fucking cherry-pick which parts of her deserve your love. You just love her. Darkness and all."

He doesn't argue.

Doesn't move.

So, I do. I turn and storm toward the exit.

"Where the hell are you going?" he calls after me.

I look over my shoulder. "To get our fucking girlfriend back. You may need time, but I don't, Cade. Figure whatever it is you need to figure out, but I'm going after her."

CHAPTER ㊳
B E L L A
N O R T H V A L E   U N I V E R S I T Y
581 DAYS SINCE ZEKE'S DEATH

We pull out of the Northvale University main parking lot when Knox hands me a black duffel from the front seat. By the time we hit the freeway, I've swapped out the showgirl for the soldier.

"You okay, Bells?" Knox calls out, trying to sound casual.

"Fine."

"Totally believable," Tex mutters from the passenger seat, not bothering to hide the sarcasm.

"Okay both of you shut it," I snap, settling back into my seat.

Tex doesn't even look at me. "We've got company."

My eyes shoot up to the side mirror. "You have got to be fucking kidding me," I say as a sleek black motorcycle weaves through traffic behind us like it belongs in a heist movie.

"Pull over."

"Bella—"

"Damn it just pull over, Knox."

Knox grumbles something about 'unhinged Russian architecture majors' but does it anyway. The van slows down and eases onto the shoulder. I'm already pushing the door open before we've come to a full stop.

The roar of the motorcycle cuts as the rider swings it around and parks a few feet behind us. He takes his helmet off.

Lex.

Hair windblown, jaw tight, icy-blue eyes locked on me like he's ready to either kiss me or kill someone for me. Probably both. I walk right up to him, heart a literal freight train pounding in my chest.

"Why the fuck are you following me?" I snap, stalking up to him like I'm about to start swinging.

Lex doesn't even blink, just tips his chin, "Nice to see you too, baby."

"I'm serious, Lex. Turn on your bike and go home. I'm busy."

"I can see that. Let me come with you."

"No way in hell."

"Why not?"

"This is a mission, dumbass. We have protocol." I say putting my hands on my hips. "You don't just waltz in like it's a damn frat party."

"I can be useful," he says with that cocky tilt of his head. "You need muscle, I *am* muscle."

"Go. Home. Lex."

"No."

"Yes."

"Nope," he says popping the p.

"God, I don't have time for this," I mumble as I pull my pistol from my holster and point it straight at his chest. His eyes flick to the barrel of the gun, then back to mine.

"There it is, baby," he murmurs. "There's the fucking darkness I knew was in you. You're just like me."

"What the fuck are you doing, Lex?"

He shrugs, casual as ever. "Look, Cade's an idiot. Love him to death but he's still an idiot. Trust me, I've been fucking him for years. I've seen him throw walls up and tear himself apart over shit that never mattered. He gets over it. He did with me and he will with you. Especially with you because you're not just some phase or fling, baby. You're the girl he's been orbit—"

"Stop talking, Lex."

He takes one step closer. I don't lower the gun.

"Go home. Now."

"Baby," Lex rasps, eyes dragging down my body then lock back with mine. "Either pull the trigger or shut the fuck up and listen to me."

My jaw clenches. Every nerve in my body is vibrating as I holster my pistol.

"What?" I snap.

His mouth twitches. "Good girl."

Before I can blink, he grabs both my wrists and yanks me into him, rough and possessive. One of his hands pins mine behind my back while the other fists my hair. He dips his head low, breathing me in like I'm his next addiction.

Then he licks my fucking neck.

A slow, filthy drag of tongue over pulse. I gasp, half-shocked, half-amused, because it's exactly what I did to him back at The Pit.

"That," he growls into my skin, "is the last time you ever walk away from us again. Do you understand me, Bella?"

My breathing's erratic. Heart is racing. Legs are shaking. The pulse between my thighs pounding. God, my fucking vagina and aggressive men I swear.

I hate him.

I want him.

I hate that I want him.

Knox steps out of the van, arms crossed, one brow raised. "Okay, as much as I'm all for whatever this is." He waves a vague hand between us. "We need to move. Clock's ticking."

"Great. I'll follow you," Lex says not even looking at Knox.

I whip my head toward him. "Lex—"

"Not up for debate, baby. Now get your sexy ass moving. We're gonna be late."

@LucaWasHere
Off to play hero with a brute in tow?
Tsk, tsk, Izzy, you should've said no.
He's loud. He's reckless. He's easy to trace.
And if you're not careful, he'll give them your face.

You think he protects you? You think he's the shield?
But war's not won in the center field.
It's silence, shadows, clever disguise.
Not fists and fury and fire in his eyes.

CHAPTER ㊴
LEX
QUEENS, NEW YORK
A SHADY AS FUCK LOOKING BUILDING...
581 DAYS SINCE ZEKE'S DEATH

We pull up just shy of the drop, parking the van and my bike in the shadows of the alley. The building looks like it's one good gust of wind from collapsing. Perfect place to do shady shit. Or get buried.

There's another car that grabs my attention. Jet black. Glossy. Expensive as fuck. Some overpriced import with bulletproof windows and a custom license plate that probably says something like *GOD-MODE,* because of course it does.

And leaning against it? Well fuck me sideways. Tall, tan, and shirtless, because apparently dress codes don't apply when you're rich and insane. Just dark jeans, combat boots, and a full dragon tattoo curling across his chest and shoulder like he thinks he's in a Marvel movie.

Asian guy. Lean, inked, and lounging like the devil himself. He's grinning like he already knows how this ends.

"Who the fuck is that?" I mutter, already annoyed.

Bella steps out of the van all lethal curves and controlled chaos. My fucking chaos. She walks straight up to him like it's nothing, like she owns the ground under her red stilettos.

The annoying half-naked dude just says, "About time," and pulls her right into him.

What the actual fuck?

She stiffens. "Not now, Laing."

Laing. *Laing?* What kind of name is that? Sounds like the villain from a sushi-themed Bond movie.

He leans down, lips at her ear, and whispers something I can't hear. Which only makes it worse.

My jaw clenches. Fists too. I'm about two seconds away from stomping over there and breaking every rib that fucking dragon's crawling over. I don't care if he's CIA, NSA, goddamn Mortal Kombat.

He touches her like that again, and I'm putting him in the ground.

"Chill, dude."

Knox. Of course.

Not now Bestie.

He steps up next to me, calm as ever. "You don't want to touch that."

"The fuck I don't," I growl, eyes locked on where Laing's still got his hand on her hip like he owns her.

"Lex. Seriously. I know we just met but, if you care about her—and I'm assuming you do, based on the whole 'licking her neck and declaring eternal possession in front of a van full of people' thing—then don't fuck up her missions."

"He touched her."

"He always touches her." Knox shrugs. "Creepy, flirty, and unfortunately... extremely useful."

I glance at him, ready to argue.

He cuts me off with a flat look. "You storm over there and punch him and derail whatever op we're doing tonight? That's ego, Barinov. And Bella doesn't have time for ego."

I swallow the fury rising in my throat, watching as she finally pulls away from Laing and says something sharp enough to wipe the smug grin off his face.

I exhale. "I don't like him."

Knox taps me on the shoulder. "Nobody does. But until she tells him to go? We're stuck with his ass."

I narrow my eyes. "Who the hell is he?"

"Laing Wei. Head of the Red Silk Triads out of Hong Kong. Took over when his father was killed. Brutal, brilliant, and tough as shit."

My head snaps toward him. "He's Triad?"

"Yeah. Usually stationed in San Francisco, but lately..." He trails off. I follow his line of sight. Bella, still standing way too fucking close to Tattooed Dragon-Dick. "...he's been hanging around New York more."

"Wonder why."

Knox smirks like he knows damn well why, and I swear to God

I nearly punch him just for that look.

Instead, I mutter under my breath, "This night just keeps getting better."

Knox clocks my glare and leans in. "Don't worry, man. Bella plays him just like he plays the rest of the world."

I grunt.

"She's in control. Always," he adds. "We've got his Black Book so he works for us until she says otherwise."

He jerks his chin toward Bella as she heads back toward us, Laing glued to her side like a damn shadow.

"She's the boss," Knox finishes. "You'd be smart to remember that."

Bella stops in front of us, calm and composed like she's not dragging a Triad kingpin around like a pet.

"Alright, boys," she says, giving Laing a side glance. "There's been a change of plans. Krolek's not here."

Knox snorts. "Lovely."

"Same plan as before," she says, cool and in command. "Tex, get into position."

"On it," Tex mutters. He's already walking away with his sniper case slung over one shoulder like it's a damn lunchbox. Guy moves like death on vacation.

Bella turns slightly, eyes scanning the rest of us. "Knox? Nate? Comms, cameras, medics and transport?"

Knox gives a quick nod. "Cameras up, audio clean. We're golden."

"Medical on standby," whoever Nate is, chimes in from the door of the van, checking something on a screen.

Bella nods. "Good."

Then, just for a heartbeat, her eyes flick to me. I don't miss it. A glance. Barely a second. But I feel it in my ribs. She turns back just as fast.

"Laing and I go in like planned. Happy couple of foster parents looking to buy and sell."

Fucking happy couple my ass.

Laing steps in close and pulls her against him, one hand low on her back. "You got it, Iz."

Iz? The fuck does this guy think he is?

Bella pulls away just enough to regain control. She doesn't say anything but the message is clear.

Good girl.

"Alright, Tex, you hear me?" she says into the comms.

Tex must respond in the comms because she continues. "Okie dokie boys," she says with a southern twang. "What's the word of the day? Tex, it's your turn to pick."

Bella sighs. "I am abso-fucking-lutely not saying that."

A few chuckles ripple through the group. Knox nearly chokes on air.

Laing of course, leans back with all the subtlety of a sledge-hammer. "What do you want it to be, Iz?"

If Mortal Kombat touches her one more time, the word of the day is going to be homicide.

"Let's keep it simple," Bella says, brushing Laing's hand off her hip. "Something we can work into a lovely husband and wife conversation."

Husband and wife. Gag.

"Baby," I pipe up, voice loud and clear. "Don't say husband and wife with this guy, it makes me want to puke."

Laing turns to give me a look. All stoic and silent and full of that smug Triad patience bullshit.

Bella rolls her eyes, but she's grinning. "Okay, boys," she says dryly. "Let's just do Paris. Quick, casual, easy enough to work into whatever lovely conversation you get us into, Laing."

She looks at Laing, but he's not looking at her. He's still staring at me. Well stare all you want, Mortal Kombat. Get a good hard look. Because one day soon when you're not useful anymore, I'll be the last thing those pretty dragon eyes ever see.

Meeting adjourned.

Laing finally puts on a shirt and buttons it up around the wire, thank fuck. If I had to stare at that damn dragon any longer, I was going to rip it off his smug chest myself.

She walks over to me. "Lex."

"Yes, baby?" I reply pulling her into me, earning a hushed mumble from Tattooed Dragon-Dick.

"Please be good and try not to screw this up for me. I've already had a shitty enough night. I will not lose these kids do you understand me?"

"You go get your kids. I'll stay with Knox."

She walks back to him. To fucking Laing. He falls into step beside her like he belongs there. I stand there, jaw locked, blood pounding, watching her hips in those leather pants that were apparently crafted to ruin my fucking sanity.

Then he does it. That smug bastard opens the car door like he's her fucking knight. Doesn't say a word. Just looks at me—*chin up, eyes cold*—and shuts the door.

Knox steps up beside me, arms crossed. "Still jealous?"

"I'm two seconds away from lighting him on fire."

Knox shrugs, totally unbothered. "Cool. I'll bring marshmallows."

I climb into the van, shutting the door a little harder than necessary. The fed guy is already there, clean-cut and all buttoned-up professionalism. He gives me a nod.

"I'm Nate," he says, offering a handshake like we're about to go over blueprints instead of busting up a creepy sale of some little kids.

"Lex," I say, gripping his hand. "Appreciate you keeping her alive."

He nods once, all serious. "Always."

I glance around. "So, uh... can I get one of those earpieces? I'd like to hear what the hell is going on."

Nate reaches for a small black comm set, starts handing it over until Knox smacks his hand away mid-pass.

"Not yet," Knox says, not even looking at me. He's laughing at the screens. "Let's let Mommy and Daddy finish their little lover's quarrel first."

I blink. "What the fuck are you talking about?"

Knox, deadpan, presses the button on the main mic. "Laing. Bella. Either kiss and make up or shut the fuck up."

He laughs and then hands me an earpiece. "There. That's better. Welcome to the team, Barinov."

He smirks. "You can listen but you don't get a mic. You've caused enough drama for one night."

"Glad to know I'm making an impact."

Nate huffs a laugh, then leans in closer to the screen. "Here we go."

Bella and Laing show up on a different cam, walking toward a run-down brick building with blacked-out windows and a rotting fire escape. I squint.

"So, what exactly is going on? Who is this Krolek?" I ask.

Knox points with a lazy finger to one of the cameras. "Bella and Laing are going in as a foster family looking to purchase some kids for their homes. Homes like the one Bella and her brothers grew up in. Ones where the kids will be abused and sold for a hefty profit."

He zooms in the on camera to get a better look of the room. "Krolek's a nasty fucker out of Eastern Europe," he says, fingers flying over the keys. "Kids, guns, flesh, you name it, he's in it. Zeke had him flagged for years, but he's slippery as hell. Rarely shows up to the buys himself."

Knox reaches for a USB drive and sticks it into a tablet. "We were hoping he'd be here tonight but that's not the case. Zeke was also pretty sure that Krolek is the one who supplied the kids for Carlos's house."

On screen, Laing's got his arm around Bella and squeezes her tight. He leans in, whispers something in her ear, and she fake-laughs like it's some romcom bullshit.

A door opens and five little tiny and scared kids are led out. All of them have to be under ten. The smallest one's holding a stuffed rabbit with one missing ear.

My stomach fucking knots. I don't know if it's the kids. Or Bella playing house with a Triad boss. Or both.

Knox's voice cuts through it. "Okay, Laing. We have a visual on the kids. Now ease him into it. Get him to put the kids back inside, I don't want them anywhere near the crossfire."

Laing starts some slow, sleazy sales pitch by talking numbers, rotation, discretion. I tune it out. I'm watching Bella. Every blink. Every shift of her weight. Every time she glances at the kids like she's about to snap someone's spine.

The muscle gets the kids back into the room. Knox leans forward. "Problem Child, you're up."

Bella's voice goes syrup-sweet. "Oh, honey! This is perfect, thank you!" she squeals, tugging Laing down into a kiss.

What the actual fuck is this girl doing? Signing Laing's death certificate is what it looks like.

Laing groans against her lips as she adds, "Ooh, but can we keep that little one? I like her. She'll be perfect for our home in Paris."

Jesus fucking Christ this is making my skin crawl, but damn if it isn't slick as hell.

I don't hear the shot. But I see it. The seller drops and hits the ground like a sack of bricks. Bella and Laing move in sync, guns already drawn, turning them on the guards without missing a beat.

Knox grins, flicking a switch. "Showtime."

Bella's voice cuts through the feed, no longer playing housewife. It's cold. Lethal. Fucking divine. "You two. Drop your guns and kick them over."

The guards freeze for half a breath, just long enough to consider testing her. Then they wise up and do exactly what she says. Smart moves.

She glances over at Laing. "Honey," she says mockingly. "Tie them up."

Laing flashes a wicked grin and does what he's told, zip-tying both men with practiced efficiency.

Bella lowers her gun. "Nate. Knox. Get in here. Let's get these kids out. We need to have a chat with our little friends here."

"I'm coming," I say sharply.

"Nope. She'll rip my balls out and gift wrap 'em for Haley's Christmas present if I let you in there. I'm talking ribbon, bow, and a glittery tag that says *'Thanks, bitch.'*"

"Good for Haley," I growl. "But I'd like to see you try and stop me."

Nate doesn't even look up. "It's fine. Let him go, Knox. I'll handle Bella."

Knox raises a brow. "You sure?"

Nate gives a slow nod.

We fire up the van and creep down the road, white chat crunching under the tires as the building fades behind us. The second we stop, all three of us pile out.

Bella's already moving. Calm, fast, and completely in control. She's guiding the kids toward safety like she's done this a hundred times. And maybe she has. But I've never seen anything like it. Watching her save them—*actually save them*—it's the best goddamn thing I've ever seen. Just pure instinct. All heart. All fire.

She's carrying the smallest one, a little girl can't be more than four. She's clinging to Bella's shoulder like she's found her forever safe place. And fuck me if that doesn't twist something brutal and permanent in my chest.

Bella crosses to us, steps right up to Nate, doesn't even glance at me. "How far out are the medics?" Right on cue, the sirens whine down the block and a rig screeches around the corner, lights blazing.

"Right now," Nate says with a short laugh.

Bella dips her head toward the little girl, "Okay sweetie. Let's get you checked out, yeah?"

The girl nods, wide-eyed and quiet. Bella walks off with her, still not looking at me. It shouldn't sting, but it fucking does.

Knox and Nate head out to help the rest of the kids. Bella hands the little girl to an EMT. The little girl tries to latch onto Bella. She must say something to calm her down, because she nods and finally lets go.

Then Tex appears, silent and lethal as ever, and walks straight to Bella. Laing joins them. The three of them start talking. Quiet. Focused.

Knox steps up beside me, hands in his pockets, watching everything unfold. "You ready for a real show?" he asks, voice low but laced with something different. Almost proud.

I scoff. "Better than all this?" I say, gesturing around at the busted building, flashing lights, and Laing's smug ass hovering way too close to my girl.

Knox tips his chin, cocky. "Just wait until we get the kids out of here."

The ambulance doors shut with a final clank, sirens fading as they roll off with the kids. A breath leaves my chest I didn't know I was holding.

"Alright. Let's go." Knox says and I fall in step beside him.

We round the side of the building and I see them. Bella, Tex, and Mortal fucking Kombat are standing in a loose arc around two metal folding chairs.

And strapped to those chairs are the remaining muscle from the seller's crew. They're sweating bullets. Eyes flicking between the three people in front of them and the corpse cooling on the concrete beside them.

One shot.

Left eye.

Whole damn socket... gone.

Damn, nice shootin' Tex.

CHAPTER (40)
BELLA
QUEENS, NEW YORK
581 DAYS SINCE ZEKE'S DEATH

"Where's Krolek?" I don't yell. I don't bark. I ask calmly. Which is exactly why both men strapped to those folding chairs start to sweat a little harder. Their gazes shift from the body slumped on the ground, to each other, and to the blood soaking into the concrete.

They don't answer. Not even a stutter. They look at him. Tex. Then at Laing. And that's their first mistake. Laing cracks his neck and steps forward.

"Yeah," he says, voice casual and almost cheerful. "You're gonna want to answer her."

Tex doesn't say a word as he walks over to the wall, crosses his arms, and leans back against it like he already knows how this ends.

Our guests still don't open their mouths.

"Fine. Guess we're doing this the fun way," I say.

BANG.

My gun kicks back. Left shoulder, only a little love tap. Our guest of honor wails.

Scarface, the other one with the jagged gash cutting across his brow shouts at me. "You crazy bitch!"

Apparently, he's not a fan of me shooting his buddy.

"Laing," I sigh, bored.

BANG.

Laing fires without hesitation. Scarface's kneecap. The snap echoes, followed by another round of screaming.

"Call her a bitch again," he grits, glaring at Scarface. He nods toward the guy that I clipped. "We've got a spare. You're not exactly necessary."

"Aww, thanks honey." I smile sweetly and blow him a kiss.

Behind me, I hear Lex mutter under his breath. Something about a dragon dick. I don't turn around. I step closer, cock my head, and speak again.

"So. Let's try this one more time, shall we? Where is Krolek?"

The one with the hole in his shoulder coughs, voice ragged. "You kill us now, fine. But if we talk? Krolek... he kills us worse."

"Well yeah," I say casually, circling them like a shark. "You may be right."

I strut over and drop into his lap like he's some dirty little throne. Straddling him. Owning the moment. I feel his whole body freeze under me—whether it's fear or arousal, who gives a shit.

I lean in, voice dropping. "Chances are, Krolek's still hiding somewhere safe in Poland." I wave my gun in the air like I'm about to give a TED Talk. "But last I checked?" My eyes lock on his. "You're not in Poland."

Then without a blink, I shift the barrel right towards Scarface's temple.

BANG.

My lap buddy screams like a little bitch.

"Now, you might want to give me what I want," I say, wiping some of the blood off my cheek with the back of my hand.

"Fuck, Iz..." Laing mutters behind me.

His eyes dart to me, confused. Probably trying to figure out if I'm going to shoot him or strip him.

Good. Let him spiral.

"See, our little arrangement doesn't have to be all bad." I stand up slow, dragging the threat across his skin with every movement. I walk over to Nate, but my gaze doesn't leave Lex.

He's leaning against the wall, arms crossed. That deadly body all relaxed and lethal. Our eyes lock, those icy-blues narrow and that damn smile widens. He's loving this.

Fucking psycho.

Takes one to raise... well, to know one.

"So," I say, tearing my eyes away and turning back to our guest of honor. "I have an idea instead."

I gesture casually to Nate, who's been quiet up until now. "You see this man here?"

The guy with the bleeding shoulder lifts his head slightly.

"He's really good at making people disappear." I pause. "Not like your buddies here." I nod to the corpses. "No, I mean safe. Tucked away. New identity, new life. Far from Krolek. Rich. Happy. Healthy. A whole new beginning."

I say it soft and slow, like a lullaby laced with poison. And I can see it, he's eating it up. The desperation. The delusion. The part of him that wants to believe there's still a way out.

He glances at the bodies beside him and licks his lips like they've gone dry. "What... what do you have in mind?"

Got him.

I tilt my head and smile. "Tex you're up."

Tex steps forward, boots slowly hitting the concrete with that calm, calculated weight of a man who's about to ruin someone's week.

Our guest stiffens. I glance at him as Tex stops just in front of him.

"Now, this is Tex," I say lightly, almost sweet. "He's very, *very* good at making sure that you're not going to lie to me. Micro-expressions and all that shit."

The man's breath catches.

"So, here's the deal," I continue, crouching just enough to meet his eyes again. "As long as everything that comes out of your little mouth from this point on is one hundred percent the truth," I pause, letting the silence press on his chest. "We'll patch you up and have you on your way before the sunrise."

His eyes dart to Tex, then back to me.

"But..." I add, straightening. "If even one syllable feels off?" I look up at Tex. He cracks his knuckles. I look back at the man. "Well then... your new beginning turns into a closed casket."

Tex grins. "Let's have a chat."

He squats in front of the guy, elbows resting on his knees. Calm. Professional. Fucking terrifying. "What's your name?"

"Piotr," the man says, voice rough with pain.

"How long you been working for Krolek, Piotr?"

He hesitates, then chokes out, "Seven years."

Tex nods slowly. "You got family?"

Piotr's eyes flicker. "Yes. Wife. And a son, seventeen."

"Back in Poland?"

He nods.

Tex raises a brow. "Yeah, I'm going to need a verbal response, Piotr."

"Yes. In Poland," Piotr says quickly.

"You ever personally hurt one of the kids Krolek brings?"

"No. Never. I... I don't touch kids."

Tex tilts his head. "Did you ever watch it happen and stay quiet?"

Piotr hesitates. "Sometimes... I look away. But never help. Never."

"Did you ever deliver one of them? Take a kid from one place to another and know what you were doing?"

Piotr swallows hard. "Y-y-yes... I knew. I don't touch, I swear on my son. But I know where I take them."

Tex studies him in silence. Just long enough to make him sweat.

Then he glances at me. "So far, so good. He's telling the truth. He's guilty as sin, but he can be useful."

I cross my arms, watching carefully. I nod.

"Okay, Piotr," Tex says, voice suddenly all business. "Here's what you're going to do. You're going to call Krolek. Tell him everything went smoothly. The transfer is on the way right now."

He nods to Knox. "Knox, send the funds."

"On it," Knox replies from behind me already tapping at his screen.

"And," Tex continues, leaning in, "you're going to tell him the wife was way wealthier than expected. Loaded. Filthy rich. And she needs girls."

Piotr frowns slightly, but Tex barrels on.

"Tell him she's a madame. Runs a private elite operation and needs high-quality girls to train. That there's no budget cap. Whatever the fuck you need to say to get that bastard into the States."

Piotr swallows hard. "Understood."

The van ride back is deadly quiet. Not unusual. Missions always leave a kind of stillness in the air, like everyone's trying to breathe without disturbing whatever just got left behind.

When we finally pull up near Lex's bike. Tex throws the van in park and turns around.

"You want us to stay? Take you back to Rosethorne?"

Lex cuts in before I can even open my mouth. "I can take her."

I glance at the matte black bike.

"You don't like bikes?" he says, cocking his head.

I lift a brow. "Didn't say that."

He turns back to Tex, cocky as hell. "I'll take her."

"Didn't ask you. I asked her."

I look between them, fighting the curve tugging at my lips. "I'm good. Go on, I'll see you guys later."

Tex nods but he's still giving Lex the side-eye. We walk toward the bike, my heels scraping against the rough, chalky gravel. The second the van disappears onto the road, tires humming into the distance, Lex grabs me.

His strong arms wrap around my waist, lifting me clean off the ground. His hands slide under my ass, holding me in place as his mouth crashes into mine. All tongue and teeth. He claims my mouth like no one ever has before. My breath catches, heart thudding in my ears. I push my hands against his shoulders, dragging my lips away.

Barely.

"Lex?" I pant. "What are you doing?"

His voice is low, wrecked. Smoke wrapped in thunder. "What I've wanted to do since the second you licked my neck back at The Pit, baby. You're fucking amazing do you realize that?"

"Put me down."

"Never," he smirks, then kisses me again, harder this time.

I laugh against his mouth. "Lex. Seriously. Put me down."

"Make me."

"Lex," I say, more stern. "Down. Now."

He finally sets me down. His arms stay locked around my waist like letting go would be some kind of loss. My hands are still on his shoulders. He clearly has no intention of letting me move them.

"You can't just do that," I say, trying to keep my voice steady.

"Do what?" he says, all faux innocence.

I glare at him. "I don't know. Pick me up. Kiss me. Hijack my missions. Completely disregard protocol."

He pulls me closer, one corner of his mouth twitching. "I'm sorry, baby. It'll never happen again."

"Yeah, right." I roll my eyes. "Like it won't happen again."

He leans in, grinning. "It will, but you'll forgive me." Then kisses my forehead.

"Cade warned me about you, you know."

"Oh yeah?" he mutters. "What'd our boyfriend say?"

"Our boyfriend said that you're impulsive," I say, lifting a brow. "Reckless. A psycho with a serious anger problem."

Lex puts a hand to his chest like I physically just wounded him. "Ouch."

"But," I add, narrowing my eyes at him, "he also said that you can be very sweet when you want to. He said you are the most loyal person in the world as long as they've earned it."

"What else?"

"How do you know there is more?"

"Because I know Cade more than anyone, now what else?"

"That you love harder, faster, and deeper than most people. And that when you attach yourself to someone, you never let them go."

"Well, he's not wrong."

I tilt my head. "How are you so okay with all of this?"

"All of what?"

I throw my hands up, exasperated. "Me. This. My past. My whole fucked-up life. How are you so calm about it when I just met you, and Cade..." My voice cracks. "Cade, who once carried me out of a party when I was sick, held my hair, cleaned me up, and never told a soul."

I suck in a deep breath. "Now looks at me like I'm some kind of monster." My voice splinters on the last word. "How does that even make sense?"

Lex leans in, voice low and oddly calm. "One, Cade doesn't

think you're a monster."

"Yes he does. He all but said it back at The Pit."

"No, he fucking doesn't, baby."

My lips press together, but I don't argue.

"And two, I'm cool with all of this." He waves his hands dramatically, mimicking my gesture from before. "Because you and me? We are way more alike than you realize."

"Bullshit," I say, arms crossed.

Lex raises a brow. "Excuse me?"

"I read your—"

"Black Book?" he cuts me off, his voice dropping an octave. "You have the Barinov Black Book?"

Shit.

I shrug. "Yeah. When Cade and I first started dating and he talked about the three of us being together, I used my resources to check you out."

He leans in, arms crossed now, full brute-mode activated.

"And what all did you find?"

"I know your dad is Daniel Barinov. Bratva royalty, up to his neck in dirty deals, sure. But that's not what keeps him up at night. It's the buildings. The steel. The lines. That obsession with control etched into every inch of concrete and glass. That's what he truly lives for, the architecture."

Lex's mouth twitches, pride flickering in his eyes.

"I know Zeke and I lived in one of his buildings. It's a fucking fortress. Every Barinov structure is. I know that at the lowest level of every single one of them there's a bunker. That's where your mom and Rez's dad have established their gun running empire all over the East Coast."

Lex leans in, smooth as always. "And Europe."

I was getting there." I nod.

I know you're an architecture major not because your mom wants you to build safe-houses for her weapons, but because your dad taught you to love the structure. The weight of something built to last."

My voice softens. "You're trying to follow his footsteps as an architect... not the other family business."

He's watching me closely now.

"I also know your mother isn't just some housewife like she wants the world to see. Or just some low level gun runner. She's the head of the New York Bratva. Not your dad. Not your uncle. *Her*. And if she ever figured any of this out, she'd probably have me killed in my sleep."

Lex's smile drops. His voice is low, certain, final. "I would never let my mother touch you, baby."

And goddammit... I smile.

"So you see," I say, trying not to yawn. "We're not the same."

Lex watches me closley.

"You want to build things," I continue. "Leave something behind. You've got a father with blueprints in his blood and obsession in his veins. Me? I don't even know who mine is." I shrug.

"You're trying not to turn into your criminal uncle or your Bratva-queen of a mother. And I... I already am a criminal. Just one with a purpose."

He tilts his head, amusement dripping off his voice. "Oh yeah, baby. Total menace. Real Bonnie-and-Clyde energy. Except you'd probably shoot Clyde for slowing you down."

I roll my eyes but he doesn't let up.

"And for the record?" He steps closer. "Your *purpose* is the only thing that matters. You think I give a shit that you broke the law to save kids? That's not criminal, that's justice, not to mention hot as hell."

"Well, hot or not," I mutter, motioning between us. "This can't happen."

"Why the fuck not?"

"Because Cade," my raw and brittle voice trembles. "He's never going to see me the same way again. Not after today. Not after everything I told him. You saw his face. You heard him." The words scrape up my throat.

"And I..." I swallow hard. "I think I lost him."

The sting in my eyes hits before I can stop it. I cover my face, but it's useless, my body's already shaking. The sob tears out, ugly and broken. "And now I'm going to have to lose you too."

Lex doesn't hesitate. He wraps his arms around me like he's anchoring me to the earth. "Baby," he breathes, tilting my chin up. "You're not fucking losing either of us. You hear me?"

I shake my head, throat tight. "He doesn't love me. Not really. He'll never trust me, not after this."

"Yes, he fucking does," Lex says fiercely. "He told me. He just needs a minute to get his shit together."

I blink up at him, stunned. "He told you he loved me?"

"Right before I stormed out of The Pit to come get your stubborn ass back."

A quiet laugh slips through my lips, more disbelief than humor. Lex leans in and kisses me, like he's trying to kiss the grief right out of me. I melt into it, into him. But when he finally pulls back, the ache returns like a wave crashing back against the shore.

"Baby, come home with me."

I look at him, everything in me screaming yes. "I can't, Lex. Not until I know Cade won't look at me like he did tonight. Like I'm a monster hellbent on revenge. Like I'm something he needs to fix instead of someone he wants to love."

I swallow hard and whisper, "Can you just take me home?"

His expression softens instantly. "Sure." He brushes a strand of hair out of my face. "But listen to me. I'm not giving up on this. I'm not giving up on us. So, you fucking promise me you won't either."

I nod, tears slipping down my cheeks. "I promise."

"Let's get you home, baby."

@LucaWasHere
Smart move Izzy, letting the brute go.
You always break the ones who know.
Told the painter truths he couldn't take.
Now look at him... ready to break.

You should've stayed quiet and sweet,
But you just had to bleed at their feet.
Now the fighter's unraveling, the artist's gone cold.

How long 'til they drop what they cannot hold?

You think they'll love the girl with knives?
The one who cuts through all their lives?
You showed your rot, your blood, your scar.
And now they know exactly what you are.

CHAPTER ㊶
CADE
MINE AND LEX'S APARTMENT
581 DAYS SINCE ZEKE'S DEATH

The glow from the city leaks in through the floor-to-ceiling windows, smearing streaks of gold and cobalt across the polished floors. The skyline is a jagged silhouette—steel and glass stretching like brushstrokes across a canvas I never seem to finish.

We're thirty-one floors up in one of Daniel's buildings. It's all sharp angles and quiet power. The open-concept apartment has high ceilings, brutalist bones, and the kind of view most people would sell their soul for.

We moved in a few months ago, sick of splitting time between Wexley and Redspire, tired of living out of bags and pretending either place really felt like home.

This one does. Or at least it used to. Now it's just... quiet. So damn quiet. I roll onto my side again, staring at the red digital numbers on the bedside clock.

2:15 a.m.

Where is he?

I check my phone again.

LEX: I'll be home soon.

That was over an hour ago. I stare at the ceiling.

What the hell have I done?

I pull up her contact, thumb hovering and heart aching. I want to call her, but what would I even say? Sorry I flinched when you said you loved me? Sorry I looked at you like you were someone I didn't recognize?

I always knew Lex had darkness and I chose him anyway. But Bella? She was supposed to be like me. Light. Soft. Safe. Not someone who could look me in the eye and confess the kind of things that'll keep me up at night.

That's the part that hurts the most, because even now, even after all of it. I still love her. I just need some time.

I squeeze the phone tighter, heart hammering.

Beep-beep.

Beep-beep

The keypad to the front door unlocks.

I sit up fast, breath uneven as I shove the covers off. The hallway light bleeds in from the cracked door. I step into the hallway, heart already racing.

He walks right past me. Doesn't look at me or speak to me. Just sets his bag down in silence, goes straight into the bathroom, and shuts the door behind him.

That soft click might as well be a gunshot to my chest. I stand there, hollow, like I broke something I don't know how to fix. And this time, I don't even know if sorry will be enough.

When he comes out he still won't look me in the eye. Lex steps around me and heads toward the bed.

"Can we talk?"

"That depends, are you still gonna bitch about Bella?" he snaps. "Because if so, I don't want to fucking hear it, Cade. Not after tonight. Not after what I just saw."

"I wasn't going to bitch about Bella. Can you at least tell me what happened?"

Lex turns. "Oh, now you care about what goes on during her missions?"

"That's not fair," I say, the words catching in my throat. "I said I needed time, not that I don't care about her."

Lex exhales through his nose, jaw clenched. "Then take your time, Cade," he grits, voice rough. "But I'm not. I'm not giving up on the fact that the three of us together could be something great. I'm not giving up on her. I'm not pushing her out."

He takes a step closer, eyes burning.

"She's had enough grief to last a hundred lifetimes. I saw her darkness, Cade. It was beautiful. She's not a monster. She's a goddamn masterpiece. The way she saved those kids tonight?"

I freeze, absolutely speechless.

"Yes, it's dark. Yes, it's violent. But so is life, Cade. And Bella? She shines through the darkness. Lives for it, in the best way possible."

His raw voice drops lower "And I hope one day, Cade." He swallows hard, just once. "I hope one day you wake the fuck up and realize it too."

"Will you please tell me?" I ask, quieter now. "Tell me what happened tonight?"

He shakes his head. "No," he says. "No, Cade. I won't."

The words land like a slap.

He walks to the bed and pulls back the covers. "I'm not gonna tell you what happened," he mutters, tossing his phone on the nightstand. "Because you need to fucking see it. With your own two eyes."

And then, just like that, he climbs into bed, turns his back to me and goes to sleep. Leaving me standing there in the dark.

Alone.

I wake up to silence. There's no weight beside me or any rustle of sheets. Just cold air and the soft hum of the city outside. I sit up slowly, rubbing the back of my neck, still sore in that way you feel after a night you can't stop replaying.

The apartment feels too still. He's gone. His duffel's gone. So is his hoodie from the back of the chair. On the dresser, there's a folded piece of paper. I cross the room barefoot and pick it up.

Gone to train at The Pit.

I'll call you later.

—Lex

I read it twice.

It's short.

Dismissive.

Lex-style polite, but it still hurts. I know what it means. He needs space from me. And the worst part is I don't blame him.

I fold the note and slip it into my pocket. Then I just stand here, breathing. Wanting to say something. To text Lex. To call Bella.

But I don't.

Because I meant what I said. I need time. And if I stay here where Lex looks at me like I've already failed, I won't get it.

So, I pack light. A few clothes. My charger. My sketchbook. Grab my keys off the counter and head back to Wexley. Just for a while.

Some distance will help.

Some time will help.

Eventually, it'll all be fine.

I hope.

CHAPTER (42)
BELLA
ROSETHORNE MANSION
WEXLEY UNIVERSITY
589 DAYS SINCE ZEKE'S DEATH

I sit on the edge of my bed, the silk comforter bunched under my fists, and stare out the window.

> LEX: So, don't be upset or freak out. I just wanted to give you a heads up in case you run into him. Cade moved back to Wexley.

I reread it three times. But the words didn't change. Cade left because of me.

That was a week ago and I still feel horrible. Like the blackness in my life is spreading, infecting everything and everyone I touch.

Lex and I have been talking and hanging out a little since the night he hijacked my mission. He puts on this whole big, tough Russian gun runner act for the world to see, but it's mostly just that. An act.

Kinda.

I mean, yeah the guy can still kick ass, take names, and look fucking hot while doing it. But underneath it all, he's a damn teddy bear.

> ME: Lex I'm so sorry. I ruined everything for you.

The dots appear. Stop. Appear again.

> LEX: Baby, you didn't ruin anything. Cade just needs time and space. That's all. He'll be fine.

> LEX: You should have seen him when I told him my mom and uncle ran guns. We didn't speak for a month.

ME: A month?! Lex, you do realize that running guns is nothing compared to what I told him? This may never actually work.

LEX: It will. Plus... while he cools down it gives you and me some time to get to know each other.

LEX: Like really get to know each other, if you catch my drift.

This man I swear.

ME: We are not going there.

LEX: Why not?

I don't respond. Not right away. I just stare at my screen, a thousand thoughts clawing their way through my brain.

The door swings open. "Leaving me on read, baby? Rude."

I jerk my head toward the door. "Lex, how the fuck did you get in here?"

He strolls into my room like he's lived here for years, all slow swagger and smug grin. Black jeans. Black V-neck that hugs his tatted arms way too well. Dark hair a little messy.

God help me.

He shrugs. "Please, baby. Like a bunch of little Legacy chicks were gonna keep me from you."

"This is Rosethorne. You can't just walk in here like—"

"Like I own the place?" he cuts in, closing the door behind him and shrugs again. "Looks like I fucking can."

"You're insane."

"Not denying it."

He starts casually walking toward me like he's got all the time in the world to ruin me.

"Lex," I warn, sitting back on my elbows. "I'm serious."

"So am I."

He reaches the bed and leans down. One hand braced beside my hip, the other brushing hair from my face.

"You okay, baby?"

"No. Not really."

He nods, gentle for once. But it doesn't last. Slowly, his cocky grin returns. "Come on. Get dressed."

"Excuse me?"

"We're going on a ride."

"Lex—"

"No arguing. You've been sulking in here all day like a damn ghost. You need out. Fresh air. Fast engine. My hands on your thighs."

I don't move, just stare at him. He narrows his eyes, not playing. "Get the fuck up, baby. I will throw your little ass over my shoulder and take you out of this mansion kicking and screaming if I have to."

I stare at him for a long beat. Then sigh. "God, you're annoying."

"And yet," he says, tilting his head, lips quirking like he knows he's right. "You're already getting up."

I wrap my arms around his waist as the engine roars beneath us. The city blurs by—lights, noise, wind in my hair, Lex's body heat pressed into mine. We ride across the bridge, down through Queens, until the streets start to quiet.

And then I see it, the skyline, wide open water. Lex parks the bike under one of those old gantry cranes and kills the engine. He hops off and holds out his hand.

"Trust me."

I take it. He leads me to the edge of a pier. No one's around. Just city lights reflected on the water.

"This is my favorite spot," he says after a long beat.

"Why?"

He shrugs. "Because even when everything's fucked up, this still looks perfect."

We sit at the edge of the water, legs dangling off the concrete ledge. The skyline stretches out across the water like a dream, all gold, silver, and sharp steel edges lit by the night.

Lex is quiet for a while. "My dad used to bring me here when I was a kid."

I glance over at him, surprised. "Yeah?"

He nods. "This was our spot. We'd grab pizza from a place down the block and sit right here."

He points toward the Empire State Building in the distance. "He'd make me name every building I could see. Then he'd quiz me on the architects. Who built what. Why it mattered."

There's something soft in his voice now. Something I wasn't expecting.

"He said you can tell who someone is by how they build."

I don't say anything. Just watch him. Lex leans back on his hands, eyes scanning the skyline like it's a blueprint only he can read.

"That one's my favorite," he says, pointing to a sleek, mirrored tower near the Chrysler. "It's a total nightmare structurally, narrow as hell, glass everywhere, not even close to practical. But it still stands. Still looks like a fucking dream."

I smile. "Let me guess. You like the ones that shouldn't exist."

He grins. "Yeah. I like the ones that break the rules and don't fall." His gaze drifts back to me. "Just like you."

Before I can say anything, his phone vibrates in his pocket. He doesn't look away from me, but his phone doesn't stop.

Buzz. Buzz.

He sighs, finally pulls it out and glances at the screen.

CADE

He flips it over face-down without answering.

"Lex," I say softly. "You should answer it."

He shakes his head once. "Not right now."

"But—"

"No." His voice is sharper this time. Firmer. "He wanted space to think about everything. So, I'm giving him his fucking space."

Lex's jaw tenses, his gaze locked out over the water like it's the only thing keeping him from falling apart. "I told him I wasn't giving up on the three of us," he says. "I wasn't giving up on you."

My heart starts pounding. Hard. Unsteady.

"Lex," I whisper.

"I had him meet you first," he says, voice low, almost like it hurts to admit. "Because I didn't want to get my hopes up. I didn't want to fall too fast for someone that wouldn't..." He clears his throat, "That couldn't..."

He stops. Runs a hand through his hair.

"But now that I'm around you?" He leans in closer. "I'm not letting you go, baby. Not now. Not ever."

I stare at him, heart still pounding.

"You said," I start, voice barely above a whisper, "you didn't want to fall for someone that wouldn't and couldn't."

He blinks, like he didn't realize he said it out loud. "Huh?"

I hold his gaze. "You said you didn't want to fall for someone that *wouldn't* and *couldn't*... what were you going to say?"

Lex looks away for a second, jaw flexing. Then back at me.

"Someone that wouldn't run away when I held on too tight, because when I fall, I fall hard," he says. "Someone that couldn't only see me as a darkness, but who could handle the darkness in me. Calm it. Tame it."

I don't move.

"I love Cade," he says, quiet but fierce. "I've loved him since before I even knew what the fuck love really was. But it was hard at first. It all scared the shit out of him. Especially when he found out what my family does."

He swallows hard.

"But you?" He leans in closer, hand sliding to my jaw, thumb brushing my cheek. "Me and you, baby... this isn't hard."

His lips hover above mine, voice barely a breath. "I have a darkness, Bella. And so do you. I saw it."

A pause.

"And baby, I fucking love it. I don't want you to hide it from me. And if it ever gets too much, I want you to come to me so I can pull you the fuck out of it. Because I'm pretty sure you are the only one that could ever fully pull me out of mine."

He brushes his thumb over my lips, gaze locked on mine, those icy-blue eyes piercing into my soul.

"And I swear to God, Bella, I'm not letting you go."

My heart stops.

So, I do the only thing I can. I lean in and kiss him. And this time, he doesn't kiss me like he's trying to own me.

He doesn't kiss me like he's starving.

He kisses me like he's home. Like maybe this is what he's been waiting for all along.

I pull back, just for a second. "Lex, I need to show you something," I say hands shaking slightly as I hand him my phone.

CHAPTER ④③
LEX
BELLA AND JOSH'S PRIVATE REHEARSAL
NOT LOOKING GOOD...
636 DAYS SINCE ZEKE'S DEATH

Bella is on the major struggle bus. She just missed the same turn again—chest too far forward, wrong arm extension—and Josh barely caught her in time.

"Sorry," she gasps. "I'm sorry. I'm just... I'm in my head."

"You want to talk about it, B?"

She shakes her head, already wiping her palms on her leggings. "Not really."

"Okay. Then get out of your head and reset. I've got you. We've done this routine a million times. Plus, if you biff that turn again, I think Javi might actually bust a blood vessel. Pretty sure I saw his eye twitching."

Bella lets out a breath. Almost a laugh. Not quite, but close.

"There she is," Josh says.

She nods. When they reset, her footing is still off and the second turn nearly sends her sideways again.

I see the clench in Javi's jaw from across the room. His heels click against the hardwood as he struts toward the edge of the practice floor, arms crossed so tight it looks like he's physically holding in a scream.

"Get out of your head," he snaps with that Spanish accent and a mouthful of sass. "This routine is lyrical, not lazy. You want to win Worlds or cry backstage? For the love of all things holy, Bella, concéntrate!"

Bella doesn't answer.

He spins on his heel and beelines straight to me. "Alright, hulking disasterpiece, what the hell is going on with my girl? A mission go bad, or did Laing say something stupid again?"

My head snaps toward him. "You know?"

"Of course I know," he says, flinging his hands like it's obvious. "I've known since Zeke died, cariño. You think I didn't notice the bruises? The missed practices? Por favor, I'm not blind."

He gestures wildly toward the floor. "She looks like a hot mess dipped in regret. She's about three turns away from popping her ankle like a bottle of prosecco. ¿Qué pasa?"

I sigh, staring at Bella as she resets again, body tight with tension.

"It's Cade," I admit. "He's been gone too fucking long and it's messing with her head. Hell, it's messing with both our heads."

"Ohhh," Javi draws out with a wince. "*Him*. That explains it."

He turns to look at Bella. "She's not the type to spiral over boys. When she dumped that pretty little basketball player, Wes, she came back the next day and danced like her ass was on fire. She looked so good I was about to call the Vatican for an exorcism."

"Yeah," I say. "But this is different. It was supposed to be the three of us. We all knew what this was. And now it's like—" I gesture at the stage. "—it's like she's waiting for him to walk through the damn door and save her."

Javi's eyes narrow. He turns, just in time to catch Bella fumble again. "Watch your damn turns, Blackwood!" he yells, snapping his fingers in the air.

He turns back to me. "If this continues, Lex, I swear on my abuela's grave I'm giving this routine to Haley. She may not be as sharp, but at least she doesn't dance like she's possessed by a ghost with commitment issues."

He storms back toward Bella and Josh. I stay back and pull out my phone.

ME: She needs you.

CADE: Why? What's going on?

ME: She's in her head. Sucking ass at a routine that's supposed to be a damn cakewalk. Javi's pissed. Josh is trying, but it's not working. You need to come home Cade.

Me: It's been too long.

CADE: I can't Lex. I'm just not ready.

ME: I miss you.

CADE: I miss you too babe.

ME: Please babe. It's been weeks. I hate sleeping alone. You know that.

CADE: Alone? You and Bella haven't...?

ME: No. "Fingers only." Damn girl is a menace. She says that she's teaching me patience and restraint. Apparently it builds character. One too many Dr. Monroe appointments if you ask me.

CADE: LOL. Sounds about right. Is it working?

ME: Fuck no. I'm dying over here babe. Plus... I'm pretty sure she is just waiting on you to come home.

ME: I love you Cade. Please come home. I fucking miss you. We need you.

ME: I need you.

ME: Please babe.

ME: Come home.

CADE: Lex, I love you and I will be back. I promise. I'm not like you, I can't just get over something like this as fast as you. Please be patient. It isn't goodbye forever, babe. You know that.

ME: Fucking feels like it Cade

ME: But ok... just hurry the fuck up!

CHAPTER ④④
LEX
FUCKING CARRINGTON ROW
BECAUSE I'M A GODDAMN GOOD BOYFRIEND.
659 DAYS SINCE ZEKE'S DEATH

"Tell me again why we had to get here this early?" I say crouched under a speaker rig holding a coil of cable. It's hot as fuck. I've already sweated through my shirt. And to top it off all, someone just spilled a Celsius on my boot. Thank you very much Little Whitmore.

This is hell. Or at least Wexley's version of it.

Knox grins from behind the soundboard, smug as always. "Welcome to the Trifecta Boyfriend Club, my guy."

I stare at him like I might throw him into the pool.

He throws me a roll of gaffer tape. "The Row Pool Party is a big deal, especially for the girls. Think of it like the Met Gala but with abs, water guns, and a lot of jello shots." He flicks a switch and the pool lights strobe. "And thanks to us, way better lighting."

"Lex, we're a brand, remember?" Ellie chirps from across the pool deck. She's arranging trays of jello shot syringes like it's a military op. Clipboard in one hand, rhinestone walkie-talkie in the other. She's in full command mode, coordinating chaos with a smile that could get her out of war crimes.

She struts past me and flicks my shoulder. "Thousands of our loving fans will be tuning in tonight to see this party. It's a big deal, babe."

"Loving fans," I mutter. "Right, like Luca."

Yeah, Bella told me all about that motherfucker after I took her out on the pier. Asshole thinks he can message her. Watch her. Obsess over her. If I ever find that fucker.

"Any luck finding our little poet freak?" I ask.

Knox twists a few dials, cycling through colors until the whole setup glows electric blue. "Nah, nothing yet. He's been quiet. Bella said he hasn't sent shit since around Fight Night. So, what, like two months? Maybe he finally found a new obsession."

"He's quiet because I messaged the asshole after our date at the pier"

Knox's head snaps up. "You what?"

"I said I mess—"

"I heard you, dumbass." He cuts me off and reaches for my phone. "Let me see what the hell you did before I have to start planning your funeral."

@BarinovUnhinged
Stay the fuck away from my girl.

"Subtle," Knox laughs.

@LucaWasHere
Ah, the brawler. You move so fast.
Tell me, Lexie... think it'll last?
Does she flinch when your temper slips?
Or just bite back between your lips?

@BarinovUnhinged
She doesn't flinch, asshole. Not with me. She leans in.
And if you ever touch her feed again... I'll find you.
Try typing with bone dust, fucker.

"Bone dust, Lex?"

"What?" I shrug as Knox just shakes his head and keeps scrolling.

@LucaWasHere
Such fury. Is that what she dreams?
All fists and fire and cracked extremes?
You don't guard her. You just burn bright.
Which makes her so much easier to watch at night.

@BarinovUnhinged
Cute poems. Real original.
All that rhyming shit just proves one thing...
You've got time to obsess, but not the balls to act.
You hide in the dark like mold behind the walls.
Say her name again and I'll make you choke on it.

@LucaWasHere
I wait in silence, sweet Lexie, still.
There's deeper power in sharpened will.
You chase her fire, you beg for her name.
But embers don't ever burn the same.

She dances for you, puts on the show,
But curtains drop, and truths still glow.
You see devotion, you taste her skin.
But memory's where I always win.

You bleed for her, wear pain with pride,
But would she fight, or just run and hide?
Go home, Lexie. Let the dream decay.
Some fires burn brighter once they betray.

@BarinovUnhinged
STAY.
THE FUCK.
AWAY.

@LucaWasHere
You bring the storm, all fists and flame,
But I was there before she had a name.
I know her hums, the way she folds,
The twelve-note rhythm no one holds.

And that, sweet Lexie, is where you fall.
You chased her light. You risked it all.

You crave her crown. You want her vow.
But we built a wall. She can't escape now.

@BarinovUnhinged
You like walls? Good. Because I'll bury you behind one.
My girl will never fear again.
Not when she knows that the monster's fucking dead.

"Smooth, Barinov," Knox mutters, tossing my phone back like it's contagious.

I catch it, shove it in my pocket, and finish taping down the last cable.

Knox shakes his head. "You're a psycho, man. Luca writes poems and you write death threats. It's like a match made in hell."

I stand, stretch out my back, and roll my shoulders. Try to breathe, and then I feel her. Like static in my blood. I don't even have to turn around. I know it's her.

Cherry vanilla. That damn scent punches me in the chest. Sweet, dark, and fucking lethal. It wraps around me, crawls under my skin, and makes the whole Row vanish.

I spin fast, grabbing her like I've been starving for a hundred years. One hand in her hair, the other locking around her waist as I slam my mouth to hers. A claim of tongue, teeth, and obsession.

My fucking girl. Mine.

My baby lets out the softest noise against my mouth, and if we weren't surrounded I'd drop to my knees right now and feast on her sweet pussy as if she's the last meal I'll ever taste. Because I know her. She's probably already soaked for me. She always is.

I pull back just barely, breathing hard. "Hey, baby."

She's flushed. Dazed. "Hey, I'm glad you're here."

"Oh yeah, me too—" Knox cuts in full of sarcasm, "—if he was actually doing anything. Bella, you're distracting my help."

I don't even look up. Just keep my hands on her. "Cool it, Bestie. I'm on my five-minute union break."

Bella arches a brow. "Bestie?"

I shrug. "Yeah. Me and Knox? We're basically bros now."

Knox groans. Ellie cackles from somewhere behind a tray of glitter shots. Bella just laughs and presses a kiss to my cheek before trying to walk away.

"Nope. Not happening," I say as I catch her wrist. "Did you miss the part about a five-minute break?"

She turns back, amused. That look on her face. All smug and sweet and half-daring me to do something about it. I grab her by the waist, pick her up, and carry her like they do in those cheesy romance movies. Like a bride being taken across the threshold of some over-priced honeymoon suite. She squeals.

"Lex!"

"What? It's the rules, baby. You're legally required to sit on my lap until the five minute buzzer goes off."

She laughs but doesn't fight me. I carry her across the lawn toward one of the cabanas near the back draped in gauzy curtains. I drop onto the cushioned bench with her still in my arms, settling her in my lap. She lands with a soft oof, hands braced on my chest. Right where I want her.

"You're ridiculous."

"Yeah." I run my hands up her thighs, slow and steady. "But I'm yours."

She freezes for half a second. I feel it. The goosebumps rising on her perfect skin. The change in her breath. The way her body reacts before her words do. Her steel-gray eyes lock on mine and I swear to God, I need her. I've never needed anything like I need her.

Not air.

Not blood.

I want her so bad it fucking hurts. Hurts to hold her. Hurts not to fuck her. Hurts to pretend that this is enough.

We haven't had sex. Not yet. She's only let me use my hands and even that feels like a gift I didn't earn.

A mercy.

A tease.

Deep down, I think she's still waiting for Cade.

I told myself I'd be patient. That I'd let her come to me. That I'd earn it. But fuck, it's torture. Because I see it in her eyes. Every goddamn time I touch her. Every time she gasps, trembling under my fingers, hips jerking, thighs shaking, and screaming, *"Lex... Oh God... Lex..."*

Seeing my girl come undone like that? It's beautiful. It's fucking ruin.

We haven't said I love you yet. Not with words. But I see it every day. I see it in the way she clings to me after shattering from my touch. The way she looks at me when she thinks I'm not watching. And how her breathing changes when I say *baby* in that voice she pretends doesn't undo her.

It fucking does.

She loves me. And she will say it. Eventually. Right before I fuck the living daylights out of her.

God, I need to get laid.

She pulls back just enough to meet my eyes. "Are you sure you're up for all of this?" she asks, voice quiet and nodding toward the pool. "You're a Hollow King, remember? You gonna be okay at a Row party, baby?"

When she calls me *baby?* Good. Fucking. Lord. My cock's hard enough to punch through concrete. Little Lex hears it and practically salutes like he's going into battle. Doesn't matter where we are—on a mission, in a Hollow King's meeting, the middle of a goddamn lecture—she says that word and I'm one breath away from dragging her into the nearest dark corner and showing her what, *baby*, really gets her.

"I'm not here for The Row." I dip my head closer, lips brushing her neck. "I'm here for you."

"Lex!" Knox yells from across the pool. "Hurry up, man. I need your help with these bar lights."

"Almost finished, Bestie," I yell back.

I drag my eyes down her body and back up, my smile pure heat. "So as you can see, I'm basically the lighting intern of the year now. Where's my reward?"

She laughs. Then she leans back just a little, still perched in my lap, her fingers playing with the edge of my collar. "You'll be rewarded. Just... promise you won't kill Cal."

My smile fades a little.

"There will be chairs tonight," she says carefully. "And knowing The Order, they'll want a lot of them."

I narrow my eyes. "Define a lot."

"Enough." She arches a brow. "Enough to keep the crowd screaming. Enough to keep The Row boys drooling. Enough to get us featured on at least twenty different high-profile Instagram and Tik-Tok accounts by midnight."

"Cool. Love that for me," I groan. "Can't wait to watch the quarterback get a lap dance from my girlfriend while I stand in the shadows like a divorced husband at his ex-wife's wedding."

"Lex," she warns, knowing that I'm seconds away from snapping. "It's all an act. What The Trifecta does. The dancing, the flirting, the games, it's just a show. Just art. None of it is real, so don't take it personal. Okay?"

"You keep calling it art, baby. But the real fucking masterpiece?" My hand slides up her waist, fingers curling into her ribs just enough to make her bite her lip. "Was the way you moaned my name when I had my fingers curled inside you last night."

Her breath stutters, just like I fucking knew it would.

"Lex, I mean it. I know how you are. I know how you get with me." She leans in and presses a kiss to my mouth. "Please. Behave. Don't make me regret bringing you here."

"I'll behave. But only because you asked. However, don't expect me to be normal about this shit. I don't do calm when it comes to you."

She kisses me again and then she slides off my lap and starts to walk toward the prep tent.

"Just remember," she calls over her shoulder, "you're the one who gets to take me home."

And fuck, if that isn't the most dangerous thing I've heard all day.

Ok... this party is unhinged. Glowing shot syringes are floating in the pool like neon mines. There's a beer pong table made entirely out of black obsidian. Somebody's already cannon-balled off the second-floor balcony into the deep end, and I'm pretty sure one of the cheer girls is giving tequila-fueled lap dances in the shallow end to every guy named Hunter or Beckett.

Carrington Row is heat, music, sweat, and wealth. It's completely drunk off itself. Loud and fucking messy. Beautiful people doing ugly shit under the illusion of power.

I'm sitting in a chair by the pool, trying my best not to start a fucking riot because she's over there now. With Callum. Red bikini top. Unbuttoned denim shorts riding way too high up those dancer thighs. Red heels that should be illegal on wet concrete. Hair in a fishtail braid. *Yeah, Ellie informed me on what that is.* Red lips. Smoky eyes locked on him as they talk across the pool by the DJ booth.

She's smiling. Laughing. Even tosses her braid over one shoulder and if she so much as touches his—

"Chill, dude." Knox's voice hits my ear. *"I can see your spiraling jealousy from here."*

Right. The comm. Apparently, being a Trifecta boyfriend now comes with a communication system. The girls. Me. Knox. Javi. Rico, love that guy ever since he gave me a shirt with my girl's face on it. Even fucking Callum and August get one tonight. We're all linked up. One shared, invisible web stretched across The Row.

Not constantly, but enough for Knox to play God with the comms and pull whatever strings he needs. He runs it like a goddamn air traffic controller. Three beeps and our mics are on. Two beeps, our walkie talkie is on. One beep and your mic or walkie just got turned off.

Says it's to *keep the chaos flowing smoothly.*

We can talk to him. If he wants someone else to hear us, he can route it through. If he wants us to shut the hell up, he kills our mic. My bestie's a genius but also a real pain in my ass.

"I'm not spiraling," I mutter under my breath.

"Oh yeah?" Knox comes back, amused. *"You've been staring at her for exactly three minutes without blinking, and I just watched you grip your glass so hard I'm surprised it's not sand."*

Across the pool, Bella tosses her head back and laughs at something Callum says.

"Motherfucker is not that funny," I mumble. "Knox, if you let him touch her, I'm swimming across this pool like Poseidon and ending his quarterback career tonight."

Knox sighs. *"Lex, you're on comm. I can play that audio back for her later."*

"You wouldn't."

"Try me."

Knox shifts from private to public. No longer in my ear and now booming across The Row through the main speakers.

"Yo, Wexley!" His voice slides through, slick with energy. "It's officially time to get this party started."

The crowd erupts. Girls scream. Guys howl. Phones light up everywhere.

I glance across the pool again just in time to see it. Callum. Sliding his arm along the back of Bella's waist like he owns the air she's breathing. He leans in, says something I can't hear, and then guides her behind the stage setup like it's just part of the plan.

My grip tightens on my glass. The comm crackles in my ear, but it's background noise now. My blood's already humming. She's walking with him. In those fucking heels. In that red bikini.

It's all an act, dude. Calm the fuck down.

"Wexley Wolves, alumni, degenerates, and everyone watching on live stream..." Knox's voice rolls over like smoke. "You've been waiting for this all week. And tonight, we kick things off the way we always do here at The Row..."

I stand up. I can't sit still anymore.

"...with the sexiest girls on the East fucking Coast.." The bass drops behind Knox's baritone like a countdown. "Nah. Fuck that." Knox laughs into the mic. "Sexiest girls in the whole damn world."

I already know what's coming next. "Make some noise for the one, the only TRIFECTA!"

Lights cut. Music slams into the first beat. And I swear to God, if Callum so much as brushes her thigh during this performance.

Spotlights hit the stage. Smoke machines kick in like we're

about to launch a goddamn concert.

Knox's voice booms through the mic, full hype mode, "First up… she's sweet, she's savage, and she's smarter than all of you fuckers… Wexley's golden girl, make some noise for Ellie Whitmore!"

Ellie steps out through the curtain, high ponytail bouncing, bright yellow and pink two-piece clinging like it's stitched to her body. She does a perfect spin and gives a little pageant wave.

"Hi babes! Thanks for coming. We've got a lot of heat for you tonight, hope you're ready to melt."

"Next up… she's the fire you wish you could handle, and the reason your boyfriend's been hitting the gym. Give it up for my girl, Haley Rosethorne!"

Haley steps through the curtain in an emerald green one piece with a plunging neckline so deep you can see her fucking navel. Her long legs and red hair a damn weapon under the lights. When she stops center stage, she flips her hair and blows a kiss right at Knox.

"Save me a drink, baby," she purrs, voice low and hot. "I'll be back to blow your… let's just say mind after I blow theirs." She winks at him.

Knox fumbles the mic for a second, then lets out a choked laugh over the speakers. "Damn, baby."

Everyone's howling now, guys pounding the air, girls screaming her name. Even I have to admit it, that was pretty hot.

Good for you, Bestie.

"And last but absolutely not least." He turns the dial to switch the lighting to red. "The center of the storm and the reason The Row hasn't slept in weeks. Make some noise for my Bestie's girl, Bella Blackwood!"

She glides out. Red heels. Red lips. That fucking red bikini top that's one string away from driving me insane. Her unbuttoned denim shorts riding low and tight.

My cock twitches.

I glare at the guy next to me holding his phone way too steady, way too long, way too angled right at her ass.

I will break your fingers, fucker.

"Thank you, Knox." She smiles toward the crowd. "Like he

said, I'm Bella. This is Ellie. That's Haley. And we are The Trifecta."
The crowd roars so loud the fucking foundation shakes.

"And here at The Row?" She paces slowly. Voice silky smooth.
"We don't just throw parties. We make memories. We make legends.
We make history."

She points at the crowd, then up to the balcony where more
Wolves are leaning over the rails with drinks in hand.

"So whether you're a Wexley Wolf, an Order God, a Hollow
King..." She looks at me and blows me a kiss.

Fucker with the phone pointed at her ass looks at me and I
think he just pissed his pants.

"That's right," I say loud enough for him and everyone else to
hear. "She's fucking mine, man."

"...or just someone lucky enough to get in, welcome to the
most elite, most dangerous, most unforgettable night of your goddamn summer!" she finishes with a smile.

I shake my head, half-laughing, half-hard. "Damn, baby," I
mutter under my breath. "You better hype up my fight night next week
like that."

"Okay, Wolves, ladies, gentlemen." A pause. Knox's grin is audible. "I think we should kick this off in style."

The lights flicker, dim. A pulse of bass hums through the pool.

"How about we start this night off with a few chairs?"

The crowd erupts. Behind the stage curtain, three tall black
chairs are carried into place by a few Wexley boys, including Callum,
who's grinning like he's about to die happy.

"Thank you, boys..." Bella says stepping towards the chairs.
"Hmm... Knox. Who do you think we should get to sit in these lovely
little chairs?"

Three chairs.

Three girls.

And three very lucky bastards about to risk their lives for *my*
view.

The crowd starts chanting names. Drunk, sloppy, and desperate. Callum slides right up beside her, wraps an arm around her waist,
and pulls her in. Too close. Too smug. Too fucking comfortable. My

jaw ticks.

It's part of the act, Lex.

Bella's still smiling, teasing him.

"Well, Bells," Callum drawls, cocky as ever. It sucks balls that this guy shares a face with one of the loves of my life.

"I can think of someone who could at least sit in your chair."

Then he picks her up. Just fucking grabs her. She gasps as her legs wrap around his waist like it's normal. Like it's fine. Her braid swings behind her, red heels glinting under the lights like weapons I should be using on him. He slides his hands around her ass and squeezes.

Good God, Cal. I will fucking murder you in your sleep.

He carries her to the chair like she's his. Sits her down so she's fucking straddling him. They both laugh.

Baby, you're going to pay for this torture.

His hands are still on her. Her thighs are wrapped around him. I can't breathe. The crowd explodes. Like this is cute. Or fun. Like they're just watching two people flirt.

What they are watching is my girlfriend signing the death warrant of yet another fucking man. Let's just put Callum Whitmore on my hit list right under Mortal fucking Kombat.

Bella laughs into the mic.

Don't you dare laugh, baby.

"Okay, okay, fine, Cal. You win." Her voice is playful and teasing. She shifts in his lap and flips her hair. She flashes that smug little smile, as if she's not setting my entire bloodstream on fire.

Like she doesn't know exactly who she fucking belongs to.

"You get a chair."

The fuck he does.

She stands slowly. Legs long. Braid sliding down her shoulder. Callum leans back, too proud of himself. Sitting there like he just won the Super Bowl, the lottery, and my girlfriend's fucking heart. Like she was ever his to begin with.

She's not. She's mine.

I don't care how slow she's moving. I don't care if she hasn't said the words yet. I don't even care that Cade's dragging his goddamn feet.

Isabella Marie Blackwood belongs to me.

I don't even register who the other two idiots are, some Wexley linebacker and a Wall Street trust fund rat. Doesn't matter. All I see is Bella. My girl. Giving a slow, filthy, teasing-as-fuck lap dance... to my sworn fucking enemy.

I swear to God, if I don't get a chair tonight then someone's leaving in a body bag.

She slides a hand down his chest and arches her back. The crowd screams. He grins like a king, and I swear if this fucking complex had weapons, there'd already be blood in the pool.

"Hey there, Lex."

Fuck me, can this night get any worse?

I turn to see Madison fucking Rae and her two carbon copies flanking her like backup dancers in a perfume ad. All three in matching black bikinis and heels like they rehearsed this in hell.

"Looks like your girlfriend is quite into Callum Whitmore tonight," her tone drips with fake concern. "That's Cade's brother, right?"

She pouts. "Oooooh. Wonder what he thinks. Where is Cade anyway? I heard he moved out. Trouble in paradise Lex, baby?"

"What the fuck are you doing here, Maddie?"

She leans in, eyes gleaming as she tries wrap her arms around my waist. I shove her off with zero grace.

"Don't even fucking try it."

She gasps, like she wasn't expecting it. "Still such a brute," she laughs, brushing imaginary dust off her thigh. "No wonder you and Bella get along. You're both so..." Her eyes flick to the stage. "...dirty."

I glance back just in time to see Bella roll her hips in Callum's lap.

Maddie leans in closer, her voice like a blade. "Oh honey, relax. We're not here for you." The bitch flashes a wicked grin. "We're here to ruin your girlfriend's night."

I turn slowly, eyes locked on her. "What the fuck did you just say?"

"She took our Fight Night, Lex." She tilts her head like a smug little devil. "Now... we're taking her party."

Two beeps. "Is that who I fucking think it is?" Knox's voice cuts into my ear like a bullet. Tense. Furious.

"Yeah, Knox," I say into my comms, not blinking. "Looks like the dethroned drama club president and her little gremlins wanna play. You think we let 'em?"

Maddie's brows pinch. "Who the hell are you talking to?"

I smile. Real slow. "Didn't you hear?" I tug the comm cord into view. "I'm part of The Trifecta Boyfriend Squad now. Complete with headset and everything, Maddie."

She scowls.

The crowd behind us explodes. The dance is over and the whole Row's screaming. Drinks fly, phones flash, people chanting, "TRI-FEC-TA".

"You're not taking this party," I say. "Because your surprise entrance just got fucking busted."

I set my drink down on the chair handle beside me, not bothering to look at her again. "Maybe try a new strategy next time, Maddie." I smirk, stepping past her like she's nothing. "This one's already dead."

CHAPTER (45)
CADE
CARRINGTON ROW
WEXLEY UNIVERSITY
659 DAYS SINCE ZEKE'S DEATH

I shouldn't be here. I shouldn't be up on the balcony of The Row, standing in the shadows, staring down and hiding like a damn coward.

Lex is talking to someone, Madison Rae, I think. And Bella's in a fucking chair, grinding on my goddamn brother. I feel sick. Like something sharp is lodged under my ribs, slicing deeper every time she moves. Every time she laughs. Every time her hands touch him like they used to touch me.

I shouldn't have come. I told them I needed time. Space. But the space is suffocating and the time feels endless. A blank canvas with no shape, no light, no color. Only a deep, aching white.

I thought maybe I could handle this. That I could be the one to walk away just for a little while. That it would help. But it hasn't. It's made everything worse.

Because distance doesn't soften anything, it only makes the jagged edges harder to ignore.

I should have stayed home tonight. Painted. Sketched. Poured all this ache into a canvas. Something safe and quiet. But instead, I'm here, watching the girl I love light the world on fire while the guy I love dances in the flames with her.

The crowd is chanting her name like she's a goddess. And maybe she is. Braid swinging, hips rolling, power carved into every motion like it was born in her bones. She's sex and starlight and danger, wrapped in a cherry red bikini and denim so short it should be illegal.

And Lex.

God. Lex is fury incarnate. Muscles tense, jaw locked, rage simmering behind those ice-blue eyes. When he moves through the crowd, they part for him like he's a fucking god descending. They should. He's the Hollow King.

And she's his queen now. Bella turns, sees him and smiles like the whole universe just spun into place. That smile, it used to be mine.

My chest fractures.

Lex reaches her, says nothing. Just lifts her up, her legs wrap around his waist as if she was made to fit there. She melts into him without hesitation. The way he kisses her like he'd go to war for her, like she's oxygen and he's drowning.

It wrecks me.

Lex was right to be mad. He was. I got over his darkness. Chose him in spite of all of it. The blood on his knuckles, the fire in his veins, and the ghosts he never talks about. I stood by him even when it meant patching up bruises I didn't cause.

So why couldn't I do the same with her? Why did I run the second she cracked open that door and let me see the part of her she's been hiding since we were teens?

I remember the first time she fell asleep on my shoulder in the back of my dad's car. I remember the nights she texted me from Ellie's room, just asking if I was awake.

I always was.

And now? Now I can't stop thinking about the way she moans when I've got her pinned. The way she comes undone for me with nothing but my mouth. The way her legs shake when she lets go of all that control, just for me.

God, I miss her. I miss him too. The way Lex holds me after he spills deep inside me. The way he fills me up until I don't know where I end and he begins. The way he says my name when he's falling apart.

What the fuck have I done?

Lex breaks away from Bella, eyes dark with something only she seems to calm. He mutters something against her lips—too soft to hear, too painful to imagine—then heads toward the DJ booth.

Bella doesn't follow him. She and the girls collapse onto the poolside loungers laughing and talking. Taking a well deserved break from the first dance of the night.

I should leave.

I should really leave.

But I don't.

I stay rooted to the shadowed balcony of Carrington Row, one hand gripping the iron railing, knuckles white, watching them like a fucking creeper.

Lex must be done with Knox now because he's headed back, eyes locked on her like she's the only person at this party who exists. I see it before she does. One second, she's laughing with Ellie and Haley near the edge of the pool. The next, Lex is behind her. He grabs her wrist and pulls her up. She spins into him, smiling because she already knows what's coming. Like she's been waiting for it.

He leans down, says something only she can hear and she nods. And then he's pulling her, again. Right past the crowd. Past the stage. Straight into one of the white-draped poolside cabanas.

The lights inside are low. Just enough to see silhouettes.

Just enough to watch.

Lex doesn't waste a second, neither does she. He presses her against the support beam, mouth crashing to hers. She rips his shirt over his head in response.

Buzz. Buzz.

ELLIE: Why are you torturing yourself?

ME: What are you talking about?

ELLIE: I can fucking see you, Cade.
You're not as stealthy as you think.

I glance down at the pool just in time to catch Ellie waving at me like she's about to drag my ass down there herself.

ELLIE: Just come down here.

ME: No, I can't and do not tell anyone I'm here.

ELLIE: Ugh! You are so dramatic.

ME: I'm dramatic? El, have you met yourself?

ELLIE: OMG Cade. Look. I know this whole thing has been hard on you. But it's officially been too long. Plus, it's been hard on all of us. And I get it, you're hurting. But we all love you. And we all love them too.

ME: I know.

Dots, dots, and more dots.
Great, she's writing a book.

ELLIE: No, you don't. You're acting like you're the only one who's ever been gutted by love. But here's the thing, big brother... you've always loved her. Since you were sixteen. You were just too chicken shit to admit it.

ELLIE: Don't even try to deny it. I remember you coming into my room after that party in Philly, pacing like a maniac because you had to go pick our drunk asses up. You were fuming... and then quiet. You sat on my bed and kept asking me how she was.

ELLIE: You've been hooked ever since. You just never had the balls to act on it. Not really. Until Lex.

ME: Don't bring him into this.

ELLIE: Why not? At least he shows up. At least he's fighting for her. You? You're hiding like a little bitch on the goddamn balcony while the girl you've always loved thinks you don't even want her anymore.

ME: El...

ELLIE: She's miserable without you, Cade. She tries to act fine. God, you know how good she is at pretending, but she's not. She talks about you all the time. Keeps finding reasons to bring you up like she doesn't even realize she's doing it.

ME: She looks happy.

ELLIE: Yeah. Surface happy. But not real happy. Not the kind of happy she was when it was you and her. Not the kind of happy where she would get that stupid sparkle in her eyes every time you walked into the room. Sure, she is really into Lex. But she loves you, you idiot.

ME: I don't want to ruin her night.

ELLIE: Then come down here and make it better.

ME: What if it's too late?

ELLIE: It's not. Not if you would stop watching her from the balcony like a Nicholas Sparks character and actually go to her.

ME: You've been waiting to use that line, haven't you?

ELLIE: For years.

I glance back up from my phone and look toward the cabanas. His hands are all over—her waist, her thighs, her ass, her ribs. Bella arches into him, one hand gripping his jaw, the other buried in his hair. Her heel slides off. She doesn't even notice.

She's not thinking about me. She's not thinking about anything. Just him. Just Lex. My stomach lurches. I should be in there.

He pulls her leg around his waist, grinding deep into her. Her lips are parted, head tilted back as he moves to her neck, biting, licking, marking her because he wants every fucker at this party to know who she belongs to.

I flinch. My chest cracks wide open, raw, stupid, and aching. I should look away, but I can't. I should've held on longer. I should've stayed. Should've told her I could love the darkness in her the same way I learned to love it in him.

Instead, I'm up here.

Alone.

Watching the two people I want more than anything fall deeper in love without me.

CHAPTER ㊻
LEX
THE CABANA AT THE ROW
FINALLY ABOUT TO FUCK MY GIRL...
659 DAYS SINCE ZEKE'S DEATH

Her nails dig into my bare shoulder as I press her deeper into the shadows. She tore my shirt off the second we stepped into this damn cabana, like she needed to feel me.

Skin to skin.

No space.

No air.

Just us.

Her thighs are locked tight around my hips, her lips swollen from my kiss. That thin red bikini is doing fuck all to hide the way her nipples are begging for my mouth. Her pulse's thudding against my lips and I can feel it. I can fucking taste it.

My girl needs me. And I need her worse. One more second and I'll be inside her. One more second and I'm not stopping.

"Lex," she breathes. "Lex... baby, stop." Her voice cuts through the haze.

Fuck.

I slow. My grip softens. She's panting now, forehead to mine, eyes fluttering open.

"We are not having sex for the first time at the damn Row," she whispers like it's a rule she made up to keep us from going completely off the rails.

I blink, still trying to catch my breath. Still rock fucking hard for her. "Seriously?" I manage, voice shredded.

Her lips twitch. "You're the one who told me you wanted to earn it, remember?"

I groan, head dropping to her shoulder. "You're actually trying to teach me patience right now?"

She hums, smug. "Character development."

I let out a strangled laugh and lift my head, brushing hair from her face. "Cruel little thing," I mutter, kissing her temple. "You know what you do to me."

Her gaze softens. "Yeah, I can see what I do to you Lex." She glances down at my cock.

"Eyes up here, baby"

"But I also know you'll wait. Now go," she says, swatting my chest playfully.

I kiss her once more—harder, deeper, starved—then pull back. "Fine," I growl. "But if your next dance involves another lap, I swear to God, Bella."

"Then maybe next time, have your bestie put you in a chair."

We step out of the cabana, her braid a little looser, lips kiss-swollen, eyes dancing with trouble. I'm smug as hell and not even trying to hide it.

"Wow," a voice cuts through the crowd. "Didn't realize The Row had added cabana rentals... or is it just fuck-and-run now?"

Bella goes still. She turns toward Maddie with that lethal calm that always comes before the storm. "Awe, Maddie Rae. Didn't get enough at The Pit, so you had to come try again at The Row?"

She tilts her head, voice pure venom. "What was it you said to me that night? Something about how I didn't belong in Hollow Kings territory?"

She looks over her shoulder at me and then back at Maddie.

"You know, from the looks of it..." She steps back into me and my arms wrap around her waist instantly. Her head tilts, resting in the crook of my neck. "...I think I belong to the Hollow Kings more than you ever did. I mean I'm basically their fucking queen now. Right Lex?"

I grin like a wolf with blood on his teeth. "That's right, baby."

"Please." She rolls her eyes. "You think riding one king's dick makes you royalty? We want a rematch."

Bella tilts her head. "A rematch? For what?"

Maddie crosses her arms. "Our Fight Night. You stole it."

Before Bella can respond, Knox's voice shouts through the party speakers. "Hold up. HOLD the fuck up. Who the hell invited the raccoons to the pool party? Maddie Rae? Is that you?"

The crowd erupts. Whistles. Laughter. People are turning, phones out, catching every second. Maddie's face twists. Fucker Callum struts over, of course. Standing just close enough to look like backup.

Bella gives a slight nod toward the DJ booth, barely perceptible unless you know her.

Knox does. He dials down the music just enough for her voice to carry.

"It's okay, Knox," Bella calls. "Apparently, The Revenants are mad at us because we stole their precious little Fight Night."

I lean into her ear, can't help the growl in my voice. "God, I'm fucking crazy about you." I feel her shiver.

"Well did you tell her that you were invited to the show by Rez?" Knox asks.

Maddie's face goes pale. "What the fuck?"

"Yeah Knox, I was getting there," Bella snaps.

Maddie scoffs, but this time her voice rises over the noise. "There is no fucking way he invited you."

I hear the three beeps in my ear, my mic is on. Guess it's my turn.

I grin.

"Yeah, Mads. We did invite them." I let that hang, then lean in just a little. "Crazy, right? Turns out The Kings and The Order actually agree on one fucking thing. And that is that my girl and her girls are the sexiest, baddest bitches in both The Row and The Pit."

She's fuming. Red in the face and trying not to explode.

In my ear, Knox's voice cuts through the static. *"Allow the rematch, Lex. Let's put on a show."*

I lean forward, eyes locked on her, voice dropping low enough to make the crowd hush. "Alright, Maddie Rae. You want a rematch?"

She lifts her chin like she's already won. "Damn right I do."

I grin and step closer until she has to tilt her head back to keep eye contact.

"Good. Because this time, you're not just dancing for bragging rights." I pause, let it hang, let her sweat. "You're dancing for your spot at *my* Pit."

Her mouth parts. The crowd starts to buzz.

I tilt my head, smirk cutting deep. "So I hope you brought backup, princess. Because tonight? I'm the only King here, and I decide who the hell gets to touch my stage."

I walk back toward my girl, wrap my arm around her waist, and pull her flush against me and kiss her. Full. Possessive. Like every camera flashing is a spotlight I own.

Maddie groans. "That's not fair!"

Bella breaks the kiss, looks right at her. "Take it or leave it, Maddie. You heard him. Lex is the rep for Hollow Kings tonight."

Then she turns to me with that fucking look. Smug, daring, and dangerous, because she's already dragging Maddie's coffin behind her.

The Barbie brigade starts squawking.

"Alright, alright, Wolves, it looks like we've got ourselves a rematch!" The crowd roars as Knox's voice booms over the speakers. "Here's how this is going down. Rules of The Row: three rounds. You know the drill."

He throws a beat drop under his words. Pure showmanship, my bestie.

"Round One... dance. Obviously. Y'all better be ready to move." Cheers. Screams. "Round Two... oh, we're micing you bitches up. Hope one of you little Revenants can sing or you're gonna crash harder than you did at Fight Night."

I glance at Maddie. She's gone pale. The bitch looks like someone just unplugged her blow dryer in the middle of Homecoming prep.

Bella is still smiling like the fucking queen she is. Calm, dangerous and unbothered. My fucking Queen. The fucking Hollow Queen. That's it, I need to make a shirt. Where the hell is my man Rico?

Knox leans into the mic, dramatic as hell. "And finally, Round Three... my personal favorite... Lip. Sync. Battle."

Now the whole pool deck's screaming. Drinks are flying, I'm pretty sure some bitch just yanked her top off and spun it around like a goddamn lasso.

Maddie stiffens. Ellie's already bouncing in place. Haley looks like she's ready to throw glitter bombs. Bella doesn't even blink. She tips her head toward the booth and calls out, "Thanks, Knox."

She turns her attention back to Maddie and smiles wide.

"You sure you still want this?"

Maddie doesn't answer. She can't. Because we all already know, she's already fucking lost.

Knox keeps the energy rolling, voice dripping with hype. "Trifecta. Revenants. You each have exactly two song lengths to pick your set list and get it up to me. Tick-tock, ladies."

Bella's already walking back toward Ellie and Haley. Her heels clicking on the pool deck.

Knox pauses, then grins into the mic. "And as for our official judge." His voice drops just enough to sound lethal. "Bestie. Front and center."

I glance up, already moving.

Knox continues, "Looks like you do get a chair after all."

I settle into the chair as if it's a throne. Spread my legs and rest my arms wide across the sides. If I'm going to be the Hollow King tonight, I might as well look the part.

Eat your heart out Whitmore.

Across the pool deck, chaos reigns. Bella, Ellie, and Haley are huddled in a circle, frantically arguing in high-speed girl code. Hands flying. Heads shaking. Bella grabs her braid, twirls it around one finger while screaming *"no, no, no"* through a laugh. Ellie screeches something. Haley claps her hands. They're glowing, laughing like its game night at home and not a war at The Row.

They're fucking radiant.

Maddie and her two soulless backups are standing stiff, glancing between each other like deer on thin ice. One of them whispers something. Maddie snaps back. Her lip gloss is smudged and her confidence shot.

Ellie takes off sprinting across the pool deck, barefoot and screaming. She runs up to Knox at the booth and waves her phone like it's the damn Constitution. He takes it, grinning like the evil genius he is, and starts cueing up their set.

The Revenants still haven't moved.

I just sit here watching the girl I love light up the whole damn night. I should feel on top of the world. But part of me still aches because Cade would've loved this.

He would've been laughing right there with them. Joking with Knox. Whispering something in Bella's ear to calm the storm she always carries in her chest. We were supposed to do this together. The three of us, a fucking family.

I glance back at Bella and something twists tighter in my chest. Round Two is singing. Can she even sing? Fuck. I don't even know. There is still so much I don't know about my girl.

Knox's voice cuts through the heavy bass and the buzz of a few hundred drunk Wolves.

"Alright, alright... Round One! Let's get this dance-off started!"

I feel the concrete shake under my boots. Knox doesn't even pause.

"Maddie Rae, since you're visiting royalty... you and your Revenants are up first."

The groan from the Wexley students says it all. But Maddie struts forward like she didn't just lose half her dignity ten minutes ago. She flips her fake-ass hair and blows a kiss toward the crowd that no one asked for.

Their song starts. And I'll be honest, it's actually not bad. Not the train wreck they pulled at Fight Night. They hit some clean moves. Maddie's got rhythm when she's not too busy being a raging bitch. I'll give her that.

But then... *bam.* The one on her left face plants out of a spin. Straight up wipes out like she stepped in oil. The whole crowd gasps.

"There they are," I mutter under my breath, sipping from my drink. "The Revenants we know and love."

Maddie tries to recover but the momentum's already dead. They finish in formation but it's tight in that try-hard way. Over-rehearsed. No soul.

The song ends. Silence. A few polite claps. One loud boo from the upper deck. Even Maddie looks like she's rethinking this whole rematch.

I lean forward in the chair. "I'll give it a six," I say casually. "Could've been a seven, but clumsy there couldn't stick the landing."

The crowd explodes. Ellie nearly falls over laughing. Haley's already miming the wipeout behind Bella's back. Bella just shakes her head at me like she's going to fuck me later for being a menace.

God, I hope so. Little Lex could use a fucking release.

"Thank you, Maddie Rae. That was... something." Knox doesn't even fake the enthusiasm. "Alright Wolves. Next up, the queens of The Row themselves... Trifecta, you're up!"

Spotlights flip to red. Bass drops. "I Look Good" by Charlie Boy hits with that filthy Texas drawl and swagger-drenched beat.

And then they appear. Bella in the middle. Ellie and Haley around her like lethal shadows. Legs for miles. Hips locked. Eyes deadly. They launch into this sexy-as-sin hip-hop routine—tight, hot, every move sharpened to perfection. Hands flying. Legs slicing. Hair whipping. They switch places on every verse in a synchronized storm.

When the part about throwing the white flag comes on, Bella reaches back and pulls out a white napkin from her shorts. Locks eyes with Maddie Rae and fucking tosses it straight at her.

It floats like a death sentence. My girl. Pure fucking fire.

And just when I think I can't take more. They come to me. Ellie and Haley flank me first. Ellie plays with my hair, Haley runs her finger up and down my arm.

Bella struts over. Eyes locked on mine as she climbs onto my lap.

Calm down, Little Lex.

"Are you trying to kill me, baby?" I growl under my breath, barely able to breathe.

She mouths a kiss, rolls her hips just once, then gets up.

"Not fair, baby. Get your ass back here."

Ellie takes her place on my lap, grinding on me for a few bars.

Then Haley climbs on, locking eyes with me as she arches her back with her hands in my hair.

Jesus Christ, I might actually combust.

"The fuck are you girls doin?"

Haley winks, gets up, and all three of them move off in perfect sync, spinning back into formation for the final run.

The Wolves lose their minds.

Knox is saying something but I can't even hear it. Those girls didn't just perform. They declared war and they looked fucking good doing it.

Knox's voice is finally audible over the crowd, "Okay, Maddie Rae. I hope one of you can sing... because we're about to mic you up."

I raise an eyebrow. "This should be good."

Ok, turns out they can't sing. Shocker.

Some off-key Britney Spears disaster mixed with breathy dramatics and a lot of awkward arm sways. Maddie's mini-me tries to riff and ends up sounding like a dying hyena.

"E for effort, Maddie Mini," I mutter. "And by E, I mean eject."

The crowd claps out of pity.

"Alright, Bella," Knox announces, "you're up, baby."

Baby? The fuck, Knox? Bestie or not, don't fucking call her that.

I lean forward in my chair, ready to lose my shit... but then the beat hits. It's twangy. Southern. Country as hell.

Maddie laughs, that grating fake cackle she does when she thinks she's won something.

"You realize Bella is literally from the south Maddie?" Haley says pure sass. That shuts her up.

I don't even know the song. Some country banger that sounds like it was made to blast from a truck at a state fair. I should really listen to their Trifecta playlist more.

Sorry, baby.

But that twang? That smooth-as-whiskey Southern heat in her voice? I've never been more mesmerized in my life. Bella belts out some hilarious lines about what women actually want from us guys.

Something about being loved when she's ugly.

Ugly? Baby, you're the most beautiful thing in the goddamn world.

She throws in something about bad hair days.

Never you, baby. You're flawless 24/7. Even in my shirts. Especially in my shirts.

She *yeahs* and points at the crowd. The crowd *yeahs* back. She's eating it up. And I love it. I fucking love it.

She stalks across the stage, teasing and singing to a few other guys.

Do I like it? No.

Do I trust her? With my fucking life.

Ellie and Haley storm the stage toward the end of the song. The three of them break into this country-style line dance shimmy-shake thing. They stomp, they spin, they turn. Bella leads it like she was born to.

Maddie's smile is gone. Her ego's dead on arrival.

Mine, however, is sky-fucking-high.

From across the room, Knox whistles low. "Damn, B. Sometimes I forget you're from the South. Then you go full southern belle on stage and suddenly I remember."

Bella flips her hair over her shoulder, smug as hell. "What can I say? Arkansas raised, New York refined."

"Alright everyone it is officially time for Round Three," Knox says, dragging it out like a showman. "Lip. Sync. Battle. You know the rules... no skipping verses and for the love of all things unholy, don't do anything that makes us want to take a damn nap."

Maddie and her Revs go first. They pick one of Taylor Swift's songs. Classic. I mean, it's good. I'll give them that. Lip sync was on point, dancing's tight, and the timing's clean.

Even Bella nods in congratulations. Ellie claps once. Haley flicks a strand of hair off her shoulder like she's bored but watching.

Knox chimes in over the mic. "Nice job, Maddie. Look at you saving the best for last. See? We Wolves don't always bite."

Maddie smiles. Smug little thing.

"Alright, Trifecta, it's your turn," Knox says, his voice echoing through The Row. "Give it up for your favorite little Wicked Witches, here to close out the night with one hell of a show."

The Row boys absolutely lose their shit when Knox says *Wicked Witches*, like they've been waiting for this all damn night. They must know something I don't.

Knox turns toward Bella. "You ready, trouble?"

Bella struts toward me, hips swaying, eyes locked on mine. Clearly already planning my funeral and my lap dance all in the same breath.

"Oh, I'm ready." She smiles. "But first, there's one rule for this song, baby."

She stops right in front of me, steel-gray eyes locked on mine, her fingers curl around the hem of my shirt. "Take it off, Lex."

I do what she says without a second thought. Because let's be honest, when my girl says jump, I ask how fucking high.

The Legacy girls go wild behind her, but I barely hear them. I'm locked on her, that wicked glint in her eyes already telling me I'm about to regret whatever she has planned.

"Ellie, tie him up."

"The fuck did you just say, baby?" I raise a brow as Ellie moves behind me, already looping my arms with my shirt.

"We can't have you ruining our dance by grabbing me the second I sit down on your lap, Lex."

Bella leans in, kisses my forehead like she's not about to emotionally castrate me in front of over a hundred people.

"So, Ellie's gonna tie you to this chair, and if you're good..." she trails off, lips tilting in that dangerous way that always means trouble. "...we might untie you later."

Oh, I'm gonna fucking explode.

The opening riff of "Shakin' Hands" by Nickelback hits and the entire Row ignites. This is obviously one of those routines. One that these girls have practiced more than their midterms.

Bella takes lead vocals, Ellie and Haley handling backup. Her eyes on me the entire goddamn time. She looks at me like she owns me.

Spoiler alert: she fucking does.

The choreography's filthy in the best possible way. The Hollywood pose line hits and Haley grabs Bella's tits right in front of me, and I swear to God, Little Lex fucking salutes. Full military-grade stand at attention.

On the first chorus, she struts toward me and drops into my lap like I'm her personal throne. And I'm just sitting here tied up, losing my fucking mind and praying I don't bust in my pants like a sixteen-year-old virgin.

Holy. Fucking. Hell.

My little Wicked Witch of the East grinds once, slow and deep, and I see stars.

"Fuck, baby. I love you so much," I moan.

She freezes. Just for a breath. Then she smiles like she didn't hear it, but I know she did. My girl's good. She doesn't break character. She just winks and struts off like she didn't just turn my brain to static.

By the time she lip-syncs the line about skirts being on piles, I'm a goddamn goner, because Jesus Christ, this girl shakes off her jean shorts and reveals a red bikini bottom that makes my dick twitch so hard I almost break the fucking chair. She drops her shorts in my lap and I about lose it.

"You've gotta be fucking kidding me," I mutter, tugging at my shirt knotted around my arms. "Goddamn baby, untie me right now."

Bella just shakes her head with that evil little smile. The song hits the next chorus and she's back on me, hips rolling, making it worse. Or better. I can't even tell anymore.

My whole body's vibrating with need. I don't even know if The Row is still watching. I don't care. My world starts and ends with her.

Near the end of the song, Ellie and Haley close in. Haley removes Bella's shorts from my lap. Ellie's behind me, working the knots loose as Bella lowers herself onto my lap again. Haley strokes my hair, giggling like she's watching a porno live.

As the lyrics talk about judges and chests, Bella nods and Ellie finally lets go.

My hands snap free and I grab Bella's throat and drag her down into a kiss that's pure possession. Tongue, teeth, everything. She wraps her arms around my neck, moans into my mouth, and I lose the last shred of control I had.

I think Ellie and Haley finish the song.

Maybe.

Hell, I don't fucking know.

All I know is I've got the girl I love riding my lap, my hands on her body, and a new favorite band.

Nickelback, you dirty Canadian bastards... I owe you one.

CHAPTER (47)
B E L L A
C A R R I N G T O N   R O W
W E X L E Y   U N I V E R S I T Y
659 DAYS SINCE ZEKE'S DEATH

The party's simmered into something soft and electric. The music's still pulsing from Knox's booth. But the craziness has faded into lazy dancing, laughter by the fire pit, and half-drunk Wolves cannon-balling into the pool.

Lex is holding me in the pool, his grip strong like if he lets go, I'll drift away. My back is pressed to his chest, his arms wrapped around my stomach, locking me in. The warm water clings to my skin like silk. But even submerged, I can still smell him—leather and spice. The addictive scent curls around me, threading through the steam, making it impossible to forget who's arms I'm in.

"You killed it tonight," he says low, voice rough from vodka and need. "You, Ellie, Haley... fuck, baby. I wanted to drag you off stage and lock you up all night."

"So dramatic."

"Get fucking used to it, baby," he says as he turns me around so I'm facing him. My arms wrap around his neck, his hands slowly slipping down to my ass before he squeezes.

A quiet laugh slips out of me. Pressing in close, I rest my head on his shoulder. He holds me there. One hand rubbing soft, slow circles down my back.

"You wanna know something," he murmurs, voice hoarse, water dripping from his jaw. "You made sense to me so fucking fast, it scared me. When I held you. When you settled into me like you'd been doing it your whole life, I knew. You felt safe, like your chaos could finally breathe. Like maybe I could hold it back for you, even just for a little while."

He takes a deep breath. "I knew this wasn't just a moment. It wasn't a passing. What I feel for you? It's permanent."

He breathes in like he's trying to slow the storm behind his eyes. "I love you, Bella."

I lift my head from his shoulder, my eyes locking into his piercing icy-blues that always see too much. My breath shudders, but I don't look away.

"I love you, Lex."

Just the truth, soft and quiet, but solid as steel between us. Raw, real, and finally said.

I feel his entire body freeze against mine. His hand flexes on my back. His breath hitches. Then he exhales, shaky, like I just undid something in him.

He doesn't say anything. Doesn't need to. He lifts a hand to my neck and pulls me up to his lips and kisses me deep. Tenderly, as if he's been waiting his whole life for me to say those words.

He lifts me out of the pool, water sliding down my legs as I wrap them around his waist. The heat rolling off his bare chest is all I need.

He carries me and sets me down by the lounger just long enough for us to dry off, grab our stuff, and change.

The music is still pulsing behind us, bodies moving under the multicolored lights, but the party is fading into a blur. I don't care about drinks or dancing anymore. I just want him.

"Where are we going?" I ask once we're on his bike, his hand already on my thigh.

Lex grins. "Home."

I arch a brow. "Redspire or Rosethorne?"

"Neither. Thought I'd take you somewhere better tonight."

We pull up ten minutes later and I gasp.

"No fucking way," I whisper as I stare up at the building in front of us. The sleek black glass, brutalist lines, and a tall steel entrance glint like a knife under the moonlight.

My building.

Zeke's building.

Home.

Lex turns off the bike and glances at me. "You good?"

"This is my building."

"What?"

I whip around to face him. "Lex. This is where I live."

He stares. "You live at Rosethorne, baby. The fuck do you mean your building?"

"I live at Rosethorne, yes but this this..." I say pointing up at the black fortress in front of us. "This is my home. I've lived here since I was fourteen. Penthouse. Forty-first floor."

"You're joking."

"No. I moved in with Zeke the night we escaped Miami. This has been my home ever since."

"You're telling me I've been living in the same building as you for months and didn't know it?"

I nod slowly, watching it all hit him.

"Wait, are you on the thirty-first floor?" I ask.

Lex's eyes narrow. "How the hell do you know that?"

"This building's unique. High demand with barely any tenant turnover." I lift a shoulder. "There's only been one new resident in the last year and a half."

He stares. I keep going.

"Nate and Tex pitched our tech to your dad years ago. Zeke helped set up the first system here. Your dad loved it, signed a contract, and now almost every Barinov-owned building in the country runs on D9 Tech... Project Dylan's own private security system."

Lex drags a hand down his face, muttering, "Jesus Christ."

"And since I technically own Project Dylan and D9 Tech," I add, crossing my arms. "I still have admin access. I get alerts when new lock codes are added and assigned to the units. I just never knew it was you and Cade. I was so busy with school and dance I never opened the file to read the names, just hit accept on the code and went on with my day."

Lex groans, tipping his head back. "So, my dad is a Project Dylan client?"

"Technically," I say with a shrug. "He thinks it's just D9 Tech. Got himself a hell of a deal on a top-tier security upgrade."

I pause, letting it hang for effect. "He doesn't know a damn thing about Project Dylan. Or that his building's security is running on the blood, sweat, and blackmail of a traumatized orphan with a Batman complex."

"Goddamn." He looks at me again. Slower this time. Like something's clicking into place.

"So, you really live in the penthouse?" he asks.

I nod once. "Yeah. Since I was fourteen."

"All this time... you were just ten floors above me."

"Guess fate's a cocky bastard."

Lex grins, pure wolf. "No, baby. I'm the cocky bastard. And fate just gave me the best fucking twist of my life. But how the hell have we never seen each other?"

I take in a deep breath and look up at the building, fighting back the sting in my eyes. "Because I haven't been back here in a very long time. None of us have."

My building... our building, I guess.

The elevator doors slide shut with a soft hiss. I glance at the glowing panel. Then back at him.

"So..." I lift my brows, trying to sound casual, but my voice comes out a little breathier than I want.

"Which floor?" I drag the question out, soft and teasing, knowing damn well what I'm doing to him right now. "Forty-one or thirty-one?"

He pushes off the wall and crowds me back against the opposite one near the access panel, palms landing beside my head.

"I want to take you home, baby." His voice is rough. Sweet teddy bear Lex is gone, replaced by the man who makes my thighs clench and my lungs forget how to work properly.

He leans in, nose brushing mine, voice nothing but a whisper against my lips. "Not the penthouse. Not some cabana at the damn Row."

His mouth barely ghosts mine.

"My home."

Then he reaches behind me and presses a button.

Thirty-one.

We get to his door and he punches in the code.

"Welcome to *Casa de Barinov,* baby," he says, sweeping his arm dramatically like he's unveiling a palace.

"You're such an idiot."

"Yeah, but I'm your idiot."

The moment I step inside, something in my chest swells. It's beautiful. All sleek and modern, a beautiful open concept with concrete floors, black steel beams, and soft amber lighting.

The space breathes in long, clean lines. Kitchen island with dark matte cabinets, bar stools that scream expensive, and a leather couch facing a modern fireplace that flickers low behind black glass.

My eyes catch on a painting above the mantle—stormy and abstract, mostly blacks and grays with jagged streaks of white slicing through it.

Cade. It's his. I'd know his style anywhere.

I walk farther in, fingers grazing the edge of the couch, the back of the bar stool, the mantle. It's all lived-in, but not messy. The way a space feels when two people are trying to make it home without saying it out loud.

I stop at the floor-to-ceiling windows and let out a quiet breath. Same skyline. Same stars. Same city pulsing beneath me.

Lex steps up behind me, wrapping his arms around my waist like he always does. His chest is warm at my back, his breath steady against my neck.

"I always loved this view," I whisper.

"How long's it been?"

"Since the funeral. I tried to come back once." My throat tightens. "I had a full-blown panic attack before I even made it past the lobby."

Lex rests his chin on my shoulder, "If you want to go up there, I'll be right with you. Every step. We'll face it together, baby."

I turn in his arms, look up at him. "I do... but not right now." I bite my lip. "I want to do something else first."

"Thank fucking God." Lex says as he lifts me off the floor and carries me to the bedroom. Kissing me the whole way there.

He lays me down gently, the mattress dipping beneath me as his hands linger a second longer than they need to. Then he straightens, yanking his shirt over his head in one smooth motion.

My eyes drag over every inch of him, those brutal arms inked with shadows, the phoenix spread between his collarbones. The sharp cut of his abs and that deep V that disappears into his shorts like it's inviting me to sin.

"Eyes up here, baby."

I laugh, breathless. Because he's right, I've been caught. When I look back up, those piercing ice-blues are locked on mine, full of fire and need.

He leans in, kissing me deep, slow at first, then harder. His hands slide under my top, fingers rough and reverent as they cup my bare breasts, thumbs brushing over the sensitive peaks until I gasp.

"You're so fucking perfect," he mutters against my lips before lifting the shirt off me entirely and tossing it aside.
His mouth trails down my neck, sucking just hard enough to leave proof. He moves lower kissing, biting, worshiping until he reaches my breasts.

He takes his time, tongue flicking over one nipple while his fingers tease the other, switching sides until I'm writhing beneath him, breath hitched and thighs already squeezing with anticipation of what's to come.

"Lex." It's barely a whisper.

He doesn't answer. Just keeps going. His mouth glides down my stomach, slow, hot, and wet until he reaches the waistband of my shorts. He undoes the button, tugs the zipper down, and starts peeling them off inch by inch, leaving a trail of open-mouth kisses down my hips, my thighs, and the inside of my knee.

Then he shifts, dragging his hands back up my legs. He grips my thighs and buries his face between them like a man starved.

"Fuck," he groans. "Baby, you taste like fucking heaven."

He's rough with it. His tongue licking and swirling, lips sucking hard, mouth pulling moan after moan out of me like a symphony.

He pushes his tongue inside me, groaning low like I'm everything he's ever wanted.

His grip tightens, fingers digging into my thighs so hard I know I'll bruise.

I don't care.

My hands fly to his hair, tangling hard as I grind against his face, chasing the explosion building fast. My pussy clenches tight as he shoves his tongue in deeper. His fingers find my clit, rubbing hard, fast circles until I break.

My body arches, shaking, mouth open in a silent scream as the orgasm crashes through me like a tidal wave. I come with his name on my lips, hands still buried in his hair like it's the only thing keeping me tethered to the earth.

I'm still shaking, still riding the last waves of pleasure when he starts kissing his way back up my body, just worshiping the aftermath.

When he reaches my mouth, he hovers there, eyes locked on mine. "Wanna know how fucking good you taste, baby?" he growls.

He kisses me deep. His tongue plunging into my mouth, letting me taste myself on him. Hot. Slick. Raw. I moan against him, already aching for more.

Lex pulls back, eyes gleaming with hunger as he sits up on his knees and stands beside the bed. I follow the motion with my eyes, still breathless as he slides his shorts down.

Holy shit.

Cade is big, no denying that. He's plenty. More than enough to leave me breathless and aching in the best possible way. But Lex is built like a fucking weapon. Thick. Heavy. Veiny. A goddamn monster.

My eyes go wide. My lips part on instinct. There is no way that thing is going to fit without splitting me in two. I bite my lip without thinking, and of course he catches it. His eyes flicking down. A wolf spotting the first drop of blood.

"Don't look at me like that, baby," he murmurs while stroking himself. "Not unless you're ready to take every fucking inch."

He climbs back over me, the tip of his cock sliding through

barely enough to tease me.

"I've been waiting for this for too damn long," he rasps.

Then he pushes in. Just the tip. Just enough to make me gasp. "Ah!" I moan.

Lex doesn't stop. Slowly, he keeps pressing forward. Stretching me inch by impossible inch.

"Oh my God, Lex. It's not... oh. Fuck. Lex, it's not gonna fit—"

"Oh it's gonna fit, baby," he growls, eyes dark with promise. "I'll make fucking sure of it."

He's big. Too big. It feels like I'm being split open, like he's claiming a space in me no one's ever touched.

My back arches. My nails dig into his shoulders, drawing blood. My body fights and gives in all at once.

"Jesus Christ," he mutters. "You're so fucking tight."

And then, he's in. All the way in and buried to the hilt. He groans like he's been starving for this, forehead dropping to mine.

My breath comes out in shattered gasps. He stays buried in me for awhile. Unmoving. Letting me feel the stretch.

"I love you so much, malyshka," he whispers as he kisses my forehead.

I blink up at him, heart doing cartwheels. "Wait, what does that mean?"

He smiles, brushing his knuckles over my cheek. "It means baby. In Russian."

I can't help the way my lips curve, soft and full of everything I feel for him. "I love you too."

Then he pulls out. Fully. Just long enough to let me catch a breath before slamming right back in. Hard. Brutal. Like he's trying to bury himself so deep I'll never forget the shape of him. Never even think of another man without feeling him first.

My entire body jolts, sending a raw scream ripping through my throat.

His rhythm is punishing. Relentless. Deep, fast, and desperate, like he's not just trying to fuck me, but he's taking what belongs to him.

"Lex, oh my God—"

"Feel that?" he growls, slamming in again, hand gripping my thigh to anchor me in place. "You feel who you belong to?"

I nod. Gasp. Moan.

"Say it."

"You. Lex, you."

"That's right, baby. This pussy's mine." He bites the word as if it's sacred. "Mine to stretch. Mine to ruin. Fucking mine."

Then his mouth drops to my breast, sucking one nipple deep into his mouth before grazing it with his teeth just enough to make me arch and cry out. My back bows off the bed, fingers clawing at his shoulders, desperate to hold onto something before I come undone.

"Eyes on me, baby," he rasps, pulling back just far enough to meet my gaze.

"I want you to fucking look at me when you come. See who does this to you, so you always remember who it is that makes you fall apart."

"Say it to me in Russian."

He grins, voice low and demanding. "Glaza na menya, malyshka."

I bite my lip, dizzy with it. "Fuck, I love when you say it like that."

His smile goes feral. "You like that, huh?"

His hips slam forward, again and again, and I shatter. Right there under his stare. My eyes lock with those wild, ice-blue ones, as the orgasm rips through me in a supernova. My legs shake, my nails dig into his back, but I don't look away.

I can't.

That's what does him in. Lex releases a low growl. His hips stutter, stammer, losing rhythm. He drops his head for a second like he's about to fall apart, but I grab his face in both hands.

"Eyes on me," I whisper, voice shaking. "That's your rule."

His mouth curls into the faintest, filthiest smile. "Yes, malyshka."

And then he breaks. His whole body tenses, a guttural sound punching from his chest as he spills inside me, deep and hot and claiming. He never stops moving, just rocks into me slower now, dragging it out. Breathing hard. Whispering my name like a prayer.

"Bella. Bella..." Like if he says it enough, the world will reset.

When it's over, he doesn't pull out. Doesn't roll away. He just drops his forehead to mine, breath tangled with mine, still inside me. Still holding me.

"I'm never letting you go," he whispers.

"Good," I whisper back.

Lex groans as he finally pulls out of me, his body still trembling from the high. I'm sore, slick, and utterly wrecked, but I've never felt more wanted in my life.

He flops down beside me, chest heaving, skin burning hot. Then he reaches for me. He doesn't say a word as he pulls me onto his chest, arms wrapping around my waist like he can't stand not touching me. I melt into him, cheek pressed to his heartbeat, legs tangled with his.

We're both sweaty, breathless, and there's a slow, messy trail of him leaking out of me. Lex doesn't care. He tucks my hair behind my ear, gaze soft now, voice low and full of something real.

"God, I fucking love you, malyshka." His fingers trace down my spine, a lazy, possessive touch. "So damn much."

I smile, still catching my breath, but he's not done.

"Bella, I—"

Beep-beep.

Beep-beep.

The front door unlocks with a mechanical click. We both freeze. I whip my head toward the door. Lex sits up, muscles taut, heart pounding under my palm.

We hear footsteps down the hall.

And Cade walks in.

CHAPTER (48)
CADE
OUR APARTMENT
659 DAYS SINCE ZEKE'S DEATH

The second I get to our bedroom, I see them tangled in each other like a painting that's been waiting to be finished. Bella. Lex. Bare skin and flushed cheeks. Her hair is a mess. Their lips red. The kind of red that only comes from kissing too hard, too deep, too real.

Bella's eyes go wide. "Cade?"

Lex moves instantly, rolling over her, instinctive as hell, arm slung across her stomach shielding her, jaw locked and bracing for a bullet I don't intend to shoot. He grabs the edge of the sheet and yanks it up, hiding their naked bodies like I haven't already memorized every fucking inch of both of them.

His back is tense. Shoulders drawn tight. Muscles coiled like a goddamn wire about to snap.

I stand there, pulse hammering in my ears and force the words out through the static.

"I'm sorry," I manage, voice rough. "I should've called."

Lex sits up some more, still holding the sheet around Bella. "This is your home, Cade. You never have to call."

His eyes meet mine. No judgment or anger, only depth. The kind that says *I still want you here.*

I look at Bella. She doesn't say anything at first. Just clutches the sheet tighter against her chest, eyes searching mine like she's not sure what I'll do.

Neither do I.

Because I don't just miss them. I love them. Both of them, more than I ever thought possible. And standing here now, seeing the way she melts into Lex, I know one thing for sure... if I walk away again, I won't survive it.

"I think I should go," her voice is soft, barely above a whisper.

"Fuck no, baby."

I hold up a hand. "It's okay. You don't have to go." My throat's tight but I push through. "I'm glad you're here. I..." The words stumble, useless. "...I wanted to see both of you."

They're still tangled in the aftermath, but all I can think about is how badly I want to be in that bed. Not watching. Not aching. With them. The way it was supposed to be.

Bella moves first. She stands, wrapping the sheet around herself like armor, but it doesn't hide much—loose, low, and barely hanging on. The kind of look that would've wrecked me couple months ago.

Hell, it still does.

She walks away from the bed, leaving Lex exposed. He has no shame as he leans back on one arm, chest rising and falling, eyes locked on her as if she's the only thing keeping him breathing.

She turns and walks toward me. There's a lump in my throat that just wont go away. She stops inches from me, clutching the sheet to her chest, hands shaking. Bracing for impact and I'm the one holding the grenade.

Her eyes are weary as they meet mine. She's scared of me. Of what I'll say. Of whether I'll break her again. And it guts me, because once upon a time, before Lex, before everything, I was the one person she was never afraid of.

Now I'm the one she's preparing to survive.

I don't know what comes over me, but I say it anyway. "Hi, sweetheart."

Her lip wobbles. She takes one huge breath, tears clinging to the corners of her eyes. And then she smiles. Hopeful, fragile, but still a smile, and fuck I almost fall to my knees right then and there.

"Hi," she whispers.

Her voice punches the air out of my lungs. I take a small step forward, instinct kicking in, but she backs up. Just a step and it nearly kills me.

"Bella," My voice cracks and I force myself to breathe. "I'm so sorry."

She doesn't look up.

"I'm sorry for everything I put you through. Sorry for pushing you. Sorry for forcing you to tell me a story that wasn't mine to know."

Her eyes are glassy now. Filling fast.

"I'm sorry I was an ass and overreacted. Sorry I walked away when you needed me most. Sorry I made you feel like you were something to fear." I swallow. "Sweetheart, I looked at you like you were a monster. And that's on me. That's my shame to carry."

Her jaw trembles.

"And I..." my voice hitches. I glance around her and look at Lex, still naked and half-sitting in bed watching silently. "...I never should've left, babe. Never should've walked away. From either of you."

I look back at her.

"I'm sorry. These last two and a half months have been torture. I've missed you both so much it's nearly killed me."

I shake my head, trying to find the words. "It was like all the air got ripped out of this world and I couldn't breathe."

From behind her, the bed creaks. Lex rises and walks up behind her, slow, quiet, and completely naked. He wraps her up in his arms and pulls her back into him, her head resting under his chin.

"So, you had your time, Cade."

I freeze. So does Bella.

"Can you still love her?" Lex rasps. "Can you still fucking love us?"

His voice is too calm, the kind of calm that warns you something's about to break.

"Knowing everything. What she's done. What we've done. What we'll keep doing if it means keeping those kids safe."

He's not asking for approval. He's drawing a line in blood and daring me to step over it.

His jaw flexes. "Can you love her—every fucking part of her—past, present, and whatever darkness comes next?"

Thick and loaded silence stretches between us.

"Because if not." Lex nods to the door. "There's the fucking door."

"Lex," Bella says trying to pull away from him. "It's ok."

"No, baby it's not." He holds her firmly in place. Dominating as ever. She gives in and leans back into him.

"So? Which is it Cade?" he asks again.

I look into her eyes, they're guarded now. But beneath the fire, I see it. The worry and the hope fighting a battle in her mind. She's begging me to stay. Begging me to grab her. To fight for us.

I take a step forward and reach for her hand. Lex moves first, gripping her tighter. Protective. Ready for a war that I caused. She lays a hand on his arm, soft and sure. Then turns around, rises onto her toes, pulls him down, and presses her forehead to his. Nose to nose. A quiet anchor to calm his storm.

"It's okay, Lex," she whispers. "Let him talk."

Lex searches her face, like he's looking for some hidden crack, but she holds his gaze. Whatever he sees there makes him nod once. He steps back and lets her go.

"I love you, Cade." Her voice is soft. Frayed at the edges. "I think I've loved you for a long time. Maybe since Nashville... I don't know."

My lungs collapse around the weight of it.

"But what you said about me," her voice shakes and it's somehow worse than if she'd screamed. "It hurt. More than I can explain."

That one lands like a fist.

"You were the last person I ever wanted to hurt with all of this, all of me." She glances at Lex. Then back to me. She's steady now. Braver than she's ever looked.

"But Lex is right." She takes a small step toward me, the sheet slipping a little, her eyes never leaving mine. "We need to know."

Her voice drops to a whisper, but it slices through me like glass. "Can you love me, all of me? Even the parts that don't fully come back from what we've done? From what I'll keep doing?"

Tears cling to her lashes, but she doesn't back down. "Can you love me, even if I never stop? Even if I keep saving kids, whatever the cost? Even if there's more blood on my hands in the future than there ever was in the past?"

"Yes."

Her eyes snap up to mine, cracked open with disbelief. And then I see it. That smile. The one that used to undo me. The one I thought I'd chased away for good.

"I love you, sweetheart."

My voice breaks and I let it. "Every fucking part of you."

I step closer and this time, she doesn't retreat. I wrap my arms around her like she might vanish again if I don't hold tight enough. Her skin's warm, breath's uneven. Her whole body's humming trying everything it can to hold back the collapse.

I lift her chin, just enough to meet her eyes. "I'm sorry it took almost losing you to finally see what I had. To realize I've been in love with you longer than I ever admitted, to myself or anyone else."

Her lips part, but nothing comes out except a soft, aching sound. A sound that tears straight through me.

"Cade," she breathes and the tears fall. One after another, like she's been holding them back for years.

God, I've missed her. And now that she's in my arms again, I never want to miss her like this again.

"I know your world is chaos. I know it's pain and grit and choices no one should ever have to make," I whisper. "But I know you. I've always known you. Maybe not every detail, but the core of you. A core that's been burned into me since the day you walked into my life in glitter boots and pure fire."

I take her hand and press it over my heart. "And this, what we have, isn't just love. It's home. It's gravity."

I'm shaking now. Voice rough, heart bare. "I want to be the one who catches you when you fall. Who stays when the shadows hit. Who holds your bloodstained hands and never once thinks they're anything but holy."

She's silent, staring at me as if she's trying to memorize every word.

"I want to be your peace, Bella. The place you breathe. The arms you run to. The man who never lets you forget that you were made for more than just surviving."

I lean in, resting my forehead against hers.

"Let me be your second chance," I breathe. "Your calm. Your fucking everything. From this moment until we're old and gray and still arguing over the fact that *Fast Five* is not the best movie in the franchise."

"Yes it is." Her laugh chokes on a sob and I know this isn't our ending. It's our beginning.

A soft sound cuts through the silence behind us.

A sniffle.

Bella and I both turn. Lex is standing there completely naked, hair a mess, eyes suspiciously glassy.

Bella blinks. "Wait... baby, are you crying?"

Lex rolls his eyes—sniffles again—and grumbles, "No, I'm not crying. You're crying, goddamn."

Bella bursts out laughing. It's that real kind of laugh, messy, pure, and loud. The kind that cracks something open inside you and puts it back together all at once.

And when I hear it. When I see her smile like that, I know.

I'm finally home.

I reach out my hand to Lex, pulling him right up behind her. His chest presses into her back. My arms still around her front. We sandwich her between us. Her body curled between mine and Lex's like she belongs nowhere else.

Because she doesn't.

Because she's ours.

I look down at her, then up at him. My voice rough. Barely holding it together.

"The two of you... you're all I ever needed. And I'm sorry I pulled away. Never again. I love you two so much."

"I love you too," she says softly, eyes shining. "We both do."

Lex wraps his arms tighter around her, leaning in with a half-smirk, half-tear. "Fuckin' right we do."

I look him up and down, completely exposed, muscles flexing like he's still on some kind of high, his cock already semi-hard.

"God, you're sexy," I say without thinking. "I fucking missed this sight."

He barely fights the grin. "Right back at you, babe."

"So, do you guys want to fill me in on everything that I've missed?" I say to the both of them.

He raises an eyebrow. "I'd rather fill something else."

Lex doesn't even give her a second to process what he just said. He lifts Bella clean off the ground, her laugh breaking loose as she squeals.

"Lex!" she gasps, half-protesting and half already melting into it.

He grabs my hand with his free one and pulls us both toward the bed.

CHAPTER ⑨
BELLA
CADE AND LEX'S APARTMENT
659 DAYS SINCE ZEKE'S DEATH

Oh my fucking God. This is really happening. I mean, I knew it could happen. Like in theory. Like in the kind of fantasy you spiral into at 2 a.m. with a vibrator and a playlist called *Men Who Could Ruin Me*.

But I was not—repeat, *not*—planning on this happening tonight.

Lex has Cade's hand. Not in a sweet, couple-y way. Not in a *let's-hold-hands-and-go-skip-through-a-field* way.

No. This man, this 6'6" muscle-bound lunatic fresh out of a sex coma, has Cade's hand in one of his, me wrapped in a sheet tossed over his shoulder in the other, and he's dragging us both toward the bed like this is some kind of deranged sex quest and we're the spoils of a goddamn war.

I'm upside down. Legs dangling. Hair everywhere.

Dignity? Don't know her.

"Lex," I gasp, trying to wriggle, which only makes it worse. "What the hell are you doing?" I say as his shoulder digs into my stomach.

He doesn't stop. Doesn't even hesitate. Just tosses back, calm as hell, "Cade asked if we wanted to fill him in on what we've been up to."

He tightens his grip. "I said I wanted to fill something in. Keep up, malyshka."

Cade chuckles behind us like this is funny. Like he isn't already halfway hard from all of this. God I'm so glad he's back. I've missed him so much. Those hazel eyes, that smile.

Lex reaches the bed and plops me down in the middle like a prize he's not done unwrapping yet. The air is snagged in my lungs, my heart is racing, and every single nerve is on fire.

I blink up at them as they tower over me. And it hits me all at once.

This is *happening.*

They're both still standing. Looming. Looking down at me like they already fucking own me.

Cade's peeling off his shirt now, slowly giving me a show he knows I've earned. That soft, teasing smile playing on his lips, the one that promises safety and destruction in the same breath... God, it ruins me.

Lex is still completely naked. Unbothered. Unapologetic. His body carved from chaos and sin, every inch of him screaming control he's barely holding onto. He looks calm, dangerously calm, but I can see it in his eyes.

That storm waiting to break.

"Malyshka," Lex says, voice low and rough. "Lay back."

My pulse jumps. I don't even question it. I slide back, easing onto the bed like I'm moving through water. My hair fans out across the sheets.

Lex climbs over me with that predator-slow crawl that has my whole body buzzing. One massive hand braces next to my head, the other skimming up my ribs until it's cupping my jaw.

His mouth crashes down on mine, hard and claiming. And God, it's everything. I whimper into his mouth, hands grabbing at his arms, his shoulders, anything I can reach, because I already feel like I'm falling.

I feel the bed move beside me. Cade. He stretches out along my side, his fingers brushing my bare hip, his voice soft against my ear.

"You okay Sweetheart?"

I nod, dazed.

"Good." Cade's lips graze my cheek. "Because I don't think either of us plan on stopping."

Lex pulls back just long enough to look down at me. His thumb drags across my bottom lip, swollen from his kiss. That icy gaze locked on mine just trying to decide which part of me to devour first.

"Lay still, malyshka," he murmurs, voice rolling like thunder. "Let me taste you a little longer."

And I do, well try to anyway. God, I try.

I fail.

His tongue moves against mine with a rhythm that makes my body jolt, and I swear I feel the asshole smirk into the kiss.

Beside me, Cade's hand drifts to my stomach, fingers light and comforting. "You're perfect, sweetheart," he says it so soft I almost miss it over the sound of Lex kissing me senseless.

Lex runs his fingers through my hair, palm cradling the back of my head. His cock presses hard against my stomach, leaving a warm trail in its wake.

"Relax, malyshka. We've got you."

Cade shifts beside me, pushing up slowly onto his knees, and I watch as he reaches for Lex. Lex pushes up to meet him.

I can't breathe.

Can't look away either.

Definitely not as Cade reaches down and starts stroking Lex's cock making it pulse right in front of my eyes.

"Fuck... Cade," Lex grits, eyes rolling back as drops of precum start to coat Cade's hand. His abs start to flex and his hips start to jerk from the pressure building inside him. "Mmmm. Babe. I missed you."

He grabs Cade by the neck and pulls him in for a kiss. It's slow at first, then deeper, hungrier. Tongues tangling from months of being apart. One of Lex's hand rises into Cade's hair, the other roaming over the ridges of his abs.

Cade moans into the kiss, but never loses his rhythm.

I bite my lip and take in a deep breath.

They both stop and look down at me.

"Enjoying the show, baby?" Lex laughs.

Cade releases Lex and leans down. His finger gently lifting my chin, turning my face toward his. His touch is soft but sure, his eyes full of something that makes my heart ache.

"Sweetheart," he whispers as he kisses me. Slowly savoring every second we've missed while apart.

While I'm kissing him, I feel warmth. Goosebumps prickle across my skin as Lex's strong hands trail upward. He takes his time, sliding a rush of heat over every inch of my stomach, savoring the feel of me.

He finds my breasts. His palms curve around them, thumbs brushing over the peaks, slowly teasing. I gasp into Cade's mouth, my back arching off the bed.

Lex growls low in approval as he leans down. He takes one breast into his mouth, the other still cradled in his hand, thumb teasing in a perfect rhythm. I nearly fall apart. Soft lips, hot tongue, and a suck that sends fire racing down my spine.

Cade pulls back just enough to watch me, his forehead pressed to mine, breath warm and shaky. I can't speak. Can barely think.

"Look at what you do to us, sweetheart," Cade says, grabbing my hand and guiding it to the thick, hard line of his cock straining against his pants. "I've been losing my mind thinking about you. About this."

I draw in a ragged breath.

"You think it's been easy for me?" He leans in closer, hazel eyes on fire. "I've been walking around with this constant ache. So hard it hurts. So full I'm losing my goddamn mind."

He squeezes his hand around mine, groaning as he grits out, "I've been holding it in, sweetheart. All of it. Every last drop. Saving it for you. For when I'm so deep inside of you, you forget those months we had apart even happened."

Lex's mouth pops off my breast with a wet sound and a surprised grunt. He stares at Cade like he just grew horns.

"Cade," he says slowly, blinking. "Did you just fucking talk dirty? Thought that was my thing."

I burst out laughing. I can't help it.

Lex turns to me, deadpan. "Okay, malyshka, who the fuck is this and what did you do with our boyfriend?"

I'm still laughing, breathless now, cheeks burning in the best possible way.

Cade just grins. "Oh babe," he says, sliding his hand up my thigh. "You haven't seen anything yet."

Lex shakes his head, eyes dark with mischief, mouth tilting into that arrogant, fuck-around-and-find-out grin I know too well.

"Well shit," he mutters, dragging his palm down the center of my body. "Now I gotta keep up," he says as his face is getting danger-ously close to my throbbing center.

I gasp into Cade's mouth as Lex goes down on me. It's noth-ing like Cade. There's no slow build. No teasing. Lex eats me like he's deprived, like it's been weeks and I'm the only thing that could ever satisfy him again.

His hands grip my thighs, spreading me wide, holding me in place. His tongue is relentless—flat and heavy one second, then sharp and fast the next. He devours me, messy and loud and obscene.

He groans into me like the taste alone is enough to make him lose control. I can feel Cade smiling against my mouth, enjoying every single second of my unraveling.

A low moan escapes Lex's mouth, his tongue circling and dip-ping, sucking hard on my clit until I cry out. He doesn't stop. Doesn't let me breathe for a single second.

"Lex!"

One of his hands slides up, fingers digging into my waist to pin me down as his tongue plunges inside me, hard and deep, then up again, back to that devastating rhythm that has my hips lifting off the bed.

"Holy fuck," I choke out, legs trembling.

Cade strokes my hair, kissing my jaw. "You're doing so good, sweetheart."

I'm close. So damn close. My hips lift into it, fingers gripping the sheets, every muscle coiled and ready to snap.

"Fuck, Lex. Baby don't stop, oh—"

"Babe," Cade says, voice calm but firm. "Stop."

My head snaps up. "What?" I pant, absolutely wrecked and suddenly furious at Cade. "Why the hell would you?"

Lex looks up, dazed and confused, mouth glistening. "What's wrong?"

Cade just grins. "Nothing's wrong, babe." He looks at me. "I just want my turn."

Lex lets out a low, dark laugh. He pushes up onto his knees and leans over me to kiss Cade, hot and open-mouthed, giving Cade a taste of me right off his lips. I moan, still breathless as Cade finally turns to me.

Cade moves between my legs, positioning himself low, hands sliding up my thighs with that signature calm control that somehow makes everything hotter.

"I love you, sweetheart," he says before he goes down.

"Ah! Cade!" I cry out, back arching. "I love you too."

It's different this time. Lex is fire, all mayhem and ruin.

But Cade? Cade knows me. He has for years. He'd spent many weeks learning me. Studying every gasp, every tremble, like I'm his favorite subject. He knows my body. Knows what makes me fall apart and exactly how to put me back together.

He licks slow. Long, deliberate strokes that drag heat through my veins. Each one laced with the kind of control that only comes from knowing exactly how to wreck me.

Then he flattens his tongue and slides it up over my clit. Just enough pressure to make my hips twitch, my hands fly into his hair, and enough to cause a broken cry to fall from my lips before I can stop it.

Because with Cade, it's never just sex. It's a symphony. And right now he's playing me like he never stopped loving the sound.

He adds a bit of pressure, circling that spot with just the right amount of friction. Not too fast. Not too light.

Perfect.

My thighs start to tremble again.

"God," I whimper, just as Cade slides two fingers inside me, curling them upward just enough to hit that damn spot that sends my head back into the bed.

A moan rips out of my throat and Lex catches it with his mouth. He kisses me deep, tongue tangling with mine, swallowing every sound I make while Cade works me over with perfection.

Cade flattens his tongue once more on my clit again, right as his fingers pump faster and hit a spot that makes my toes curl. I can't hold it in any longer. I shatter completely, the sound muffled by Lex's tongue.

The pressure starts to fade. My limbs go limp, lungs heaving. Cade gently slips his fingers from me, kisses the inside of my thigh, and then slowly crawls up my body savoring every inch.

He presses a kiss to my stomach. Then my chest. Then my lips.

"I missed you," Cade whispers, softly kissing me.

I wrap my arms around him, completely breathless. "I missed you, too."

He leans in and kisses my nose, then sits back and removes his sweats, still grinning.

Lex is on the bed beside me, bare, gorgeous, and lethal. He props himself up on one elbow, his free hand brushing back my hair, fingers trailing along my cheek and my throat. He leans in and kisses just below my jaw, like he's staking a claim without saying a word.

Cade moves between my legs. He leans down, kissing my mouth first. Then my neck. Then the curve of my breast as he lines himself up and looks me in the eyes.

I smile back at him. He positions his cock at my entrance and thrusts inside. The stretch is familiar, a slow, sweet burn I've come to crave. He slides in inch by inch, hazel eyes locked on mine, his hands gripping my hips like he's afraid I might float away.

"Fuck," I whisper, arching up into him.

He lowers himself over me, his body covering me and rests his forehead on mine as he begins to move—deep, slow thrusts that fill me perfectly, over and over.

It's everything I know with Cade, steady, loving, and safe.

But this time, there's more. This time, we're all here.

Together.

"You're so fucking beautiful like this," Lex rasps. "Taking him so well, malyshka."

Cade groans softly at the words, his rhythm picking up just slightly, hips rolling with practiced precision. "You feel amazing, sweetheart," he moans. "You always do."

My hands grip Cade's back as he claims me with every thrust, his rhythm pounding through me while Lex's mouth leaves a trail of fire across my skin.

Cade picks up his pace, just a little. Each thrust still deep and controlled, but faster now. His hips roll with a rhythm that has me clinging to him, moaning against his neck.

"God, Cade," I breathe.

His hands tighten on my hips. "Come here, sweetheart."

He sits up, pulling me with him, and I follow instinctively—chest pressed to his, arms wrapped around his shoulders as he shifts his weight. Then, in one smooth, practiced motion, Cade flips us, guiding me onto him, my knees straddling his thighs, all while keeping his cock perfectly buried deep inside me.

I gasp, the stretch even deeper from this angle and grip his shoulders, barely able to breathe.

"We've really perfected that, babe," I whisper.

Cade groans, hands steady on my waist. "Practice makes perfect, sweetheart."

Lex moves beside us, fully upright now. One hand trails up my spine, then slides down again, with fingers that graze the dip of my back before resting low, possessive, comforting. His.

The other wrapped around his length, stroking with long, slow passes as he watches me ride Cade with that icy, hungry gaze

Cade's lips brush my jaw, his voice spent. "Take what you need, sweetheart."

He lays back and I start to move. Slow at first, rolling my hips in a steady rhythm that makes Cade's head tip back and his hands tighten on my waist.

"Fuck," he groans. "Just like that, Bella."

I grind down, changing the angle, gasping as he hits that spot inside me that makes me tremble. Cade meets me thrust for thrust, his hazel eyes locked on mine, completely lost in it.

Lex comes up behind me, heat radiating off his body, that fucking monster of a cock dragging across the curve of my ass as he presses up against me.

"Jesus," I breathe.

His hands slide around my front, his fingers kneading, thumbs brushing my nipples until they ache. He leans in, his lips ghosting over my neck before he bites down gently, sucking hard enough to make me whimper.

"Couldn't stay away," he growls against my skin. "Watching you ride him is the hottest thing I've ever seen."

Cade's watching us now, his lips parted, face flushed and pupils so wide they swallow the color. "God, you guys," he says, voice breathless, broken. "This is gonna make me come."

Lex chuckles behind me, low and sinful. "Good. That's the whole damn point, babe."

He rolls his hips forward, dragging his cock between my ass cheeks, while his hands keep moving. Pinching, teasing, and claiming every inch of me. I moan, caught between them, unraveling in the best way possible.

Lex's hand slides down between my legs. He finds my clit with perfect aim, fingers moving in tight, skilled circles, slick and fast, matching the rhythm of my hips.

"Fuck, Lex," I choke out, the stimulation almost too much.

"I've got you, malyshka."

Cade's hands squeeze my waist, his breath stuttering. "Jesus Bella, I'm not gonna last."

And neither am I. The blinding pleasure slams into me, my body locking down around Cade's cock, thighs shaking, a moan ripping out of me so loud it doesn't even sound human.

"Cade, oh!"

"That's it, baby," Lex growls from behind me. "Give it to him."

Cade lets out a strangled noise, a curse and my name tangled together as he thrusts up hard one last time and shatters, loud, wrecked, and entirely undone beneath me.

Lex doesn't stop moving his fingers on my clit, drawing out every beautiful wave of pleasure, his other hand tight on my breast, mouth still pressed to my neck.

I collapse forward onto Cade's chest, panting, trembling, my body still twitching with aftershocks. Cade's arms wrap around me, holding me tight as he kisses my temple, his heart racing under my palm.

And Lex?

Still watching us.

Still hard.

Still waiting for his fucking turn.

CHAPTER ⑤⓪
L E X

~~MINE AND CADE'S APARTMENT~~

ALL OF OUR FUCKING APARTMENT.
OUR BABY'S GONNA MOVE IN...

659 DAYS SINCE ZEKE'S DEATH

Well that was the hottest fucking thing I've ever seen in my twenty-two years of living on this planet. Bella riding Cade like she owned his fucking dick. Those perfect tits bouncing in my hands while she moaned Cade's name as he fell the fuck apart beneath her.

Yeah. That's going to be seared into my skull for fucking ever. Cade better paint that shit so we can hang it above our goddamn bed.

I'm still hard as granite, cock aching, every muscle in my body tight with restraint. Watching the two loves of my life come together, all while I had my fingers on her clit and my mouth on her skin made me nearly lose it right then and there.

Bella finally collapses onto Cade's heaving chest, both of them panting, exhausted, and completely gorgeous.

I give them a second. Just a breath.

"Now it's my turn, baby."

Bella lifts her head, still dazed, lips parted. She rolls off Cade, her body flushed and trembling. I watch every damn inch of her move like I've earned it.

Cade slides over to the side, completely spent, a slow smile curving across his lips as he drags the back of his hand over his mouth.

"All yours, babe," he says with that lazy, fucked-out voice of his I love so much. Then he glances over at her. "Good luck, sweetheart."

Bella chokes out a breathless laugh. Her hair is a mess and somehow she's still the sexiest thing I've ever seen with those steel eyes, perfect lips, and smile that would rival any goddess. She turns her head and looks at me and I know I'm a goner.

She's flat on her back now, legs splayed open, skin blushed and glistening, hair tangled across the pillow like something out of a fucking wet dream.

And me? I'm on my knees between my girl's thighs, cock hard

and throbbing, every second I'm not inside her feels like a personal goddamn tragedy.

I look down at her. She just smiles and nods once.

Message fucking received, baby.

I grab her hips, line myself up and thrust into her in one, fierce stroke.

"Oh, God!" Bella cries out beneath me, her back arching, a loud moan ripping from her throat that shoots straight through me.

"That's right, malyshka. I'm your God now. Me. Fucking Me." My own groan is guttural, instinctive, and torn from somewhere deep.

"Jesus fuck, malyshka..." I grit out as I still inside her for just a second, letting the feel of her soak through my bones. "You feel so good I might fucking lose it already."

She's tight, hot, perfect.

Made for this.

Made for me.

"You're taking me so well," I tell her as I start to move my hips, grinding into her with ruthless precision.

I drop down over her, my forearms bracing on each side of her head, and I kiss her hard. It's teeth, tongue, and breathless groans. Her lips part beneath mine and she gasps into the kiss, hands flying to my back, nails digging into my shoulders, matching the marks she carved in me earlier.

"Lex," she chokes out between breaths. "It's so... so full I can't."

I thrust harder. Deeper.

Mine.

Every sound, every inch, every fucking breath.

Mine.

"Take it, malyshka," I growl against her mouth. "You can fucking take it."

Cade shifts beside us, his head turning toward the sound of her voice, a flicker of concern crossing his face like he wants to step in. Like he's not sure if it's too much for her.

But he doesn't move as I keep driving into her, my hips snapping, her body arching into mine. She needs me this way, rough. She needs my darkness to drown out her own.

She moans, loud and raw, the sound shooting straight through my spine. I drop my mouth to her chest, tongue dragging across one nipple before I suck it deep, biting gently, then harder. Her whole body jerks beneath me.

"LEX!" She screams it like it's the only word she remembers. The only name that matters. And fuck, I'll never get tired of hearing it like that.

I feel her pussy clenching around me, that perfect squeeze, that telltale quake of her thighs, she's right there, so close.

"Time to play a little game, malyshka," I say to her with a wicked smile.

"Just think of it as a little punishment for teasing me and giving me a raging case of blue balls pretty much daily. For only letting me touch you with my hands and nothing else. For what was it you called it again?"

I tilt my head. "Right, building fucking character."

"Oh shit," Cade mutters.

I pull out. Hard. Fast. Leaving her empty and gasping.

"Come here, Cade."

He sits up, already moving toward me. I grab the back of his neck, pull him in, and kiss him deep, filthy, and raw.

I make sure she sees it.

All of it.

I pull back and run my thumb across his bottom lip. "I'm gonna need you to wrap those perfect lips around my cock, Cade."

"Oh really?" he grins.

"Right fucking now, *baby*."

"Mmmm," Cade moans.

It kills him when I call him, *baby*. One of his biggest weaknesses, actually. Makes him hard as a fucking rock and I love it.

He reaches down and fists my cock, stroking it few times. My hips jerk as he teases the crown with his thumb, his hazel eyes never leaving mine.

God, that unbroken stare. I fucking missed this. Missed him.

"You're perfect, you know that right?"

"You like that, Lex?"

"God, Cade," I moan and nod as he squeezes Little Lex, bringing his other hand up to cup my balls. We both look down and watch as my dick slides in and out of his hand, pulling another moan from deep within me every time he squeezes.

"Put it in your fucking mouth, babe," I order. "Don't make me say it again."

He leans down slowly, licks his lips, and drags his tongue up and down the length of me, taking extra time licking and sucking the head.

I groan as he starts swallowing the precum dripping on his tongue. He gives a few more licks before guiding Little Lex deep into his hungry mouth, moaning as it hits the back of his throat.

"That's it baby," I grunt out as I fuck his throat, grabbing a fistful of his hair while locking eyes with Bella.

"Take it, all of it."

God my fucking dick in Cade's mouth, absolute fucking heaven every damn time. He knows just what to do to drive me batshit crazy. He picks up his pace, sucking and licking Little Lex until I'm about to lose all sense of control.

"Fuuuuuck, Cade. You feel so good, baby."

He releases my dick to look up at me.

"Missed you too, baby," he says with a wink and that stupid smile I love so much.

He starts to move back down to finish the job, but I grab his shoulders to stop him.

"As much as I love my dick down your greedy little throat, I have another idea I need your help with."

I look down at Bella, spread out, wrecked. I flash her a wicked, predatory grin.

"Hold her arms down for me."

Cade blinks. "Lex?"

I don't break eye contact with her. "Now, Cade."

He laughs, low and amused, but he fucking listens. He grabs both of Bella's wrists, pulls them above her head, and pins them to the mattress. She squirms beneath us, breathless, eyes wide, lips parted like she doesn't know whether to scream at me or beg me to continue.

I thrust back inside her so hard that she winces. I'm all the way in, bottomed the fuck out, buried so deep. Fucking perfect. She gasps, legs wrapping around my waist instinctively.

Cade is still holding her down like the good boy he is. I pound into her relentlessly, dragging her right back to the edge. Her body tightens again, shaking, and I can feel her walls start to flutter around me.

"Lex. Lex, ah I—"

And then I pull out.

Again.

She looks up at me, pupils wide and completely ruined. Completely pissed.

"Bastard," she snaps, trying to catch her breath.

Cade leans down, still holding her by the wrists, and grins with a voice that is all fake concern. "Now sweetheart, be nice."

I stare down at her, chest heaving, cock throbbing, still slick and aching to be back inside where it belongs. "Say you're sorry, Bella," I growl, hands wrapped around her hip, holding her still.

"Are you fucking kidding me right now, Lex?" She glares up at me, eyes flashing with fury. She tries to free her arms, but Cade's grip only tightens.

Good boy.

She rolls her eyes. "Fine. I'm sorry, *Bella*," she says sweetly.

Cade fucking loses it. He starts laughing, hard, head dropping between his shoulders as he tries to catch his breath.

"That's not fucking funny, Cade" I snap, even though my lips twitch.

Cade lifts his head, still grinning. "You had to see that coming." He looks between us, amusement all over his face. "You two are basically the same person."

I narrow my eyes at her. She just bats her lashes and shrugs all innocent.

I reach down and wrap my hand around her throat, cutting off her air. Her eyes snap wide.

Is that fear?

No, of course not. That is fucking lust. Pure, molten, fuck-me-now lust. My baby likes it.

"Say you're sorry."

It's a game now for her. I can see it in her eyes. She doesn't speak. Doesn't even blink. Those gray eyes hold mine just daring me to break first.

"Harder," she whispers.

Fuck me.

"Oh my God." Cade lets go of her wrists, shaking his head like this is the most ridiculous and hottest shit he's ever seen. His ass is mine later for laughing and letting her go, but whatever.

The second he releases her, she moves. Some slick-ass ninja shit. She shifts her hips, flips her body, and suddenly she's on top of me, straddling my thighs like she's been planning this for days.

"Damn, baby," I mutter, half breathless. "Good moves." I narrow my eyes at her. "Like some crazy ass jujitsu shit."

She shrugs and then it hits me.

"Oh hell no." I stare up at her, rage in my eyes. "I swear to God, if that Mortal Kombat Tattooed Dragon-Dick Laing of yours taught you—"

She leans forward, wraps her fingers around my throat and squeezes. Hard. She leans in close. Her lips just above mine, eyes full of smoke and vengeance.

Cade groans from beside us. "Fuck, sweetheart."

"You say anyone's name in this bed other than Cade's or mine," she whispers low, sultry, and sharp enough to scar. Her grip tightens. "And we're gonna have real problems... baby."

Oh, fuck no. She thinks she's in control. Thinks she can climb on top and talk shit without consequences.

Cute. Fucking cute.

"Fuck this," I growl.

I wrap my arms around her waist, shift my hips, and flip her ass right back underneath me where she belongs. Just like it's a goddamn wrestling match.

She squeals, half-shocked, half turned-on, laughing through it like she knows exactly what she just started. I pin her down, one arm on her thigh, the other gripping her wrists above her head, and look down at her, panting.

"Little Miss Controlling Ass thinks she runs the show," I mutter, grinding my cock against her soaked pussy but not slipping in, not yet.

"You got jokes huh, malyshka?"

From the side, Cade's watching, breathless again, smiling like this is the best porn he's ever seen.

Bella looks up at me, unbothered as hell. She tries to sit up, probably to throw another line, maybe wrestle again, who the fuck knows with this girl. But no. Not this time. I shove her back down hard enough to make the mattress groan.

My hand wraps around her throat, tighter this time so I can feel how her pulse spikes beneath my fingers. I thrust back inside her. One brutal, full stroke. She gasps. Her whole body arches off the bed, a choked moan leaving her lips.

I don't stop. I can't. I fuck her hard and relentless. God, it feels so good. So right. Her pussy clamps around me like it's trying to hold me there, like it fucking knows I belong there. She's writhing beneath me, gasping, straining with tears starting to form in the corners of her eyes.

"Lex, oh! Lex!"

Releasing her neck, I slow my rhythm, still deep inside her. Letting her feel it, but not how she wants. Not the way she needs.

Her eyes fly open, wide and confused. "Ah! What the fuck?"

"Say it," I growl.

"Say what?" she barks back

"Say you're sorry for making me ache for you for so goddamn long, and I'll let you fucking come, malyshka."

She looks over at Cade. He laughs and shakes his head. She turns back to me. Her eyes lock on mine.

"Fine!" She rolls her eyes. "I'm sorry," she says with a voice dripping in sarcasm.

"Thank you, malyshka. That's close enough," I say as I snap my hips forward, plunging deep inside her. She moans, back arching, hands gripping Cade's arm. I don't stop.

We move together, grinding and holding eye contact. Trying to brand it into each other.

She's close again, I feel it. The way her legs tense, the way her walls grips my dick like a fucking vice.

"Oh my god, Lex! Baby, I'm gonna come."

"Then fucking do it, malyshka," I snarl. "Come all over my cock."

She wraps he legs around me, digging her heels into my lower spine. She screams. Head thrown back, body shaking, every muscle clenching around me.

"Glaza na menya, malyshka. You know the rules."

She obeys and locks her eyes back on mine as everything inside her shatters.

I lose it.

My vision blurs. I thrust once, twice, three times. I unload inside her with a roar that tears out of my chest. The kind that makes your throat raw and your body collapse.

I slowly pull out, gentler with her this time. Her body shudders beneath me, still twitching with the last waves of pleasure.

I lay down beside her, the adrenaline finally bleeding out of me. I reach for her, arms open, and she doesn't hesitate. My girl melts into me like her body knows exactly where it belongs.

Her head rests against my chest, fingers tracing slow, lazy patterns across my ribs. Like she needs the contact. Needs me.

She throws one leg over mine, anchoring herself to me. And I can feel it, feel her. The proof of what just happened, warm and sticky, leaking out of her and soaking into the sheets. Proof she's ours.

I breathe her in. Her hair. Her skin. The mix of cherry vanilla, sweat, sex, and home. And fuck, I've never felt more whole.

Cade slides in close behind her. One arm drapes over her waist, his face tucked into the back of her neck. She's between us now.

Held. Surrounded. Ours.

Three bodies tangled together.

One fucked-up, beautiful mess.

No words.

No doubts.

Just heavy breaths, full hearts, and sleep that finally comes easy.

The three of us together.
Intertwined.
For fucking ever.

CHAPTER (51)
BELLA
MINE AND ZEKE'S PENTHOUSE
660 DAYS SINCE ZEKE'S DEATH

The keypad blinks back at us just waiting for me to enter four little numbers. My fingers hover over the buttons, but I can't move. I just stare, frozen in place. It's been forever since I've stood here. Since I even looked at this door.

Behind it is everything I've been avoiding. Every memory, every ghost. Every second of my life that shattered the night Zeke didn't come home to me.

"Sweetheart," Cade's voice is soft and gentle. His hand grazes my lower back. "You okay?"

I nod once but it's a lie. My fingers tremble as I reach for the first number. I pull back, shake my hands, flex my fingers, and try to muster up some shred of confidence to hit the buttons.

I look up and shake my head. "I thought I was," I whisper. "But this... this feels like opening a tomb."

Lex steps beside me, broad and silent. His eyes scan the hallway and then land on me. "We don't have to go in. Not if it's too much, baby."

"No. I need to."

Lex kisses the back of my neck. "We've got you, baby. All the way through."

I inhale deep. Then slowly put my finger on the keypad and enter the code.

Beep-beep.

Beep-beep.

I press the door open and take a step inside. It looks the same as the day I left.

We walk in slow silence across the dark wooden floors. My fingers trail the edge of the kitchen counter as my eyes scan everything. The spiral staircase that leads up to our bedrooms. The oversized couch. The coffee mug still on the end table. Time never moved here.

It just froze.

I drift toward the couch, spotting the plush blanket I left crumpled there that last night. I pick it up, press it to my face, and close my eyes. I bite the inside of my cheek hard, willing myself not to fall apart. Not yet.

But then I see it. The fireplace mantle and the photo still resting there. It's a picture of me and Zeke. Smiling and happy after a Homecoming halftime show when I danced for the Vixens. His arm is slung over my shoulder, mine around his waist, like we belonged together in every lifetime.

Brother and sister.

Best friends.

Family.

"I can't do this," I say under my breath.

I turn away, eyes burning and walk straight to the window. Seeing the view, our view breaks me in half. I can't contain it anymore and drop to my knees. The blanket slips from my hands as I cover my face and sob, raw and silent like my lungs don't work. Grief eating me alive from the inside out.

Warmth washes over me as Cade crouches behind me. His hand is on my back, voice low and tender as his words tremble. "If I could take this pain from you, I would. Every ounce of it."

Lex moves with quiet strength, his arms slipping around me. "Come here, baby," he murmurs. He lifts me up, holding me like a baby, and carries me to the couch. Easing me down into his lap, he tucks me into his chest and holds me.

There, surrounded by the two men I love, I shatter completely. For the first time since I left this place, I let myself grieve. And it hits like a tsunami crashing into a quiet village. No warning or protection. Just total and inescapable devastation.

I wipe my eyes, still sniffling, voice hoarse. "Thank you," I whisper. "For being here with me."

Lex presses a kiss to the top of my head, his arms tightening like he never plans to let go. "Always, baby," he says. "Even if we have to hold you through hell, we'll be right here."

Cade slides closer, his hand brushing mine. "You're not alone anymore, sweetheart," he says quietly. "You never have to carry this grief by yourself again. You've got both of us for every heartbreak, for every tomorrow."

"I love you both so much."

"We love you too, baby." Lex says softly.

"Always," Cade adds.

When I finally start to breathe, I turn my head toward the window, eyes tracing the skyline. "I really did love it here. Not at first, though. I gave Zeke a hard time. I was a bratty fourteen-year-old when we got here. Called it Gotham Tower."

I let out a soft, shaky laugh. "He hated it when I said shit like that. Said this place was a fortress, not a comic book lair. But he was kind of a Batman. Always watching. Always protecting. Always one step ahead."

Lex's hand rubs slow circles on my back. "Sounds like he was a hell of a big brother," he says, voice low and steady.

"He was," I whisper. "Do you guys want me to show you around?"

"Of course," Cade says as takes my hand to his mouth and kisses it softly.

I show them around. I point out the built-in espresso bar and the fingerprint-secured wine cabinet armory.

"Tex called it multi-functional," I say dryly.

Lex barks a laugh, "We're totally putting one of these downstairs."

We step out onto the rooftop terrace and I pause for a second, breathing it in. The view, the breeze, the skyline, it's all exactly as I remember it. But nothing hits me quite like walking into my room.

Cade's the first to speak, voice low and full of wonder. "It's beautiful..."

His artist eyes sweep over everything. The soft lighting, the layered textures, the hand-painted mural stretching across the entire back wall. Razorback Stadium. Every seat, every shadow, every blade of grass. Perfect.

"The detail," he says as his eyes scan the mural. "It's like we're standing on the field."

I nod, arms wrapping around myself. "It was my favorite place in the world."

"You used to talk about it all the time. The chants, the way the air smelled before kickoff."

A soft laugh escapes me. "And how I swore the 50-yard line had magic in it."

My throat tightens. "Zeke had it painted for me when we moved here. Said if I couldn't go back, he'd bring it to me instead."

We all go quiet. Just breathing it in.

DING.

NATE: Krolek is stateside.

Lex is already watching me, his body on alert. "What is it?"

I turn the screen toward him.

Cade straightens. "What's going on?"

"You sure you want to see the other side of me?"

DING.

@LucaWasHere
So, the princess crawled back to her knights, I see.
Two blades at her side, swearing loyalty.
One paints her grief, while Lexie breaks bone.
But neither of them know she dies alone.

So kiss your boys and play pretend,
But I'm the start. I'll be the end.
Mine in madness, mine in flame.
And when I come? You'll moan my name.

"Goddamn, I thought we were done with this asshole."

Lex grabs his phone from his pocket and fires back a message. "Fuck this shit. If he wants to play poet, so can I."

@BarinovUnhinged
You talk like a poet. You stalk like a ghost.
But behind that screen, you're all empty boast.
You watched? Congrats. That's all you'll do.
Because while you hide, I'll protect her too.

We don't run scared. We don't play games.
And when we move? We don't miss names.
So keep typing, creep. You're not that clever.
Step any closer and I'll end this forever.

He hits send. "There. Take that, Dr. Seuss." Lex turns to me, fire in his eyes. "Forget him, baby. We've got bigger shit to deal with. Girls to save, an op to plan. Let's go."

CHAPTER ⑤②
CADE
DITMAS PARK, BROOKLYN
667 DAYS SINCE ZEKE'S DEATH

The mansion looks untouched. Like someone packed a suitcase and vanished. Perched on a wide, tree-lined street in Ditmas Park, the house is stately and pristine—fresh paint, manicured hedges, iron gate still working.

"This place just foreclosed a couple weeks ago," Knox mutters from the van, fingers flying over the keyboard. "Bank never even changed the locks."

He zooms in on a floor plan glowing across the screens. A four-story Victorian dream turned nightmare. Still fully furnished. Perfect cover.

"Tex is in position," Knox says, tone clipped. "Laing, Bella, you're clear to enter. Remember, Krolek thinks this is his chance to move up in the world. He's looking to supply your clubs, so play it smooth."

Nate chimes in, "Bella, make it clear you're asking for a sample of the girls. We still don't know where he's keeping them, so don't pull the trigger unless you have eyes."

Knox exhales into the mic, the calm before the storm. "Keep it sexy. Convincing."

We're watching from the van parked three houses down, hidden under a veil of shadows and outdated neighborhood neglect. Lex leans forward in his seat, jaw tight, eyes locked on the tablet like he could burn a hole straight through the screen.

"I fucking hate this part of the job," he growls low, voice strained. "It's bullshit that I couldn't go in there with her but Mortal fucking Kombat can. I swear to God if Dragon-Dick so much as—"

"Drop it Lex," Nate pipes up, clearly annoyed with our presence.

"Did you just say Dragon-Dick?" Knox laughs.

"If the name fucking fits."

"They're in," Nate says, completely ignoring Lex and Knox's banter.

In the weeks I was gone, Lex didn't just stick around. He carved out a place in Bella's world like he'd always belonged there. Like he was built for it.

He's practically part of The Trifecta family now. Ellie and Haley laugh at his jokes as if he's always been in the group. Knox calls him ride or die. Coach Javi trusts him with lighting cues and drills. Rico even tosses him fabric swatches for costume input. The crowds love him. The girls love him more.

And Bella looks at him as if he's gravity.

But what kills me most is that he's been on multiple Project Dylan missions. Missions where he got to see her at her fiercest. Not just dancing or teasing or breaking hearts, but burning the whole world down to save the innocent. Leading. Commanding. Conquering.

He watched her walk through hell and drag light out of it.

And I missed it. I missed her. The real her. The one who doesn't flinch. The one who carries scars and still fights like the world's worth saving.

Lex got to stand in the glow. He got to hold that flame.

I look at the screen, Bella and Laing are in the entry way of the mansion. She's breathtaking. Her dress is sculpted elegance and danger sewn in black satin. Strapless with a slit that cuts nearly to her hip. It fits like it was poured onto her. The fabric catches the soft hallway light and turns it into something sinful—shadows and shine tracing the curves of her body with every step. A damn weapon dressed for war.

Laing's right beside her, looking just as sharp. Sleek dark suit, perfectly tailored, no tie, and shirt unbuttoned just enough to flash that damn dragon tattoo on his chest like he's proud of it. And he should be, I guess. The guy's infuriatingly good-looking.

And yet all I see are his fingers anchored to the small of her back, pressing just a little too low. Too territorial and intimate. Like he's earned the right to touch her like that.

He hasn't.

I can appreciate a beautiful man. I'm an artist, I get it. But the second he forgets where he stands, I'll happily remind him.

Lex mutters beside me. "Fucking Mortal Kombat-ass prick."

Knox glances up from the screens.

"You good?"

"No," Lex growls. "He touches her like that again—"

"Not the time," I cut in. But my voice is tight as well, because it's not just Lex losing his composure. Being forced to watch the woman we love play pretend in a way that makes my skin crawl is almost enough to make me lose mine too.

She approaches the man at the center of it all, Krolek. Tall, late fifties, slick gray suit and a shark smile. He's holding a glass of something expensive, surrounded by men who look exactly like him. All masks and monsters.

"Please," Krolek gestures to the leather chairs next to him. "Sit."

Laing drops into one of the oversized armchairs and pulls Bella down onto his lap like it's her rightful place. My stomach twists.

Krolek leans forward, swirling his drink with lazy curiosity. "Laing Wei. All the way from Hong Kong. Now how the hell did you manage to land a piece of ass like this for a wife?"

Laing gives a modest shrug and runs his hand up Bella's bare thigh, squeezing as he gets to the top of the slit in her dress. "I just got lucky," he says. "But truth is, she found me in one of her clubs in San Francisco."

Lex stiffens beside me.

Laing continues, his tone smooth, casual, and way too damn convincing. "One of her girls was giving me a dance, but I couldn't keep my eyes off her. This sexy thing was over there at the bar drinking with some Russian prick."

Lex's fists slam against his thighs. "Motherf—"

Knox elbows him hard. "Cut it out. It's part of the plan. Krolek's Polish, he hates Russians. That line just bought us credibility. It's not a pissing contest."

Bella laughs softly, tilting her head toward him like it's a fond memory. "Baby, I've told you a million times. It was just business."

"Business or not, he was touching what I wanted and I couldn't have it." Laing slides his hand up her back and curls his fingers into the back of her neck, dragging her down to him and kisses her. Not a peck. A full-on, open-mouthed, possessive-as-hell kiss that sends Lex surging up in his seat like he's ready to tear through the van wall.

"Don't," I warn, grabbing his arm.

"I will kill him," he growls. "I will fucking kill him."

Back inside, Bella finally pulls back, her lips still parted, gaze lazy and dangerous. "We're absolutely crazy for each other," she purrs as her hand trails across Laing's chest.

Lex looks like he's about to have an aneurysm burst.

"After San Francisco, we expanded. Three exclusive clubs right here in the city. All of them discreet, profitable, and dripping in indulgence."

She gives a slow and sinful smile, the kind that melts resistance and commands attention.

"Think of The Obsidian... only with better dancers, higher stakes, and pleasures most men don't even know they need, until we show them."

Laing's hand slides up and down her thigh. He leans in, mouth brushing her ear. "That's right, baby," his voice low and filled with heat. "They come once and then they always come back for more."

Bella laughs and tilts her head, giving him access to her throat. He takes it, lips brushing her neck in a way that feels far too real for comfort. My fists tighten and the pressure in my jaw could cut diamonds in half.

She leans toward Krolek, just enough for him to get a perfect view down her dress. "We're hosting a private party for our most elite clients next month. All we're missing..." Her cherry-red lips part, voice sultry. "...are the right girls."

She doesn't sound like Bella. She sounds like the woman monsters trust.

Over the comms, Tex crackles in, amused. *"It's working. I can see the fucker's dick getting hard from here. She's almost got him."*

Lex mutters from beside me, clearly over this, "God I hate this fucking van."

I glance over, then back at the screen. "She's got this," I say tightly, though it's more for my own reassurance than his. Because right now, I don't know what's worse. Watching Bella become someone so terrifyingly seductive or knowing her and Laing play this part a little too well.

"I can get you the girls," Krolek says, his Polish accent curling around every word. "You tell me what you like. Age. Look. Temperament. I will make it happen. Quickly."

Laing nods, smooth as ever. "Perfect." He leans back and grins. "We are, however, looking for a very specific flavor."

He glances at Bella, eyes gleaming. "My lovely bride here has high standards for our clubs. Before we make any kind of commitment, she'll need a little preview. A sample. Just to make sure the product matches the price."

"Ah, of course. I understand completely."

He turns, barking something in Polish to the man near the door. The command is short, clipped, and efficient. The man nods once, then mutters into a walkie.

A minute passes before the far door creaks open.

Five girls step in. They can't be older than nineteen. Most are probably closer to sixteen. All of them are dressed as if they've been shoved through a glam factory—cocktail dresses, sky-high stilettos, glossy curls and makeup applied to hide the fear in their faces. But it's still there. In the eyes. Hollow. Haunted.

They line up like inventory.

Krolek gestures toward them with a grand sweep of his hand. "Please. Inspect."

Bella elegantly stands. Laing joins her. Together they walk the line, her hand brushing his chest like they're at some sick designer showcase.

"What the hell is going on?" I whisper.

"She's inspecting them," Knox replies. "Making sure they fit her brand. She's not Bella right now, Cade. She's a goddamn madame."

Bella pauses halfway down the row. Turns to Laing. "Sit."

He drops back into his seat without a word.

"Good boy." She winks, which earns her a chuckle out of Krolek.

She turns to a tall brunette in a hot pink dress. "You. Come here."

The girl hesitates. Eyes flick to Bella, then Laing, then to Krolek. Her lip trembles.

She doesn't move. So, Bella does instead.

SMACK.

The slap echoes through the mansion. Gasps fill the van.

"Keep it cool," Knox growls. "It's all part of the plan. She has to sell it."

Bella straightens, expression unreadable. Her tone, however, is razor-sharp. "I thought you said your girls were well-trained. Obedient." She tosses a cold glare at Krolek. "This one clearly is defective."

Krolek chuckles, the sound oily and smug. "She's new." He tips his glass again, eyes dragging across Bella like she's the main course on his menu. "She just needs a little discipline."

"I don't tolerate disobedience in my clubs," she says towards the brunette.

"But when you behave, we reward you very well," Laing adds with a wink and a sleazy grin toward the girls.

Some of them start to tremble.

"Dragon-dick creep," Lex whispers under his breath.

Bella steps away from the brunette and stops in front of a blonde in a green strapless dress. "Open your mouth."

The girl obeys. Bella crouches slightly, inspecting her teeth with a practiced eye.

"Honey, come here."

Laing rises and wraps himself around her waist from behind, his chin brushing her shoulder. "What do you think, baby?" He says as he kisses her cheek.

Bella hums like she's admiring art. "I like these four."

She nods down the line. "The bitch up front needs to be taught some manners."

She flashes Krolek a tight smile.

"Good thing your good at getting bad girls to behave, baby," she says as she turns and wraps her arms around Laing's neck pulling him down for a kiss. Its sweet, intimate. Annoying as hell.

"We'll take them."

Krolek grins clearly thinking he just sealed a deal with the devil. "Perfect."

"Laing," Bella says sweetly, still wrapped in Laing's arms. "Can you call Kenji and have him come grab the girls while we finish up?"

"Sure thing, baby." Laing presses a kiss to her forehead before pulling out his phone. He walks casually toward the front hall, speaking in soft Mandarin.

A few seconds later, another man enters. Early thirties, sharply dressed, sunglasses still on despite the dim lighting inside the mansion. He gives a curt nod.

"You five," Bella calls to the girls. "Go with Kenji to the car. We'll finish up here and be out soon."

They follow him in a line. Cows to the slaughter.

"If they give you any lip Kenji," Bella adds, all sugar and sadism. "Feel free to break them in."

My gut twists. I know it's an act. I know it's part of the plan, but hearing her talk like that, watching her play this role, it hits somewhere deep. This is the world she had to learn to survive in. This is the darkness that she had to hide from every night.

Bella and Laing return to Krolek, calm and composed like they just stepped out of a boardroom instead of a trafficking transaction.

"Now, where were we?" Krolek says, licking his bottom lip like a goddamn predator.

"We'll need at least fifteen girls per club," Bella says, her voice low and authoritative. "Three clubs in New York, one in San Francisco. Let's start there for now."

Krolek grins. "That's a lot of pussy, sweetheart. But for you?" He leans back with a sleazy chuckle. "Anything."

"*Girls are secured,*" Kenji says through the comms.

"Bella," Knox says into the mic. "The girls are safe. It's showtime."

"Showtime?" I whisper under my breath.

Bella doesn't miss a beat. "So, Krolek," she says. "I know it's a strange question, but I'm always a little skeptical in my line of work. Comes with the territory, I guess."

She tilts her glass, eyes on him. "I like to know who I'm doing business with. Personality type, behavioral patterns, how likely someone is to stab me in the back once the deal closes."

Krolek chuckles politely, still trying to place her.

"So... what's your sign?"

He blinks, confused. Bella just flashes that razor-edged kind of smile that says she's already won and he just hasn't realized it yet.

"I don't actually believe in horoscopes," she continues, idly twisting the diamond ring on her finger. "I just think it's fascinating how people see themselves. What mask they choose to wear."

She lets the silence stretch. Lets him squirm. "Go on," she coaxes softly. "Indulge me."

Next to me, Lex mutters under his breath, "Jesus Christ, she's terrifying."

He's not wrong, but fuck, I've never loved her more.

Krolek finally laughs, forced and brittle. "Cancer," he says, raising his glass. "Emotional. Loyal. Sensitive." He smirks. "Or so they say."

Bella tilts her head, eyes glittering. "Cancer," she echoes. "So deep down, you're just a soft little crab with a hard shell and mommy issues?"

His smile falters. "I prefer protective."

"Mmhmm." Her voice purrs like silk over a knife's edge. "Cancers always do."

He narrows his eyes, intrigued despite himself. "And you?" he asks. "What's your sign?"

Bella leans back, gaze unflinching. A slow, knowing smile curves her lips.

"Scorpio."

The word barely leaves her mouth before the shot cracks through the comms. Krolek stiffens—eyes wide, glass shattering from his hand—then drops face-first onto the marble floor.

"Damn, Tex. The throat, that's brutal!" Lex says with admiration.

One of Krolek's guards reaches for his gun.

BANG.

He drops before he can aim. The other guard shot him. Why? I have no idea. He then lowers his weapon and says something in Polish to the rest of the room. The other men freeze, get to their knees, and put their hands in the air.

Thank you, Piotr," Bella says.

The man nods.

"Nate, get Piotr out of here. Tex, beautiful shooting, as always. Laing honey, tie them up. Knox, I'm coming out."

And just like that, Bella returns. No more deep-voiced seductress. No more calculated madame. Just her. the girl who destroys monsters for a living. And I've never seen anyone more terrifying or more breathtaking in my life.

CHAPTER ⑤③
BELLA
DITMAS PARK, BROOKLYN
667 DAYS SINCE ZEKE'S DEATH

The night air hits me like a slap to the face. My heels scrape against the stone as I step off the porch and make my way toward the black SUV parked by the curb. Kenji stands watch by the front, arms folded and eyes scanning the street like he's waiting for war.

I open the door slowly. The brunette I had to slap recoils so hard she nearly hits her head on the window. Her eyes are wide and terrified. She curls her shoulders inward bracing for another hit.

"Hey," I say softly. "It's okay. You're okay. What's your name?"

She doesn't move. Just stares at me confused and scared. "Lilly," she says so quietly I barely hear it.

"I'm sorry I had to hit you, Lilly," I tell her, crouching down a little, lowering my voice like I would for a child. "We had to sell it. Krolek had to believe that I wanted to buy you. The whole thing was just an act."

Lilly's brow furrows. "What do you mean?"

"I mean we're not who you think we are. My name is Bella and we're here to get you home. All of you."

There's a long pause. Then one of the other girls, a redhead in a silver dress, starts crying. Big, gulping sobs that she tries to hold in with the back of her hand. Another follows, clinging to her friend like she might collapse.

"You're safe now," I whisper. "I promise."

I glance back at the house. Tex is already sweeping the scene. Knox's van is pulling up behind us, headlights off so the girls stay calm.

"I need you to get out of the car," I tell the girls gently. "We're going to have to get your information so we can find your families. We've got a change clothes for you, water, blankets, whatever you need."

They don't move right away. So, I offer a hand to the Lilly. She hesitates at first but then takes it.

"Look," I say, nodding over my shoulder as the black van rolls to a stop beside us. "That's our team. You're not alone anymore. We're going to get you girls home."

By the time I get the girls out of the SUV, Nate and Knox are walking up to us with duffel bags of clothes, bottles of water, and blankets.

Knox sets the bag down and looks at me. "You ok, Bells?"

"Yeah, this is Lilly. Lilly this is Knox and this is Nate. They are going to get you all taken care of. They'll help you find your families."

The girls behind me nod and Lilly smiles.

I walk away, the pressure of the night starting to build. The slap, the feel of Laing's hands on me, the things I had to say. The show I had to put on. The kill shot. All of it starts to crash down on my chest like a weight I can't breathe under.

And then there's Cade. He saw it all. Every calculated move. Every lie. Every seductive word that wasn't me.

My hands begin to shake.

I look up and see them. Lex is already moving fast. I pick up my pace until I'm practically crashing into him. He scoops me up, wrapping one arm around my waist, and the other cradling the back of my head.

"Are you okay, baby?"

"No." The word comes out hoarse. "I hated being the one to put fear in those girls' eyes. When I opened the van door, the way they looked at me. The way she flinched? All I could see was me flinching from Carlos's belt in Miami."

The pressure rises again and my hands start to shake harder. I can't stop them.

"Baby," Lex whispers, catching them, pulling them to his chest. His ice-blue eyes lock with mine. "You saved them. That's all that matters."

Behind him, Cade stands silent, watching. The worry crawling up my spine sharpens. He hasn't said a word, just stands there taking it all in.

Tears burn behind my eyes. Fear coils tight in my ribs. The

fear that he'll walk away again. That seeing this version of me, the one Lex has already made peace with, will be too much for him.

But he doesn't move away. He steps forward and reaches out his hand. When I place my hand in Cade's, his breath catches. Then he pulls me in and slides one hand to the back of my neck and crashes his lips against mine.

He finally pulls back and presses his lips to my temple. "I love you, sweetheart."

The breath I didn't realize I'd been holding slips out of me in a shudder.

"I love you too," I whisper into his chest.

"You were extraordinary."

My lips part, but no sound comes out.

"Lex was right when he said he didn't need to tell me about all of this," he says. "He was right that I needed to see it with my own eyes. And what I saw tonight, it wrecked me. In the best way."

He cups my cheek, his thumb brushing along my skin with a gentleness that breaks me even further.

"I used to think the line between darkness and light was something you had to pick a side on. But you move between them like you were born to. You walk into shadows and come back with the broken. You turn pain into power. Grief into justice."

Footsteps crunch behind us. Laing strolls toward us like he didn't just spend the last hour with his hands all over me, playing a role only one of us enjoyed a little too much.

"Dragon motherfucking," Lex growls. Then hauls off and punches Laing straight in the face.

"Lex!" I gasp.

Cade yanks me into him just as Laing stumbles back, a hand to his jaw. But he doesn't fight back.

"Nah, it's okay, Iz."

He winces slightly but gives Lex a nod. "I deserved that."

Red and blue lights flicker at the end of the road. Laing glances back at them, then turns to us one last time. "That's my cue," he laughs, gesturing to the car that Kenji is already sliding into. Laing winks, lip bleeding just a little. "Try not to miss me too much."

"You feel better?" I ask.

"Not even close, baby," Lex says as he wraps an arm around my shoulders.

"Menace," Cade mumbles.

"You love me. Both of you." Lex says, pressing a kiss to the top of my head.

We walk toward the line of police cruisers. The flashing red and blue lights casts our shadows in a purple hue across the pavement. Lex's arm is still wrapped around my shoulders, his thumb absently brushing against my collarbone like he's trying to soothe the weight of everything we just did. Cade walks on my other side, close but silent. His hand grazes mine every so often like he's not sure if I need space or anchoring.

One of the NYPD officers is talking to Lilly, she's nodding her head to his questions. He looks up and we make eye contact.

There is an instant familiarity about him I just can't shake.

The way he stands.

His emerald green eyes.

His dark hair is streaked with gray, but then I see it.

The scar curling down on his left forearm.

The scar he would never talk about.

"Bella?!" he shouts.

"Oh my God." I whisper.

"Bella! Oh my God! Bella!" Completely forgetting about Lilly, he sprints to me.

"Baby, who is that?"

I drop Lex's arm and take off running. We collide halfway across the sidewalk, crashing into each other like we've waited a lifetime for this moment. His arms lock around me with bone-crushing strength and we fall to our knees in the grass.

I'm sobbing. He's sobbing.

His badge digs into my shoulder, his gun belt bruises my hip, but it doesn't bother me. I'd take a thousand bruises to be here in this moment, safe in the arms of the man who helped raise me. The man who loved me like his own.

"You're okay," he chokes, pulling back to frame my face with shaking hands. "Jesus, Bella, I thought we lost you. I thought—"

"I missed you so much." I nod through my tears. "But, I couldn't risk looking, there's a lot you don't know... and I-I didn't know if you were still—"

"We never stopped looking," he says. "Never. We tried to find you, Sugar Bear. They said you were placed in the southeast, but everything went dark after that. I didn't know where to start."

I sob harder, clutching his jacket like I'm ten years old again.

Behind us, Lex and Cade stand frozen. Watching us and confused as hell. I don't care, because for the first time in years, part of me feels like that little girl again.

The one who used to ride on Uncle Jack's shoulders through Razorback Stadium on game days.

CHAPTER ⑤④
L E X
K I N G S L E Y   F I E L D
W E X L E Y   U N I V E R S I T Y
ABOUT TO WATCH OUR GIRL KILL IT!
675 DAYS SINCE ZEKE'S DEATH

The crowd's already loud and the game hasn't even started. I lean forward in my seat on the front row, arms resting on the steel barrier as I watch the chaos unfold below. The Wexley Wolves haven't taken the field yet but the real show's already begun.

The Trifecta.

They're lined up in front of the student section, posing for photos like goddamn celebrities, and honestly, they might as well be.

Little girls in mini Trifecta shirts bounce on their toes, ponytails flying, glittered cheeks catching the light. One's holding a sign that says, *I wanna be Bella when I grow up,* and I swear, my heart does a weird fucking thing in my chest.

Because there she is.

My girl.

Laughing, radiant, and absolutely untouchable in her black and burgundy Trifecta uniform. Signing autographs with that signature smile, crouching down to pose with a group of middle schoolers, then standing and tossing her hair like the main character in every fantasy I've ever had.

She's safe. She's smiling. After everything she just did. After everything we all just went through. She should be wrecked, but somehow, she's right here stronger than ever. And now, she's got family back in her corner.

Uncle Jack showed up like a ghost from the past and changed everything. They've had lunch a few times, catching up. She told him about her life and I can tell it's been good for her.

It was hard on the guy, especially since his wife died a few years back. I don't know the whole story, I don't need to. All I care about is that she's got another family member back.

He knows about why Henry can't come to her performances. Vince and all that shit. It killed him. Apparently, he and Henry are still pretty tight. Jack was hurt that Henry never told him about their reunion at Bella's high school graduation, but he understood in the end.

He is the reason for all the NYPD presence at the field tonight. Something about protecting his Sugar Bear, which is adorable.

Tried to call her that the other night while I was balls-deep and feeling sentimental. Let's just say she throat-punched me mid-orgasm.

Lesson learned.

Cade's beside me, drink in hand and looking just as obsessed as I feel. I glance over at him. He catches me looking, lifts his chin in that quiet way he does, and interlocks his fingers in mine.

She finally breaks from the crowd, waving to a few more people yelling her name like she's the goddamn quarterback instead of the girl who's about to steal the halftime show. She gives a little finger wave and a wink to some frat guy in a Wexley jersey, then rolls her eyes when he stumbles into his friend trying to blow her a kiss.

My fucking girl.

She makes her way toward us, hips swaying, that show-day glow still clinging to her skin. Then she drops herself right onto my lap. One arm around my shoulders, the other hand still clutching a Sharpie like she's ready to sign my damn soul next.

She kisses me. Not a peck. Not some PG, camera-safe shit. No, this is slow, teasing, and deep enough to make my pulse glitch and my brain short-circuit. By the time she pulls back, I'm already gripping her thighs just trying to remember what oxygen is.

She looks at me like she knows exactly what she just did. The little tease. Eyes lit up, smile wicked and sweet all at once.

I drag my hands up her thighs and over her waist. "You kiss every fan like that, or am I just the lucky bastard in the front row?"

"Just you," she whispers, smirking. "Though one kid said if I kissed him, he'd get his dad to buy me a beer."

I bark out a laugh, tilt my head, and give her a look that says *don't test me.*

"Tempting offer," I say, sliding my hand a little higher. "But if his old man shows up with that beer, he's losing a few teeth."

She grins. "Jealous much?"

"Always, baby," I admit, grinning back. "It's part of my charm."

She turns her attention to Cade and before the poor bastard can even say hi, she leans in and kisses him too like she's grounding herself in him.

Cade grips the edge of his seat as if he's not sure if he wants to stay upright or drag her ass straight into his lap. Can't say I'd blame him if he did.

"Hey," she says, brushing her nose against his like they're the only two people here. "Missed you."

"Not possible," he breathes back.

The guy fucking melts. Right there. Right in front of me. His whole face softens like she just flipped a switch inside him.

Bella lights up instantly as Savannah and Clay slide into the row behind us. Savannah wraps her arms around Bella's shoulders from behind and gives her a tight squeeze.

"Sweetheart, that outfit is dangerous," she teases, flicking the end of Bella's burgundy crop top. "One more inch and half the student section would've passed out."

Bella grins, tossing a wink over her shoulder. "Just wait 'til you see the other ones. Rico went crazy for tonight."

Clay huffs out a low laugh. "And here I thought this was a football game, not a fashion show."

"There's a little bit of that too, Dad," Bella jokes, nudging her knee against mine.

She says it so easily—*Dad*—like it's always been his name. I'm not mad. Not at her. Clay and Savannah gave her a home when no one else did. But it still hits somewhere low in my chest. A quiet reminder that she's woven into Cade's world in a way I'll never be.

Bella turns to me, resting her chin on my shoulder. "Wait, I thought your dad was coming?"

"He is," I say, pulling my phone from my pocket and checking a text. "He's trying to find a parking spot. Last I heard he was stuck behind a beer truck full of Row boys tailgating like it's the damn Super

Bowl."

Bella laughs, but there's a flicker of worry in her eyes. "I'm kind of nervous to meet him."

"Baby, he's gonna love you. Trust me."

She opens her mouth to protest, but I cut her off before the spiral can start.

"My dad's the good one," I say with a grin. "He loves three things in life—classic architecture, high-stakes poker, and sexy women who are smarter than him."

I shoot her a look, cocky as hell. "You're all three, baby. Built like a masterpiece, impossible to read, and guaranteed to ruin him."

She laughs but I can tell she's still overthinking.

"He's cool," I say more gently. "Way cooler than I deserve. Mom couldn't make it tonight. Something about a meeting with my uncle, which is most likely Bratva code for selling a missile system to a dictator with a yacht."

Bella snorts, her body relaxing against mine. "Great. Can't wait for that family dinner."

"Hey," I say, curling my arms tighter around her waist. "You've survived shootouts, CIA-grade ops, Laing, and Fight Night, baby. You can handle my dad. He's just... human."

My thumb drags lazy circles over her thigh. "You weren't this nervous meeting Cade's parents."

"That's because she met my parents when she was a teenager," Cade says, sipping his beer. "Back before she was dancing in outfits that could get her arrested in half the country."

He shoots her a look. "Speaking of getting arrested, remember when you and Ellie accidentally ended up in Canada?"

Bella bites her lip, trying not to laugh. "It was supposed to be a road trip to Buffalo."

I raise a brow, grinning. "You crossed into Canada by accident, baby?"

"They didn't even realize until customs had them detained," Cade says, shaking his head. "Two teenage girls, zero map skills, and a trunk full of snacks like they were prepping for a zombie apocalypse."

Bella shrugs, pure mischief. "We made it back."

"Barely," Cade says. "My parents were losing their minds and you were like, 'but the maple syrup was worth it.'"

"Zeke almost killed me that weekend."

Two quick beeps crackle in our ears. *Walkies live.*

Knox's voice comes through, crisp and controlled. *"Mic check, everyone."*

"Hugh?"

"Everything's good up here in the booth, Knox," Hugh replies, already half distracted by his soundboard.

"Javi?"

"Claro, mi amor. And if anyone ruins my formation tonight, I swear to God, I'll retire mid-routine."

Knox snorts. *"Lex?"*

"Present, Bestie."

"Cade?"

"All good."

"Josh?"

"Ready and caffeinated."

"Sam?"

"Yep. Let's go make 'em sweat."

"Drake?"

"Yo. Been ready for hours."

Knox's tone shifts, more playful. *"Hales?"*

"Yes, lover," Haley purrs through the mic.

"Ellie?"

"Ready!" she chirps cheerfully.

Knox pauses, the smirk in his voice audible. *"Problem Child?"*

"Yes, Knox," Bella deadpans, rolling her eyes even though he can't see it.

"Alright, girls," Knox says, clapping once. "Stretch it out, shake it off, and make 'em remember tonight."

A single beep cuts through the line. *Earpieces off.* Showtime.

Bella rises, adjusting her top as she stands between us. She leans down first to Cade, brushing a kiss against his lips, slow and sweet, the kind of kiss that lingers in your bloodstream.

"Wish me luck."

"You don't need it, sweetheart."

Then she turns to me. I grab her waist before she can even lean down and pull her in for a kiss that's a little longer, a little deeper. She tastes like cherry gloss and adrenaline.

"Stretch good, baby," I growl against her mouth. "I'll be watching every damn move."

She grins, pulls back just enough to wink at both of us, then spins on her heel and jogs toward the sideline where Ellie and Haley are already starting warm-ups.

Josh is down on one knee beside her now, helping her stretch out her hamstrings. Bella's flat on her back, one leg extended while he gently pushes the other toward her chest. She's talking to him, smiling, laughing, and totally relaxed. One hand's on her calf. His other one moving way too high up her thigh.

I shift in my seat.

Cade side-eyes me. "Don't start."

"I'm not," I lie.

Josh adjusts her leg and she winces, biting her lip. He says something that makes her laugh again, and my jaw tightens so hard I hear it click.

Yeah. I'm definitely starting. But before I can stand, I hear a familiar voice behind me.

"Jesus, Lex. You'd think the Bills were playing here tonight."

I turn just as my dad walks down the steps toward us, looking like he just stepped out of a Manhattan architect's boardroom instead of pulling up to a college football game. Black button-down with sleeves rolled to the elbows, sunglasses tucked into the neck of his shirt, designer messenger bag slung over one shoulder like he didn't just spend twenty minutes circling for parking.

"Hey, Dad," I say, standing just long enough to pull him into a quick hug.

"Cade." He nods. "Good to see you again, son."

"You too, Daniel," Cade replies with a respectful smile.

Dad drops into the seat beside me and glances around the packed stadium. "This place is a damn zoo. How many people go to this school?"

Cade shrugs. "Not this many. They're not just here for football."

He nods. "Right. You said your girl's dancing tonight. So where is she?"

I point toward the field. "Right there, Dad. The one on her back being stretched out by Captain Too-Happy-With-His-Hands."

He follows my gaze. "Damn, men. Your girl's hot."

"Mmhmm," I nod, eyes still locked on her. "Black hair, long legs, cherry-red lipstick. A goddamn dream."

We watch her for a beat in silence. She looks over and catches us staring. Her eyes land on me first and then slide to the man sitting beside me. I can see it instantly, the flicker of nerves across her face. She tries to smile, but it falters at the edges. Still, she gives us a little wave.

I raise my hand in return, giving her the softest look I can manage, silently telling her she's okay. That we're right here.

She looks back at Josh and says something I can't hear. And yeah, I'm still watching his hands. But now I'm watching hers too, and I see that little tremble in her fingers.

"She nervous?" Dad asks, softer now.

"Yeah, first time meeting you has got her twisted up."

He exhales slowly. "She's got nothing to worry about."

"You'll like her," I say without looking at him. "But she's been through hell, Dad. And somehow, she's still soft. Still fire. Still standing."

He places a hand on my shoulder and gives it a firm squeeze. "Good. You two deserve a girl like that."

I feel the tightness in my chest ease. Even though I still want to break Josh's fingers.

Dad leans forward, elbows on his knees, eyes scanning the field like he's trying to understand what all the fuss is about. "So explain this to me," he says, nodding toward the cluster of girls stretching near the end zone. "What makes their dances so special? I mean, don't get me wrong, I'm all for tight uniforms and a little choreography, but this... this feels different."

"It is," I say, already half-smiling. "This isn't just cheer or dance. It's a performance. A full-blown production. Think halftime at the Super Bowl meets a damn Broadway show."

Cade chuckles. "He's not exaggerating."

He points again, this time at the three girls in different crop tops. "Why do those three look different from the rest?"

"Because they are different," Cade says. "That's The Trifecta."

Dad raises a brow. "Sounds like a great bourbon."

"Sounds like trouble," I add with a grin. "But nah, it's Bella, Ellie, and Haley. Coach Javi started grouping them together their freshman year and couldn't separate them after that. They've got chemistry no one else can touch."

"They choreograph most of their own routines now," Cade adds. "They draw crowds to practices and trend online every time they perform. There's a reason the rest of the team wears matching basic gear and the three of them have their own. They've basically become their own brand around here."

"They're not just dancers," I say. "They're the act. Legacy's the team, but The Trifecta's the show."

He watches for a beat, then leans back in his seat. "Damn. No wonder you look like you're ready to throw hands with the guy stretching her out."

Cade laughs under his breath. I just shrug.

"I'm fine," I lie, eyes narrowing at Josh again.

"You're in love, son" he says, not even looking at me. "That's what that is."

The stadium lights dim just slightly, enough to make the jumbotron glow brighter, casting a cool electric haze over the field. The crowd's already loud, but when the PA system crackles and Hugh's voice booms out across Kingsley Field, the whole place vibrates with energy.

"Alright, Wexley fans!" Hugh's voice is pure stadium hype, loud and smooth. "We've got a sold-out crowd tonight for the first home game of the season here at Kingsley Field!"

Cheers erupt, echoing through the stands like thunder.

"Your Wolves are taking the field against the Northvale University Titans, undefeated last year, and ready to prove they've still got it."

Booing breaks out in the student section.

Hugh's voice cuts through the roar again, this time with a grin so wide you can hear it. "Hey, Bella! You girls about ready to get this show on the road?"

On the sideline, Bella turns and flashes a wicked little smile toward the announcer's box, blowing a kiss in Hugh's direction. The camera catches it and plasters her face across the jumbotron, larger than life.

Right next to me, Dad leans in with a raised brow. "Wait, are the girls mic'd up?"

"Hell yeah, they are."

"You serious?"

"I told you," I say, jerking my chin toward the field where the girls are finishing stretching, shaking out nerves like they're about to walk into battle. "It's a whole damn show, Dad."

The girls start heading down to the walkway in front of the stands. Right in front of us. Bella takes the center. Hair in perfect waves, black and burgundy top hugging her like a damn dream. Ellie and Haley on her left and right, all three of them standing with that signature Trifecta confidence, like queens about to burn down a kingdom.

"Hey there, Hughy!" Bella calls, strutting across the walkway in front of our row. "God, I've missed you. It feels so good to be back at Kingsley Field." She pauses for the crowd to react.

She's close now. Too close. One arm's length away from me in that little crop. I nearly grab her ass and pull her onto my lap where she belongs, but I restrain myself.

Barely.

She starts pacing slow, owning the space like a born performer. "So, Hughy, how have you been? How was your summer?"

"It was great. The wife and I took the kids to Ireland for a few weeks. What about you girls?"

Bella twirls with one of her curls and flashes a smile. "Oh, nothing major. Just the usual—dancing, laying out by the pool at The Row working on our tan..." That gets a loud pop from some of The

Order sitting in the student section.

She pauses. "Oh my God, Hughy, I totally forgot to tell you!" She says with the sass and excitement of someone gossiping with a girlfriend at brunch. "So, you know how we get to perform at The Row parties, right?"

"Yeah, of course!" Hugh says. "The Order should be grateful you girls show up. Y'all make their Row parties worth something. I hope they are paying you well."

Bella laughs. "Right? Make sure you tell that to Cal and Augie," she says pointing over her shoulder. "Anyway, we were at the end of summer pool party and guess who showed up."

Ellie takes the cue, stepping forward. "The disgusting Revenants." The stadium boos on instinct.

Haley adds, "Yeah. Maddie Rae stomped up like, 'You girls are so mean, you took Fight Night from us!' Blah blah bullshit. Then challenged us to a rematch."

Hugh chuckles. "So, what'd you do?"

Bella flips her hair and steps center. "What we always do, kicked ass while shaking ass."

Cade laughs beside me.

"Three rounds. Three wins. You should've seen it," Ellie beams.

"I'm honestly not surprised," Hugh says. "But hold up girls, did you just say you stole a Fight Night?"

"We didn't steal it, Hughy," Ellie's sassy ass cuts in.

"Yeah, we earned it. We were invited to dance by one of their Hollow Kings. It's not our fault that The Revenants suck," Haley says, eyes on me now as she points in my direction. "Just as Bella's new boyfriend, he was there."

Right then, Knox steps up to the girls. "Excuse me, what exactly are you all doing?"

Bella rolls her eyes. "What does it look like, Knox. We're having a conversation," she says in an annoyed tone. The crowd roars again.

"Well, how about we dial back the girl chat and get a little more dancing, yeah?" Knox says, dry as ever. "You're supposed to be hyping up the Wolves, not hosting late a night podcast."

Ellie groans. "Ugh, buzzkill, you're no fun. We haven't seen Hughy all summer!"

Bella sighs. "Sorry, Hughy... duty calls."

And with that, all three of them take off toward the student section while the rest of The Legacy gets into formation on the field.

Knox shakes his head and as he walks off. An exasperated mutter comes over the speakers one last time, "I swear to God, these girls..."

Dad shakes his head in disbelief. "What was that?"

I laugh. "That was part of the show. They don't just dance. They run the field. Interact with the crowd during timeouts, halftime, you name it."

The second the girls take their places in front of the student section. Bella motions for them all to sit down. They listen to her.

Cade leans over beside me, watching the crowd sit down with a brow arched. "I guess they all know something we don't."

Pitbull's "I Believe That We Will Win" hits the speakers—loud, electric, and pulsing with adrenaline. The Trifecta doesn't move at first. Bella just steps forward, and lips Pitbull's lines to the student section.

Her mouth syncs perfectly to the lyrics about fear and what they are going to do about it. She paces in front of the students, eyes fierce, chin high, and locking eyes with the shirtless Order guys on the front row with W-O-L-V-E-S painted on their chests.

When she gets to the end of the line and mouths and rise, the three girls all motion for the students to stand up like a damn pastor calling the invitation at the end of a sermon.

The crowd stands and completely erupts. "I Believe!" chants thunder from the student section to the top row. Fans bang on bleachers. Flags wave. The little girl with the Bella sign loses her shit. Even the damn concession guys stop what they're doing.

Dad leans forward, wide-eyed. "Holy fuck, son your girl..." He shakes his head, grinning like a lunatic. "Goddamn."

"Yeah. She does that," I mutter, jaw ticking with a twisted kind of pride.

The girls run to the field and take their places in front of Josh,

Drake, and Sam. The guys lift them in the air as the next round of chants begin. While the guys hoist them into the air, the girls point toward the tunnel and the stadium detonates.

The Wexley Wolves burst onto the field like an army breaking formation. Helmets flashing under the floodlights. Smoke cannons firing from the end zone. The crowd goes feral. Drums, chants, horns, and thousands of voices vibrating the bleachers.

Bella's the first to hit the turf. She and the girls sprint toward the Wolves' huddle, sneakers kicking up turf pellets and static under the lights. She slips right between the shoulder pads and helmets like she belongs there. Like the entire goddamn team takes orders from her.

The beat hits that line about showing up and showing out and she doesn't hesitate. She grabs August by the chest pads and yanks him down so they're face-to-face. The crowd's roaring, cameras flashing, but all I see is her—wild, fearless, commanding.

She shouts something in his ear, pure fire and authority. August just grins, nodding like the maniac he is. A soldier taking orders from his sexy as hell general.

I've never seen anything hotter in my life.

Across the field, the Titans look like they're going to shit their pants. Well, some of them at least.

Not my Hollow Kings brothers. DeShawn and Chase are on the sideline hyping themselves up like the psychos they are. Rez just has his eyes focused on Bella, shaking his head and grinning from ear to ear. Bastard.

The huddle breaks into synchronized jumps, fire in their eyes and of fucking course it's Callum who is jumping with my girl in his arms like he's king of the world.

"Fuck that guy," I mutter under my breath.

Dad laughs, clapping once. "Well, that's one way to start a damn game."

The refs head toward midfield, the Wolves and the Titans following in behind him. The captains line up for the coin toss. All eyes shift to the center of the field.

Except mine.

Because The Trifecta just disappeared into a black tent on the sideline like they're pulling off some sort of magic trick. Rico screaming in Spanish so loudly we can hear his dramatic ass from here.

Dad leans forward, squinting. "What is that? Where'd they go?"

Cade exhales slowly. "Costume change."

The tent flaps open, and fuck me. Bella leads the pack, hair in a sleek high ponytail, dripping with attitude. She's traded the flashy Trifecta uniform for black spandex shorts and a tiny top styled into cropped version of a Wolves' football jersey. And plastered right across her chest, bold and unforgiving...

#7. Callum's number.

Clay whistles like he just saw the winning Powerball numbers. "Well, I'll be damned! That's my quarterback's number, isn't it?"

"Holy. Fucking. Shit. She has Callum's number on her tits. Goddamn it," I groan as I run my hand down my face.

Cade leans over. "I don't like it either, but it makes sense, babe."

"What part of our girl's tits being branded with another man's number makes any fucking sense, Cade?"

He grabs my thigh. "Three star players. Three Trifecta. It boosts school spirit. You know the drill."

I glare back down at the field where Bella's strutting like she owns every blade of grass. Ellie's got August's number stretching across her chest. Haley has Jalen's. All three girls flanked by their stunt guys again like this is round two of domination.

I grit my teeth and mutter, "Tell me again why I can't go down there and staple my number across her goddamn soul."

Cade chuckles, not helping. "One, because you don't have a number. Fighters don't have jerseys. And two, because it's a performance, not a mating ritual, babe."

I cross my arms. "Feels like both."

The scoreboard lights flash as the buzzer sounds and Kingsley erupts with cheers. The Wolves are up. Callum's already pounding his chest like he just secured a playoff berth. Typical.

I'm mid-eye roll when I notice Bella standing directly in front of me at the railing, her arms crossed loosely over her chest, looking out into the crowd searching for something. Ellie and Haley are perched behind her, legs swinging over the edge, smirks on their faces like they know something I don't.

"What's up, Bells?" Hugh asks over the speakers.

"Oh, nothing," she calls back, her tone casual. But her eyes don't stop scanning. "Just looking."

"For what?" Hugh asks.

She tilts her head slightly. "I'll know when I see it." Then she gasps, loud enough to cut through the music and crowd. "Ah! There!" she yells, pointing. "Girls, look!"

Haley and Ellie jump off the rail, all three of them zeroing in on the middle of the stands behind us like predators locking onto prey. Bella takes off up the stairs.

"What the hell is going on?" Dad leans in, brows raised.

"I have no clue," I mutter, sitting up straighter.

Suddenly, Bella's coming down the stairs with a tiny human in her arms, a literal child, as if this is just something she does on the daily. The little girl is in a pint-sized Trifecta uniform, complete with glitter face paint and a bow that's nearly the size of her head.

"Bella, why are you kidnapping a child?" Hugh says through the speaker.

"I'm not kidnapping her Hughy. I have an idea, just give me a second."

Bella stops right in front of our row, cradling the girl on her hip like she's been doing it for years. The other girls come up behind them.

"Hey guys," Bella says, motioning toward the three Legacy stunt dudes. "Come here."

They hustle over immediately.

Bella adjusts the little girl on her hip slightly to talk to her. "Hi, sweetie. What's your name?"

The little girl shyly leans in and says, "Millie."

Bella beams and looks to the crowd. "Everyone say hi, Millie!"

"Hi Millie!" the crowd echoes back.

Bella shifts her weight, carrying Millie back and forth in front of our section like she's giving a speech at the damn UN. "Millie here wants to be in The Trifecta tonight. Right, babe?"

Millie nods with all the force of a kid who believes this moment is her actual Disney moment.

"Okay, so we're gonna teach you how to fly. You think you can do that?"

Millie nods again, braver now. Bella kisses the top of her head.

"Fuck," I mutter under my breath. "Why does Bella holding a kid do things to me?"

Cade leans over, voice low and mocking-sweet. "Because you've officially crossed over into softdom. Welcome, babe."

Bella sets Millie down gently. "Alright Millie. First, you're going to practice with us girls, okay?"

The Trifecta help guide Millie up into a little cradle lift. Nothing too high, just enough for her to squeal and wave. She lands perfectly and immediately throws her arms around Bella's neck.

"You're a natural," Bella says, laughing.

"Okay, now the boys are gonna do it," she adds, adjusting Millie's bow. "They're stronger than us."

Millie gives a determined nod and Josh lifts her up into the air like she's made of light. The crowd loses it. When she comes back down, Millie runs to hug all three girls before her mom comes down from the stands, misty-eyed and overwhelmed. The Trifecta wraps around her. Posing with the pint-sized cutie for pictures, letting her shine like the tiniest queen in the stadium.

Dad exhales next to me. "Well, I'll be damned. They really do run this place."

The game's back in full swing. The crowd's roaring and the stadium lights blaze down like we're in a damn NFL arena. My bestie really is a master with lighting. The Wolves are up, but barely. Titans aren't giving them an inch. The tension's thick enough to cut with a knife.

"That's pass interference, Ref!" Bella shouts from her spot on the sideline, hands cupped around her mouth. "Throw the damn flag!"

Dad chuckles beside me. "Your girl's got some lungs on her."

"Oh hell yeah, she's competitive as fuck. Fits right in, huh?"

The flag flies a second later.

"Thank you!" Bella shouts again.

"Definitely Barinov material." Dad laughs, shaking his head looking both impressed and slightly terrified.

"So... where exactly is Mom?"

Dad exhales through his nose. "Moscow. With your uncle."

"Of course."

"Big deal, apparently. Some multi-million-dollar shipment going south. They're trying to smooth things over before anyone starts shooting each other in a boardroom."

I groan, rubbing a hand over my jaw. "I just really wanted her to be here to meet Bella. She's so close with Cade's family. Hell, she's practically a Whitmore. Calls Clay *Dad* and everything, and I just... I just wanted that for us."

Dad nods slowly, watching Bella scream at the field again as Callum narrowly misses a sack from Rez.

"Run the damn ball, Cal!" she yells, stomping once like it'll help move the chains.

"She's a firecracker," Dad says, then turns back to me. "Alright, here's the deal, son. When your mom gets back, I'll talk to her. We'll set something up. Brunch, maybe. You know how much she loves a good brunch. The woman can't say no to a white tablecloth and bottomless mimosas."

I huff a soft laugh. "Thanks, Dad."

"TOUCHDOWN, WOLVES!!!"

The crowd explodes. Bella and the girls jump into the air as if they just won an unlimited shopping trip on Fifth Avenue, hair flying, fists in the air.

"Alright Wexley fans, it's halftime here at Kingsley Field! Your Wolves are up and if the second half is anything like the first, we're in for one hell of a finish!" The crowd roars. Horns blare. And from the sound of it, no one's sitting down.

The Trifecta hits the field in front of the full Legacy squad and it's pure sex in motion. "Dirrty" by Christina Aguilera blasts through the speakers and the stadium damn near combusts. The bass shakes the bleachers and those girls move like they were born for the spotlight.

Hip rolls. Hair whips. Sweat catching in the lights. The guys launch them into the air. The whole thing is choreographed mayhem. It's sharp, dangerous, impossible to look away from. They own every inch of turf like it's a stage built just for them.

And then, God help me, Josh grabs the edge of Callum's jersey on Bella and rips it clean off. Beneath it is the tiniest Trifecta bikini top I've ever seen. Burgundy with black straps that cross low on her back, hugging her like sin itself.

I choke on a laugh, eyes wide. "You've got to be fucking kidding me," I mutter under my breath, grabbing my phone.

ME: Are you trying to kill me man?

RICO: I knew you'd get a kick out that.

ME: You insane little bastard.

RICO: You loved it and you know it.

The song ends in a blur of lights and adrenaline. The girls start back up the stairs toward the student section, swagger in every step, high-fiving fans and soaking in the moment. Ellie twirls a little flag some kid gave her, Haley's tossing compliments like candy.

Bella breaks away. She turns and starts walking straight toward us.

"Hell of a show out there, Bells," Clay says from behind Dad.

"Thanks," Bella laughs as she sits down on my lap.

"But let's talk about Cal for a second," Clay continues, already in football dad mode. "What the hell is he doing out there? Kid's built like a linebacker and still won't run the ball."

She exhales and slides closer, shaking her head.

"Right? The defense keeps giving him these massive holes. It's like Moses parting the Red Sea and your boy just stands there. Rez nearly laid his ass out that last drive."

Cade snorts. "You should coach him."

"We'd be up by like fourteen if I was, Cade." Bella laughs. "They're playing scared."

Clay grumbles. "Damn shame. That last red zone stall made me want to kick my own son's ass."

"Maybe he'll get it together this half. If not, I'm suiting up," she says, sass returning in full force.

"You'd look hot in pads, baby."

She rolls her eyes at me, but smiles, finally relaxing as she tucks herself under my arm.

I nudge her gently. "Baby, there's someone I want you to meet."

She looks up and I tilt my head toward the man sitting beside me. "This is my dad. Daniel Barinov."

Her spine straightens just a little, lips parting as she reaches out. "It's nice to meet you, Mr. Barinov."

My dad chuckles, taking her hand with a warm smile. "Please, call me Dan."

"Okay," she says, cheeks tinting pink. "Nice to meet you, Dan."

He grins, eyes flicking over to me for a second before turning back to her. "So... I've heard a lot about The Trifecta," he starts. "But when these two said it was a show?" He lets out a low whistle. "I didn't believe them. Thought they were just bragging about their girl."

I glance at Cade, who hides a grin behind his cup.

"But then you came out there, struttin' across that field like you owned the damn place, commanding the crowd, making them feel something? That wasn't just dancing. That was performance, it was pure power."

"Wow. Thank you. That... that means a lot."

"It should. I've seen a lot of things, but it's rare to see someone move people like the way you girls do."

"She does it to me every day," I say casually, brushing my

thumb along her waist. "Drives me absolutely insane."

She laughs, swatting at my arm and I catch her hand just to kiss the back of it.

"Excuse me?" A woman stands there nervously, holding the hand of a little girl, probably five or six, in a glittery Trifecta jersey and a huge burgundy bow. The girl is gripping a sign with sparkly letters that say *BELLA BLACKWOOD IS MY SPIRIT ANIMAL!*

"Would it be possible to get you to sign her poster?"

Bella's whole face lights up. She turns fully, crouching down so she's at eye level with the little girl. "Hey there, sweetheart. What's your name?"

"Sophie," the girl says shyly.

"Well, Sophie," Bella says, taking the Sharpie from Sophie's mom. "This might be the coolest sign I've ever seen."

She signs it, adds a little heart, and then gently tugs the edge of Sophie's bow. "I think you're gonna be better than me one day," she whispers.

Sophie beams and waves back to us as her mom walks her back to their seats.

Two short beeps cut through the noise. *Walkie's on.*

"Bella," Knox's voice crackles in our ears. *"You about ready?"*

"Yeah, I'm ready. Where do you want me?"

"Just stay there with Lex. That'll actually work perfect, if Lex behaves."

"I always behave, Bestie"

Knox laughs, *"Alright everyone, lets get ready. It's time to fly."*

One Beep. *Earpieces off.*

"What was that about?" Cade asks, leaning in.

Bella's eyes flick toward the field, then back to us, that little smile tugging at the corner of her mouth. "I guess it's time for us girls to fly."

Before either of us can ask what the hell that means, Ellie and Haley come running over from the other side of the bleachers, glowing with post-performance adrenaline.

"Ready, bitches?" Ellie says with a wicked grin.

Over the loudspeakers, Hugh pipes up again. "That was one hell of a performance, girls."

Haley looks up toward the booth. "Thank you, Hughy!" She pauses and glances toward Bella who's firmly planted on my lap. "Um... Bella... what are you doing?"

Bella doesn't even look at her. She just keeps staring at me, smiling into my eyes. "Sitting with my man. Taking a little break. What does it look like, Hales?"

Ellie folds her arms and leans in dramatically. "Well, I've got bad news."

Bella quirks an eyebrow. "What kind of news, El?"

"Nope." Ellie shakes her head and jerks her thumb at Haley. "Hales, you tell her. He's your boytoy."

"Ugh, Knox wants us to fly," Haley grimaces.

Bella freezes. Then slowly stands and looks between them. "Yeah, no. Not happening. Do you remember the last time? That did not..." she cuts the words dramatically, spinning toward the crowd with a hand to her chest. "...did not end well."

Laughter ripples across the stands.

"Well," Haley says, "he said we have to."

Bella tosses her hands up. "And who exactly died and made Mr. DJ the boss of us?"

Hugh's voice cuts in over the mic, perfectly timed, "I don't know, Bella I think you should give it a try."

She gasps like he just committed treason. "Stay out of it, Hughy! These feet?" She points down at her black Nikes. "Stay. On. The. Ground."

Right on cue, the student section starts chanting: "FLY! FLY! FLY! FLY!"

Bella rolls her eyes and groans. "Ugh, fine. But if I die, I'm haunting all of you."

She starts walking toward the field, calling back over her shoulder, "I swear to God, if Josh drops me and I have to miss Regionals because I'm in a neck brace, I'm gonna send Lex to kick his ass."
The crowd explodes with laughter.

"Did she just say my name over the fucking speakers?"

Cade snorts beside me. "Yup."

Bella turns toward Ellie first. "Alright, El, you're up."

Ellie flashes a confident grin, then sprints toward Sam. He launches her like a missile. She spins in the air, legs tucked, arms perfectly aligned, and then lands gracefully in his arms, hair whipping around her as she sticks the pose.

Bella claps, cheering. "Wooo! Okay, girl, look at you with that triple back-spin-tuck-swan-dive or whatever the hell that was! Nice job! Everyone give it up for Ellie Whitmore!"

The crowd roars.

"Alright, Hales. Show 'em how it's done."

Haley takes off and Drake launches her so high it's like gravity's optional. She flips midair and lands in his arms with a wink that's pure hellfire. Front row loses their minds. Can't blame them.

Bella whistles. "Damn, okay. Little aerial queen over here. Give it up for Haley Rosethorne!"

Then she turns to the crowd with that trademark look. "There ya go, Knox. We flew. Goodnight." She turns on her heel and starts walking away.

Knox's voice crackles over the stadium speakers. "Um... Problem Child, aren't you forgetting something?"

Bella doesn't even look back. "Nope. You said fly. We flew. End of story."

I grin, arms crossed. "She's such a pain in the ass."

Dad nudges me with his elbow. "Yeah, but she's your pain in the ass."

Knox sighs dramatically over the mic. "I meant all of you. That includes you, Bella."

Bella spins around mid-step, eyes wide. "Ugh!" She storms back over to the guys, stomping like a bratty toddler. She pauses just in front of Josh and the guys, glaring up at them. "If you drop me, I can guarantee I will end you."

Then she hesitates, half-turning to glance back at the stands. "Do I really have to?" she says to no one in particular, voice pitched for drama.

Ellie and Haley laugh, in perfect unison, "Just do it, Bella!"

Bella rolls her eyes, then mimics them in the most exaggerated, mocking tone. "Just do it, Bella. Just be brave, Bella. Just leap through the sky, Bel—"

Before she can finish, Josh nods to the others, and they launch her. She flies. I mean, flies. Spins at least three times midair, legs tucked, arms out, and long, black hair trailing behind her. I don't even know what the hell the move is called.

I feel Cade stiffen beside me and hear him whisper, "Holy shit."

They catch her clean and she bounces upright like she's on springs.

"Oooh, good job boys," she calls out with a grin, brushing invisible dust off her shorts. "Would've hated for my boyfriends to have to bury you for breaking my spine."

"Give it up for Bella Blackwood!" Ellie screams to the crowd.

Fourth quarter. 30 seconds left. Wolves are down by a field goal.

The student section's losing their minds. Bella, Ellie, and Haley are posted up in front of them, leading chants with the rest of The Legacy. Bella's got her pom on one hip, other hand cupped to her mouth as she screams encouragement like she's the one calling the plays.

Her phone buzzes in my pocket.

I glance at the scoreboard, 20 seconds.

Handoff to Cal.

I pull the phone out. It's a message from a name I'd sell my soul to Satan himself just to erase.

@LucaWasHere
Nice flying, Izzy. You really soared.
Uncle Jack cheered like he's been restored.
His little Sugar Bear, back in his grip.
All pride and joy on a fucking power trip.

But sugar melts when the flames grow near.
Don't get too comfy, don't keep him dear.
Luck runs out and when it does,
You'll learn who watched, who always was.

"TOUCHDOWN WOLVES!" Hugh yells over the speakers and the crowd erupts.

Cade's on his feet. Fireworks go off above Kingsley Field. What a fucking game. The fans are screaming. The team's rushing the field.

But me? I'm staring at the message on Bella's screen. I pull out my phone to send a quick message to our resident stalker poet.

@BarinovUnhinged
You want to whisper? I'll roar through blood.
I've bled in the Pit, you'll drown in the mud.
Say Jack's name again, I'll carve it in bone.
She's mine, motherfucker, back the fuck off what I own.

CHAPTER (55)
BELLA
BRUNCH AT THE BARINOV'S
694 DAYS SINCE ZEKE'S DEATH

The wind catches the hem of my coat as we climb the limestone steps, that crisp autumn bite teasing my skin. Rust-colored leaves crunch under Lex's boots beside me. The trees along the iron gate blaze in orange and gold. From the looks of it, even nature knew it needed to dress up for Irina Barinov.

Holy hell, this house. Massive, yeah, but not the cold, concrete palace I expected from a Bratva queen. It's all warm stone and curved archways, tall black-framed windows gleaming against the sunlight. Everything is symmetrical and precise. Way too perfect and beautiful to be accidental.

Ellie picked my outfit. She said I needed to look *fall-chic but terrifyingly expensive.* So here I am in a cinnamon-brown fitted midi dress, belted tight at the waist, tall suede boots, and a maroon coat that swishes behind me with each step. My hair's curled into glossy waves, my earrings are tiny gold daggers, and my nerves are about to explode.

What was supposed to be a calm brunch with the Barinov's somehow snowballed into a full-scale family summit. Barinovs, Whitmores, and me thrown right into the center. While I'm glad to have the Whitmores here for moral support, it all still seems like too much.

Thankfully, Tex is here too. My family. Not that he's happy about it. I had to talk him into coming—*under protest, obviously*—but after that last message from Luca, I didn't want to show up completely unguarded.

I've pulled back a little from Uncle Jack and Daddy lately, just enough to create some distance. A few calls, a couple quick check-ins. No more lunches. My gut's been buzzing and I've learned not to ignore it.

We've added a few extra security details around them too. Nothing dramatic. Only for precaution.

And I know Luca's probably just being his usual creepy self. Probably bluffing. Probably nothing. But if it's not. If he's more than some cyber-stalker with a bad poetry habit then I'd much rather feel paranoid than sorry.

I wanted them here today, I really did. But until I know more, I'm not risking anything. Especially not for mimosas and finger sandwiches, no matter how damn good they probably are.

We barely make it past the front doors and into the towering foyer before Tex stops beside me. "Bella, can I talk to you for a second?"

I pause mid-step and glance up at Lex. "Give me a minute," I tell him gently.

He leans down and brushes a kiss against my forehead. "I'll be right inside, baby."

I smile and turn to Tex. "What is it?"

He doesn't answer right away. His jaw's locked, eyes scanning the hallway like the walls might close in on us. "We shouldn't be here."

"What do you mean?"

"Just trust me, Bella. You and I," he grits, pointing between us. "Should not be inside the Barinov estate."

Something in his tone slices right through me. "What are you not telling me, Tex?"

His nostrils flare. "Drop it. Let's just go." He reaches out like he's going to take my arm and pull me with him, but I step back, yanking away from his grip.

"Tex, it's just brunch," I snap. "What's the worst thing that could happen?" I don't give him time to answer. I link my arm through his and start walking. He stiffens beside me but follows, tension radiating off him in waves.

We turn into the grand living room, high ceilings, gold trim, and oil paintings that are probably older than the country. The instant we cross the threshold, everything halts. A champagne glass slips from someone's hand and shatters against the marble.

"James?"

I follow the sound to the far side of the room and there she is. Irina Barinov. Lex's tall, elegant, and lethal Bratva Queen mother.

She's wearing tailored ivory trousers that fall perfectly over pointed nude heels and a pale blue silk blouse tucked in. Her white-blonde hair is swept into a polished twist, not a strand out of place. Everything about her is expensive and terrifyingly beautiful, like fall in Manhattan with a gun in its purse.

And... she's staring at Tex as if she just saw a ghost.

I blink at him. "Tex, why did she just call you James?"

He still doesn't look at me. No answer. Just a muscle ticking in his jaw.

I don't even realize that Lex has moved until I feel him beside me, one hand resting lightly on the small of my back.

Irina tears her gaze from Tex—*James?*—and looks at me. Dead in the eyes. Something flashes behind her ice-blue eyes, shock, calculation.

Recognition?

She looks back at Tex like they're having an entire conversation I can't hear. A silent war written in stares and unsaid things.

"Hello, Irina," Tex says.

"Okay. Someone better start talking. Tex, how the fuck do you know my mom?"

"It's been a long time," he says quietly to Irina, ignoring Lex completely. His voice sounds different. Lower. Rougher.

Her chin lifts, spine straightening like a blade. "It has," she says and then points toward me. "And do you want to explain this to me?"

I turn toward Tex, eyes searching his face, but he still won't look at me. His focus is locked on her. Like I don't even exist.

"Tex," I whisper.

Nothing.

Irina steps forward. "Is this... Is this her?"

"What the fuck are you two talking about?" Lex growls beside me. "Mom, this is Bella. Mine and Cade's girlfriend."

Irina turns back to me, really looks at me, and I swear something breaks behind her perfect icy expression.

"Izzy?" she breathes.

My jaw drops. "Okay, seriously, would one of you like to tell me what the hell is happening right now?"

"Scandalous," Ellie mumbles under her breath.

Savannah sighs, gently smacks her arm, and whispers, "Darling, not now."

Lex's hand tightens on my waist.

Tex finally turns to face me. "There was a reason I didn't want to bring you here."

I throw my arms out. "Would someone please just tell me who the fuck Izzy is and why you all keep staring at me like I'm about to sprout wings and float through the ceiling?"

Irina takes a slow step toward me. I instinctively back up, pressing into Lex's chest. His hand slides to my hip, steadying me, but even he feels tense. Like he's bracing for a bomb.

Irina doesn't stop. Her heels click softly on the polished floor, her silk blouse catching the light as she narrows the space between us. Her gaze is locked on my face like I'm a damn puzzle she's been trying to solve for decades.

She lifts a hand to my hair, brushing it behind my ear as her voice softens. "You look just like her."

"Like who?" I ask.

"Your mother."

My knees almost give out. "You knew my mother?"

Irina nods slowly. "Yes. I knew your mother. Izzy was my best friend in the entire world."

"Izzy?"

Her lips press into a bittersweet smile. "Isabella," she says softly. "You were named after her."

My heart stumbles.

Then the expression on her face hardens. Ice snapping beneath the weight of fury. She turns fast on Tex.

"And you," her voice turns lethal. "You told me you lost her." She steps in closer and gets straight into his face. "You told me she was gone. That you couldn't find her. That every search was a dead fucking end."

Irina's voice is bitter and cold, her hand shaking as she points toward me. "Which I can see now was a complete lie."

My stomach drops. The SUVs at the funeral. The constant fear from Mama. The whisper-warnings about staying hidden from someone.

My pulse races. "Tex?"

He doesn't meet my eyes. Just runs a hand down his face like he already knows he's been caught.

"What is she talking about?" I press. "What does she mean you lost me?"

"Bella..." he starts, but Irina slices right through.

"Your mother," she says, eyes blazing, "was everything to me. We ruled The Revenants together before that name meant what it does now. She was like a sister. Fierce. Wild. Brilliant."

Irina's voice drops lower, more bitter. "She danced at The Obsidian. Before she knew what it really was. Before she understood who Roman Russo really was."

I glance at her. "The club owner?"

Irina's gaze hardens, the chill of it cutting through the air. "He's a monster," she says evenly. "Head of the Italian Mafia here in New York. Owns The Obsidian, buried beneath his luxury hotel, NOX."

She pauses, almost savoring the word. "And below that lies his kingdom. The casino. His sick little playground where he and his Italian brutes convince themselves they own this city."

She takes in a deep breath.

"We all went to school together," she says finally, her voice quieter now. "Daniel. Roman. Me. Izzy."

The name falls like a confession.

"He always had a thing for her," Irina continues, a faint ache threading through her words. "Hired her to dance at his club. And she... she loved him. God, she loved him."

For a heartbeat, she closes her eyes. Just once, like the memory still cuts deep. "But he was already promised to an heiress back in Rome," she says, the warmth fading from her tone. "Old money. Old power. A marriage that would fortify the Russo empire."

Irina exhales slowly. "And when your mother found out she was pregnant with his child..."

Her voice falters.

"She ran," she whispers. "Left me a note saying she was sorry. That she had to disappear before Roman could get to her. That she was terrified he'd take you from her."

Her voice finally cracks. "She died in that hospital giving birth to you."

No one moves. No one breathes.

"I sent James," she whispers, nodding toward Tex, "to find you. To bring you back to me. To raise you. To keep you safe from that monster."

She looks at me and then at Lex, who hasn't moved an inch from my side. And then back to me. "You were supposed to be mine to protect."

I turn to Tex slowly. My voice is barely audible. "Is that true?"

He finally looks at me. "I found you when you were three," he says, his tone low and heavy. "You were at a Razorback game with Henry and Jack. I watched you from a few rows back. You were laughing, wearing this cheerleading outfit and dancing like the world had never hurt you."

His voice thickens. "You were happy, Bells."

He glances at Irina. "I told Irina that I was having trouble finding you. That the trail was cold. But it wasn't. I just... I couldn't do it."

"You couldn't do what?" I whisper.

"I couldn't rip you from that home. From him. From your family. The last time I ever saw you in Arkansas was the day of Elise's funeral."

I feel like I'm spinning out of control.

"Moved back to Texas. Started over. Met Nate, did what I did best... and well... you know the rest."

I can't speak. Can't move. I just stare at him. At *James*. The man who saved me and lied to me all at once.

I swallow hard. My voice cracks. "But you never told me who I was."

He sighs. "Zeke didn't want—"

"Hold on," I cut him off. "Are you saying that Zeke, as in my big brother, knew who I really was."

"Yes, he found out when he..." He looks around not knowing if he should say anything else.

"Just tell me Tex, please."

He leans in and whispers in my ear so no one else can hear, "When he found Roman Russo's black book on his father's laptop."

My legs start to give out.

Luckily, Lex steps forward and braces me. "What do you mean Bella was yours to protect, Mom?"

Irina tears her gaze away from Tex and finally meets her son's eyes. "You were still a baby, Aleksandr. Your father and I were having complications trying for another child."

Her voice softens, just a fraction as she looks at me. "Izzy was my best friend. My sister in every way but blood. We had this plan... to raise you both together. You and Isabella. Just like she and I had grown up. Side by side. Always."

She swallows hard. "When she died, I was devastated. I still had you, but I couldn't lose her daughter. I needed to find her. To keep that promise to Izzy. I sent James to do it because I couldn't leave you here alone, you were too little."

"You wanted to raise us as... *siblings*?" Lex asks, face scrunched in disgust.

Ellie's voice cuts through the tension from behind. "Well, damn," she says, eyes wide. "That would've made things very awkward at fight night."

Lex chokes out a sound—half laugh, half groan.

I shoot Ellie a glare, but there's no real heat in it. Just the chaos of a world that suddenly doesn't make sense.

"None of this is how it was supposed to happen."

I nod slowly, voice cool. "Yeah. I'm getting that a lot lately."

My chest feels tight. Too many stares. Too many secrets. Too many goddamn truths I wasn't ready to hear.

"I think I just need some air," I say, backing up a step toward the hallway.

Lex straightens instantly. "You want me to come with you?"

I shake my head, already pulling my phone from my pocket. "No. I'll be okay. I just... I'll be right back."

His eyes search mine like he doesn't believe me, but he nods. "Okay, baby. Don't go far."

I nod once and slip out into the hallway, the polished floor cold under my boots, the sound of chatter and tension muffling behind me as my fingers fly across the screen.

> ME: Get me the fuck out of here. Right now!!

> CAL: Where are we going?

> ME: To have a chat with my father.

> CAL: You sure about that, Bells?

> ME: I need to know, Cal. I need answers.

> CAL: I'll meet you outside.

NOX - Manhattan, New York

Cal doesn't say a word as we pull up at NOX. He throws the car in park, gets out, and falls into step beside me like a silent shadow. We cut through the grand lobby, following the signs toward *The Obsidian*. The hallway is darker here, lit with red back lights and humming with low bass that pulses through the floor like a heartbeat.

When we reach the heavy black doors, the bouncer shifts to block us. "We're not open."

I don't back down. "I want to see Roman Russo."

He crosses his arms. "He's not taking visitors."

I meet his stare. "Then tell him..." I step forward, chin raised. "His daughter, Isabella, is here to see him."

The bouncer hesitates, then reaches for his earpiece. A few seconds later another bouncer comes out, older than the first. His eyes widen when he sees me, a flicker of recognition flowing through his face.

Apparently I really do look like her.

"Follow me."

Cal and I exchange a glance and then we're moving deeper into the belly of the beast.

The Obsidian is bathed in red light, glowing like danger itself. Shadows crawl along the black marble walls, flickering with the pulse of low, sensual music. A massive bar stretches across the left side, all obsidian stone. The dance floor is jet black glass, reflecting the ceiling's web of chandeliers like liquid ink. Black tables with crimson candles scatter the room, sleek and silent and ready to host sins.

It's beautiful.

It's deadly.

And it's his.

We're led down a private hallway of mirrored walls with no visible cameras. Everything looks curated and cold, until we stop in front of a thick, matte black door.

The bouncer knocks once, opens it, and gestures us inside.

Roman Russo sits in his leather chair, still and poised with a glass of something dark swirling between his fingers like it's an extension of his control.

He isn't what I expected. Not some fat old mobster. Not a cold, gray ghost from my nightmares. He's... hot. Unsettlingly hot—which, yes, I realize is weird as hell considering the DNA situation—but seriously, the man looks *good*. The kind of man women whisper about in stories they're not supposed to tell.

Black hair swept back with just enough silver at the temples to make it worse. And a damn jawline that could've been carved from marble. A black dress shirt, top buttons undone, sleeves rolled to his forearms like power's just another accessory.

He looks up slowly. Like he already knew I'd walk in, like I'm the last move in a game of chess he's been playing for years. His steel-gray eyes assess me sharply. The same as mine. Just one glance and something old and heavy settles between us.

The guy doesn't look like a father. He looks like the villain in every good girl's fantasy.

He rises, smooth and unhurried, like a predator dressed in

precision. He steps around the desk, closing the distance one measured stride at a time. When his hand starts to lift—maybe to touch, maybe to test—instinct takes over.

I draw my gun and shove it right in his face.

Cal chokes behind me. "Shit, Bella! When the fuck did you get a gun?!"

Roman doesn't flinch. His steel eyes lock on mine and something changes in them, something slow, sad, and certain.

"You really are her," he says quietly.

"Apparently," I reply coolly.

His gaze flicks past me to Cal. "And who are you?"

Cal straightens. "I'm her backup."

I roll my eyes. "Settle down, secret service."

Roman's mouth tugs, just barely. "There's no need for theatrics or weaponry," he says calmly, glancing at the gun in my hand. "You are safe in here. Please, sit."

I hesitate. Just for a breath. Then lower the gun and sink into the chair across from him. Cal silently follows.

Roman watches me like he already knows the questions. Hell, he's probably been waiting to answer them his whole life.

"I heard Irina's side of the story," I say, keeping my gaze locked on his. "So what's yours?"

A small smile curves his lips. "Oh, I'm sure Irina had quite a lot to say."

He leans back on his desk. "Irina, Daniel, Izzy, and I all went to Northvale together," he begins, voice low and steady. "We were thick as thieves... mostly. But Izzy—"

A weighted exhale falls from his lips. "I loved her. More than anything in the world."

My jaw tightens. "Then why didn't you fight for her?"

"I did. As much as I could. But I was promised to someone else, Luciana Bellanti. Rome. My father's final demand. Your grandfather's dying wish."

He gives a faint, tired smile. "Marrying her tied the Russos to one of the oldest bloodlines in Italy. Power. Legacy. Stability. All the things our family thought mattered."

Something flickers behind his eyes, grief, regret, maybe both. "But none of it mattered to me. I just wanted Izzy."

He pauses. "After graduation, I hired her to dance at The Obsidian. It was the only way I could keep her close without starting a war within my own family. We were careful. Quiet. Madly in love."

He looks away, the faintest tremor in his voice. "Luciana was in Rome most of the time, so it was easy to pretend. Until it wasn't." He hesitates.

"Until she got pregnant," I finish softly.

He nods. "She was terrified. Not of me, I think. Of what we'd done. Of what she might lose if she stayed. Maybe she didn't believe I'd choose her."

His gaze meets mine, steady and full of ghosts.

"Or maybe she didn't trust herself."

He exhales slowly, the sound more confession than breath.

"Your mother had a complicated relationship with her emotions," he says quietly. "She could be warmth and laughter one moment, then turn cold enough to freeze the air in her lungs. On stage, she called herself Raina... and sometimes, I think she *became* her. It was like Izzy was the light she showed the world and Raina was the darkness she couldn't escape."

His gaze drifts past me, lost in memory.

"Izzy was light. Joy. Love. Everything I ever wanted." He takes a deep breath. "But Raina... she carried the fear. The rage. The control. She never believed I loved Izzy. Thought I wanted to own her, tame her."

He swallows hard, jaw tightening. "We fought about it constantly. She said I was just like my father, power-hungry and cruel. And when Izzy got pregnant..." His voice fractures. "I think that was the moment she finally broke. Raina took over. And Izzy never came back."

When he finally looks at me, his steel-eyes are raw with regret, like the truth still bleeds when he speaks it. "I think it was Raina who ran that night... not Izzy."

Thick, dense silence presses down. "If you loved her that much, why didn't you go after her? Look for her, look for me?"

"I did," he says quietly, voice threaded with regret. "I found the love of my life dead on a cold steel slab at a hospital and you were gone. No one would give me any answers."

He stands up and starts to pace. "For years. I had two of my best men on it. One of them was named Malik Carter—brilliant man, genius with computers. He traced every lead, every record, every file he could get his hands on."

The name hits me like a gunshot to the chest. I swallow hard. "Malik. Carter?"

"Yes," Roman nods, leaning back on his desk. "He finally found something after a few years of searching. He and his wife, Kathryn, were on their way back to New York to show me when their plane went down somewhere over Pennsylvania."

My stomach drops. My lungs stop working.

"They left behind a son," Roman continues, his brow creasing. "Ezekiel, I think. I met him once, at the funeral. Good kid. Proud. Strong. Stood tall even when his world was falling apart."

The room blurs around me.

No. No, no, no.

Zeke.

Roman knew them. Knew Zeke's parents.

My hands start to shake.

Roman exhales slowly. "After that... things got complicated. I still had people searching, but every lead went cold. Somewhere along the line, the trail eventually just died. Even my contacts inside the NYPD couldn't pull anything up. It was like you vanished into smoke."

"So, you just gave up?"

"I was grieving," he says quietly. "I had lost Izzy. I lost you. And I lost the only version of myself that was ever good."

I blink. Hard. Everything's wrong. The floor. The lights. The way this office smells like smoke and legacy.

Cal notices. "Bells, are you ok?"

I can't answer. I just shake my head, the pressure pushing behind my ribs. "No," I whisper. "No, I'm not okay."

Roman quickly stands and crouches in front of me like he's seen this before. Like he's helped someone come down from an emotional high that rips them to their core.

"Breathe, child," he says softly. "You're safe now."

"NO!" I shout, leaping to my feet. The chair skids out and crashes to the floor. "Don't. Don't tell me to breathe. Don't act like you know me. Don't act like this is normal."

I'm spiraling. Shaking. Heat in my chest, ice in my spine.

"I'm sorry," I choke. "I can't... I can't do this right now. This was a mistake." I look at Cal, desperate. "I need to get the hell out of here."

I bolt.

The second the doors of NOX close behind me, I suck in a mouthful of air like. Cold fall wind hits my face and I don't even care that my makeup is probably ruined. My chest is rising too fast, my breath is shallow and uneven as I pace the sidewalk. My boots click against the concrete like they're keeping time with my spiraling.

Cal wraps me up in his arms. "Bells..." he says gently, stroking my back. "C'mon. Just breathe, alright? You're okay. You got out of there."

"No, I didn't," I whisper. "I just learned that my entire life is built on fucking ghosts."

My phone dings in my coat pocket.

LAING: 2 kids. 81st and Columbus. Looks like an abusive dad. It'll be in and out. You coming?

I look up at Cal.

"I need you to take me somewhere real quick."

CHAPTER ⑤⑥
L E X
MY PARENTS' HOUSE
FREAKING THE FUCK OUT!
694 DAYS SINCE ZEKE'S DEATH

Bella's been gone too long. I glance toward the foyer where she disappeared to get some air. My gut's already twitching. She said she just needed a second. Said she'd be right back. But my girl doesn't go silent. Not like this.

The room behind me is a fucking circus. Mom dropped a bomb and walked off like it wasn't nuclear. Cade's pacing, Tex is muttering threats to himself, and Dad is pouring bourbon like it's water. I'm two seconds away from throwing someone through a window when Ellie skids into the doorway like she just ran a damn marathon.

"Uh... guys?" She's pale. Blue eyes wide. "So, Bella's gone."

Everything stops.

"And so is Cal."

Tex is the first to move. "Gone?" he snaps.

Cade steps forward, voice furious. "You mean left? As in walked out? Alone?"

"I don't know!" Ellie throws her hands up, pacing. "I went to check on her. Door was open. No Bella. No Cal. And I looked outside, Cal's car is gone too."

My heart drops. I'm already pulling out my phone, calling.

Ring. Ring. Ring.

Hey it's Bella. Sorry I missed your call, but leave a message and I'll call you back. Kisses!

"Fuck."

Cade's doing the same thing. "Cal's not picking up either."

"Fuck!"

Tex is barking into his phone now. He's got Knox on the line, trying to ping her last location. Ellie's on the verge of tears, rambling about how Bella looked pale when she went out for air. Savannah's got her hand on her chest like she might faint. And my mom—*my fucking mother*—is standing off to the side like she didn't just set off the grenade that blew this whole day to hell.

"She said she just needed a minute," I mutter, trying to not lose my goddamn mind. "She said she'd be right back."

"It's been over an hour," Cade replies, looking just as worried.

Tex cuts in, still on the phone. "Knox has nothing yet. She must've disabled the GPS on her and Callum's phones so no one would follow them. But he's working on traffic cams to find Callum's car. We'll find her."

"We better. Because if—"

I'm interrupted by Cade's phone vibrating on the marble island. He glances down.

"Oh my God," he says as the color drains from his face.

I step in front of him. "What?"

He holds it up.

CAL: Look bro, sorry I left with your girl, but something's off. She's not okay. You guys need to get here right now 81st and Columbus.

I don't even think. I grab my helmet and leave.

Baby, what the fuck did you walk into?

I'm flying through the city. Don't remember how I got here. Don't care. My girl said she needed air and now she's gone. I can feel it in my chest, pounding with every second that ticks by.

Please be alive. Please be fucking alive.

When I hit 81st and Columbus, I nearly crash the bike. There's a body on the steps. Blood everywhere. Callum's slumped against the curb, bleeding. And Bella—

No.

She's being dragged. Kicking and screaming. He's got her by

the waist, hauling her toward a blacked-out SUV.

Out of nowhere... *BANG.*

His fucking head explodes. Drops like a sack of bricks. Bella crumples with him.

"MALYSHKA!"

I'm off the bike, sprinting. My knees hit the pavement hard.

She's shaking. Dazed. But she's breathing. I grab her. Pull her into me.

"You're okay. I've got you. I've got you."

"Lex?"

"Yeah, malyshka. I'm here," I say as she clutches my jacket.

We hear footsteps as he walks up. Calm. Slow. A king surveying his battlefield.

Roman Russo.

She sees him and stiffens. "You?" she breathes. "You followed us?"

He crouches.

I shift, putting myself between them. "Back. The fuck. Off."

"I'm your father, Isabella. It's my job to keep you safe."

Tex and Cade come flying in behind us. Tex sees Roman and loses it. He tackles him. "Get the fuck away from her!"

Roman slams into a car. Tex pulls a gun on him.

"Tex, no!" Bella screams, lurching from my arms. "Don't shoot him! He saved me!"

He doesn't move.

"Tex," she says again. Quieter. "Please. He saved me."

Slowly, his hand lowers and she collapses back into me. But then Callum groans and Bella spins.

"Cal!" She runs to him, helps him sit up. "I'm so sorry, are you okay?"

He winces. "Yeah. I think. Just... What the hell happened?"

Tex steps in. Gun still tight in his grip. "Yeah, Bells. What the hell is this?"

Bella straightens. "It was a trap."

I stalk closer. "What?"

She meets my eyes. "I got a text. From Laing. He said two kids.

Abusive dad. In and out. Clean. We got here, no kids. No anything. Just an ambush. I got the one who hit Cal, but I just wasn't fast enough for the other one."

She shakes her head. "I should've seen it. I'm sorry, Cal."

"Laing set you up," I growl. "That motherfucker is dead. I'll carve that damn dragon off his chest myself."

Roman steps forward. "If this man betrayed you, I'll deal with him."

Tex snaps, "You won't touch shit."

Buzz. Buzz.

Bella pulls out her phone and gasps.

@LucaWasHere:
Oh Izzy, baby, so quick to accuse.
But your dragon-tatted plaything was just our bait to use.
You think he set the trap in your name?
Sweetheart, nothing in this game is tame.

I almost had you. So close. So near.
Heartbeat racing, edge of fear.
But Daddy dearest stepped into frame.
Always the hero, always the same.

Lexie was late, he nearly lost.
You slipped right through and look at the cost.
He swings, he guards, he plays the brave.
But I see the cracks he'll never save.

So let him chase, let him play pretend,
But Lexie's nearing his bitter end.
He should go home and stop wasting his breath.
Before I show him the shape of death.

I grip her arm. "We're done. You're not staying out here where poet boy can see."

The door slams behind us. I throw my helmet so hard it bounces off the wall. Cade winces. Bella flinches. She still hasn't said a word since we left that sidewalk.

Good. Because if she opens that pretty mouth right now, I might say something I won't come back from. Or worse, pull her into my arms and never let her leave them again.

She walks inside like a ghost. Bruised, bleeding, silent. And I swear to fucking God, I'm two seconds from losing it.

"You should've fucking told me."

She stops in the center of the room, arms crossed tight like she's holding herself together by threads. "Lex—"

"No," I cut her off. "You don't get to do that. You don't get to lie, disappear, and then act like this is just another fucking mission."

Cade steps forward and tries to be the buffer. "Lex, maybe just let her—"

"Don't." I jab a finger at him. "You didn't see what I saw. You didn't watch her get dragged across the pavement like a rag doll while some fuck tried to throw her into a car like she was cargo."

Bella's chin lifts. But she still doesn't speak.

"You could've died, Bella," I bite out. "You think this is just another chapter in your tragic little war story? That this is some heroic solo mission? What the fuck were you thinking?"

Still.

Fucking.

Silent.

I step forward. "Do you get it? If I was ten seconds later. If Russo..." A deep breath shudders through me. "If Russo hadn't showed up, you would've been gone. Disappeared. Or worse."

"She was just trying to—" Cade cuts in.

"She should've had backup," I snap.

"I did have backup," she says, voice firmer now. "I thought Laing would be there. And I had Cal."

"You had *Cal?*" My voice rises. "The guys a quarterback. What the fuck was he going to do, throw a spiral at the guy? Bella, come on.

He's not built for this."

"Stop, Lex." Her voice cracks. "Just stop."

I'm too worked up to stop. My fists are clenched, my chest is tight, and my blood's a wildfire. I want to grab her, scream at her, kiss her until she remembers who the fuck she belongs to.

I roll my shoulders to try to calm the fury rising within. "We can't lose you, baby. I can't. You matter too damn much."

She lets out an empty, broken laugh. "You think I don't know that? You think I didn't want to tell you? You think I didn't want you there?"

"Then why didn't you?" Cade asks, stepping beside me. Calmer now, but just as wounded.

She spins on both of us. "Because I knew you wouldn't let me go to The Obsidian. You'd try to stop me. And I had to see him."

I pace a few steps away, trying to hold back the rage clawing up my chest.

She comes after me, eyes blazing. "I didn't ask for any of this! I didn't ask to be born to a ghost. To find out my mom was just as broken as me, or have Roman fucking Russo show up dropping bombs about knowing Zeke's family!"

Her hands fly out, voice cracking. "Everything's twisted and connected and fucked, and I don't even know who to trust anymore!"

Her voice finally breaks, soft and shaking. "I don't even know who I am."

She falls to her knees. Like the weight of it all finally cracked her open. Her knees slam the floor.

I've seen this before—after ops, after trauma. When her emotions crash into her all at once and she can't breathe through them.

Cade's faster than me. He drops beside her in an instant, pulling her in. "Hey. Hey. It's okay," he whispers. "You're okay, sweetheart."

She clutches his shirt, sobbing. Fingers in her hair, clawing at her chest like she's trying to crawl out of her own skin.

I stand there frozen. Watching her fall apart in his arms. Watching him hold her. Watching him completely fail to calm her the fuck down.

I drop down beside them and shove Cade back without even looking at him. "Get off," I growl.

He doesn't argue. Just backs up because he knows he isn't what she needs right now. Not for this. He's the calm. The light.

But the part of her unraveling on this floor? That storm inside her? That belongs to me. Only I can bring her back from that edge.

I've been doing it for months, after every mission, every panic spiral. Every time she broke down over him, over their breakup, over everything. *Me.* I'm the one who holds her when she falls apart. The one who knows exactly how deep that darkness runs and still doesn't flinch.

I wrap my arms around her, staking a fucking claim. Bella thrashes, wild and clawing, but I don't let go.

"Breathe," I whisper, my mouth at her temple, my grip iron. "Breathe with me, baby."

Her fists slam against my chest—once, twice, again—until she breaks. Just fucking breaks. All that fire, all that fury, melts into sobs as her body caves into mine.

I tilt her chin up, force her to look at me. Her eyes are wild. Shattered. Full of betrayal and grief and something darker, something that looks a hell of a lot like surrender.

"Everything's broken," she whispers.

I nod once, firm. "Yeah. It is."

Her breath shakes. "And I'm not okay."

I lean in, nose brushing hers. "Neither am I, baby."

Her fingers fist in my shirt like she's drowning. "I need—"

"I know."

I crush my mouth to hers. It's not soft. Or sweet. It's a desperate, full-body, bone-deep need to feel something other than this black hole inside us. She kisses me back like she can't breathe and I'm the only air she'll ever get again.

My hands are everywhere, her back, her waist, gripping her thighs as I lift her off the ground. She wraps around me, trying to fuse our skin together.

I slam her into the wall. She gasps against my mouth. "Lex."

"Tell me to stop."

She doesn't.

I rip her dress over her head. It tears. She doesn't care. She yanks my jacket and shirt off, digs her nails into my chest like she's trying to claw her way inside. We're fire and gasoline. Rage and grief. Two storms colliding.

I bite down on her neck and she moans as her hands go to my belt. Fumbling. Shaking.

"I need you," she pants. "Right now."

I growl against her skin. "You have me."

My pants hit the floor. Her panties follow.

I don't wait. I line up, grab her hips, and slam into her in one hard, unrelenting thrust. Her scream is sharp. Raw. And it rips straight through me. She digs her heels into my back and throws her head back against the wall. I fuck her like I'm trying to erase the last twenty-four hours. Like I'm trying to make her feel alive, feel safe.

"Mine," I growl against her skin, lips brushing the sweat-slick curve of her throat. "You hear me, malyshka? Mine."

"Yes," she gasps.

And then I lose it. I drive into her with the kind of brutal rhythm that doesn't ask, it takes. Her nails claw into my back drawing blood, but I don't stop. Not when she cries out. Not when her entire body arches under me like she's breaking apart from within.

I grip her jaw, force her eyes back to mine. "Look at me."

Her pupils are blown wide, lips swollen from my kisses. "Lex..."

"Come with me," I rasp, breath ragged. "Glaza na menya, ma-lyshka."

She shatters right there under me. Her steel eyes locking with mine. Her lips cursing my name.

I go with her, everything in me snapping loose as I bury myself deep and shatter so hard that I see the fucking stars. I stay there, forehead pressed to hers, both of us wrecked. Still moving. Still needing. Because even after all of that, I'm not fucking done.

I kiss her mouth, her cheek, her shoulder. I grip her hips and keep moving, slower now, grinding into her like I can rewrite every terrible thing that happened today. Like I can fuck the memory of that man's hands off her skin or even just pull her back from the edge one thrust at a time.

Cade's in the room. I know he is. I can feel his presence—tight, still, watching.

But right now, this is mine. She's mine.

Her legs wrap tighter around me, like she knows. Like she needs this just as bad.

"Say it," I whisper. "Say you're mine, malyshka."

"I'm yours, Lex," she breathes, breaking again. "Always."

"Now. Promise me you will never do anything that reckless ever again, not without me, baby."

"I promise."

CHAPTER ⑤⑦
BELLA
REGIONAL COMPETITION
MANHATTAN, NEW YORK
702 DAYS SINCE ZEKE'S DEATH

The dressing room smells like hairspray, body glitter, and straight-up ambition. It's complete insanity backstage. Girls darting between lighted mirrors, lashes flying, spray bottles misting, topped off with Javi and Rico yelling at us all in a Spanish fury.

Rico's on a rampage with the outfits, slinging custom garment bags as if it's fashion week and he's behind schedule.

"Haley, teal. Ellie, pink. Bella, purple."

Javi bursts through the door in a whirlwind of cologne and chaos, waving a clipboard above his head. "Legacy!" he calls, eyes already scanning for strays. "I've got the schedule."

He stops in front of us, dramatic as always. "Alright, mis estrellas, listen up." He points the clipboard at Haley first. "Legacy opens, which means mi fuego, you better burn that stage down. It's your routine, Hales. No pressure, just perfection, ¿sí?"

Then he spins to Ellie, eyes gleaming. "And you, Miss Whitmore, your solo's up against Maddie Rae. I want her crying into her rhinestones by the second eight-count, understood?" He clutches his chest dramatically. "Vamos, princesa, make me proud."

He turns to me with a wicked grin. "Bella, you and Josh, ay Dios mío, my favorite duet, my little center-stage sinners. Don't make me regret pairing you two. I want passion, drama, fuego y pecado, all of it."

He claps his hands once, loud enough to rattle the mirrors. "And Trifecta, you close. Big finish. Smoke. Flames. Tears. Make the judges need therapy, ladies. This isn't just Regionals, bebés. This is war in sequins."

Ellie practically glows. Haley cracks her neck like she's about to body-slam someone. Josh gives me a wink from across the room.

Javi claps his hands again, louder this time. "Alright, team. No pressure, but I want gold in every category. I want them begging for an encore. I want tears, real tears in the judges' eyes."

He leans in close, voice dropping low. "Now, get out there and don't you dare fuck this up."

He spins on his heels and disappears through the curtains like a man walking into his own telenovela finale.

No pressure or anything.

Hair and makeup are working their magic around us, a well-oiled glam machine. I sit in front of the mirror, lips parted slightly as someone lines them in deep wine-red. I look like power and temptation stitched in silk and sequins.

But underneath it all, I'm fraying. These last few days have been a goddamn blur. Emotionally, physically, and to be honest... sexually.

Lex has literally fucked me senseless on every surface of their apartment. Kitchen counter. Living room couch. Bathroom vanity. Pinned against the window with the entire city of New York watching.

Even up against Cade's massive bookshelf like we were reenacting some dark, twisted version of *Beauty and the Beast*—only this time, the Beast whispered in Russian and fucked like a god.

Cade walked in halfway through that one. Didn't even blink. Just loosened his tie, sat down in that big leather chair of his, and started stroking himself while he watched us like we were art. Then he joined in. Took his time going down on me while Lex whispered filth into my ear and held my wrists above my head.

I think I blacked out at one point. In the best way.

Lex even read us poetry after. I'm not kidding. Completely naked. His voice all low and raspy. But it didn't last long, he got distracted by my breasts and Cade's dick and made us both come before he even hit the second stanza.

They keep asking me to move in. Cade with his soft eyes and slow hands. Lex with his dirty promises and unrelenting need. And God, I want to. I want them.

But something still holds me back...

Don't get me wrong, I love them. So much it aches. So much it terrifies me. But something's still off. The weight of everything I've learned—the Barinovs, the Russos, Zeke, the *Izzy* of it all—it's sitting in my chest like lead. And every time I try to exhale, it's still there.

Heavy, sharp, and fucking suffocating.

Irina keeps asking me to meet her for coffee. *"Just a quick talk,"* she says. She looks at me like I'm Izzy and it freaks me out. I don't like it. I'm not ready to unpack all of that. Not with her. Not yet. So, I keep dodging and keep making excuses.

Lex doesn't push but I can feel the disappointment every time I turn her down. He wants me to have with Irina what I have with Savannah, some kind of maternal connection.

But it's different. I've known the Whitmores since I was fourteen. There's history there. Real love. The kind that grew over late-night kitchen raids and family lake trips, long before any of us realized how much we'd come to matter to each other.

And then there's Roman. He's here, somewhere out in the crowd. We've been texting a little since he saved my life. Since he knelt in the street like some mafia vigilante dad and painted the sidewalk with a stranger's skull. He wants to be part of my life now. Says he doesn't want to waste another second.

Cade told me to invite him to Regionals. Said it'd be low pressure. Not a dinner or a sit-down where we'd have to talk the whole time. Just a seat in the crowd. He could watch, cheer, and then leave.

Luca's been quiet all week. Not a single message. Which freaks me the hell out. I've been on edge—paranoid, checking corners, and flinching at shadows. Always waiting for the next move.

Which is so not me. I feel like I'm going soft after meeting the guys. Like the badass who shot Carlos in the dick is slowly slipping away.

Dr. Monroe calls it progress. Says my nervous system is finally coming down from the survival mode I've been stuck in for years. That I'm starting to *process the trauma*. Whatever the hell that means.

All I know is, I don't like feeling exposed and vulnerable. Vulnerable gets you killed.

So maybe I shouldn't have, but I called Uncle Jack the next day. Told him what happened, minus the skull-splattering part. I just said things got tense and I was safe now. Told him not to tell my dad, just to say I called and everything was okay.

He agreed.

Then, of course, he went and called Lex and Cade. Apparently, they're best buddies now. Bonded over football, bourbon, and their shared obsession with keeping me alive. They made a whole safety plan for The Trifecta and everything.

Jack couldn't make it today. It's the anniversary of Aunt Claire's death this weekend and Daddy decided to fly him to Arkansas for a fishing trip.

So to be safe, Jack sent a few of his buddies from the NYPD to be stationed all over this place. Plain-clothes officers. Canines. Probably snipers on the roof if I had to guess.

And I know it's probably for the best, but it's also a reminder that I'm not safe.

Not really.

Not even here.

Not even now.

"Bella," Rico says, pulling me away from my thoughts.

He crouches down in front of me, voice gentle now. "You good, baby?"

I nod. "Yeah. I'm just... breathing."

He gives me a knowing smile. Then leans in, pulling the strap of my costume onto my shoulder, fixing it with the kind of care most people reserve for religious artifacts.

"Breathe all you need," he whispers. "Then go out there and burn the fucking floor down."

We're lined up in the wings now, the stage buzzing with nerves, victory sweat and enough glitter to choke a rhinestone. The crowd's still electric from the last routine and the judges are scribbling so fast their pens might catch fire.

Ellie's already holding her first-place plaque, bouncing in her heels with that megawatt smile that makes everyone around her look dim by comparison. She nailed her solo—clean lines, impossible turns, and that damn near airborne back bend she only pulls out when it counts.

Legacy took first too, which means Haley's been insufferable since they announced it. She keeps flashing her gold medal like it's a weapon, flipping her hair and throwing fake kisses into the crowd like a cheerleader on a Red Bull bender. I love her for it and I'm so proud of her. That dance was her baby and it was amazing.

Josh and I took first for our duet. Not that I ever doubted it. That routine was sex, strength, and in perfect sync. He lifted me like I was made of smoke and I gave the judges just enough eye contact to make them feel it. When they said our names, he picked me up and spun me like it was prom night.

Now it's just The Trifecta left.

My fingers are ice. My thighs ache. And I feel like if they say anyone else's name, I might actually break down in the middle of this stage in front of the entire New York dance elite.

The announcer taps the mic. "And now," she says, smiling at the judges' table, "for the final and most competitive category of the day, Small Group: Collegiate Division."

Javi's behind us, hands clenched so tight his knuckles are white. Rico has both hands clasped most likely praying to the gods of fringe, rhinestones, and rhythm.

My heart pounds.

"In third place..." the announcer begins, dragging it out like this is The Hunger Games. "...The Revenants from Northvale University!"

A smattering of polite claps echoes through the crowd as The Revenants step forward, their smiles so tight they might crack. Maddie stands just a few feet away, her crown slipping, her pride bleeding out in silence. She looks like she just swallowed glass.

The announcer smiles, flipping open the final card like she's about to crown Miss America. "And in first place..."

I grab Haley's hand. She grabs Ellie's. All three of us are locked in a death chain of sequins and nerves. It's between us and this team of Boston who performed a lyrical routine that was crazy beautiful.

I'm sweating bullets and deep down I know the announcer is

trying to pause for dramatic effect, but if she doesn't open her mouth soon I'm gonna—

"From Wexley University, The Trifecta!"

The crowd erupts. Rico screams louder than the announcer. Javi full-on jumps. I don't think I've ever seen the man's feet leave the floor before. Haley shrieks. Ellie throws her arms around me. We're hugging and crying and laughing all at once as someone shoves a plaque in our hands.

I can feel it in my chest, this isn't the finish line. Not even close. It's not over. Regionals may be a win, but we're still a long way from Worlds.

Nationals is next, and if we think tonight was a fight? The next round is war.

The competition's only going to get harder.

The pressure sharper.

The target on our back, bigger than ever.

CHAPTER (58)
CADE
REGIONAL COMPETITION
MANHATTAN, NEW YORK
702 DAYS SINCE ZEKE'S DEATH

She walks out like a goddess. Glitter on her cheeks, lipstick slightly smudged, and eyes wild from adrenaline. Her hair is teased to hell, smile a tad crooked as if she just survived war and still won the crown. Which, she did. I step forward and hand her the bouquet of white daisies that I've been holding like a damn security blanket. Her face softens the second she sees them.

"Awe, Cade!" she breathes. "I love you." She throws her arms around my neck and pulls me in for a kiss. It's fast and sweet and still somehow short-circuits my brain.

Lex shows up a second later like he always does, heat and chaos wrapped in leather and spice. He loops an arm around her waist, claiming his territory.

"We did it!" She smiles.

Mom's voice cuts through like a horn at rush hour. "You three! Get together. I need a picture."

Lex groans. "Seriously?"

"Yes, seriously. This is history."

Ellie's already dragging Cal into the next shot while Mom aims her phone at us. "Cade, stand a little closer. Lex, less serial killer, more supportive boyfriend. Bella honey, try not to look like you just got railed backstage."

Lex smirks. "Can't help it."

"Lex," I mutter.

"What? I'm just saying her glow is *real*, babe."

Before I can fire back, he grabs Bella by the chin and pulls her into a very deep kiss. Like, unnecessarily deep. Like, *Jesus Christ, people are watching* deep.

Mom snaps the photo anyway. "Perfect. Looks like a promo for a very sexy HBO show."

Bella's cheeks flush but she doesn't step away.

"Alright, Whitmores, I need all three of you together. Family shot!" Mom calls, already waving her phone like a damn paparazzi.

"Baby, that's our cue," Lex says, tugging Bella out of the shot.

I drag my feet behind Ellie and Cal, throwing on my best son-of-the-year smile while we shuffle into place. We've taken about twelve photos already, but apparently this is the official one, so Mom's not playing around.

We're standing there, grinning like the perfect little family, but all I can focus on is them. The two loves of my life. Lex's hand on her hip. Bella's fingers curled in his shirt. Whispering. Laughing.

God, I love them. Even when they're being ridiculous. Even when they're driving me insane. Even when I feel like I'm the only one who hasn't quite figured out how to breathe without them.

I look away and that's when I see him. Roman Russo. Striding through the crowd like he owns the damn building, like he built it brick by brick with blood and threats. Jet-black suit cut razor-sharp across a frame that could snap a man in half. Shoulders broad. Hands steady. One gripping an enormous bouquet of blood-red roses. The other swinging loose. His steel-gray eyes are locked and loaded on Bella.

It takes everything in me not to step in front of her. Not to shield her from the man who made her, lost her, and now, God help us, wants her back. I don't like the man. Don't trust him. And I hate that the loves of my life both come from dangerous families who could swallow them whole all while calling it *protection*.

Bella steps forward to meet him. Their voices blur. He hands her the roses. She hesitates but then takes them. Her smile flickers on, too polite. Too practiced. She's not okay, not even close.

Lex slides up beside me, silent for a beat, then nods toward them. "You're staring, babe."

"Yeah. I know."

"You want me to go punch him?"

"I want you to move her to another country."

Lex chuckles under his breath. "Same. He wants to play daddy of the year, but he knows nothing about her. I mean he brought her roses, babe. Roses. Her literal least favorite flower in the world. Fuckers not gonna last."

I let out a small laugh.

"But hey, at least this is better than dinner at our place. Can you imagine that guy walking through our door?" He makes a disgusted face. "No fucking thanks."

"It's not our place yet, babe."

"Semantics."

I glance over at Bella again—still talking to Roman, still holding those damn roses—and something tightens in my chest. "What do you think is holding her back, Lex?"

He sighs. Then steps in, wrapping his arms around me from behind like he can shoulder the question for me. "I don't know, but we'll get her to move in, Cade."

I lean back into him, let the weight of us settle. "I love you, Lex."

Lex presses a kiss to my neck. "I love you too, babe."

Bella walks back over with tense shoulders and arms full of flowers. Unsure of what to do with any of it, herself included.

"You okay, sweetheart?" I ask, brushing a strand of hair from her face.

She nods. "Yeah. It's just... awkward. Talking to him."

Lex and I both go still.

"I don't know," she continues. "It's weird. He says all the right things, but I still feel like I have to put on a mask around him. Like I can't be myself. It feels like a weird first date or something."

Lex groans. "Baby, please don't talk about dating your dad. It makes me want to punch things."

She laughs and leans in, pressing a kiss to his cheek. He lets out a soft grunt and slides an arm around her waist, tugging her in as close as the flowers will allow.

"But," she says, tilting her head, "since he's trying to win the Dad of the Year Award, he offered to let us use The Obsidian for my birthday. He said what's his is mine. So, anytime I want to use it, or NOX, I can. Just have to say the word."

Ellie overhears and shrieks. "Shut up. Shut up. Shut up. Shut up! Are you serious?!"

Bella laughs. "Yeah, so... I guess you should probably get planning."

"AHHHH!" Ellie spins in a full circle like her soul just left her body.

Lex grins. "Careful, Barbie. You're gonna pull a hamstring."

"Excuse you," Ellie gasps, fanning herself dramatically. "This is history in the making, Lex."

Bella arches a brow, fighting a smile. "So, you're in?"

"In?" Ellie grabs her phone. "I'm already texting Knox. We need lighting, fog machines, stage setups, security, costumes, backup dancers. Oh! And we need strip—

"Whoa." I lift a hand. "Can we maybe not have strippers at the party my girlfriend is starring in?"

"Ugh!" Ellie shrugs. "Fine. Sexy firemen then."

Lex snorts. "Better. Less competition."

"Ah! Bells, we are so going to do some Taylor performances."

"No, we are not," Bella says dryly.

"Oh, come on!" Ellie throws her hands up. "You and I both know two things."

She ticks them off on her fingers. "One, some of your best, and I mean best dances are to Taylor Swift songs. That *Midnight Rain* contemporary on the rain stage with Josh? Perfection. Literal goosebumps every time. It's probably going to win you two a world championship one day."

Then she leans closer, lowering her voice like she's sharing state secrets. "And two, you are a closet Swiftie. Don't even try to deny it. I saw your face in New Orleans last October at her concert. The lights, the dancing, the friendship bracelets," she gasps. "You ate it up, babe. Ate. It. Up."

"Okay, fine," Bella says, sighing. "We can do one Taylor song. One. But no, and I mean no, rain stage at my party, El."

"Ugh! Why not?" Ellie whines.

"Because I'd rather not be dripping wet at my own party," she shoots back.

Bella catches Lex's smirk forming. "Don't say it, Lex. I swear to

God, do not fucking say it."

We all start laughing.

"Aww, baby, you know me so well."

"Wait, what about The Row's party that night?" I ask.

Ellie scoffs. "Fuck The Row. This is The Obsidian. And it's ours for the night for Bella's twenty-first birthday. On fucking Halloween, Cade!"

Bella's eyes go wide and I swear even Lex winces. The idea of Ellie Whitmore unleashed with that kind of venue and theme? Yeah, no one's surviving this.

Cal strolls over, catching the tail end of her screech. "What's this about The Obsidian?"

Ellie spins on him, a twister in heels. "Bella's birthday. There. Halloween night. Cancel everything. I need your guest list by tomorrow."

Cal lifts a brow, hands in his pockets. Not fazed at all. "Great. We'll be there."

"Fucking perfect," Lex mutters behind me. Like the words themselves taste like blood and bile on his tongue. Bella grabs his hand before he can spiral.

"Just like that," I say, looking at Cal. "What about your big Row party?"

Cal shrugs like it's no big deal. "I'll just bring them all to you, Bells." He winks and strolls off.

Lex blows out a breath and shakes his head. "This is gonna be a goddamn disaster."

"Costumes!" Ellie screams, dragging Bella away. "We need costumes!"

"If she puts me in tights again, I'm burning the building down," Lex says as we watch them walk off.

"Think we'll survive this?"

He huffs. "Only if there's vodka. A shit-ton of vodka, Cade."

CHAPTER 59
BELLA
ASHMOOR HALL
WEXLEY UNIVERSITY
708 DAYS SINCE ZEKE'S DEATH

After competitions, it's basically tradition. A full lock down at Ashmoor Hall. No spectators. Not a single distraction. Only us, the mirrors, Knox, and Javi with his clipboard of doom. He calls it *Refinement Week*. I call it soul murder with an 8-count.

We've spent the entire week picking apart Regionals, getting new assignments for Nationals, and drilling every single number until we bleed perfection. Once Javi's satisfied, he'll let us back into the basketball arena for public practices. Cue the groupies, the chairs, the photographers, and most importantly... Lex and Cade.

Which is exactly why Lex has been insufferable this week. Every day he gripes about being *'banned from the building'*. That it's *'not fair'* that Knox gets to come inside when he and Cade don't.

And no matter how many times I try to explain to the man that Knox has been our tech-guy-slash-manager since day one, Lex still acts like he's being personally victimized by the dance gods.

"Just let me stand in the corner, baby. I'll be quiet. Silent. Mute. I swear on my dick," he whined to me yesterday as I was trying to head into Ashmoor Hall.

In his defense, he's under a lot of pressure at Northvale. The Hollow Kings' Donor Fight is tomorrow night and things have been tense. Rez and Lex both have a lot riding on it. Rez has been shielding him from most of the politics, but Lex still carries it. I see it in the tight set of his jaw, the weight in his shoulders, he's stressed.

And while technically I'm just supposed to be there to dance, let's be real, I've had my hands in this thing since that first Fight Night. Rez wanted a Row-level spectacle in The Pit and that's exactly what we're bringing.

The Trifecta has performed at every Fight Night this semester. Lex thrives on it. Says it's the reason he's still undefeated this season.

Every time I step out in one of Rico's custom sets with *Property of Lex Barinov* across my chest, or every time I strut past the edge of that ring and catch his eyes, he turns into something feral.

He says I flip a switch in him, that watching me dance before he fights makes his blood sing. That I'm his own personal war cry. The rhythm of my hips is the reason his fists find their mark.

He's insane, but it's kind of cute.

Knox runs the lights and announces the show now like it's his full-time job—barking cues through his headset, stealing the damn spotlight with every intro. He calls us *The Knockout Queens,* which Lex fucking loves, and somehow always times the bass drop to hit the exact second our heels hit center ring.

Tomorrow's Fight Night could make or break everything for The Hollow Kings. Rez wanted big names this time. Brutal ones. Fighters with international pull and a reputation for blood. No more college athletes or frat boys pretending to be gangsters. He wanted the kind of men whose names make people scream.

And for that, he came to me.

Lex told his cousin a little about me. Not the full *my girlfriend hacked into the family's Black Book* part, but enough. Rez thinks my underworld connections start and end with Roman Russo, and we didn't exactly correct him.

We made a deal. The lineup stays secret until Knox calls their names tomorrow night. No leaks. No whispers. The less anyone knows, the louder the chaos hits. Only my fighters, Cade, Rez, Knox, and I know who's stepping into that ring.

And Rez is right, this crowd doesn't want a fair fight. They want carnage wrapped in velvet. Violence with a price tag. They have no idea what's coming. Let's just say, tomorrow night's going to be one hell of a show.

Buzz. Buzz.

"Hey, what's up?" I answer.

"Just making sure you still want me to do this tomorrow?"

"Yes. We need a solid fight. You and Lex will give the donors the show they've been waiting for. The one they'll be happy to put their money on."

"You sure? Is he going to be okay with it?"

I roll my eyes. "He'll be fine. Shocked and totally pissed at both of us, but fine. Look, we need big time fighters. You've got the skill, the reputation, and just enough drama to make it interesting. Plus, you can technically be considered an international fighter and that's what Rez wants. So, don't be late."

"You want me to hold back?"

I laugh. "No. I want you to fight hard. For real. Give them a show."

"Understood," he exhales through his nose. "I won't disappoint you."

I hang up, heart already racing as I get in the car to head to Dr. Monroe's office.

Dr. Monroe's Office - Manhattan, New York

Dr. Monroe doesn't even bother with pleasantries today. He just watches me with that unreadable calm, pen resting against his notepad waiting for a confession.

"I'm assuming this isn't about dance," he says finally.

"Not directly." I shift in the chair. My thighs stick to the leather.

I hate this room.

"But still a performance," I mutter.

His brow lifts just slightly. "Go on."

"There's a fight. A big one."

He already knows what that means. He doesn't ask.

"The Northvale donors will be there," I continue, voice flat. "All of them. Or enough to make it matter. And this time... I'm part of the show."

His pen moves once, barely. "You'll be performing? That's not unusual. Don't you girls always dance?"

"We do, but this time it's different. I'm more like orchestrating the fights." I force a breath. "The fighters I picked, they're brutal. They are all going to make a statement."

"But you're worried."

I nod. "Because Lex doesn't know who he is fighting against. And when he sees him... he's going to lose his shit."

Silence.

"He's already walking a tightrope," I whisper. "This might snap whatever thread he's holding onto."

Dr. Monroe doesn't move. "You've seen him spiral before."

"Yeah." My throat tightens. "But not like this. Not with me in the middle of it."

He waits.

I shake my head. "He won't see it coming. Not until the second he lays eyes on my fighter. And by then, it'll be too late. The donors will be watching. Cameras. Eyes. Money on the line."

He scribbles something, then asks, "Who is he?"

I hesitate. "Someone deeply invested in earning my trust and respect."

His brow lifts.

"Let's just say... he has a lot to prove. To the donors. To Lex. To me."

"You trust him?"

"Not completely," I say honestly. "But I trust how badly he wants me to accept him, how badly he wants me to like him."

Dr. Monroe watches me for a beat. "So, you're handing that kind of power to a man you don't trust, while keeping the one you do in the dark. Why?"

"Because it has to be real," I say, and the words feel heavier than I mean them to. "The fight. The rage. The outcome. They're not going to buy it if it feels staged. These people bet with blood in mind."

Dr. Monroe's expression doesn't change, but his pen pauses. "So, you're using Lex's reaction as part of the strategy."

"I mean I don't really want to, I hate it."

He waits.

I sigh. "But yeah... it helps. His jealousy. His fury. He's already half feral when it comes to me or Cade. This will push him the rest of the way."

"And you're okay with that?"

"No." The word rips out of me before I can stop it.

He watches me. Silent. Waiting.

I look down at my hands. "I can handle it."

"That's not what I asked."

I exhale, jaw tight. "I'll do what I have to. I always do."

"And what will that cost you this time?"

I pause. "Maybe him."

"Lex?"

I nod. "I'm just worried he's going to hate me for it. For keeping it from him. For setting him up to snap in front of everyone. And when he finds out what I have to do to sell it..." my voice trails off.

"What exactly do you mean by that? Sell it?"

"I mean I can't just stand in the corner and cheer like normal. I have to make it look personal. Like I'm emotionally invested in the other side, in all of my fighters. All night long. I have to be touched, teased, claimed, if that's what it takes."

His brow lifts slightly. "So, your plan is to exploit his possessiveness."

"To make sure the donors believe it? Yes." I meet his eyes. "Because if they believe it, they'll invest. If they invest, Rez and Lex can breathe."

Dr. Monroe leans forward slightly, voice softer now. "Bella, what you're about to do."

I stare at the edge of his notepad, letting the silence drag.

He nods slowly. "Just make sure you're not the one who ends up bleeding for it."

The Pit – Northvale University
Donor Fight Night
709 Days Since Zeke's Death

Cade and I step into The Pit, the underground already humming with Fight Night electricity. It's two hours before the doors open, but mayhem is already in full swing. Knox is in the lighting booth, barking into his headset. Rico is backstage, flinging costume racks and shouting at the poor hair and makeup crew to stop fucking up his vision.

Rez walks up, stretching his neck like he's already halfway through warm-ups. "Hey, B. Look, I just wanted to say thanks for everything you've done to make tonight happen."

"I did it for Lex."

He nods. "I know." He glances toward the ring. "So, let's go over the plan."

I tip my chin, voice cool. "Fight One: Hollow King Chase Cooper vs. Caleb Briggs."

Rez raises a brow. "Who the hell is Caleb Briggs?"

"He's from Knoxville, Tennessee," I say, casually brushing off the not-so-international part. "Leader of the Ashen Sons."

"Yeah... I've heard of them. Gun runners. Midwest all the way down to Mexico. And how do you know him?" he asks.

I just smile. "That's not important. Just know he wants something from me and this fight is my price."

"Let's just be clear on something," Cade cuts in.

"Every one of the four fighters she brought in tonight wants something from her, Rez," he adds while wrapping an arm around my waist. "And to get it, they're going to have to put on a damn good show for her."

"Damn, B. Lex said you had connections." Rez smirks. "Fight Two?"

"Hollow King DeShawn Reyes versus Tatenda Khoza."

"Khoza?" Rez clears his throat. "As in Jackals of Johannesburg, Khoza? How the fuck did you got someone from Blood Diamond country to show up to The Pit?"

"He was already stateside." I shrug.

"Fuck, okay." Rez gives a low and impressed nod. "And my fight... are you sure about that one?"

I grin. "Awe, Rezy. Are you scared?"

"Fuck that," he snaps, shaking his head. "But still, that man's a beast."

Cade chuckles, then looks at me more seriously. "In all honesty, sweetheart, the one we should be worried about is Lex's fight. Are you sure this isn't a mistake?"

I pause, then smile slow. "I'm sure, babe. We needed a showstopper for the main event. And the two of them? They're going to give us the fight of the year. Plus, you know that my prize fighter will do anything for me right now. So, when I told him he was going up against my boyfriend..."

Cade's brow lifts. "He agreed?"

"Hesitated at first," I admit. "But yeah. He agreed. Said he'd do it just for me."

Rez cracks his knuckles. "Alright. I'm gonna go warm up and pretend I'm not about to get my ass handed to me by one of the biggest criminal leaders in the world. Thanks for that, B."

"I'm going to go check on Knox," Cade says leaning down, brushing a kiss against my cheek. "He's running half this place solo, and I'm afraid if one light is off during your performance, Rico and Javi might actually commit a felony. You go check on Lex, I'm sure he needs to burn off some steam before the fight."

I grab his wrist. "Babe, come with me. It's more fun when it's all three of us."

He grins, leans in, whispering low and hot against my ear. "As much as I'd love to fuck the hell out of both of you right now back there..." His voice turns teasing. "We've got a show to run, sweetheart. Lex needs this night to be a win. So, helping Knox is how I help him."

I sigh but nod. He cups my face and kisses me.

"I love you," I whisper.

"I love you, sweetheart," he says, already pulling away.

CHAPTER ⑥⓪
LEX
THE PIT
ABOUT TO MAKE FUCKING HISTORY.
709 DAYS SINCE ZEKE'S DEATH

For tonight's Donor Fight, they've separated the fighters—our side versus Bella's mysterious imports. No sneak peeks or scouting your opponent. None of the normal shit. Usually, we get to see who we're up against. Watch their style, size, and see if they're more speed or brute force.

Not tonight. Rez and Bella have been on lockdown about this shit for weeks. Between the lighting, the music, and the crowd, it's been anarchy in the best way.

I love that Bella and my cousin are finally getting close. Feels like she's becoming a real part of my family. We've spent so much time at The Row and at Wexley, that being back at Northvale feels almost like coming home.

Across the room, Chase is stretching his neck while DeShawn throws combos into the air like he's already in the ring. Hollow Kings warming up. Focused. Silent.

There's a whole-ass table in the corner loaded with protein bars, fresh fruit, sandwiches, and electrolyte drinks. Knox might run the lights, but Ellie made sure the bodies holding the lights aren't going pass the fuck out.

Rez walks in, wiping his hands on a towel and claps both palms down on my shoulders. "You ready for tonight?"

I crack my neck and roll my shoulders back. "Born ready."

He nods once, then starts to turn, but I catch him with a look.

"Seriously... gimme a clue, Rez. Who the hell am I fighting?"

Rez laughs. "Nah, man. It's better if you don't know."

"You say that like I'm not walking into a damn blindfolded brawl."

"You'll be fine. You're Lex Barinov. Punch first, ask names later."

I snort. "That's not inaccurate."

"Plus, your girl scares the shit out of me," Rez adds, tilting his head toward the door. "She may be small, but if I even thought about snitching on the lineup, she'd probably castrate me in my sleep."

"Jesus, Rez."

He grins. "And smile while doing it."

"Sounds about right," I mutter, shaking my head with a half-smile. "She's terrifying."

He leans against the wall, looking almost proud. "Seriously though, B's been busting her ass for this. She's got half the city wrapped around her finger and the other half begging for scraps."

Before he can continue, the door creaks open. "Okay, boys. Out. I need to talk to my boyfriend."

Rez whistles as he grabs his water. "Alright, I'm gone. Try not to get him too worked up, B. He's still gotta fight later."

She walks toward me, hips swaying, those steel eyes already locked and loaded. I drop the protein bar and wrap her up the second she's in reach, arms caging her tight like I've been waiting all day to breathe her in.

"Hey, baby, about fucking time you got back here."

She tips her head back, flashing a grin that could raise the dead. "I can't stay long. Rico needs me in hair and makeup, and I still need to check on my fighters. Make sure they're all ready to go."

I groan, dragging my hands down her spine. "Baby, who are these guys?"

She leans in, lips brushing my jaw. "Let's just say they're the kind of men who'll bring in big money from your donors." She rises on her toes and kisses the tip of my nose. "And put on one hell of a show while doing it."

I narrow my eyes. "That sounds like code for *not your normal Row boys.*"

She lifts her chin, eyes gleaming like she planned this whole damn ambush. "It is. So, you better be ready, baby."

Then she slips out of my arms with that lethal little wink that always scrambles my brain. "Because they are. And I'll make you a deal..."

She pauses and lets it hang there. "If you make your fight a fight to remember... if you win, if you beat my fighter. I'll do what you've been asking of me for weeks."

My heart stops.

"I'll come home for good," she says softly. "I'll move in, Lex."

I swear to God, I forget how to breathe. One second, I'm standing there like a cocky bastard about to go punch someone's face in, and the next I'm a goddamn wreck.

My chest expands like I just took my first breath in years. I rake a hand through my hair, trying to process the words that just left her mouth.

She'll come home for good. To us. To Cade. To me.

"Fuck," I whisper. "You serious?"

"Just win the fight, Barinov."

She turns to leave, but I grab her by the wrist, tugging her back into my space.

"No, no. You don't get to walk away from me like that."

She smiles, slow and sinful. "Oh baby, I'm not walking away." Her fingers trail down my chest, slipping beneath the hem of my shirt, tracing the lines of muscle as she drops to her knees in front of me.

"Bella..." My voice is hoarse, breath catching. "What are you doing?"

She glances up with dark, playful eyes. "Oh, you know, just helping you work out a little pre-fight stress. It was Cade's idea." She pulls my shorts down to the ground, eyes widening as she bites the side of her lip.

My heart is hammering, hands fisting at my sides as her fingers move slow, teasing my cock. It pulses in her hands.

"You want me to stop?" she asks, cocking her head, the ghost of a smirk on her lips as she runs her hand up the length of me.

"Fuck no," I growl, jaw tight, eyes locked on her like she's the only thing that exists. "Baby, you touch me like that and I'm gonna forget there's even a fight tonight."

She hums, pleased, and I black out for a second as her mouth finds me. Her tongue glides from the base to the tip and I let out a moan. I brace a hand against the wall trying to stay upright while she ruins me.

"Jesus, baby. Mmmm..."

She takes me in and moans around me, deep and needy, and I swear my knees almost buckle. My hand slides to the back of her head, steadying myself. Her cherry-red nails bite into my thighs. The sight of her on her knees, lips wrapped around my cock, and her eyes starting to water nearly undoes me.

"Fuck, baby," I grit out, my voice raw. "You're gonna make me lose it."

Bella doesn't slow down. She picks up her pace, sucking and licking me like she's starving and I'm her favorite meal on the goddamn planet.

A few more strokes and I'm right there on the edge of unraveling. My hips jerk forward, and her eyes meet mine. She gives me the look. That wicked, gorgeous, wreck-me look.

It's over.

I groan her name as I come, spilling deep down her throat. And of course, like the perfect fucking angel-devil she is, she swallows every drop. Doesn't flinch. Never stops. She keeps her eyes on me the entire time.

I reach down, lift her effortlessly, and crash my mouth to hers. The kiss is messy, desperate, our breaths tangled and harsh. I taste myself on her tongue, which only starts to wake Little Lex back up.

"That was fun," I say, trying to catch my breath.

She laughs. "I knew you had some pre-fight stuff to burn off, baby."

That word... *baby*. Damn it. I'm already hard as steel again, because apparently Little Lex has zero concept of self-control around this woman. I yank her leggings off. Then pick her ass up and slide my hands beneath her thighs. She wraps around me, her legs tightening at my waist as I push into her in one smooth, deep thrust.

Her head falls back. "Lex, ah! This was supposed to be about you, not me."

I growl into her neck. "You are about me. Every fucking inch of you."

I move with hard, fast thrusts that knock the breath from her lungs. That force her to feel every inch of me. I hold her in the air like she weighs nothing, like she belongs nowhere else but right here. In my arms. Around me. On me. With me.

Her nails rake down my back, leaving red trails I'll feel for days. Her breath stutters against my ear. Each drive of my hips rip a moan from her throat, each sound mine.

I can't stop. Won't stop. Not until she breaks apart in my arms. Not until her body screams my name.

She shatters with a cry that punches the air from my lungs. Her legs tighten around me, and I let go, grunting through clenched teeth as I spill inside her. We collapse into it, a tangled heap of sweat and skin. Her head rests against my shoulder. My arms lock around her like she's the only thing holding me together.

"I love you," I whisper, brushing her tangled hair off her face.

She looks up, cheeks flushed, lips still kiss-swollen and smiles that damn smile that always floors me. "I love you too, Lex."

She bends to grab her clothes, slips her leggings back on, and smoothes her crop top over her ribs. The second she reaches for the door, I tug her back into my arms and kiss her once more slow, deep, and hungry all over again.

"Baby," she laughs against my mouth. "I have to go. Rico's waiting and you need to start warming up. Plus, I still need to go check on my fighters."

"I don't want you to go," I mutter, burying my face in her neck.

"I'll see you soon," she says, lips brushing my ear. "I'll be the one with your name plastered on my chest."

I stare at the door she disappeared through, already missing her, and the second I remember what she's off doing—checking on *her* fighters—something primal flares in my chest.

Our girl is so moving in tonight.

The four of us Kings sit in the warm-up room, glued to the screen like a bunch of restless wolves. They stream the event back here so we don't lose our damn minds waiting for our fights. Usually, it's background noise. Not tonight. Not with her out there.

The lights in The Pit drop to blood red and Knox's voice rips through the sound system like thunder. "Ladies and gentlemen, welcome to the biggest goddamn fight in The Pit's history!"

The crowd ignites.

"But before we bring out our fighters, I wanna introduce my favorite ladies. I like to call them the Knockout Queens of our Hollow Kings... The Trifecta!"

The crowd damn near explodes when the girls walk out.

Fuck. Me. Knee-high leather boots. Black one-pieces that shimmer like a goddamn midnight dare and dip so low I can see the curve of Bella's sternum from here. Side cutouts, fishnet tights. Rico, you genius, insane little bastard. You actually did it. My girl looks like war and a wet dream had a baby.

"Thank you, Knox. We're happy to be here. And Knox was right, we do have one hell of a show for you tonight," Bella says toward the crowd.

"Damn, cuz. Your girl is fine as hell. Look at those – "

I snap my head toward Rez. "Watch it."

Rez laughs. "Chill. I'm just giving you props."

"Give me props silently," I growl, eyes locked back on the screen.

Knox leans in, "Did I hear right earlier, Bella? This a Bella vs. Rez kind of Fight Night?"

"Yeah, Knox. Tonight's a little different than your usual brawls here at The Pit. Rez has his Hollow Kings fighters..." she turns and winks at the camera. "And I have mine."

Laughter from the crowd. Cheers. Roars.

But all I hear is *mine*. She's calling them hers.

"Now, I don't mean my Row boys like usual," she adds, teasing. "Tonight, I brought backup."

My jaw tightens.

Knox raises a brow. "Wait, Bella, are you saying these aren't Wexley football guys?"

Bella smiles like she's the villain in every guy's favorite movie. "Nope. And these aren't your average campus jocks either. I brought with me some of the biggest, the baddest, the sexiest—"

"Baby." My voice comes out rougher now. She's playing cute, but I'm about ready to start walking out there grab her and drag her ass out of the ring caveman-style.

"—fighters from all across the world."

Rez elbows me with a smug-ass grin. "Surprise! Your girl's insane."

Knox is losing it. "Holy shit, Bells."

Bella shrugs, loving every second of this. "Let's just say I made a few calls."

Knox whistles. "Well damn. I think it's time we get this show on the road. What do you say, girls? Want to dance to kick things off?"

The crowd loses it.

Music hits. Lights drop. And then they move. The Trifecta hits center ring like they've been training for this their whole lives, slinking, grinding, flipping their hair like sirens. It's sexy as hell, choreographed with pure seduction. Bella's hips roll. Her fingers trail down the curve of her thighs.

The girls are killing it, the donors are eating it up, but all I can think about is how she keeps calling those mystery fighters *hers*. Like they matter. As if they're not about to get wrecked the moment they step into my ring with me.

Knox's voice booms through the arena, slick and cocky like he's narrating a damn UFC pay-per-view. "Okay, Bella. Since your boys are the visitors tonight, let's go ahead and bring out the Hollow King for Fight One!"

I snort, watching it all unfold on the screen. "Quit fucking calling them her boys, Knox."

Chase stands up and heads for the door, prepping for his entrance.

"Coming in hot, representing the Hollow Kings and Team Rez, we've got your crowd favorite, your middleweight champ, Chase Cooper!"

Chase charges out like he's already won, throwing his hands up for the crowd and bouncing on his toes. Back here in our holding room, DeShawn claps and hollers. I stay silent. Focused.

"Alright, Bella," Knox teases. "You want to do the honors or should I?"

She smiles like she's five seconds away from setting the whole ring on fire. "Go ahead, Knox."

"Okay, everyone. First up on Team Bella we've got one crazy-ass-cowboy straight outta Knoxville, Tennessee..."

I lean forward. "She brought a fucking cowboy?"

Knox hypes it up. "The leader of the Ashen Sons himself. Caleb Briggs!"

Briggs struts into The Pit like it's his goddamn show—jeans, tight black shirt, boots, black Stetson. He heads straight for Bella and wraps her in a hug that lasts a full three seconds longer than it should. My jaw tightens and I'm two seconds away from throwing a chair.

Rez just laughs. "Maybe you should get a cowboy hat, cuz."

DING.

I hate to admit it, but the cowboy can fight. He's fast, clean, and strategic. Chase lands a few, but Briggs dominates from start to finish. Ten minutes in and Chase is flat on the mat, sucking air while Briggs tips his damn hat like he's in a country music video. Then winks at my fucking girl when she gets in the ring to raise his arms in victory.

Knox's voice reverberates through the speakers. "Well, apparently cowboy's got some moves, because Caleb Briggs just made Chase Cooper look like a little bitch. And that's saying something!"

Rez whistles low. "Well shit, looks like it's Bella: 1, Me: 0."

I don't say a word, because I'm too busy wondering who the hell Bella brought into my kingdom. And how many of her boys think that they get to touch what's mine.

Knox's voice cuts through The Pit smooth like a shot of top-shelf tequila. "Alright! Next up, fighting for Team Rez, we've got the man with hands like hammers and footwork like a panther... DeShawn Reyes!"

DeShawn jogs into the ring, hyped up and cocky, pumping up the front row.

"And now..." Knox drags it out for the drama. "Fighting for Team Bella, coming to us all the way from Johannesburg, South Africa the one, the only... Tatenda Khoza!"

I freeze. "Did he just fucking say who I think he did?"

Rez nods, slow. "Yeah. He did. How exactly does your girl have all these contacts?"

I just shrug, grinning like this is all one big inside joke. "She's Bella Blackwood, man. Queen of chaos. Apparently, international chaos."

But I know better. I know these names. Briggs and Khoza are Black Book names. Khoza's not just some underground fighter. He's a blood diamond enforcer with ties in all of South Africa.

Holy shit.

If all her fighters are Black Book guys Team Rez doesn't stand a chance tonight.

"Who the fuck did this girl pick for me?" I say under my breath.

Khoza enters the ring like a damn showman. All swagger and precision. The guy is built like a fucking tank, pure muscle and no bullshit. Skin like burnished bronze, veins and ink running down his arms like warning signs. Shaved head, jaw cut from stone, brown eyes that say he's seen hell and walked out bored.

DeShawn is fucked.

DING.

Khoza plays the crowd, lets DeShawn land a few hits early on, probably to sell the fight better. He's keeping it tight and technical. In complete control.

Bella's yelling from the sideline, calling out combos and reading openings, and it's not my favorite thing to watch. Seeing her that locked in for another man's fight?

No. Fucking. Thanks.

DING.

The men return to their corners. Bella walks right up to Khoza, leans down, and whispers something in his ear. He looks up at her and smiles with blood in his teeth.

Then she kisses his goddamn forehead. I snap the neck off my beer bottle against the edge of the bench, slicing open my palm.

Rez doesn't even flinch. "Looks like your girl's really good at playing the crowd... and her fighters."

I glare at him.

"I did tell her I needed to sell this," he adds, smug as hell.

DING.

Round Two starts and ends in under sixty seconds. Khoza drops DeShawn so hard, it echoes through The Pit. Bella jumps in the ring all smiles as she raises yet another one of her champions hands in victory.

Then the motherfucker lifts Bella into the air like she's his fucking prize. I shoot to my feet, fists balled tight. "Baby, I swear to God."

"Shit, Bella: 2. Me: 0." Rez says, shaking his head.

Knox's voice cuts in again over the crowd.

"Alright folks, we're gonna take a quick intermission. Grab a beer, kiss your girl, and we'll be right back with the final two fights of the night!"

Yeah. Great. Only problem is my girl's too busy being worshiped by international criminals to remember who the fuck she belongs to.

Buzz. Buzz.

BELLA: How you liking the show so far?

> ME: Oh you mean the part where you let blood diamond boy carry you like a damn trophy? Yeah... Love it. Super romantic, baby.

BELLA: Oh, don't be jealous. Rez wanted great fights for the donors and that's what I gave him.

> ME: You brought Black Book guys.

BELLA: We needed big names... so yeah.

> ME: Who the fuck am I fighting Bella?

BELLA: You'll see. Gotta get back out there. Fight 3 is about to begin. I love you!! And remember what I said...a fight to remember, baby. Or I don't move in Kisses!!!!

I stare at the screen. "Oh, I'll fucking give you a fight to remember."

For the second half of the night, Rico clearly said go harder and hotter. Now the girls are in tight black leather shorts that are basically thongs, skimpy, ripped black cropped bralettes with *Hollow Kings* in red bold script across the front.

Bella's says *Certified Lex Addict* in glittering blood-red across her chest that makes my lungs forget how to function.

Rez walks up behind me, eyeing the shirt and raises a brow. "Damn. That's one way to stake a claim."

I turn, jaw ticking. "You ready?"

Rez runs a hand over his head. "To be honest? I'm nervous as fuck for who Bella picked for me. I mean... the guy's a damn beast."

I narrow my eyes. "So let me get this straight. I'm the only one who doesn't get to know who the fuck I'm up against?"

Rez grins. "Yep. Main Event's gotta kill it, man. Shock factor. Make the donors go feral. And your girl?" He nods toward the screen where Bella's commanding the crowd. "She's killing it. Got the donors eating out of her gorgeous little hands. Tonight's a huge success because of her, you should be proud. I know I sure as hell am."

Knox voice booms through the crowd. "Alright Hollow Kings, you know him, you fear him, make some noise for none other than Damien motherfucking Reznikov!"

Rez jogs into the ring, shaking out his arms, all swagger and steel. The crowd roars, hungry for violence.

Knox grins. "Well Rez. Bella. It looks like Team Bella is up 2-0."

Bella strolls up to Rez, all hips and hellfire. "No hard feelings, Rezy," she purrs, tapping him on the cheek. "Looks like my guys are just better than your little Hollow Kings."

Knox raises an eyebrow. "Alright, Bella, let's not get ahead of yourself. And fighting for Team Bel—"

She holds up a hand, stepping forward with a wicked glint in her eye. "No, no, Knox. I think I'll take it from here."

She turns toward the crowd. "Alright, Northvale," she says, voice dripping in pure sass, "I know you've seen some insane fights tonight. Blood, sweat, and maybe a few concussions."

A ripple of laughter and shouting rolls through The Pit. She smirks, pacing the ring slow, letting the tension stretch.

"But this one?" she says, stopping dead center, eyes glinting beneath the strobes. "This one's personal."

The crowd stills. She raises a hand, palm out to calm an audience she fully intends to destroy. "Fighting tonight for Team Bella..." she pauses, letting the silence crackle, then tips her head toward the entrance.

"The biggest, baddest Italian I've ever met. The man who taught New York to bleed power and called it business..."

Her voice drops, deadly intimate. "My father." Then she explodes, pointing toward the tunnel as the bass hits. "The one. The only. Roman Russo!"

The crowd detonates.

I freeze. "Shit. She brought fucking Russo to this?"

Rez's head jerks toward her. The crowd is standing. Phones everywhere.

And there he is, tall, tan, sleeves rolled up, eyes like polished obsidian. Roman walks in like he owns the damn world. Kisses Bella on the cheek and gives the crowd a single nod before turning toward Rez.

DING.

Roman strikes first, vicious and clean. A body shot that thunders through The Pit, followed by a backhand elbow that splits Rez's lip open within the first ten seconds.

Rez doesn't flinch. He wipes the blood away with the back of his hand and grins like he's been waiting for this exact brand of punishment. Then he unloads. Fast jabs. Low kicks. Feral speed and no hesitation.

By round two, The Pit's a madhouse. Donors shouting, bills flying, the air thick with sweat and blood. Rez is on a tear now. Fast, relentless, and unpredictable. He feints left, then lands a brutal hook to Roman's ribs that echoes through The Pit. Roman grunts and is forced back a step. Probably the first time anyone's ever pushed him like that.

Rez doesn't let up. He's all motion and fury, fighting like the world owes him a debt he intends to collect tonight. He drives Roman into the corner, shoulders and fists colliding in a blur of muscle and rage.

Bella's voice cuts through the noise. "Come on, Roman!" she yells, hands cupped around her mouth, eyes bright. Like this is her moment. Her war. Her family name bleeding across the mat.

Then the final round hits. Roman circles, shoulders rolling, breath steady. Rez wipes the blood from his mouth and spits it onto the mat, grinning like a man who refuses to die quietly.

Roman lands first, a brutal cross that cracks against Rez's temple. Rez staggers, blinks through the daze, then roars and drives forward anyway, throwing wild, furious punches that barely miss. The crowd's screaming, half for him, half for the king.

He clips Roman's jaw hard, but it only wakes the devil. Roman's eyes go dark. He steps in, slams a knee to Rez's ribs, followed by an elbow to the face that snaps his head back. Rez tries to swing again, but his footing's gone.

Roman seizes the opening. One clean, devastating right hook. Years of violence and control exploding in a single strike. The crack echoes through The Pit like a gunshot. Rez drops hard.

The crowd roars. Bella launches into the ring like she's been waiting her whole life to do it. She throws her arms around Roman, lifts his hand high, as if she's presenting the crowned King of Italy to his adoring court.

Knox laughs through the mic. "Okay it looks like that's Team Bella, three. Rez, zero. Rez, love ya man... but I hope your cousin can bring it in the main event."

I stand. Roll my neck and crack my knuckles. "Oh, I'll fucking bring it, Bestie."

The crowd's still losing it's mind over Roman's win when Knox's hyped voice slices through the chaos.

"Alright, Pit fans, don't sit your pretty asses down just yet, because it's time for the main event!" The lights strobe. The bass drops. "You've seen blood, you've seen fire, but you haven't seen him."

The arena plunges into darkness. Then the lights flare red. The

Pit glows like the mouth of hell.

"Fighting tonight for Team Rez. The undefeated, unhinged, undisputed Hollow King himself... Lex Barinov!"

The roar's deafening. I roll my shoulders and walk into the ring. The red lights washing over everything, hot and heavy, like I'm walking straight into fire. My blood is already simmering.

She saunters toward me like nothing about this is war. "Now, baby," she says sweetly, "I know tonight we're technically on opposite sides, but I just wanted to wish you good luck." She starts to walk away.

Fuck that. I grip her waist and pull her in, slamming my mouth onto hers in a kiss so deep, so filthy, half the damn crowd forgets to breathe. I don't care. Let them watch.

"Okay you two," Knox yells through the mic. "Get a fucking room. Bella... you're up, babe."

She pulls back, smug as hell, lips red and swollen, "Good luck, baby." Then she turns and struts to center of the ring like it's her fucking throne.

The red lights start to fade. A single bright, golden spotlight lands on her. Mine and Cade's Queen reclaiming her stage. "Alright everyone. I saved my absolute best, sexiest, and favorite fighter for last."

The gold spotlight on her flickers twice, then fades to electric blue—cool, seductive, pulsing to the beat of the bass. The Pit transforms, washed in sapphire light that ripples over the crowd like water.

"Fighting tonight in our main event for Team Bella, all the way from Hong Kong..."

No. Fucking. Way.

"...the leader of the Red Silk Triads..."

Baby. Don't you dare say it.

"...Laing Wei!"

Tattooed Dragon-Dick comes strutting in like a damn god. Shirtless, of fucking course, inked from neck to hip. That massive dragon gleaming under the blue lights like liquid metal. The whole place goes silent for a second. Then mayhem erupts.

He walks straight to her. Wraps his arms around her waist

and grabs her by the fucking ass. She doesn't push him away. She just places a hand on his chest dragging her finger up and down the dragon and smiles into his eyes.

"Glad you could make it, Laing."

"Aw, Iz, I wouldn't miss this for the world." He looks over at me and does that stupid chin up thing as if to say, *hey dude.*

"Dead," I grit. "You're fucking dead."

I start forward but Knox stops us. "Ok boys, back up. Save it for the fight."

Bella walks over, slow and wicked, her eyes on me the entire time. "Fight to remember, baby." She kisses me on the cheek. And then she's gone.

Out of the ring.

Leaving me alone.

Staring down the man who used to fuck our girl.

DING.

I don't wait. No bow. No circling. I'm on him. Fist to jaw. Elbow to ribs. A slam that rattles his spine. Laing takes it, grinning like the sadistic bastard he is. He ducks my next punch and drives his knee into my gut, catching me off guard.

"So, does Iz scream your name and call you her god when your buried balls deep inside her, or is that just saved for me?"

"Motherfucker." I swing again and miss. He clips my jaw with a hook that snaps my head to the side. Blood hits the mat. Might be mine. Might be his. Doesn't matter.

We trade blows like it's a religion. Nothing held back. Forgetting everything around us the crowd, the donors, the fucking cameras. Just him and me and a centuries-old rage in my chest I didn't even know I had until I saw him touch her.

"You think she chose you?" he spits, ducking under a wild right. "She'll always come back to me. Ladies love the dragon." He winks at Bella.

I slam my fist into his ribs—once, twice—until I feel something crack. Laing snarls, headbutts me square in the temple and I stumble back.

"She likes a little danger, Barinov," he taunts, breathing heavy but still grinning. "That's why she keeps crawling back to me."

I lunge again. We're in a frenzy now. Fists, knees, sweat, and blood. All of it blending like warpaint.

"She doesn't come back to you, Laing. She comes on me. And that's the only fucking comeback that matters."

DING.

We break apart, barely, and I slam back to my corner. Rez comes at me with a towel.

I shove it away.

Across the ring, she's in Dragon Dick's corner. Wiping his mouth with a towel. Leaning in. Talking. Her hand on his shoulder like he's hers to steady.

My girl.

MY. FUCKING. GIRL.

"Calm down, dude," Rez mutters. "This is part of her plan."

"Plan?" I spit. My jaw is a hinge about to snap.

Rez nods, hands gripping my shoulders. "I told her we needed something that would kill it. Raw. Real. She knew Laing would get under your skin more than anyone and force a good fight out of you."

He laughs. "She was right. This is the best fight of your life."

His words are supposed to settle me, but the sight of Laing pulling her onto his lap—her not moving, not pushing him off—slides like ice into my veins. For a second the world narrows to her curve over that fucking dragon and the stupid, smug look on Laing's face.

I'm out of my chair before I even know I'm moving. "Fuck this." My voice cuts the noise. "Start round two, Rez."

DING.

Laing charges and this time, he's faster. Meaner. Ready. His fist connects with my rib cage. Another to the jaw. He spins, elbows me across the face and I stumble back, vision ringing with heat.

My knee hits the mat hard. Palms down. Blood dripping onto the floor. He laughs.

"Is that all you've got, Barinov?" Bella says standing ringside, arms folded across her chest, eyes locked on mine.

Then she smiles. Not at me. At him. "Laing... what are you waiting for?" Like she wants *him* to win.

I fucking lose it. I launch off the mat like a missile. Tackle Mortal Kombat into the side of the ring. He tries to throw me off. Too late, I grab his shoulders and drive my knee into his stomach. My elbow slams into his temple.

"She's not yours," I growl. "She'll never fucking be yours."

"You sure about that?"

He headbutts me. I taste blood again. The rest is a blur. We trade savage blows. My knuckles are torn open. His cheek is split and his left eye is starting to swell. My ribs burn like fire. His shoulders are dragging. By the time the bell rings, we're both soaked in sweat and blood, breathing like bulls, but neither one of us down.

DING.

Bella's still in his corner. Laughing. Smiling. Like this is a fucking game. She presses the towel to Laing's chest, whispers something that makes him grin. My jaw locks so tight it aches.

Rez leans on the ropes beside me, all calm steel. "He's quick," he says, voice low. "Don't give him the rhythm. Make him chase you."

I spit blood, drag in a breath that burns. Across the ring, Laing rolls his shoulders, loose and cocky, that smirk just begging me to lose it.

Rez slaps my arm once. "You've got the reach. Use it, Lex. Watch that left knee. It twitches before he swings. You catch that, he's yours."

I nod, eyes fixed on the bastard across from me.

DING.

Laing doesn't charge this time. No, the fuck-face is calm and loose. His stance drops, low and fluid, and then... *bam!* Some freaky jiu-jitsu shit.

He wraps low, flips me. I hit the mat hard, breath punched out of my lungs. It's the same damn move that Bella used on me in bed.

This fucker taught her that.

"You bastard." I grit out as the fury takes over. I snap. I fight with every ounce of rage in my bloodstream. Wild. Barbaric. Blow after blow. Elbow, hook, uppercut, anything that makes Laing bleed.

But the asshole just smiles, bleeding through his teeth.

"She's always liked it rough," he hisses, blood slick on his tongue. "Didn't think you had it in you, Barinov. I'm surprised a Russian nobody like you could even satisfy her."

Something inside me detonates. I explode into him. Fist to face.

CRACK.

His nose breaks beneath my knuckles with a wet, brutal snap. Blood pours instantly, running down his lips like war paint.

Bella slams her palms against the mat. "Come on, Laing!"

She's shouting for him. For fucking Dragon-Dick! The crowd erupts, but all I see is red, and I'm not just talking about Mortal Kombat's nose. Laing stumbles back, blinking through blood, and I charge again.

Left hook. Right elbow. Knee to ribs. No rhythm. No technique at this point. Just rage.

DING.

We're in our corners, blood in my mouth and fire in my veins, when I see her. Bella. Walking across the ring like she owns it, because at this point every goddamn inch of this fucking Pit belongs to her now.

Knox crackles over the speakers. "Uh, Bella... what do you think you're doing?"

She waves him off, keeping her steel eyes locked on me. "Nothing, Knox. I just need to have a little chat with my boyfriend."

Laing laughs at the world *boyfriend*. Asshole.

She steps into my corner, face inches from mine, and suddenly everything fades. There's only her. My girl. My fucking queen.

Her voice drops soft and low as she sits down on my lap, taking the towel from Rez and wiping blood off me.

"Hey, baby." Knox must have turned off her mic because her voice isn't flowing through the speakers anymore.

"Hey," I rasp, throat raw. "You here to finally take my side?"

She smiles. "Baby, I'm always on your side. Just a show remember, we had to sell it. Donor Fight and all. And it's been one hell of a show, Lex. You're doing great."

My chest heaves. "But?"

"But," she whispers, brushing her lips across my cheek running a finger down my chest stopping right at the top of my shorts, "I think I'm done with the show now. I've seen enough."

I blink. "What?"

She leans in, straddling my lap like there's not hundreds of people watching us. "I'm ready to go home now. To our home. You earned it, Lex."

My heart stops. I grab her waist, pulling her in forehead to forehead. "Just give me one more second, malyshka," I growl. "Then we go home."

"Make it quick, Barinov." She presses a light and sweet kiss to my nose. And then she turns, walking back toward *him*.

DING.

I don't wait. I fucking launch. One left hook to the jaw that makes Laing stagger. He tries to pivot but I'm already on him. A savage right. A few knees to the ribs. And then one brutal shot to the temple.

He drops. Cold. Bloody. Unmoving.

The Pit erupts.

Bella jumps into the ring before Knox can even speak. She grabs my hand and throws it in the air. I barely hear the crowd. I pick her up, wrap her legs around my waist, and claim her mouth right there in front of everyone.

"Mine," I rasp.

Laing pushes himself up on one elbow, blood streaking his face as he stands. He glances at Bella, then at me, and holds out his hand. I hesitate. Tighten my grip on her.

Bella nods once. A silent thank you. He nods back. Just once. I shake his hand and then he walks away without a word.

I turn my eyes back to my girl. Her arms are locked around my shoulders. Her face still flushed. I kiss her again, slower this time.

"Let's go home, baby."

@LucaWasHere
Nice match, Lexie. Such brutal flair.
But victory's cheap when she isn't aware.
Had to taste her past to stoke your flame.

Kissed her ghost just to earn your name.

You swing for blood when she draws the crowd.
But tell me, Lexie, you proud or just loud?
She cracked her smile to rattle the night,
While you stood tall on borrowed fright.

Predictable. Soft beneath the bark.
You only shine when the room goes dark.
You think she's yours? You think she chose?
But you're just the thorn not the fucking rose.

So heed this warning, laced in spite,
Let her move in, and I'll snuff out your light.
You let her settle or let her taste your name,
And I'll paint the walls with what's left of your shame.

The game is changing. I'm realigning my path.
But don't mistake silence for mercy or wrath.
Bow out, Lexie. Go home. Stay smart.
Before I tear your little kingdom apart.

@BarinovUnhinged
Cute verse, Luca. Real bold of you.
But you rhyme like a bitch, and we both know it's true.
You stalk. You whine. You beg for a taste.
But I've already claimed what you'll never replace.

You talk big shit through a goddamn screen.
But I'm the storm. You're the roach between.
So send another poem. Send a prayer.
But know this, coward, I'll always be there.

CHAPTER ⑥1
BELLA
THE OBSIDIAN
721 DAYS SINCE ZEKE'S DEATH

The days after the Donor Fight were a damn whirlwind. Biggest event in Northvale history, and Rez is still riding the high. He's practically been begging me to keep supplying him with more of my fighters. Doesn't care how I get them, he just wants them. Bad.

Khoza and Briggs both came up to me after asking to earn their Black Books back by working in The Pit. I told them I'd think about it. O'Malley caught wind of it and now he wants in too. I guess brawling for blood is easier than chasing intel. Still, if they want redemption, they're going to have to work hard for it.

Daniel and Irina were at the fight too. Apparently, Irina wasn't too thrilled that Roman showed up. She texted me the next day, trying to be all sweet and motherly. Said something about how, when I become a Barinov, my allegiance better lie with the Russians and not the Italians.

Bitch, I'm not even engaged. I've barely unpacked my shit. Chill. Plus, my allegiance will not be to the Russians or the Italians. It'll be to Lex. To Cade. To me. Our family. Plus, the ice bitch didn't even mention Cade in her little *allegiance threat* and that pissed me the fuck off.

Lex saw the text thread and absolutely lost it. He went off on his mom, told her to back the hell off. Then Daniel called and apologized on her behalf. The whole thing was a mess. She'll pay for that tonight. Ellie and I made sure of it.

Speaking of Lex... The Donor Fight turned that man into a straight-up savage. We got back to our apartment and he absolutely wrecked me on the kitchen counter. Didn't even take his boots off. Just ripped my shorts off, yanked my panties down, and growled, *"Mine."*

Then he threw me on the bed and ravaged me all over again while Cade watched. Grabbed my throat so hard I nearly blacked out.

He finally dragged Cade into it. Told him to *"get on your knees and taste what belongs to us."* And Cade did.

Good lord he did.

Cade went down on me like he was starving. But of course, Lex has zero patience, so he fucked Cade senseless while Cade's mouth was still on my clit, unraveling me molecule by molecule. I swear Cade's tongue anywhere near my pussy should be fucking illegal.

And then, Lex fucked me. Again. Hand fisted in my hair, whispering the filthiest things I've ever heard. Let's just say, when one of your boyfriends has the sexual stamina of a Roman god and a high pain tolerance, everyone walks away a little bruised and blissed-out.

By the time it was over, I could barely walk. Pretty sure I limped into practice with a bruised vagina and zero regrets.

And yeah... I'm officially out of Rosethorne. Moved into the apartment on the thirty-first floor with the guys. Between Lex, Cade, Knox, Nate, and Tex, they had me packed and relocated in under twenty-four hours. Like a damn tactical unit. A dangerous, lethal, extremely attractive moving squad.

Home Sweet Home. I'm sure our resident stalker-poet will have a very unhinged opinion about that any minute now.

And thanks to our stalker-poet and his lovely increasing threats, we've got NYPD stationed nearby and some of Daniel Barinov's men doing incognito surveillance from time to time. Guys in plain clothes who look like they belong but don't say much. Just in case.

Still, part of me keeps brushing it off. *"He's probably just some basement-dwelling freak who gets off watching girls from behind a screen,"* I told Cade last night. *"If we ignore him long enough, he'll get bored and crawl back into whatever Reddit-thread-from-hell he came out of."*

Of course, Lex didn't love that plan. Mostly because he keeps writing back. I wish I were kidding. It's like a damn rhyme-off at this point. Every time Luca drops a new horror poem into my DMs, Lex responds with threats that sound like they belong in a Bratva edition of Dr. Seuss.

The other night he actually paused mid-mission to ask me, *"What rhymes with decapitate?"* I told him *medicate*, and now I'm scared it's going to end up in a courtroom transcript.

"*Stop baiting him,*" Cade told him. "*He wants a reaction. He wants power. If you keep giving it to him, babe, he's never going to go away.*"

Lex just shrugged. "*He wants a stage. I'm giving him a grave.*"

God help me, I think he meant it as romantic.

So, yeah. We're fine. Everything's fine. Totally normal relationship stuff. Just a girl, her two guys, and the anonymous psycho-poet watching them from the shadows.

"Ah! I can't believe this party is finally happening!" Ellie squeals.

"Yeah, thanks again for helping me switch the theme last minute," I say, tugging the strap of my heel tighter.

She waves me off with one manicured hand. "Please. Anything to take down the Ice Bitch Witch of Moscow. She's going to choke on her judgment tonight."

Haley's in the corner, sharpening a gold hairpin like she plans to actually stab someone with it and honestly, I hope she does.

I'm in front of the mirror, one leg propped on the velvet bench, lacing gold heels around my thigh like I'm getting ready for war. Because I am. Tonight isn't just a party. Tonight... is karma.

"Move your asses, goddesses!" Rico declares, bursting through the door like he's got Jupiter on speed dial. "This isn't Mount Olympus, bebés. This is Capitoline Hill, and we are not losing the war for best dressed, ¿entendido?"

He's wearing an emerald blazer over black mesh, six necklaces, and the expression of a man who's holding the world together with willpower and setting spray.

"Final rundown. Ellie, you are *Venus*. Glow like a whore in candlelight and make every man here want to cry into his wine. You've got the blush satin with the chainmail hips and the sheer train that flutters like sin. Got it?"

"Already crying, darling," Ellie says while applying mascara. "I look like sex and regret."

"Good. Haley, you're *Diana*, huntress of my dreams and destroyer of frat boys. Looking beautiful in emerald silk with the twin leg slits and the fake bow that could still take out a man's ego from twenty feet away."

"Perfect. I love shredding men's egos." Haley grins, adjusting the strap of her dress.

"Let's see," Rico says, ticking off fingers like a general reviewing his troops. "Callum and The Order will be stationed at the bottom of the stairs as your Roman guards. Lex is *Mars*, God of war."

"Obviously," Ellie laughs, tossing her curls.

"And Cade... *Apollo*. God of the sun, art, music, and swoon-worthy jawlines. I already checked in on your boys and baby girl, damn. If they had a thing for Barcelonans, you'd be in some serious trouble." He fans himself dramatically, then winks. "Luckily for you, they're fully booked and aggressively loyal."

Rico's voice softens. "And you, my beautiful little rage monster, are *Nemesis*. Vengeance. Balance. Divine retribution in thigh-high stilettos."

He walks toward me slowly, almost reverently, and adjusts the gold chain belt hanging low across my hips. His fingers are gentle, surprisingly so. "Black and crimson. Gold blade charms. Cape that flows when you turn. You look like a weapon. Because you are, darling."

I arch a brow. "You gonna cry, Rico?"

"Bitch, I might." He flicks my hip. "You look like justice."

"She looks like she's about to eat Lex alive," Ellie calls from across the room.

"She always does," Haley mutters, not even looking up.

Rico claps like he's summoning a storm. "Alright, divas—¡ojos aquí!" he calls, snapping his fingers.

"Haley enters first, then Ellie. Bella, you come down last, obviously, like the goddess you are. Roman will escort you. Knox has the spotlight cues locked and loaded. And when you hit that floor?" He grins, wicked and proud. "The room will stop breathing. So do us all a favor and don't eat shit in heels."

Rico takes a swig from his flute and struts toward the door. "Ten minutes, goddesses. This world isn't ready." He slams it behind him.

For a second, it's quiet. Just the low hum of music from the club floor below, muffled by velvet and walls. Ellie hums something under her breath. Haley exhales and starts curling her lashes.

And then the door opens again, softly as Roman steps inside. He doesn't say a word. Doesn't need to. His presence fills the room like smoke.

He's dressed in black and gold, a custom-tailored suit with a single drape over one shoulder that glints like woven sunlight. A golden cuff wraps around his left wrist. A laurel crown rests lightly in his dark hair. He looks like power made flesh.

He's Jupiter tonight. The King of the Roman gods. Rico's idea, although it totally fits him.

"You look just like your mother," he says quietly. "Absolutely stunning."

I swallow once. "You clean up nice."

There's a beat of silence. Not awkward, not really. Not anymore.

I glance at him. "Thanks for the venue. And Fight Night. And for saving my life. And for not, you know... pushing this whole father-daughter thing." I hesitate. "You've been cool about it and I know that can't be easy for you."

"Isabella, I don't want to be another man trying to claim you. You've had enough of those."

He tilts his head slightly, something flickering behind his eyes. "When you're ready, I'll be here. Until then, I'll settle for standing beside you and reminding the world whose blood made you."

He takes a deep breath and almost smiles. "I used to dream of this, you know. Walking you down those stairs. Letting the world see who you are."

I hold his gaze. Steel to steel. "And who am I?"

Slowly and regally, he walks forward until he's looming over me. Then he leans down just enough to whisper, "A goddamn reckoning, my daughter."

CHAPTER (62)
LEX
THE OBSIDIAN
OUR GIRL'S TWENTY-FIRST BIRTHDAY PARTY.
721 DAYS SINCE ZEKE'S DEATH

The music's low, the bass rolling like a slow punch to the ribs. Just enough to keep the crowd restless. Spotlights drift in lazy golden arcs across The Obsidian floor, catching on sequins, skin, and too many damn champagne flutes. Candles flicker in glass towers, throwing dancing shadows across the wall. Velvet ropes pulse around the raised VIP section, packed with Wexley's elite—football kings, trust fund brats, and Row royalty posing like they're running the goddamn world.

Savannah's sipping something pink and dangerous. Clay's half-listening to Dad talk shop about glass-reinforced concrete. Mom's looking around like she doesn't want to be here. And Cade's beside me, shoulder to shoulder, radiating that golden calm that drives me insane in the best and worst ways.

I'm dressed as Mars, Roman war god. Ellie put Rico in charge of all our costumes for tonight. Black leather harness. Burgundy-lined cape slung off one shoulder. Bracers. Boots. Blood-red paint streaked across my cheekbone like a warning.

Savannah raises her glass toward us, "So, what exactly are we all supposed to be tonight? Gladiators? Gods? Gold-plated sex cult?"

Clay chokes on his drink. Mom doesn't blink.

Dad glances over my outfit with an arched brow. "Roman military meets couture runway?"

Cade laughs under his breath and lifts his glass. "Bella and Ellie's idea. Rico's vision."

They all turn to me. I lean back, stretching my arm across the red velvet booth, and let the words hit slow. "They picked the theme, *Roman gods and goddesses*. Said if the Italians, the Russians, and the Whitmores were all gonna show up in one room, they might as well worship something. Might as well worship the birthday girl, and I for one can't agree with her more."

Mom exhales like she's trying not to roll her eyes. Savannah full-on grins. "She's not wrong," Savannah says. "She looked divine at the fitting. What's she coming down as again?"

I drag a thumb across my jaw, watching the staircase. "Nemesis."

Dad grins slightly. "The goddess of vengeance?"

"Balance. Justice. Retribution. Our fucking girl."

Cade sets his drink down a touch too carefully. "Her and Ellie came up with the idea after Fight Night. Changed the entire theme and everything in less than a few days. I've never seen Rico work so hard in his life."

"I didn't know there were so many curse words in the Spanish language," I laugh.

I glance over at Mom. She's trying to keep her face neutral, sipping her wine like it doesn't taste like guilt. Too late. That's what you get for cornering one of the loves of my life with your loyalty speeches and backhanded warnings. Like Bella owes you something.

You push Bella into a corner and she doesn't run. She doesn't cry. She fights back. With couture, theatrics, and a guest list that could ignite a war. This whole party is a middle finger dipped in gold leaf.

"Smart theme," Dad offers. "Classical. Commanding. I like it. It's very Bella."

Mom hums her agreement. "It's... dramatic."

I look at her, but she can't meet my eyes. Good. Because what really pissed us off wasn't the whole *pick a side* bullshit. It was the way she erased Cade from the picture like he's just an accessory. Like Cade and the Whitmores weren't even a side for Bella to pick from in the first place. Like our love for him isn't real enough to count.

Savannah, who's always two steps ahead of everyone's bullshit, arches a brow at Mom. "Well, Bella's nothing if not decisive," she says smoothly. "She knows exactly who she belongs to."

That hits. A little too hard, because Mom flinches. Just barely.

Clay lets out a low whistle. "So, who's walking her down tonight? I'm surprised you guys aren't over there at the bottom of the stairs."

Cade's quiet. So, I answer.

"Roman." I take a slow sip of my drink, then set it down with a dull clink. "He's playing Jupiter, king of the Roman gods."

Mom stiffens.

"Jesus. That girl knows how to throw a party," Clay says as Callum and his stupid Order bros walk down the stairs dressed as Bella's personal guards.

Savannah hums. "No. She knows how to rule a kingdom."

The music shifts, subtle, but powerful. The kind of tone change that hits your spine before your ears.

Knox's voice crackles over the speakers, smooth as ever. "You've seen the warriors. Now bow to your gods."

A hush falls across the club floor. Students in designer togas, leather straps, and gold crowns all suddenly going still. Spotlights cut through the dark, golden beams slicing air like blades.

"Please welcome the goddesses of Wexley," Knox's voice booms over the speakers. "Descending from Capitoline Hill, your huntress and your heart-breaker... Haley, the goddess Diana, and Ellie, the goddess Venus. Try not to worship too loudly."

The crowd's eyes lock on the stairs as Haley and Ellie appear first. Draped in emerald and blush. The girls glide down like royalty, all fire and gold, heading straight toward Callum and the rest of The Order.

"And now," Knox says, voice dropping into something reverent, almost unholy, "Capitoline bows to vengeance. To power. To the storm and the silence. Our gods of the night, Jupiter and Nemesis."

The spotlight sharpens dead center on the top of the stairs and there she is. Bella, on the arm of Roman Russo. The fucking King and his heir. The goddamn goddess of vengeance.

"Bow to your gods," Knox commands.

Everyone drops. Toga after toga, head after head. The Roman guards kneel. Even Dad dips his head slightly.

I glance toward my mother, she doesn't move. "She certainly knows how to make an entrance," she says, clipped.

"Yeah," I mutter. "She always does."

Bella reaches the bottom step. Roman kisses her cheek softly and steps away as Josh, Drake, and Sam, dressed in black and gold Roman guard uniforms, move out from the shadows. They take their positions in front of the girls.

A soft piano. A single voice. "Ordinary" by Alex Warren begins to play. The girls move like smoke and fire. Lifted and spun across the floor with reverence and precision. Every sway of their skirts looks like a painting torn to life—gold catching light, fabric slicing the air like blades. Arms stretch like wings. Heels land with surgical control. It's not a dance. It's a declaration.

Bella is dead center. Josh lifts her high as her head tilts back. Her cape unfurling behind her like a black flame. Our girl commands the floor.

That line that talks about praying at the altar hits and all three guys drop. Right there at their goddesses' feet. Knees bowed. Heads down.

Then, on the next beat, they launch the girls skyward. Bella soars. Arms wide. Cape arcing. Her eyes fierce and untouchable. And for a second, everything disappears, the crowd, the noise, even the war in my chest. It's just her, midair. Like vengeance incarnate wrapped in power and golden fire.

"Jesus Christ," I say leaning toward Cade.

Cade leans in just slightly, voice quiet but full of awe. "This isn't just a performance, Lex. It's pure art."

And when they hit that final note, arms extended, backs arched, and heads tilted to the ceiling like they were born from constellations, the room explodes in screams and cheers. Savannah wipes a tear and mutters something about *"never seeing anything so divine."*

"Give it up for our goddesses!" Knox yells over the chaos. "I'd like to give a shout out to our birthday girl, Bella! Happy 21st babe." He raises his glass toward her. "It's Halloween, and we are at The Obsidian! So I think it's about time we get this party officially started!"

The lights drop again, then flicker back to life with a strobe-pop blast as the beat shifts. Something bass-heavy and dirty kicks in, a club remix of, "Where the Party At" by Jagged Edge, pulses through the speakers like a heartbeat on cocaine.

The crowd surges. Bodies move. Glasses clink.

Bella's still glowing under the lights, standing with Ellie and Haley in the middle of it all like they're carved from gold and sex and sin. The Order boys are around them, drinking, cheering, trying not to look like they're dying to be picked for the next dance.

Too bad for them. This one's already claimed.

"That's our girl," Cade mutters beside me.

"Yeah," I growl. "Let's go mark that shit."

We move through the crowd like sharks cutting water—slick, silent, lethal. People step back, eyes flicking toward us, but no one stops us. No one even tries.

Bella spots us just before we reach her, those eyes snapping to mine like a fuse being lit. Her lips curl, all spark and challenge. I don't stop walking. Just grab her waist, spin her around, and pull her straight into me. Her ass grinds against my hips like she knows exactly what I need.

"Jesus, baby," I growl into her ear, hands sliding low. "You know what you do to me?"

"You planning on showing me properly?"

"I'm planning on ruining you," I whisper, teeth grazing her jaw. "Right here. On this floor. Let them all watch."

Her breath stutters. But she doesn't stop dancing.

Cade steps in front of her, smiling soft and dangerous in a way people always underestimate. He runs a hand down her side, just brushing her hip. "You were unreal tonight, sweetheart. Like something a man would paint and never recover from."

She laughs. Sharp and hot and wicked. And then we're moving with her, sandwiching her, syncing to the beat like we've done this a hundred times. My hands on her thigh riding up the slit in her dress. Cade's on her waist. Her body sliding between us like we were built for this.

A few songs in, the lights flash again. Floodlights swing toward the DJ booth, and Knox cuts the track with one arm raised like a damn prophet of the party gods.

"Alright, alright, alright! Shut the hell up for one second!" he yells over the crowd. "Let's give it up for the birthday girl!"

The room explodes. Cheers. Screams. August yells *"Queen*

shit!" from the bar.

I've still got Bella in my arms, one hand wrapped around her waist, the other resting low on her thigh. She looks up at the booth with parted lips, hair sticking to her neck like silk.

"Okay, Bells," Knox grins into the mic. "So, here's the deal. Your boys Drake, Sam, and Josh have a little birthday challenge for you. Straight from the Roman gods themselves."

The crowd goes nuts.

"Each one of them picked a dance. A solo. A moment. A test, if you will. And you, goddess? You're the fire they wanna survive."

Bella's shaking her head, but she's laughing. Bright. Dangerous.

"So, what do you say, Nemesis?" Knox calls, leaning into the mic. "You in?"

She tips her head back, still in my arms, and flashes the kind of grin that gets men in trouble in every mythology. Then nods.

"Alright then bitch, get out there," Knox yells, hyping the crowd. "Sam, you're up first! Everybody clear the floor. 'Cause the God of Fire himself, Vulcan, commands it!" Knox hits a button and fire erupts from behind the DJ booth.

The dancers scatter. Cade grabs her hand and pulls her out of my grip, spinning her once before letting her go with a quiet whisper I can't quite catch.

She walks straight into the center of the floor. All eyes on her. Sam steps out of the dark to meet her, grinning and carrying a pair of her boots in his hands.

The lights stay low as Knox begins again. "Now we all know Sam is the softie of the group. Don't lie, bro, we've seen the playlists. So, he went a little easy on you, Bells."

The crowd laughs. Bella turns toward Sam with a curious smile, brows lifting when she notices the boots.

"He wanted to give you a little piece of Arkansas for your twenty-first," Knox says "So brace yourselves, Wolves because the goddess of vengeance is about to go southern on our asses. Bella, switch those heels for your Luccheses real quick, and let's show these people how y'all dance back in the country shall we?"

Ellie shrieks next to Cade. "OH MY GOD YESSSS!"

"Dancin' in the Country" by Tyler Hubbard, full country bass and boot-stomp rhythm hits over the speakers.

Haley's screaming. Ellie's jumping up and down, hands on Cade's shoulders. Bella's eyes go wide. Sam just smiles, takes her hand, and pulls her in like he's been rehearsing this in secret for weeks.

They start with a tight two-step, left-right-left, hips swaying, boots sliding. Bella grins full and open and blinding. He sweeps her off both feet. She lets herself go. Spins. Drops. Laughs. Sam twirls her once, then twice, then catches her by the waist and dips her like they're the last couple on a honkytonk dancefloor at closing time.

Ellie leans in toward Cade, eyes misty, smile wild. "Look at our little country queen! Reminds me of Nashville," she whispers, voice cracked with pride.

I can't look away. The second the song ends, the crowd goes insane.

Bella's cheeks are flushed, smile still lingering. She starts walking back toward me and Cade on instinct, but Knox's voice cuts in sharp over the mic. "Whoa whoa whoa, Bella! You're not done yet."

She freezes mid-step.

"Drake! Get your ass out here!"

The crowd screams as Drake emerges from the shadows, a devilish grin plastered on his face. He's dragging a fucking chair to the center of the floor.

My spine snaps straight. "Oh, hell no."

Drake plops down in it, legs wide and full of confidence.

"Alright, goddess," Knox says, trying not to laugh. "You know this song. I've seen you do it. Usually on a Row boy or two, but your boy Drake specifically requested this one for himself."

Bella's face lights up. Part surprise, part challenge.

"So let's see that *Booty Work!*"

I step forward, rage crawling up my throat like a wildfire. Cade grabs me by the front of my harness and yanks me back into him, locking his arms around me. "Breathe, she comes home with us," he says, calm but firm.

My fists clench as Bella walks to the chair like she's walking into a confession booth. Her hips rolling and her eyes locked on Drake like he's already been sentenced. She straddles the chair. Spins. Drops low.

Ellie and Haley burst out from the wings. Bella's shrieking backup dancers summoned by Satan himself.

"Fucking Christ," I mutter.

The Trifecta takes over. Bella center, the other two flanking her. Hands on knees. Hips circling. Hair flying. It's not just sexy. It's raw, choreographed sin. And I hate how much I love it. Because it's brilliant, because it's perfect. Because she looks like she's made of fire and sweat and silk and ruin. I just wish it was *me* in that goddamn chair.

"Woah! How about that?" Knox roars over the crowd, voice ragged with laughter. "Sam gave us heart, Drake gave us heat..."

He pauses, just enough to let the tension breathe. "Josh. You're up, man."

Josh strides out, smug grin and flexed confidence, dragging out not one, but two more chairs to the dancefloor.

Cade's hand tightens on my arm like he already knows I'm about to launch myself into the center of the floor.

"What the actual fuck," I mutter.

"Lex," Cade warns.

"Goddesses," Knox purrs into the mic, drawing the word out. "Please... take a seat."

The girls glance at each other, then laugh and strut toward the chairs like this is just another rehearsal. Bella sits center. Ellie and Haley beside her. The room practically combusts when the first beat of "Pony" hits the speakers.

"No fucking way. This is going to be some Magic Mike shit, Cade."

The guys move slow as predators. It's ridiculous. It's obscene. It's... working. Josh drops to his knees between Bella's thighs and the crowd loses its mind.

She laughs, head thrown back. It's the sound that tips me over the edge.

"Jesus," I mutter, dragging a hand through my hair. "She's

gonna kill me."

Then the chorus hits and the girls flip it. Bella shoves the chair back with her heel, stands, and pushes Josh down into it. Ellie and Haley doing the same to Sam and Drake. The crowd screams.

She swings a leg over his lap, grinding once before twisting off and ripping one of his gold chest straps free. She holds it up high, shimmering in the light, and smirks like a goddess collecting spoils.

The lights hit her, gold and sweat and vengeance. She looks right at me and smiles that wicked little smile.

"That little tease," I hiss.

Cade laughs beside me quiet, breathless, and in awe. "Yeah," he says. "God, I love her."

Knox breathes into the mic, half-laughing, half-exhausted. "Somebody give it up for those performances. I mean damn, talk about divine intervention. That was some godly shit."

The crowd screams again. "Alright Obsidian, you know what to do. Dim it down, turn it up, and find someone worth sinning with." The lights drop low. A new beat slides in, smooth, deep, and filthy slow. I cut across the floor before anyone else can even blink and grab Bella right out of Josh's arms, dragging her into me like the past fifteen minutes didn't just fry my entire nervous system.

Her breath catches as I press her full to my chest, my hand firmly cupping the back of her neck. "Baby," I growl, leaning down, lips brushing hers. "You are in some serious trouble."

She pulls back, grinning against my lips. "Jealousy looks good on you, God of War."

"You haven't seen how good it feels," I murmur, voice low, dragging her into a sway with me as the music pulses around us.

She smiles, body loose between us. We dance like that for a few songs, dirty and sensual. I press against her from behind, fingers laced at her waist, letting my breath drag down the back of her neck.

The beat fades, the tempo slowing, dim lights shifting to a warm gold. The next track is the kind of song you sway to with someone you don't ever want to let go of. Bella exhales, her body melting back into mine, and Cade slides in close, arms wrapping around her from the front. All three of us dancing together. No theatrics, no grind. Only the kind of closeness that makes the whole room disappear for a little while.

We're still on the dance floor when Knox's voice cuts through the music. "Hey yo Bella! Your boy Cade has a special request."

She turns toward Cade, brow raised. "What?"

Cade doesn't miss a beat. Just lifts her hand to his lips, "You remember Nashville, sweetheart?"

CHAPTER ⓺⓷
C A D E
T H E   O B S I D I A N
721 DAYS SINCE ZEKE'S DEATH

The first notes of "Nobody" by Dylan Scott drift through the speakers. Bella freezes in my arms, pupils blown wide.

"Oh my God, Cade," she breathes. "I can't believe you remember this."

I tighten my grip on her waist, guiding her into the sway. "How could I forget? This was the moment you taught me how to dance."

She laughs under her breath, head shaking softly. "Yeah, I know. But still... you didn't even want to be in Nashville. You and Cal were so mad at us."

"Not at first," I admit, brushing her hair behind her ear. "But I honestly ended up never wanting to leave."

She pulls me in for a quick kiss before I spin her out and back into my arms. Her laugh curls down my spine. We keep moving to the rhythm, the world fading around us.

"Sweetheart," I rasp, voice low against her temple, "I think Nashville was the first time I stopped seeing you as Ellie's friend and started seeing you as you."

Her gaze flicks up to meet mine.

"I mean, I never acted on it or anything. I was unsure. Nervous," I admit. "But I really think that night was when I first started to truly fall in love with you, Bella."

She gives me that smile, the one that's only ever been mine. "I love you so much, Cade."

"I love you too, sweetheart," I press a kiss to her forehead. "When we're finished, Lex and I need to give you your present."

Her brows lift, just slightly. "My present?"

"We won't be gone long," I add.

When the song is over, I grab her hand, motion for Lex, and we lead her off the floor like gods claiming what's ours.

The door clicks shut behind us, cutting off the thump of the bass and the roar of the crowd. It's quieter back here, just the three of us and the aftershocks of too much dancing, too much adrenaline, and too much of her.

"So, this where I get ravished?" she asks with a smirk.

"Eventually," Lex laughs behind her.

"But first," I say, catching her hand, "you sit."

She tilts her head, eyes narrowing, but she listens. Bella drops onto the couch beside the mirrored wall, legs crossed, dress hitched just enough to wreck me. God, she's beautiful.

I reach for the package I stashed earlier, carefully wrapped in black linen and tied with burgundy silk. "Close your eyes."

She smiles softly, eyes shining. "You're lucky I trust you." And then closes them.

I lay the present on her lap. "Okay," I say quietly. "Open."

She unties the ribbon and unwraps the linen. Her eyes flutter open and then freeze. She doesn't speak. Barely breathes.

The painting stares back at her—bold, intimate, raw.

It's the three of us. She's front and center, naked in a sea of white sheets. Everything is black and white except her blood-red lips. Soft. Open. Her eyes are half-lidded, mouth caught in that breathless moment between surrender and command.

Lex is beside her on the left. His hand wrapped around her throat, squeezing just enough to mark possession, his tongue brushing the side of her neck.

I'm on the right. My arm slung across her chest, shielding her from view. Protecting her. Claiming her. Kissing her cheek like a man who would kill for her without hesitation.

Three bodies.

One moment.

Eternal.

Her breath stutters. She lifts a hand, fingertips grazing the edge of the canvas like it might bite. "You painted this... for me?"

"For us," I say softly. "But yeah. It's yours."

Tears gather at the corners of her eyes, catching the light like broken glass.

Lex leans in behind her, looking over her shoulder and lets out a deep breath. "Babe..." he growls, voice thick. "That's going over our bed. Dead center. So, I can see it every single time I'm fucking the shit out of both of you." He steps around and pulls me forward, crashing his mouth against mine. It's rough. Messy. Perfect.

Bella doesn't move at first. She just stares at the painting like it's breathing. Like it might speak before she can. A tear slides down her cheek, slow and silent.

"Cade..." Her voice shakes around my name. She rises, cradles the painting in both hands, and then looks up at me like I just gave her the moon. "I don't have words. I love it. I love you."

My chest tightens.

She sets it down, leans in and kisses me, her fingers curling in my hair like she never wants to let go.

When we finally break apart, I clear my throat and nod toward Lex. "Babe..." I say, still trying to catch my breath. "Show her your present."

Lex grins, full of pride, and pulls off the harness across his chest.

Bella tilts her head. "What are you doing?"

He unbuttons the front of his black shirt and pulls the fabric apart, just enough to reveal the fresh ink over his heart. It's the same style as the one on her shoulder. Same wisps of smoke trailing behind the letters. Same bold, black lines that pulse with meaning.

But instead of a Z, it says *Bella*.

Simple. Permanent. And hers.

She gasps. Then covers her mouth with both hands in shock.

"Lex..." She walks toward him slowly, like she's afraid the moment might vanish if she moves too fast. He doesn't say anything.

Not at first.

"I didn't want initials. Didn't want anything vague. I wanted you. Right here." He taps his chest. "Because that's where you've lived since the second I saw you, malyshka."

Bella blinks hard. Then reaches out and touches the skin just beside the tattoo. She looks up at him and the space between them disappears. Their lips crash, fierce, full, breathless.

Lex lifts her up, hands on her thighs, her dress slipping...

The door slams open. "Okay, Jesus Christ!" Ellie stands there with a hand over her eyes. "Can't you two sex gods wait like an hour? Maybe till you get home? Or even the damn car?"

Bella groans and lets her head falls against Lex's shoulder. "El—"

"Nope. Save it. Come on, we need to go change. It's time to make the Ice Bitch Witch of Moscow cry."

Lex laughs, full-on and unfiltered. "What did you just say?"

Ellie grins unapologetically. "You heard me."

Bella slides out of Lex's arms, smoothing her dress down, and turns back to both of us with a watery eyes and a bright smile. "I love you both so much."

We head back to the club—Lex pulling his shirt closed again, me grabbing the painting to keep it safe. The music's already fading from the song and the crowd's resetting. The entire Legacy dance team is out there on the floor looking like they know exactly what's about to go down.

Knox leans into the mic with that cocky little smirk he wears like armor. "And now, for their final performance... the goddesses of Wexley want to offer a very special dedication. This one's for Karma."

The lights shift in an instant and vivid teal, pink, and purple flood the room. Bella's colors. Their colors.

Gasps ripple through the crowd as the Wexley Legacy girls, draped in white togas just seconds ago rip them off in sync, revealing a new layer beneath: yellow and orange fringe dresses all rhinestoned and gleaming.

"Guess were switching from Roman gods to Latin flair," Lex laughs beside me.

Then the music hits, Taylor Swift's "Karma." A revenge anthem so pointed, it might as well come with a blade.

Everyone's eyes are painted at the stairs waiting for The Trifecta's entrance, but no one's walking down the stairs. No, they enter from the side. Right by Irina's table.

Bella in purple fringe, glitter clinging to her collarbones like stardust. Skin glowing. Eyes lethal. She struts out first, followed by Ellie in flamingo pink, and Haley in bright teal. Bold and sexy dresses designed for maximum impact.

"Damn, Rico," Lex mutters beside me grinning. "Nice work, man."

The girls don't glance at Irina. They don't need to. Their entire existence right now is a fuck you wrapped in silk, fringe, and rhinestones.

I glance toward the VIP section just in time to see Irina sit up stiff. Rigid. Furious.

Perfect.

Because I hate the way she talks to Bella. Like she needs to make make some insane choice between everything, Roman, The Barniovs, herself. Like our love, this chaotic, beautiful, dangerous love between the three of us is a threat instead of something sacred.

I hope every beat of this song wrecks her.

Lex wraps his arms around me from behind, lips brushing my ear. "These girls making me a Nickelback fan and now a Swiftie. Goddamn."

I nod, my eyes on Bella as she twirls, smiling like a secret that's begging to be broken.

When the song talks about the different things that Karma is, Bella starts to move throughout the crowd while the rest of the girls keep dancing. She works the crowd like she's been in show business her entire life. She can't help but laugh and it takes my breath away seeing her this happy. Seeing her truly in her element, it's everything.

When it gets to the final part, the girls are all in the center of the dance floor again. The song says something about how Karma is some kind of queen and all the girls kneel at The Trifecta's feet, creating a beautiful sparkling sea of yellow and orange.

And then when it says something about a guy and a screen, they all point to the screens behind the bar—where *Obsidian* has been flashing all night— it glitches once. Then it reappears as a massive photo. A photo my mom took. Bella, Lex, and me at Regionals.

"Damn, Bestie. Nice work Knox." Lex huffs a laugh.

Then they all jump up and finish the dance. The room erupts into screams and applause. Cameras flash. I glance toward Irina, she's frozen. Completely still. Her lips are white from how tightly they're pressed together.

And right beside her, my mom is grinning from ear to ear. Like she's been waiting for this moment all night long.

By the time Bella reaches us, her skin is flushed, but her smile is pure murder. She didn't just dance tonight. She made a queen fall. Karma's a bitch Irina, a bitch named Isabella Marie Blackwood.

"You guys see her face?" she pants, breathless from the routine.

"Pretty sure Mom cracked a tooth trying not to hiss."

Bella grins and slides into my side just as her phone vibrates in Lex's pocket.

His whole body stiffens. "What the fuck?" He pulls it out, reads the screen, and groans like it physically hurts him.

Bella lifts her brows. "Who is it?"

"Mortal Kombat."

Her expression changes instantly. Curiosity, caution, and something colder underneath.

"Happy Birthday, Iz. Sorry I missed the party. Had an important meeting in Hong Kong—" He stops. Snorts. "Of course you did."

"Lex," I say, tired already. "Just finish it."

He grits his teeth and keeps going. "But don't think I didn't get you something. Sabine's keeping it safe for me... oh and tell your boyfriend I want a rematch."

He flips the phone around to show us the location. "Warehouse 29-A. Brooklyn."

Bella frowns. "Do you think he's serious?"

"That motherfucker wants a rematch? I'll give him one. I'll tie him to the goddamn scaffolding and see how much blood he's willing to spill for a round two."

"Lex." Bella gripes. She yanks the phone from his hand and stares at the address again. "What do you think it is?"

Lex shrugs, still fuming. "Could be a trap."

"Or a gift," Bella mutters. "He said he got me something."

"He also said Sabine's guarding it," I say, already pulling up the map on my phone. "Which means it's definitely not something legal."

Bella looks up at me. That fire's back in her eyes, even under the exhaustion. The mission in her blood. The pull she can't resist.

"So?" she asks softly.

I tilt my head. "So, let's go find out, sweetheart."

CHAPTER ⑥④
BELLA
WAREHOUSE 29-A
BROOKLYN, NEW YORK
721 DAYS SINCE ZEKE'S DEATH

We pull up to the warehouse that Laing texted us, no longer in costume. I'm in ripped jeans, a yellow crop top, and my leather jacket. Battle gear, birthday edition. Lex is in his usual black jeans, black V-neck, and black boots, because God forbid the man own anything with color. And Cade, sweet Cade, is in worn jeans and a hoodie, the drawstring twirling around his fingers like he's trying to focus.

Tex is already waiting outside, leaning against the wall like a dark omen. "Hey," he says. "Happy birthday, Bells."

"Thanks," I reply, eyeing the warehouse door behind him. "You been inside?"

He shakes his head. "No. I was waiting on you."

"Laing didn't by chance tell you what the hell it is?" I ask.

"No, I asked him after you called," he snorts. "Dipshit just said Sabine was holding it. Whatever the fuck that means."

I glance between the guys, then back at the door. "Alright. Let's do this."

Tex's eyes flick to Cade. "You sure you want him here?"

Cade's voice is calm, but sharp. "You're not going to stop me."

Tex grunts. "Didn't say I would. Just asking if you need a minute to cry or stretch or whatever it is your people do before a showdown."

"Let it go, Tex," Lex snaps.

Tex rolls his eyes and turns toward the door. "Alright then. Hope he can stomach whatever we're about to walk into."

The rusted door creaks open as Jacques, one of Sabine's guys, nods at me and steps aside.

"Welcome, chérie," Sabine calls from across the room. "And happy birthday, Isabella."

She's draped in shadow and gold, standing beside a chair at

the center of the warehouse.

"Sabine," I say, voice steady but low. "What is this?"

She tilts her head and gestures slowly, and that's when I see him. Tied to a chair. Mouth taped. Eyes wide. Sweat pouring down his face like it's holy water and he's already seen the Devil.

And wrapped around his neck, coiled like a noose from hell, is none other than Celeste. Sabine's massive soul searching snake. Her iridescent scales shimmer like golden sunlight under the low light as her tongue flicks lazily near his ear. Reading him. Judging him. Deciding if he's worth the breath he's still taking.

"Is that a—" Cade starts.

"Happy birthday to me." I cut him off. "Thanks, Laing."

His eyes go wide when he sees me stalking toward him. Lex and Cade hang back a step. Tension rolling off them like heat, as if they are unsure if they should stop me or help me.

Or just let me burn.

Sabine steps up beside me, calm as ever, and slips a sleek, silver blade into my hand. Behind me, I hear Cade suck in a breath.

"You ready for your revenge, baby?" Sabine purrs.

I smile without looking away from him. "Let's begin."

I crouch a little in front of him, my blade catching the light.

"Hello, Vince."

He thrashes in the chair, trying to shake off the massive snake coiled around his neck, but it's no use. Celeste holds steady.

"This is Celeste," I say, waving a hand lazily toward the thick, iridescent coils around Vince's throat. "She's a lovely little friend of mine."

His eyes bug. He's sweating bullets and I swear I can smell the fear ripple off of him.

"She's got this little gift, kind of like a special magical power," I add, voice syrupy sweet. "Sabine, care to explain?"

Sabine grins slow and wide. "Of course."

She walks toward Vince, heels clicking like it's his judgment day. "See here," she drawls in that perfect Cajun lilt, "my girl Celeste's got a bit of voodoo in her blood. Special power passed down from my mama's mama."

I cross my arms and say with my best southern drawl, "Celeste can read the souls of men."

Sabine nods, her dark-brown eyes gleaming. "That's right, cher. Evil don't hide from her. She knows what's rotten. What's twisted. What's worth savin' and what ain't."

I glance at Vince, who's gone ghost white. Celeste's tongue flicks near his jaw.

"And trust me," I say, stepping a little closer. "She works. Your buddy Carlos? Pure fucking evil. Celeste didn't hesitate when she looked into his dirty little soul."

Behind me, Lex lets out a low huff of a laugh. I glance back at him. He mouths, *"I fucking love you,"* and all I can do is smile.

Vince is shaking now. Literally vibrating in the chair, sweat dripping down his temples, duct tape barely holding back a scream.

Sabine leans in beside me. "So, we're gonna have Celeste take a lil' peek inside you, mon chou."

The snake rises higher, her body tightening slightly. Her glittering eyes meet Vince's. And for one heartbeat, everything stills. Then she turns her head toward Sabine.

I grin, teeth bared. "This is the best part."

Sabine gives a slow nod and Celeste strikes. Fangs sink into Vince's neck like they were meant to live there. He screams, muffled by the tape, whole body thrashing like a man on fire.

Lex's voice cuts through the chaos, low and amused. "Goddamn, baby."

CHAPTER 65
CADE
WAREHOUSE 29-A
BROOKLYN, NEW YORK
721 DAYS SINCE ZEKE'S DEATH

"Goddamn, baby," Lex mutters beside me as the snake sinks its fangs into Vince's neck.

Celeste, they said. That thing is a monster—thick and glistening like it slithered straight out of hell. Bella doesn't even flinch. She just stands there, dead calm, watching Vince squirm under the snake's hold.

"Really should've seen that one coming," she shrugs as if she's just commenting on the weather.

"Come here Celeste," she says reaching for the snake. She lets it curl around her arm like it belongs there. Like she belongs to something darker now.

She walks the creature over to Sabine, who looks like some kind of voodoo queen from a fever dream. Her eyes glassy with thrill, as if this is all just foreplay before the real storm hits.

Bella turns toward Vince, Tex steps up beside her on instinct. "Now, Vincent... if I take the tape off, you gonna behave?"

He is drenched in sweat, trembling like a coward. His eyes dart to Sabine. Then to the snake still hissing in her arms. Then back to Tex. Not looking at Bella, not even once. Apparently, that pisses Tex off because he punches him clean across the jaw.

I wince. Lex exhales a deep breath he's been holding since we got here.

Tex growls, "Answer her. Yes or no. Are you going to behave?"

Vince nods, chest heaving. His eyes flick to Bella again, begging this to stop.

Tex looks at her. They don't speak. They don't need to. These two know each other so well they can have a full conversation just on looks alone. She nods and Tex rips the duct tape off his mouth.

Vince gasps and then spits, "You fucking bitch, let me—"

A cruel and unhinged laugh escapes Bella's beautiful face. It's almost gleeful, like she's finally snapped and decided to make art out of this madness.

"Now, Vincent. What did I just say?"

Tex doesn't wait. Another punch. This one splits Vince's lip, leaving a crimson trail down his chin.

I glance at Lex. His fists are clenched and his jaw is locked so tight I can hear the grind of his molars from here. His eyes haven't left Bella, not once. He wants in. Bad. This is killing him to stand back here with me on the sidelines instead of up there in the action.

Vince finally shuts his mouth. Smart move.

Bella steps in closer, lowering her voice. "I've waited a long, long time for this."

Her fingers trail to the inside of her wrist, brushing the small tattoo. *Dylan*. Vince, the sick bastard, smiles when he sees it. Laughs when he sees Dylan's name on her wrist.

Something dark flashes through Bella's eyes. There is no hesitation when she lifts the knife Sabine handed her earlier and drives it deep into his shoulder.

Vince screams, ragged and violent. "You little fucking bitch!" he roars, spitting blood across the concrete. "I will kill you."

Bella tilts her head. "Like you killed my brother?"

Vince freezes for a heartbeat, then smirks. "Which one?"

Tex's fist cracks across his jaw before he can finish the grin.

Vince spits blood, laughing through it. "Still a touchy subject I see," he chokes out. "But no, I didn't kill the mutt. Didn't even have a hand in that explosion. But I heard about it. Hell, I got off on that shit. Watched it like a damn highlight reel."

The room goes still. Bella's jaw tightens, but her voice stays calm. Too calm. "You watched my brother die?"

"Over and over and over. I had my men get me the security footage from Chicago." He grins wider, teeth pink with blood. "Should've been me though. Would've been one hell of a show."

Bella leans into the blade, tearing through muscle as she twists. "Vincent," she murmurs. "You really don't learn, do you?"

He glares up at her, eyes wild. "I told you the truth, what else do you want, bitch—"

"Okay, fucker," Lex lunges, explosive beside me, pure violence in motion.

Tex is faster. He throws an arm across Lex's chest, holding him back like a damn wall. "Not yet, Lex," he shouts, voice calm but firm. "She decides when we act. You understand?"

Bella's head tilts, just a notch. "Tex, let him go," she says quietly before turning her steel gaze to Lex. "Baby, come here."

Lex stalks toward her, every step a threat wrapped in black.

Bella turns back to Vince like she's hosting a fucking dinner party. "Vincent, this is Lex. One of the loves of my life."

She steps aside, giving Lex a full view of the man who once had her price tag. "And I don't think he likes you calling me a bitch very much. That right, baby?"

Lex doesn't say a word. Doesn't have to. His eyes are pure murder, slow, and personal. I've seen Lex mad before, but this is something darker, something completely terrifying.

Bella drops into a crouch, inches from Vince's blood-slicked face. "So, Vincent," she whispers, "I'm going to need you to say you're sorry."

He glares. A seething beast ready to snap.

Bella rises and turns to Lex. She grabs him by the collar, pulls him down, and kisses him like she wants Vince to choke on it. Like the kiss itself is a weapon.

When she finally breaks the kiss, her lips brush his and she breathes, "Baby... it's your turn."

Lex snaps. He lunges, and then it's just fists. Fist after fist after fist. Every single one landing with a sickening crack. Vince's face caves under the force. Blood splatters the floor. His nose collapses, his jaw twists sideways. Bella's blade still juts from his shoulder like a goddamn flag.

"Lex," Bella says, gently now. Calm again. "That's enough, baby."

His fist rears back. And for a second, I don't think he's going to stop. But he does. His arm drops, breath ragged, chest heaving. His jaw clasped so tight it looks carved from stone.

I just stare with my mouth open, because I've never seen anyone stop Lex mid-rage. Not Rez. Not any of the Hollow Kings. Not even Daniel. No one.

But Bella just says his name and the beast folds entirely.

Bella steps forward, hand soft against his jaw. "Thank you, baby."

Sabine lets out a wicked little laugh. "Ooooh, baby girl, did you ever get yourself one hell of a man." She glances at me. "Two of them, from the looks of it."

Bella walks over to her, calm and composed now like none of this touched her. Like she's washed it off already. "Sorry, Sabine. Where are my manners? That one's Lex," she says, laughing and nodding toward the man still seething by the chair.

"And that one..." she looks at me "...that one's Cade."

I glance at Lex. His eyes haven't left Vince. Not once. He's one twitch away from shattering something. There's heat rolling off him in waves. Raw, heavy, and volatile waves. He's still in it. Still on that razor's edge between control and detonation.

And I'm just standing here trying to remember how the hell we got here. How the girl we swore to protect turned into a storm dressed in silk. And why watching her own this room, own him, makes me want her even more.

Even when I know it's going to break us all.

CHAPTER ⑥⑥
LEX
WAREHOUSE 29-A
BROOKLYN, NEW YORK
ABOUT TO LOSE MY SHIT.
721 DAYS SINCE ZEKE'S DEATH

I can hear Bella talking to Sabine behind me. She's making introductions or some shit. Playing polite. But I can't fucking see her.

All I see is him. Vince. The man who carved pain into our baby's life like it was his right. The man who abused her little brother. Who set off a chain reaction that ended with Dylan in the ground. The man who bought Bella. Put a price on her like she was inventory. Like she was his to use. His to own.

Bella let me have a taste of vengeance. One hit. Two. Five. But it's not enough. Not nearly fucking enough. I want back in. I need back in. I need to end him. Crack every bone in his face and let his body rot in this concrete tomb.

She walks back into my line of sight, eyes locked on mine, then grabs my face and kisses me again like she's desperate. Like I'm the air and she's drowning. I know what this is. She's doing it to piss off Vince, the sick bastard who thought he could ever touch her.

So, I kiss her back. I pull her into me tighter, feasting on her tongue like I'll never get enough. Because I will never get enough of this woman.

She pulls back just an inch, breathless. "I love you, Lex."

"I love you too, malyshka."

Then she turns, smooth as ever, and rips the blade out of Vince's shoulder. His screams echo off the walls but refrains from calling her a bitch this time. She crouches in front of him again, and I catch the flick of Vince's eyes. Down her goddamn shirt.

I step forward, fast and ready to rip his throat out, but she feels me. She always does. She glances back.

"What is it, Lex?"

"The fucker's looking down your shirt, baby. He should know by now you're mine. He doesn't get to look at what he'll never have."

Bella turns back to Vince. "Now, Vincent were you violating my privacy?"

Vince shakes his head frantically.

She clicks her tongue. "Well, then are you calling the love of my life a liar?"

He doesn't answer. Doesn't dare. Bella rises slowly, the queen of death, and walks over to me. She hands me her knife, calm and deadly.

"Baby, two times for a lie. No more, no less, and no vital organs. We're taking our time with my old friend, remember?"

I nod. "Yes, baby." I don't delay. One stab deep into the opposite shoulder. He howls. Another straight through the palm of his hand. He screams like a little bitch.

"Motherfucking psycho," he spits through the blood. "You're just her goddamn lap—"

Before I can even lunge again, Bella is there. She walks up to him, boots clicking against the concrete.

"What did you just say?" she asks softly, tilting her head.

Vince shuts up. Mouth clamped tight. But it's too late. Bella doesn't dare break eye contact as she reaches out and gently takes the knife from my hand. Then she presses the tip right in front of Vince's eye.

"Answer me, Vincent!" she roars.

He gulps, trembling. "I-I didn't mean—"

"Sabine?" Bella calls out without looking away from him.

"Yes, baby?"

"Can you bring Celeste here for me?"

"Of course, child." Sabine steps forward, and God help me, she's smiling like this is some sort of Sunday brunch. She places Celeste right into Bella's waiting hand.

The creature winds around her with a slow grace, like it knows it's part of the performance. Part of the punishment. Celeste curls up her arm, across her shoulders, down her waist, claiming her like the darkness does.

And somehow, I'm hard. Terrified? Sure. Turned the fuck on? Absolutely. Nemesis. Fuck, that costume was perfect. Our girl is vengeance.

Bella crouches again, face level with Vince. "Vincent," she murmurs. "If you think you can talk to my man like that we're going to have a real problem."

Then she drops Celeste right onto his lap. Vince loses his fucking mind. Screaming. Thrashing. Pleading. But he can't move, he's tied too tight. Celeste slithers slowly across his thighs, unbothered by his movements.

Bella watches it all. Unmoved. Like a queen watching the consequences of her wrath play out in real time.

I hear Cade shift behind me. He's getting tense. His breathing's uneven. He's hanging on by a thread.

I glance at Bella, my voice low. "Baby... maybe Tex should take Cade back to the car."

Tex steps in like a loaded weapon, getting right in my face. "What did you say, Lex? You don't get tell her what to do. She is in charge here. What fucking part of that do you not understand?"

I don't flinch. Don't blink. I'm not afraid of him. But I am trying to protect the man Bella loves. Hell, the man *we* love, because this shit's only about to get darker.

Bella steps between us, placing a hand on Tex's chest. Her touch is soft, but her presence is iron. "Tex, it's okay. I'll handle it."

He nods and takes a step back.

She turns to Cade. "Cade now's your chance. Do you want to stay? Because from here on out it's only going to get worse. Vince isn't leaving this building."

Cade takes a step toward her. "Sweetheart, I want to stay. I told you, darkness and light. All of you. I love all of you. I'm in. Forever." He pulls her in and kisses her like it's the last thing tethering him to this world.

Sabine lets out a low, delighted chuckle. "Ooooh, chérie... you one lucky lady."

"Yes. Yes, I am."

Vince is still losing his damn mind in that chair. Celeste is wrapped around his torso, squeezing with slow intent. Her body gleams under the low light, her tongue flicking in and out like she's testing the air for fear.

And she's finding plenty.

"Get it off me! Get it the fuck off me!" Vince screeches, squirming, legs kicking against the chair legs.

He's sweating like a pig, tears streaking down his blotchy face. The same face that once smirked through a deal to buy our girl. The same hands that hurt her family. The same monster who made her little brother bleed from the inside out. Now he's being judged by something primal.

Bella stalks back to him. Every step she takes toward Vince, he flinches harder knowing damn well his life expectancy is running short.

"Now, where were we?" Bella tilts her head at Vince, then looks to Sabine with a polite smile. "Sabine, would you mind taking Celeste off our little friend here?"

Sabine nods, amused. "Of course, baby."

Bella's eyes stay locked on Vince. "But just so we're on the same page," she adds, her voice dipping into something cold and final. "From here on out, if you lie or if you call me any names, you don't get my knife. You get Celeste."

Vince stiffens like a fucking corpse reanimated. He nods fast, eyes darting toward the snake as Sabine slowly unwraps her. He's shaking. Not from the blood. Not from the blade. But from her.

That snake scared him more than any of us ever could and Bella saw it. Filed it away and weaponized it. Sabine cradles Celeste like she's holding royalty and steps back into the shadows.

Bella stands tall, smooths her hands down her top, and claps once. Light. Chipper. Fucking terrifying as hell.

"Alright! Here's what we're going to do," her voice is pure mockery. "Think of this as your confessional. Your last rites. Your come-to-Jesus whatever the fuck you want to call it."

Vince squints, confused. "What are you talking about?"

Tex huffs a dark laugh from behind me. Clearly, they've played this game before.

Bella doesn't miss a beat. "Tex?" she says sweetly, holding out her hand like she's inviting him to dance. He quickly steps up and takes it.

"You wanna be the priest tonight or should I?"

Tex grins. "Oh, I think I'll be the priest." He spins her once and dips her low like they're on a dance floor. "You sit and enjoy the show instead, Bells."

Bella's smile grows. She turns and walks toward the wall, boots echoing like gunshots against concrete. She grabs a metal chair and drags it slowly, scraping all the way across the floor until it screeches to a stop in front of Vince. She flips it around, straddles it backward, knife still in hand, and just watches him.

Cade moves up beside me, his arms crossed tight. He's trying to stay calm, but he's breathing through his nose like a goddamn bull.

Sabine slinks up on my other side, Celeste curling around her arm like liquid muscle. She leans in close and whispers in my ear, "You're gonna love this part, chéri."

The snake hisses, whispering secrets just for me.

Sabine chuckles. "She likes you. Sees your darkness, but she's intrigued by your soul... wants to know it." She leans in closer still, and murmurs something low in French Creole. I don't understand all of it, but one word cuts clean: *l'ombre*. The shadow.

Tex steps up behind Vince, places both hands on his shoulders, fingers digging in like steel. "Vince, we gather you here tonight for your final trial," he says, voice cool but loaded. "Now's the time. Is there anything you'd like to confess?"

Vince's breath rattles in his chest. His eyes bounce from Tex, to Bella, to the snake, to Sabine, and back to Bella. Then he snaps. "You fucking psychopathic bunch of lunatic freaks!"

Sabine tsks, clicking her tongue in disapproval. "Wrong answer, chéri."

She sets Celeste on Bella's shoulders. The snake slithers up and over, draping itself like a scarf across our girl's collarbone, curling at her throat. Bella doesn't move. She reaches up and runs her fingers down Celeste's spine like it's the most natural thing in the world.

Vince trembles. Palms sweaty, face pale, bleeding and broken.

Bella leans in. Sweet and fucking adorable. "Now, Vincent, I think you can do better than that."

Vince startles. "What do you want me to say?" he snaps, voice cracking.

Tex circles him like a shark, calm but deadly. "The truth, Vince. The truth about it all."

Vince blinks, confused, like he doesn't know which truth they mean.

"We want you to confess what you had planned for Bella. What you and Carlos said to make Zeke black out in a fit of rage that night in Miami?"

I can feel Cade tense up beside me, bracing for an impact he already knows is coming. Bella must feel it too because she leans back slowly in her chair and locks eyes with Cade.

"I'm okay, sweetheart," Cade says through a nod.

She nods back, then looks back at Vince. "Go on."

He starts mumbling. Rambling nonsense. His eyes flick to the snake, then to the blood drying on his shirt. He's unraveling. He can't focus on anything other than Celeste wrapping around Bella's shoulders.

"Lex, baby."

"Yes?" I answer, already stepping forward.

"Hold Celeste for me."

I reach down and take the snake from her shoulders. She coils around my arm like she knows me. Like she recognizes the fury boiling beneath my skin. The kind of rage that doesn't come with shouting, but with silence.

Bella crouches low again, knife dragging up the inside of Vince's thigh, voice turning to pure ice.

"Go on, Vincent."

"I was... I was..." he stutters.

Tex growls and grips his shoulders tighter. "Today, dumbass."

"Fine, you want to know what I was going to do to the little bitch?" Vince spits, voice shaking. "I was going to make the mutt watch me fuck her right in front of him. Watch while his little sister broke in half around my cock."

He laughs, a wet, broken sound. "Then I was gonna take her home. Chain her up. Fuck her until she forgot her own name. Sell her if she bored me. Maybe kill her. Maybe not."

His eyes flare. The madness bleeding through. "All I know is that bitch right there is fucking mine. Bought and paid for. Signed on the dotted line. Mine."

Silence. No one breathes. Cade's jaw locks so hard I swear I hear it crack. I don't even feel Celeste on my arm anymore. All I see is pure red-hot rage.

Sabine steps forward, eyes narrowed and unflinching, as she gently lifts the snake from my arm. "Here, *l'ombre,*" she says softly. "Let me hold her. I have a feeling you're going to want your hands free for this next part."

I nod. Because she's right. Hearing Vince call Bella his. Hearing his plans for her. I'm done. He's fucking dead.

Bella calmly stands, unshaken by Vince's words. She steps between us and Vince and stares him down like she's already counted the seconds left in his life.

"Mine? You say that word like it means something. But you see, Vincent, I think the two of them might have a difference of opinion on who I actually belong to."

She looks at me. I'm fuming. Barely holding it together. But I won't touch him. Not until she tells me I can.

Bella nods at me, and my voice cuts through the room like a goddamn blade, low, dangerous, and absolute.

"You never owned a fucking thing, Vince. Least of all her." I take a step closer. "She's not yours. Never fucking was." Another step. "You didn't earn her. You didn't touch her. You didn't even get close."

My chest heaves. "You know why?" I tilt my head, eyes locked on the bastard who thought he could claim her. "Because she got out and she chose us."

I let that hang in the air, heavy enough to crack bone. "That's what kills you, isn't it? The fact that you had to buy what we were given." I let out a humorless laugh. "Fuck, looking at you now, I bet you've had to pay for every piece of ass you ever got."

I lower my voice. "But Bella? She picked Cade. She picked me."

I tap my chest, voice rough. "She looked at everything we are, all the wreckage and all the rage and said yes."

I pause and exhale slowly. "That's love, motherfucker." I lean in, eyes blazing. "That's real."

Sabine lets out a low, throaty laugh from beside me. The kind that coils around your spine. "Mmm, baby," she says, eyes gleaming with something between reverence and thrill. "That right there? That's the kind of love women pray for in dark corners and forgotten churches. The kind they write spells for. Bleed for. The kind that don't break when the fire comes, it rises with it. Burns with it."

Bella nods, satisfied. Then turns to Cade. "Cade?"

"You still don't get it, Vince," he says, stepping forward. "All you ever did was circle her light, trying to find a way to smother it. You thought fear could make her small, that you could break her. You thought ownership could make her yours."

He shakes his head and huffs through his nose. "But she doesn't break that way. She never did. You didn't destroy her, Vince. You defined her. Every threat you made just showed her how to become stronger. Showed her exactly what she doesn't want in this world."

Cade looks at me. I nod, damn near in tears. He turns back to Vince. "Bella chose us, and we'll spend every breath proving she made the right choice."

He takes another step, close enough for Vince to see the conviction in his hazel eyes. "Lex and I will be right here. Every. Damn. Day. Making sure your name stays buried in the dark where it belongs. Making sure your shadow never even grazes her light again."

Cade pauses, fists balled at his sides.

"You wanted power. You wanted to own her. But the only thing you'll ever be remembered for is failing to touch the kind of woman even gods envy."

His words settle over the room like a slow-burn spell. The air itself seems to hold its breath. Even Vince finally shuts the hell up.

Next to me, Celeste lifts her head, tongue flicking toward Cade like she's tasting the air around him. Sabine watches with a slow, knowing smile. "Ahh, this one loves true. Not with fire, but with root. Deep, old, and hard to kill. That's the kind that grips you tight when the storm won't pass."

Cade lets out a shaky breath at Sabine's words. I swear, he looks at Bella like he already knew that and just needed the universe to say it out loud.

Sabine steps closer, Celeste still curled around her shoulders like a crown of serpents and looks at me... then at Cade. "She's blessed to have y'all. And you? You're blessed 'cause she chose you. Don't let the gods forget it."

Bella turns back to Vince, smiling like this is just a game she's already won. "I am theirs, Vincent. In every way that matters. And definitely not yours. Never was. Never will be. No matter how much you paid or what you signed on Carlos's pathetic little dotted line."

She leans in close, her voice a whisper sharpened to a blade. "But you know what I will be?" A pause. "I'll be the last face you ever see, Vincent."

She straightens, eyes flicking to me, then Cade. "That is... after I let the loves of my life have a little fun with you first."

The second she gives the word, something in me snaps. There's no more holding back. No more breathing through the rage. Tex clamps his hands on Vince's shoulders like he knew I was about to explode. And thank fuck he does, because if Vince were loose right now, I'd tear his spine out through his throat.

I move in, fast, fists already flying. The first hit lands square on his jaw. The second, his ribs. I hear something crack. Good.

"You think she belonged to you?" I spit, my voice hoarse with hate. "You think that you bought her? Claimed her?"

I grab him by the throat, slam him back against the chair, and keep swinging.

"No. You don't get to say her name. You don't even have the right to breathe her air."

Vince is coughing blood now, spitting teeth between screams. And I don't care. I don't fucking care. One more punch. One more crack.

Behind me, I hear Cade, his breath uneven. He's not ready yet. Still processing. Still on the edge of the dark. But I live here in the darkness, here in the abyss with Bella.

Tex lets out a laugh. "Damn, Barinov. Looks like you got some demons to exorcise."

"Yeah," I growl. "And this fucker just volunteered to be my altar."

"That'll do, Lex." Bella's voice slices through the red haze in my head, soft but absolute. My fist freezes mid-air. I step back, chest heaving, blood dripping from my knuckles. Vince's face is unrecognizable now—swollen, broken, a portrait of everything he's done finally coming back to bury his ass.

Bella steps forward, calm as ever as Tex straightens behind Vince and claps a hand on his ruined shoulder.

"Well Bells," he drawls, "final judgment?"

Bella tilts her head. Her smile is ice. "Oh, he's guilty, alright."

Tex laughs. Bella laughs. And it's terrifying. The sound of two wolves finding joy in the slaughter. She turns to Sabine and nods once.

Sabine just raises a single finger. "Jacques," she says coolly.

The door creaks open and Jacques walks in, quiet, casual, like this is just business. He's carrying a red container and a silver lighter.

Bella takes a step back. I move to her left, Cade to her right. We're an unshakable wall around our girl. Sabine and Celeste stand beside me, Celeste hissing low, like she knows what's coming. Tex falls in next to Cade, eyes fixed on the scene like he's watching a sermon.

Jacques doesn't as a word as he uncaps the can and starts pouring it over Vince's slumped body. The bastard twitches. Groans. But he doesn't beg. He knows it's over. Gasoline splashes across his shirt, his hair, the concrete floor beneath him.

Then the click of the lighter.

A spark.

A flame.

And then—*whoosh*.

Fire consumes him. He screams. The sound is music to my ears.

I reach over and thread my fingers through Bella's, squeezing tight and anchoring her to the moment she's been chasing for years. She doesn't flinch, never peels her eyes from the flames.

And then I feel it, Cade reaching across her, grabbing her hand from the other side.

No words. Only heat and silence and the sound of monsters and nightmares finally burning.

And I know what's coming. I know I'll have to pick up the pieces of her that will shatter the moment we get home. The moment it all hits her, but I don't care. She got her vengeance. She got her revenge.

For Dylan.

For Zeke.

For her.

CHAPTER ⑥⑦
C A D E
O U R   A P A R T M E N T
722 DAYS SINCE ZEKE'S DEATH

We walk back into the apartment without saying a word. It's nearly two a.m. and we all are exhausted. I drove us home from the warehouse, hands white knuckled on the wheel, trying not to look in the rearview mirror. Bella was curled up in the backseat, quietly pressed into Lex's side, his arm around her shoulders like a shield. None of us spoke, we just let the weight of the night sink in.

Now, she walks through the door like a ghost. She shrugs off her leather jacket, lays it over the counter without a care. Then she disappears into the bathroom. The door clicking shut behind her.

Lex and I stand there in the entryway, both of us still catching our breath.

"You okay?" he asks, his voice low.

I don't answer right away. I don't know how. Finally, I shake my head. "I don't know. That was..."

"Brutal?" he offers. "Unrelenting?" He looks toward the closed bathroom door, then back at me.

"That was Bella. That's her darkness, Cade. The part most people don't see until it's too late. The part she's had to bury so deep just to survive. Tonight? That was justice fucking served. Raw, real, and unapologetic revenge."

I run a hand through my hair, trying to steady myself. "Are you gonna go in after her?"

"No, babe. You are."

I blink. "Me?"

"She already knows I can pick up the pieces," he says. "I've done it. I know how to hold her through it all when she breaks." He glances toward the closed bathroom door. "But this time, you need to."

Lex steps closer, voice soft but steady. "She needs to know both of us can pull her back from it. When the emotions get too strong, she needs to know that she doesn't have to fight them alone. If she's going to let you have all of her, you must see all of her. And still choose stay."

My throat goes dry. "But what do I do? How do I help her? I'm not you, babe."

Lex leans in and presses a kiss to my cheek. "You go in there and you figure it out."

He walks into the kitchen like nothing happened. Like he didn't just hand me the most important moment of my life. He grabs a glass and pours himself a drink while rubbing a hand over his face.

I go over and stand at the bathroom door, staring at it like it's a locked vault that I don't have the code for. Thick steam silently curls out from beneath it. My fingers hover over the knob. I turn it and step inside.

The room is heavy with heat. The mirror's fogged over. She's on the shower floor naked, knees pulled in, back to the tile, the spray pouring over her like it's supposed to cleanse her of everything. She doesn't look up. She just sits there. Her arms wrapped around herself like she's trying to hold her soul together.

I undress, then slide the door open, and step inside. I drop to my knees in front of her, voice barely above a breath.

"Hi, sweetheart."

She lifts her head. Her eyes are wrecked. Red, panicked, swimming in unshed tears.

"I had to do it," she chokes out. "I had to. For what he did to me. For," her fingers drift to her *Dylan* tattoo. Her voice breaks. "Please don't hate me, Cade. Please, please don't leave me."

I wrap my arms around her, pulling her in, skin to skin, heart to heart. Water soaks us both, warm but unrelenting.

"Hey," I whisper, holding her tightly. "Shhh. I've got you."

She starts to shake in my arms as the tears start to flow faster.

"Shh," I whisper into her hair. "Just breathe, sweetheart. I've got you."

She gasps against my shoulder, her body vibrating. I stroke her back slowly, trying to anchor her as her tears flow freely.

"You did what had to be done," I say against her temple. "And I'm so proud of you."

She lets out a sob. This one different. Softer. She melts into me, letting me carry her weight. Eventually, she looks up. Eyes glassy.

"You're not scared of me?"

I shake my head. "Never." I lift her chin to make her look at me. "I love you."

She stares at me like she doesn't deserve it. "Cade, I love you too."

I lift her off the ground in one smooth motion. Her legs wrap around my waist, her arms around my neck, and I pin her gently to the shower wall, kissing her like my life depends on it. Her fingers clutch at my shoulders, holding on as if I'm the only thing keeping her alive.

I pull back. I set her feet down, slow and careful, like she's made of something sacred. And then I drop to my knees.

"Cade..."

I look up at her, hands caressing their way up the backs of her thighs. "I've got you, sweetheart."

I lean in, tongue tracing her heat, already slick and begging for me. I start slow—soft circles with gentle pressure—until I feel her knees start to tremble. Her fingers thread desperately into my hair, but I don't stop. I don't rush. I know her. I've learned every inch of her body like it's art. Like it's holy. I know exactly how to make her come undone with my mouth. And I do, while savoring every second of it.

Because this isn't just lust.

This is love.

This is *mine*.

I flatten my tongue, dragging it slow and deep before thrusting it inside her, licking her open and tasting her like she's the only thing I've ever wanted. Her moan echoes off the steam-slicked tiles.

I look up at her, eyes locked with hers, my mouth still warm from her skin. I pause just long enough to whisper, "I love you so damn much, Bella."

Then I dive back in, sucking her clit like a man starved, needing only her to survive. She rides my face like it's the only way she remembers how to feel. Her moans grow louder, sharper.

"Oh, Cade." My name falls off her lips like a prayer.

Her fingers tighten in my hair, and I feel it. The way her thighs start to twitch against my shoulders. The way her hips jerk just slightly, chasing every flick of my tongue.

She's close. So damn close I can almost taste it.

"Cade," she gasps, her voice cracking.

I slide one hand up to her hip, the other gripping the back of her thigh to steady her.

"It's okay, sweetheart," I murmur against her skin. "Let go for me, *baby*."

She does.

Her entire body seizes for half a second, then shatters. A strangled cry rips from her throat as her orgasm slams through her. Her knees almost give out, but I hold her firm, tongue still working her through every wave, every aftershock. She shakes against me, her hands flying to the slick tiles behind her searching for something to ground her.

But it's me. I'm her anchor. And I've never loved her more than I do in this moment—naked, raw, broken and still completely glorious. I press one last kiss to her inner thigh before standing slowly. Watching as she sags back against the wall, chest heaving, cheeks flushed, eyes glassy with tears and relief.

A low whistle breaks the silence. "Well, that was fucking hot as hell," Lex says, his voice full of that wicked cocky humor that only he could pull off after a night like this.

Bella leans her head back against the tile, still catching her breath. I glance down at her and she meets my eyes, lips twitching into a small, exhausted smile.

We both look toward Lex and just shake our heads. He's already opening the shower door, naked and shameless. His hand wrapped firmly around his cock stroking himself for the world to see.

"You gonna stand there stroking it or get in here and do something with it, babe?" I taunt.

He steps in like a wolf, ice-blue eyes locked on Bella before crashing his mouth to hers with a hunger that makes my breath hitch all over again. God, I'll never get used to this, to them. Watching them. Loving them.

Lex lifts her up, pins her to the tile, and drives into her with one brutal thrust that has her crying out into his mouth.

I wrap my hand around myself, because there's nothing more beautiful than watching Bella unravel, especially at Lex's hands. The way she clings to him. The way he holds her like a sinner clutching salvation.

"God you guys," I moan, stroking myself, eyes never leaving them. "A masterpiece the two of you, I could watch this all day."

Water rushes over them, cascading like it's trying to wash away the madness we just survived. But it can't. Nothing can. This right here, this is how we heal. Together. With our mouths, hands, and hearts intertwined as one.

Lex lets out a deep groan as he finishes, burying his face in Bella's neck as her fingers claw into his back. He lowers her slowly, carefully, like she's the most precious thing on earth. She almost slips but Lex steadies her, then glances at me.

Before I can speak, he pulls me in, grabbing the back of my neck and pressing his mouth to mine. I melt into it.

Bella's soft voice cuts through the steam.

"Lex..." She bites her lip, all wicked and sweet at the same time. "Turn him around. Hold him still for me." Lex grins, already gripping me. And I swear to God, I don't know what I did in a past life to deserve this kind of love but I'm never letting it go.

Lex's hands tighten around my arms, turning me toward Bella as my back hits his chest. I feel his hungry breath ghost against my neck.

"Hold still, Cade" she purrs, sinking to her knees in front of me.

My heart is already pounding. She looks up at me. Her eyes, dark with mischief and fire, locking with mine as she licks her lips. She doesn't blink as she slowly takes me into her mouth.

It's not just the heat or the pressure or the way her tongue swirls around the head of my cock, it's the look. That unbroken stare. Like she's branding me from the inside out. Like she's saying *this is mine* without ever having to utter a single syllable.

Lex's lips find my neck just as she sucks me in deeper. His

kiss open-mouthed, teeth grazing just enough to make me groan. My fingers twitch at my sides. I want to grab her hair, want to bury myself deeper, but I can't move. Not when Lex is holding me like this. Not when Bella's mouth is full of me.

She hums around me and I swear the tiles behind her spin. Lex growls softly against my skin sending vibrations running straight through me. This is more than sex. This is worship. It's war. It's art in its rawest form, crafted with teeth and tongue and a crown of steam.

Bella pulls back slowly, lips wrapped tight, tongue flicking just beneath the head. Then she goes down again, deeper. And deeper. Until her nose brushes my skin.

"Fuuuuck, Bella," I rasp, barely breathing.

Lex's voice is low in my ear. "Our baby's so damn good at this, isn't she Cade?"

I nod, jaw tight, moaning as she bobs her head with ruthless grace. Like she's the one in control. Like she knows she could ruin me right here in front of the man who already owns half my soul.

I feel Lex hardening behind me, his cock pressed thick and full against the curve of my ass. He's still holding my arms, still watching Bella take me apart with her mouth, and now he's ready to wreck me too.

"Seriously, babe," I pant, breathless, not even pretending to hide the grin in my voice. "How the fuck do you get so hard this fast?"

Lex chuckles low, biting at my shoulder. "That's what you two do to me. You want me calm then you better stop being so fucking beautiful."

His hand slides between us, slick fingers spreading me open with a practiced ease that makes my spine arch.

Bella pulls back for half a breath, eyes still locked on mine as her hand replaces her mouth, stroking me in a tortuously slow rhythm.

"You ready for him, sweetheart?" she asks, all sweet and sinful.

I nod.

"Good," she winks and wraps her lips back around me just as Lex pushes one finger deeper inside. I hiss. Another joins, stretching me further. And then, with one brutal, perfect thrust, he buries himself deep inside me until I'm so full of him that I might burst.

"Fuck," I growl, voice strangled.

"That's it, Cade," he grits, his voice rough as gravel. "Feel me. Take me. You're mine now. Both of you. *Mine*."

Then he starts to move, slow at first, dragging out each thrust like he wants to memorize the sound it pulls from my throat.

The pressure builds with every push, every grind of his hips. The heat of his skin, the slight burn as he moves deeper, the rasp of his breath on my neck, the faint tremor in his hands... It's everything I've ever wanted.

Bella moans around me. Like the sound of his voice does something to her too. I lose focus, the pleasure ricochets from her mouth, to his hips, to every inch of me like I've been lit from within.

Lex leans forward, his chest pressed against my back, his teeth grazing my ear. "You feel that, Cade?" he rasps, voice breaking on a groan. "That's what it means to be ours. Every inch of me, inside you, inside her. That's what we are. One."

He thrusts harder now. Faster, deeper, each movement rougher than the last until I can't tell where his rhythm ends and mine begins. The sounds blur—his growl, her moans, each of their names falling from my lips.

"God, Lex..." I choke out.

He bites down on my shoulder just as he slams into me again. "Come for us," he growls. "Right down our girl's throat while I fill your ass up, Cade. Right fucking now, baby."

Baby, that fucking word. That's all it takes. I come undone with a shattered groan, hips jerking forward into Bella's waiting mouth, Lex's cock slamming deep one final time as he spills inside of me.

We all stay there frozen in that moment. Water cascading down. Steam rising. My body held between the two people I love more than anything in the world. There's no beginning or end. Just breath and heat and skin, the three of us tangled in something that feels infinite.

In this moment, we're not separate. We're not broken. We're one.

We step out of the shower, dripping and breathless, steam

still curling in the air like smoke after a storm. Towels hang forgotten. None of us rush. There's no shame left between us. Just skin, trust, and the kind of peace you only get after breaking apart together.

Bella reaches for her pants, still pooled on the floor near the vanity. She bends to dig through the pocket.

SMACK

Lex's palm playfully connects with her bare ass.

"Jesus," she mutters, half laughing as she shoots him a look over her shoulder.

I grab a towel and run it through my hair. "You ever not grab her ass, babe?"

"Nope," Lex replies casually, already reaching for his own towel.

Bella pulls her phone from the pocket of her pants, screen lighting up in her hand. But then she stops. Her entire body stills. Her smile fades as her grip tightens.

"What is it?" I ask, stepping forward.

She doesn't speak. Just stares at the screen.

"Baby?" Lex says, voice suddenly flat. "Who is it?"

Bella's face pales as she scrolls, then turns the screen toward me, her fingers gripping it tight. She swallows hard, eyes darting toward the door like she's expecting a shadow to move.

"We need to call Knox. Now."

@LucaWasHere
So bold of you—unchained, untamed.
Letting Lexie and Whitmore stake their claim.
Looks like Vince lit up like a birthday spark.
Fitting for a girl who forgets the dark.

Cute show in the shower, all steam and skin,
But let me remind you, I'll always win.
I saw every twitch beneath that flame.
Lexie's hands, all shaking with shame.

Whitmore, a muse of soft regret.

They touch, but I own every breath they get.
They think they've won, but I never tire.
I wait in the quiet. I sharpen the wire.

So lose the dead weight or I'll make my art.
One stroke for the body, two more for the heart.
Tell Whitmore to paint the scene just right,
A Whore in Ashes. A Lover's Blight.

I'll frame it in silence, dripping red,
For every truth you choked instead.
No Lexie. No Whitmore.
Only our twelve notes, Izzy, and a goddamn war.

Attached is a video of Bella on her knees. My hands in her hair, my eyes shut. Lex behind me, in the fucking shower.

　　Just now.

CHAPTER ⟨68⟩
BELLA
OUR APARTMENT
722 DAYS SINCE ZEKE'S DEATH

Knox shows up less than fifteen minutes later, looking like he just rolled out of a spy thriller. A black duffel slung over one shoulder full of wires, USB drives, tiny sensors, metal rods, a tablet, two burner phones, and what might be a pair of night-vision goggles. He doesn't say a word, just walks in, drops the bag on the kitchen counter, and starts working.

I sit on the couch between Lex and Cade, their bodies shielding mine like twin anchors. My hands are pressed down on my legs, trying to still the tremble in my knees.

Lex notices first. His hand slides onto my thigh, warm and solid. "Baby, it's okay. Knox'll get it all figure it out."

"He wants me away from you," I whisper.

My voice cracks on the last word as I clench my hands together, digging my nails into my palm, trying to breathe. But the panic's already crawling up my spine, coiling behind my ribs.

Knox walks back in like clockwork, calm as hell, and drops a small silver pin onto the coffee table with a *clink*. "I found this facing the shower."

In the sudden stillness of the room, that small piece of metal feels heavier than any gun. Lex has started pacing, his hands balled into tight fists. Cade remains frozen in place, his gaze locked on the pin. I feel like a phantom in my own body, observing a nightmare that belongs to someone else.

"I thought he was just a creep," I whisper. "Just some sadistic loser who got off on writing poems and watching from the dark. But this?" I run my hands through my hair. "This means he was here. He was inside our house."

Cade stands, every muscle is stiff with dread.

"We baited him," his voice is raw. "All those messages... we thought we were outsmarting him. But we gave him what he wanted."

Lex punches the wall, fist going straight through the drywall with a deafening crack. Plaster dust rains down, clinging to his skin, mixing with the blood already welling from his knuckles.

Knox looks up from the tangle of gear on the floor, his eyes sharp and haunted. "Alright," he says quietly. "This is what we're gonna do."

He stands and wipes his hands on his jeans. "I'm going to sweep every inch of this place," he says, already scanning the room like he's mapping a plan. "Then Rosethorne. Then The Pit and every other building tied to your names."

He looks up, jaw tight. "But I want the three of you out of here. Now."

His voice softens, but only barely. "Somewhere safe. Somewhere you choose. No routines. No patterns. No one else knowing." He pauses, meeting each of our eyes in turn. "Not even me."

Lex shakes his head. "We can't just run."

"Yes, you can," Knox snaps, louder than before. "You're not thinking straight."

Knox rubs the back of his neck. "This isn't some Instagram creep in a basement anymore, Lex."

He points toward the bathroom. "He watched you. In the shower. He got close enough to plant a camera in your goddamn bathroom and none of us knew."

Knox's eyes narrow, voice dropping to a low, grim edge. "That means he's either a ghost..." He looks straight at me. "...or someone you've already let in."

My mouth goes dry. "Knox, you said you're checking Rosethorne?"

"Yeah, there, The Pit, anywhere I can fucking think of at this point."

"The Masquerade. Maybe... maybe we should cancel," I say softly.

"No fucking way." Lex's voice snaps through the room like a strike of lightning. "We're not canceling. You girls have been working your asses off for this. You've been prepping since summer for it. I'm not letting that fucker take it from you, not a chance."

Knox drags a hand down his face, exhaling hard. "Lex is right, the Masquerade's weeks away. We've got time to figure this out, lock the systems, and trace every feed. But right now..." He gestures toward me. "Right now, we keep her breathing and we keep her hidden until I know how deep this goes."

"Between all of our connections, we can keep you safe, baby," Lex's jaw flexes. "I'll call Jack. I'll call in the Bratva if I have to. Hell, I'll even call Tattooed Dragon-Dick to come stand watch at the goddamn door."

Cade lets out a soft breath, somewhere between a chuckle and a wince.

I nod. "Let me make a call, I think I have a place we can go."

NOX

We walk into the presidential suite at NOX and my jaw hits the floor. It's massive. Bigger than our apartment. Hell, bigger than most houses. Dark wood floors stretch beneath soaring ceilings. Floor-to-ceiling windows looking out over the city, glittering like a spilled bottle of diamonds. There's a sleek fireplace, a marble bar with crystal decanters, velvet seating, and a king-size bed so grand it looks like royalty should sleep in it.

I catch a glimpse of the bathroom through a cracked door. Black stone, gold fixtures, and a tub big enough to swim laps in.

Roman steps in behind us, motioning around with a casual wave of his hand.

"Make yourselves comfortable. This suite is yours for as long as you need it."

I turn toward him, softening my voice. "We really appreciate you letting us stay here."

He gives a small nod. "Anything for you, Isabella. NOX is yours anyway, same as The Obsidian."

Lex huffs under his breath behind me, muttering something like *fucking great* as he sets down his bag.

Cade slides up next to me, voice gentle. "Here, sweetheart. Let me take this." He takes my suitcase from my hand and carries it toward the bedroom. I catch the curve of a smile on his lips as he looks around. "Damn. This place is insane."

Roman's voice breaks through my thoughts. "I'll let you get settled. But Isabella..." He waits until I look at him. "...I'd like for you to join me for breakfast in the morning. If that's all right."

Before I can even respond, Lex steps forward like a wall. "If she goes, we all go."

Roman lifts a brow, amused but unfazed. "Very well. The offer still stands."

We'll see you downstairs in the morning." I reach out and gently place my hand on his arm. "Thank you again. I mean it, Roman."

His eyes glance to where my hand touches him and then up to my face. There's something there, flickering just behind the surface. Not anger. Not even disappointment. A small, quiet ache. A silent wish for the words I didn't say.

Dad.

Father.

But I can't. Not yet. Maybe not ever. I drop my hand. Roman gives a single nod, then steps out of the suite, the door clicking softly shut behind him.

The restaurant inside NOX is exactly what you'd expect from Roman Russo—sleek, shadowed, and decadent. Glass chandeliers hang like icicles over velvet booths. Even at nine a.m., candlelight flickers against silver flatware. A wall of windows lets in just enough gray Manhattan light to remind you this isn't a dream. It's a kingdom.

And he's the king.

Roman's already seated when we arrive in the corner booth. I slide in. Cade sits beside me, Lex across, already looking annoyed. "Thank you for coming, Isabella," Roman says smoothly, lifting his coffee. "I know things have been... tense."

Lex scoffs. Cade lays a hand on my thigh under the table.

"We appreciate the suite," I say. "And the sweep of the floor. I know you didn't have to."

"You're my daughter. What's mine is yours."

Lex huffs, loud and unbothered. "You keep saying that. Feels more like what's yours is yours, and we're just lucky to be breathing in your orbit."

"Lex," I warn, gentle but sharp.

"You're fiercely protective. I respect that. But all I want is to get to know my daughter. All of her. And if that means tolerating your brooding scowls and bone-deep distrust, so be it."

Lex leans forward. "You want to know her? Start by telling her the truth about why she was raised in hell. Why it took twenty years and a damn body count for you to show the fuck up."

Roman exhales through his nose, like he's holding back a thousand answers. "I told Isabella when she and Cade's twin came to see me, I did try. I put my best men on it. The trail went cold."

His voice roughens, words scraping as they come out. "It was like she vanished into thin air. One day there were whispers, the next nothing. Leads ran dry and all I was left with was silence."

My stomach turns. I push my coffee away. "So, what do you want from me, Roman? Just to make up for lost time? Or is there more?"

His expression softens just slightly. "I want to know you. Your favorite color. What you're afraid of. What makes you laugh."

"There isn't much to tell," I admit. "Favorite color is blue. I grew up in the system. I got out with help from my bro—"

I stop myself. Zeke. The Black Books. Not yet.

Roman notices. "You can talk to me, Isabella. You can trust me."

Lex mumbles something under his breath.

Roman turns to him, voice like silk pulled tight. "I see Irina has filled your head with fury toward me. But don't be so quick to judge what you don't understand, Aleksandr."

Lex's shoulders go rigid. I reach for his hand instinctively. He softens. Roman sees it. The way Lex breathes easier at my touch. The way Cade leans in. The way we exist in an orbit around each other, gravity and chaos bound by love.

"It's just Bella. And just call him Lex."

Roman inclines his head. "Understood. My apologies."

I let out a shaky breath. "I'm just... not ready to unload my whole therapy file at breakfast."

He smiles, just slightly. "That's fair. But when you are ready, I'll be here."

"Thanks."

"Your performance at Regionals was inspiring, Bella. I have never been so proud of anything in my life."

Something tight in my chest tugs loose. "Thank you. Would you like to come to a practice sometime? It might be fun. You could see a bunch of different routines."

Lex tries to hide a wicked grin and fails. "You sure you want him watching you do a chair routine on me, baby?"

Cade groans. "Lex."

"What?" Lex shrugs. "He wants to know our lives. That's a big fucking part of it, babe."

Roman chuckles behind his fist. "I do own a nightclub, Lex," he says, the corners of his mouth curving. "Trust me, I'm well acquainted with chair routines."

A faint smile tugs at his lips—part pride, part mischief. "And after watching your birthday performances at The Obsidian, I think I've already seen a few things I can't unsee."

He pauses, taking a sip of coffee before adding, "Still, I would be delighted to come to a practice. I'm headed to Rome soon for business. I'll be gone for awhile, but when I return..." He meets my eyes. "...I'd love to attend."

"I'd like that," I say softly.

"So, Lex, Cade. How do you plan on keeping my daughter safe now that this man has been inside of your home? Is there something I can do?"

Lex stiffens. "It's being handled. We don't need your help."

Roman raises an eyebrow. "It never hurts to have more protection. Bella, I can get you a bodyguard. I can get all of you a bodyguard, round the clock protection."

"Not necessary," Lex snaps. "I will keep her safe."

"Of course," Roman says, tone unreadable. "But sometimes the best security is layered. If you change your mind let me know."

I squeeze Lex's hand across the table. Cade rubs his hand on my thigh under the table. I feel like I'm splintering in three directions.

Roman rises. "Well, thank you for meeting with me, Bella. I really should be going. I've got a plane to catch. If you need anything at all, you call me."

I nod.

The second he's gone, I sag against the booth, head tilted back, eyes fluttering shut for just a second.

My phone buzzes. I grab it out of my bag, expecting to see a message from Knox or Ellie, maybe even Coach Javi. But instead, it's from him.

@LucaWasHere
While Daddy flies and Wolves all bite,
I'll slip beneath the ballroom light.
But masks won't hide what's mine by thread,
You'll feel me, love, before I'm dead.

So, look for me at your Winter Ball,
I'll blend right in, for I've watched you all.
A dance, a drink... a little gift.
Just one more crack before the shift.

My blood turns to ice. My stomach drops.

I don't realize I've gone pale until Cade says, "Bella?" and Lex snatches the phone out of my hand.

"He's coming to the Masquerade," I say again, barely recognizing my own voice. "Luca. He's going to be there."

Lex stares at the screen like he's ready to snap it in half.

Cade's jaw tightens. "How the hell can we stop him if we don't even know who he is?"

Lex finally speaks, and when he does, it's all steel and storm.

"We do know something. We know he's coming. That means we've finally got the upper hand."

"How is that the upper hand?" I ask.

"Because now we bait him, baby. We draw him out from behind his damn screen."

Lex looks at me, deadly calm. "We use the Masquerade. Every camera, every angle, every blade we can pull from the shadows. He thinks he's crashing our night?" A dark smile tugs at his lips. "Let's make it his fucking funeral."

I exhale shakily, but it doesn't settle the dread coiling in my stomach.

Lex leans forward, eyes meeting mine. "As much as I hate saying this, baby. Call them all."

I frown. "All?"

"All of them. Every ally, every name from every book. Nate, Jack, Tex—hell, even fucking Laing."

My eyebrows shoot up.

"I don't like him. I don't trust him," Lex growls. "But I'd rather deal with that smug asshole breathing down my neck before I let Luca lay a hand on yours."

"Okay, I'll call them."

His tone softens just barely. "This is the moment we stop reacting, baby. From here on out, we hunt."

CHAPTER ⑥⑨
B E L L A
R O S E   O F   T H O R N S
M A S Q U E R A D E   B A L L
W E X L E Y   U N I V E R S I T Y
756 DAYS SINCE ZEKE'S DEATH

The dressing room glows with soft golden light, but the air is tense, electric. My hands tremble slightly as I tighten the silk ribbon at the back of Ellie's gown. She's quiet. Unnervingly quiet, not the normal stream of sass and sparkle I'm used to.

"You okay?" I ask, smoothing the satin over her shoulders.

She glances at me in the mirror. Her bright blue eyes wider than usual.

"Yeah. Just... Sabine keeps looking at me like she's picturing my autopsy."

I glance over. Sabine stands perfectly still in the corner. Her red gown clinging to her like blood on bone. She hasn't said a word since we walked in. Just watching. Observing like a damn hawk in bright red lipstick.

"She's weird," Haley mutters from behind me while adjusting her emerald earrings. "Hot. But definitely weird."

"It'll be fine," I say softly, turning back to the mirror. "We've got eyes on us already."

Our gowns shimmer in the candlelight. Ellie in golden-pink tulle, Haley in rich emerald velvet, and me in blood red. Floor-length, with off-the-shoulder sleeves and a low back. A crimson satin mask rests beside me on the vanity, waiting. Unarmed and exposed, but stunning nonetheless.

"I hate not being able to carry," I mutter.

Tex's voice crackles in my comm, low and steady. *"Front perimeter is locked. Kenji just checked in. Everyone's in position. You're clear to go when Javi gives the signal."*

Nate follows a second later. *"Copy that. Ballroom is full. Roman's still on his way from Italy. Rez and Khoza have the VIP section on their radar. O'Malley's got the roof. Daniel and his men are covering the exits. Laing's got the main floor. Briggs just took the upper balcony and Jack's got the lobby on lockdown."*

"It's time," Sabine says handing me my mask.

We file out of the dressing room, masks in place, heels clicking down the corridor like the beginning of a march.

Cade's calming voice hums in my comm. *"Just breathe, sweetheart."*

Lex follows, lower. Darker. *"No one's getting near you, baby. Not tonight."*

The strings swell as we glide in, the hem of my gown sweeping the marble. Ellie spins past me, her dress blooming like a sunflower, a flash of golden silk and pink rhinestones catching the light. Haley follows, her emerald skirt flickering like a flame, all sharp turns and clean lines.

Josh, Drake, and Sam meet us at the center, crisp in their black suits and matching masks. Hands join. Steps align. The dance turns formal for a beat, a beautiful waltz of poise and precision that holds the room captive.

We spin in pairs, then break apart only to reform in new lines, new shapes. The floor becomes a chessboard and we're the queens of the night.

The violins hit a crescendo. Josh lifts me into a half spin and for a moment, I'm flying, one hand reaching, one heart pounding, the whole world suspended in awe.

And then we descend into the final sequence. Our hands linked, gowns sweeping, and heads high. A single turn. A final beat. Silence.

The ballroom erupts into applause. We bow. Not too long, just enough to show grace and not surrender. Enough to let them know we own this room.

Let the night begin.

The lights dim lower. A bass-line hums through the floor as Knox transitions from orchestral elegance to a darker, sultrier beat. Strobe lights pulse to life overhead, washing the ballroom in flashes of violet and gold. The masquerade becomes a glittering club in a matter of seconds

Lex finds me first, peeling me out of the crowd with one strong hand on my waist. He doesn't speak, just pulls me into his chest and starts to move with me. The tempo doesn't matter. I follow him instinctively, heart hammering against the bones of my corset.

Cade joins from behind, brushing my hair off my shoulder, lips ghosting over the shell of my ear. "You killed it, sweetheart."

They move with me as if I'm their axis. Lex leading with a grounding confidence, Cade swirling behind me with care. Their hands trail down my arms, across my hips, up to my neck. I almost forget where we are.

"Tell me you wore this corset for me," Cade whispers, lips teasing against my neck.

"I wore it so our Hollow King would cry," I shoot back.
Lex lets out a short laugh. "That's the spirit, baby."

Over the comms, Nate's voice crackles through. *"North corridor clear."*

"Rooftop's all good, no bogeys up here," O'Malley chimes in, his Irish accent curling around the words like a pint at the end of a long night. *"Quiet enough to hear a bloody pin drop."*

"Lobby's clean," Jack says, clipped and calm.

A beat of silence, then Sabine purrs through the channel, *"Perhaps his soul caught wind of what's waiting here and decided to stay dead. Even shadows fear fire, no?"*

Lex snorts. Cade shakes his head. I exhale a laugh as some of the tension finally bleeds off me. Maybe she's right. Maybe Luca chickened out. Maybe we finally got ahead of him.

"Second sweep of VIP. All secure this side," Khoza's deep, baritone voice says over the comms. *"No eyes, no movement. We're good. Sawa? You see anything shift, even a shadow and you call it in. Hatuchezi tonight."*

Laing crackles in over the line, dry as ever. *"Good God, man. English, please. Some of us barely passed high school."*

"Means we don't play, mate. So, keep your eyes sharp... or stay out of my fucking way."

Lex spins me again, pulling me close so I'm flush against his chest and leans down until his lips are right at my ear. "You know," he murmurs. "If he doesn't show, we should celebrate."

Cade steps in behind me, hands at my waist. "Oh, we're celebrating either way. You're ours tonight, sweetheart. All night long."

I close my eyes for just a second, letting myself sink into the warmth of them, the safety. The rhythm. Their touch.

Laing cuts in over comms, *"Don't suppose I get a dance after that performance? Maybe a kiss? Come on, Iz, I wore the nice suit."*

Lex snarls immediately, "Back the fuck off Mortal Kombat."

Tex deadpans, *"Laing, don't make me shoot you from here."*

Ellie laughs softly in the background. *"I'm starting to like him."*

"He's too reckless for you, baby girl," Sabine replies flatly.

I glance up toward the balcony, then to the VIP and the main entrance—Jack, Briggs, Daniel, even Kenji and Khoza are posted everywhere, eyes sweeping the crowd like lions in tuxedos.

I lean into Lex and whisper, "Still feel like we have the upper hand?"

His eyes flick down to mine. "We have everything we need."

Lex spins me, catches me, and dips me low with a cocky grin. "You know, we never actually told you."

"Told me what?"

"How much we love you."

My chest tightens. "I know you do."

Lex tilts his head. "No, you don't, baby. You think you know, but you haven't even scratched the surface."

I bite my lip, trying not to cry, trying not to crack open under the weight of the emotion in his voice.

There's a sudden sharp crackle in my ear. Static. Interference. Followed by an annoyingly smug voice.

"Hey, Iz. Laing again," he says over the comms, tone lazy like he's lounging poolside with a drink. *"Real touching moment out there. Had me reaching for tissues and all that shit."*

Lex groans but Laing just laughs. *"Easy, champ. Still sore from the last time you turned me into street art? Good hit, by the way. Real poetic. Let's run it back sometime. You know, for old time's sake."*

"*Laing,*" Nate snaps, "*shut the hell up and keep the damn line clear before I throw your ass into the Hudson.*"

A sharp feedback blares through the main speakers. The lights freeze mid-strobe. Then his voice fills the air. Low. Rhythmic. Filthy with glee.

"Izzy…
Such a pretty little puppet, dressed up just right,
You twirled in your chains under chandelier light.
Mask on your face, but I know what's beneath,
A smile full of lies and a mouth full of teeth."

I stop breathing. Cade's hand clamps at my waist. Lex goes rigid, scanning.

"Shame your brother wasn't there to see,
Zeke always loved a good tragedy.
Might've clapped 'til his hands turned red,
If he weren't so busy being dead."

"What the fuck," Cade growls, tucking me behind him like I'm still that fifteen-year-old girl he used to drive across state lines for.

Lex shoves someone aside, barking into his mic, "Knox. Shut it down. Now."

"*I'm locked out!*" Knox snaps back through the comms.

"You're searching for me now, aren't you?
Lexie's eyes cut the room in two.
Whitmore's poised, so tense, so brave,
But heroes don't dance on the edge of a grave.

No, no, no… don't look below,
I'm not the dark you think you know.
I am the stage, the silent scream,
The puppet master in your dream."

"Who the fuck is that, Lex?" Rez snaps.

Briggs growls, *"Who's watching the girls?"*

"I'm heading back to the roof!" O'Malley shouts. *"Keep your eyes peeled, yeah?"*

"I said I'd dance, and dance I will.
The room goes on, the air goes still.
You twirled in silk with eyes shut tight,
While something darker kissed the night."

"Dressing room's clear, bébé. Haley and Ellie are both safe. For now," Sabine says.

"Lock the doors. No one in or out until we catch this bastard," Jack grits.

"But you looked so beautiful. Haunting. Divine.
Like death dressed up in something fine.
I almost felt it—something cruel,
Till you smiled at him like I'm the fool."

Lex is circling me like a shield. Cade's back is pressed to mine.

Laing growls, *"Oh, this motherfucker's gonna die slow."*

"Shame your brother missed the scene,
He always knew what shadows mean.
Maybe he watches. Maybe he hides.
Maybe he waits on darker tides."

My vision tunnels and my knees go weak.

"Because not everything is what it seems,
Not every grave holds silent screams.
And not every ghost you thought had died,
Stayed in the dark where secrets hide."

Knox curses, fingers flying. *"I'm still locked out you guys."*

"We're getting her out. Now," Lex rasps, grabbing my wrist. But the voice isn't done, and I can't move.

"Takes one to raise one, that much is true.
He trained the monster that now lives in you.
But Eden's not built with fire and bone.
It starts with a whisper when you're all alone."

My throat tightens. My heart shatters.
Tex scans the area. *"Does anyone have a fucking visual?"*

"Zeke taught you to run. I taught him to crawl.
He wept like a dog at the edge of it all.
But death is a tale for the ones who grieve.
Your ghost still listens. He just won't leave."

Cade leans into me. "Bella, sweetheart, breathe. Look at me. Breathe."

"You flinch from my flame, but it's always been yours.
Etched into blood, behind hidden doors.
Your brother now bears it, deep in his bone.
And soon, little Izzy, he won't be alone.

A collar of fire, a whisper, a code.
He walks where I lead, down every dark road.
Tick... tick... like a bomb in his head.
Your brother is breathing, but better off dead."

Nate whispers, *"That's not possible."*

"But enough about him. Let's talk about you.
About the lies you wear and the games you do.
You let them touch you, pretend they belong.
But that's not love, sweetheart. That's playing along.

Lexie and Whitmore. So noble, so blind.
Thinking they've tamed what already is mine.
But wolves don't keep angels. They break their wings.
And I've clipped enough to know these things."

Lex snarls before the last word even fades. His mask is off now—literally, figuratively—jaw clenched, fury carved into every line of his face. "I'm gonna kill him," he growls. "I don't care who he is, I'll tear him apart."

Cade's hands are shaking. He turns toward Knox's booth and shouts into the comms. "Kill the feed! Knox, shut it off!"

"No signal override," Knox responds, tight and tense. *"I've fucking unplugged everything up here and it's no use. He's hijacked the entire system."*

Lex's eyes snap to the crowd, then to every balcony, every shadow. "Then where the fuck is he?"

"You screamed for them, now didn't you, pet?
While Lexie bit and Whitmore sweat.
You arched for them, a perfect prize.
Did they see me in your hungry eyes?

You moaned so sweet, you begged so loud,
Pressed to the glass, so fucking proud.
But right before you fell apart,
You whispered my name. From the dark.

Every thrust they gave, I kept the score.
Every bruise, every cry, I wanted more.
They worship your body and kiss every scar.
But only I know who you really are.

This isn't revenge. This is divine.
A holy reset. A sacred sign.
I gave you mercy. I gave you years.
Now I'll take back what bled through tears."

"Lex, Cade get her the fuck out of here!" Tex screams.
Lex pulls on my arm, but my feet won't move.

"So go check the table, wrapped in red,
Something borrowed. Something bled.
No ribbons, no card, no soft disguise.
Just truth we carved and severed ties."

The voice cuts out. Silence crashes over the room like a wave.
And then I run.
"Malyshka, no!"
Lex's voice booms behind me, but I don't stop. My heels echo against the marble as I race toward the gift table, one long rectangle draped in white satin, buried under towers of champagne flutes and ribboned boxes.
Except one.
Wrapped in blood-red paper. No name. No bow. I reach for it with shaking fingers. I know I shouldn't. But I already know it's for me. I rip the paper. The box opens and I scream. The sound tears from my throat, raw and feral, as I stumble backward.
"Oh my God..." Cade breathes behind me, voice strangled.
Lex is there in an instant. "Malyshka, come here!" he barks, yanking me into his arms just as my knees give out. He spins me away from the table, shielding my body with his own. My fists slam into his chest, desperate to claw my way back, to see it again, to *unsee* it.
But it's too late.
I saw it.
"JACK!" Lex shouts over the stunned silence, voice slicing through the ballroom like a gunshot. "TEX! WE NEED YOU! NOW!"

My breath won't come, it sticks like glass.
A jagged burn I can't surpass.
I try to breathe, but every try,
Feels like a scream I cannot cry.

The ballroom blurs, too loud, too bright.

Then fades to black and steals the light.
The people vanish. The music dies.
I'm drowning in my own disguise.

Lex is talking. I see his face.
But all I hear is empty space.
His voice, a hum inside his chest.
A lullaby I once possessed.

Cade's hands, steady, hold my own.
But I'm not here. I'm skin and bone.
I'm glass. I'm smoke. A haunted hum.
I'm all the things I can't outrun.

Slipping under, gone from sight,
Bury the day, embrace the night.
Where mercy rots, the heart turns black,
And madness grows, there's no way back.

PART 3

CHAPTER ⑦⓪
LEX
OUR APARTMENT
SCARED TO FUCKING DEATH
2 DAYS SINCE THE MASQUERADE

"Knox, this isn't fucking working," I mutter, dragging a hand down my face. My jaw's so tight I can barely get the words out. "You need to take over."

Haley's arms cross over her chest, her voice is soft, trembling at the edges. "Yeah, babe. Lex is right. She needs you. It's been two days. You have to bring her back."

Knox doesn't move. He just stares at the couch like it's holding a bomb. "I don't know if I can," he says finally and the defeat in his voice makes my stomach turn. "Look at her. She hasn't moved. Hasn't eaten. She hasn't even blinked since yesterday."

"She did this after Zeke," Haley whispers, voice cracking. "You were the one who got through to her. You pulled her out."

She presses her knuckles to her mouth, trying to hold it together. "Please, Knox. Help her. I can't," her voice breaks completely. "We can't lose her."

"That was different, Hales," he says, his voice shakes just barely, but enough to make me look at him. "Last time she never saw Zeke's body. Never saw the blood. The damage. Just a closed casket and a thousand things left unsaid."

He swallows hard, jaw gritted like it hurts to speak. "This time... she saw him. She held it. In her hands." He glances toward the couch, where she sits in the same damn spot she collapsed in two nights ago. "Right when she was finally starting to connect with him after all these years."

His voice drops to almost nothing. "She held her father's head in her hands."

A beat of silence.

"I'm worried that there isn't anything left inside of her for me to pull out this time."

Footsteps pad softly across the floor. Ellie appears beside us, her makeup smeared, blonde curls dull and flat like the air's been drained out of her too. She's holding a bottle of water in both hands, fingers wrapped so tightly around the plastic it crinkles.

"She wouldn't drink it," she says quietly. "I tried. Sat next to her for like fifteen minutes." The tears start to fall from her deep blue eyes. "She just... looked right through me."

I swallow hard. My pulse is hammering behind my eyes.

Dr. Monroe steps forward from the back wall, hands folded, shoulders tense under his dark green sweater. He's been here the whole time, watching. Waiting.

Completely fucking failing.

"I'm sorry," he mutters, head shaking. "I don't know what else I can do. If we can't get her to eat or drink... if she won't talk to me, won't let me in." He pauses, then says it straight. "We're going to lose her."

My chest caves at his words. Then I hear it, soft, broken, and almost under her breath. That low and steady hum.

"Hmm... hmm... hmm...

Hmm... hmm... hmm...

Hmm... hmm... hmm...

Hmm... hmm... hmm..."

Twelve notes. Just like Luca warned.

Something in Cade snaps. "Just fucking do it, Knox!" he roars, voice sharp enough to slice the air in half. Everyone freezes. Even Tex looks over. Cade's fists are shaking, his chest heaving like he can't get enough air.

"I don't care what you have to do. Beg, scream, slap her out of it. Just get her back!"

He storms past me, nearly shoulder-checking the counter, pacing like a caged animal. His hands go to his head gripping his hair, clawing through it like he's seconds away from shattering.

"Bring her back to us," he mutters again, quieter this time, hands braced on the wall like it's the only thing holding him upright. "Please, Knox."

Knox exhales, shoulders sinking. "I'll go try again."

He walks toward the couch taking slow, measured steps like he's approaching a crime scene. Bella hasn't moved. Not once. Still curled up where she first sat two nights ago, like she's been carved out of stone. She's in one of Cade's old hoodies now, sleeves bunched at her fists. No makeup. No shoes. Just... hollow.

Sabine and the girls got her inside and changed. Haley held her up while Ellie wiped the blood from her palms. Sabine whispered something in Creole while she pulled the pins from her hair. They got her out of the gown. Cleaned the smudged lipstick. Then she sat down on the couch and hasn't moved since. She just stares out the window toward the city.

Knox lowers himself to the floor in front of her, cross-legged, just like he did yesterday. "Hey, B..." he tries, voice soft. "It's me again."

Nothing.

Cade drifts over to me, silent at first. His gaze doesn't leave her.

"She looks like she's already gone," I mutter.

"She's not," he says automatically, but his voice falters at the end. "She can't be."

"Then where the fuck is she, Cade?"

Haley whispers next to us, "It's like Zeke died all over again. Like he took whatever was left of her with him and now..."

"Now there's nothing left." I say.

She doesn't argue. Just nods. Barely.

Knox keeps talking, still gentle, still useless. Her eyes don't move. Her chest barely rises.

Tex's phone buzzes on the counter. "Yeah?"

A pause.

"Okay... Yeah... Thanks, Jack. Keep me posted."

I turn to him. "Any news?"

"NYPD questioned every single person at the Masquerade. Nothing. No witnesses. No footage. No one saw a damn thing."

He slips the phone back into his pocket. "Jack's gonna head over to her dad's place now. See if he can find anything useful."

I nod, barely. "This has to work."

There's a knock at the door. Nate opens it and he walks in.

Roman Russo.

Impeccably dressed.

Calm and fucking alive.

"You shouldn't be here." My voice comes out low. Too calm. Too even. A warning before the detonation.

He just stands there, looking past me and at her. At Bella still curled on the couch. Still broken.

I lunge forward and slam him into the wall so hard the pictures rattle off the nails. "You shouldn't fucking be here!" I shout, fists bunching in his suit jacket. "She didn't deserve this!"

He grunts but doesn't fight back.

"It should've been you," I snarl. "Not her father. Not Henry. It should've been your fucking head in that box!"

"Lex!" Cade shouts.

Khoza's already moving. Rez crosses the room in three strides.

Dad's behind me in a flash. "Lex. Son, breathe. Stand down."

I don't hear him. I can't. My vision's gone red, hands shaking, pulse roaring.

"Let me go!" I bellow, trying to shove free.

Rez pins my left arm. Khoza grabs my shoulder. Dad wraps me in a brutal hold from behind.

"Get off me!" I roar, body straining. "She's broken because of him!"

Sabine steps forward and presses a hand to my cheek and somehow, everyone goes still. "Your rage won't heal her," she says. "Your fury will not sew her soul."

I freeze.

"She does not need your fire right now, *l'ombre*," she murmurs, fingers still warm on my skin. "She needs your tether. The part of you that wraps around her and holds her to this world. That is your offering. That is your gift."

I'm breathing hard. Glaring over her shoulder at Roman. But I stop fighting.

She nods and drops her hand. Dad lets go first. Then Rez. Then Khoza. No one speaks. Roman straightens his jacket but doesn't say a word.

"Balcony," Sabine says, tilting her head toward the door.

Cade is already there, sliding the door open. We step outside. I lean on the railing, fingers digging into it. I can't fix this. I can't fight this. And for the first time in my life, I don't know what to do.

Cade shuts the balcony door behind us, sealing off the silence. Cold night air cuts through my shirt, but I barely feel it. I'm burning from the inside out. Cade stands a few feet away, staring out at the city like it might offer answers.

It won't.

Not tonight.

I press my palms flat to the stone ledge. Try to steady my breathing. Try to find a rhythm. It doesn't do shit.

Sabine steps forward. The hem of her dress whispers against the floor as she moves toward us, like she's walking onto sacred ground. "You're both breaking," she says simply.

Cade turns to her. "Because we're losing her."

"She's not yet lost, Cade" Sabine says. Her eyes flick to the window behind us, to the shape on the couch that hasn't moved in two days. "She is... drifting. Between this world and the next."
My stomach twists.

"Then how do we pull her back?" Cade asks. "Tell us, Sabine. We'll do anything."

"She will not come back with noise. With logic. With fire. For her spirit is no longer in a place of reason." She steps closer, looking between us like we're pieces of some ancient ritual. "You must meet her there in the darkness. Where the soul bruises and the spirit hums beneath the skin."

I shake my head. "You're talking about her heart, her soul. What if we can't reach it?"

Sabine places a hand over my chest, fingers splayed. "Then you'll bleed with her."

I sink to my knees. It happens so fast. One second I'm standing. The next, I'm on the cold stone floor, hands gripping my hair, throat closing. "We can't lose her," I whisper, shaking. "I can't. Not like this."

Cade kneels beside me, wrapping an arm around my back, anchoring me as I fall apart. "We won't." But I hear the fear in his voice too.

Sabine kneels in front of us, her hands warm and steady on both our chests. Her eyes go half-lidded, like she's seeing something none of us can. "You boys, you ain't just her lovers. You're her line of life. Her weight in this world."

Her fingers press a little deeper, right over our hearts. "You're the fire and the flood. Her balance and her madness. The pull in her bones when the dark starts whisperin'. You two boys are the gravity in her chaos."

She leans in close, eyes glowing like coals. "If you don't show her the path back, she won't find it. She'll keep wandering' through shadows, lookin' for a door that ain't there."

I lift my head, tears streaking my face. "How?"

Sabine's gaze softens, "Once she is truly broken, your boy Knox will call to her and have her face the truth. But it is you she must follow once he's through," she says, eyes locking on mine.

She rises slowly, silk swaying with the wind. "She will walk through hell if she knows that you, *l'ombre*, are waiting on the other side."

Cade lets out a bitter breath, shaking his head. "She's already broken, Sabine. You saw her. You saw what all of this did to her."

Sabine turns to him with a strange calm, like a storm speaking through still waters. "No, chéri. You do not yet know what broken is," her voice lowering into something thick and ancient. "She is breaking, yes. Not broken. Not yet. What you see is the storm building. The waves rising."

She lifts a finger, tapping it gently to Cade's chest. "Your girl's still raining on the inside, mon loup. And if you don't let it pour out of her... she'll surely drown in the silence instead."

Cade flinches, like the words hit bone. Sabine turns back to me, eyes dark and full of something older than language.

"She must shatter, you must let her," Sabine says looking deep into my eyes. "And when she does—when the scream tears through her soul like a wildfire—that is when you call. That is when she will hear your voice, *l'ombre.*"

She closes her eyes for a beat, like the wind itself is listening. Then she exhales and straightens, silk whispering around her ankles as she rises.

"Now come. This cold ain't no friend to men with hearts already splintering'. Wind like this gets in your bones and makes the sorrow stick."

She taps her fingers twice against the railing, sealing in her words. "Inside now, before the chill makes ghosts of the living. We got work to do."

We step back inside. The warmth doesn't help. The air in here is thicker than outside, like grief left to rot in silence.

Knox is still crouched in front of her, hands wringing, voice raw. He doesn't even glance up. "It's not working," he mutters. "Trying to pull her back like last time... it's not fucking working."

He looks up now, eyes bloodshot. "Back then, there was something. Sadness. Grief. Pain I could feel, something I could grab. There were so many emotions with Zeke I could pull out of her."

His hands shake. "But this?" He takes a shallow breath. "There's nothing. No fear. No sadness. Just a void. She's just... gone. It's like talking to a corpse with a heartbeat."

Knox looks away, defeated. "I don't..." He looks up at Sabine, eyes pleading. "I just don't know what else to do."

Sabine glides forward toward Bella and leans down carefully without touching her. "You must find one, Knox," she says. "You need one flame to light the way. One crack in the armor to bring her back."

"I don't know what she has left. She's already shut down. She's empty! What the hell am I supposed to even reach—"

"Rage." I cut in. "She'll always have rage." The words punch out of me before I even think.

Sabine's head tilts slowly. A smile pulls at the corner of her mouth. "Yes, *l'ombre,*" she breathes. "Rage, the old fire. The sleeping wolf. That surely still lives."

Knox stares at me. Then gapes at her.

"Rage, are you serious? You want me to wake up rage? Have you met her? Do you know what she'll do to me if I poke that bear and she actually feels it?"

He gestures toward Bella, still motionless on the couch. "How the hell am I supposed to pull rage out of her and still keep my head—or my dick—intact?!"

Sabine clicks her tongue once, sharp as bone.

Knox shuts up immediately.

"Rage is not what we should pull out of her," Roman says quietly. "Her mother—"

"You don't get a vote here!" I snap.

Roman's eyes flick to me. "I'm her father."

"You may be her *father*..." I take a step forward. "...but you don't know her. You don't love her." My voice cuts through the room, ice-cold. "So, no. You don't get a fucking vote."

Roman opens his mouth to respond, "She doesn't—"

"You speak of blood, and yet you do not know her soul." Sabine steps forward, her presence cutting through the room like a blade as she locks eyes with Roman. "And for that you will not speak again."

Roman freezes.

Then she turns to Knox. "The path is chosen." Her voice drops even lower, but it echoes through the air. Each word vibrating through my soul.

"There is one among us who bears the flame.
To call her back, to speak her name.
One who can shake her to the bone,
And break the silence with a scream alone."

Her gaze sweeps the room like a slow-moving spell.

"And only then will the tether hold steady.
Only then, Knox, will she be ready.
To hear your voice, to feel your touch,
To come back those she loves so much."

Sabine turns to me and Cade. "I'm sorry, *l'ombre*. But what must be done to awaken her cannot come from love.

For your love runs deeper than the sea,
Darker than bone magic, older than the oldest tree.
It would die in her place without a second breath.
But love like that, chéri, can't hold back death.

To wake the rage, no love can stay.
The ones who soften must fall away.
Regret, guilt, mercy, let them die.
She'll rise in ruin, not lullaby."

Her head lifts. And then she nods. To *him*.
Mortal.
Fucking.
Kombat.
Laing strolls over like he's the final boss, sleeves pushed up just enough to show the tail end of that smug-ass dragon. He's calm, which somehow pisses me off more. All that military-grade posture and ice-cold stillness, like he's already calculated the next ten moves on the board.

"I'll do it, Sabine," he says. "I can bring her back."

My brain doesn't even register the words before my body explodes. "The fuck you will!"

I charge him, but Cade catches me by the chest.

"Get him away from her!" I roar, shoving against Cade's hold, eyes wild. "You think he's the one?! You want that asshole anywhere near her? Touching her?"

Laing doesn't move. He just watches me like he's waiting for me to get it all out.

"She's not yours to break. You so much as breathe wrong and I will put you through the fucking wall!"

Briggs and Khoza step in fast, grabbing my arms before I can lunge again.

"L'ombre, you cannot be the flame tonight.
Her wrath needs cold, not warmth or light.
You are the end, her soul's last breath.

But first she must dance with rage and death."

"I swear to God," I twist hard, chest heaving, vision swimming. "I'll kill him."

"You can try." Laing shrugs. "After I bring your girlfriend back."

From the corner, Dr. Monroe stands up so fast his chair tips. "Nope. No. I will not be present for this voodoo-rooted, rage-fueled exorcism!" he announces, waving his hands in the air. "This is beyond my license. Beyond therapy. Beyond reality. I'm a doctor, not a damn soul wrangler!"

Nobody stops him. All eyes are on her. All tension points toward what's coming.

Sabine turns back to Laing.

"She will hate you. She may fight.
May draw blood in the dying light.
But if her soul begins to burn,
The path will open. She may return."

Laing nods.

Behind me, Cade's breathing. Heaving. My chest is heaving. I don't feel right. My own skin is a prison I'm desperate to escape. The impulse is a raw, primal roar inside me to stop this. Shut it down. End this now before he even thinks about fucking touching her.

This isn't some prophecy. It's just betrayal. Right now. Right here. And it's all I can focus on. But I can't move. Because deep down, I know Sabine's right. And that's the part that fucking kills me.

I'd do anything to get Bella back. Burn cities. Break gods. Drag her soul out of hell myself if I had to. But I can't. Because right now love isn't the weapon she needs.

And fuck me, that might be the cruelest part of it all.

CHAPTER ⑦⑴
CADE
OUR APARTMENT
2 DAYS SINCE THE MASQUERADE

The silence is a canvas, and the quiet is a deeper, more brutal kind of noise than any storm could ever be. Bella still hasn't moved, not even a breath of a tremor. She's a sculpture of grief on the couch, all sharp edges and delicate, curled-up lines. A piece of art frozen in its own story, and none of us have the heart to look away.

Knox clears his throat. "Sabine... take the girls upstairs. Please."

Sabine clicks her tongue. "I'm not leaving until Bella has returned. Not a second before."

Briggs steps forward. His quiet, calm certainty is a weapon more potent than any shout. "I'll take them," he states, his gaze sweeping over the room. "I'll keep them safe."

Knox nods. "Thank you."

The girls don't move. They don't want to leave her—hell, none of us do—but they know. This isn't something you watch. Not if you care about her. What's coming, it's raw and ugly. The kind of pain that leaves scars you can't see.

Laing's the only one who can take her there. He's built for it, calm and unflinching. He's the kind of man who knows exactly how to pull the rage out of someone without worrying about what comes next.

I hate him for it. I hate that he is the one that is going to do this.

But, more than anything, I hate that I'm grateful he's here.

Briggs appears in the doorway and holds a hand out for the girls. "Come on, Ellie. Haley."

Haley brushes a kiss to Bella's temple, whispering something none of us hear. Ellie squeezes my arm as she walks by.

The second the door clicks behind them, Knox turns to Khoza and Rez and gives them a quick nod. They move toward Lex. One to the left. One to the right.

He stiffens instantly. "The fuck is this?"

"Lex," Knox says gently. "You can't interfere."

Knox turns to Tex next. "Stand by Cade."

Tex steps forward without a word and stands at my side like a goddamn wall.

Knox breathes in deep. Looks at all of us before looking at her. "Okay." He nods once, a curt and final motion. "Laing... you're up."

Before Laing can move, Roman steps forward from the corner, voice clipped and too calm to be anything but uneasy. "Are we sure this is the right plan?" he says. "There has to be another way."

The room freezes. Every breath held.

Daniel turns toward Roman. His tone is bone dry, laced with steel. "Back down, Roman. This is family business."

Roman's jaw tightens. "I am her family, Barinov. She's my daughter."

Lex snaps before anyone else can. "Not right now you're fucking not." His voice is a sharp, explosive weapon. The kind of sound that makes the air pull back.

"Right now, she needs us," Lex growls. "Not some ghost with perfect suits and a twenty-year absence." He takes a step forward, Rez and Khoza tensing instantly. "So, unless you've figured out how to crawl inside her soul and pull the trauma out with your bare fucking hands, sit the fuck down and shut up."

Roman's face tightens but he doesn't move.

"And if you're so desperate to help..." Lex adds, voice a dangerous whisper, "...go guard her friends with Briggs. That's about all you're good for right now."

Roman doesn't argue. Doesn't defend. He doesn't need to. He just stands there, outnumbered and outmatched, a ghost in the flesh who knows the fight was lost long ago.

Lex turns back to Bella, his chest heaving. Every shallow breath he draws is a fresh spark against his already very short fuse.

Knox lifts his chin. "Laing. Now."

Laing moves slowly, like a man approaching an altar, or a bomb. He crouches in front of Bella, balanced on the balls of his feet.

"Hi there, Iz," he murmurs, like they're old friends catching up.

She looks right through him. Staring out at the skyline slicing through the dark. Twinkling lights of a world she can't reach anymore.

Laing hums low under his breath as he starts unbuttoning his shirt.

Lex stiffens behind me. "What the fuck are you doing?"

Laing doesn't stop. His voice is calm, but every syllable drips with calculated chaos. "You want rage, Lex? You want to pull her out of the dark?"

He pops another button.

"Then you need someone who's known her long enough to know just how to get under that perfect little skin of hers."

Another button.

"Someone who knows just where the fire's buried, and how to pour gasoline on it."

Lex takes a step forward, but Rez moves fast and grabs him by the shoulder and yanks him back.

"Not now," Rez hisses.

Lex's jaw flexes so hard I swear I hear his teeth grind. But he doesn't move. Not toward Laing, anyway.

Laing just smiles like a wolf about to bite. He slips his shirt off slowly, daring someone to stop him.

He touches her. Softly. He brushes a hand down her cheek like he's petting a memory. She doesn't react. Then his fingers shift, hooking under her chin.

"Fucking look at me, Iz." Laing jerks her chin up with a brutal force. Her head snaps back like a doll's. Her eyes meet his. Blank. Empty.

He leans in, breath hot and venomous. "Daddy's head in a box was all it took to break you?"

He sneers, withdrawing his hand from her chin as if he'd just touched something foul. "You're weak. Pathetic. Just a scared little girl pretending she runs this empire. But you own nothing, Iz. Nothing."

Still nothing. Not a twitch. Not a breath.

Lex snarls behind me, low and brutal. "I swear to—"

Rez grabs him by the collar, dragging him back just as Lex starts to step forward. "Lex, enough."

I can feel the storm radiating off him.

The bastard, Laing, just smirks. He plants a hand on Bella's shoulder and shoves her backward into the couch. Hard. She folds like paper. Limbs limp, eyes glassy. A marionette with cut strings.

Laing swings one leg over her lap and straddles her. "C'mon, Iz." His tone all sing-song and sadistic. "You can't play dead forever."

His hands move again. Up her arms. Over her shoulders. Fingers dragging slow and wrong across her. He stops at the hem of her hoodie. "Take it off. Let's see what's left under all that grief."

She doesn't move. So, he does it himself. Grabs the fabric. Yanks it hard up and over her head in one swift, violent pull. He tosses it to the floor like garbage.

Still, she doesn't flinch. Doesn't blink. Just sits there, exposed and silent.

Laing stares at her. Waiting.

CRACK.

He slaps her across the face. The sound echoes like a gunshot. Her head whips sideways. A red mark blooms across her cheek.

But still, nothing.

I see Lex snap, Khoza and Rez slam into him again.

"Let me go," Lex seethes. "I'll kill him."

Laing leans in again, breath thick with power. "C'mon, Iz. I know you're in there. You wanna hurt me? Do it. You wanna scream, break, fight? Fucking do it. Give me the fire. Show them you're still a queen."

Bella just sits there, exposed in her black bra and leggings, her pale skin. An unnerving contrast to the blankness of her stare. From behind me, a low, deadly sound tears from Lex's throat. It's the kind of sound meant to kill. Rez stiffens, his entire body going taut and rigid in anticipation.

Tex shifts, his weight poised. His eyes lock on me, ready to act if my own rage breaks loose.

Laing doesn't even look back. He leans in. Trails his fingers down her collarbone. Over her ribs. Then down her arms, slow and sickening. "You remember how to feel, Iz?" he whispers. "Or did they bury that with your old man's head?"

Lex is shaking. His fists are clasped so tight his knuckles have gone bloodless. "Touch her again," he growls, "and I swear to God—"

Rez gets in his face before he can lunge. "Cool it," Rez snaps. "Or you're gonna go join Briggs upstairs."

Laing's hand drifts back up. Slides over the swell of her chest—just enough to spark a reaction. Just enough to make all of us want to kill him.

But she breathes, a sharp, quick inhale. It's the first real movement in two days. We all freeze.

"There she is." Laing's voice drips with something between mockery and obsession.

He crouches closer, fingers trailing the waistband of her leggings like he owns her. Like she's just a shell to peel open. "Sitting there like a pretty little corpse. Still breathing, but barely."

He brushes her hair behind her ear, taunting like he's petting a doll right before snapping its head off. "You're warm. That's something, I guess. Can't say how long it'll last."

"Enough!" Roman barks from the corner.

But Bella doesn't move. Not even a flicker.

Laing straightens. Rolls his neck as if he's warming up for a fight.

"Fuck it."

He grabs her. One hand clamped around her arm, the other locking tight at her waist. He rips her off the couch like dead weight and drags her across the apartment. Slams her face-first against the wall before anyone can move.

"GET OFF HER!" Lex lunges.

Rez and Khoza slam into him from both sides, locking him down. Nate rushes in behind them, arms braced against Lex's chest as he thrashes like a wild animal.

Laing doesn't even glance back at the commotion. His body pins Bella to the wall. One arm cages her wrists. The other slides up, fingers wrapping around her throat.

"No daddy. No brother. No fucking Russian guard dogs. Just me now, Iz."

He leans in, lips brushing her ear. "I'll ruin you so thoroughly, they won't recognize what's left."

Bella doesn't respond. So, he presses closer.

"I will take every piece you've got buried in that twisted little head of yours. Rip it out. Break it in front of them. Make them watch while I make you beg."

Still, no reaction. His hand dips lower, hovering just above the waistband of her leggings.

"You want to play dead? Fine. I'll fuck the life back into you."

Bella slams her head backward into his face. The crack of bone-on-bone echoes through the apartment. Laing stumbles, blood gushing through his teeth. Bella spins on him, eyes wild, chest heaving, fists already cocked.

He grins through the blood. "Finally."

All hell breaks loose. Bella lunges with no hesitation, no strategy. Just rage. Pure, savage rage. She drives her fist into his jaw so hard his head snaps sideways. He absorbs it, laughs, and swings back, but she's faster. Duck. Jab. Hook. Another punch to the gut.

Laing grunts, stumbling again. He wipes the blood from his mouth, still grinning.

"C'mon, Iz. Hit me harder. Show the room who you really are."

She doesn't answer. Just steps in and drives her knee into his ribs. Again. And again. He collapses to one knee, gasping. This isn't a spar anymore, it's a purge. She's exorcising something, bleeding it out through her fists.

Laing grabs her leg, pulls her off balance, and slams her to the floor. The whole apartment shakes. He scrambles on top, forearm pressed to her chest.

"What do you think your little boytoys over there will think of you," Laing growls, "after they watch me—"

She drives her elbow into his face. Blood sprays. She rolls them, slamming him into the ground. Climbs on top, one hand wraps around his throat, the other slams down into his ribs, once, twice, three times.

Laing doesn't even glance back at the commotion. His body pins Bella to the wall. One arm cages her wrists. The other slides up, fingers wrapping around her throat.

Bella's hand tightens around his throat. Her teeth are bared, eyes wild and burning. She leans down, voice shaking with fury. "Touch me again, Laing" she whispers, deadly calm. "And I'll snap your windpipe and watch you die smiling."

Laing coughs, blood bubbling at his lips, but he doesn't flinch. Doesn't move. Just... smiles. Like this was his sick and twisted master plan all along.

Roman takes a slow step forward. "Isabella."

She doesn't look at her father. Her hand still tightly locked around Laing's throat.

"This isn't the fight that matters."

Still nothing. Laing's face is starting to turn red.

"Let him go," Roman says, softer now. "Don't give him the power to pull you under."

Her fingers twitch.

"You've already survived worse, daughter."

And for just a second, her hands loosen. Not much. But enough to know she heard him.

Knox steps forward. Voice firm, but kind, "That's it, B. Let him go. You won, babe."

Her eyes flick between Laing and Knox.

"C'mon, Bella. You've already proved your point, he's still bleeding and you're still standing. You got him. Now come back to us. To Ellie, to Haley. To Lex and Cade. To your family. We need you, Bella."

He looks at me and Lex. "They need you, Bella."

She lets go. Laing chokes, coughing, rolling to the side. Bella stumbles backward, breath ragged, and hands shaking. She drops to her knees like the wind's been ripped out of her. She's breathing like she just crawled out of hell. Her chest is heaving. But she's here.

She's back.

Sabine steps forward like she's been waiting patiently on fate to cue her. She kneels beside Bella, not rushing or speaking at first.

Then she reaches out and gently takes Bella's hand in hers.

"Bienvenue, ma belle. Welcome back, baby girl."

Bella looks at her, dazed. Alive.

Sabine nods once, like she sees the flicker behind those eyes and it's enough. "You still got a long way to go, Bella," she says, voice thick with soul. "But you just took the first step."

She brushes a thumb over Bella's knuckles. "That rage you feel burnin' inside? Don't run from it. Don't bury it. Hold it. Let it be your fire."

She glances toward Knox, then back to Bella. "'Cause he's not done yet. That boy's still got work to do."

Sabine rises slowly, never letting go of Bella's hand until she has to. "Come now, baby girl," she whispers, guiding her toward the couch and helping through the aftershock. "Let's sit you down. One storm at a time."

She eases Bella into her spot, tucks her hair behind her ear like a mother might, and steps back without another word.

CHAPTER ⑺
LEX
OUR APARTMENT
FROZEN IN FUCKING PLACE
2 DAYS SINCE THE MASQUERADE

She's breathing. Fucking breathing. And I still can't move. Not because Rez, Khoza, or even Nate are holding me back—they let go the second she headbutted Laing in the face. No. I'm frozen because I'm scared if I take one step, I'll shatter whatever the hell this is.

She's on the couch now, chest rising like she just clawed her way back from the grave. Sabine tucks her hair behind her ear, calm as if she didn't just watch Bella drag herself out of the dark with blood on her knuckles.

Knox steps in front of her slowly. Drops to a crouch, level with where she's curled on the couch. "Welcome back, B," he says gently. "You know what we have to do."

In an instant, the fire in her eyes dies out. Fear rushes in, sharp enough to cut and real enough to gut me. Her lips part, head tilting like she wants to say something, but the words get trapped somewhere between her chest and throat.

Her gaze finds his. Then mine. Shakes her head once... twice... slow, trembling. A single tear carves down her cheek, and it feels like it burns right through me.

"I don't want to," she whispers. Her voice is so small it makes me want to tear the world apart. "Please... don't make me."

Knox doesn't back down. "Bella, it's time."

She shakes harder. Her knees start to draw in.

Knox's voice stays low, but firm. "We have to face it. You know the drill. It's the only way forward. Just like last time."

She's folding into herself. Sabine moves first, quiet and calm. She crosses the room with a soft gray blanket I didn't even see her grab. She kneels beside Bella like she's approaching a wounded animal and drapes it over her shoulders. She pulls the ends tighter and rests a hand against Bella's cheek.

"Even the fiercest spirits gotta be held sometimes, bébé," she murmurs, voice low and hushed but heavy with that bayou rhythm. "Let it break. Then rise up meaner."

Bella curls tighter into herself, knees to chest beneath the blanket, hands gripping the fabric like armor. "I can't," she chokes out. "Please, Knox. I can't. I can't do this."

"It's the only way."

I twitch. My jaw flexes. My breath sharpens. Say the word. Just fucking say the word and I'll carry her out of here myself.

Knox must sense it because he looks up at me and shakes his head once. Not yet.

He turns back to her. "You have to face it, Bella. We all do."

She's slipping. And all I can do is watch.

"Bella," he says softly, "what happened? Tell me what happened."

She shakes her head fast. "I can't. I can't—" Her voice cracks as the tears finally come.

"Just breathe, Bella."

"I can't," she sobs. "Please. I need them, Knox. I need..." she's breathing so fast, I'm afraid she's going to hyperventilate. "...need him."

I move toward her. One step, two, but Rez is already reaching for me.

"She needs me. She fucking needs me, Rez."

He grabs my arm tight enough to bruise.

"Motherfucker, let me go," I snarl, ready to tear through him.

"No," he grits. "Let him work."

Knox presses forward, his tone firmer now. "Bella, I'll give you what you want. I'm not keeping him from you. But you have to face it first. That's the only price. Face it, let it in and it'll all be over." His hand rests gently on her knee.

"Quick and easy," he says.

But nothing about this feels easy.

"I can't," she cries. "I c-c-can't."

"Why not, Bella?" Knox presses. "Why not?"

"Because it's my fault!" she screams, her voice echoing off the walls. "It's my fault Daddy is dead!"

The words crack the whole room in half. Sabine gasps. My stomach drops. Cade makes a broken sound next to me, eyes never leaving her.

"I didn't listen, I didn't believe him. Knox he warned me, and I kept. I kept."

"Kept what?" Knox asks softly. "Kept what, Bella?"

"I kept disobeying him," she sobs, voice small and trembling, almost like a child's. "I stayed with them." Her breath hitches, sharp and uneven. "I chose to love them."

Another sob. "And he, he killed my daddy, Knox."

Her voice cracks on *daddy*. "He killed my daddy because... Because I didn't listen."

She shakes her head, tears streaking down her face. "He told me to stop, and I—" Her breath shudders out. "—and I didn't stop."

She folds forward, words dissolving into gasps. "I'm sorry... I'm sorry." Her voice breaks completely. "Daddy... I'm sorry."

My chest feels like it's being peeled open. Every word slices deeper. Every sob burns straight through my bones, through my fucking soul.

Knox flinches, just once. Then he surges forward, hands framing her face. "No," he says, loud and clear. "Bella, no."

She's falling apart.

"You listen to me right now," Knox says. "Luca is a monster. And yeah—we're going to find him. Lex will find him. Lex will *kill* him. I promise you that. But you don't get to do this to yourself. Not today. Not ever. None of this is on you."

She's shaking so hard it looks like she's trying to vibrate herself out of existence.

"Do you hear me?" he goes on, voice ragged. "You chose love. That's not weakness. That's the bravest thing anyone can do. You fought to feel joy, Bella. And he, he couldn't stand it. So, he tried to kill it. But that's on him. Not you. Never on you, babe."

Her lips are trembling. Her hands curl tighter. Knox touches her cheek.

"Let it out. Grieve. Scream. Fall apart if you have to. But don't you dare carry this alone. Don't you dare fucking blame yourself for what happened."

She lets out a sound that destroys me, half scream, half sob. Knox finally nods at us.

That's all I need. I tear out of Rez's grip and drop to my knees in front of her. "I'm here," I whisper. "I'm fucking here, malyshka."

She collapses into me. Arms clinging. Fists pounding weakly at my chest until they ball in my shirt and stay there. Cade drops beside us, fast but quiet. One hand wraps around her waist. The other grips my shoulder.

"We've got you," he whispers to her. "We've got you, sweetheart."

She cries. God, she cries. Like she's trying to empty every scream she's swallowed since that red-wrapped box hit the floor.

"I've got you, malyshka," I whisper again. "We're not letting you go."

Cade pulls us tighter. Her body trembles between us. And for the first time since that fucking poem... she's here. Not the ghost. Not the weapon. Not the survivor. Just Bella. Just our girl.

Broken, but alive.

Fayetteville, Arkansas
7 Days Since Henry's Death

It's cold as fuck. Sky's the color of ash. Trees stripped bare like bones. And the wind apparently has a point to prove. It's cutting right through my coat, my skin, my goddamn soul. Like it knows I don't deserve the warmth today. Like it's punishing me for even stepping outside.

The air's too still. Too quiet. The kind of silence that feels wrong. Like the world's bracing for something. Or mourning something it already lost. Either way, it matches the weight sitting on my chest.

Bella hasn't moved in ten minutes. She's just sitting here, one hand in mine, the other in Cade's, her eyes locked on the polished casket in front of her like she might shatter if she blinks. Her black coat is buttoned tight to her chin, her hood is pulled up around her hair, but her cheeks are still raw from the wind.

She's crying silent tears. The kind that sneaks down without warning and leaves tracks on her skin.

The pastor's voice is steady behind the pulpit, something about comfort and peace and eternal life and all that shit. About how Henry Harrington was a good man. A brave man. A family man. A man who loved his daughter more than life.

Bella flinches at that part. I squeeze her hand. Cade does too.

Everyone and their brother is here. Jack's sitting next to Cade. Ellie and Haley sit one row behind us with Knox seated at their center. Javi and Rico stand with their hands clasped in front of them, heads bowed.

There are about twenty or so bundled-up strangers in uniform, Fayetteville Fire Department standing proud in their dress blues.

The entire Wexley football team showed up, lined shoulder to shoulder behind the Legacy girls. And behind them, a wave of old Razorbacks, former teammates of her dad's, big and broad and broken-eyed as they watch their fallen brother's casket being lowered into the earth.

The Whitmores came, somber and elegant. Tex is next to them in black with his arms crossed. Nate, sharp in a coat and scarf, jaw locked like he might kill someone just for breathing too loud.

Briggs, O'Malley, Khoza, Laing, and Sabine all made the trip.

Even my parents came down.

Roman didn't come. Cade and I told him not to. Told him that she just lost her father and didn't need to deal with another one at his funeral. He agreed. For once, he fucking listened.

She sniffles beside me. Still staring. Her fingers squeeze mine back. God, I fucking love her. And I hate that she has to wear black today. Hate that this is how her story with him ends—in a cemetery full of despair and solemn words, with no chance to say goodbye. No chance to scream. Just a casket, a cold wind, and a pain so sharp I can feel it in my spine.

I look down at her.

At her lashes soaked with tears.

At the tiny wrinkle in her brow that hasn't faded since the night of the masquerade.

At her breath fogging in the cold.

She's here. She's alive. But she's a long way from okay. And we're not going anywhere. Cade and I will walk every mile of this grief with her, carry the rage if she can't. We'll wait for her when the world doesn't, and never let go.

And Luca. Luca is going to die. By *my* fucking hands. Because I've seen her break before, but never like this.

Not gutted.

Not hollow.

Not lost to the point where even her fire went dark.

Once was too many.

This? This was unforgivable.

CHAPTER ⑦③
BELLA
OUR APARTMENT
63 DAYS SINCE DADDY'S DEATH

"Ah! Cade," I moan, voice breaking as he sucks my clit between his lips, tongue flicking in brutal, punishing circles that make my hips buck against his mouth.

His fingers are inside me, curling just right, dragging over that perfect spot again, and again, and again. I'm soaking his hand, writhing, desperate, my thighs trembling as the pressure coils tight.

He groans into me, hungry, feral. "That's it, sweetheart. Come for us. Let go... for me."

Lex's mouth crashes into mine, claiming and wild, like he can taste every bit of what Cade's doing to me. He pulls back, breathing hard, then dips lower, wraps his lips around my nipple and bites. I cry out, grabbing at Cade's thick hair while grinding up into his mouth.

Lex growls, dragging his teeth along my skin. "You're so fucking perfect like this," he rasps. "Come on, baby. Let us have it. Let us wreck you."

I nod. My whole body's trembling now. The pressure between my legs climbs, tightens, coils into a need that steals the air from my lungs.

"Her love was a weapon,
Her heart the disease."

The voice slices through my mind like a whisper from hell. I blink. They're gone. Gone. The warmth, the mouths, the hands. I'm alone. In our bed in our apartment.

But the sheets are sticky and dark. I throw the comforter back and stagger out of bed, nearly slipping. My breath catches in my throat.

There's blood. Everywhere. It's soaked into the white sheets. Spattered across the walls. Footprints in it. My footprints.

"Now she lies in their blood,
Kneeling low in the flood."

"No, no, no, no..." I whisper, stumbling barefoot into the living room, clutching the wall for balance. The copper stench hits me like a punch to the face.

Zeke's body is on the couch. Eyes open. Mouth parted. His chest torn apart. Ribs cracked. One hand still stretched toward me. Daddy's next to him. Slumped in his recliner. A bullet wound in his left temple. Blood soaking the collar of his Razorback T-shirt.

I choke on a sob and run to the front door, slipping in the wetness. I fumble with the handle, yank it open, and trip.

I land hard. The wind knocks out of me as my spine hits the floor. My palms slap wet tile. I scramble to sit up, breath stuck in my throat.

And then I see them, Cade and Lex, bleeding out in the doorway. Cade's throat is carved wide open, nearly ear to ear. A gaping smile of death. His body twitches once, just once, as if trying he's to reach me before everything inside him pours out in thick, pulsing crimson waves. His eyes are already glassy. Gone.

Lex. God, Lex. His face is a horror show. One eye swollen shut. Blood smeared across his jaw where his lip's been split open. His arms are outstretched like he tried to shield Cade. Like he fought as hard as he could and still lost. There's a knife buried in his stomach.

My knife. Handle up. Twisted in deep.

Blood floods beneath him, seeping between floorboards. A shimmering lake that stretches toward me, coming to claim me now too.

"She killed them with kindness, then painted in red.
Their hearts left to wither, their bodies left dead.
She opened her legs with a whisper, a lure,
And shattered their souls with a touch they thought pure."

Lex's head jerks, just slightly. A muscle spasm. Or the last flicker of life.

I scream so hard my throat tears. Because I loved them. Because I should've saved them. Because I can still see Luca in my mind, his smug fucking grin while he carved them open just to leave me this picture.

> *"You clawed for some salvation,*
> *but I promised damnation.*
> *You don't get to choose, my little whore.*
> *You're not theirs. You're mine forevermore."*

I crawl forward, sobbing, slipping in blood—*their blood*—trying to get to them, but it's already too late. Lex's chest doesn't rise. Cade's hand is still.

And I'm still alive. I slam the door shut, screaming as the lights flicker red. The hallway stretches. Warps. Bleeds. Their voices echo now. Zeke, Daddy, Cade, and Lex all calling my name. Accusing. Dying.

I run. But the blood is everywhere. Flooding the apartment. Rising past my ankles. Drenching the walls. Filling my mouth. I'm choking on it, grasping at my throat.

> *"You'd think you'd learn, but you never see.*
> *I'll take every soul 'til there's no one but me.*
> *So cry, Izzy. Bleed. Beg and crawl,*
> *Because I'll burn your little world just to watch you fall."*

"No! NO!" I grab my head, nails digging into my scalp as Luca's voice laughs through my mind. I fall to my knees, sobbing, shaking, begging for someone, anyone, to make it stop.

I jolt awake.

Sweating. Gasping. Clawing at my throat like I can still taste blood. I throw the blankets off, stumble out of bed, and run.

CHAPTER ⑦④
LEX
OUR APARTMENT
STILL NOT GETTING ANY FUCKING SLEEP.
63 DAYS SINCE HENRY'S DEATH

"Baby?" I call after her, but she's already gone, bolted straight into the bathroom like the devil himself is clawing at her heels. The door slams shut behind her.

Cade's already halfway out of bed beside me, bare feet on the floor.

"You go," he mutters, calm but tight. "Pull her back in. I'll make her some tea."

The second I step inside the bathroom heat punches me in the face. The shower is on full blast, steam fogging up the mirror, turning the air thick and wet. She's on her knees under the spray, scrubbing her hands raw. Her arms. Her chest. Anywhere she can reach. Scrubbing like she's trying to wash off blood that isn't there.

It's been two months since we buried her dad. Since the night she shattered in our arms. She has good days, some good nights. But this one's not good, it's the kind that rips her straight out of bed drowning in sweat and memories.

She hasn't let us close since that night. Not really. Says she's fine, but I see it in her eyes. The distance. The guilt. She won't kiss us and sometimes she flinches if we touch her too long.

And I get it. I fucking get it. She doesn't want to blame us, but she does. Thinks if she hadn't loved us—hadn't asked Cade to come watch her dance—maybe her dad would still be alive. Maybe Luca wouldn't have slipped through the cracks.

She hasn't said it out loud. Doesn't have to. I see it every time she won't meet my eyes. Every time she avoids Cade's touch. Every time she locks herself in the bathroom like she can outrun the guilt.

And now, with the whole *maybe-my-brother-is-fucking-alive* twist? Yeah. That sure as hell isn't helping.

Tex and Nate are convinced Zeke is alive. They say it's the only thing that makes sense. That no one could pull off this level of surveillance and all this precision without Zeke's help.

Zeke was the mastermind behind the Black Book network and Project Dylan. The king of shadows. The ghost in every system. If Luca's operating like this, it's because Zeke gave him the fucking keys.

After the funeral, Knox went into Zeke and Bella's penthouse. Opened some hidden server buried in a false wall behind the bookshelf, some serious Mission Impossible shit. Racks of black towers, blinking lights, heavy-duty cooling fans that never stop humming. The thing looked like it could launch a goddamn satellite.

They were locked out. Access fucking denied. Not even Knox could crack it, and that bastard can get into the Pentagon if you give him five minutes and a shitty Wi-Fi signal. Bella sat there for hours, trying every password she could remember. Birthday combos. Inside jokes. Stupid shit only she and Zeke would've known.

Nothing worked.

And then she remembered something that Zeke had told her in that hell house they used to call a home. When they were still kids, still surviving he'd told her and Dylan they'd escape one day. Zeke took an old map out of a drawer in the kitchen, laid it out, and told Bella to close her eyes and point.

She did.

Costa Rica. That's where her finger landed. That was his promise. Costa Rica would be where he'd take them and start a new life.

And that motherfucker made the password *Costa Rica*. Like some twisted breadcrumb trail, left just for her. The second she typed it in, the server unlocked. Every door flew open.

And buried deep in the data, there it fucking was. The damn timestamp. The exact moment the password was changed lined up with the same day she got her first message from Luca.

So either Zeke's been in that penthouse or he hacked it remotely from wherever he and "Luca" are hiding.

There's no denying it anymore. Zeke isn't dead. He's alive. And he's playing the game. Hell, he's the mastermind behind the whole game.

Bella refuses to believe it. Says maybe he's being forced, that her brother would never hurt her.

I wish I could believe that. I really do. But I'm not blinded by that sibling-bond bullshit. There is no Luca. There's only Zeke. And this is some sick and twisted brother-sister love-hate betrayal dressed up as a creepy Edgar Allan Poe poetry shit.

Looking back at the messages, it all makes sense now. The way "Luca" knew things about her no one else could possibly know. No one but him.

So when I find Zeke, when I catch him, I will kill him for everything he's put her through. But I'm not saying that to my girl. I won't be the one to rip her progress to shreds. Not when she's finally starting to come back. Not when we've finally gotten a piece of her light again.

Especially since that fucker hasn't made a move or said a single word since his creepy poem at the masquerade.

"Baby," I say again, softer this time.

She doesn't hear me. Or maybe she does and just can't stop. Her hands are shaking. Her skin is red and raw, and yet she keeps scrubbing like the water's not hot enough to burn it all away. I step into the shower. Fully clothed. Doesn't fucking matter.

I crouch in front of her and take her wrists gently. She jerks back at first, eyes wild like she doesn't recognize me. Like she's still trapped in whatever nightmare ripped her out of our bed. But then her gaze clears and the moment she realizes it's me, her whole body trembles.

"Look at me," I say, voice low but sharp enough to cut through the static in her head. "Your hands, they're clean. You're clean. It's not real. You hear me? It was just a bad dream. You're safe, baby. I'm right here."

Her eyes finally meet mine. Wide and bloodshot. But something alters behind them, a thread snapping back into place. Her breath shudders and a sob punches its way out of her throat. She crumbles forward into me.

I catch her. My arms lock tight around her shaking body. I hold her to my chest like I'm trying to fuse us together.

"I've got you, baby," I whisper into her soaked hair. "You're alright. You're home."

She doesn't run. Doesn't flinch. She pulls into me. Her hands fist the back of my drenched shirt.

And that? Fuck, that's new. Usually when we try to pull her back from the edge, she fights us. She turns to ice or fire, shoves us away, shuts down, and disappears behind those walls she's built to survive.

But not this time. This time, she chooses me. She lets me hold the weight with her. Lets me carry it. And for the first time in weeks, maybe longer, she lets herself rest. Just for a second. Just long enough for me to feel her heartbeat press against mine.

I scoop her up, skin flushed from the heat, hair dripping down her spine. She curls into me on instinct. I grab a towel from the rack, set her down and wrap it around her slow and gentle. I guide her out, one hand steady on her back, the other gripping her hand tight.

The apartment's still dark. The only light spilling from the kitchen where Cade's already there, leaning against the counter. A mug waiting with steam curling into the air. His eyes find us, find her, and everything in him softens.

I'm soaked. She's soaked. We're both dripping across the hardwood, leaving a mess I don't give a single shit about, because she's still holding my hand. And that's all that matters right now.

"Hey sweetheart," Cade says softly, stepping forward. "Chamomile. Extra honey."

She pauses, just for a second, then takes the mug. Her fingers wrapping around the warmth like it might keep her from falling apart again.

"Thanks," she whispers. "And... I'm sorry."

She sinks down onto the barstool, eyes locked on the steam. Cade and I both freeze.

"I'm sorry for being this much. A mess. A burden. Just too much."

I shake my head. "You're not too much, baby."

Cade exhales slowly and steps closer, voice quieter but no less certain. "You've never been a burden, sweetheart. You're everything. Brave, brilliant, beautiful, and still standing. That's not too much. That's miraculous."

"We've got you," I say. "Always."

She blinks fast, eyes glassy.

I reach out and tuck a damp strand of hair behind her ear.

"You wanna talk about it?"

She nods slowly. "It was... Luca. And blood. Everywhere. I thought I was in bed with you. With both of you. But it wasn't real. It got all twisted. Zeke. My dad. Then you. All of you, you were dead."

She starts to shake, staring straight ahead and not looking at us at all. "And he was there. In my head. In my body. Like he'd taken over everything."

Cade's behind her in a second, arms sliding around her waist from behind. She stiffens for a beat but doesn't pull away. I meet his eyes over her shoulder. He sees it too. The tiniest crack in her wall.

Bella shifts slightly, her back still pressed against Cade's chest, his arms wrapped around her like a safety belt. She sets her mug down with a quiet clink, then lifts one hand, resting it lightly on Cade's forearm.

"You're still coming later today, right?"

Cade's arms tighten. "Hell yeah, sweetheart."

"Always, baby," I say. "We've been at every practice and we're not stopping now."

She nods and talks about Nationals, the nerves, the doubt. But when I tell her she's still the best damn dancer I've ever seen... she smiles. And fuck, it hits me so hard I nearly die. That smile. The one we haven't seen since before the funeral. Since before her world cracked in half. It's small. Soft. But it's real.

Cade presses a kiss to her temple from behind. She turns and reaches for me. Her fingers trace along my jaw, brushing up to my cheek like she's relearning the shape of me.

"I love you," she whispers.

Jesus Christ, I'm not okay. My heart fucking shatters. I grab her hand and kiss it. I breathe against her skin. "I love you so much, baby."

But then I feel it, the smallest flicker of hesitation in her. That split-second edge of fear under her skin. I pull back and rest my forehead against hers. My chest is burning, but I won't rush her. Not now.

Not when she's barely putting herself back together.

So, I do the only thing that makes sense. I hook one arm under her thighs, the other behind her back, and I lift her into my arms.

She gasps, soft and startled. "Lex..."

"I've got you," I whisper.

Cade's right behind me as I carry her down the hall. I push our bedroom door open and ease her onto the bed like she's made of glass. She looks up at me, and for a split second, I see all of it—the war still going on behind her eyes. The guilt. The fear. The way she's still trying to believe she didn't cause this, that she's not cursed, not poison.

I kneel down beside the bed, kiss the letters on inside of her wrist. "We don't have to do anything. We're not here for that. We're here for you, baby."

"I know," she says softly. And this time, I believe her.

I tuck the blankets around her, every motion slow and reverent. She reaches for me before I can pull away.

"Stay," she whispers.

"Always." I strip off my wet clothes and crawl in behind her.

Cade climbs in on the other side, his hand brushing hers beneath the blanket. And for the first time in weeks, she lets us both hold her.

Wexley, University

"How's she doing?" Knox asks, eyes focused on the DJ booth as he twists a knob and taps his tablet. The bass thumps softly through the arena, testing the levels. The lights above us shift, casting streaks of gold and crimson across the polished wood floor of the gym.

"The nightmare hit around three a.m.," I say, rubbing the back of my neck. "It was bad. Like, screaming-in-the-shower bad. But it's the first one in a few days. They're starting to space out again."

Knox nods, flipping a switch and watching as one of the overhead lights flicker into place. "How do you think she's gonna do with all this?"

I glance out at the stands as the doors open. People start trickling in—students, teammates, Legacy alumni, coaches, random fans of the Trifecta. Haley's already bouncing around, greeting people like it's her birthday while Ellie's directing traffic like a damn campaign manager.

"I'm hoping," I say, voice rough and tired. "The music. The crowd. The noise. Maybe it brings her back, even just a little... especially once she realizes that it's all for her and her dad. We got a glimpse of the real her last night. She let us hold her in bed. All three of us, just holding on."

"That's a start," Knox says, watching a stagehand haul in a rack of folding chairs. His tone is gentle, but he doesn't look at me when he says it. Probably doesn't want to see how fucked I look right now.

"I know it is," I mutter, jaw tight. "But damn, Knox. This is killing me. I miss her so much. And she's still right here. Right in front of me and I just can't fucking reach her."

The DJ setup clicks as another bassline hums through the air, vibrating the floor beneath our feet.

"I know, man," Knox says after a beat. "I'm so sorry. I can't imagine what you and Cade are going through. Or what she's dealing with. But your family is strong. The strongest out of all of ours. You three will make it through this. I know you will."

I nod, swallowing hard. "Thanks, Bestie."

That gets a dry chuckle out of him, even as he flips open a crate of mic packs and starts organizing them. "Oh, I meant to tell you," he adds. "Since this is basically a party-practice, you're going to be in charge of her chair stuff today."

I arch a brow. "Her chair stuff?"

"You know what I mean," he says. "I'm letting you decide if she does the chair routine or not and who's in it. I don't want to push her. If she starts spacing or looks even remotely off, just give me the signal. We'll cut the bit and let Haley and Ellie finish it out."

"Thanks, Knox. I appreciate that." I glance down at the floor, watching a few stage markers being laid out. "That means a lot."

By now the stands are almost half full. People keep filing in, more than I expected. Rico, Javi, and some of the Legacy freshmen are weaving through the crowd, handing out folded burgundy shirts. Every single one of them is the same.

Dad had the University of Arkansas do a rush order on a custom shirts for us. All the shirts look like replicas of a Razorback football jersey complete with HARRINGTON and 17 on the back.

It's a tribute. A quiet, powerful one. Something Bella doesn't know about yet.

Cade and I take our seats in the front row, right where she'll see us the second she walks out. I can't sit still, my leg's bouncing and my eyes scanning every inch of the gym like I'm waiting for a bomb to drop.

The place is packed now. Legacy's stretching, their warm-up jackets half-zipped, hair slicked back, and ready to perform. Javi's pacing, muttering in Spanish. The bleachers are vibrating with the low thrum of conversation and anticipation.

Next to me, Dad leans forward, elbows braced on his knees like he's gearing up for war. Mom reaches over him and squeezes my arm. She's been softer lately. Warmer. Like she's finally seeing Bella for who she is. I just hate that it took a dead father and a broken girl to get her to act like a fucking mom.

On Cade's other side sit Cade's parents, dressed like they're attending a silent auction instead of a tribute dance. And just one seat down from Clay, sitting with his elbows on his knees and his jaw like stone?

Roman fucking Russo.

Yeah. That Roman. He asked to come. Insisted, really. Said he wanted to see his daughter dance, for Henry. Cade and I told him no. Twice. But he showed up anyway. Said he'd stay in the crowd and stay out of her face.

She's not ready. And if he tries to push her, I'll drag him out of this arena by his throat.

The gym gets louder, cheers and whistles echo now as people realize it's almost time.

Knox throws me a look from the DJ booth. Everything's on standby.

My phone vibrates. I glance down.

BELLA: I need you.

My throat closes. Cade's already leaning toward me, like he felt the shift in my entire body.

"What?" he asks.

I show him the screen. He doesn't wait, just stands. I'm already moving. Elbowing through the crowd. Past the line of Legacy girls waiting to go on.

We push past the last curtain and step into the narrow backstage corridor just in time to see her. Bella stands near the mirror wall, her back half-turned as Ellie adjusts her earring and Haley smooths down the edge of her outfit.

But it's the outfit that nearly kills me.

A beautiful black and burgundy one-piece, short as sin, dripping in fringe that shimmers with every movement. Her legs look a mile long, those toned thighs wrapped in knee-high black boots, dusted with burgundy glitter that catches the backstage lighting like fire. Her hair's curled and wild, lips painted a deep bruised red. She's chaos and elegance and danger wrapped into one lethal vision.

She turns and the second her eyes land on us, her whole face softens. Thank fuck. She walks straight toward us no second-guessing and throws her arms around both of us in one tight, trembling hug.

"I can't do this," she whispers. "I'm so nervous. I don't get nervous, that's not me."

"Breathe, baby," I say, cupping her face, gently pulling her back just enough to see her. "You're okay. You've got this. You're not alone."

She sucks in a breath, then steps back and her gaze drops to our chests. "What are those?" she asks, squinting at our shirts.

Shit.

Cade looks at me *like you wanna handle this or should I?*

"Uh..." he clears his throat. "Well. That was supposed to be a surprise."

"Surprise," I say quickly, shrugging. "My dad had 'em made. Custom Razorback shirts. You know, for your dad. Thought it might... help a little bit."

Her eyes dart between us, wide and already glassy.

"Guys! That's amazing. I love them!" she says, and then she grabs my shirt, yanks me down, and kisses me.

No warning. Just mouth on mine, fierce and hot and fucking alive. Her lips crush into mine. Months of silence and guilt burn off in the heat of it. My hands fly to her waist, holding her close, bracing myself before I float right off the earth.

Then she breaks the kiss, turns to Cade, and pulls him in too, just as greedy, just as desperate. He groans into her mouth, palms cradling her cheeks like she's something breakable and sacred.

We hear Knox announce Ellie, Haley, and the rest of the Legacy.

"Will you guys go out there with me? I know I'm supposed to sing to kick today off, but like... I might need a little push. A gentle shove. Or, you know, Cade you could drag me out by the hair, Lex throw me over your shoulder like a neanderthal. We've got options," she smiles and shrugs.

We both laugh and holy shit, it's real. A joke. She's joking. Cade brushes his thumb across her cheek. "Oh my god. Our girl's joking."

Before she can answer, two beeps. *Walkie on.*

Knox's voice crackles through the comms. *"Alright, Bella. Everyone's in place. You about ready to come out, babe?"*

She looks between us, then nods. Her chest rises and falls with a deep breath and something in her eyes sharpens. Like a match finally finding flame.

She straightens her spine and shakes out the last bit of nerves. "Yeah, Knox," she says. "I'm ready."

The lights in the gym dim suddenly, then flash back to life in deep red and bright white, slicing through the space in rhythm with the bass Knox drops over the speakers. The crowd erupts, that pulsating pre-show buzz sweeping through every seat.

"Alright, Wexley, this is it. The official dress rehearsal for Nationals. You've already met The Legacy. You've already fallen for our girls Haley and Ellie."

The lights pulse once, twice then the red intensifies, spotlighting the center of the court. "But now... it's time."

Another bass drop. The crowd leans forward.

"Time to meet the one you've heard about. The one you've seen run this floor like it's her own personal kingdom." A beat of silence. A slow rise of tension. "The center of the storm. Give it up for the one and only Bella Blackwood!"

The roar hits like a wave.

Bella flinches, just barely. But we've got her. Cade and I tighten our arms around her, one on each side, her fists gripping our arms like lifelines. We guide her forward, step by step, onto the court.

Onto her throne. The lights follow us as we walk, three shadows cast in scarlet and white, like a coronation. Her head held high, that shimmery burgundy-and-black outfit catching every ray of light.

When we hit center court, she halts. The spotlight finds her. And for a split second, the whole damn world goes quiet.

"You've got this, baby."

CHAPTER ⑦⑤
B E L L A
W E X L E Y   U N I V E R S I T Y
63 DAYS SINCE DADDY'S DEATH

"Alright everyone," Knox's voice echoes across the gym, "listen up." A few people whistle and cheer from the bleachers, but he lifts a hand to quiet them. "This one's a little different."

I pull in a breath and steadying myself at half court.

His tone shifts, softer, but still strong. "Today's not just a dress rehearsal for Nationals. It's not just warm ups before tonight's Row party at the Catacombs. Today is a celebration of this team, this girl." He points to me. "And her dad."

The gym quiets.

"Henry Harrington was the kind of man who showed up. To every game. Every performance. Every moment that mattered. So today, we show up for his girl."

Don't cry, don't cry, don't cry. Just breathe.

"And y'all better behave, because if any of you make her cry, I swear to God, Lex will kick your ass, Cade will paint your tombstone, and I'll DJ your funeral."

The gym's still echoing with laughter when Knox lifts the mic again, that smug little smirk stretching across his face like he's been dying to drop this bomb.

"Now Bella..." he says, dragging it out like it's a game. "Before you start shaking your sparkly ass out here and stealing the show, some of our Wolves have a little surprise for you."

Cal and August start to walk out on the court and stand beside me.

"Alright, Wexley," Knox booms, voice bouncing off every wall like a damn cannon. "We know you know this one, because we all practiced it, so it's time to..." He raises his hands in the air. "CALL. THOSE. HOGS!"

"Oh my god," I whisper.

"WOOOOO. PIG. SOOIE!"

My heart stutters. My breath gets stuck somewhere between my ribs.

"WOOOOO. PIG. SOOIE!"

It's like a freight train of memories—game nights, lake weekends, Razorback red everywhere. Daddy yelling louder than anyone else in the stadium.

"WOOOOO. PIG. SOOIE! RAZORBACKS!"

The gym explodes. And I break. Tears hit my cheeks and my knees almost buckle. It's perfect. It's Arkansas. It's Daddy.

Cal opens his arms and I walk right into them as he lifts me in the air.

"Told you we had you," he says, holding me tight.

"This was your idea?" I cry.

"For you, Razorback."

I try to laugh, but it comes out like a sob. "My dad would've lost his mind."

"Then we nailed it."

Knox clears his throat again, trying to keep it together. "Alright, Cal, you and August take your fine-ass selves back to the bleachers."

Cal kisses my forehead. August grins and salutes me before jogging off, dropping back into their spot with the rest of the football guys. I wipe under my eyes, sniff once, and glance over at Knox.

He gives me a small nod, mic still in hand. "Bella, head on out to the front walkway."

The front walkway cuts between the edge of the court and the first row of bleachers, right where they're all sitting. Lex. Cade. The Whitmores. The Barinovs. Roman.

Shit, this a mistake, I can't do this.

"Where I'm From" by Jason Michael Carroll starts to play. I try to hold back the tears. I lock eyes with Lex. He nods once, calm and steady. I look at Cade, he smiles back at me.

No, they're here. I can do this.

When I hit the first chorus, I start walking. Slow, easy steps across the front walkway, heels clicking against the metal walkway, the sound drowned beneath the music and my heartbeat.

God, Daddy, I hope you're watching, because I don't know how to do this without you.

When I sing about moms and dads being together since high school, my gaze finds Savannah and Clay—forever sweethearts. She blows me a kiss and I smile through the lump in my throat.

I keep singing. My voice stays steady, even when my hands tremble. And, when I reach the part that talks about brothers, I stop walking.

Zeke, please... if you're out there, please be the good guy. I can't survive this if you're not.

Lex reaches out and rubs my thigh, just once. Like he knows I'm balancing on the edge of a thought I'm terrified to fall into. It's enough. The storm inside me stills.

Then I hit the part about going home to family and friends, and I don't hold back. I belt it out with my southern twang thick, raw, and real. That Arkansas grit lives in my bones, and it rises in every note.

Memories of my life in the south rushes through me. And all I can do is smile. It probably doesn't sound like much to some people here from New York, but it's where I'm from and in this moment I'm damn proud of it.

When I get to the line about the quarterback and the home-coming queen, I look up. Straight into the rafters. Straight into heaven. And I point.

To Mama.

To Daddy.

To everything that made me, *me.*

My breath trembles, but my spine stays straight. I turn toward the girls, ready to return to formation, ready to move on. But then I see it.

The jumbotron.

It's changed. It's me and Daddy. Little me in pigtails, grinning with gap teeth. Daddy spinning me barefoot in the kitchen, both of us laughing. Him lifting me onto his shoulders at a Razorback game, red foam finger in my tiny hand. My birthday. My dance recital, me in a sparkly tutu, him in a suit and tie, kneeling down so we're eye level.

My graduation party. Us in New York when Zeke flew him in for the Fourth of July.

Every photo a memory. Every one a wound.

Lex and Cade come up behind me like they felt the second my heart cracked open and realized I needed their touch. They don't say anything. Just wrap around me. One arm each. Holding me like they've got me. Like I'm safe. Like I'm home.

I lean back into their warmth. "How?" I whisper.

"I called Jack," Lex's voice is low against my ear. His lips brush my temple as he tightens his hold. "Told him you'd need this."

His fingers find mine, threading through, palm to palm, and he squeezes. Steady. Sure. I close my eyes and breathe them in.

The gym erupts in cheers. And Knox's voice fills the space, thick with emotion, "Give it up for Bella Blackwood, y'all."

Lex kisses my forehead, "Breathe, just breathe. You're home, baby."

After we run through a couple of our routines for Nationals and Worlds, the crowd starts buzzing again. My chest is heaving from the last routine. We hit every beat, every powerful flip, every clean turn.

"Alright, alright, enough practice for a little while." The crowd whistles and claps, but Knox keeps going. "I mean, y'all killed it. Tens across the board. First place at Nationals and Worlds without a doubt."

Someone in the stands yells, "Trifecta for life!"

I roll my eyes, grinning.

"But..." Knox drawls, and the noise dips just enough for him to keep going. "I think it's time for something else. Something fun. Something filthy."

The Row boys go feral.

"I think it's time we give the people what they want..." He pauses dramatically. "Trifecta, I think we give them a damn chair."

They lose it in an absolute uproar. Cal is on his feet. August's shirt is halfway off.

Knox just laughs into the mic. "Okay, okay! Freshmen, go grab me one of our signature chairs." Knox turns to me, still amped. "Bella, since today is about you, you're doing the chairs. I'm gonna let you pick the song."

I laugh, shaking my head as everyone screams louder.

"But," Knox holds up a finger. "There's a catch."

Oh no.

"Lex gets to pick who goes in the chair."

I whip my head toward him. Lex is leaning forward in his seat like he's been waiting for this moment. A cocky, lethal look staining his face. Like he already knows he's won. He stands slowly with his eyes locked on me.

Of course he'd pick himself. There's not a single universe where Lex Barinov watches me do a chair routine and doesn't claim the seat for himself. Asshole. God, I love him so much.

"First chair goes to Cade."

Holy shit.

The crowd howls. Cade gives Lex a look—part mock-offended, part amused—but he's already standing. He brushes a hand across the low of my back as he walks past.

I smile and run over to tell Knox my song choice. Knox grins like he's been waiting all day for this. He paces in front of the booth. A ringmaster about to unleash hell.

"Alright everybody shut up!"

The crowd just gets louder. He laughs, shaking his head.

"The queen has spoken." He bows to me. "And she picked a good one for you, Cade."

Cade throws a lazy salute from the chair, already lounging like he was born for it.

"But first things first," Knox adds. "You know what's coming, dude."

Cade raises an eyebrow like he's playing dumb.

The Legacy girls scream at the top of their lungs, "TAKE IT OFF!"

I shrug at Cade and wink. Cade tips his head back laughing,

hands going to the hem of his shirt as the opening beat of "Lollipop" by Lil Wayne drops. He pulls it off in one smooth motion, tossing it toward the bleachers. He opens his arms like a sacrifice to the gods.

"Let's go, sweetheart," he drawls it out, voice full of smug heat.

I strut toward him with a grin that says I already own him.

This dance is usually split between me, Ellie, and Haley. Rotating through the chair, switching places, and building tension. But today it's just me. One queen. One chair. One man. I adjust on the fly improvise the gaps, slide into every beat.

The music pulses, the bass drops, and I sink onto Cade's lap. I straddle him slow, one hand dragging up his chest, the other threading through his hair just to tug. A teasing little pull. He leans back and lets me, smiling like the smug bastard he is. I stare straight into those hazel eyes.

"Damn, sweetheart," he breathes, low and rough, "I missed you."

I slide off him like liquid silk, letting the next part of the routine take over. It's flirtatious and filthy—hips rolling, fingers dragging down my own body, teasing him, teasing the whole crowd. They eat it up.

Cade just licks his lips, soaking it all in like I'm his personal religion. God, the way he looks at me like I'm still whole. Like I never broke.

I strut back over and sink down onto Cade again, grinding to the final beat. The Trifecta's no touching rule is so not happening. Cade's hands are on me the whole time, palms sliding up my thighs and fingers tracing my waist.

When he runs his hand down my spine, I arch. Goosebumps erupt across my skin. He laughs. That cocky, low laugh I forgot I loved so much.

I've missed my guys. Their hands, their heat, the way they orbit me like I'm their sun.

I've missed this too. The music. The movement. The way the bass crawls under my skin and rewires everything I thought I couldn't feel. The way the beat takes over, louder than my thoughts, steadier than my heartbeat.

The song ends, but he doesn't let me go. He pulls me deeper into him like I'm something sacred. And when his lips find mine, it's soft and sweet. That low, burning ache we never really lost. Like his mouth remembers every version of me it's ever kissed.

I smile against his lips. "So, should I just sit here a minute, you know…" I drag one finger down his chest, stopping just above his belt, "…until you cool down?"

He grabs my hand, heat flaring in his eyes. "Sweetheart," he rasps, "you are going to be the death of me."

"I love you, Cade."

"I love you more, Bella."

Knox's voice crackles over the mic, grinning. "Whew! Somebody remind me what the hell happened to the no-touching rule?" The crowd laughs. "Damn, Bella… that was hot."

Knox runs his hands through his hair. "And Cade, you might want to just sit there for a little bit, buddy."

CHAPTER ⑯
LEX
WEXLEY UNIVERSITY
HARD AS GRANITE AFTER WATCHING BELLA RIDE CADE...
63 DAYS SINCE HENRY'S DEATH

Cade drops back into the seat next to me, breathless and flushed, hair a mess from Bella's hands. He's got that dazed, lovesick look on his face and I can't even blame him.

I nudge his knee. "You good?"

He lets out a low laugh, still catching his breath. "Barely."

I flash a wolfish grin. "You looked like you were thoroughly enjoying yourself."

"Yeah, thanks for that." His grin fades into something softer. "Lex... I think she's back."

That gets my attention. I turn fully toward him. "You think?"

He nods, eyes still on the court. "The way she looked at me. The way she moved. That little smirk she gave right before she climbed onto my lap. That was her, babe. That was our girl."

I take a deep breath, watching Bella reset with the rest of Legacy for the next number. She's laughing with Ellie, tossing her hair over her shoulder. There's a glint in her eyes I haven't seen in too damn long.

"I don't know. It could just be the dancing. She always lights up when the music hits."

"It's more than that," Cade says, squeezing my thigh. "She didn't just perform. She played with me. With the crowd. She was teasing, flirting, confident as hell. That spark in her eyes, it wasn't fake."

I glance at him. "You really think she's back?"

"I think she's healing and not just surviving. Babe, she's living."

The weight of that hits me hard. For so long it's just been about keeping her afloat, keeping her from drowning in everything she lost. But now she's swimming on her own again. Even if just for a night.

I let out a breath and reach over, interlacing my fingers with his. "God, I hope you're right."

He squeezes my hand, warm and steady. "I am."

On the court, the girls launch into a new Latin routine and Bella takes center like she was born for it. Her body rolls with every beat, hair whipping, a playful smile tugging at her lips that's real. She looks like fire and freedom. We both sit there, hands locked, watching the girl we love burn up the floor.

"She's back," Cade says again, this time with quiet certainty.

Knox's voice cuts through the gym, the music fading out behind him. "Ellie, you and Hales need to run your duet for Worlds backup. Let's see it clean. Bella, take a damn break and go sit with your boys. I'm pretty sure after that chair routine with Cade, Lex is feelin' a little lonely."

Cade barks out a laugh, elbowing me. "You okay, babe? Feeling neglected?"

I smirk, eyes locked on Bella. "Neglected isn't the word... more like starved."

Bella walks up and sits her pretty little ass in my lap. "Hey, baby," she says, a little breathless, a little smug.

I grab the back of her neck and pull her down, crashing my mouth against hers. There's no teasing in this kiss, fuck a gentle lead-in. I kiss her like she's the surface after too long in the deep.

Her lips part for me instantly. My fingers thread into her hair, and I tilt her just the way I like. Deep. Demanding. Desperate to feel her. Even more desperate to see for myself if Cade is right. When I pull back, my chest is heaving and not from the damn heat in this gym.

"You're really back, malyshka," I breathe, eyes wide.

She doesn't answer with words. She grabs the front of my shirt, yanks me in, and kisses me harder. Dirtier. She sucks my bottom lip into her mouth and bites down, slow and sharp, and I groan. My cock twitches under her ass. Fuck, she knows what she's doing.

"I'm back, baby."

She turns around and leans back against me, settling into my lap with this casual confidence like she owns the whole fucking world. Like I'm her throne and she's finally come home to it. We sit there locked together, her spine against my chest, watching her best friends take the floor.

In the middle of Ellie and Haley's number she sits up, eyes flicking toward Knox at the DJ booth.

"Now?" she says quietly, like she's confirming something. "Okay, who's bringing it out there?"

I blink, confused as hell, until I realize she's talking to Knox on the damn walkie.

"Okay yeah," she nods again, then turns to me.

"I need to go change."

I don't move. "No."

"Lex."

"Baby."

"Lex."

I tighten my grip around her waist. Not about to let her go and give her a chance to disappear again.

"Lex," she says again, exasperated, but fighting a smile.

Then she turns to Cade.

"Cade. Will you please tell our brute of a boyfriend to let me go so I can go change."

Cade chuckles and shoots me a look. "Let her go, Lex."

My grip tightens dramatically like I'm some damn villain in a melodrama. "I'd rather die."

Bella laughs, leans back, and presses a kiss to my jaw, then swivels to Cade and kisses him too, just as quick.

"I'll be right back," she says, flashing that look that always promises trouble.

As Ellie and Haley finish their number, the gym roars with applause. The Legacy boys push out this massive square stage onto the center of the court. It's heavy, reinforced, covered in black panels, and raised just enough to feel like a pedestal. Callum and August start going crazy in their seats.

"What the hell is that?" I ask, glancing at Cade.

He shrugs. "I've never seen it before."

I tilt my head. "You think this is that rain stage thing she told Ellie not to bring to her party?"

Cade's brows lift. "Oh, shit. Maybe."

The gym lights drop as she steps out from behind the curtain. Barefoot and in a sheer lavender dress clinging to every perfect line of her body. It looks like something out of a dream, short and gauzy, layered like petals. Her skin glows under the pale lights, her hair pinned half up with soft waves spilling down her back.

She looks like a fucking ballet fairy. If that fairy was carved out of every dark craving I've ever had.

Josh meets her at center court and takes her hand. They walk in sync up the steps to the stage. The only lights still on are two soft blue beams hitting the square platform.

The first notes of "Midnight Rain" by Taylor Swift echo across the gym. I lean forward in my chair, elbows on my knees, eyes locked on our girl. She moves like the song is hers. Every extension of her leg, every turn of her neck, every flick of her fingers, it's beautiful.

Josh lifts her and spins her into a dip that makes the crowd gasp. Her back arches, her arms stretch, her feet graze the surface like she's gliding on water.

When the chorus hits, so does the rain. Water pours down from hidden slats above the stage, soaking them in seconds.

My phone is already up. Because holy shit. That's our girl dancing barefoot in the rain. Drenched in lavender. Spinning and bending and swaying with this haunting kind of beauty that belongs on a stage in Paris, not a college gym. I can't stop watching her.

"She's unreal," I mutter, still recording. "Like, not even real. That's goddess-level shit."

Cade nods beside me, just as gone. By the time the song fades, she's breathless and soaked to the bone. Hair clinging to her back and her dress plastered to her glowing skin. And fuck, she's smiling. Like this was all some sort of a release and not a performance.

The crowd just sits there, not clapping and utterly stunned. Then someone yells and the whole place erupts. She steps down from the rain stage completely soaked, shining, fucking breathtaking, and starts walking back toward us, squeezing water from her hair.

But Knox's voice booms over the speakers before she can even reach the edge of the court. "Uh-uh. Bella Blackwood, where you goin'? You're not done."

She stops mid-step, blinking up at the DJ booth like she misheard him.

"Excuse me?"

Knox grins, one hand cupping his mic, the other throwing her a challenge. "I said I'm calling you out, bitch. Lip sync battle. You and me. Right here. Right now."

Cade laughs beside me. "Oh my God."

I lean forward. "He's actually lost his mind."

Bella wipes water from her eyes. "Knox, I'm soaked."

"And your point?" he fires back. "What, you scared?"

She lets out the most dramatic sigh I've ever heard with Broadway-level dramatics. Then shrugs off her drenched lavender dress and tosses it to the floor.

My jaw drops. "What the fuck are you doing, baby?!"

"Holy shit," Cade mutters beside me. "I knew she had Rico make her some more fight night outfits, but damn."

Yeah. Damn is right. A Rico original—purple, glittery, and skin-tight—but it's the word across her chest that nearly knocks the air out of me.

BARINOV. In black rhinestones. Right over her heart.

Ellie jogs out from the sideline, carrying a pair of purple and black heels and a towel. She tosses the towel at Bella's head.

She flashes me a wink, slow, smug, and fucking lethal, like she knows she just branded my name across her chest and lit my soul on fire doing it.

Then she cracks her neck and glares up at Knox. "Okay, fucker. Let's go.".

Knox points to his backup DJ. "Hit it."

"Right Thurr" by Chingy blasts through the gym like it's 2004 again. What follows is chaos. Glorious, ratchet, Wexley-certified chaos. They switch off verses, each one trying to out-perform the other. Bella goes full stripper squat during her first chorus, throwing her hair like it's a weapon. Knox tries to mimic it, fails spectacularly, and the whole gym loses their minds.

They do finger guns, body rolls, exaggerated air-humps. Knox even rips off his shirt halfway through and twirls it like a damn heli-copter. Bella mocks him right back, throws invisible money at him, then turns around and twerks like the floor is her stage and the devil's her hype man.

I think I black out somewhere around that part. Cade's crying from laughter beside me.

When its over, Bella and Knox hug like the insane duo they are, arms flung, laughing, and still half-wet from the rain stage. She wipes her face with the towel one more time, cheeks flushed and glow-ing like she just conquered the damn world.

Knox leans back into the mic, echoing through the gym speak-ers like it's his own personal concert. "Alright everyone, Thank you all for being here! We will see you tonight at the Pulse at the Catacombs!"

CHAPTER ⑦⑦
B E L L A
W E X L E Y   U N I V E R S I T Y
63 DAYS SINCE DADDY'S DEATH

The girls and I change, grab our bags, and slip into our sneakers before pushing out the back door of the gym. It's golden hour. That early-evening glow that makes everything feel like a movie.

And waiting just outside is our army. Lex. Cade. The Whitmores. The Barinovs. Hell, even Roman. All of them, every single one.

Lex sees me first. He breaks from the group and walks straight toward me as if I'm the only thing that matters.

He wraps an arm around my waist and pulls me in tight. "You were incredible."

I smile up at him, still catching my breath. "Yeah?"

"Yeah, baby." He leans in, rasping deep against my ear. "I've never wanted to fuck you and worship you at the same time so badly in my life."

I bite my lip. "Later."

Then Cade steps up on my other side, all soft eyes and crooked grin. "You were magnetic, sweetheart. Like glow in the dark, steal the breath from the room kind of magnetic."

"Thanks," I whisper, brushing my fingers over his chest. "I missed this."

Daniel whistles low behind them. "If that performance was you at practice... I'm terrified to see Nationals."

Clay chuckles, eyes twinkling. "Y'all need to come choreograph my next office holiday party. We've got a folding chair and a fog machine. I'll pay you in tequila and regrets."

Ellie flips him off. Haley curtsies.

Then Irina speaks, and everything stills just slightly. "That rain number," she says coolly. "It was... beautiful."

"Thanks." I nod.

I turn and see Roman. He's standing a little ways off, watching quietly. Black dress pants, a fitted button-up with the sleeves rolled just enough to feel intentional. The top few buttons are undone, collar relaxed, trying maybe a little awkwardly to look more like a dad than a kingpin.

His hands stay in his pockets. His eyes, those steel-gray eyes, are locked on me. Steady. Quiet. And for once, not cold. Just... waiting. Like he's not here to command. Like he's just hoping I'll choose to walk toward him.

I take a slow breath and step forward. Lex's hand catches mine. I glance back. He looks tense, his body wanting to move before his brain tells it to.

"It's okay, baby," I whisper, squeezing his hand. "I'll be right back." I nod toward my bag on the ground. "Grab my bag?"

He grunts, still not letting go.

I press a kiss to his cheek. "Promise."

He lets go. I walk toward Roman slowly, legs still wobbly from the dances and the adrenaline crash.

"Hey," I say quietly.

Roman smiles. "You were amazing, Bella."

My breath catches. Not at the words, but the way he says them, he means them. Like he's proud of me.

"The way you moved, the emotion in it. It wasn't just a routine. It was something else. Like watching someone bring the storm to life."

He runs a hand through his black hair. "You remind me so much of your mother when you dance."

That hits harder than I expect. I nod, swallowing past the sudden ache in my throat.

"Thank you. I just wish I could have known her."

"She was fierce," he adds, almost to himself. "Didn't care what anyone thought. But onstage, she was unforgettable."

I glance down at my shoes, then back at him.

He clears his throat, shifting slightly. "I know you're headed to your party tonight and I wanted to ask, if it's alright, I'd really like to be there."

My face pulls into something between confusion and horror. "Wait, what? Roman, it's a college party. A real one. You absolutely do not need to be there."

"No, no, no," he says quickly, hands lifting in surrender. "Not like that. Not to, I don't know, crash it or hang out or whatever the hell you kids do these days."

He takes a breath. "I mean for protection."

That stills me. He takes a careful step closer. "I know Luca's been quiet lately and maybe it's nothing. But I'd feel a hell of a lot better knowing someone was keeping an eye on you. Just in case."

I cross my arms. "I've got Lex. And Cade."

Roman tilts his head. "And most likely, you'll all be drunk as shit."

I blink.

"And I'm not judging," he adds. "You deserve to blow off some steam. But if anything were to happen tonight, I just want to be close. Out of sight. Out of the way. But there."

I hesitate. "Lex will lose his shit if he sees you there."

"I'll stay hidden," he says. "Promise."

I sigh. "Fine. But don't hover. And for the love of God, don't get into a staring contest with anyone."

His lips twitch like he wants to laugh but doesn't. Then he steps forward just a little. A tentative movement. He reaches for me and I tense.

He stops immediately. Hands lowering like I slapped them. "Sorry. I... I'm sorry."

"No," I say quickly, shaking my head. "It's okay. I'm just not ready for that yet."

He nods, gaze dropping. "I understand."

A long beat passes between us. Heavy but not sharp. More like a silence we both don't know how to fill yet.

"I'll see you there," he says finally. "And Bella?" He meets my eyes again. "You really are unforgettable, daughter."

I bite the inside of my cheek, then nod. "Thanks, Roman."

His jaw flexes. And then he turns, quiet and composed, and walks back to his car.

🖤🖤🖤

The Catacombs – Carrington Row

The Catacombs isn't your average basement. They're a kingdom carved beneath Carrington Row. Exposed brick. Concrete floors slick with decades of spilled drinks and louder sins. Purple and gold LED strips run along the ceiling beams, casting a low, pulsating glow. The main room is massive, speakers already thumping low bass like a heartbeat.

But just off to the side is the real prize, The Trifecta's Get-Ready Room. My personal favorite. Vintage vanity mirrors, string lights, racks of costumes, a couch that's seen everything but judgment. It smells like perfume, body glitter, and secrets that never leave this room.

I'm curled on Cade's lap on the couch, arms draped around his neck. His hand absently tracing my thigh like muscle memory when a water bottle hits my chest mid-thought.

"Hydrate or die, bitch," Knox announces from the doorway, cocky as ever, "because tonight y'all are gonna get lit or some shit."

I snort and grab the bottle. "Charming as ever, DJ Asshat."

Cade leans in, voice warm against my ear. "I missed this."

I bump my forehead against his. "Same."

The door swings open and Lex walks in, a brown paper bag in one hand. August trailing behind with a tray of stacked containers like a waiter on steroids.

"Room service, ladies and gents," August calls.

Lex ignores him, eyes locked on me. "Eat up, baby," he says leaning down to press a kiss to my mouth slow and sweet, but laced with something dark and hungry underneath. "Carbs. You're gonna need 'em."

Haley swoops in like a seagull. "Please tell me that's pasta."

"It's literally nothing but carbs," August groans, setting it down. "Barinov wouldn't let me bring anything green except one Caesar salad."

"Because that shit doesn't count when the girls are going to be seventy-five percent tequila by the end of the night." Lex says, already opening my container and handing it to me like the world's hottest personal chef. "Now eat. Or I'm feeding you myself."

"Tempting," I murmur, popping open the lid. "But then I'd probably choke and die and you'd never get the release you've been waiting weeks for, baby."

Cade chuckles beneath me, arms wrapping tighter around my waist. "Can confirm. Girl's a menace with noodles."

Lex quirks a brow. "Bet she's—"

August cuts him off and groans. "Ugh, can you three not."

"Don't start Augie," Ellie warns from the vanity, fluffing her hair like it's war prep. "They're in a good mood. Let them flirt with carbs and each other."

"Thank you, Little Whitmore." Lex says to Ellie causing her to roll her eyes.

"Hydrate, Problem Child," Knox adds. "You're the host tonight. No dying before midnight."

I salute him with the bottle. "Yes, Dad."

The room's buzzing by the time we finish our dinner. Haley is already fixing her makeup, Ellie's blasting music off her phone, and August is bitching about the lighting in his corner. It feels like before. Like the version of us that used to live for nights like this.

Knox slams a bottle of tequila onto the counter. "Alright, bitches and bastards. Time to pregame properly."

August claps his hands. "Finally."

He lines up eight glitter-rimmed shot glasses, Wexley Wolves decals and all. He pours generously, spilling half of it with chaotic flair.

"Hey," Cade says, reaching for a towel. "You're wasting it."

Knox shrugs. We all grab our glasses.

Ellie lifts hers first, a wicked glint in her eyes. "To chaos."

Haley bumps hers. "To the baddest Wolves in the den."

Cade raises his and nods toward me. "To getting her home in one piece."

Cal grins. "To whatever happens, happens. We all remember the Hamptons."

August bows. "To Queen Bella."

Knox throws both hands in the air like he just dropped the

bass. "To tequila, bitches!" he yells, spinning around like he's on stage at Coachella. "Tonight's forecast? 100% chance of blackouts."

Lex lifts his and looks straight at me. "To the girl who brought the whole damn pack to its knees."

They all look at me. "To you all, to my family. I don't know how I would have gotten through all of this without each and every one of you. I love you guys."

We throw them back in unison, the tequila burning down like liquid regret. Ellie and Haley dart to the mirror for last-minute touch-ups and to put on our new outfits. Cal heads upstairs to hype the crowd and Knox grabs his mic and heads toward his booth.

Lex pulls me aside, one arm around my waist, backing me into the brick wall with no apology. His mouth brushes my ear. "Can't wait to get you home, baby. That chair routine? That rain dance? Wearing my name like it's your goddamn birthright? Yeah. I've got plans for you."

I smirk, tilting my face up to his. "You better."

He groans, then crashes his mouth against mine—fast, hard, dirty. Like a promise. When he pulls back, his voice is rough. "Fuck, I love you."

"I know," I whisper, lips brushing his. "Now go before I forget we have a party to host, I need to change."

He grins and backs off just as Cade grabs my hand and Ellie calls out, "Boys, get out!"

CHAPTER ⑦⑧
LEX
THE CATACOMBS
HOPING MY BESTIE PUTS ME IN A CHAIR TONIGHT...
63 DAYS SINCE HENRY'S DEATH

The Catacombs might be under the Row, but it's got its own pulse. Brick archways. Candelabra sconces lit with flickering purple LEDs. Glow shots lining the bar in a candy-colored arsenal. The DJ booth is up on a balcony and Knox is already leaning over it about to baptize the room in chaos.

Cade stands next to me, one arm slung around my waist, drink in his other hand. His shirt's half unbuttoned. God he's hot. His hazel eyes are scanning the room like he's waiting for her.

The lights flicker from violet to gold and then Knox's baritone booms through the speakers in a fucking thunderclap. "YO WEXLEY!" he shouts, mic hot and hyped. "Welcome to the hottest, dirtiest, wildest night of the semester... The Pulse at the Catacombs!"

The crowd explodes. Drinks fly, bodies jump, and the room shakes. Cade and I yell with them, caught in the current.

Knox grins down at us from the booth. "You came for a party, you came for heat, and baby, we don't disappoint. So, let's give it up for the Queens of Wexley. The wolves who wear stilettos and set fire to the floor every damn time."

The bass cuts, just for a second. Then it kicks back hard as he growls into the mic, "THE TRIFECTA."

Spotlights blast from the side curtain. And then they walk out. All three of them in shredded black leather pants with slits riding high and hugging every curve. Boots tall enough to kill a man's ego. And tops of bright yellow leather, cropped tight across their chests. Their names stamped across their tits in bold black letters like glittering warning labels.

The second they hit center stage, Knox leans over the mic, grinning like a proud dad and a reckless best friend all in one.

"Damn, girls," he drawls, fanning himself with a folded napkin like he's about to pass out. "Bella, baby, how you feelin' tonight?"

I raise a brow and shout toward the booth, "Chill it with the baby, Bestie."

The crowd laughs. Cade huffs a quiet chuckle beside me.

Bella just rolls her eyes, grinning like a menace. "It feels great to be back down here at the Catacombs!" she shouts, voice full of power, hips cocked, that signature sass in her smile. "But tonight isn't just any other Row party. No, tonight is a celebration."

The room leans in.

"A celebration for us getting ready to fly out in a few days to Dallas for Nationals sure, but it's more than that."

She turns toward the side entrance, eyes flashing. "Javi, get the hell out here!"

Javi steps out from the shadows, hands raised like a rockstar, laughing as he makes his way to center. He's in a dark pink button-up and tight jeans, hair slicked back, looking equal parts salsa god and frat party MVP.

Bella steps aside, letting the spotlight hit him before continuing.

"Tonight is a very special night," she says, that grin growing wicked. "Because tonight is Coach Javi's fortieth birthday! And we are here to party."

People stomp, scream, and throw napkins in the air like it's confetti.

Bella lifts a hand. "Millennial style! We're talking throwbacks. The shit you and Rico danced to in clubs when you thought Bluetooth was peak technology. We've got Latin. Hip-hop. Fusion mashups. All your favorite songs, all night long. We even got a few combos we've been saving just for you."

Javi's beaming, full-on, glowy, and emotional dad-vibes.

Cade leans closer to me, voice low. "Our girl's taking her life back, Lex."

I nod, watching her, chest full and tight all at once.

Knox grabs the mic again, hyped like he's about to launch into orbit. "That's right, Javi. This night's for you. This night's for The Legacy. This night's for The Trifecta!"

He slams his hand down on the soundboard. "Let's get this show on the road, 'cause it's about to get fucking crazy down in this bitch!"

The music slams into gear. Lights strobe—green, gold, and electric violet—flashing off the stone walls like we're in some underground rave version of Olympus. The Catacombs are alive. Sweaty. Hyped. Ours.

Knox grabs the mic again, already laughing. "Well the truth is, we couldn't get Mr. Worldwide to show up for your birthday, Javi. Trust me, Ellie tried."

The crowd howls. Ellie bows dramatically, blowing kisses from her place on stage.

Knox grins. "But this? This is the next best thing."

The beat drops, "Greenlight" by Pitbull, and the room erupts.

Bella throws her head back and lets the music pour through her like liquid fire. Ellie and Haley join her, sexy as ever, all three of them in perfect sync like they've been waiting months to unleash hell.

Red lights. Green lights. Flashing with every beat like the whole damn Catacombs is pulsing in sync with the music and the girls are killing it—hip rolls, drops, and smiles that could start wars.

Buzz. Buzz.

REZ: Ready?

ME: Go.

The crowd suddenly parts. Like Moses and the goddamn sea. Out from the shadows step Rez, Chase, and DeShawn, my brothers, my Hollow Kings. They're in black and gold, striding through the dance floor like they own the fucking underground. The girls freeze mid-routine, jaws dropping as if we just called in backup from Hell.

Knox—*bless his dramatic ass*—kills the music. "What the actual fuck," he yells into the mic. "Is that who I think it is?" His voice shoots through the speakers. "Lex, Bestie, are we getting crashed by your Kings?!"

Three beeps in my ear, *mic is on.*

"Nah, Knox." I smirk. "You said this was a party to celebrate our girls…" I nod toward Bella, who's still frozen in place, eyes wide, chest heaving from the last chorus. "So, I brought my guys here to help."

She turns to me and for a second, I think she might cry. Then she smiles. Soft. Real.

Knox grins like a madman. "Well then, welcome to the Combs, Kings!" He slams the button. "Girls, hit it!"

The lights sync back to the music, green to red, red to green. The beat picks back up and the girls drop into the final chorus, energy exploding off them like fireworks.

Rez and the boys move toward us, hype-man level swagger, nodding in rhythm. Chase points at Ellie. DeShawn mouths something at Haley. Rez just watches Bella, eyes locked like the protective wolf he's always been.

Cade turns to me, stunned. "You planned this?"

I nod. "Yep."

"For her?"

I glance at our girl, surrounded by love, soaked in sweat and strobe lights, more alive than I've seen her in months.

"All for her," I say. "I figured she needed all of our family here."

Knox smiles, still breathless from the last number. "Damn girls. That's one way to make Mr. Worldwide proud."

The crowd howls.

"But I got an idea…" He turns toward some Legacy girls. "Freshmen! Bring us out three chairs, please!"

I blink. "Oh shit… here we go."

Rez raises a brow. "What the hell are the chairs for?"

Cade leans in. "If I had to guess…" he says, cutting a glance toward me then back to Rez. "They're for you."

Knox grins wide. "Kings, welcome to our kingdom of temptation and sexiness here at Wexley. Since you're our guests of honor tonight, you get the first chairs."

Cade laughs, smug. "Told you."

The crowd parts again as three chairs are carried out and dropped center stage.

Knox grins. "Ladies, go pick your King."

Bella doesn't hesitate. She grabs Rez by the arm and pulls him toward the middle chair. Ellie loops her arm through Chase's. Haley grabs DeShawn, who just laughs and follows like a man walking straight into the fire.

Rez lowers into the chair, arms spread cocky. Bella steps forward, slow and lethal.

"Bella?" Knox calls into the mic. "You wanna explain the rules to your guests?"

"Sure thing." She turns to face the crowd. "Hey guys. Thanks for being here."

She spins and sinks into Rez's lap. My jaw clenches. She leans in close, too close, and grabs a handful of his shirt.

"No shirts allowed, Rezy."

"Fucking hell, baby," I blurt out under my breath.

Whistles, screams, and chants echo throughout the Catacombs. Ellie's already yanking Chase's shirt over his head. Haley's got DeShawn laughing as she pops his buttons one by one.

Ellie winks. "That's rule one, boys."

Haley chimes in, pointing at Rez. "And rule two? We touch you. You don't touch us. Especially you, Rez. Lex already looks like he's about to combust and that is not a good combo."

Laughter rolls through the Catacombs like a damn wave.

Cade bumps my arm and mutters, "Relax, big guy. She's just getting her power back."

And he's right. Because even though my fists are clenched, and even though I'm two seconds from throwing Rez through the wall, Bella's not breaking. She's playing. She's in control.

"Hot in Herre" by Nelly starts playing.

I groan. "You've got to be kidding me."

Cade grabs my arm, firm. "Relax," he says, not even looking at me. His eyes are glued to the stage like the rest of the damn world.

The girls reach for their hips. RIIIIIP. The leather pants come off in one fluid motion. Velcro. Fucking Rico and his custom designs. Underneath are tiny and tight black leather shorts that look like they were painted on.

The Kings' eyes go wide. Rez's jaw drops. Chase mutters something under his breath and DeShawn just starts praying.

I feel the heat spike in my chest. *Mine.*

They strut forward in sync, circling the chairs like predators, each movement sharper than the last. Teasing. Tempting. Deadly. They're not sitting yet, just dancing around the guys, hips swaying, and eyes locked.

They finally drop and sink onto the Kings' laps with the kind of confidence that could ruin lives. The guys lean back like gods getting worshiped. Every single one of them cocky, wild-eyed, grinning like devils and not to mention probably hard as fuck in those chairs.

Knox's voice cuts back over the mic, still laughing. "Jesus Christ, Rico, how the hell did you even design those pants? Velcro?! You sick genius. Give it up one more time for The Trifecta and their Kings!"

The crowd roars.

"And now..." Knox drags the pause for drama. "Let's open this floor up, baby. I want bodies grinding, sweat flying, and memories y'all regret in the morning!"

The music shifts to something dirty and thumping. Rez is the first to stand, yanking Bella up with him as the crowd floods the floor. She laughs, hair flying as he spins her. Rez wraps an arm around Bella's waist. His hands are low and their bodies are pressed chest to chest. Their hips are moving like the beat's wired deep into their bones.

Nope.

I move. I don't storm in. I don't need to. I just appear, sliding up behind her like smoke and shadow, tugging her out of Rez's arms with one hand around her hip.

Mine.

Rez grins. "Damn, B," he says, backing off with hands up. "Didn't know your man had a sixth sense for jealousy."

"Please. He's got a radar locked on my ass 24/7."

Chase winks at Cade. "Better keep up, pretty boy."

Cade just shrugs, stepping in on her other side, pulling her close from the front. And just like that we're back. Me and Cade, her shadows, her gravity. One behind and one in front. Our hands on her hips, her shoulders, and running them down her thighs.

She leans her head back into my chest.

I lean down, mouth at her ear. "Gonna get you home and fuck the shit out of every inch of you, malyshka"

She laughs, gasps, really. I bite down on her collarbone, just enough to leave a mark. Cade's hands slide lower, guiding her hips against his. I match the rhythm from behind—slow, filthy, fucking perfect.

She turns between us.

Our girl.

Our chaos.

Ours.

CHAPTER ⑲
CADE
THE CATACOMBS
CARRINGTON ROW
63 DAYS SINCE HENRY'S DEATH

The dancing slows down as Knox cuts the music, breathless from laughing and yelling over the mic all night. "Alright, alright," he pants into the mic. "Girls, go get changed for Fusion #1."

Bella turns to me and Lex, cheeks flushed, hair a wild, sweaty mess. She grins. "Don't miss me too much."

Lex tugs her in, kissing her hard. "Go kill it, baby."

She turns to me, softer. "You good?"

I nod, brushing hair from her face. "I love you, sweetheart."

She kisses me quick and then disappears to the changing room with Ellie and Haley.

The floor's still packed, but it's different now. Softer. Lit with a blue glow and dripping with anticipation. Lex pulls me toward the center, music still thumping under the buzz of the crowd.

It's just the two of us now, moving to the beat, swaying in sync. His hands slide to my hips. My fingers knot in his shirt. We dance together for awhile, his forehead presses against mine.

"I love you, babe," he rumbles.

I smile. "Yeah, I know. I love you too."

"This reminds me of the first time we danced together," he says quietly.

"At Northvale?"

He shakes his head, faint grin tugging at his mouth. "Nah. Your artist showcase a few days after we met at The Pit Freshman year. You had charcoal on your hands and pretending you weren't nervous, but you were. They played some indie song about hurricanes and heartbreak."

I laugh. "You remember the song?"

"I remember every second of that night," he says, eyes dark and soft all at once. "You wouldn't look at me at first. Then the lights hit and you finally did. You smiled. Like I hadn't already fallen for you sexy ass three songs ago."

"I thought you said you fell for me at The Pit."

"Yeah, I did. Lost the fucking fight because of your sexy ass remember?" he shakes his head and smiles. "But that dance was when it sealed the deal for me, Cade. That dance was when I knew I wasn't ever going to let you go."

My throat tightens. "You said something that night."

He nods slowly. "Yeah. I told you that you were gonna ruin me." His grin fades, voice dropping lower. "Guess I was right."

"Lex..."

He brushes his thumb over my jaw, a quiet sigh slipping out. "You've always been the calm after my fights, Cade. My first good thing."

I press my forehead against his. "And you're the chaos that makes me feel alive."

He lets out a soft laugh, small and real. "Guess we're still the same."

"Guess we are."

He kisses me like he's trying to memorize the taste of the past and the present at the same time. The noise around us fades until it's just this. His heartbeat. Mine. The pulse of the bass keeping time with both.

Over the speakers, Knox's voice crackles back to life.

"Alright Javi, it's time, baby! The girls have cooked up a little something for you. Millennial fusion dances. Their way of saying happy birthday to the best dance coach in the world."

The crowd cheers. Lex throws an arm around my neck, head leaning on my shoulder like a lazy, drunk lion.

"Rico made their costumes," Knox adds, "I mixed the music and trust me, it's a whole production, man. But first, you know what time it is. Sit your little Latin birthday ass in this chair right here."

Javi appears from the shadows. Dragged into the spotlight by two football players, laughing and protesting the whole way.

"Get back out here, girls!" Knox yells.

Ellie struts out first, bouncing in skirt that's a flirty swirl of bright yellow, glitter catching the lights with every step. Her top is a tiny yellow and orange sparkling crop that makes the crowd whistle and holler like they've already lost their minds.

Haley follows, hips swinging, skirt lime green, top hugging her in all the dangerous ways. Her smirk screams trouble. The green makes her red hair look even more unruly, like someone lit a match and dared the room not to stare.

Bella's in hot pink and purple, Rico's twisted idea of a birthday gift to every man in this room. Glittery mini so short it's criminal, a tiny top that clings to every inch of her abs like it was sculpted there. Her long black hair is curled and wild, bouncing with each step like it knows how lethal she is. She's color, mayhem, and sex appeal wrapped in sugar and steel. And she knows it. Hell, she owns it.

Lex groans beside me. "What the hell, she looks like the sexiest Barbie I've ever fucking seen."

Knox grins like a game show host. "Ok Javi, this one's from Ellie."

The beat kicks in. Backstreet Boys mixed with some Britney Spears hits. It's pure early 2000s fun. All bouncy, playful, and iconic. Ellie eats it up, flirty and sassy. Javi is singing along with an enormous grin on his face.

Rez walks off and cuts through the crowd. He walks right up to Knox, mid-performance. I squint.

"What's he doing?"

Lex, arms still slung around my shoulders, snorts. "Who the fuck knows."

The guys talk for a second. Rez says something low, Knox raises a brow and then lets out this laugh that practically screams *bad idea accepted*. They do one of those bro handshake-high-five–pull-you-in things that's way too choreographed for comfort.

Knox runs a hand through his hair, already hyped, muttering, *"You're a fucking menace, man,"* like that's a compliment. Rez just walks back toward us, smug as hell.

Lex stares at him. "What was that all about?"

Rez grins. "You'll see soon enough."

Lex's jaw tightens. I feel it in the way his arm locks just a little tighter across my chest. The song ends. The crowd loses it. Javi is beaming, chest puffed like he just won coach of the millennium.

Knox grabs the mic again. "Alright, Javi! Happy damn birthday, you little legend. Now Bella, sweetheart, don't go too far..."

Bella freezes mid-step, caught on her way backstage. She turns slowly, eyes narrowing.

Knox keeps going. "You've got a request. One of our guests wants a dance and I couldn't say no."

Lex's whole body tenses beside me. "No the fuck he didn't."

Rez steps back into the light, all swagger and smug satisfaction. Bella blinks, caught off guard. He leans in, mouth close to her ear, and whispers something to her. Whatever he says pulls a real laugh from her, bright and unguarded.

Knox waves them into place. "Alright you two, don't make me regret this... *Danza Kuduro,* let's go!"

The beat slams through the Catacombs. Bella and Rez move like they've done this a thousand times. All hips, hands, tight turns and locked eyes. Latin dance with a street edge. She dips, he spins her. She rolls her hips, he mirrors it move for move.

"He can dance?" I ask, stunned.

Lex groans. "Yeah. His mom was big in ballroom back in Moscow. Fucking unfair."

I nod slowly, watching Bella absolutely own it. "Yeah, but that? That's not rehearsed."

"Nope. That's pure improv. Fucking Rez and our girl, damn."

Rez drags his hands down her arms, their bodies brushing too close. She's grinning, flushed, and glowing. That kind of happy that only happens when she's in her element. The music pulses into a rapid cha-cha, hips locking and snapping, feet moving in sharp, flirtatious sync. It's fast, hot, full of turns and playful tension, every beat matched with a flick of her wrist or a dip that nearly sends her to the floor.

Knox is cracking up. "Holy Russian shit, Rez! Bestie, your boy's got moves!"

Lex groans again. "I'm gonna kill him."

Knox leans into the mic. "Ladies, time to go get ready for Haley's birthday surprise."

"You good?" I ask, passing him a beer.

He chugs half, wipes his mouth, and growls, "I swear to God, if Haley's present is anything like what I'm imagining, I'm gonna need ice packs. Plural."

After a song or two, I hear Knox through the beat. "Okay, Wexley, I hope y'all are ready, because this next performance is a personal request from our resident redheaded heart breaker. And my baby said go big or go the fuck home."

The lights dim. The bass hits right as the girls step back out. Bella and Ellie in plunging black one-pieces cut so deep they flirt with scandal. Slits down to their damn belly buttons, torn fishnets painted across long, toned legs, and knee-high boots that strike the ground like a fucking drumbeat. Their eyes are smoky, hair wild. Untamed halos of heat and hunger. They don't just look like sin... they wear it like armor.

Haley's in the same cut, but hers is blood red, criminally bold, the kind of color that doesn't just turn heads but instead owns the room. She's pure disruption, grinning like she lit the match and dares you to ask what's burning.

Lex chokes beside me. "I called it. Go get the ice packs."

I grin. "They do look good."

"Good?" he barks. "The girls look like every filthy thought I've ever had and I've had more than my share."

Javi's already laughing and shaking his head when the girls drag him out to the chair center stage. He tries to protest, but it's no use. Haley plants a kiss on his cheek and he goes red.

"Ok Javi, here's a special fusion straight from Haley's brain to your bloodstream."

It's filthy. A hurricane of hips and legs and hair and attitude. They surround Javi like he's prey and they're the wolves. Bella runs her hand down her own thigh. Ellie licks her lips. Haley spins, drops low, and then pops up with a wink that sends the whole place into a meltdown.

Chase saunters over with DeShawn, both whistling low.

"Yo," Chase says, eyes locked on Ellie. "The fuck y'all feeding these girls?"

"Violence and glitter," I tell him.

DeShawn elbows Lex. "Damn, Barinov. That's your wifey up there? Shit."

Lex doesn't even blink. "Yeah. Keep your paws off or I'll break your fingers."

DeShawn laughs. "Heard."

Lex exhales like he's being tortured. "I swear on every Black Book in this world, I'm not making it to the end of the night. You better hold me back if she comes off that stage looking at me like that."

"You want me to hold you back or hold you down, babe?"

Lex shrugs, eyes never leaving her. "Both."

The lights flash. The song ends. Javi is blushing so hard I think he might pass out.

Knox's voice cuts through the noise like a firework, "All right, Wolves, dance floor's open! Let's make this place pulse!"

"Badd" by the Ying Yang Twins starts booming through The Catacombs and the dance floor fills. Lex doesn't say a word. Just knocks back a shot, grabs my hand, and pulls me toward the floor with that look on his face. That *mine* look.

Yeah, I know it well.

Bella's already moving, hips still riding the rhythm from that last set, hair wild, eyes glowing. Lex catches her by the waist and pulls her flush against him. His mouth drops to her ear. I can't hear what he says, but whatever it is makes her smile and laugh.

Then she leans back, hooks her arm around his neck, and says loud enough for both of us, "Yeah... but I'm your bad bitch."

Lex leans in to kiss her, his hand gripping her jaw, thumb brushing her cheek, and then he's sucking on her bottom lip, biting just enough to make her gasp.

My dick twitches just watching them. God, it's been so long. Too damn long since I've felt her this close. Since I've had both of them like this. The heat. The chaos. The way we fit. I missed this. I missed her, missed us.

She spins, grabs my shirt in both fists, and yanks me into the fire. Our lips crash, fast and messy, and I swear I taste tequila and trouble. Her hands are in my hair. Mine are already on her waist. Lex moves in behind her, sliding his palm up her spine, and suddenly the three of us are pressed together, moving as one.

Her hips grind into me, then into him, then into both of us. Lex kisses her shoulder, growls something low into her neck. She laughs and throws her head back like she was made for this.

I can't stop touching her. Lex leans forward, grabs my jaw, and kisses me like a promise. Then he's back on her, hands everywhere, and I'm right there with him. We're on fire. No rules. No shame. No space.

We're still tangled up in each other when Rez shows up on the dance floor with DeShawn and Chase, each of them holding two shots like they've just walked out of a damn music video.

"Gentlemen," Rez grins, handing a shot to Lex, one to me, and the last to Bella. "And Bella." He winks at her, the cocky bastard.

He raises his glass. "To Lex and Cade, for having the sexiest and deadliest woman in this whole damn city. You ever let her go, I'm first in line."

Bella rolls her eyes but she's grinning. Lex growls something under his breath, but we all clink glasses and knock the shots back.

It burns.

Worth it.

Knox's voice crackles over the speakers again. "Alright, ladies, it's time to get ready for Bella's fusion. Let's make it unforgettable."

Lex doesn't miss a beat. He catches her by the waist, pulls her in tight, and whispers something against her skin, something I can't hear that makes her laugh. Loud and real. The kind of laugh that sounds like a damn miracle after everything she's been through.

She turns to me, eyes soft but sparkling. "I'll be right back," she says, placing her empty shot glass in my hand.

Lex grips Rez's shoulder with a nod. "Appreciate you making the trip, cousin. Wouldn't have felt right without you here."

Rez gives him a chin lift, voice low. "Wouldn't miss it. Bella on that floor? Damn."

DeShawn claps Lex on the back, laughing. "Yeah, I swear she had you moving faster than I've ever seen."

Lex smirks. "She keeps me sharp. But don't get it twisted, I'm still the one running The Pit."

Chase whistles low, shaking his head. "King of the Pit, sure. But letting Rez spin her around like that?"

Lex's laugh is dark, unbothered. "Spin her, dip her, whatever, doesn't matter. I'm the one she screams for when the music stops."

I lean back, watching them talk like war buddies post-battle, all while pretending they aren't secretly terrified of the girls about to walk back out here.

Knox steps up, grinning like he's about to cause an earthquake.

"Alright," he calls out, voice cutting through the noise. "We've had some flirty... and some sexy... millennial fusions tonight, but this one? This one's gonna be the dirtiest."

Lex, arms crossed beside me, lets out a low whistle. "Now we're talking."

DeShawn shouts from behind us, "Why the hell have you never brought us here before, Lex?!"

Lex shrugs, smug as shit. "Didn't wanna ruin y'all."

Knox laughs into the mic. "Some of you might know that our girls don't just own The Row. They also own Northvale's Pit."

The reaction is immediate. The Hollow Kings lose their damn minds. Lex fist pumps the air like this is fight night and Bella just laid someone out with a blade to the jugular.

Knox keeps it going. "So Rico's been busting his ass getting these girls some brand-new outfits for fight night. Wanna see 'em?"
The place goes wild. Knox throws a hand toward the curtain. "Then bring 'em back out... Lex's Knockout Queens, The Trifecta!"

Holy hell. They walk out, and I swear the floor shakes.

Cut-off jean shorts that barely qualify as legal. Black cowboy boots stomping like a warning. And the tops? God help us all. Ellie's in a tiny yellow halter that says *"Rez Wrecked Me"* across the front. Rez is howling, damn near tears in his eyes.

Haley's is lime green with *"Why Choose?"* in glitter, complete with Sharpie arrows. One pointing left that says *Chase*, the other to the right that says *DeShawn*. The boys lose it. DeShawn's laughing so hard he nearly drops his beer.

But then Bella steps out and Lex stops breathing. Red. Fiery. Blinding. Sinful. And across her chest, bold black letters scream, *"Lex's Bitch."*

Lex stares, eyes narrowed at her like he's ready to throw hands with anyone who looks too long. "I'm gonna fucking explode."

I laugh. "In your pants?"

"In my soul," he hisses.

Knox throws his hands up as the crowd starts chanting. "And now," Knox shouts over the mic, "Nickelback, baby. A filthy mashup of some of their greatest hits."

The beat slams—gritty, heavy, unapologetic—and my heart punches my ribs. She did this for me. Nickelback. My favorite band. My guilty pleasure, my no-shame soundtrack.

She remembered.

The girls own the stage like they've got a patent on lust and I'm gone. Absolutely fucking gone.

Lex groans beside me, tilting his head back like he's in physical pain. "Fucking Canadian rockers corrupting my soul. I swear to God, Cade, I'm about five seconds from dragging her off that stage and letting the song finish without her."

I watch her look over, straight at us and smile.

"Make it three," I counter.

CHAPTER ⑧⓪
LEX
THE CATACOMBS
ABOUT TO MURDER CALLUM WHITMORE... AGAIN.
63 DAYS SINCE HENRY'S DEATH

The last beat of the Nickelback mashup slams into the floor like a meteor. The crowd's still roaring when Knox steps up to the mic again.

"Trifecta, stay on the floor."

The girls freeze and then all three of them start laughing as three burgundy and black high-top tables are wheeled onto the dance floor.

Cade leans in. "Are they gonna dance on the tables?"

"Holy hell, these girls... goddamn."

Knox grins like a demon. "Ladies, you know what time it is."

They each step behind one of the tables. The crowd roars louder as three of Wexley's finest start strutting out—Callum, August, and the tight end, Jalen.

They each take a spot in front of a girl, and of fucking course, Callum goes to Bella's table. Then three Legacy girls come out carrying trays stacked with neon-colored shot glasses, ten on each tray.

Cade stiffens beside me, eyes locked on Bella. "This is not going to end well. Last time she took shots with Cal, they ended up skinny-dipping in the Hamptons."

"The fuck they did."

"Relax, babe. It was years ago. And technically, I think it was her idea."

Knox is grinning like a lunatic. "Wexley, it's time to find out if our Trifecta can out drink some of our big, bad Wolves!"

"Big, bad fucking mistake," I mutter.

"Shots" by Lil Jon hits like a brick wall. The lights flicker red. The first round goes down like liquid fire and the crowd screams: "ONE!"

The girls grind up against their football players like this is foreplay and the shots are the warm-up. Bella's got her back to Callum's chest, dancing to the beat, her head tilted, laughing. He leans down to say something in her ear, and I swear to God I see red. Haley's practically straddling Jalen now. Ellie's got August eating out of her hand, literally.

The second shot hits. "TWO!"

I'm gripping my cup so tight it might snap. Cade puts a hand on my shoulder.

"She's just having fun," he says gently, but his eyes are on Callum too.

By the third shot, Bella drops to her knees in front of him when the song talks about sucking cocks. The crowd goes nuclear as Callum pours a shot straight into her mouth and then throws his head back to down his own.

"THREE!"

"Three," I mutter. "Fucking three."

Cade barely glances at me, already reading the tension in my jaw.

"How many more until we hit Hamptons level?" I snap, the words edged with ice.

He lifts a brow. "Four, maybe five. Depends if that's bourbon or tequila in those shot glasses."

I glare across the room as Callum grabs another. "Cool," I grit. "Guess I'll start digging Cal's grave now."

Rez appears beside me. "Man, seems like everyone in this damn place wants a piece of Bella's ass."

"I'll fucking kill them all," I growl.

Rez laughs. "Relax. She's yours. Look at her damn tits, Lex… She's yours."

"SHOTS!" Cheers erupt from the crowd singing along to the song.

Shot four. The girls are grinding again, sweaty, wild, an un-fucking-touchable.

The floor pulses. "FOUR!"

Cade exhales hard. "Four."

I nod once. "One more and we're pulling her off the damn table."

He smirks, but there's zero humor in it. "You or me?"

I crack my neck. "We'll flip a coin."

Cade laughs and shakes his head. "Hope Cal's wearing a cup."

Bella's legs are around Callum's waist as he lifts her in the air, spinning her like a prize. Ellie's laughing, her head thrown back in August's arms. Haley's got Jalen by the jaw and is whispering something I'm sure is insanely filthy.

"FIVE!"

Cade mutters, "We've officially entered Hamptons level."

"If she takes that top off, I'm throwing hands. And then a table. And then Cal off the roof."

I'm about to rip the floor up, but then Bella's eyes flick to me just for a second and she smiles. And it's like everything else disappears. All the noise, the bodies, the chaos. She sees me. Only me. The tension in my chest eases.

Yeah, this party's out of control. Yeah, I want to body check Callum through the fucking wall. But our girl is taking her life back. And fuck... she's never looked hotter.

Buzz, Buzz

DAD: Your girl's probably going to need to be carried out of here. But goddamn, you picked a good one.

I snort, biting back a grin. "Yeah. I know."

He's standing in the shadows by the bar, disguised in jeans and a fitted jacket like he's just another partier. After the masquerade, there was no chance in hell I was letting her walk into this place without backup. So yeah, my dad's here. Watching. Guarding.

Knox opens the dance floor back up. Rez sprints out first like the cocky bastard he is, grabbing Bella by the waist and spinning her around like he owns her. She laughs—head thrown back, eyes lit up— and for a split second, the rage is back.

"Fuck that shit," I growl, already moving.

Cade's hand clamps down on my arm.

"Lex. Give them a minute," he says low in my ear. "He's your family and they're friends. You should've seen how much work they did together for your Donor Fight."

I grit my teeth. I watch Rez plant himself behind her and start grinding. I can't breathe. My hands ball into fists. My girl, my fucking girl, is letting him. She's laughing, sweaty, glowing, letting the music take her like it's nothing.

By the second chorus, I'm done. "Can I go now?"

"Go get our girl."

I bolt. Cross the floor in four strides and grab her by the waist, yanking her out of Rez's hands and spinning her around to face me. Her eyes go wide, then dark as her smile spreads.

"Yeah, malyshka. You know what time it is." I pull her against me, grinding with her to the beat, hands gripping her hips like handles. Cade slides in behind her, all smooth and heat, hands already in her hair.

"Goddamn, you look so good," I murmur, biting at her earlobe. "You know I almost decked him for that, right?"

She laughs, breath hot in my mouth. "I was just dancing."

Cade pulls her hair aside and kisses her neck. She moans low and dirty right against my lips.

I groan. "Bourbon?"

She nods and jumps up, arms locking around my neck, legs cinching my waist. Her cowboy boots smack my thighs as she grinds against me, like she's riding me in our bed and not in the middle of a dance floor with half of Wexley watching.

Cade's watching her too, eating it up. His eyes are blazing and his dick is probably hard as concrete.

Yeah, our girl's feelin' it now. Tipsy, high off the night.

She's back.

Rico, our resident rhinestone warlock and part-time hydration fairy, comes sprinting across the dance floor like a man on a mission. He's got a tray of water bottles in hand and muttering something about electrolytes and lawsuits. He doesn't stop moving, just tosses one bottle to each of the girls with damn near perfect precision.

"Hydrate or die, bitches!" he shouts.

Without missing a beat, all three of them raise their bottles and chorus back in unison, "Yes, Dad!"

They blow him kisses and start chugging like their lives depend on it. Bella leans back just enough to drink without spilling, still wrapped around me like a fucking vice. I don't let her go. Not even a little. She finishes the water, wipes her mouth with the back of her hand.

She leans in close, lips brushing my ear as her arms tighten around my neck.

"I have a surprise for you," she whispers, all soft and sweet, with something devilish hiding underneath it.

"What is it?"

Her smile curves against my jaw. "Shhh," she teases, breath warm. "I'm not supposed to tell."

Then she giggles—*giggles*—and that damn Southern accent starts slipping through like honey seeping into cracked wood.

"You'll see soon enough, baby."

God damn it, I love her. Out of the corner of my eye, I catch something moving. Josh, Drake, and Sam wheeling something big up the corridor of The Catacombs, trying to be sneaky but failing miserably.

Knox's voice blares over the speakers, smug as hell. "We have a special king in the building tonight..." The lights shift, a spotlight sweeping over and stopping on me. "Mr. Lex Barinov, leader of our distinguished guests... the Hollow Kings."

Cade claps a hand on my back, grinning. Bella's trying to hold it together, biting her lip like she's not the one who planned all this.

"And I think it's time," Knox adds, "that he gets himself a goddamn chair."

"About fucking time," I mutter, cracking my neck.

Bella snorts and covers her mouth, shaking her head. "You're impossible."

The Row boys start screaming, losing their minds as the three Trifecta stunt dudes wheel something out from the shadows.

"The rain stage?" I ask, eyes narrowing.

"Surprise!" she squeals.

The guys roll it into place, center of the floor, that slick, raised platform with mist sprayers lining the edges. A single chair gets set in the middle and Knox calls out again.

"Alright, King Barinov. Get your ass up on that throne."

I move to go, but Bella grabs my hand and yells for the whole combs to hear, "What are the rules of my chairs, King Barinov?"

I grin. Slow. Dirty. Then reach down and strip my shirt off, dragging it over my head, baring every scar, every fight, every inch of Bratva ink under the spotlight.

The screams get louder. Bella catches my shirt one-handed and waves it like a victory flag. She tosses it to Cade, then saunters up behind me, her boots echoing off the platform.

I drop into the chair, legs wide, body humming. I lean back, spread my arms along the edge of the chair like I own the damn world.

Bella climbs the stage with that fucking look, the one that says you're mine, and I know that I'm already fucked. Then she turns to the crowd, hands on her hips.

"I need a belt!"

"What did you just say, baby?"

The crowd screams. August's already halfway up the platform, grinning like the devil child he is. He unbuckles his belt and hands it over with a bow.

"Anything for you, Queen Bella."

"Thanks, Augie," she purrs. Then hands it off to Ellie with a wink.

My heart's pounding now. "Baby... what are you doing?"

Ellie leans down, brushing her hair over one shoulder as she whispers instructions into my ear. She tightens the belt around my wrists, snug behind the chair.

"Got it, Lex?" Ellie asks.

I nod once.

"Alright, Wexley..." Bella says, voice like gasoline on an open flame. "It's officially time for a *Love Game*."

The place erupts. The water kicks on, mist and rain soaking everything in seconds. The synth hits fills the air, bass thick enough to crush a ribcage.

Fuck. Me. The girls circle me. Bella front and center. Ellie to my left, Haley to my right. Fingertips dragging over my shoulders and chest, teasing and claiming. Bella sinks between my knees completely drenched. She's glowing, her eyes gleaming like she already knows exactly how I'll break.

She slides her hands up my thighs. Her nails scratch across my jeans, right over the bulge that's aching now, and I swear to God if there weren't 200 people watching I'd rip through these restraints and—

"Un-fucking-tie me," I growl.

Haley leans down, puts her lips to my ear. "Shhh..." she whispers. "Be a good King."

They keep moving. Teasing and grinding around me. Ellie and Haley's hands are everywhere, my chest, my hair, my neck.

And fucking Bella... she's between my legs, her fingers closing around my cock over my jeans. She squeezes, once, twice and my hips jerk. My breath leaves my body in a sharp hiss.

She doesn't stop. I'm not gonna make it. Every second is agony. Sweet, torturous heaven. I can't hear shit except the thunder of the beat and the heat of her body pressed between my legs.

As the song winds toward the end, Ellie steps behind me. Her breath is hot against my ear. "You remember what to do?"

I nod as Ellie starts to untie the belt.

Bella takes a step back. I rise. The chair creaks as I stand, slow and predatory. Water pouring over my shoulders, the belt falling away, hitting the stage with a wet slap.

She keeps backing up, step by step, like a dare. My boots echo over the platform, stalking her in time with the rhythm.

I take one step forward.

She takes one step back.

The smirk on her lips grows, like she's not scared, like she's starving for me to catch her. The lights flare blood-red.

Her voice cuts through the air, *"A LOVE GAME!"*

That's it. I lunge. She squeals as I grab her. My hands slide under her thighs as I hoist her up, legs locking around my waist like they fucking belong there.

She's drenched, panting, laughing, and then I kiss her. No. I devour her. Mouths clashing. Tongues tangled. Her hands in my wet hair, tugging. My fingers grip her thighs so tight they'll leave bruises.

And she loves it.

The rain hits harder. Steam rises off our bodies. Her head drops back as I kiss down her throat, teeth scraping her skin, biting into the edge of her collarbone like a claim. She's moaning in my arms for all of Wexley to see.

Ellie and Haley dance around us like sirens, spinning, flipping their hair, lost in the beat, but all I see is her.

The room explodes. The chant hits before Knox can even finish the damn announcement. "HOLLOW KINGS! HOLLOW KINGS!"

The floor shakes. The Catacombs roar. And I swear for a second, I forget I'm soaked, fucking hard, and on the verge of taking my girl on this stage in front of everyone.

Because all I can do is look.

Bella's still in my arms, breathing heavy, smiling like she owns the fucking world. Ellie and Haley spin around us, glitter catching the lights like fire. The boys from The Row are banging on the rails, the Kings are chanting along with The Order, and Knox's voice is drowned out by sound.

And I realize, they did this. This war that's been boiling for years—Northvale vs. Wexley, Titans vs. Wolves, Hollow Kings vs. The fucking Order? These girls squashed it.

All of us... Rez. Callum. August. DeShawn. Knox. Chase. Me and Cade. We're all here, together. The Trifecta didn't just start a movement, they fused kingdoms.

I press my lips to her temple, still holding her like a lifeline. "Fuck, baby," I whisper, voice rough with pride. "You realize you girls turned a rivalry into a reign?"

Knox's voice rips through, still laughing from the chants. "How about tonight, y'all?!"

Three chairs are brought out to the end of the dance floor.

"Ladies," Knox grins, "we need you to take your seats. So yeah, King Barinov... you're gonna have to put her down."

She looks at me with that wicked little smile, teeth on her bottom lip.

"This isn't another Magic Mike thing, right?" I mutter as I set her down, reluctantly.

She just winks. The girls strut to their chairs and sit down.

Cade walks over and leans in close, lips grazing mine. "You look like you want to devour her."

"I want to do a hell of a lot more than that," I growl back, pulling him in for a kiss. "To both of you."

He smiles and wraps his arms around my waist.

"Ok everyone! In just a few days, these queens fly out to Dallas for Nationals!"

The crowd screams. Whistles. Chants. Someone even rings a damn cowbell.

"And here at Wexley," Knox continues, "school spirit is mandatory as fuck. So, our Wolves... they've got something to say to their girls."

"I Believe That We Will Win!" Pitbull's remix slams through the speakers.

Callum, August, and the rest of the Wexley football team explode out onto the floor like it's game day at Kingsley Field. Full-blown hype mode. They form a circle around The Trifecta, jumping and chanting. Bella puts a hand over her heart, eyes glassy.

Cade nudges me, shouting over the music. "We doing this or what, King?"

We both charge the floor, barging into the circle, grab Bella and lift her off the ground as the chant builds around us. Ellie's crying from laughter. Haley's screaming with joy. I look over to see Rico and Javi smiling from ear to ear, wiping tears out of their eyes.

"Now this is how you hype up a dance team," Rez says walking up to me and joining in the on the chaos.

Home - about to finally give Little Lex the release he's wanted for fucking ever!
64 Days Since Henry's Death

She's slung over my shoulder like a sack of tipsy, glitter-drenched potatoes, singing what I think is Luke Bryan but might also be a hymn. Or a threat. Hard to say with that accent of hers curling around every note.

"She always get this southern when she's wasted?" I ask as I unlock the apartment, steadying her with one arm.

"Only when she's drunk and safe," Cade mutters, hauling the duffels behind me. "Last time I heard it this strong was back in Nashville."

I grin, because yeah, tonight was a fucking win. Our girl laughed, danced, owned every inch of The Catacombs. She was fire. She was back. I carry her into the bedroom and she mumbles something about bourbon and boots before flopping onto the mattress face-down, still in my hoodie and her leather shorts.

"She gonna get under the covers?" Cade asks.

"She was," I mutter, brushing hair off her cheek. "Now? Dead to the world."

We exchange a look, the one that says we've been waiting all goddamn night to finally touch her. After the dances, after *Love Game,* after her cowboy boots dug into my back while she moaned into my mouth.

My cock twitches.

Cade groans.

"Five minutes," I say. "We grab the rest of her shit, come back, wake her up soft. Real soft."

"Deal."

We sprint down to the car like two dudes chasing a holy relic, grab The Trifecta's luggage mountain, and drag it all back up. I'm sweating. Cade's cursing. But we're hyped. Ready.

And then I open the door. She's curled on her side, snuggled in my hoodie, one boot still on.

Dead.

Ass.

Asleep.

Mouth open. One arm hanging off the bed. A little snore. I just stand there, staring at her. Cade walks in behind me, sees the scene, and literally wilts.

"You've got to be kidding me."

"Yeah, I'm gonna punch a wall."

"She moaned my name like two hours ago, Lex."

"She rode me like a mechanical bull to Ludacris, Cade."

We both just stare. Then I sigh, step forward, and slowly pull off her other boot. She doesn't move. Cade gently covers her with the blanket. She snuggles deeper into the pillow, letting out a tiny content hum.

I press a kiss to her temple and whisper, "Sleep, baby." Then I turn around and adjust a very angry Little Lex like a soldier defeated.

Cade's right behind me, muttering, "Blue balls are a hate crime."

We fall into bed beside her, staring up at the ceiling in silence.

"So, you wanna rock-paper-scissors for who gets the cold shower first?" Cade whispers.

"Fuck that. We both suffer."

CHAPTER ⑧⑴
BELLA
HOME
64 DAYS SINCE DADDY'S DEATH

"Is she dead?" Knox's voice rings out from the kitchen, way too loud for someone not being murdered.

"No," Cade says, pouring himself a cup of coffee. "She groaned when I opened the blinds. Then threatened my bloodline."

"She's alive," Lex mutters, padding down the hall shirtless, still towel-damp with a hand raking through his hair. "Just currently in a bourbon-and-glitter-induced coma. Caused by way too many shots, rainwater, and one too many lap dances."

Knox snorts. "Y'all were five seconds from banging on the dance floor. Again."

"She was... enthusiastic," Cade laughs.

"Enthusiastic?" Lex scoffs. "She bit me, Cade."

Knox tosses a gummy worm at him. "You looked like you were gonna break the floorboards of the damn rain stage. Spontaneous combustion is real."

Lex shrugs, rubbing the back of his neck. "I'm fine. Not sure about my jeans though."

"Pretty sure Bella's the one who shredded them," Cade adds, casual.

Lex grins. "Worth it."

My phone buzzes violently on the nightstand, followed by more, then more. I groan from under a mountain of pillows, one eye barely cracking open.

ELLIE: Um... where is Bella?

HALEY: Yeah, group chat is sooo DEAD without her.

ELLIE: Also?

ELLIE: Why did I wake up in DeShawn's shirt??

HALEY: Girl, you STRIPPED YOURSELF on the Pit mat.

ELLIE: Lies.

HALEY: Rez had to cover your ass with a Trifecta fight night banner.

KNOX: Confirmed. I have the video.

ELLIE: You're all fake as hell for letting me live like this.

LEX: She's still passed out.

ELLIE: UGH. I miss her chaos.

ELLIE: Also… do we think I'm dating DeShawn now?

HALEY: You literally proposed and kissed his biceps.

ELLIE: SHUT UP

HALEY: It was lowkey romantic.

CADE: Correction Hales, it was lowkey creepy.

Footsteps thud outside the room. The door creaks open and Lex pokes his head in, smirk locked and loaded. Cade follows, armed with a water bottle and a bag of sour gummy worms.

I groan from the blankets. "No."

"Dramatic much?" Lex says, strolling in. "You danced for six hours, took who knows how many shots, and rode me like a damn rodeo queen in front of half of New York."

"You make it sound like a felony," I croak.

"Oh, it was," he says, flopping down beside me. "Still recovering. I'm pretty sure I pulled a hip."

Cade gently pulls the covers down and hands me the water.

"Hydrate or die, bitch," Lex says in his best Rico impression.

I glare and whisper, "Everything's too loud. Even your jawline is loud."

Lex barks a laugh. "You'll live."

I sigh, cracking the bottle open. "This is what victory feels like? Bourbon and bruises."

They settle in beside me, heat radiating on both sides like living heating pads. Lex draws lazy circles on my thigh.

Cade kisses my hairline. "We canceled everything today," he says softly.

"We leave for Nationals in a couple days," Lex adds. "Thought we'd hang, pack, maybe watch Ellie spiral about her new fake fiancé."

"Oh my God," I groan into Cade's shoulder. "That's gonna be a whole-ass telenovela."

Cade grins. "With fight rings instead of wedding rings."

Lex deadpans, "Til bruises do us part."

I laugh, then wince. "Ow. Even my laugh is hungover."

The door creaks open again, because Knox doesn't believe in knocking. He just strolls right in, sunglasses already on, backpack slung over one shoulder. "Alright, I'm out," he announces. "See you degenerates at the airport." He eyes me sprawled like a corpse. "Bella, sweetie... try not to barf on anything important. Like Cade's shirts. Or Lex's ego."

With a groan, I blindly grab the nearest weapon—my water bottle—and hurl it at his head. It thuds against the door frame.

"Whoa! Friendly fire!" Knox ducks, laughing. "Look likes your arm is still working. Impressive."

I flip him off. "Get out," I croak, burrowing deeper into the blanket.

"Love you too," he calls as he backs down the hallway. "Remember, hydration and vibes only, bitch." The door clicks shut behind him.

Lex snorts. "He's lucky you didn't hit him."

"Please. If I wanted to hit him, he'd still be on the floor. I was aiming for his ego," I mutter, curling into Cade's side like a hungover goblin.

Cade stretches beside me, rubbing the sleep from his eyes. "You want me to make you something to eat?"

"Oh my God. Yes. Anything greasy and terrible for me. Bonus points if it's covered in syrup and regret."

He bends down to kiss my temple. "Back in a few, sweetheart."

I watch him walk out shirtless, yawning, muscles flexing with every lazy stretch. I'm already picturing pancakes, bacon, hash browns, the works.

The second the door shuts, Lex props himself up on one elbow, eyes glinting, mouth already curved with that unmistakable look. The look that says there is trouble brewing and he's fully aware of it.

"Damn, baby..." he drawls.

I blink at him. "What now?"

He reaches out, brushing hair off my face, knuckles grazing my cheek like he's trying to kill me with slow affection. "You were so sexy last night. That damn top? Lex's Bitch?" He groans like he's physically in pain. "I nearly lost it. I was five seconds from pulling you off that table and fucking you over the DJ booth."

I laugh, voice still scratchy. "We'd get banned from The Row."

"We'd get crowned, more like it." He leans in, mouth brushing my jaw. "And get this, my dad saw it."

"Wait. What?"

He grins. "Yeah. He was there. Lurking in the shadows like a Bond villain. Said, and I quote, *'My son's girl might need to be carried out, but at least she's the hottest one in the building,'* or some shit like that."

I smack his chest. "Lex! You didn't tell me your father was watching!"

He shrugs like it's nothing. "He was impressed."

I groan, burying my face in my hands. "That makes two of them. Roman was there too."

Lex rears back. "Excuse me?! Why was that fucker there?"

"Chill, baby. He was doing his whole mafia-Batman thing. Perched near the exit, glaring at anyone who breathed near me."

Lex blinks, then snorts. "What the fuck kind of weird parent trap spin-off shit did we end up creating?"

We both start laughing. Which is a mistake. Laughing hurts. Everything hurts. But I'm still giggling when he slides closer, pressing a kiss to my neck.

His hand slips under the hoodie I stole last night—his hoodie, oversized and warm and totally mine now. "Seeing you in this does things to me, baby."

"I'm literally dying," I mutter. "My soul is ninety percent bourbon and bad decisions."

"And yet you're still the hottest fucking thing in this city."

He pulls the hoodie up, exposing my bare skin, and lets out a low groan. His mouth finds my collarbone, kissing lower, dragging his tongue over the edge of my breast until his lips close over my nipple. My gasp echoes, sharp and needy, as my fingers thread into his hair.

He groans into my skin. "You're gonna kill me, baby. I swear to God, you're gonna end me."

"You sound so sad about it."

"I'll die with a smile," he growls, sliding a hand down to grip my thigh.

Just as I arch into him—

"Well, that's just rude."

We both freeze.

Cade stands in the doorway holding a full plate like a disappointed husband who just walked in on his cheating wife. "Didn't even wait for me? Sent me off to make you food while you guys jump each other's bones without me."

Lex lifts his head. "You made pancakes?"

Cade rolls his eyes. "Yes. For her. Not for your sex-demon-ass."

I yank the hoodie back down, cheeks on fire. "It wasn't... I mean technically we didn't finish, or start really."

"Uh-huh." Cade hands me the plate and flops down beside us.

I immediately inhale a strip of bacon like I've been starved for months. "God, I love you," I mumble around the grease.

He kisses my cheek. "Love you too, sweetheart."

Lex wipes his mouth and drapes an arm around my waist, smug. "Ditto."

We eat in sleepy silence, sun streaking across the bed, our legs tangled like it's just another lazy morning.

Cade licks syrup off his fork. "So, what exactly should we expect at Nationals?"

I pause mid-bite, raise an eyebrow. "Pain. Glitter. Probably Hales getting into a fight with someone's mom."

"And my sister?" he asks.

"Oh, she'll cry backstage, threaten to quit, then pull off a perfect triple flip into a death drop like the drama queen she is."

Lex grins. "Can't wait."

"Yeah, Nationals is no joke." I take another bite of pancake, swallow hard. "It's two full days. Big groups and solos only dance once. They win, they go to Worlds."

I exhale, leaning back against the headboard. "But trios and duos? You have to kill it on day one and land in the top three just to earn a shot to dance again on day two. Then on day two, you have to win first place before you can make it to Worlds."

Lex raises an eyebrow, swirling syrup on the plate. "So no pressure at all. Just survive the bloodbath, then do it again, only flawlessly on a bigger stage with judges breathing down your neck." He leans in and winks. "Good thing pressure looks good on you, baby."

"And the guest judge?" I groan, stabbing my pancake like it owes me money. "Fucking Alejandro Miguel Santibañez. The Latin dance god. The man could choreograph a salsa with his eyes closed and still make it sexier than half the shit we've done all season."

They both look at me like I'm speaking in a foreign language.

"Ugh! He's only one of the biggest Latin choreographers in the world. He's a living legend. I'm so nervous! Especially since the Trifecta's doing two Latin numbers. If we screw up even a little, he'll see it."

Cade sets down his fork and looks at me with those damn hazel eyes. "Hey, sweetheart. You're ready for this. You girls have trained harder than anyone I've ever seen. He's not gonna see a flaw, Bella. He's going to see fire."

Home
Later that Night

Cade's dinner was insanely delicious. Some creamy garlic pasta that melted in my mouth, a crisp lemony salad, and homemade bread that made me moan indecently at the table.

He just raised an eyebrow and said, "Told you I remembered your favorite."

Now we're camped out on the couch like heathens with a movie playing that none of us are actually watching. My feet are in Cade's lap. Lex is behind me, sprawled out, one arm draped over the back cushion the other around my waist. His fingers drift lazily across my shoulder, tracing invisible lines. I melt into the touch, eyes fluttering closed.

"You full, baby?" Lex murmurs, voice low against my neck.

"Stuffed," I whisper, barely able to breathe.

He chuckles. "Not yet, you're not."

I feel Cade tense a little beside me with anticipation as Lex's hand slides down skimming my collarbone, then lower, slipping beneath the edge of the hoodie. His palm brushes the curve of my waist and I lean back into him like muscle memory. He presses a kiss just below my ear.

Cade watches us in silence, his fingers tightening on my ankle like he's holding back. I reach for him and that's all it takes.

Lex grips my hips, pulling me further onto his lap as Cade leans in from the front. They take turns fiercely kissing me, hungry for more. Cade shifts his weight, his fingers curling around the hem of Lex's hoodie, my hoodie now, and lifts it slow. Inch by inch. My bare skin catching the light.

Nothing underneath.

Lex sees it and groans like I just knocked the wind out of him. His hands are on me instantly, sliding over my ribs, up my back, his mouth following in hot, open kisses.

"God, malyshka," he breathes against my spine, every word

vibrating against me. "I need you so fucking bad right now."

I tilt my neck, offering it to him like a dare. "Then what are you waiting for, King?"

He growls—*actually fucking growls*—and scoops me into his arms. Cade's already up, following with that quiet intensity in his hazel eyes. The kind that makes my whole body hum.

Lex sets me down at the edge of the bed, his hands lingering as he pulls back just long enough to strip off his shirt. Cade does the same. I slide back across the bed, propped up on my elbows, letting them look at me. Letting them want me.

Lex climbs onto the bed from one side, Cade from the other. Two sets of hands, two sets of fingers trailing all over my body leaving hundreds of goosebumps in their wakes. Two mouths kissing up my legs, my hips, my stomach like I'm something holy. Like they've been fasting for months and I'm their first taste.

Cade presses a kiss just beneath my belly button, then another, slower. My breath hitches. Cade's fingers hook into the waistband of my shorts and drag them down, his lips trailing after them in slow, reverent kisses down my thighs. My head falls back against the pillow as Lex takes my hand, lacing our fingers together and placing a small kiss on the writing on my wrist.

The silk sheets kiss against my skin like cool water, every inch a reminder that I'm bare, open, theirs. Cade's hands slide up my thighs. His mouth is heat and heaven, tongue flicking, licking, and sucking. He groans like the taste of me is the only thing keeping him alive. He sucks in my clit, gently, slowly, and bites just enough to make me cry out in ecstasy.

"Cade!"

Lex takes my chin, turning my face toward him, the scent of dark spice and leather hitting me all at once. His eyes blaze into mine, claiming my soul as he kisses me. Tongue, teeth, everything I've been aching for.

Cade's hand slides between my thighs, two fingers slipping deep inside me with practiced ease. I groan into Lex's mouth, my body arching like it's chasing lightning. He pulls back just enough, icy-blues locked on mine.

"That's right, malyshka, Let it out."

Cade's fingers move slow and deep, every curl hitting just right, while his tongue circles my clit with the kind of pressure that makes stars explode behind my eyes. My breath stutters. My body trembles as I grind down against his mouth, chasing every flick, every stroke, every wave of heat he's building in me—like he knows exactly how to unmake me piece by piece.

"Ah, Cade! Oh!" I cry out as my orgasm crashes through me. Lex eats the sound with another kiss.

"God, malyshka," he whispers, thumb brushing my cheek as I come down from the high. "You're so beautiful when you fall apart. I'll never get tired of watching you come all over our man's mouth."

Cade rises between my legs, hazel eyes full of fire and reverence, his skin glowing in the soft lamplight. He stands up and slowly removes his shorts revealing his already hard and throbbing cock. He reaches out for my hands, pulls me up chest to chest and wraps his arms around my waist.

"I love you, sweetheart," he whispers as he kisses me on my forehead.

"I love you, too."

"Lex, babe, lay down." Cade orders.

Lex obeys, grinning from ear to ear.

"Sweetheart, it's your turn," he says to me with a smirk as he turns me around so I'm facing Lex sprawled out on the bed in front of us.

I don't say a word. Just pop the button of his shorts and tug the fabric down, slow and teasing. He lifts his hips to help, eyes on me like I'm the only thing keeping him breathing. My hand wraps around his thick velvety length and he lets out a sound that's half moan, half curse, his hands fisting the sheets.

"Fuck, malyshka," he groans, head falling back against the pillow.

His hips twitch into my palm, his breath stuttering as I stroke him in long, smooth passes. A rhythm that's more torture than relief. He's watching me now, eyes dark and hungry, hand sliding into my hair like he needs something to hold on to.

"You trying to kill me?" he rasps, voice wrecked.

"Not yet," I whisper, leaning in to kiss just beneath his hip bone, lips grazing sensitive skin.

His abs tighten. He moans again, louder this time, and I swear the sound alone makes my thighs press together. Every ounce of control he usually holds so tight is slipping, melting into the heat between us.

"I missed your hands, missed you."

I glance up at him through my lashes, lips brushing his skin, hand still stroking. "Baby, then don't look away."

The scent of him fills my lungs leather, spice, and something darker, something that's only his. My lips part. A deep and guttural groan escapes his lips. One hand fisting the sheet, while the other tangles in my hair.

"Fuck, malyshka... look at you," he moans. "So good for me. Always so goddamn good."

His voice is pure wreckage of smoke, rust, and want. Each word slamming low in my stomach. I take him in deep, his back arching as I pump his cock in and out. I pick up my pace and his grip on my hair gets tighter.

"Malyshka, oh fuck."

I feel Cade behind me, teasing my entrance with the tip of his cock. I let out a moan around Lex when Cade thrusts into me from behind. Stretching me inch by inch until I'm completely full.

He moves with long, sensual thrusts. His hips rolling in a rhythm that's more art than urgency. Every inch of me claimed, every gasp drawn out like music only they know how to play.

Cade's fingers slide between us, finding my clit with ruthless precision. He rubs slow, punishing circles that sync with every motion of his hips, the rhythm steady and maddening.

I cry out against Lex, the sound muffled by the weight of him on my tongue.

Still, I don't stop. I suck harder, deeper, my mouth greedy for every groan he gives me. My hand claws up Lex's chest, nails dragging desperately across his skin. The pressure behind me is building fast, white-hot and unstoppable.

"Fuck, malyshka," Lex growls. "You two... oh my God."

I'm so close. Overwhelmed, stretched, consumed, and completely filled by the loves of my life. Cade's hands grip my hips and his pace picks up behind me, deeper, harder, his breath hot against my back. I can feel him throb inside me, every inch pulsing with need. He's close.

"God, sweetheart," Cade rasps, voice thick with need, "I'm gonna come."

His grip tightens on my hips, grounding himself, anchoring us both to the edge of something neither of us wants to come down from. Every thrust drives deeper, faster, like he's memorizing the shape of me from the inside out.

I gasp, one hand tangled in the sheets, the other still pressed to Lex's chest, nails digging into muscle as Cade's other hand finds my clit again, circling just right.

"Cade," I breathe, still muffled from Lex's cock down my throat. The pressure coils tight in my spine, heat crashing like a wave behind my ribs.

"I've got you," he whispers, lips brushing my shoulder. "Come with me, sweetheart."

And I do. My breath stolen, everything unraveling inside me. Cade groans behind me, low and broken, his rhythm faltering as he follows me over the edge, hips stuttering, body flush against mine.

Lex looks down, his fingers still in my hair. "Fucking art, the both of you," he rasps. "But you're not done yet malyshka, get the fuck up here and sit down."

I release Lex's cock slowly, dragging my tongue along the length as I pull back, teasing him with one last lick from base to tip. Then I rise and straddle his hips. I hover just above him, not sinking down. Not yet.

His eyes flare. "Malyshka, what are you doing?"

I drag the head of his cock toward my pussy, teasing, grinning. "Just taking you in. Little by little."

"Sit the fuck down, malyshka," he growls, voice already wrecked.

I tilt my head, all fake innocence. "You remember that one

time you edged me, like, a million times until I apologized for something that wasn't even my fault to begin with, baby?"

Behind us, Cade huffs a laugh. "Oh shit."

Lex's jaw ticks. "Malyshka, do not play with me right now. Sit. Down."

"No," I purr, biting my lip as I rock my hips just enough to make him twitch, only taking the head of his cock inside me. "I don't think I—"

"Bella," he cuts me off. "Shut the fuck up and sit down, right now."

Lex's hands fist the sheets, his icy eyes dark and desperate.

I shake my head.

"Cade," he grits out, not looking away from me. "Help me out. Sit our girlfriend the fuck down."

"Cade, don't you dare!" I snap at him over my shoulder.

He steps up and places his hands firmly on my hips. "Sorry, sweetheart," he laughs, not sounding sorry at all. "But after last night? You teasing us all night just to pass the fuck out, giving us both a raging case of blue balls? I'm with Lex on this one."

He kisses my neck and pulls me down in one smooth, unforgiving motion, until Lex is completely buried all the way inside of me.

"Ah! Traitor!" I cry out, breathless, head tipping back against Cade's shoulder.

"Thanks, babe," Lex moans sitting up, arms wrapping tight around my waist. His mouth crashes into mine. His kiss is all tongue and hunger, stealing every breath as he thrusts up into me deep, perfect, and entirely overwhelming. My body arches against him, chasing every movement, every sound, every inch of him.

"Ah! God, Lex," I gasp, wildly clawing at his shoulders as the unstoppable rhythm builds.

He groans low against my neck, his grip bruising, his pace ruthless.

"You feel so good, malyshka," he growls, voice rough and ragged.

He pushes deeper, pulsing inside me as his own release hits. His teeth find my neck. He bites down with a moan just hard enough to leave a mark. A promise. A claim.

Lex lays back and I collapse against his chest, breathless and wrecked, every part of me humming with heat and heartbeats. His arms stay around me, holding me tight like I'm something sacred. Like I'm home.

Cade slides in quietly beside us, one warm arm curling around my back, his lips brushing the crown of my head. The bed shifts under our tangled limbs—sweaty skin, tangled sheets, quiet laughter and soft exhales. A mess. A miracle.

We don't say anything. We don't need to.

Because for the first time since Daddy died. For the first time in what feels like forever, I feel whole again. Not fixed. Not healed completely. But held. Loved.

Home
66 Days Since Daddy's Death

I'm halfway in a suitcase and one minor crisis away from losing it.

"Where's my second set of fishnets?" I mumble, digging through a pile of bodysuits. "Not the shredded ones, the performance pair. The ones that don't scream, *I blacked out and fought a raccoon*"

"Check the hamper," Cade calls from the closet. "You wore them the other day at practice for Javi's salsa gauntlet."

Lex lifts his head from where he's sprawled on the rug, halfway through packing his duffel. "Hold up, we have gauntlets now?" His eyes flick to me instantly, brow raised. "How the hell did I miss that?"

I toss another skirt across the room. "You didn't, baby. You were too busy watching me dance to notice what Javi called it."

Lex grins, shameless. "Damn right. You in heels? That's the only thing I'm ever paying attention to." He leans back on one elbow, tongue running across his bottom lip. "You could dance the Macarena and I'd still be hard as fuck."

I finally spot the fishnets dangling off the headboard like some kind of lacy war trophy and groan. "Why are they up there?"

Lex shrugs. "Because you wore them up *there*."

Cade chuckles from the closet.

"Good times, baby." Lex grins.

I shake my head and stuff the fishnets into my bag. "God, we are not normal."

"Speak for yourself, baby. I'm the picture of mental stability."

"Your suitcase is filled with protein bars, brass knuckles, and three different colognes."

"Exactly. Essentials."

Cade emerges with an armful of folded outfits. "You don't have to bring everything, you know, sweetheart. We'll only be gone a few days."

"Tell that to my anxiety," I mutter, zipping a garment bag with way too much force.

Cade crosses the room and presses a kiss to my temple. "Hey. We've got this. You've got this."

I exhale. "Yeah. I just... I want it to be perfect. If we don't win at Nationals, we don't go to Worlds. I don't want to screw it up. And what if the judges hate me? The fact that he's going to be on the panel scares the living shit out of me."

"You won't," Cade says gently. "And they won't. You're going to kill it. All three of you."

Lex flops onto his back, eyes on the ceiling. "If that bastard even thinks about looking at you the wrong way, I'm filing a formal complaint."

"Lex..."

"I'm serious, baby. One head tilt, one smug little look, lick of his lips, and I'm dragging his ass off the panel myself."

I toss a balled-up sock at his head.

He catches it midair, smug as hell. "Ha! Still got it."

"You're ridiculous," I laugh.

Cade nudges my suitcase closed and latches it for me. "Go triple-check your makeup bag, sweetheart. I already pre-packed snacks and chargers. I'll go take the rest of the bags to the car."

I exhale and smile at him. "How are you so perfect?"

"Lex packed vodka and a switchblade," he laughs. "I packed trail mix and your travel migraine kit."

Lex lifts a pointed finger toward Cade. "Balance."

The limo eases to a stop at the edge of the private tarmac just as the wind decides to attack. Winter in New York has an unforgiving bite to it. The kind of cold that slices straight through your coat, your sweater, and your soul.

I yank my beanie down tighter over my ears and brace against the gust as the door opens. Ellie hops out first, bundled in a sherpa-lined cream jacket that makes her look like some golden Upper East Side snow bunny.

Haley follows, her long burgundy coat cinched tight at the waist, wind catching the ends like a damn runway moment. Rosethorne royalty in full winter glam.

Cade steps out of the car, steam curling off his coffee like he conjured the cold just to look that good in it. He's wearing a tailored black wool coat that is so perfect it should come with a warning label all sharp at the shoulders, cinched at the waist, and the collar popped against the wind. Underneath, his gray hoodie peeks out casual and effortless, just like him.

Then there's Lex.

A walking storm cloud. Hood up. Shoulders squared. Black gloves on those hands that have ruined me more times than I can count. His coat's some Bratva-grade winter armor, still open just enough to show a glimpse of the Phoenix on his chest.

He looks pissed at the cold. Pissed at the wind. Pissed at the fact that his boots are probably too nice for this tarmac. But mostly, he looks hot enough to melt the damn snow.

"Why the hell do people not believe in heated sidewalks?" Lex grumbles.

"Because then you'd have nothing to complain about," Cade replies, smirking. "Plus, aren't Russians supposed to love the cold?"

Lex levels him with a dead stare. "Fuck that shit. I'm two seconds away from turning back and throwing hands with winter."

Ellie huffs. "You two sound married."

Haley adds, brushing snow off her coat, "Well they're kind of Bella-married. So, the bickering tracks."

Lex just grins and drops his arm around my shoulder. "Where's our ride, baby?"

I nod toward Project Dylan's newest sleek black jet sitting just past the security gate. A predator on the tarmac. Minimalist silver markings. Custom tail number. No logo. Just danger and speed wrapped in matte black.

Cade whistles low. "Jesus, Bella. That's not a jet. That's a damn Batmobile with wings."

"Don't get hard over it," Lex says, dragging his duffel. "We're not even on board yet."

The hangar doors slide open with a mechanical hiss. And as if summoned by Satan himself, out strides Eric, looking like he just walked off the set of *Top Gun: Apocalypse*. Leather bomber jacket worn like a second skin, scuffed combat boots pounding across the concrete with swagger, and Ray-Bans hiding eyes that have probably seen war, whiskey, and way too many bad landings.

He's got that unshaven, vaguely feral, *I've survived three plane crashes and one bar fight this week* kind of energy. A crooked grin plays on his mouth, equal parts cocky and unhinged.

"Bells!" he calls. "You brought the whole damn entourage."

Lex's eyes narrow. "Who the hell is that?"

"That," I say, grinning, "is Eric."

Lex raises a brow. "Pilot Eric?"

"Yup," Cade says without hesitation, already looking worried.

"The one who flew you and Zeke out of Thailand on three minutes' notice?" Lex asks.

"The one and only," I reply, already bracing.

Lex squints. "Didn't he get kicked out of the FAA's database for hacking it so he could change his pilot's license to say *Sky Daddy?*"

Cade sighs. "Also, true."

Right on cue, Eric laughs, "Welcome to Air Chaos, motherfuckers! Trademark pending."

Lex stares. "Absolutely not."

Eric points at him. "You must be the Russian mafia boyfriend."

"Bratva," Lex deadpans.

"Same difference." Eric shrugs, then turns to Cade with a shit-eating grin. "Ah, Cade Whitmore. Still sour over Cabo?"

"Cabo is the reason I have turbulence-induced PTSD, Eric."

"Son, I'm the reason you survived that turbulence. You're fucking welcome."

Lex frowns. "Wait, you guys went to Cabo?"

Eric waves a hand. "Not technically. But hey, great trip right?"

Cade mutters, "You said we were flying to Cabo. We landed in the Midwest during a heatwave."

I nudge him with my elbow. "To be fair, the barbecue was worth it."

Eric claps his hands. "And the mechanical bull. Don't forget the mechanical bull, man."

Cade shoots him a look. "I threw up on that mechanical bull."

"And yet, you got back on. That's grit, son."

Lex just stares. "Nope. I'm not getting on a plane flown by a man who renamed himself Sky Daddy and caused a federal cyber investigation just to impress his Tinder date."

Eric beams. "She did swipe right."

Lex crosses his arms. "We're going to die."

I smile and lock my arm through his. "But we'll die with legroom, baby."

Eric turns to the girls and bows dramatically. "Ladies. Haley Rosethorne in the flesh, sexy as ever. Ellie Whitmore, lovely to see your sassy ass again."

Eric stares at the mountain of bags being loaded onto the jet. "Damn, how many days are we gone again? Thought we were flying to Dallas, not staging a fashion coup."

Ellie flips her hair. "You think this level of fabulous fits in a carry-on?"

I raise a brow. "Would you rather we under packed and complained the whole time?"

Eric raises both hands. "Shit, no. Just praying there's still some fuel left after lifting all this."

Knox jogs past with a garment bag slung over his shoulder. "Don't worry, Cap. I only brought essentials."

Eric eyes the gold embroidery on the bag. "Is that sequined lingerie?"

"Stagewear," Knox says with a wink. "Very essential."

Cade laughs, stepping around a rolling trunk. "I only brought one bag."

Lex snorts behind him. "Yeah. And half of it is snacks for her."

Eric nods at me. "Well, she is the type to kill over a granola bar."

Lex smirks, pulling his hood down. "Damn right."

"Alright, psychos. Let's haul ass before this snow picks up and they shut down our runway. Dallas Love Field waits for no drama queen."

CHAPTER ⟨82⟩
C A D E
N A T I O N A L S   D A Y   1
D A L L A S ,   T E X A S
70 DAYS SINCE HENRY'S DEATH

If backstage had a soundtrack, it'd be heavy breathing, rapid Spanish, and the occasional high pitched scream.

"¡Pelo mojado?! ¿Estás bromeando?!" Rico is in full meltdown mode. Which, to be fair, is his default setting, but today it's nuclear.

Controlled chaos, if you tilt your head and squint hard enough. Glitter dust in the air, curling irons sizzling, and half-dressed dancers darting like stage-trained banshees. Top it all off with Rico screaming in Spanish from atop a folding chair while waving what might've once been Haley's backup costume.

"¡¿Dónde está el sujetador con los flecos?! I swear to God, if you lose one more sequin—!"

I duck just in time as a rhinestone belt flies past my face. We've just come off The Legacy group number. Bella had landed her last center lift like she was born under a spotlight, not raised in shadows. Ellie stuck her triple pirouette and Haley threw in a midair hair flip that Knox swore deserved its own slow-mo reel. They crushed it.

And now we were twenty minutes out from The Trifecta's first set, a Latin fusion trio that has Javi pacing like a lunatic and Rico clutching rosary beads backstage.

And through it all, there's Bella. She's ripping off her Legacy set like a woman on a mission, the deep burgundy sequined top already halfway over her head.

"Lex, shoes! Cade, get the purple! Javi, for the love of God, breathe! And someone find Haley's earring before Rico throws himself into traffic."

"Wait! What earring?" Haley calls from her chair, spinning as her curls are set with surgical precision.

Bella's already stripped down to pasties and briefs, standing with one foot braced on a bench like some glittering Amazon general, sweat clinging to the lines of her back with glitter still dusted across her collarbone from the group number.

Lex is on his knees at her feet again, silver stilettos in hand, muttering something about worship and war zones. I grab the next outfit off the rack and damn near forget what breathing is.

The dress is... lethal. Saturated amethyst so rich it glows under the fluorescents. Rhinestoned fringe down one hip, a slit so high I'm surprised it doesn't require a license, and a neckline deep enough to start a scandal. Backless, shoulder-baring, and bold.

I hold it out. "Your gown, m'lady."

"You two are way too into this," she laughs pointing a finger between me and Lex.

"Rico will cut us all if we don't get you into this in the next ten seconds," I counter.

Lex steadies her as she steps in. I guide the fabric up over her hips, careful with the fringe. She finishes securing the hidden side clasps herself, then plants a hand on my shoulder so Lex can zip up the back.

"You're stressing," I say, brushing a stray hair out of her face.

Bella's voice tightens. "He hates Latin fusion. Hates trio sets. With my luck, probably hates purple fr—"

Lex cuts her off. "Baby. Breathe."

She looks at him and for a second the mask drops. She's not center-stage Bella. Not the storm. Just a girl trying to measure up.

"You're not dancing for Santibañez," I say gently, adjusting one of her earrings. "You're dancing for the girls next to you. For Javi. For you."

"And for me," Lex adds. "Because watching you dance is the only religion I believe in."

Bella laughs. Just a little, but it's real.

Hair and makeup rush her. The twin glam artists from hell, curling her high pony into a sleek bounce while reapplying highlighter and triple-lashing her eyes. Someone shoves a water bottle into her hand.

"Baby, even my mother's impressed."

Bella's head snaps toward Lex. "I thought just your dad was

coming."

He shakes his head. "Nope, she's here too. Second row, dead center. Right behind the judges. Wearing that icy blue silk bullshit she saves for executions and weddings."

Bella freezes.

Lex adds, "She's... being her usual terrifying self. But she didn't blink during Legacy. Didn't look at her phone. Didn't whisper to Dad. She watched you. Every step."

Bella swallows.

Lex continues, quieter now. "When the lights came up, she said, and I quote, *'She commands well. Dangerous.'*"

She stares at him like he just told her she was being reviewed by a war council.

Lex shrugs. "That's the Bratva version of a standing ovation."

She turns to me. "Do you really think it's gonna land?"

I crouch beside her makeup chair, locking eyes with her. The lights above us catch the shimmer on her cheekbones like warpaint made of stars.

"It's not going to land," I say. "It's going to burn."

"Great, like crash and burn?" she whispers.

"No, sweetheart," I say taking her shaking hands in mine. "Like make Santibañez question his entire career."

"Like make my mom blink," Lex adds.

She takes in a deep breath. "Don't go far," she pleas.

"Front row," I say. "We'll be louder than Javi."

"You better be louder than Rico," she mutters.

"Impossible," Lex deadpans.

The headset tech calls two minutes. Hair and makeup back off. The insanity ebbs around her like a tide pulling out to sea. Ellie and Haley are already standing near the wings, breathing in sync. Bella rises, smiles at us, and nods before heading over to the girls.

We weave our way through the velvet ropes again, slipping into our seats just as the lights dip and the crowd quiets. Knox leans back to let us through.

Front row is packed now, everyone's here. My parents are to my right, Mom's hand resting on Dad's arm, both of them dressed to the nines. Mom's wearing a sleek navy jumpsuit with diamond studs and a glass of white wine that somehow hasn't spilled through everything. Dad's in a tailored black suit, proud and beaming, already clapping before anything's even started.

Cal's leaned forward two seats down, elbows on his knees, jaw set in quarterback-mode. August is bouncing his leg like he's the one about to go out there and dance.

And then there's Roman. Perfect suit. Calm, cool, collected. Hands folded in his lap like he's watching his daughter take the throne he always knew she'd claim. His eyes track movement across the stage, then flick toward Lex. Just once.

Lex doesn't look back. He drops into the empty seat beside me, jaw tight. I don't need to ask. I can feel it, that quiet storm that always brews behind his eyes whenever Roman's around.

Irina and Daniel sit directly behind us, second row.

She leans forward, just a little, and says over my shoulder, "How's she looking back there, Cade?"

Before I can answer, Lex beats me to it voice dry and a little too loud. "Like a red flag with my name on it."

Daniel clears his throat. Mom chokes on her wine. Irina just hums, like that's exactly the kind of answer she expected from her son.

"She's good," I say, glancing toward the wings where Bella's just stepped into position with Ellie and Haley. "She's steady. She'll be okay."

I pause, then add under my breath, "We've just gotta make it through today."

Daniel leans forward now, brow furrowed. "Why just today?"

Lex finally turns his head. "Because today's when it counts."

I nod. "Trios and duos have two rounds. Only the top three from each category qualify for tomorrow's finals. If they take first tomorrow, then they get go to Worlds."

Dad lets out a low whistle. "No pressure."

Callum grins, all cocky confidence. "We win or we pack."

Daniel leans in a little closer, voice mild but curious. "And the solos? The big groups? How do they work?"

"They dance once," I say. "Solos and full-group routines are one-and-done. If you place top in either, you get your spot at Worlds."

"Ellie's a shoe-in," Lex adds, still watching the wings. "Her solo's ranked first in prelims and trending higher. Judges love her."

"Legacy's group set could go either way," I admit.

"That's not the one they care about," Lex finishes.

Daniel raises a brow. "No?"

Lex shakes his head. "It's the trio. That's the one that matters."

I nod, eyes drifting back to the stage. "They've danced solos. They've danced in groups. But The Trifecta? That's different. They're not just teammates, they're family."

"They want Worlds," Lex says softly, almost like it's a prayer.

"Those girls," I say, "are sisters. And they want it all."

The opening chords of *Mi Gente* snaps through the sound system like a shot of adrenaline as the girls step forward. Bella center, Ellie and Haley on the sides like a perfectly calibrated V-formation in violet and silver fringe. The moment they hit the first count, it's not chaos anymore. It's precision. Fire and control in every step.

They don't just dance to the beat, they shape it. Cha-cha and salsa footwork flickers beneath them, sharp and cut like glass. Their arms slice the air, fluid and fast. Feet pivot and snap through lightning-fast directional shifts, turns that land clean.

There's a beautiful chemistry to their movements. To the way they react to each other mid-spin. The unspoken sync in their spacing, the collective inhale before every dramatic pause. Like one organism split into three.

Judges are scribbling. Even the hardass ones. Their brows furrowed and nodding like they just got hit with something they didn't expect. The judge on the left looks like he's already added them to the winner's sheet. The blonde woman beside him mouths *wow*.

And then there's him, Santibañez. The Latin ballroom tyrant. The one Bella is so terrified of. He's not writing. He's watching, and not in the way he watched the Phoenix girls before. Those poor dancers who got a whole head shake and a scribble mid-performance. No, this time he leans forward, elbows on the table, lips parted just slightly. Like he's... enchanted.

Lex notices too. "Is he—?" he whispers.

I nod. "Hooked."

"Thank fuck."

The final combo hits and Bella spins through a tight double, landing in perfect stillness as Ellie and Haley mirror her pose. They strike the final line together, all heels and presence and glitter that somehow feels like war paint.

Mom exhales. "That girl's a weapon."

Dad whistles low. "That's the one they wanted, huh?"

"That's the one that matters," I say.

Lex lets out a breath. "Okay, yeah, they killed that."

"They owned that," I correct.

Lex stands, brushing off his hands like he's just watched a full-blown military op go down. He turns to me with that half-wild gleam in his eye, the one that only shows up when Bella dances or when someone threatens one of our lives.

"You ready to head backstage?" he asks.

"Yeah."

"Let's go help our baby get ready for her duet."

Backstage is quieter now. No screaming. No rhinestones flying through the air. No Rico having a religious crisis. Just the low whirr of a blow dryer in the corner. Soft murmurs from a nearby coach. Someone adjusting a lighting cue over comms.

The storm has passed and Bella is standing dead center in the calm. She's still in the trio set, glittering purple fringe clinging to her skin, heels steady, but there's sweat beading down her spine and a flush in her cheeks that has nothing to do with the routine. Lex tosses her a towel, and she catches it midair without looking.

"That felt... good," she says, chest rising and falling like she's waiting for someone to tell her she imagined it.

Lex is crouched by her duffel, digging out the heels for her duet. "He didn't blink, baby."

Bella freezes. I step forward, kneeling beside her as she swaps out her shoes.

"Santibañez," I clarify. "He didn't write. Didn't check his watch. Didn't even breathe for half of it."

Lex straightens. "He watched you like you girls were on fire."

Bella swallows. Her hand pauses on the strap of her heel.

"Phoenix girls before you?" Lex adds. "He shook his head mid-routine and started writing in block letters like he was filing a restraining order."

I give her a small smile, low and steady. "You all had him frozen, sweetheart."

She exhales like she's been holding that breath since the moment she stepped onstage. "Yeah?" she asks, voice barely there.

Lex's voice softens. "Yeah. You wrecked him. All three of you did."

Her eyes flick up, darting between us, and for the first time tonight, she lets herself smile. Not for the crowd. Or for the judges. Just for us. "I've got one more, then we're done for the day."

Lex hands her the water bottle. "Then we eat. And breathe. Maybe even sit down."

I fasten the last strap on her shoe and look up. "You've got this duet in the bag."

"Top three, or nothing," she says.

"No," Lex replies, stepping into her space. "Top one."

She grins, grabs both of our hands, and squeezes once, a silent thank you.

We're back in our seats by the time the stage lights shift to that muted lavender wash, soft and moody, like twilight slipping into memory.

Bella walks out. Her hair is curled and pinned to one side, just loose enough to bounce with each step, styled like a vintage starlet on the edge of rebellion. Her dress flows like smoke, soft lavender layered in sheer chiffon, catching the light like it was dipped in silver. It hugs and releases in perfect places, trailing behind her like it's always been part of her.

Josh steps out beside her. He's shirtless with black pants sharp at the hip with a single lavender stripe wrapping his thigh like brushstroke on canvas. Her light. His shadow.

The music builds delicate strings layered over soft, rising power. This isn't Trifecta's Row Party chaos. This is something quieter, more intimate and aching. A ballet of breath and longing.

Bella falls into the movement like she's made of it. Every line is liquid. Every reach, every lift, every extension is purposeful. Josh mirrors her like a whisper. She glides across the stage, turns into his arms, unravels midair and lands as if gravity was just waiting for her permission.

Lex leans forward beside me, already filming. "I love the sexy dances," he says under his breath. "And the chair ones? Don't get me wrong, they kill me. But this? Our girl dancing like a damn princess up there?" He exhales slowly. "Does things to me, babe."

I can't even look away to answer. My throat's already tight. "She's... everything," I whisper.

Beside me, Mom exhales softly. "She's beautiful, son. She's going to make a beautiful bride."

"Mom—"

She tilts her head. "Tell me I'm wrong."

Then she turns her attention to me, her hand sliding over to find mine. "I always saw it, you know," she says gently. "The way you looked at her."

I glance over, caught in the moment, in the sound, in the swell of music that feels like it's stitching itself through my chest.

"Even when you were younger. That first time she came over with Ellie... she was this little spitfire. Busted-up knees from dance, messy hair, yelling at Cal for calling her short. And you just watched her. Like she was a thunderstorm rolling through your ribs."

I laugh quietly. "I didn't even know I was doing it."

"Oh, we did," she says. "You were sixteen. She was bubbly and crazy. And you? You were calm, Cade. But the second she walked into a room, you lit up."

Onstage, Bella floats into a turn—her arms extended, her eyes distant and soft—like she's dancing through the dream of a girl who used to sit on the floor of my studio and watch me paint for hours.

"She used to sneak into your studio," Mom says, like she's reading my thoughts. "Said she was hanging out with Ellie, but she always ended up with you. Curled up on the floor, head on her knees, just watching you paint. She wouldn't even talk. Just sat there like your silence was the only place she could breathe."

"She never said anything."

"She didn't have to." Mom squeezes my hand. "She calmed when you were around. She's always been like that with you, Cade. Even when she didn't know why."

I blink, jaw tight. The music swells.

"She's loved you since she was a child," Mom whispers. "She just didn't realize that's what it was then. But I knew."

Onstage, Josh lifts Bella again like she's glass and air. She folds into him, then pushes away in a spin, her lavender dress trailing behind her.

"She's always been it for you," Mom says. "You think you're just now falling? Baby, you've been gone for a long, long time."

Lex nudges my shoulder. "Hey. Not to kill the mother-son-moment, but I'm pretty sure she just hit a turn I don't think was anatomically possible."

Mom laughs through her tears and rests her head against my shoulder. I feel it right in the center of my chest. Like everything I've ever felt for her is rising all at once, impossible to contain.

Mom squeezes my hand again, softer now. "She's going to be your wife." The word lands heavy. Not as a dream. As a truth.

"She already is, in all the ways that count," she continues. "Not just yours, I know that. She's Lex's too. And somehow, the three of you make that work. Not just... messily, or halfway. Really work."

I don't say anything. My eyes glued to Bella as she moves like the music is being born under her feet.

"She loves Lex fiercely, but she leans on you in a different way. She always has. You ground her, Cade. You always have."

"She grounds me," I admit quietly.

Mom smiles. "That's how I knew. Not just that she'd be part of your life, but that she'd change it. Make it deeper. Quieter. Real."

I glance down at our hands. "It's not traditional."

"No, not really," she says. "But, it is true and that is what matters most."

Bella lifts her arms in a slow turn, the light catching the lavender of her dress like stained glass.

"She's not just your girl," Mom whispers. "She's your future. Both of yours. And I've never seen you happier, either of you."

I look over at her, my voice barely audible. "You're really okay with all of it?"

"I love you, Cade. I love who you love. Lex, Bella, and the family you three are creating, that's the only part I care about."

Lex leans over. "She's still killing it," he says, nudging me lightly. "Can we marry her onstage? Is that allowed, Savannah?"

Mom laughs, eyes misty. "You boys better start planning. Because when she's ready, she's not going to walk. She's going to run down that aisle."

The final notes hits like a breath held too long. Bella lands in Josh's arms, arms still extended, her dress fanned around her like a ripple in time. The lights dim, soft and golden, catching just enough shimmer on her skin to make her look unreal.

I'm on my feet before I even realize it. Lex is right beside me, shouting something in Russian that's probably obscene and beautiful at the same time. Knox lets out a whoop. The rest of the family follows. Callum and August with both fists in the air, Dad clapping so hard I think Mom might cry again.

Lex wipes at his cheek with the back of his hand, then immediately scowls and mutters, "Fucking allergies."

As expected, my sister took first in her solo and Josh and Bella took first in their duet. There wasn't single person in this room who doubted it, and there sure as hell wasn't a judge who looked remotely surprised when their names were called.

The announcer clears his throat as the cheers fade. "And now... what you've all been waiting for..."

The audience leans in. Lex nearly vibrates beside me.

"It's time for the Trios." The screen lights up again.

"Our top five placements for trio performances..."

I feel Lex shift beside me, and I don't blame him. I can feel it too, the pulse in the air, the weight in my chest.

"In fifth place... Pulse Academy from Los Angeles." Polished, clean, technically strong, but forgettable. The three girls step forward, trying not to look disappointed.

"In fourth place... Boston Elite." I'm surprised they didn't place higher to be honest.

"Thank fuck, they get to dance tomorrow," Knox mutters.

"In third place... Crescendo School of Movement from Chicago." Big stage presence. Great musicality. But they weren't the story tonight.

That leaves two. The Trifecta and a trio from New York Performance Conservatory who performed a clean, jazz-contemporary hybrid that hit hard but didn't really linger.

Bella, Ellie, and Haley are standing close, fingers tangled together in a chain I know none of them want to break. Ellie's biting her lip. Haley's staring straight ahead like she's daring them to say any other name. Bella's face is unreadable and her hands are trembling.

"And in first place..."

I shift in my seat.

"From Wexley University... The Trifecta!"

The house explodes. The entire audience is on their feet. And the fancy judge she was so scared of stands for the first time during the awards. No clapping. He rises slowly, deliberately, and gives one sharp, approving nod, the kind that says this wasn't good. This was great.

Lex slaps my shoulder so hard I flinch. "They fucking did it!"

"They get to dance tomorrow," I say, barely able to speak around the lump in my throat. "They really did it."

CHAPTER (83)
BELLA
DALLAS, TEXAS
70 DAYS SINCE DADDY'S DEATH

The top floor of the restaurant Savannah reserved feels like something out of a dream, all glass and height and whispered wealth. The city of Dallas stretches out below us in a glittering sprawl, lights blinking like a sea of stars scattered upside-down. Floor-to-ceiling windows wrap the circular space, curving with the slow, almost imperceptible rotation of the room. Every angle offers a different constellation of skyline, skyscrapers lit up in blues and golds, highways glowing like arteries in motion.

Inside, the restaurant is all quiet elegance. Sleek walnut tables. Black velvet chairs. Soft jazz curling through hidden speakers like smoke. There's the faint scent of citrus and expensive wine in the air, layered over candle wax and wood polish. Each place setting is pristine—crystal glassware, weighty silver utensils, and linen napkins folded with military precision, like someone ironed them into submission.

I'm seated between Cade and Roman.

Lex is directly across from me, a wall of black-on-black elegance with the top of his shirt slightly undone, all heat and carved jaw tension. Daniel sits next to him, calm as ever, and Irina is perched on Lex's other side like a marble queen draped in—*shocker*—ice-blue silk. Her posture is flawless. Her silence is louder than anything she could say.

Cade's hand rests lightly on the back of my chair, his fingers brushing the bare skin of my shoulder every so often. I keep my shoulders squared, my smile smooth, my breathing even. And I do my best not to spill anything on this dress.

It's strapless, deep burgundy silk that clings and sweeps in all the right places. Ruched along the side, slit high enough to show thigh when I cross my legs. I know it's borderline scandalous. I also know Irina hasn't stopped side-eyeing me since I sat down, her lips pressed in a line so sharp it could probably cut glass.

Which only makes me love this dress even more.

Daniel is talking to the waiter, ordering a bottle of Barolo. Cade's flipping through the menu, but I already know what I want.

"Old fashioned," I say when the server stops by, flashing a soft grin. "Extra orange peel, please."

Clay chuckles. "That's my girl."

Roman lifts a brow. "Strong choice."

I shrug. "Learned it from Clay."

The waiter nods and heads off, menus disappearing with him. Conversation dips for a moment, the quiet hum of the restaurant filling the space—silverware clinking, low jazz bleeding through the speakers, the scent of seared steak and truffle pasta curling in the air.

By the time the drinks arrive, the tension's already softened. Daniel's chatting with the sommelier, Clay's trading a story with Roman, and I'm trying not to inhale the bread basket before the entrées show up.

A few minutes later, the food arrives. Plates gliding onto the table one by one, each one a small work of art. Steam curls upward, carrying the smell of garlic and herbs, butter and wine. Forks scrape, glasses clink, someone laughs softly down the table. For a moment, everything feels easy. Warm light, good food, and the rare quiet that settles over people who finally have nothing to survive for a few minutes.

"Alright," Clay says, adjusting his cufflink. "What's the lineup for tomorrow?"

I take a sip, my voice a little hoarse. "Just two more. One trio. Latin. Faster, sharper, more grounded. It's a firestorm if we hit it clean."

Savannah leans in with a smile. "After what we saw today? I have no doubt. You girls were stunning. That trio... I've never seen chemistry like that."

Ellie beams, "This one's even hotter, Mom."

I nod. "We've been sitting on it all season. Javi saved it for Nationals on purpose."

Lex grins. "He's a bastard. I respect it."

"And the duet?" Clay asks, looking toward me.

"Me and Josh close the entire day with our *Pillowtalk* routine."

"It's slower," Ellie adds, "but it simmers. Way darker than tonight."

Lex grins, not even pretending to behave. "My baby's sexy in that one. Like fucking foreplay on a stage."

Cade groans. "Lex."

Lex shrugs, completely unapologetic. "What? We're all family here. And by now, I think it's safe to say everyone knows how the three of us are."

"Good lord," I mutter, taking another drink.

Ellie grins and points at me with her straw. "He's not wrong. There's enough sexual tension in your trio to power a small country. I'm just glad it's somewhat choreographed now."

Savannah's cheeks turn pink, but she's still smiling.

Clay just raises a brow and mutters, "Remind me to keep the grandkids far from the Nationals footage."

Roman leans in, voice low, calm. "You were extraordinary tonight."

I meet his eyes and this time, I let it sit there a moment. Let the words land. "Thank you," I say quietly. "For being here."

His brows lift slightly, surprised. I reach out and rest my hand on his.

"I mean it," I add. "You didn't have to show up. But you did. You've been showing up, you keep showing up. For me."

Lex doesn't move but I feel the shift across the table, the tension pulling tight through his shoulders. His jaw clicks once and he takes a slow sip like it might keep him from exploding.

Roman smiles and it's not the polished, intimidating one he usually gives. It's quieter. Gentler. "I wouldn't have missed it," he says. "But Bella, when we're back in New York, I'd like you to come by The Obsidian. There's something I want to talk to you about, something I want to give you."

Lex leans forward. He doesn't say a word, but his silence is louder than anything.

I nod, slow and steady. "Okay. I'll come by when we're back." Roman's smile lifts again. "That sounds perfect." He picks up his drink, swirls it once. "How are you feeling about tomorrow?"

I let out a slow breath. "Honestly? I don't know. I saw the line-up. It looks like three Latin routines. Everyone's trying to impress the guest judge. Our piece is good, it is, but…"

"But?" he prompts gently.

"It's not really my call," I admit. "And I just want to make sure we stand out. This round matters. It can make or break us for Worlds in Paris, and I'm not sure doing what everyone else is doing is the right move."

Roman tilts his head. "You're strong. If you feel something's off, why don't you change it?"

I laugh and shake my head. "Because you've clearly never met Javi."

He starts to say something else, but is interrupted by Ellie's loudmouth.

"Wait!" Ellie shrieks, pointing across the table. "Do you all re-member the Range Rover?"

I nearly choke on my pasta. "Oh no. Here we go."

"The Range Rover?" Daniel asks, arching a brow.

"The girls stole my son's car," Clay replies sipping his drink.

Cal's already grinning. "You didn't even steal the right fucking car, Bells."

Cade sets his fork down slowly and looks at me. "That was my car."

"We were sixteen," I say, smile creeping up like it's got a ven-detta. "Barely even a crime."

"You stole my birthday present."

"We thought it was Cal's," Ellie says with a dramatic shrug.

"He drove the white one," Cade grits out. "You jacked mine and took it to a bonfire in the Hamptons."

I grin, utterly unbothered. "It was a really good bonfire."

"You came back at two a.m. with sand in the floorboards, a dented mirror, and someone else's hoodie in my backseat."

Cal snorts. "You mean Micah's hoodie? She wore that thing for like two months."

Roman leans forward, sipping his scotch, eyes flicking to me. "You stole a Range Rover?"

"It was more like a creative borrowing situation," I say sweetly.

Daniel raises a glass toward Cade. "I'm just impressed she brought it back."

"They abandoned it in the driveway with the engine still running!" Cade says, scandalized.

Savannah covers her mouth, laughing. "Give them a break, they were only sixteen."

"And completely feral," Cade mutters.

Roman tilts his glass toward me. "Remind me to never give you keys to anything that has significant value."

"No promises," I shoot back, raising my brows.

Lex stills. Not obvious or loud, just a sharp little shift in his jaw and a flick of his eyes toward me like the idea of me in another guy's hoodie might kill him on the spot. I don't say anything, but I see it. The tension. The tick in his temple.

Clay leans in. "You posted a photo of you two standing on the hood. Tagged *Hamptons Vibes*."

I shrug. "Got good engagement."

Cade nudges me gently, eyes warm. "Sweetheart, remember when Ellie had a crush on your brother?"

Ellie groans. "Cade!"

He raises a hand in mock defense. "What? I barely knew the guy. Just remember her begging you to bring him to that one pool party."

"She made brownies," I say, pointing my fork at Ellie. "Bribery in its purest form."

Ellie hides behind her wine glass. "He was hot and mysterious and he fixed my laptop without making me feel stupid."

Cade chuckles. "You swooned because he knew how to bypass parental controls."

"Don't mock my type." Ellie laughs. "He was kind. Always made me feel safe."

Cal groans. "Good God. What is with you two and brothers?"

That breaks the tension. Laughter spills out across the table. Ellie snorts into her wine, Cade covers his face with his hand, and even Roman's mouth twitches like he's trying not to smile.

Cal leans back, eyes gleaming. "Yo. Speaking of you girls and terrible boyfriend choices—remember the prep school twins?"

"Absolutely not." I groan immediately.

Ellie covers her face. "Cal, shut up."

"They had a band," he says, already cracking up. "Remember? A fucking band."

"They had a damn publicist," Cade mutters.

I smile into my drink. "They were entrepreneurial."

"They wore matching pastel polos," Ellie says. "Like... daily."

"Had a driver named Philippe," Cal adds.

"Oh my God," I laugh. "Philippe used to give us snacks from that chauffeur cooler."

"Bells, remember when they tried to serenade us at that rooftop party?" Ellie asks.

I snort. "Mine played the violin."

Cal claps. "The violin! That's right! You dated the one who brought a Stradivarius to that party."

"His name was Preston," I add. "He told me I had a vintage soul."

Cade nearly chokes on his drink. "Babe, he literally cried when you ghosted him."

"Please, he cried when I asked for still water."

Lex leans forward, finally speaking. "Wait, how long did this... violinist era last?"

I glance at him at him, eyes glittering. "About two months. I ended things when he tried to quote Hemingway during a massage."

Savannah laughs, wine glass tilted. "I vaguely remember that one. Didn't he send you monogrammed love letters?"

I nod. "Scented. With a wax seal."

Clay mutters, "Christ."

Cal grins across the table, apparently wanting to keep the chaos going strong. "Remember St. Barts?"

"Oh my God, iconic." I raise my glass toward him.

"Oh my God, illegal," Cade adds, already laughing.

Ellie's wheezing before he even finishes. "Oh my God, the jet skis!"

"The ones you two stole," Cade says, jabbing his fork in mine and Cal's direction.

"We borrowed them," I say sweetly. "For a sunrise joyride."

"You crashed into a wedding," Cade deadpans.

"It was a small wedding," Cal says, shrugging.

"A destination wedding," Ellie snorts. "You soaked the little ring bearer."

"He forgave me." I wave a hand. "I think."

Roman raises an eyebrow, watching me with dry amusement. "You stole jet skis?"

"Allegedly." I flash him a grin. "We were never charged."

Lex huffs across the table. He hasn't touched his steak in minutes.

Clay leans back with a sigh. "All I remember is getting a call from resort security saying my son and Bella were racing jet skis through a wedding ceremony."

"You stormed down the beach in linen pants and no shoes," Savannah laughs. "Yelling something about diplomatic immunity."

"I was trying to save the brand," Clay says, dry as ever. Then he looks at me. "You looked me dead in the eye and asked if dessert was worth an international scandal."

"It was," I say without missing a beat.

Ellie gasps. "You still had seaweed in your braid when we got back to the cabana."

"And you made me promise not to tell your brother," Cal adds.

Cade rolls his eyes. "You two gave the hotel staff a panic attack."

"We returned the jet skis," I argue.

"They were beached," Cade fires back. "With coral damage."

"We left a note," Cal says, like that makes it any better.

"A note that said, *'our bad, love you, mean it,'*" Cade mutters.

Daniel chuckles quietly from his end of the table. "Sounds like a very thorough legal defense."

Roman's mouth twitches. "Did you at least win the race?"

"I did," I say smugly.

"She cheated," Cal says.

Savannah shakes her head and takes a sip of wine. "No one else would've dared pull that stunt and still gotten dessert."

"You mean the coconut tart?" I ask. "I'd commit crimes for that tart."

"You did commit crimes for that tart," Cade says flatly.

"That's love," I say, tipping my glass to him.

Everyone's laughing again—Cal's head tilted back, Ellie wiping her eyes, Savannah glowing with amusement, and Clay shaking his head like he still can't believe he funded the whole vacation.

Roman lifts his glass toward me in a mock toast. "Well. That explains the reports."

Across from me, Lex hasn't said a word. But I can feel him watching. And I already know what's coming.

I text him under the table.

> ME: Bathroom. Now. Don't make me drag you, baby.

Three seconds later, his chair scrapes back. I wait a beat before slipping away, careful not to draw attention.

By the time I push into the bathroom down the hall, he's already there—arms tense, jaw tight, pacing like a caged animal.

I shut the door softly behind me and lean against it. "Okay, spill it, Barinov. What's wrong?."

He doesn't look at me. "Nothing."

I scoff. "Nope. Try again. I know you too well to buy that bullshit. You've had that storm cloud face since the appetizer course."

Silence.

I step closer. "You look like you did that week I banned sex until Cade got back from that gallery show in L.A."

"That wasn't a sex ban. That was psychological warfare, baby. You wore those little shorts knowing damn well I was one wrong move away from taking you on the floor at The Pit."

"Exactly," I say, folding my arms. "So, talk to me. What's going on?"

Lex leans back against the bathroom counter and crosses his arms. "I just really hate this part of the night," he mutters.

"What part?"

His gaze drops to the floor. "The whole 'remember when' bullshit. It always happens when we have dinner with Cade's family." He drags a hand through his hair. "The Whitmore stories. The vacations. The fucking shared history."

Lex lets out a low breath, eyes flicking up to mine. "Cade fits into your world like he was made for it. I'm the outsider," he says quietly. "Just the guy who showed up late to the damn party."

My chest tightens. "Lex..."

"I know what we have is real," he says, voice rough. "But it still fucks with me, baby. Every time one of you says 'remember when,' it's like I'm being reminded that there's a version of you and Cade I never got to meet. A life I'll never touch. I can't compete with that."

I step between his legs, take his hand. "Hey, you don't have to compete."

He lets out a bitter breath. "Feels like I do."

"Fine," I say, lifting my chin. "You want a remember when? I'll give you one."

I step even closer, fingertips trailing up his chest. "Do you remember when I saw you for the first time, because I do."

Lex's brow furrows. "Fight night?"

I laugh softly. "No, dumbass. It was at Ellie's eighteenth birthday. You and Cade showed up way late. You were in a leather jacket, brooding like the storm you are. I remember thinking you looked like trouble."

His mouth tugs at the side. "I was trouble."

"Not arguing about that. But I was so jealous of Cade for the way you looked at him. You were dangerous. Hot. Clearly into him. And all I could think about was how you'd never even glance at me."

Lex tilts his head. "Didn't know you noticed me back then."

"I did," I say, honest and steady. "Even when I shouldn't have."

His eyes soften. "Guess I was blind."

I smile. "At least you see me now."

Lex's jaw flexes, and I know he's trying to keep it together, so I keep going. "Remember our first date?"

"You mean when I hijacked your mission with Mortal Kombat and turned it into a flirt-off with bullets?"

I roll my eyes. "No. Our real first date. A couple nights after. You picked me up outside Rosethorne like we were about to rob a bank."

"Because we kind of were," he grins. "That reservation wasn't even mine, *Mrs. Voronina-Belyakov*."

"You were blasting Russian rap in that sleek black McLaren like you were auditioning for *Fast & Furious: Bratva Drift*."

"Baby, you wore that red leather jacket," he says, eyes dancing. "Looked like sex bottled up. What did you expect?"

"And you took me to that rooftop in Tribeca. The one with the string lights, the private chef, and a violinist playing *Toxic* on a loop."

Lex snorts. "An underrated classic."

I huff out a laugh. "We didn't talk about missions. Or Cade. It was just you and me. Champagne and bad decisions."

He grows quiet. Eyes locked on mine.

"And then..." I say softly, "remember a week or so later when I was spiraling and convinced Cade was never coming back to us? You didn't try to fix it. You just put me on your bike and drove us to Cooper's Beach at two in the morning."

"Because you breathe better by the water."

I nod. "And you always give me the ocean, Lex. You know me better than you think, baby and we haven't had nearly as much time as Cade and I."

I rest my head on his shoulder, then glance up with a teasing smile. "Remember that night in Central Park?"

Lex groans. "When you threatened to kill me if your heels got ruined?"

"They were Giuseppe Zanotti."

"You were wearing white in the rain, malyshka. You really think I wasn't gonna make a move?"

"You spun me like a lunatic under that streetlamp."

"You laughed." He shrugs.

"You kissed me like the world was ending."

He leans in. "It was raining. You were soaked. I have no regrets, malyshka."

I grin. "It was perfect. Just you, me, and the rain."

Lex exhales slowly, the tension bleeding out of him.

"I remember the first time I knew I loved you," I say.

His brows lift. "Was it at he pier?"

"No. That's when I started to fall for you, yeah sure. But the night I knew for sure, was in Boston at The Liberty Hotel."

Lex stiffens slightly. He remembers.

"We'd just rescued those kids. That hell house in Roxbury," I say. "You, me, the guys, and O'Malley. We got them out. Every last one of them."

"O'Malley's fucking insane."

I smile faintly. "He still saved your ass."

Lex huffs a quiet laugh. "Yeah, well. Only after nearly blowing the damn house up with all of us still inside."

"Either way, he still saved your ass. Afterward, I shut down. Shut myself in the hotel bathroom. I couldn't breathe. Couldn't move. I didn't want to be strong. Not for you. Not for anyone. I just wanted the world to stop spinning for a minute. Just long enough for me to remember who I was without the mission."

Lex pulls me into his chest like he needs to feel my heartbeat against his own chest.

"You didn't knock," I whisper, voice catching on the memory. "You just came in. Sat beside me. Said nothing. Matched every breath like it was the only way to keep me tethered to the world."

Lex doesn't speak, but his eyes are locked on mine like he's back there too.

"You didn't try to fix me. Didn't ask what was wrong. You just... stayed. In the dark. In the silence. You made it safe for me to fall apart."

My fingers trail up his chest with a slow reverence.

"That night, was the first time I knew. Really knew. That I loved you."

His jaw tightens.

"Because you didn't save me like a hero. You held me like a man who'd already made room in his soul for all of my wreckage."

He says nothing, but his grip on me tightens.

"You've been my oxygen ever since, Lex," I whisper.

His jaw works like he's fighting everything he wants to say.

"Remember when you took me to Northvale to show me your senior project?"

"The Blackwood?"

"Yeah. The Blackwood. A whole hotel. Your senior project isn't just a sketch or a floorplan. It's a monument. A skyrise dripping in black marble and steel. Brutal, stunning... you."

He exhales through his nose, like he wants to downplay it, but I know him too well. The pride is there, just under the surface. Like a flame he's still learning how to let burn.

"You said it looked like us," he says.

"I did. Because it felt like us. The way the shadows wrapped around the glass. The sharp edges and warm spaces. That rooftop suite with the black infinity pool—"

"With the underwater speakers," he adds, voice lower now. "Because you said you wanted to float and still feel the music."

I smile. "And the dance studio on the 22nd floor. You designed a fucking dance studio, Lex."

He shrugs, but his hand finds mine. "Had to give my baby a stage."

I laugh under my breath. "You didn't build me a stage, Lex. You gave me a cathedral."

He goes quiet again for a second. "I'm going to build it, malyshka."

I blink up at him.

"The Blackwood," he continues, eyes locked on mine. "It's gonna be real. Maybe not tomorrow, maybe not next year. But I will build it. Our hotel. Our home. I want you dancing in the lobby barefoot and Cade painting masterpieces on the rooftop terrace. I want the world to know that it's ours."

"I believe you," I whisper.

His thumb brushes the back of my hand.

"You know what else I remember?" I ask, leaning closer.

He lifts a brow, the corner of his mouth twitching. "Baby if you say the drafting table, I'm gonna need a cigarette."

"No, after that. After we messed up all your blueprints and I was laying on your sweatshirt on the floor, hair a mess, mascara halfway down my face..."

His voice drops into a hush. "You said you felt like the world finally made sense."

I nod. "Because it did."

Lex swallows hard.

"I remember how you looked at me that night," I say, voice soft. "Like I was the last piece of a puzzle you didn't even know you were trying to put together."

He doesn't answer. Just pulls my hand up and presses a kiss to my wrist, just below the edge of my bracelet. A kiss so tender, it feels like it rewrites the rage inside him. Like it melts it.

"I've been spinning all night," he admits. "That duet, the trio, Roman, fucking everything. But you..." His forehead presses to mine. "You bring me back, malyshka. Always."

"That's what love is supposed to do, Lex. So you see," I say, brushing my fingers against his cheek, "we may not have years of re-member whens, but we've got a ton of really good ones that matter just as much."

He's quiet. Then, softly, he whispers, "Yeah. We really do."

I nudge his chest. "Now get it together, Hollow King."

His slow, wicked smirk returns, the kind that curls with smoke and danger. In a blink of an eye, his mouth is on me, hot and unre-lenting. His hands drag me backward toward the door, slamming the lock with one swift flick before he presses me against the cool marble counter. It's too fast, too hungry, but that's us. Fire with nowhere to go.

Lex grips my thighs, lifts me like nothing, and sets me down hard on the counter. The silk of my dress slides up in waves as he steps between my legs, hands rough, hungry, already searching—

And then he freezes. His fingers halt mid-motion.

His eyes flick up to mine, dark and electric. "Where the fuck are your panties?"

"In this dress? There's no way I could possibly hide a panty line."

The sound he makes isn't human. A low, vicious growl rips from his chest like it physically hurt him not to know that sooner.

"Fuck, malyshka."

His hands grip my thighs harder, like he doesn't know whether to drop to his knees and feast, or bend me over right now and ruin us both.

"You've been walking around all night with nothing under this?" he rasps, voice shredded with disbelief and lust. "Sitting next to Cade. To Roman. Like this?"

"I wore it for you, baby. The dress, it's all for you."

"Fuck," he groans, already sinking to his knees. "Look at you."

"Lex—"

His mouth is on me before I can finish. His tongue, his fingers, all of it demanding. It's messy and hot and perfect. My hands slam back against the mirror, head tipping as he devours me like it's the only way to make it through the night.

I gasp, legs shaking. "You.... are insane. Oh!"

He grins against me. "You love it."

My release hits violently, shattering through me as I grind down on his mouth, fingers curling in his hair like lifelines.

He stands, wipes his mouth with the back of his hand, eyes dark as sin. Then he's undoing his belt, fast and impatient. He grabs me by the hips and yanks me forward, lined up, breathing hard.

I pull him in with a fistful of his shirt and kiss him as he sinks into me with one punishing thrust. We both moan. The rhythm starts hard and stays harder. The sound of skin, the slam of hips, the scrape of my heels against the counter. His hand cups the back of my neck. Mine claw at his back. His forehead presses to mine.

"Mine," he growls. "Say it."

"Yours," I pant. "Always."

He slams into me again.

"Fucking say it louder, malyshka."

Another thrust.

"Yours, Lex. I'm yours," I cry out.

The heat rises like wildfire. My breath's a mess. His jaw is clenched. His fingers bruise into my hips.

"I love you, malyshka," he grits. "So goddamn much."

"I know. I love you too."

My second orgasm slams into me without warning, the kind that punches the air from my lungs and leaves my whole body shaking. He follows a beat later, gasping into my neck like I stole the last bit of his oxygen.

"I needed this," he says.

"I know. Me too."

His voice comes quieter now, hoarse. "I'm still building that hotel, you know."

"You fucking better," I whisper.

I stand, tugging my skirt back into place. "Let's get back to dinner before Ellie comes charging in here like a Gucci-clad hurricane."

Lex keeps one hand low on my back as we walk back to the table, guiding me with that quiet possessiveness that always makes me feel claimed and loved.

When we reach our table, I pause in front of my seat between Cade and Roman. Lex pulls the chair out, but instead of walking to his, he drops into mine, legs spread wide and pulls me straight into his lap. I settle back against him, not fighting it.

Cade doesn't say a word. He shoots a warm and knowing smile and reaches out to squeeze Lex's hand where it rests on my thigh. Lex links their fingers silently.

Across the table, Ellie arches a perfectly sculpted brow. "Well, finally. Thought maybe you two were christening the damn bathroom."

"We did."

The table freezes.

Lex leans back. "She screamed my name twice. Maybe three times. I lost count."

"Lex!" I hiss, cheeks flaming.

He just grins. "What? Don't act shy now, malyshka. They should know how fucking perfect you looked with your dress around your waist and my hands on your thighs."

Ellie shrieks. Cade groans and drops his face into his hands. Cal laughs so hard he nearly chokes. "Jesus Christ, man."

"He's your problem now, Cade." Daniel mutters from across the the table.

Roman lifts his glass, slow and thoughtful. "Bold. Looks like she chose well." His eyes lock on Lex's in a warm and measured, but non-confrontational stare. "Don't ever disappoint her."

Lex holds his gaze. "Never."

Ellie fans herself with a napkin. "Okay, seriously? You two need a 12-step program and a cold shower. In that order."

Savannah lifts her wine. "Honestly, I'm just impressed you made it back to the table with your outfit still intact."

Clay chuckles, easy and proud. "Well she's practically a Whitmore now. We always bounce back fast."

A few people laugh. Glasses clink.

Irina's voice is quiet but cold as ice. "Barinov."

Lex goes still. Cade's glass pauses mid-lift.

Cal—*oblivious or just plain ignoring Irina*—leans forward with a grin. "Wait. Nashville."

Lex leans in, eyes narrowing with a smirk. "There it is. I've been waiting for someone to finally bring up this legendary Nashville story you all whisper about but never fucking explain."

He turns to me, eyes gleaming. "What'd you do, malyshka? Burn something down? Steal a stage?"

Ellie gasps. "Oh my God, the concert trip! Lex, you'll love it."

Cade groans. "You mean the trip where you two said we were going to Cabo and we landed in Tennessee?"

Lex blinks. "You thought you were going to Cabo?"

Cal nods, completely unbothered. "They conned Eric into flying us out."

Lex's brow lifts. "Wait. Sky Daddy Eric?"

Cal points. "The one and only. Didn't ask a single question. The psycho just fueled the jet, cranked a playlist, and loaded it with drinks and snacks for the girls."

Cade cuts in. "Yeah, except he took a huge fucking detour that left us stranded in Nassau for two days before we even got to Nash-ville."

"He said the universe needed us to vibe longer," Ellie says, mimicking Eric's stoner tone perfectly.

Savannah groans. "That man is a walking liability."

Lex's laughs "That guy's a nut job."

Roman raises a brow. "And you trusted him with an interna-tional flight?"

"He's FAA-certified... ish," I mutter, sipping my drink.

Lex shakes his head. "I'm never getting on a plane again with any of you ever again."

Clay chuckles. "You're not truly family until you've almost been deported because of Sky Daddy."

Cal grins. "Anyway, the girls told us it was a beach week..."

"Yeah," Cade mutters, "and instead we ended up at a Jason Aldean concert. In Nashville. In the middle of July."

Ellie points her fork at him. "You had a great time."

Cade's smirk is dry. "Sure. Right after Eric tried to kill us in the air, I got second-degree sunburn, nearly passed out from heatstroke, and your drunk friend spilled beer on my new boots."

I nudge him. "I taught you to two-step."

"You spun me like I was auditioning for the Grand Ole Opry," he says, mouth twitching.

"It was cute," Ellie adds. "Until Tucker showed up."

Cade's jaw ticks. "Ugh. The bull rider."

Lex raises a brow, intrigued. "Tucker?"

Cal's already laughing. "Some guy Bells met at the concert. In-vited us to a bonfire after party."

"He was nice," I say sweetly.

"He was clingy," Cade mutters.

Ellie grins. "Cade went full-on bodyguard mode when Tucker kept trying to dance with her."

Lex's eyes cut to Cade. "Really?"

Cade shrugs, smooth. "Didn't like the way he kept touching her."

I glance between them, biting back a laugh. "Babe, you shoved the guy into a hay bale, went full on Lex-mode and everything."

"Good job, babe. Making me proud," Lex hums, amused. "So what happened to this Tucker guy?" he asks, eyes flicking to me.

I lean back into his chest, swirling the ice in my glass. "No idea."

"She ghosted him," Ellie grins.

Lex's mouth twitches. "You ghosted a bull rider, baby?"

"He said I had buckle bunny potential," I reply. "I panicked."

Cal snorts. "He sent you that belt buckle in the mail."

Cade arches a brow. "And you kept it."

"It was cute!" I protest. "I wore it with my cutoff shorts."

Ellie fans herself. "It was a look."

Lex groans under his breath. "Jesus Christ, baby, are you talking about the one you wore—"

"Yep," Cade says cutting him off and smirking.

Lex sets down his glass with a thud. "That buckle's not surviving the week. When we get back home, it burns."

Cade leans back, smug as hell. "Easy, babe. You're gonna break your glass."

"Not if I break this Tucker fucker first," Lex growls as laughs break out around the table.

"Pretty sure that was the last time I saw you before you disappeared off to Wexley and fell for this guy," I say, nodding between Cade and Lex. "We barely talked at all my senior year."

Cade's smile falters just slightly. "Shit. You're right." His eyes flick over mine, softer now. "I think I was so wrapped up in school and everything else I didn't even notice how far apart we got."

That's when Clay raises his glass, the soft clink drawing everyone's attention.

"Alright everyone, glasses up. To the ones we've lost," he says, voice steady. "To the ones who fought their way back. And to the ones who walked in later but still made this place feel like home." He looks around the table, gaze lingering just a second longer on Lex. "May it hold."

Glasses lift. Drinks swirl. Crystal kisses crystal.

And as the sound fades, Lex leans in—his lips brushing my

temple, voice low enough only Cade and I can hear.

"Home," he whispers.

CHAPTER ⁨84⁩
BELLA
NATIONALS DAY 2
DALLAS, TEXAS
71 DAYS SINCE DADDY'S DEATH

The final notes of *Pillowtalk* fade into a wall of sound, the crowd exploding as if we just ripped the stage in half. Josh's hand slides around my waist and he spins me one last time with a grin that's all teeth and triumph. My body's still humming, chest rising and falling with adrenaline, heart slamming like the bass line still hasn't stopped.

We did it. Every beat landed. Every touch, every breathy grind and whispered hip flick, we didn't just dance it. We devoured it.

Which is why we always save the best dances for day two. Because day two is when the bodies are tired, the routines blur, and the judges start forgetting who's who. That's when you hit them with a set that grabs them by the throat and doesn't let go. That's when you bring fire.

Josh and I book it off the floor, lungs heaving, laughing like idiots as the stage doors close behind us. I practically collapse into him for a second, both of us slick with sweat, buzzing from the high.

Josh shakes his head, beaming. "That," he pants, "was nasty. In the best possible way."

I nod, still catching my breath.

He groans dramatically, pressing a hand to his chest. "I'm scared to walk back out there. Your Russian's gonna kill me."

I grab a towel from the rack and wipe the sweat from my chest. "Please. Lex knows this is all fake. He's seen us practice that grind in the mirror like fifty times."

Josh grins. "Yeah, fifty times, five hundred times, he still looks at me like he wants to run me over with his motorcycle."

I toss the towel at his head. "Shut up."

He ducks it, then sobers just slightly. "But for real, he good? You good?"

I glance up at him. "Yeah. I mean, he's probably going to corner you later and say something vaguely threatening in Russian, but yeah. We're good."

Josh exhales, pushing a hand through his sweaty hair. "Okay. I just... wanted to check. I know things are different now. You've got your guys. And I'm not trying to overstep."

"Things are different," I say, softer this time. "But not with you, J. You've always been my constant. My partner. My friend. Nothing about this, any of this, changes that."

His shoulders drop, tension bleeding out. "Good. Because honestly, you're the only one who can handle my dramatic ass."

"Right? As if anyone else would let you add that extra body roll mid-routine."

He laughs. "What can I say? The people deserve flair."

I bump him gently with my shoulder. "Well, lucky for you, I'm not going anywhere."

He stares at me for just a few seconds too long.

"What?" I ask.

He shrugs. "I haven't seen you this happy in... well, ever. You weren't like this with Wes."

Something shifts in my chest.

"You must really love them," he adds, voice quieter now. "Lex and Cade. Both."

I pause, fingers curling around the edge of the water bottle I'd just grabbed. "Yeah. I do."

Josh smiles, genuinely proud. "Good. You deserve that kind of love after all the shit you've been through."

"Thanks, J."

He slings an arm around my shoulder again. "Now let's go cool off before your Hollow King puts me in a headlock."

We practically crash into Coach Javi. "¡Dios mío!" he breathes, pressing both hands to his heart like I just proposed. "That was sex on stage. Pure sex. That is how you open day two."

Josh and I both pant-laugh, adrenaline still pounding. "We'll take that," I grin, grabbing the sheer robe and wrapping it around my chest. "Felt good out there."

Javi nods, still glowing. "Felt legendary."

But as he walks off toward the music director, I catch a glimpse of the monitors backstage. Another trio's out there, all red fringe and hair flips. Latin number. Again. The choreography is amazing, but the energy in the judges' box?

Flat.

The female judge leans back with her arms crossed, not even writing. Santibañez has his elbow on the table, jaw in hand, eyes glazed like a dad forced to watch dance recitals for six hours straight.

I scan the floor backstage. Dancers are everywhere stretching, braiding, icing knees. I spot Javi near the wings and weave through the chaos.

"Javi!"

He turns just as I reach him, eyebrows up.

"We have a problem," I say, breathless but firm. "Trio's up in less than twenty and we're about to blend."

Javi tilts his head. "What do you mean blend?"

I point to the monitor. "They're over it, Javi. The judges. The Latin routines."

He turns and watches. The dancers on stage are good—great, even—but the energy just isn't there. One judge yawns into their hand. Another taps their pen against their scorecard with the bored rhythm of someone counting ceiling tiles.

"They're tired," I add. "Every team is doing the same thing. The same look, the same footwork, the same damn hip circles."

Javi frowns, arms folding across his chest. "But our trio is solid. You've rehearsed it for weeks."

"I know." I look at him, eyes steady. "But solid isn't going to get us to Worlds. Not if they stop watching halfway through."

He studies the screen again. Silent. We both watch as the guest judge leans back and actually mouths something to the lead judge, something that makes the man shake his head and shrug.

"I'm not trying to undermine you," I say quickly. "But we're running out of chances. You put me in the center for a reason, right?"

He doesn't answer at first. But his jaw tightens.

"I'm saying," I continue, "trust me. Let me fix this."

"You want to change the routine, mija?" he asks, quiet, incredulous.

"Full scrap," I say, breath still sharp but steady. "New music. New outfit. Start fresh. But with a dance we already know is solid, Javi. One of ours. One that we know already hits hard." I step closer, eyes locked on his. "We can beat every one of those Latin routines with our own fire, you know we can. You taught us how."

Javi watches the stage again, then the judges. "You think you can pull that off in under twenty minutes?" he asks, one brow arching.

I lift my chin. "I know I can. With Rico on costumes and Knox on audio? Please. That's dream team energy. Just give me the green light."

He stares at me for a long second, arms crossed, foot tapping, like he's debating whether to hug me or throttle me. Then he exhales slow and dramatic, like he's in a telenovela.

"Madre de Dios, you remind me of me when I was twenty-one," he says, eyes narrowing. "Bossy. Bold. Ridiculous. And, unfortunately, probably right."

"So that's a yes?"

He sighs, tosses his hands in the air. "Fine. Go. Get your tech wizard. I'll find Rico and warn the stage manager we're throwing the whole damn script out the window."

"Thank you," I say, grabbing his arm. "Seriously. You won't regret this."

"Oh, I better not," he calls after me, already spinning on his heel like he's halfway down a runway. "Because if this crashes and burns, Bella Blackwood." He points at me, eyes wide. "I swear on every rhinestone in Rico's closet." He clutches his chest, like he's invoking a saint. "I will make you choreograph all of Legacy's Christmas pieces next year."

He starts pacing dramatically, counting on his fingers. "And I mean all of them. Elementary schools. Retirement homes. Random street corners in Times Square. I will personally glue a reindeer hat to your head and make you teach a routine called '*Jingle Bell Rock: The Remix.*' With tap shoes. In the snow."

He spins at the end of the hallway, finger raised like a villain in a holiday musical. "Candy cane unitards, Bella. Unitards. Don't tempt me."

"Love you, Javi!" I yell over my shoulder, already dialing Knox.

He shouts back something in Spanish I'm pretty sure is profanity.

CHAPTER 85
LEX
NATIONALS DAY 2
DALLAS, TEXAS
PRAYING WE GET TO GO TO PARIS...
71 DAYS SINCE HENRY'S DEATH

Knox answers his phone two seats down with a sharp, "Hey, B. What's up?"

Cade and I both glance over.

"What? Are you for real?"

He shifts forward in his seat, elbow on his knee, hand over his mouth like he's trying not to laugh. "What'd Javi say?"

A beat. Then he snorts. "You sure? 'Cause that's a ballsy-ass move, bitch. Even for you."

"Did he just call her a—"

Cade glances at me. "Don't."

I ignore him.

But before I can stand up and explain to Knox how many teeth he doesn't need, the guy mutters, "Yeah yeah, I'm on it. Bye," and hangs up.

He bolts upright, already moving past the rows of seats, muttering something under his breath.

I lean forward. "What the hell was that, Knox?"

He waves me off without even looking. "I'll be right back. Your girl's changing shit. I'll explain when I get back."

And he's gone, cutting across the back of the room toward the sound booth, pulling a flash drive from his hoodie and handing it off to the tech guy like it's a damn mission drop.

Cade shifts beside me, eyes narrowed. "What the hell is Bella doing now?"

I stare at the stage, then the booth, then back again. "No idea," I mutter. "But apparently, something."

The lights are still low. The announcer is stalling. The judges lean back in their seats, clearly drained after two full days of almost all

Latin routines. A few of them look like they could nod off right there. One guy's literally pinching the bridge of his nose.

Cade exhales. "She's not actually gonna change the routine this late, right?"

I don't answer. I just lean back in my chair and stare at the stage waiting for the chaos to begin.

Knox comes back out and drops into his seat, glitter on his cheeks like he's just escaped a diva-fueled war-zone.

Cade leans toward him. "Okay, tell us what the hell is going on."

Knox exhales like he just survived a hostage negotiation. "Bells says the judges are zoning out. Two full days of pretty much constant Latin and they look like they're about to fall asleep in their shrimp cocktails. So, they're flipping the script."

Cade blinks. "Flipping?"

"Literally." Knox jerks a thumb toward backstage. "Right now, as we speak. They're changing the choreo, the outfits, the hair. I just heard Rico screaming '*If one more bitch asks me to hot-glue anything in the next thirty seconds, I swear I will light myself on fire.*'"

"What the fuck did she change it to?" I ask.

But before Knox can answer, a voice booms through the speakers. "Now entering the floor. From Wexley University, The Trifecta."

Every head turns. And then, holy fucking shit. The girls step out. Gone are the rhinestones and feathered skirts and in their place are fight night legends.

Ellie's in high-waisted black leather pants with thigh slits that leave nothing to the imagination, paired with a cropped black tee that reads *REZ IS MY REASON* in screaming red block letters. Her curls are slicked high, lips cherry-glossed, grin lethal.

Haley struts next to her in skin-tight black leather shorts and a ripped tee that says *CHASIN' DESHAWN* in the same dripping font, hair in two sleek braids, eyes smoky enough to set off a fire alarm.

Then Bella. Fuck. Me.

Red leather pants like second skin, her black combat boots gleaming under the stage lights. Her shirt is a blood-red crop cut to show skin, ink, and attitude. Across the chest in bold black lettering: *I*

COME HARDER FOR THE HOLLOW KING. with a small black heart icon under it like a fucking signature.

I actually choke as "Disco Inferno" begins.

Knox leans forward and mutters, "Rico deserves a raise and a restraining order."

I just grip the seat like it's holding me back from charging the stage. "She's a goddamn genius,"

Cade whistles. "Damn, sweetheart."

"This is gonna kill me," I mutter.

Cade raises a brow. "It's Nationals, babe. This is branding."

"But if she so much as glances at that guest judge."

"Santibañez?" Knox snorts. "Dude, he's gay."

"I don't care. If she licks him like she did me on fight night—"

"You'll what?" Cade asks, fighting a smile.

I glare straight ahead. "I'll jump the goddamn rail."

Cade claps me on the shoulder. "At least let her win first."

She and the girls hit the floor in perfect sync, hair whipping, knees sliding, and bodies hitting those accents like the music's wired straight into their veins. It's *Disco Inferno* reborn, same fire and sin, but stripped down and polished to something meaner, cleaner, and twice as hot.

The lights flash gold and crimson, strobes chasing over their skin. Sweat gleams down the curve of her throat. When she drops into that body roll—slow, controlled, teasing the crowd before snapping back up into a punch of choreography—it's game over.

The judges lean forward. The audience loses their rhythm trying to keep up. The final bass drop hits, and the girls freeze in place. Their shoulders heaving, eyes electric, completely drenched in heat and hunger and every drop of power that routine could possibly hold.

The arena fucking erupts.

And the judges. Those bored, stiff-ass fossils who looked like they were counting ceiling tiles fifteen minutes ago are on their feet. Clapping. Even that tight-ass guest judge, Alejandro Whatever-The-Fuck, is smiling like Bella just made his whole damn month.

"Dudes... I think we're going to Paris," Knox says, voice hushed but hyped.

Cade exhales a breath like he's been holding it the entire performance. "They did it."

The announcer's voice comes through the speakers, cutting clean through the roar. "Can we have all of our trios return to the floor for final scoring."

The three trios stand center stage beneath the blazing lights.

Ellie, Bella, and Haley huddle tight in the middle—arms looped, foreheads pressed together, shoulders shaking with adrenaline and hope.

The crowd is buzzing. No one's sitting. Every flash from every phone screen catches like lightning on Bella's red top and all I can do is stare at her.

The announcer steps up with the envelope.

"Don't stall. Just say it. Say it, dude." I mumble under my breath.

"In third place... representing the Caldera School of the Performing Arts..."

Bella's arms tighten around Ellie and Haley. The three of them rock slightly on their feet, locked together like war-sisters on the edge of legend.

My heart's pounding.

"And in first place, headed to Paris, France for Worlds..."

A pause.

The longest fucking pause of my life.

"...Wexley University's The Trifecta!"

Ellie screams first. Bella tackles her. Haley grabs them both. They drop to the floor in a tangle of leather, shrieking and laughing and crying. Javi launches from the wings like a damn missile, colliding with them in a full-body hug, yelling something about diva angels sent from choreography heaven. Rico's right behind him, half sobbing, half fixing Ellie's top mid-celebration.

Cade fists my shirt and pulls me in, hard. I grab his jaw. His mouth crashes into mine. Hot. Desperate. Triumphant.

When we break, breathless, Cade grins against my lips. "Well, babe," he pants, "looks like we're flying to Worlds."

I snort. "With Sky Daddy."

He groans. "God help us all."

We start to move toward the stage, shoving past the crowd of dancers and parents. Security tries to block us at the edge of the stage, but before I can lay the fucker out, Bella sees us coming and screams.

"LET THEM UP!"

Knox is already one step ahead, tossing a badge and yelling something about VIP clearance. Within seconds, we're onstage. Bella launches herself at me, arms around my neck, legs around my waist.

"We did it!" she yells, tears streaking her face.

I spin her. "Damn right we did, baby."

CHAPTER ⑧⑥
BELLA
NOX
76 DAYS SINCE DADDY'S DEATH

We're going to Worlds. Ellie is dancing. Josh and I are dancing. And most importantly, The Trifecta is dancing. I still can't believe
it. In just a couple months we are going to be dancing our hearts out in
freaking Paris, France. Like, the Eiffel Tower, crepes, leather jackets,
hot baguette boys, *Paris.*

The last few days have been complete and utter chaos. We flew
home straight after the win, high on adrenaline and victory. We turned
the private jet into a sky-high party. I'm talking glow sticks, champagne, playlist battles, and Rico threatening that if anyone spilled on
his vintage fur coat one more time, he'd jump... midair.

Sky Daddy Eric strolled out of the cockpit halfway through the
flight, shirt half unbuttoned, tequila in one hand, aviators still on. He
grinned at the cabin like we were all his adoring fans.

"Relax, kids. We're on autopilot. This baby practically flies
herself."

Cade glanced up, face blanching. "Eric, that's not exactly comforting."

Eric only winked, leaning over to blow him a tequila-soaked
kiss. "Come on, Picasso. Don't be so uptight. You made it to Worlds.
Live a little."

Cade stared. "Didn't you install the autopilot system yourself?"

"Sure did. Named her Lucille."

Lex sat up in an instant. "The fuck do you mean, named her?"

"Because she deserves one," Eric said solemnly, taking another swig like that settled the matter.

Lex muttered, "I knew we should've driven."

Eric was already strolling down the aisle like a runway model.
"Relax, boys. FAA cleared me last month. Well. Mostly."

"Mostly?" Cade yelped.

"I passed the vibe check," Eric shrugged.

Lex tightened his seatbelt so hard it squeaked. "What vibe? Unhinged chaos?"

"Exactly." Eric raised his tequila. "Air Chaos, baby. Trademark pending."

Knox, from the back row, lifted a lime wedge and toasted him. "My king."

"Okay, no," Cade said, visibly sweating. "Knox, don't encourage him."

Eric turned to me. "Wanna co-pilot, Blackwood? I'll let you push the shiny buttons."

Lex growled, "Touch one fucking switch, baby, and I swear I'll throw Eric out of this plane."

Eric saluted us. "Anyway, congrats on making it to Worlds. Try not to crash the penthouse when you land. I'm out." And then he vanished back into the cockpit for the rest of the flight.

Cade immediately grabbed a whiskey and threw it back. "If we survive this, I'm never stepping foot on a private jet again. I'm flying Delta. I want peanuts and a crying toddler."

Lex raised a brow. "Middle seat?"

"Middle seat."

"Layover?" Lex asked.

"Give me five."

And then the crazy began. Six hours of zero sleep, shots, loud music, and bad decisions.

When we got home, sweet Jesus, the sex. Reuniting with my guys after Nationals was like lighting a match in a room full of fireworks. Lex had me against the glass wall of our suite before my heels even came off—his voice all low Russian growl, his hands rough and greedy.

Cade didn't even wait for the bed, just pulled me down onto the fur rug in front of the fireplace and made love to me like the world could fall apart around us and he'd still only see me.

It was messy. It was perfect.

And now we're here. Standing in the marble lobby at NOX, staring at the gilded elevator doors like they're about to swallow me whole.

Lex steps forward, blocking the elevator with his body. "Baby. Let us come with you."

I shake my head. "No. He said he wanted to talk to me alone." Lex's jaw ticks. "Who gives a flying fuck what he wants? Let us come."

Cade steps between us, calm as ever. "Lex."

But Lex doesn't back down. "I don't like it. He's a manipulative bastard. You shouldn't be alone with him."

I sigh. "We really connected at Nationals. He's... trying." My voice dips. "And he's the only parent I have left."

That softens them both. Just a little.

"Look," I say, reaching for their hands. "If I'm not back down in thirty minutes, you can come barge in like the overprotective psychos I know and love."

Lex narrows his eyes. "Ten."

"Twenty," I counter.

"Ten," he snaps again.

Cade holds up a hand. "Fifteen."

We all look at each other.

"Fine," Lex and I say in unison.

I pull them both in. "I love you."

Cade kisses my forehead. "We'll be right here."

Lex tugs my wrist, pressing his lips to my knuckles. "Fifteen minutes, baby."

And then I step into the elevator.

Roman's office is quiet. Dark wood and heavy with silence. He stands as I enter, warmth flickering in his eyes. "I'm glad you came."

I offer a soft smile. "Me too. Thanks again for coming to Nationals. It meant a lot to me, having you there."

He walks around the desk, motions for me to sit. "It meant a lot to me, too. Watching you dance was something else. Thank you for allowing me to be there."

I sit. "Well, we had to make sure you got your money's worth."

That earns a low chuckle. "You're as dangerous as your mother was. Maybe more."

He lifts a folder from the desk. Thick. Formal. My pulse picks up.

"I wanted to talk to you about something. Something real," he begins. "I once told you that NOX and The Obsidian were yours if you wanted them. And I meant it. These." He gestures to the documents. "Are the formal deeds. Transfer agreements. Corporate control. Everything I've built, tied up in the shell corps and offshore trusts, all of it."

I stare. "What are you saying?"

"I want to name you, my heir. Publicly. Formally. Isabella Marie Russo. You can keep using Blackwood or hyphenate it, that's all up to you. Just legally on paper, I'd love for you to become a Russo. My daughter."

The words land like bricks.

"Don't worry about the businesses or any of that just yet. I'm still here, so legally we'd be co-owners. But when the time comes?" He shrugs lightly. "It'll all be yours."

My heart is thudding now. "Roman, that's—"

"Big. I know." His gaze softens. "But so are you. You're not a little girl anymore, Bella. You're a force. You're fire and legacy and blood. You are mine. And I think it's time that the world knows it."

His eyes drift toward the window, watching The Obsidian below. "I just wanted to give you something. After all the years I wasn't there for you."

My phone buzzes in my pocket.

LEX: Clock's ticking baby

I roll my eyes, then glance up at Roman. "I don't know what to say."

My throat tightens. My chest too. Roman stays calm and doesn't rush me, watching with a still patience.

"I just..." I blink fast, trying to keep it together. "You're the only parent I have left. And ever since you saved my life, something changed."

Roman's jaw ticks. His gaze drops for half a second, then lifts again, sharper now.

"I know we were texting and calling before, but now it feels different," I whisper. "Like it's not just about filling the silence anymore. Every time we talk, it gets more real. More... ours."

His fingers drum once on the desk, then still.

"Then in Dallas, we actually sat down and talked, really talked. And when it came time to stand up to Javi about switching the dance..." my voice falters. "It was your voice in my head. Your voice gave me the courage."

The corner of his mouth moves, something between pride and pain.

"You're the reason I changed that routine. You're the reason we're going to Paris, Dad."

The word slips out before I can stop it.

Roman—*Dad*—freezes. Like it's the one thing he never thought he'd hear from me. His eyes go glossy, but he blinks fast, swallowing it down like a man not used to being handed softness.

I take a deep breath and look up at him, our steel eyes locking. "I would love nothing more than to be your daughter."

His breath is jagged and unguarded. Like the words hit someplace he thought had gone numb. "Really?" he whispers.

I nod, but it's barely a movement. "Yeah. I mean it. You've shown up for me in ways I never thought I'd get again. And I know I'm not ready to give up the Blackwood name... not yet. Not formally. That name is Zeke. It's who I became because of him. I just, I need more time with that. Is that okay?"

He doesn't hesitate. "Take all the time you need."

My hands tremble, but I don't care. I don't even look at the paper. I stand and walk straight into his arms. He catches me like he's been waiting his whole life for this very moment.

The sobs hit messy and fast. Years in the making. His arms tighten around me, one hand cradling the back of my head. The other gripping around my back like a shield. He silently breathes with me, kissing the top of my head.

I finally pull back. My face is a wreck. Mascara's smudged, cheeks wet, lips trembling. But his eyes are glassy too, jaw clenched like he's holding back everything he's never said. He carefully reaches out, thumb brushing a tear from my cheek with a reverence that cracks something wide open in me.

When I turn toward the desk my hands are still shaking. The paper silently waits, heavy with everything it means. Roman stays behind me, a steady presence at my back. The warmth of a father that I thought I'd never get to feel again.

I pick up the pen. And for a second, I just stare at the line. Then I sign it.

Sharp.

Final.

Mine.

The ink bleeds like a vow. His hand lands on my shoulder, strong and silent.

Something catches my eye on his desk. A photograph framed in gold. A photo of Roman standing beside another man. Tall, lean, and in a NYPD uniform. Grinning. Confident. Familiar.

My stomach drops.

"Dad. Who's this?"

Roman glances over. "Hmm? Oh. That's an old friend of mine, Luca. He was my mole inside the NYPD. Had him on the ground looking for you after you were born. Before everything fell apart and the trail went cold. Haven't seen him in years."

My mouth goes dry.

My vision tunnels.

Emerald eyes.

Dark hair.

Scar on his left forearm.

The one he never talked about.

I can't breathe. I take a step back.

"Dad... that's not—"

"You really shouldn't have seen that, Sugar Bear."

My spine locks. "Jack—"

BANG.

The shot rings out like thunder.

Roman stumbles, blood blooming across his chest like a dark rose. He collapses onto the desk, eyes wide. "B-bella," he breathes.

"Dad!"

I hear the click of a gun and then the voice that lives in my nightmares.

"Hello Izzy, my little pet."

CHAPTER (87)
LEX
NOX
FOURTEEN MINUTES AND FIFTY-SEVEN SECONDS,
FIFTY-EIGHT, FIFTY-NINE...
76 DAYS SINCE HENRY'S DEATH

"Time to go," I say, already moving."

"Lex," Cade's voice cuts in behind me.

"No." I snap, grabbing his arm. My eyes never leave the elevator. "We're going up there. Now."

The elevator doors open with a cheery little ding that feels like a fucking insult.

We step out and I freeze. There's blood on the floor.

"Jesus," Cade breathes.

Three guards, one slumped and one face-down. Silent. Motionless. The one by the bar... he's gone. The crimson halo under his head is still spreading.

"No," I whisper.

We take off in a full sprint, the echo of our steps bouncing like gunshots off the marble. I slam through Roman's doors so hard they rattle the walls.

"MALYSHKA?!" My voice cracks. "BELLA?!"

Roman's slumped across his desk, chest heaving, blood soaking through his button-down in waves.

Cade barrels in behind me, eyes wide. "Oh my God."

"Where is she?!" I scream, rushing to Roman, grabbing his collar. "Where the fuck is she?!"

His head lolls. His lips are pale.

"Bella!" Cade shouts, already tearing open doors, checking behind furniture, throwing open the balcony over looking The Obsidian.

She's not here. She's not fucking here.

"Roman, look at me!" I'm shaking him now, blood slipping through my fingers like water. "Where is she? Where the fuck is she?!"

He blinks. Once. Twice. "She's... gone," he rasps. The words are barely audible.

He collapses. Limp. Heavy.

"NO—NO, NO, NO, Stay with me!" I shake him harder. "Don't fucking die on me, you don't get to die yet! Where did she go?!"

Cade stumbles back, horror flooding his face. "Lex..." His voice is thin. Broken. "She's not here. She's gone."

I can't breathe. My vision blurs.

I grab the edge of the desk, knuckles white. "She was just here."

"I know."

"She was just here, Cade!"

"I KNOW!" He chokes on the word. It splinters in the air between us.

A slow, hot roar starts building in my head. My lungs burn. My hands are covered in Roman's blood. Bella's black cherry and smoked vanilla scent still lingers in the room. Her voice, her laugh—it's still in the fucking air.

And now she's gone.

"No," I whisper.

I drop to my knees and for the first time in years, I scream.

@LucaWasHere
Hi there Lexie. Did you miss me?

She whimpered once—your name, I think.
But then she bled, and couldn't blink.
So soft. So still. So easily mine.
Your little queen, now mine redefined.

You played the game. You lost the piece.
Our board belongs to something carved from your unease.
We don't bluff. We don't forgive.
She's with us now. And she'll learn to live.

You touched her once and called it fate,
But I'll be the one to detonate.
She wears my collar. Bears my name.
So go home, Lexie. You've lost the flame.

Her screams? A symphony of purest art.
Each note a promise we'll tear apart.
So gather your kings, your knives, your pride,
But the girl you loved already died.

And Lexie? Sweet Lexie, you better sleep tight,
Because tomorrow, my game finally ignites.
One door opens. One rule breaks.
Let's see how much your kingdom shakes.

[Attached Image]

A dim, grainy photo taken from the front seat of a SUV. Bella lies unconscious in the back. Her hair is messy, matted with blood from a wound at her hairline. One cheek is bruised, her lips parted slightly.

www.ingramcontent.com/pod-product-compliance
Lightning Source LLC
Chambersburg PA
CBHW021930110726
47901CB00003B/782